ROBERT MUSIL

THE MAN

WITHOUT

QUALITIES

ALFRED A. KNOPF ⸎ NEW YORK 1995

A SORT OF INTRODUCTION
PSEUDOREALITY PREVAILS
INTO THE MILLENNIUM

TRANSLATED FROM THE GERMAN BY **SOPHIE WILKINS**
EDITORIAL CONSULTANT: **BURTON PIKE**

FROM THE POSTHUMOUS PAPERS

TRANSLATED FROM THE GERMAN BY
BURTON PIKE

ROBERT MUSIL

THE MAN

WITHOUT

QUALITIES

ALFRED A. KNOPF   NEW YORK 1995   I

A SORT OF INTRODUCTION

AND

PSEUDOREALITY PREVAILS

TRANSLATED FROM THE GERMAN BY
SOPHIE WILKINS
EDITORIAL CONSULTANT: **BURTON PIKE**

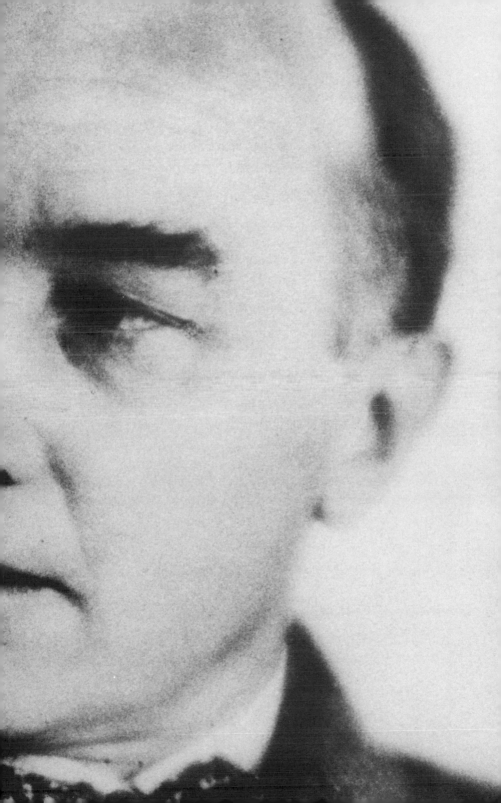

THIS IS A BORZOI BOOK
PUBLISHED BY ALFRED A. KNOPF, INC.

Copyright © 1995 by Alfred A. Knopf, Inc.

All rights reserved under International and Pan-American Copyright
Conventions. Published in the United States by Alfred A. Knopf, Inc.,
New York. Distributed by Random House, Inc., New York.

Originally published in German as *Der Mann ohne Eigenschaften*
by Rowohlt Verlag, Hamburg, in 1952 and 1978. Copyright © 1952, 1978 by
Rowohlt Verlag GmbH.

Library of Congress Cataloging-in-Publication Data
Musil, Robert, 1880–1942.
[Mann ohne Eigenschaften. English]
The man without qualities / Robert Musil ; translated from the
German by Sophie Wilkins and Burton Pike.
p. cm.
ISBN 0-394-51052-6
(boxed set)
I. Title
PT2625.U8M313   1995
833'.912—dc20   92-37943
CIP

Manufactured in the United States of America

Published April 30, 1995
Second Printing, June 1995

CONTENTS

PART II: PSEUDOREALITY PREVAILS

PART I

A SORT OF INTRODUCTION

1

From which, remarkably enough, nothing develops

A barometric low hung over the Atlantic. It moved eastward toward a high-pressure area over Russia without as yet showing any inclination to bypass this high in a northerly direction. The isotherms and isotheres were functioning as they should. The air temperature was appropriate relative to the annual mean temperature and to the aperiodic monthly fluctuations of the temperature. The rising and setting of the sun, the moon, the phases of the moon, of Venus, of the rings of Saturn, and many other significant phenomena were all in accordance with the forecasts in the astronomical yearbooks. The water vapor in the air was at its maximal state of tension, while the humidity was minimal. In a word that characterizes the facts fairly accurately, even if it is a bit old-fashioned: It was a fine day in August 1913.

Automobiles shot out of deep, narrow streets into the shallows of bright squares. Dark clusters of pedestrians formed cloudlike strings. Where more powerful lines of speed cut across their casual haste they clotted up, then trickled on faster and, after a few oscillations, resumed their steady rhythm. Hundreds of noises wove themselves into a wiry texture of sound with barbs protruding here and there, smart edges running along it and subsiding again, with clear notes splintering off and dissipating. By this noise alone, whose special quality cannot be captured in words, a man returning after years of absence would have been able to tell with his eyes shut that he was back in the Imperial Capital and Royal City of Vienna. Cities, like people, can be recognized by their walk. Opening his eyes, he would know the place by the rhythm of movement in the streets long before he caught any characteristic detail. It would not matter even if he only imagined that he could do this. We overestimate the importance of knowing where we are because in nomadic times it was essential to recognize the tribal feeding grounds. Why are we satisfied to speak vaguely of a red nose, without specifying what shade of red, even though degrees of red can be stated precisely to the micromillimeter of a wavelength, while with something so infinitely more complicated as what city one happens to be in, we always insist on knowing it exactly? It merely distracts us from more important concerns.

So let us not place any particular value on the city's name. Like all big cities it was made up of irregularity, change, forward spurts, failures to keep step, collisions of objects and interests, punctuated by unfathomable silences; made up of pathways and untrodden ways, of one great rhythmic beat as well as the chronic discord and mutual displacement of all its contending rhythms. All in all, it was like a boiling bubble inside a pot made of the durable stuff of buildings, laws, regulations, and historical traditions.

The two people who were walking up one of its wide, bustling avenues naturally were not thinking along these lines. They clearly belonged to a privileged social class, with their distinguished bearing, style of dress, and conversation, the initials of their names embroidered on their underwear, and just as discreetly, which is to say not for outward show but in the fine underwear of their minds, they knew who they were and that they belonged in a European capital city and imperial residence. Their names might have been Ermelinda Tuzzi and Arnheim—but then, they couldn't be, because in August Frau Tuzzi was still in Bad Aussee with her husband and Dr. Arnheim was still in Constantinople; so we are left to wonder who they were. People who take a lively interest in what goes on often wonder about such puzzling sights on the street, but they soon forget them again, unless they happen to remember during their next few steps where they have seen those other two before. The pair now came to a sudden stop when they saw a rapidly gathering crowd in front of them. Just a moment earlier something there had broken ranks; falling sideways with a crash, something had spun around and come to a skidding halt—a heavy truck, as it turned out, which had braked so sharply that it was now stranded with one wheel on the curb. Like bees clustering around the entrance to their hive people had instantly surrounded a small spot on the pavement, which they left open in their midst. In it stood the truck driver, gray as packing paper, clumsily waving his arms as he tried to explain the accident. The glances of the newcomers turned to him, then warily dropped to the bottom of the hole where a man who lay there as if dead had been bedded against the curb. It was by his own carelessness that he had come to grief, as everyone agreed. People took turns kneeling beside him, vaguely wanting to help; unbuttoning his jacket, then closing it again; trying to prop him up, then laying him down again. They were really only marking time while waiting for the ambulance to bring someone who would know what to do and have the right to do it.

The lady and her companion had also come close enough to see something of the victim over the heads and bowed backs. Then they stepped back and stood there, hesitating. The lady had a queasy feeling in the pit of her stomach, which she credited to compassion, although she mainly felt irresolute and helpless. After a while the gentleman said: "The brakes on these heavy trucks take too long to come to a full stop." This datum gave the lady some relief, and she thanked him with an appreciative glance. She did not really understand, or care to understand, the technology involved, as long as his explanation helped put this ghastly incident into perspective by reducing it to a technicality of no direct personal concern to her. Now the siren of an approaching ambulance could be heard. The speed with which it was coming to the rescue filled all the bystanders with satisfaction: how admirably society was functioning! The victim was lifted onto a stretcher and both together were then slid into the ambulance. Men in a sort of uniform were attending to him, and the inside of the vehicle, or what one could see of it, looked as clean and tidy as a hospital ward. People dispersed almost as if justified in feeling that they had just witnessed something entirely lawful and orderly.

"According to American statistics," the gentleman said, "one hundred ninety thousand people are killed there every year by cars and four hundred fifty thousand are injured."

"Do you think he's dead?" his companion asked, still on the unjustified assumption that she had experienced something unusual.

"I expect he's alive," he answered, "judging by the way they lifted him into the ambulance."

2

HOUSE AND HOME OF
THE MAN WITHOUT QUALITIES

The street where this little mishap had occurred was one of those long, winding rivers of traffic radiating outward from the heart of the city to flow through its surrounding districts and empty into the suburbs. Had the distinguished couple followed its course a little longer, they would have come upon a sight that would certainly have pleased them: an old garden, still retaining some of its eighteenth- or even seventeenth-century character, with wrought-iron railings through which one could glimpse, in passing, through the trees on a well-clipped lawn, a sort of little château with short wings, a hunting lodge or rococo love nest of times past. More specifically, it was basically seventeenth-century, while the park and the upper story showed an eighteenth-century influence and the façade had been restored and somewhat spoiled in the nineteenth century, so that the whole had something blurred about it, like a double-exposed photograph. But the general effect was such that people invariably stopped and said: "Oh!" When this dainty little white gem of a house had its windows open one could see inside the elegant serenity of a scholar's study with book-lined walls.

This dwelling and this house belonged to the man without qualities.

He was standing behind a window gazing through the fine green filter of the garden air to the brownish street beyond, and for the last ten minutes he had been ticking off on his stopwatch the passing cars, trucks, trolleys, and pedestrians, whose faces were washed out by the distance, timing everything whirling past that he could catch in the net of his eye. He was gauging their speeds, their angles, all the living forces of mass hurtling past that drew the eye to follow them like lightning, holding on, letting go, forcing the attention for a split second to resist, to snap, to leap in pursuit of the next item . . . then, after doing the arithmetic in his head for a while, he slipped the watch back into his pocket with a laugh and decided to stop all this nonsense.

If all those leaps of attention, flexings of eye muscles, fluctuations of the psyche, if all the effort it takes for a man just to hold himself upright within the flow of traffic on a busy street could be measured, he thought—as he toyed with calculating the incalculable—the grand total would surely dwarf the energy needed by Atlas to hold up the world, and one could then estimate the enormous undertaking it is nowadays merely to be a person who does nothing at all. At the moment, the man without qualities was just such a person.

And what of a man who does do something?

There are two ways to look at it, he decided:

A man going quietly about his business all day long expends far more muscular energy than an athlete who lifts a huge weight once a day. This has been proved physiologically, and so the social sum total of everybody's little everyday efforts, especially when added together, doubtless releases far more energy into the world than do rare heroic feats. This total even makes the single heroic feat look positively minuscule, like a grain of sand on a mountaintop with a megalomaniacal sense of its own importance. This thought pleased him.

But it must be added that it did not please him because he liked a solid middle-class life; on the contrary, he was merely taking a perverse pleasure in thwarting his own inclinations, which had once taken him in quite another direction. What if it is precisely the philistine who is alive with intimations of a colossally new, collective, ant-like heroism? It will be called a rationalized heroism, and greatly admired. At this point, who can tell? There were at that time hundreds of such open questions of the greatest importance, hovering in the air and burning underfoot. Time was on the move. People not yet born in those days will find it hard to believe, but even then time was racing along like a cavalry camel, just like today. But nobody knew where time was headed. And it was not always clear what was up or down, what was going forward or backward.

"No matter what you do," the man without qualities thought with a shrug, "within this mare's nest of forces at work, it doesn't make the slightest difference!" He turned away like a man who has learned to resign himself—indeed, almost like a sick man who shrinks from every strong physical contact; yet in crossing the adjacent dressing room he hit a punching bag that was hanging there a hard, sudden blow that seemed not exactly in keeping with moods of resignation or conditions of weakness.

3

EVEN A MAN WITHOUT QUALITIES HAS A FATHER WITH QUALITIES

When the man without qualities had returned from abroad sometime before, it was a certain exuberance as well as his loathing for the usual kind of apartment that led him to rent the little château, a former summer house outside the city gates that had lost its vocation when it was engulfed by the spreading city and had finally become no more than a run-down, untenanted piece of real estate waiting for its value to go up. The rent was correspondingly low, but to get everything repaired and brought up to modern standards had cost an unexpectedly large sum. It had become an adventure that resulted in driving him to ask his father for help—by no means pleasant for a man who cherishes his independence. He was thirty-two, his father sixty-nine.

The old gentleman was aghast. Not really on account of the surprise attack, though that entered into it because he detested rash conduct; nor did he mind the contribution levied on him, as he basically approved of his son's announcing an interest in domesticity and putting his life in order. But to take on a house that had to be called a château, even if only in the diminutive, affronted his sense of propriety and worried him as a baleful tempting of fate.

He himself had started out as a tutor in the houses of the high aristocracy while still working for his degree, and he had continued tutoring even as a young law clerk—not really from necessity, for *his* father was quite well off. But those carefully nurtured connections

paid off later on when he became a university lecturer and law professor, and they led to his gradually rising to become the legal adviser
to almost all the feudal nobility in the country, although by this time
he had no need of a professional sideline at all. Even long after the
fortune he had made could stand comparison with the dowry
brought him by his wife—the daughter of a powerful industrial family in the Rhineland, his son's mother, who had died all too soon—he
never allowed these connections, formed in his youth and strengthened in his prime, to lapse. Even after retiring from his practice, except for the occasional special consultation at a high fee, the old
scholar who had achieved distinction made a careful catalog of every
event concerning his circle of former patrons, extended with great
precision from fathers to sons to grandsons. No honor, wedding,
birthday, or name day passed without a letter of congratulation from
him, always a subtle blend of perfectly measured deference and
shared reminiscence. He received just as promptly in return brief
letters of acknowledgment, which thanked the dear friend and esteemed scholar. So his son was aware, from boyhood on, of the aristocratic knack for meting out almost unconsciously and with
unfailing condescension the exact degree of affability called for, and
Ulrich had always been irritated by the subservience of a man who
was, after all, a member of the intellectual aristocracy toward the
owners of horses, fields, and traditions. If his father was insensitive
on this point, it was not because of any calculation; it had been a natural instinct for him to build a great career in this way, so that he
became not only a professor and a member of academies and many
learned and official committees but was also made a Knight, and
then a Commander, the recipient of the Grand Cross of various high
orders. His Majesty finally raised him to the hereditary nobility, having already previously named him to membership in the House of
Lords. There the distinguished man joined the liberal wing, which
sometimes opposed the leading peers; yet none of his noble patrons
seemed to mind or even to wonder at this; they had never regarded
him as anything but the personified spirit of the rising middle class.
The old gentleman participated keenly in the technical work of legislation, and even if a controversial issue had him voting on the liberal
side the other side bore him no grudge; their sense of the matter was,
rather, that he had not been invited to join them. What he did in

politics was no different from what he had always done: combine his superior knowledge—which sometimes entailed working toward a gentle improvement of conditions—with the demonstration that his personal loyalty was always to be relied upon; and so he had risen quite unchanged, as his son maintained, from the role of tutor to the upper class to that of tutor to the Upper House.

When he learned about his son's acquisition of the château it struck him as a transgression against limits all the more sacred for not being legally defined, and he rebuked his son even more bitterly than on the many previous occasions he had found it necessary to do so, almost in terms of prophesying a bad end of which this purchase was the beginning. The basic premise of his life was affronted. As with many men who achieve distinction, this feeling was far from self-serving but consisted in a deep love of the general good above personal advantage—in other words, he sincerely venerated the state of affairs that had served him so well, not because it was to his advantage, but because he was in harmony and coexistent with it, and on general principles. This is a point of great importance: even a pedigreed dog searches out his place under the dining table, regardless of kicks, not because of canine abjection but out of loyalty and faith; and even coldly calculating people do not succeed half so well in life as those with properly blended temperaments who are capable of deep feeling for those persons and conditions that happen to serve their own interests.

4

IF THERE IS A SENSE OF REALITY, THERE MUST ALSO BE A SENSE OF POSSIBILITY

To pass freely through open doors, it is necessary to respect the fact that they have solid frames. This principle, by which the old professor had always lived, is simply a requisite of the sense of reality. But if there is a sense of reality, and no one will doubt that it has its justification for existing, then there must also be something we can call a sense of possibility.

Whoever has it does not say, for instance: Here this or that has happened, will happen, must happen; but he invents: Here this or that might, could, or ought to happen. If he is told that something is the way it is, he will think: Well, it could probably just as well be otherwise. So the sense of possibility could be defined outright as the ability to conceive of everything there might be just as well, and to attach no more importance to what is than to what is not. The consequences of so creative a disposition can be remarkable, and may, regrettably, often make what people admire seem wrong, and what is taboo permissible, or, also, make both a matter of indifference. Such possibilists are said to inhabit a more delicate medium, a hazy medium of mist, fantasy, daydreams, and the subjunctive mood. Children who show this tendency are dealt with firmly and warned that such persons are cranks, dreamers, weaklings, know-it-alls, or troublemakers.

Such fools are also called idealists by those who wish to praise them. But all this clearly applies only to their weak subspecies, those who cannot comprehend reality or who, in their melancholic condition, avoid it. These are people in whom the lack of a sense of reality is a real deficiency. But the possible includes not only the fantasies of people with weak nerves but also the as yet unawakened intentions of God. A possible experience or truth is not the same as an actual experience or truth minus its "reality value" but has—according to its partisans, at least—something quite divine about it, a fire, a soaring, a readiness to build and a conscious utopianism that does not shrink from reality but sees it as a project, something yet to be invented. After all, the earth is not that old, and was apparently never so ready as now to give birth to its full potential.

To try to readily distinguish the realists from the possibilists, just think of a specific sum of money. Whatever possibilities inhere in, say, a thousand dollars are surely there independently of their belonging or not belonging to someone; that the money belongs to a Mr. Me or a Mr. Thee adds no more to it than it would to a rose or a woman. But a fool will tuck the money away in his sack, say the realists, while a capable man will make it work for him. Even the beauty of a woman is undeniably enhanced or diminished by the man who possesses her. It is reality that awakens possibilities, and nothing would be more perverse than to deny it. Even so, it will always be the same possibilities, in sum or on the average, that go on repeating themselves until a man comes along who does not value the actuality above the idea. It is he who first gives the new possibilities their meaning, their direction, and he awakens them.

But such a man is far from being a simple proposition. Since his ideas, to the extent that they are not idle fantasies, are nothing but realities as yet unborn, he, too, naturally has a sense of reality; but it is a sense of possible reality, and arrives at its goal much more slowly than most people's sense of their real possibilities. He wants the forest, as it were, and the others the trees, and forest is hard to define, while trees represent so many cords of wood of a definable quality. Putting it another and perhaps better way, the man with an ordinary sense of reality is like a fish that nibbles at the hook but is unaware of the line, while the man with that sense of reality which can also be called a sense of possibility trawls a line through the water and has no idea whether there's any bait on it. His extraordinary indifference to the life snapping at the bait is matched by the risk he runs of doing utterly eccentric things. An impractical man—which he not only seems to be, but really is—will always be unreliable and unpredictable in his dealings with others. He will engage in actions that mean something else to him than to others, but he is at peace with himself about everything as long as he can make it all come together in a fine idea. Today he is still far from being consistent. He is quite capable of regarding a crime that brings harm to another person merely as a lapse to be blamed not on the criminal but on the society that produced the criminal. But it remains doubtful whether he would accept a slap in the face with the same detachment, or take it impersonally as one takes the bite of a dog. The chances are that he would first hit back and then on reflection decide that he shouldn't have. Moreover, if someone were to take away his beloved, it is most unlikely that he would today be quite ready to discount the reality of his loss and find compensation in some surprising new reaction. At present this development still has some way to go and affects the individual person as a weakness as much as a strength.

And since the possession of qualities assumes a certain pleasure in their reality, we can see how a man who cannot summon up a sense of reality even in relation to himself may suddenly, one day, come to see himself as a man without qualities.

5

ULRICH

The man without qualities whose story is being told here was called Ulrich, and Ulrich—his family name must be suppressed out of consideration for his father—had already given proof of his disposition while still on the borderline between childhood and adolescence, in a class paper on a patriotic theme. Patriotism in Austria was quite a special subject. German children simply learned to despise the wars sacred to Austrian children, and were taught to believe that French children, whose forebears were all decadent lechers, would turn tail by the thousands at the approach of a German soldier with a big beard. Exactly the same ideas, with roles reversed and other desirable adjustments, were taught to French, English, and Russian children, who also had often been on the winning side. Children are, of course, show-offs, love to play cops and robbers, and are naturally inclined to regard the X family on Y Street as the greatest family in the world if it happens to be their own. So patriotism comes easily to children. But in Austria, the situation was slightly more complicated. For although the Austrians had of course also won all the wars in their history, after most of them they had had to give something up.

This was food for thought, and Ulrich wrote in his essay on love of country that anyone who really loved his country must never regard it as the best country in the world. Then, in a flash of inspiration that seemed to him especially fine, although he was more dazzled by its splendor than he was clear about its implications, he added to this dubious statement a second, that God Himself probably preferred to speak of His world in the subjunctive of possibility (*hic dixerit quispiam*—"here someone might object that . . ."), for God creates the world and thinks while He is at it that it could just as well be done differently. Ulrich gloried in this sentence, but he must not have expressed himself clearly enough, because it caused a great uproar and nearly got him expelled from school, although nothing happened because the authorities could not make up their minds whether to regard his brazen remark as calumny against the Fatherland or as blasphemy against God. At the time, he was attending the Theresianum, that select school for the sons of the aristocracy and gentry that supplied the noblest pillars of the state. His father, furious at the humiliation brought upon him by this unrecognizable chip off the old block, packed him off abroad to a Belgian town nobody had ever heard of, where a small, inexpensive private school run on shrewd and efficient business lines did a roaring trade in black sheep. There Ulrich learned to give his disdain for other people's ideals international scope.

Since that time sixteen or seventeen years had passed, as the clouds drift across the sky. Ulrich neither regretted them nor was proud of them; he simply looked back at them in his thirty-second year with astonishment. He had meanwhile been here and there, including brief spells at home, and engaged in this or that worthwhile or futile endeavor. It has already been mentioned that he was a mathematician, and nothing more need be said of that for the moment; in every profession followed not for money but for love there comes a moment when the advancing years seem to lead to a void. After this moment had lasted for some time, Ulrich remembered that a man's native country is supposed to have the mysterious power of making the mind take root and thrive in its true soil, and so he settled there with the feeling of a hiker who sits down on a bench for eternity, but with the thought that he will be getting up again immediately.

When he set about putting his house in order, as the Bible has it, it turned out to be the experience he had actually been waiting for. He had got himself into the pleasant position of having to restore his run-down little property from scratch. He was free to follow any principle, from the stylistically pure to total recklessness, free to choose any style from the Assyrians to cubism. What should he choose? Modern man is born in a hospital and dies in a hospital, so he should make his home like a clinic. So claimed a leading architect of the moment; and another reformer of interior decoration advocated movable partitions in homes instead of fixed walls so that people would learn to trust their housemates instead of shutting themselves off from one another. Time was making a fresh start just then (it does so all the time), and a new time needs a new style. Luckily for Ulrich, the little château already had three styles superimposed on one another, setting limits on what he could do to meet all these new demands. Yet he felt quite shaken by the responsibility of having the opportunity to renovate a house, what with the threat hovering over his head of "Show me how you live and I will tell you who you are!"—which he had read repeatedly in art magazines. After intensive study of these periodicals he decided that he had best take the extension of his personality into his own hands, and began to design his future furniture himself. But no sooner had he come up with an impressively massive form than it occurred to him that something spare, and strictly functional, could just as easily be put in its place; and when he had sketched a form of reinforced concrete that looked emaciated by its own strength, he was reminded of the thin, vernal lines of a thirteen-year-old girl's body and drifted off into a reverie instead of making up his mind.

He was in that familiar state—not that the occasion mattered too seriously to him—of incoherent ideas spreading outward without a center, so characteristic of the present, and whose strange arithmetic adds up to a random proliferation of numbers without forming a unit. Finally he dreamed up only impracticable rooms, revolving rooms, kaleidoscopic interiors, adjustable scenery for the soul, and his ideas grew steadily more devoid of content. He had now finally reached the point to which he had been drawn all along. His father would have put it something like this: "Give a fellow a totally free hand and he will soon run his head into a wall out of sheer confusion." Or this: "A man who can have anything he wants will soon be at a loss as to what to wish for." Ulrich repeated these sayings to himself with great enjoyment. Their hoary wisdom appeared to him as an extraordinary new thought. For a man's possibilities, plans, and feelings must first be hedged in by prejudices, traditions, obstacles, and barriers of all sorts, like a lunatic in his straitjacket, and only then can whatever he is capable of doing have perhaps some value, substance, and staying power. Here, in fact, was an idea with incalculable implications. Now the man without qualities, who had come back to his own country, took the second step toward letting himself be shaped by the outward circumstances of life: at this point in his deliberations he simply left the furnishing of his house to the genius of his suppliers, secure in the knowledge that he could safely leave the traditions, prejudices, and limitations to them. All he did himself was to touch up the earlier lines, the dark antlers under the white vaultings of the little hall, the formal ceiling in the salon, and whatever else that seemed to him useful and convenient.

When it was all done he could shake his head and wonder: "Is this the life that is going to be mine?" What he possessed was a charming little palace; one must almost call it that because it was exactly the way one imagines such places, a tasteful residence for a resident as conceived by furniture dealers, carpet sellers, and interior decorators who were leaders in their fields. All that was missing was for this charming clockwork to be wound up, for then carriages bringing high dignitaries and noble ladies would come rolling up the driveway, and footmen would leap from their running boards to ask, looking Ulrich over dubiously: "Where is your master, my good man?"

He had returned from the moon and had promptly installed himself on the moon again.

6

LEONA, OR A CHANGE IN VIEWPOINT

Once a man has put his house in order it is time to go courting. Ulrich's girlfriend in those days was a chanteuse in a small cabaret who went by the name of Leontine. She was tall, curvaceously slender, provocatively lifeless, and he called her Leona.

He had been struck by the moist darkness of her eyes, the dole-fully passionate expression on her handsome, regular, long face, and the songs full of feeling that she sang instead of risqué ones. All these old-fashioned little songs were about love, sorrow, abandonment, faithfulness, forest murmurs, and shining trout She stood tall and lonely to the marrow on the tiny stage and patiently sang at the pub-lic with a housewife's voice, and even if something suggestive did slip in now and then, the effect was all the more ghostlike because she spelled out all the feelings of the heart, the tragic as well as the teas-ing, with the same wooden gestures. Ulrich was immediately re-minded of old photographs or engravings of dated beauties in ancient issues of forgotten women's magazines. As he thought him-self into this woman's face he saw in it a large number of small traits that simply could not be real, yet they made the face what it was. There are, of course, in all periods all kinds of countenances, but only one type will be singled out by a period's taste as its ideal image of happiness and beauty while all the other faces do their best to copy it, and with the help of fashion and hairdressers even the ugly ones manage to approximate the ideal. But there are some faces that never succeed, faces born to a strange distinction of their own, unyieldingly expressing the regal and banished ideal beauty of an earlier period. Such faces wander about like corpses of past desires in the great void of love's traffic, and the men who gaped into the vast tedium of Leontine's singing, unaware of what was happening to them, felt their nostrils twitch with feelings quite different from those aroused by brazen petite chanteuses with tango spit curls. So Ulrich decided to call her Leona and desired to possess her, as he might have wanted to possess a luxurious lion-skin rug.

But after their acquaintance had begun, Leona developed another anachronistic quality: she was an incredible glutton, and this is a vice whose heyday had passed a very long time ago. Its origin was in the craving she had suffered as a poor child for rich, costly delicacies; now, finally liberated, it had the force of an ideal that has broken out of its cage and seized power. Her father had apparently been a re-spectable little man who beat her every time she went out with ad-mirers, but she did it only because there was nothing she liked better than to sit at one of those sidewalk tables in front of a little pastry shop, spooning up her sherbet while genteelly watching the passing parade. It could not be maintained that she took no interest in sex, but it could be said that she was, in this respect as in every other, downright lazy and hated to work. In her ample body every stimulus took an astonishingly long time to reach the brain, and it happened that her eyes began to glaze over for no apparent reason in midafternoon, although the night before they had been fixed on a point on the ceiling as though she were observing a fly. Or else in the midst of a complete silence she might begin to laugh at a joke she just now understood, having listened to it days ago without any sign of understanding it. When she had no particular reason to be otherwise, she was completely ladylike. She could never be made to tell how she had got into her line of work in the first place. She apparently did not quite remember this herself. But it was clear that she regarded the work of a cabaret singer as a necessary part of life, bound up with everything she had ever heard about greatness in art and artists, so that it seemed to her altogether right, uplifting, and refined to step out every evening onto a tiny stage enveloped in billowing cigar haze to sing songs known for their heartrending appeal. If things needed livening up a bit she did not, of course, shrink from slipping in something gamy now and then, but she was quite sure that the prima donna at the Imperial Opera did exactly the same.

Of course, if the art of trading for money not the entire person, as usual, but only the body must be called prostitution, then Leona occasionally engaged in prostitution. But if you have lived for nine years, as she had from the age of sixteen, on the miserable pay of the lowest dives, with your head full of the prices of costumes and underwear, the deductions, greediness, and caprices of the owners, the commissions on the food and drink of the patrons warming up to their fun, and the price of a room in the nearby hotel, day after day, including the fights and the business calculations, then everything the layman enjoys as a night on the town adds up to a profession full of its own logic, objectivity, and class codes. Prostitution especially is a matter in which it makes all the difference whether you see it from above or from below.

But even though Leona's attitude toward sexual questions was completely businesslike, she had her romantic side as well. Only with her, everything high-flown, vain, and extravagant, all her feelings of pride, envy, lust, ambition, and self-abandonment, in short, the driv-

ing forces of her personality and upward social mobility, were anchored by some freak of nature not in the so-called heart but in the
gut, the eating processes—which in fact were regularly associated in
earlier times and still are today, as can be seen among primitives and
the carousing peasantry, who manage to express social standing and
all sorts of other human distinctions at their ritual feasts by overeat-
ing, with all the side effects. At the tables in the honky-tonk where
she worked, Leona did her job; but what she dreamed of was a cava-
lier who would sweep her away from all this by means of an affair as
long as one of her engagements and allow her to sit grandly in a
grand restaurant studying a grand menu. She would then have preferred to eat everything on the menu at once, yet the pain of having
to choose was sweetened by the satisfaction of having a chance to
show that she knew how one had to choose, how one put together an
exquisite repast. Only in the choice of desserts could she let herself
go, so that reversing the usual order she ended up turning dessert
into an extensive second supper. With black coffee and stimulating
quantities of drink Leona restored her capacities, then egged herself
on through a sequence of special treats until her passion was finally
quenched. Her body was now so stuffed with choice concoctions that
it was ready to split at the seams. She then looked around in indolent
triumph and, though never talkative, enjoyed reminiscing about the
expensive delights she had consumed. She would speak of *Polmone à
la Torlogna* or *Pommes à la Melville* with the studied casualness with
which some people affectedly let drop the name of a prince or a lord
of the same name they have met.

Because public appearances with Leona were not exactly to Ulrich's taste, he usually moved her feedings to his house, with the antlers and the stylish furniture for an audience. Here, however, she felt
cheated of her social satisfaction, and whenever the man without
qualities tempted her to these private excesses with the choicest fare
ever supplied by a restaurant chef she felt ill-used, exactly like a
woman who realizes she is not being loved for her soul. She was a
beauty, she was a singer, she had no reason to hide, as several dozen
men she aroused every evening would have testified. Yet this man,
although he wanted to be alone with her, would not even give her the
satisfaction of moaning "Leona, you devil, your ass is driving me
crazy!" and licking his mustache with desire when he so much as

looked at her, as she was accustomed to expect from her gallants. Although she stuck to him faithfully Leona despised him a little, and Ulrich knew it. He also knew well what was expected of him, but the days when he could have brought himself to say such things and still had a mustache were too long gone. To be no longer able to do something one used to be able to do, no matter how foolish it was, is exactly as if apoplexy has struck an arm and a leg. His eyeballs twitched when he looked at her after food and drink had gone to her head. Her beauty could be gently lifted off her. It was the beauty of that duchess whom Scheffel's Saint Ekkehard had carried over the convent's threshold, the beauty of the great lady with the falcon on her glove, the beauty of the legendary Empress Elizabeth of Austria, with her heavy crown of braids, a delight for people who were all dead. And to put it precisely, she also brought to mind the divine Juno—not the eternal and imperishable goddess herself, but the quality that a vanished or vanishing era called "Junoesque." Thus was the dream of life only loosely draped over its substance.

But Leona knew that such elegant entertainment entitled the host to something more than a guest who was merely there to be gaped at, even when he asked for nothing more; so she rose to her feet as soon as she was able and serenely broke into full-throated song. Her friend regarded such an evening as a ripped-out page, alive with all sorts of suggestions and ideas but mummified, like everything torn from its context, full of the tyranny of that eternally fixed stance that accounts for the uncanny fascination of tableaux vivants, as though life had suddenly been given a sleeping pill and was now standing there stiff, full of inner meaning, sharply outlined, and yet, in sum, making absolutely no sense at all.

7

IN A WEAK MOMENT ULRICH
ACQUIRES A NEW MISTRESS

One morning Ulrich came home looking a mess. His clothes hung in shreds, he had to wrap his bruised head in a cold towel, his watch and wallet were gone. He had no idea whether he had been robbed by the three men with whom he had got into a fight or whether a passing Samaritan had quietly lifted them while he lay unconscious on the pavement. He went to bed, and while his battered limbs, tenderly borne up and enveloped, were restored to being, he mulled over his adventure once more.

The three heads had suddenly loomed up in front of him; perhaps he had brushed up against one of the men at that late, lonely hour, for his thoughts had been wandering But these faces were already set in anger and moved scowling into the circle of the lamplight. At that point he made a mistake. He should have instantly recoiled as if in fear, backing hard into the fellow who had stepped into him, or jabbing an elbow into his stomach, and tried to escape; he could not take on three strong men single-handed. He resisted the idea that the three faces suddenly glaring at him out of the night with rage and scorn were simply after his money, but chose to see them as a spontaneous materialization of free-floating hostility. Even as the hooligans were cursing at him he toyed with the notion that they might not perhaps be hooligans at all but citizens like himself, only slightly tipsy and freed of their inhibitions, whose attention had fastened on his passing form and who now discharged on him the hatred that is always ready and waiting for him or for any stranger, like a thunderstorm in the atmosphere. There were times when he felt something of the sort himself. Regrettably, a great many people nowadays feel antagonistic toward a great many other people. It is a basic trait of civilization that man deeply mistrusts those who are outside his own circle, so it is not only the Teuton who looks down on the Jew but also the soccer player who regards the pianist as an incomprehensible and inferior creature. Ultimately a thing exists only by virtue of its boundaries, which means by a more or less hostile act against its surroundings: without the Pope there would have been no Luther, and without the pagans no Pope, so there is no getting away from the fact that man's deepest social instinct is his antisocial instinct. Not that Ulrich thought this out in such detail, but he knew this condition of vague atmospheric hostility with which the air of our era is charged, and when it suddenly comes to a head in the form of three strangers who lash out like thunder and lightning and then afterward vanish again forever, it is almost a relief.

In any case, facing three such louts, he apparently indulged in too much thinking. For although the first one who jumped him, anticipated by Ulrich with a blow on the chin, went flying back, the second, who should have been felled in a flash immediately afterward, was only grazed by Ulrich's fist because a blow from behind with a heavy object had nearly cracked Ulrich's skull. Ulrich's knees buckled, and he felt a hand grabbing at him; recovering with that almost unnatural lucidity of the body that usually follows an initial collapse, he struck out at the tangle of strange bodies but was hammered down by fists growing larger all the time.

Satisfied with his analysis of what had gone wrong as primarily an athlete's slipup—anyone can jump too short on occasion—Ulrich, whose nerves were still in excellent shape, quietly fell asleep, with precisely the same delight in the descending spirals of fading consciousness that he had dimly felt during his defeat.

When he woke up again he checked to make sure he had not been seriously hurt, and considered his experience once again. A brawl always leaves a bad taste in the mouth, that of an overhasty intimacy, as it were, and leaving aside the fact that he had been the one attacked, Ulrich somehow felt that he had behaved improperly. But in what way? Close by those streets where there is a policeman every three hundred paces to avenge the slightest offense against law and order lie other streets that call for the same strength of body and mind as a jungle. Mankind produces Bibles and guns, tuberculosis and tuberculin. It is democratic, with kings and nobles; builds churches and, against the churches, universities; turns cloisters into barracks, but assigns field chaplains to the barracks. It naturally arms hoodlums with lead-filled rubber truncheons to beat a fellow man within an

inch of his life and then provides featherbeds for the lonely, mistreated body, like the one now holding Ulrich as if filled with respect
and consideration. It is the old story of the contradictions, the incon-
sistency, and the imperfection of life. It makes us smile or sigh. But
not Ulrich. He hated this mixture of resignation and infatuation in
regard to life that makes most people put up with its inconsistencies
and inadequacies as a doting maiden aunt puts up with a young
nephew's boorishness. Still, he did not immediately leap out of bed
when it looked as though he were profiting from the disorderliness of
human affairs by lingering there, because in many ways it is only a
premature compromise with one's conscience at the expense of the
general cause, a short circuit, an evasion into the private sphere,
when one avoids doing wrong and does the right thing for one's own
person instead of working to restore order in the whole scheme of
things. In fact, after his involuntary experience Ulrich saw desperately little value even in doing away with guns here, with monarchs
there, in making some lesser or greater progress in cutting down on
stupidity and viciousness, since the measure of all that is nasty and
bad instantly fills up again, as if one leg of the world always slips back
when the other pushes forward. One had to find the cause of this, the
secret mechanism behind it! How incomparably more important that
would be than merely being a good person in accordance with ob-
solescent moral principles, and so in matters of morality Ulrich was
attracted more to service on the general staff than to the everyday
heroism of doing good.

At this point he went back in his mind to the sequel of last night's
adventure. As he regained his senses from the beating he had suffered, a cab stopped at the curb; the driver tried to lift up the
wounded stranger by the shoulders, and a lady was bending over him
with an angelic expression on her face. This child's picture-book vision, natural to moments of consciousness rising from the depths,
soon gave way to reality: the presence of a woman busying herself
with him had the effect on Ulrich of a whiff of cologne, superficial
and quickening, so that he also instantly knew that he had not been
too badly damaged, and tried to rise to his feet with good grace. In
this he did not succeed as smoothly as he would have liked, and the
lady anxiously offered to drive him somewhere to get help. Ulrich
asked to be taken home, and as he really still looked dazed and help-

less, she granted his request. Once inside the cab, he quickly recovered his poise. He felt something maternally sensuous beside him, a fine cloud of solicitous idealism, in the warmth of which tiny crystals of doubt were already hatching, filling the air like softly falling snow and generating the fear of some impulsive act as he felt himself becoming a man again. He told his story, and the beautiful woman, only slightly younger than himself, around thirty, perhaps, lamented what brutes people were and felt terribly sorry for him.

Of course he now launched into a lively defense of his experience, which was not, as he explained to the surprised motherly beauty, to be judged solely by its outcome. The fascination of such a fight, he said, was the rare chance it offered in civilian life to perform so many varied, vigorous, yet precisely coordinated movements in response to barely perceptible signals at a speed that made conscious control quite impossible. Which is why, as every athlete knows, training must stop several days before a contest, for no other reason than that the muscles and nerves must be given time to work out the final coordination among themselves, leaving the will, purpose, and consciousness out of it and without any say in the matter. Then, at the moment of action, Ulrich went on, muscles and nerves leap and fence with the "I"; but this "I"—the whole body, the soul, the will, the central and entire person as legally distinguished from all others—is swept along by his muscles and nerves like Europa riding the Bull. Whenever it does not work out this way, if by some unlucky chance the merest ray of reflection hits this darkness, the whole effort is invariably doomed.

Ulrich had talked himself into a state of excitement. Basically, he now maintained, this experience of almost total ecstasy or transcendence of the conscious mind is akin to experiences now lost but known in the past to the mystics of all religions, which makes it a kind of contemporary substitution for an eternal human need. Even if it is not a very good substitute it is better than nothing, and boxing or similar kinds of sport that organize this principle into a rational system are therefore a species of theology, although one cannot expect this to be generally understood as yet.

Ulrich's lively speech to his companion was probably inspired, in part, by vanity, to make her forget the sorry state in which she had found him. Under these circumstances it was hard for her to tell whether he was being serious or sardonic. In any case it might have seemed quite natural, perhaps even interesting, to her that he should try to explain theology in terms of sport, since sport is a timely topic while nobody really knows anything about theology, although there were undeniably still a great many churches around. All in all, she decided that by some lucky chance she had come to the rescue of a brilliant man, even though she did wonder, betweenwhiles, whether he might have suffered a concussion.

Ulrich, who now wanted to say something comprehensible, took the opportunity to point out in passing that even love must be regarded as one of the religious and dangerous experiences, because it lifts people out of the arms of reason and sets them afloat with no ground under their feet.

True enough, the lady said, but sports are so rough.

So they are, Ulrich hastened to concur, sports are rough. One could say they are the precipitations of a most finely dispersed general hostility, which is deflected into athletic games. Of course, one could also say the opposite: sports bring people together, promote the team spirit and all that—which basically proves only that brutality and love are no farther apart than one wing of a big, colorful, silent bird is from the other.

He had put the emphasis on the wings and on that bright, mute bird—a notion that did not make much sense but was charged with some of that vast sensuality with which life simultaneously satisfies all the rival contradictions in its measureless body. He now noticed that his neighbor had no idea what he was talking about, and that the soft snowfall she was diffusing inside the cab had grown thicker. So he turned to face her completely and asked whether she was perhaps repelled by such talk of physical matters? The doings of the body, he went on, were really too much in fashion, and they included a feeling of horror: because a body in perfect training has the upper hand, it responds automatically in its finely tuned way to every stimulus, so surely that its owner is left with an uncanny sensation of having to watch helplessly as his character runs off with some part of his anatomy, as it were.

It indeed seemed that this question touched the young woman deeply; she appeared excited by his words, was breathing hard, and cautiously moved away a little. A mechanism similar to the one he had just described—heavy breathing, a flushed skin, a stronger beating of the heart, and perhaps some other symptoms as well—seemed to have been set off inside her. But just then the cab stopped at Ulrich's gate, and there was only time for him to ask with a smile for his rescuer's address so that he could thank her properly. To his astonishment, this favor was not granted. And so the black wrought-iron gate banged shut behind a baffled stranger. What she presumably saw were the trees of an old park rising tall and dark in the light of electric streetlights and lamps going on in windows, and the low wings of a boudoir-like, dainty little château spreading out on a well-shorn emerald lawn, and a glimpse of an interior hung with pictures and lined with colorful bookshelves, as her erstwhile companion disappeared into an unexpectedly delightful setting.

So concluded the events of last night, and as Ulrich was still thinking how unpleasant it would have been if he had had to spend more time on yet another of those love affairs he had long since grown tired of, a lady was announced who would not give her name and who now entered his room heavily veiled. It was she herself, who had not wanted to give him her name and address, but had now come in person to carry on the adventure in her own romantically charitable fashion, on the pretext of being concerned about his health.

Two weeks later Bonadea had been his mistress for fourteen days.

8

KAKANIA

At the age when one still attaches great importance to everything connected with tailors and barbers and enjoys looking in the mirror, one also imagines a place where one would like to spend one's life, or at least where it would be smart to stay even if one did not care for it too much personally. For some time now such an obsessive daydream has been a kind of super-American city where everyone rushes about, or stands still, with a stopwatch in hand. Air and earth form an anthill traversed, level upon level, by roads live with traffic. Air trains, ground trains, underground trains, people mailed through tubes special-delivery, and chains of cars race along horizontally, while express elevators pump masses of people vertically from one traffic level to another; at the junctions, people leap from one vehicle to the next, instantly sucked in and snatched away by the rhythm of it, which makes a syncope, a pause, a little gap of twenty seconds during which a word might be hastily exchanged with someone else. Questions and answers synchronize like meshing gears; everyone has only certain fixed tasks to do; professions are located in special areas and organized by group; meals are taken on the run. Other parts of the city are centers of entertainment, while still others contain the towers where one finds wife, family, phonograph, and soul. Tension and relaxation, activity and love, are precisely timed and weighed on the basis of exhaustive laboratory studies. If anything goes wrong in any of these activities the whole thing is simply dropped; something else or sometimes a better way will be found or someone else will find the way one has missed; there's nothing wrong with that, while on the other hand nothing is so wasteful of the social energies as the presumption that an individual is called upon to cling for all he is worth to some specific personal goal. In a community coursed through by energies every road leads to a worthwhile goal, provided one doesn't hesitate or reflect too long. Targets are short-term, but since life is short too, results are maximized, which is all people need to be happy, because the soul is formed by what you accomplish, whereas what you desire without achieving it merely warps the soul. Happiness depends very little on what we want, but only on achieving whatever it is. Besides, zoology teaches that a number of flawed individuals can often add up to a brilliant social unit.

It is by no means certain that this is the way it has to be, but such ideas belong to those travel fantasies reflecting our sense of incessant movement that carries us along. These fantasies are superficial, restless, and brief. God knows what will really happen. Presumably it is up to us to make a new start at any given moment and come up with a plan for us all. If all that high-speed business doesn't suit us, let's do something else! For instance, something quite slow-moving, with a veiled, billowing, sea-slug-like, mysterious happiness and the deep, cow-eyed gaze the ancient Greeks admired. But that is not how it really is; we are at the mercy of our condition. We travel in it day and night, doing whatever else we do, shaving, eating, making love, reading books, working at our jobs, as though those four walls around us were standing still; but the uncanny fact is that those walls are moving along without our noticing it, casting their rails ahead like long, groping, twisted antennae, going we don't know where. Besides, we would like to think of ourselves as having a hand in making our time what it is. It is a very uncertain part to play, and sometimes, looking out the window after a fairly long pause, we find that the landscape has changed. What flies past flies past, it can't be helped, but with all our devotion to our role an uneasy feeling grows on us that we have traveled past our goal or got on a wrong track. Then one day the violent need is there: Get off the train! Jump clear! A homesickness, a longing to be stopped, to cease evolving, to stay put, to return to the point before the thrown switch put us on the wrong track. And in the good old days when the Austrian Empire still existed, one could in such a case get off the train of time, get on an ordinary train of an ordinary railroad, and travel back to one's home.

There, in Kakania, that state since vanished that no one understood, in many ways an exemplary state, though unappreciated, there was a tempo too, but not too much tempo. Whenever one thought of that country from someplace abroad, the memory that hovered before one's eyes was of white, wide, prosperous-looking roads dating from the era of foot marches and mail coaches, roads that crisscrossed the country in every direction like rivers of order, like ribbons of bright military twill, the paper-white arm of the administration holding all the provinces in its embrace. And what provinces they were! Glaciers and sea, Karst limestone and Bohemian fields of grain, nights on the Adriatic chirping with restless cicadas, and Slovakian villages where the smoke rose from chimneys as from upturned nostrils while the village cowered between two small hills as if the earth had parted its lips to warm its child between them. Of course cars rolled on these roads too, but not too many! The conquest of the air was being prepared here too, but not too intensively. A ship would now and then be sent off to South America or East Asia, but not too often. There was no ambition for world markets or world power. Here at the very center of Europe, where the world's old axes crossed, words such as "colony" and "overseas" sounded like something quite untried and remote. There was some show of luxury, but by no means as in such overrefined ways as the French. People went in for sports, but not as fanatically as the English. Ruinous sums of money were spent on the army, but only just enough to secure its position as the second-weakest among the great powers. The capital, too, was somewhat smaller than all the other biggest cities of the world, but considerably bigger than a mere big city. And the country's administration was conducted in an enlightened, unobtrusive manner, with all sharp edges cautiously smoothed over, by the best bureaucracy in Europe, which could be faulted only in that it regarded genius, and any brilliant individual initiative not backed by noble birth or official status, as insolent and presumptuous. But then, who welcomes interference from unqualified outsiders? And in Kakania, at least, it would only happen that a genius would be regarded as a lout, but never was a mere lout taken—as happens elsewhere—for a genius.

All in all, how many amazing things might be said about this vanished Kakania! Everything and every person in it, for instance, bore the label of *kaiserlich-königlich* (Imperial-Royal) or *kaiserlich* und *königlich* (Imperial *and* Royal), abbreviated as "k.k." or "k.&k.," but to be sure which institutions and which persons were to be designated by "k.k." and which by "k.&k." required the mastery of a secret science. On paper it was called the Austro-Hungarian Monarchy, but in conversation it was called Austria, a name solemnly abjured officially while stubbornly retained emotionally, just to show that feelings are quite as important as constitutional law and that regulations are one thing but real life is something else entirely. Liberal in its constitution, it was administered clerically. The government was clerical, but everyday life was liberal. All citizens were equal before the law, but not everyone was a citizen. There was a Parliament, which asserted its freedom so forcefully that it was usually kept shut; there was also an Emergency Powers Act that enabled the government to get along without Parliament, but then, when everyone had happily settled for absolutism, the Crown decreed that it was time to go back to parliamentary rule. The country was full of such goings-on, among them the sort of nationalist movements that rightly attracted so much attention in Europe and are so thoroughly misunderstood today. They were so violent that they jammed the machinery of government and brought it to a dead stop several times a year, but in the intervals and during the deadlocks people got along perfectly well and acted as if nothing had happened. And in fact, nothing really *had* happened. It was only that everyone's natural resentment of everyone else's efforts to get ahead, a resentment we all feel nowadays, had crystallized earlier in Kakania, where it can be said to have assumed the form of a sublimated ceremonial rite, which could have had a great future had its development not been cut prematurely short by a catastrophe.

For it was not only the resentment of one's fellow citizens that had become intensified there into a strong sense of community; even the lack of faith in oneself and one's own fate took on the character of a deep self-certainty. In this country one acted—sometimes to the highest degree of passion and its consequences—differently from the way one thought, or one thought differently from the way one acted. Uninitiated observers have mistaken this for charm, or even for a weakness of what they thought to be the Austrian character. But they were wrong; it is always wrong to explain what happens in a country by the character of its inhabitants. For the inhabitant of a country has at least nine characters: a professional, a national, a civic, a class, a geographic, a sexual, a conscious, an unconscious, and possibly even a private character to boot. He unites them in himself, but they dissolve him, so that he is really nothing more than a small basin hollowed out by these many streamlets that trickle into it and drain out of it again, to join other such rills in filling some other basin. Which is why every inhabitant of the earth also has a tenth character that is nothing else than the passive fantasy of spaces yet unfilled. This permits a person all but one thing: to take seriously what his at least nine other characters do and what happens to them; in other words, it prevents precisely what should be his true fulfillment. This interior space—admittedly hard to describe—is of a different shade and shape in Italy from what it is in England, because everything that stands out in relief against it is of a different shade and shape; and yet it is in both places the same: an empty, invisible space, with reality standing inside it like a child's toy town deserted by the imagination.

Insofar as this can become visible to all eyes it had happened in Kakania, making Kakania, unbeknownst to the world, the most progressive state of all; a state just barely able to go along with itself. One enjoyed a negative freedom there, always with the sense of insufficient grounds for one's own existence, and lapped around by the great fantasy of all that had not happened or at least not yet happened irrevocably as by the breath of those oceans from which mankind had once emerged.

Events that might be regarded as momentous elsewhere were here introduced with a casual *"Es ist passiert . . ."*—a peculiar form of "it happened" unknown elsewhere in German or any other language, whose breath could transform facts and blows of fate into something as light as thistledown or thought. Perhaps, despite so much that can be said against it, Kakania was, after all, a country for geniuses; which is probably what brought it to its ruin.

9

THE FIRST OF THREE ATTEMPTS TO BECOME A GREAT MAN

This man who had returned could not remember any time in his life when he had not been fired with the will to become a great man; it was a desire Ulrich seemed to have been born with. Such a dream may of course betray vanity and stupidity, but it is no less true that it is a fine and proper ambition without which there probably would not be very many great men in the world.

The trouble was that he knew neither how to become one nor what a great man is. In his school days his model had been Napoleon, partly because of a boy's natural admiration for the criminal and partly because his teachers had made a point of calling this tyrant, who had tried to turn Europe upside down, the greatest evildoer in history. This led directly to Ulrich's joining the cavalry as an ensign as soon as he was able to escape from school. The chances are that even then, had anyone asked him why he chose this profession, he would no longer have replied: "In order to become a tyrant." But such wishes are Jesuits: Napoleon's genius began to develop only after he became a general. But how could Ulrich, as an ensign, have convinced his colonel that becoming a general was the necessary next step for him? Even at squadron drill it seemed often enough that he and the colonel did not see eye-to-eye. Even so, Ulrich would not have cursed the parade ground—that peaceful common on which pretensions are indistinguishable from vocations—had he not been so ambitious. Pacifist euphemisms such as "educating the people to bear arms" meant nothing to him in those days; instead, he surrendered himself to an impassioned nostalgia for heroic conditions of lordliness, power, and pride. He rode in steeplechases, fought duels, and recognized only three kinds of people: officers, women, and civilians, the last-named a physically underdeveloped and spiritually contemptible class of humanity whose wives and daughters were the legitimate prey of army officers. He indulged in a splendid pessimism: it seemed to him that because the soldier's profession was a sharp, white-hot instrument, this instrument must be used to sear and cut the world for its salvation.

As luck would have it he came to no harm, but one day he made a discovery. At a social gathering he had a slight misunderstanding with a noted financier, which Ulrich was going to clear up in his usual dashing style; but it turned out that there are men in civilian clothes also who know how to protect their women. The financier had a word with the War Minister, whom he knew personally, and soon thereafter Ulrich had a lengthy interview with his colonel, in which the difference between an archduke and a simple army officer was made clear to him. From then on the profession of warrior lost its charm for him. He had expected to find himself on a stage of world-shaking adventures with himself as hero, but now saw nothing but a drunken young man shouting on a wide, empty square, answered only by the paving stones. When he realized this, he took his leave of this thankless career, in which he had just been made lieutenant, and quit the service.

10

THE SECOND ATTEMPT. NOTES TOWARD A MORALITY FOR THE MAN WITHOUT QUALITIES

But when Ulrich switched from the cavalry to civil engineering, he was merely swapping horses. The new horse had steel legs and ran ten times faster.

In Goethe's world the clattering of looms was still considered a disturbing noise. In Ulrich's time people were just beginning to discover the music of machine shops, steam hammers, and factory sirens. One must not believe that people were quick to notice that a skyscraper is bigger than a man on a horse. On the contrary, even today those who want to make an impression will mount not a skyscraper but a high horse; they are swift like the wind and sharp-sighted, not like a giant refractor but like an eagle. Their feelings have not yet learned to make use of their intellect; the difference in development between these two faculties is almost as great as that between the vermiform appendix and the cerebral cortex. So it was no slight advantage to realize, as Ulrich did when barely out of his teens, that a man's conduct with respect to what seem to him the Higher Things in life is far more old-fashioned than his machines are.

From the moment Ulrich set foot in engineering school, he was feverishly partisan. Who still needed the Apollo Belvedere when he had the new forms of a turbodynamo or the rhythmic movements of a steam engine's pistons before his eyes! Who could still be captivated by the thousand years of chatter about the meaning of good and evil when it turns out that they are not constants at all but functional values, so that the goodness of works depends on historical circumstances, while human goodness depends on the psychotechnical skills with which people's qualities are exploited? Looked at from a technical point of view, the world is simply ridiculous: impractical in all that concerns human relations, and extremely uneconomic and imprecise in its methods; anyone accustomed to solving his problems with a slide rule cannot take seriously a good half of the assertions people make. The slide rule is two systems of numbers and lines combined with incredible ingenuity; the slide rule is two white-enameled sticks of flat trapezoidal cross section that glide past each other, with whose help the most complex problems can be solved in an instant without needlessly losing a thought; the slide rule is a small symbol carried in one's breast pocket and sensed as a hard white line over one's heart. If you own a slide rule and someone comes along with big statements or great emotions, you say: "Just a moment, please—let's first work out the margin for error and the most-probable values."

This was without doubt a powerful view of what it meant to be an engineer. It could serve as the frame for a charming future self-portrait, showing a man with resolute features, a shag pipe clenched between his teeth, a tweed cap on his head, traveling in superb riding boots between Cape Town and Canada on daring missions for his business. Between trips there would always be time to draw on his technical knowledge for advice on world organization and management, or time to formulate aphorisms like the one by Emerson that ought to hang over every workbench: "Mankind walks the earth as a prophecy of the future, and all its deeds are tests and experiments, for every deed can be surpassed by the next." Actually, Ulrich had written this himself, putting together several of Emerson's pronouncements.

It is hard to say why engineers don't quite live up to this vision. Why, for instance, do they so often wear a watch chain slung on a steep, lopsided curve from the vest pocket to a button higher up, or across the stomach in one high and two low loops, as if it were a metrical foot in a poem? Why do they favor tiepins topped with stag's teeth or tiny horseshoes? Why do they wear suits constructed like the early stages of the automobile? And why, finally, do they never speak of anything but their profession, or if they do speak of something else, why do they have that peculiar, stiff, remote, superficial manner that never goes deeper inside than the epiglottis? Of course this is not true of all of them, far from it, but it is true of many, and it was true of all those Ulrich met the first time he went to work in a factory office, and it was true of those he met the second time. They all turned out to be men firmly tied to their drawing boards, who loved their profession and were wonderfully efficient at it. But any sugges-

tion that they might apply their daring ideas to themselves instead of
to their machines would have taken them aback, much as if they had
been asked to use a hammer for the unnatural purpose of killing a
man.

And so Ulrich's second and more mature attempt to become a
man of stature, by way of technology, came quickly to an end.

11

THE MOST IMPORTANT ATTEMPT OF ALL

Thinking over his time up to that point today, Ulrich might shake his
head in wonder, as if someone were to tell him about his previous
incarnations; but his third effort was different. An engineer may understandably become absorbed in his specialty instead of giving himself up to the freedom and vastness of the world of thought, even
though his machines are delivered to the ends of the earth, for he is
no more called upon to adapt the daring and innovative soul of his
technology to his private soul than a machine can be expected to
apply to itself the differential calculus upon which it is based. But the
same cannot be said of mathematics, which is the new method of
thought itself, the mind itself, the very wellspring of the times and
the primal source of an incredible transformation.

If it is the fulfillment of man's primordial dreams to be able to fly,
travel with the fish, drill our way beneath the bodies of towering
mountains, send messages with godlike speed, see the invisible and
hear the distant speak, hear the voices of the dead, be miraculously
cured while asleep, see with our own eyes how we will look twenty
years after our death, learn in flickering nights thousands of things
above and below this earth no one ever knew before; if light,
warmth, power, pleasure, comforts, are man's primordial dreams,
then present-day research is not only science but sorcery, spells
woven from the highest powers of heart and brain, forcing God to

open one fold after another of his cloak; a religion whose dogma is permeated and sustained by the hard, courageous, flexible, razor-cold, razor-keen logic of mathematics.

Of course there is no denying that all these primordial dreams appear, in the opinion of nonmathematicians, to have been suddenly realized in a form quite different from the original fantasy. Baron Münchhausen's post horn was more beautiful than our canned music, the Seven-League Boots more beautiful than a car, Oberon's kingdom lovelier than a railway tunnel, the magic root of the mandrake better than a telegraphed image, eating of one's mother's heart and then understanding birds more beautiful than an ethologic study of a bird's vocalizing. We have gained reality and lost dream. No more lounging under a tree and peering at the sky between one's big and second toes; there's work to be done. To be efficient, one cannot be hungry and dreamy but must eat steak and keep moving. It is exactly as though the old, inefficient breed of humanity had fallen asleep on an anthill and found, when the new breed awoke, that the ants had crept into its bloodstream, making it move frantically ever since, unable to shake off that rotten feeling of antlike industry. There is really no need to belabor the point, since it is obvious to most of us these days that mathematics has taken possession, like a demon, of every aspect of our lives. Most of us may not believe in the story of a Devil to whom one can sell one's soul, but those who must know something about the soul (considering that as clergymen, historians, and artists they draw a good income from it) all testify that the soul has been destroyed by mathematics and that mathematics is the source of an evil intelligence that while making man the lord of the earth has also made him the slave of his machines. The inner drought, the dreadful blend of acuity in matters of detail and indifference toward the whole, man's monstrous abandonment in a desert of details, his restlessness, malice, unsurpassed callousness, money-grubbing, coldness, and violence, all so characteristic of our times, are by these accounts solely the consequence of damage done to the soul by keen logical thinking! Even back when Ulrich first turned to mathematics there were already those who predicted the collapse of European civilization because no human faith, no love, no simplicity, no goodness, dwelt any longer in man. These people had all, typically, been poor mathematicians as young people and at school. This

later put them in a position to prove that mathematics, the mother of
natural science and grandmother of technology, was also the primordial mother of the spirit that eventually gave rise to poison gas and
warplanes.

The only people who actually lived in ignorance of these dangers
were the mathematicians themselves and their disciples the scientists, whose souls were as unaffected by all this as if they were racing
cyclists pedaling away for dear life, blind to everything in the world
except the back wheel of the rider ahead of them. But one thing, on
the other hand, could safely be said about Ulrich: he loved mathematics because of the kind of people who could not endure it. He
was in love with science not so much on scientific as on human
grounds. He saw that in all the problems that come within its orbit,
science thinks differently from the laity. If we translate "scientific
outlook" into "view of life," "hypothesis" into "attempt," and "truth"
into "action," then there would be no notable scientist or mathematician whose life's work, in courage and revolutionary impact, did not
far outmatch the greatest deeds in history. The man has not yet been
born who could say to his followers: "You may steal, kill, fornicate—
our teaching is so strong that it will transform the cesspool of your
sins into clear, sparkling mountain streams." But in science it happens every few years that something till then held to be in error suddenly revolutionizes the field, or that some dim and disdained idea
becomes the ruler of a new realm of thought. Such events are not
merely upheavals but lead us upward like a Jacob's ladder. The life of
science is as strong and carefree and glorious as a fairy tale. And Ulrich felt: People simply don't realize it, they have no idea how much
thinking can be done already; if they could be taught to think a new
way, they would change their lives.

Now, it is a question whether the world is so topsy-turvy that it
always needs turning around. The world itself has always had a two-
fold answer to this question. From the beginning of the world most
people, in their youth, have been in favor of turning the world
around. They have always felt it was ridiculous the way their elders
clung to convention and thought with the heart—a lump of flesh—
instead of with the brain. To the young, the moral stupidity of their
elders has always looked like the same inability to make new connections that constitutes ordinary intellectual stupidity, and their own

natural morality has always been one of achievement, heroism, and change. But they have no sooner reached their years of accomplishment than they no longer remember this, and even less do they want to be reminded of it. Which is why many of those for whom mathematics or science is a true profession are bound to disapprove of anyone taking up science for reasons such as Ulrich's.

Nevertheless, experts judged his achievements in this third profession, in the few years since he had taken it up, to have been not inconsiderable.

12

THE LADY WHOSE LOVE ULRICH WON AFTER A CONVERSATION ABOUT SPORTS AND MYSTICISM

It turned out that Bonadea, too, yearned for great ideas.

Bonadea was the lady who had rescued Ulrich on the night of his ill-fated boxing match and who had visited him the next morning shrouded in veils. He had baptized her Bonadea, "the Good Goddess," for the way she had entered his life and also after that goddess of chastity whose ancient temple in Rome had become, by an odd reversal of fate, a center for all the vices. She did not know that story. She was pleased at the euphonious nickname Ulrich had conferred on her, and wore it on her visits to him as if it were a sumptuously embroidered housedress. "Am I really your good goddess," she asked, "your own *bona dea*?" And the correct pronunciation of these two words demanded that she throw her arms around his neck and lift her face up to his with a gaze full of feeling.

She was the wife of a prominent man and the fond mother of two handsome boys. Her favorite phrase was "highly respectable," applied to people, messengers, shops, and feelings, when she wanted to praise them. She could utter the words "truth, goodness, and beauty" as often and as casually as someone else might say "Thursday." Her intellectual needs were most deeply satisfied by her concept of a peaceful, idyllic life in the bosom of her family, its radiant happiness toned down to a gentle lamplight by the hovering presence far beneath of the dark realm of "Lead me not into temptation." She had only one fault: she could become inordinately aroused at the mere sight of a man. She was not lustful; she was sensual, as other people have other afflictions, for instance suffering from sweaty hands or blushing too readily. It was something she had apparently been born with and could never do anything to curb. Meeting Ulrich in circumstances so like a novel, so firing to the imagination, she had been destined from the first moment to fall prey to a passion that began as sympathy, then led, after a brief though intense inner struggle, to forbidden intimacies, and continued as a seesaw between pangs of sinful desire and pangs of remorse.

But Ulrich was only the most recent of God knows how many men in her life. Once they have caught on, men tend to treat such nymphomaniac women no better than morons for whom the cheapest tricks are good enough and who can be tripped up in the same way time and again. The tenderer feelings of male passion are something like the snarling of a jaguar over fresh meat—he doesn't like to be disturbed. Consequently, Bonadea often led a double life, like any other respectable citizen who, in the dark interstices of his consciousness, is a train robber. Whenever no one was holding her in his arms, this quiet, regal woman was oppressed by self-hatred for the lies and humiliations she had to risk in order to be held in someone's arms. When her senses were aroused she was subdued and gentle; her blend of rapture and tears, crude directness shadowed by predictable remorse, mania bolting in panic from the lurking depression that threatened, heightened her attraction, arousing excitement much like a ceaseless tattoo on a drum hung with black crêpe. But between lapses, in her intervals of calm, in the remorse that made her aware of her helplessness, she was full of the claims of respectability, and this made life with her far from simple. A man was expected to be truthful and kind, sympathetic toward every misfortune,

devoted to the Imperial House, respectful toward everything respected, and, morally, to conduct himself with all the delicacy of a
visitor at a sickbed.

Not that it made any difference if these expectations were disappointed. To justify her conduct, she had made up a tale of how her
husband had caused her unfortunate condition in the innocent early
years of their marriage. This husband, considerably older and physically bigger than she, was cast as a ruthless monster in the sad, portentous account she gave to Ulrich during the very first hours of their new
love. It was only sometime afterward that he discovered that the man
was a well-known and respected judge, of high professional competence, who was also given to the form of hunting that consists in the
harmless gunning down of wild game; a welcome figure at various
pubs and clubs frequented by hunters and lawyers, where male topics
rather than art or love were the subject of conversation. The only
failing of this rather unaffected, good-natured, and jovial man was
that he was married to his wife, so that he found himself more often
than other men engaged with her in what is referred to in the language of the law courts as a casual encounter. The psychological effect of submitting for years to a man she had married from motives of
the head rather than the heart had fostered in Bonadea the illusion
that she was physically overexcitable, and fantasy made it almost independent of her consciousness. She was chained to this man, so favored by circumstance, by some compulsion she could not fathom;
she despised him for her own spinelessness and felt spineless in order
to despise him; she was unfaithful to him as a means of escape but
always chose the most awkward moments to speak of him or of their
children; and she was never able to let go of him completely. Like
many unhappy wives, she ended up with an attitude—in an otherwise
rather unstable personal environment—determined by resentment
of her solidly rooted husband, and she carried her conflict with him
into every new experience that was supposed to free her from him.

What could a man do to silence her lamentations but transport her
with all possible speed from the depressive to the manic state? She
would promptly charge the doer of this deed with taking advantage
of her weakness and with being devoid of all finer sensibilities, but
her affliction laid a veil of moist tenderness over her eyes when she,
as she put it with scientific detachment, "inclined" to this man.

13

A RACEHORSE OF GENIUS CRYSTALLIZES THE RECOGNITION OF BEING A MAN WITHOUT QUALITIES

It is not immaterial that Ulrich could say to himself that he had accomplished something in his field. His work had in fact brought him recognition. Admiration would have been too much to ask, for even in the realm of truth, admiration is reserved for older scholars on whom it depends whether or not one gets that professorship or professorial chair. Strictly speaking, he had remained "promising," which is what, in the Republic of Learning, they call the republicans, that is, those who imagine that they should give all their energies to their work rather than reserve a large part of them for getting ahead. They forget that individual achievement is limited, while on the other hand everybody wants to get ahead, and they neglect the social duty of climbing, which means beginning as a climber so as to become in turn a prop and stay to other climbers on the way up.

And one day Ulrich stopped wanting to be promising. The time had come when people were starting to speak of genius on the soccer field or in the boxing ring, although there would still be at most only one genius of a halfback or great tennis-court tactician for every ten or so explorers, tenors, or writers of genius who cropped up in the papers. The new spirit was not yet quite sure of itself. But just then Ulrich suddenly read somewhere, like a premonitory breath of ripening summer, the expression "the racehorse of genius." It stood in the report of a sensational racing success, and the author was probably not aware of the full magnitude of the inspiration his pen owed to the communal spirit. But Ulrich instantly grasped the fateful connection between his entire career and this genius among racehorses. For the horse has, of course, always been sacred to the cavalry, and as a youth Ulrich had hardly ever heard talk in barracks of anything but horses and women. He had fled from this to become a great man, only to find that when as the result of his varied exertions he perhaps could have felt within reach of his goal, the horse had beaten him to it.

No doubt this has a certain temporal justification, since it is not so very long ago that our idea of an admirable masculine spirit was exemplified by a person whose courage was moral courage, whose strength was the strength of a conviction, whose steadfastness was of the heart and of virtue, and who regarded speed as childish, feinting as not permissible, and agility and verve as contrary to dignity. Ultimately no such person could be found alive, except on the faculty of prep schools and in all sorts of literary pronouncements; he had become an ideological phantasm, and life had to seek a new image of manliness. As it looked around, it found that the tricks and dodges of an inventive mind working on logical calculations do not really differ all that much from the fighting moves of a well-trained body. There is a general fighting ability that is made cold and calculating by obstacles and openings, whether one is trained to search out the vulnerable spot in a problem or in a bodily opponent. A psychotechnical analysis of a great thinker and a champion boxer would probably show their cunning, courage, precision and technique, and the speed of their reactions in their respective fields to be the same. It is probably a safe assumption that the qualities and skills by which they succeed do not differ from those of a famous steeplechaser—for one should never underestimate how many major qualities are bought into play in clearing a hedge. But on top of this, a horse and a boxer have an advantage over a great mind in that their performance and rank can be objectively measured, so that the best of them is really acknowledged as the best. This is why sports and strictly objective criteria have deservedly come to the forefront, displacing such obsolete concepts as genius and human greatness.

As for Ulrich, he must even be credited with being a few years ahead of his time on this point. He had conducted his scientific work in precisely this spirit of improving the record by a victory, an inch or a pound. He meant his mind to prove itself keen and strong, and it had performed the work of the strong. This pleasure in the power of the mind was a state of expectancy, a warlike game, a kind of vague masterful claim on the future. What this power would enable him to accomplish was an open question; he could do everything with it or nothing, become a savior of mankind or a criminal. This is probably the nature of the mind that provides the world of machines and discoveries its constant flow of new supplies. Ulrich had regarded science as a preparation, a toughening, and a kind of training. If it turned out that this way of thinking was too dry, hard, narrow, and blinkered, it would have to be accepted, like the grimace of extreme exertion and tension that show on the face when the body and the will are being pushed to great accomplishments. He had for years gladly endured spiritual hardship. He despised those who could not follow Nietzsche's dictum to "let the soul starve for the truth's sake," those who turn back, the fainthearted, the softheaded who comfort their souls with spiritual nonsense and feed it—because reason allegedly gives it stones instead of bread—on religious, metaphysical, and fictitious pap, like rolls soaked in milk. It was his opinion that in this century, together with everything human, one was on an expedition, which required as a matter of pride that one cut off all useless questions with a "not yet," and that life be conducted on a provisional basis, but with awareness of the goal to be reached by those who will come after. The fact is, science has developed a concept of hard, sober intelligence that makes the old metaphysical and moral ideas of the human race simply intolerable, even though all it has to put in their place is the hope that a distant day will come when a race of intellectual conquerors will descend into the valleys of spiritual fruitfulness.

But this works only so long as the eye is not forced to abandon visionary distance for present nearness, or made to read a statement that in the meantime a racehorse has become a genius. The next morning Ulrich got out of bed on his left foot and fished halfheartedly for his slipper with his right. That had been in another city and street from where he was now, but only a few weeks ago. On the brown, gleaming asphalt under his windows cars were already speeding past. The pure morning air was filling up with the sourness of the day, and as the milky light filtered through the curtains it seemed to him unspeakably absurd to start bending his naked body forward and backward as usual, to strain his abdominal muscles to push it up off the ground and lower it again, and finally batter away at a punching bag with his fists, as so many people do at this hour before going to the office. One hour daily is a twelfth of a day's conscious life, enough to keep a trained body in the condition of a panther alert for any adventure; but this hour is sacrificed for a senseless expectation, because the adventures worthy of such preparation never come along. The same is true of love, for which people get prepared in the most monstrous fashion. Finally, Ulrich realized that even in science he was like a man who has climbed one mountain range after another without ever seeing a goal. He had now acquired bits and pieces of a new way to think and feel, but the glimpse of the New, so vivid at first, had been lost amid the ever-proliferating details, and if he had once thought that he was drinking from the fountain of life, he had now drained almost all his expectations to the last drop. At this point he quit, right in the middle of an important and promising piece of work. He now saw his colleagues partly as relentless, obsessive public prosecutors and security chiefs of logic, and partly as opium eaters, addicts of some strange pale drug that filled their world with visions of numbers and abstract relations. "God help me," he thought, "surely I never could have meant to spend all my life as a mathematician?"

But what had he really meant to do? At this point he could have turned only to philosophy. But the condition philosophy found itself in at the time reminded him of the oxhide being cut into strips in the story of Dido, even as it remained highly doubtful that these strips would ever measure out a kingdom, and what was new in philosophy resembled what he had been doing himself and held no attraction for him. All he could say was that he now felt further removed from what he had really wanted to be than he had in his youth, if indeed he had ever known what it was. With wonderful clarity he saw in himself all the abilities and qualities favored by his time—except for the ability to earn his living, which was not necessary—but he had lost the capacity to apply them. And since, now that genius is attributed to soccer players and horses, a man can save himself only by the use he makes of genius, he resolved to take a year's leave of absence from his life in order to seek an appropriate application for his abilities.

14

BOYHOOD FRIENDS

Since his return, Ulrich had already been a few times to see his friends Walter and Clarisse, for these two had not left town, although it was summer, and he had not seen them for a number of years. Whenever he got there, they were playing the piano together. It was understood that they would take no notice of him until they had finished the piece; this time it was Beethoven's jubilant "Ode to Joy." The millions sank, as Nietzsche describes it, awestruck in the dust; hostile boundaries shattered, the gospel of world harmony reconciled and unified the sundered; they had unlearned walking and talking and were about to fly off, dancing, into the air. Faces flushed, bodies hunched, their heads jerked up and down while splayed claws banged away at the mass of sound rearing up under them. Something unfathomable was going on: a balloon, wavering in outline as it filled up with hot emotion, was swelling to the bursting point, and from the excited fingertips, the nervously wrinkling foreheads, the twitching bodies, again and again surges of fresh feeling poured into this awesome private tumult. How often they had been through this!

Ulrich could never stand this piano, always open and savagely baring its teeth, this fat-lipped, short-legged idol, a cross between a dachshund and a bulldog, that had taken over his friends' lives even as far as the pictures on their walls and the spindly design of their arty reproduction furniture; even the fact that there was no live-in maid, but only a woman who came in daily to cook and clean, was part of it. Beyond the windows of this household the slopes of vineyards with clumps of old trees and crooked shacks rose as far as the sweeping forests beyond; but close in, everything was untidy, bare, scattered, and corroded, as it is wherever the edges of big cities push forward into the countryside. The arc that spanned such a foreground and the lovely distance was created by the instrument; gleaming black, it sent fiery pillars of tenderness and heroism out through the walls, even if these pillars, pulverized into a fine ash of sound, collapsed only a hundred yards away without ever reaching the hillside with the fir trees where the tavern stood halfway up the path leading to the forest. But the house was able to make the piano resound, forming one of those megaphones through which the soul cries into the cosmos like a rutting stag, answered only by the same, competing cries of thousands of other lonely souls roaring into the cosmos. Ulrich's strong position in this household rested on his insistence that music represented a failure of the will and a confusion of the mind; he spoke of it with less respect than he actually felt. Since at that time music was, for Walter and Clarisse, the source of their keenest hope and anxiety, they partly despised him for his attitude and partly revered him as an evil spirit.

When they had finished this time, Walter did not move but sat there, drooping, drained and forlorn on his half-turned piano stool, but Clarisse got up and gave the intruder a lively greeting. Her hands and face were still twitching with the electric charge of the music, and her smile forced its way through a tension between ecstasy and disgust.

"Frog Prince!" she said, with a nod backward at the music or Walter. Ulrich felt the elastic bond between himself and Clarisse tense again. On his last visit she had told him of a terrible dream in which a slippery creature, big-belly soft, tender and gruesome, had tried to overpower her in her sleep, and this huge frog symbolized Walter's music. The two of them had few secrets from Ulrich. Now, having barely said hello to Ulrich, Clarisse turned away from him and quickly back to Walter, again uttered her war cry—"Frog Prince!"— which Walter evidently did not understand, and, her hands still trembling from the music, gave a pained and painfully wild pull at her husband's hair. He made an amiably puzzled face and came back one step closer out of the slippery void of the music.

Then Clarisse and Ulrich took a walk through the slanting arrows of the evening sun, without Walter; he remained behind at the piano. Clarisse said:

"The ability to fend off harm is the test of vitality. The spent is drawn to its own destruction. What do you think? Nietzsche maintains it's a sign of weakness for an artist to be overly concerned about the morality of his art." She had sat down on a little hummock.

Ulrich shrugged. When Clarisse married his boyhood friend three years ago she was twenty-two, and it was he himself who had given her Nietzsche's works as a wedding present. He smiled, saying:

"If I were Walter, I'd challenge Nietzsche to a duel."

Clarisse's slender, hovering back, in delicate lines under her dress, stretched like a bow; her face, too, was tense with violent emotion; she kept it anxiously averted from her friend.

"You are still both maidenly and heroic at the same time," Ulrich added. It might or might not have been a question, a bit of a joke, but there was also a touch of affectionate admiration in his words. Clarisse did not quite understand what he meant, but the two words, which she had heard from him before, bored into her like a flaming arrow into a thatched roof.

Intermittent waves of random churning sounds reached them. Ulrich knew that Clarisse refused her body to Walter for weeks at a time when he played Wagner. He played Wagner anyway, with a bad conscience; like a boyhood vice.

Clarisse would have liked to ask Ulrich how much he knew of this: Walter could never keep anything to himself. But she was ashamed to ask. So she finally said something quite different to Ulrich, who had sat down on a small nearby mound.

"You don't care about Walter," she said. "You're not really his friend." It sounded like a challenge, though she said it with a laugh.

Ulrich gave her an unexpected answer. "We're just boyhood friends. You were still a child, Clarisse, when the two of us were already showing the unmistakable signs of a fading schoolboy friendship. Countless years ago we admired each other, and now we mistrust each other with intimate understanding. Each of us would like to shake off the painful sense of having once mistaken himself for the other, so now we perform the mutual service of a pitilessly honest distorting mirror."

"So you don't think he will ever amount to anything?" Clarisse asked.

"There is no second such example of inevitability as that offered by a gifted young man narrowing himself down into an ordinary young man, not as the result of any blow of fate but through a kind of preordained shrinkage."

Clarisse closed her lips firmly. The old youthful pact between them, that conviction should come before consideration, made her heart beat high, but the truth still hurt. Music! The sounds continued to churn toward them. She listened. Now, in their silence, the seething of the piano was distinctly audible; if they listened without paying attention, the sound might seem to be boiling upward out of the grassy hummocks, like Brünnhilde's flickering flames.

It would have been hard to say what Walter really was. Even today he was an engaging person with richly expressive eyes, no doubt about it, although he was already over thirty-four and had been for some time holding down a government job vaguely concerned with the fine arts. His father had got him this berth in the civil service, threatening to stop his allowance if he did not accept it. Walter was actually a painter. While studying the history of art at the university, he had worked in a painting class at the academy; afterward he had lived for a time in a studio. He had still been a painter when he moved with Clarisse into this house under the open sky, shortly after they were married. But now he seemed to be a musician again, and in the course of his ten years in love he had sometimes been the one, sometimes the other, and a poet as well, during a period when he had edited a literary publication with marriage in mind; he had then taken a job with a theatrical concern but had dropped it after a few weeks; sometime later, again in order to be able to marry, he became the conductor of a theater orchestra, saw the impossibility of this, too, after six months, and became a drawing master, a music critic, a recluse, and many other things until his father and his future father-in-law, broad-minded as they were, could no longer take it. Such older people were accustomed to say that he simply lacked willpower, but it would have been equally valid to call him a lifelong, many-sided dilettante, and it was quite remarkable that there were always authorities in the worlds of music, painting, and literature who expressed enthusiastic views about Walter's future. In Ulrich's life, by contrast, even though he had a few undeniably noteworthy achievements to his credit, it had never happened that someone came up to him and said: "You are the man I have always been looking for, the man my friends are waiting for." In Walter's life this had happened every three months. Even though these were not necessarily the most authoritative people in the field, they all had some influence, a promising idea, projects under way, jobs open, friendships, connections, which they placed at the service of the Walter they had discovered, whose life as a result took such a colorful zigzag course. He had an air about him that seemed to matter more than any specific achievement. Perhaps he had a particular genius for passing as a genius. If this is dilettantism, then the intellectual life of the German-speaking world rests largely upon dilettantism, for this is a talent found in every degree up to the level of those who really *are* highly gifted, in whom it usually seems, to all appearances, to be missing.

Walter even had the gift of seeing through all this. While he was, naturally, as ready as the next person to take credit for his successes, his knack for being borne upward with such ease by every lucky chance had always troubled him as a terrifying sign that he was a lightweight. As often as he moved on to new activities and new people, he did it not simply from instability but in great inner turmoil, driven by anxiety that he had to move on to safeguard his spiritual integrity before he took root where the ground was already threatening to give way under him. His life had been a series of convulsive experiences from which emerged the heroic struggle of a soul resisting all compromise, never suspecting that in this way it was only creating its own dividedness. For all the time he was suffering and struggling for his intellectual integrity, as befits a genius, and investing all he had in his talent, which was not quite a great talent, his fate had silently led him in an inward full circle back to nothing. He had at long last reached the point where no further obstacles stood in his way. The quiet, secluded, semi-scholarly job that sheltered him from the corruptions of the art market gave him all the time and independence he needed to listen exclusively to his inner call. The woman he loved was his, so there were no thorns in his heart. The house "on the brink of solitude" they had taken after they married could not have been more suitable for creative work. But now that there was no longer anything left to be overcome, the unexpected happened: the works promised for so long by the greatness of his mind failed to materialize. Walter seemed no longer able to work. He hid things and destroyed things; he locked himself in every morning, and every afternoon when he came home; he went for long walks, with his sketchbook shut; but the little that came of all this he never showed to anyone, or else tore it up. He had a hundred different reasons for this. His views also underwent a conspicuous change at this time. He

no longer spoke of "art of our time" and "the art of the future"—
concepts Clarisse had associated with him since she was fifteen, but
drew a line somewhere—in music it might be with Bach, in literature
with Stifter, in painting with Ingres—and declared that whatever
came later was bombastic, degenerate, oversubtle, or dissolute. With
mounting vehemence he insisted that in a time so poisoned in its intellectual roots as the present, a pure talent must abstain from creation altogether. But although such stringent pronouncements came
from his mouth, he was betrayed by the sounds of Wagner, which
began to penetrate the walls of his room more and more often as
soon as he shut himself in—the music he had once taught Clarisse to
despise as the epitome of a philistine, bombastic, degenerate era but
to which he was now addicted as to a thickly brewed, hot, benumbing
drug.

Clarisse fought against this. She hated Wagner, if for nothing else
for his velvet jacket and beret. She was the daughter of a painter
world-famous for his stage designs. She had spent her childhood in
the realm of stage sets and greasepaint; amid three different kinds of
art jargon—of the theater, the opera, and the painter's studio; surrounded by velvets, carpets, genius, panther skins, knickknacks, peacock feathers, chests, and lutes. She had come to loathe from the
depths of her soul everything voluptuary in art, and was drawn to
everything lean and austere, whether it was the metageometry of the
new atonal music or the clarified will of classic form, stripped of its
skin, like a muscle about to be dissected. It was Walter who had first
brought this new gospel into her virginal captivity. She called him
"my prince of light," and even when she was still a child, she and
Walter had vowed to each other not to marry until he had become a
king. The story of his various metamorphoses and projects was also a
chronicle of infinite sufferings and raptures, for all of which she was
to be the trophy. Clarisse was not as gifted as Walter; she had always
felt it. But she saw genius as a question of willpower. With ferocious
energy she set out to make the study of music her own. It was not
impossible that she was completely unmusical, but she had ten
sinewy fingers and resolution; she practiced for days on end and
drove her ten fingers like ten scrawny oxen trying to tear some overwhelming weight out of the ground. She attacked painting in the

same fashion. She had considered Walter a genius since she was fifteen, because she had always intended to marry only a genius. She would not let him fail her in this, and when she realized that he was failing she put up a frantic struggle against the suffocating, slow change in the atmosphere of their life. It was at just this point that Walter could have used some human warmth, and when his helplessness tormented him he would clutch at her like a baby wanting milk and sleep; but Clarisse's small, nervous body was not maternal. She felt abused by a parasite trying to ensconce itself in her flesh, and she refused herself to him. She scoffed at the steamy laundry warmth in which he sought to be comforted. It is possible that that was cruel, but she wanted to be the wife of a great man and was wrestling with destiny.

Ulrich had offered Clarisse a cigarette. What more could he have said, after so brusquely telling her what he thought? The smoke from their cigarettes drifted up the rays of the evening sun and mingled some distance away from them.

How much does Ulrich know about this? Clarisse wondered on her hummock. Anyway, what can he possibly know about such struggles? She remembered how Walter's face fell apart with pain, almost to extinction, when the agonies of music and lust beset him and her resistance left him no way out. No, she decided, Ulrich couldn't know anything of their monstrous love-game on the Himalayas of love, contempt, fear, and the obligations of the heights. She had no great opinion of mathematics and had never considered Ulrich to be as talented as Walter. He was clever, he was logical, he knew a lot— but was that any better than barbarism? She had to admit that his tennis used to be incomparably better than Walter's, and she could remember sometimes watching his ruthless drives with a passionate feeling of "he'll get what he wants" such as she had never felt about Walter's painting, music, or ideas. Now she thought: "What if he knows all about us and just isn't saying anything?" Only a moment ago he had, after all, distinctly alluded to her heroism. The silence between them had now become strangely exciting.

But Ulrich was thinking: "How nice Clarisse was ten years ago— half a child, blazing with faith in the future of the three of us." She had been actually unpleasant to him only once, when she and Walter had just got married and she had displayed that unattractive selfishness-for-two that so often makes young women who are ambitiously in love with their husbands so insufferable to other men. "That's got a lot better since," he thought.

15

CULTURAL REVOLUTION

Walter and he had been young in that now-forgotten era just after the turn of the last century, when many people imagined that the century was young too.

The just-buried century in Austria could not be said to have covered itself with glory during its second half. It had been clever in technology, business, and science, but beyond these focal points of its energy it was stagnant and treacherous as a swamp. It had painted like the Old Masters, written like Goethe and Schiller, and built its houses in the style of the Gothic and the Renaissance. The demands of the ideal ruled like a police headquarters over all expressions of life. But thanks to the unwritten law that allows mankind no imitation without tying it to an exaggeration, everything was produced with a degree of craftsmanship the admired prototypes could never have achieved, traces of which can still be seen today in our streets and museums; and—relevant or not—the women of the period, who were as chaste as they were shy, had to wear dresses that covered them from the ears down to the ground while showing off a billowing bosom and a voluptuous behind. For the rest, there is no part of the past we know so little about, for all sorts of reasons, as the three to five decades between our own twentieth year and the twentieth year of our fathers. So it may be useful to be reminded that in bad periods the most appalling buildings and poems are constructed on principles just as fine as in good periods; that all the people involved in destroying the achievements of a preceding good epoch feel they are improving on them; and that the bloodless youth of such inferior periods take just as much pride in their young blood as do the new generations of all other eras.

And each time it is like a miracle when after such a shallow, fading period all at once there comes a small upward surge. Suddenly, out of the becalmed mentality of the nineteenth century's last two decades, an invigorating fever rose all over Europe. No one knew exactly what was in the making; nobody could have said whether it was to be a new art, a new humanity, a new morality, or perhaps a reshuffling of society. So everyone said what he pleased about it. But everywhere people were suddenly standing up to struggle against the old order. Everywhere the right man suddenly appeared in the right place and—this is so important!—enterprising men of action joined forces with enterprising men of intellect. Talents of a kind that had previously been stifled or had never taken part in public life suddenly came to the fore. They were as different from each other as could be, and could not have been more contradictory in their aims. There were those who loved the overman and those who loved the underman, there were health cults and sun cults and the cults of consumptive maidens; there was enthusiasm for the hero worshipers and for the believers in the Common Man; people were devout and skeptical, naturalistic and mannered, robust and morbid; they dreamed of old tree-lined avenues in palace parks, autumnal gardens, glassy ponds, gems, hashish, disease, and demonism, but also of prairies, immense horizons, forges and rolling mills, naked wrestlers, slave uprisings, early man, and the smashing of society. These were certainly opposing and widely varying battle cries, but uttered in the same breath. An analysis of that epoch might produce some such nonsense as a square circle trying to consist of wooden iron, but in reality it all blended into shimmering sense. This illusion, embodied in the magical date of the turn of the century, was so powerful that it made some people hurl themselves with zeal at the new, still-unused century, while others chose one last quick fling in the old one, as one runs riot in a house one absolutely has to move out of, without anyone feeling much of a difference between these two attitudes.

If one does not want to, there is no need to make too much of this bygone "movement." It really affected only that thin, unstable layer of humanity, the intellectuals, who are unanimously despised by all those who rejoice in impregnable views, no matter how divergent from one another (the kind of people who are back in the saddle today, thank God); the general population was not involved. Still, even though it did not become a historical event, it was an eventlet, and the two friends, Walter and Ulrich, in their early youth had just caught its afterglow. Something went through the thicket of beliefs in those days like a single wind bending many trees—a spirit of heresy and reform, the blessed sense of an arising and going forth, a mini-renaissance and -reformation, such as only the best of times experience; whoever entered the world then felt, at the first corner, the breath of this spirit on his cheek.

16

A MYSTERIOUS MALADY OF THE TIMES

So they had actually been two young men, not so long ago—Ulrich thought when he was alone again—who, oddly enough, not only had the most profound insights before anyone else did, but even had them simultaneously, for one of them had only to open his mouth to say something new to find that the other had been making the same tremendous discovery. There is something special about youthful friendships: they are like an egg that senses in its yolk its glorious future as a bird, even while it presents to the world only a rather expressionless egg shape indistinguishable from any other. He vividly remembered the boy's and student's room where they had met whenever he returned for a few weeks from his first outings into the world: Walter's desk, covered with drawings, notes, and sheets of music, like the early rays of the glory of a famous man's future; facing it, the narrow bookcase where Walter sometimes stood in his ardor like Sebastian at the stake, the lamplight on his beautiful hair, which Ulrich had always secretly admired. Nietzsche, Peter Altenberg, Dostoyevsky or whoever they had just been reading had to resign

themselves to being left lying on the floor or the bed when they had
served their purpose and the flood of talk would not suffer the petty
interruption of putting a book tidily back in place. The arrogance of
the young, who find the greatest minds just good enough to serve
their own occasions, now seemed to Ulrich strangely endearing. He
tried to remember these conversations. It was like reaching on awakening for the last vanishing, dreamlike thoughts of sleep. And he
thought, in mild astonishment: When we were assertive in those
days, the point was not to be right—it was to assert ourselves! A
young man needs to shine, far more than he needs to see something
in the light. He now felt the memory of the feeling of being young,
that hovering on rays of light, as an aching loss.

It seemed to Ulrich that with the beginning of his adult life a general lull had set in, a gradual running down, in spite of occasional
eddies of energy that came and went, to an ever more listless, erratic
rhythm. It was very hard to say what this change consisted of. Were
there suddenly fewer great men? Far from it! And besides, they don't
matter; the greatness of an era does not depend on them. The intellectually lackluster 1860s and 1880s, for instance, could no more prevent the rise of a Nietzsche or a Hebbel than either of these men
could raise the intellectual level of his contemporaries. Had life in
general reached a standstill? No, it had become more powerful!
Were there more paralyzing contradictions than before? There could
hardly be more! Had the past not known any absurdities? Heaps!
Just between ourselves: people threw their support to the weak and
ignored the strong; sometimes blockheads played leading roles while
brilliant men played the part of eccentrics; the good Germanic citizen, untroubled by history's labor pains, which he dismissed as decadent and morbid excrescences, went on reading his family magazines
and visited the crystal palaces and academies in vastly greater numbers than he did the avant-garde exhibitions. Least of all did the political world pay attention to the New Men's views and publications;
and the great public institutions resisted everything new as if surrounded by a *cordon sanitaire* against the plague. Could one not say,
in fact, that things have got better since then? Men who once merely
headed minor sects have become aged celebrities; publishers and art
dealers have become rich; new movements are constantly being
started; everybody attends both the academic and the avant-garde

shows, and even the avant-garde of the avant-garde; the family magazines have bobbed their hair; politicians like to sound off on the cultural arts, and newspapers make literary history. So what has been
lost?

Something imponderable. An omen. An illusion. As when a magnet releases iron filings and they fall in confusion again. As when a
ball of string comes undone. As when a tension slackens. As when an
orchestra begins to play out of tune. No details could be adduced
that would not also have been possible before, but all the relationships had shifted a little. Ideas whose currency had once been lean
grew fat. Persons who would before never have been taken seriously
became famous. Harshness mellowed, separations fused, intransi-
gents made concessions to popularity, tastes already formed relapsed
into uncertainties. Sharp boundaries everywhere became blurred
and some new, indefinable ability to form alliances brought new people and new ideas to the top. Not that these people and new ideas were
bad, not at all; it was only that a little too much of the bad was mixed
with the good, of error with truth, of accommodation with meaning.
There even seemed to be a privileged proportion of this mixture that
got furthest on in the world; just the right pinch of makeshift to bring
out the genius in genius and make talent look like a white hope, as a
pinch of chicory, according to some people, brings out the right coffee flavor in coffee. Suddenly all the prominent and important positions in the intellectual world were filled by such people, and all
decisions went their way. There is nothing one can hold responsible
for this, nor can one say how it all came about. There are no persons
or ideas or specific phenomena that one can fight against. There is no
lack of talent or goodwill or even of strong personalities. There is just
something missing in everything, though you can't put your finger on
it, as if there had been a change in the blood or in the air; a mysterious disease has eaten away the previous period's seeds of genius, but
everything sparkles with novelty, and finally one has no way of knowing whether the world has really grown worse, or oneself merely
older. At this point a new era has definitively arrived.

So the times had changed, like a day that begins radiantly blue and
then by degrees clouds over, without having the kindness to wait for
Ulrich. He evened the score by holding the cause of these mysterious
changes that made up the disease eating away genius to be simple,

common stupidity. By no means in an insulting sense. For if stupidity, seen from within, did not so much resemble talent as possess the ability to be mistaken for it, and if it did not outwardly resemble progress, genius, hope, and improvement, the chances are that no one would want to be stupid, and so there would be no stupidity. Or fighting it would at least be easy. Unfortunately, stupidity has something uncommonly endearing and natural about it. If one finds that a reproduction, for instance, seems more of an artistic feat than a hand-painted original, well, there is a certain truth in that, and it is easier to prove than that van Gogh was a great artist. It is also easy and profitable to be a more powerful playwright than Shakespeare or a less uneven storyteller than Goethe, and a solid commonplace always contains more humanity than a new discovery. There is, in short, no great idea that stupidity could not put to its own uses; it can move in all directions, and put on all the guises of truth. The truth, by comparison, has only one appearance and only one path, and is always at a disadvantage.

But after a while Ulrich had a curious notion in this connection. He imagined that the great churchman and thinker Thomas Aquinas (d. 1274), after taking infinite pains to put the ideas of his own time in the best possible order, had then continued through history to go even deeper to the bottom of things, and had just finished. Now, still young by special dispensation, he stepped out of his arched doorway with many folios under his arm, and an electric trolley shot right past his nose. Ulrich chuckled at the dumbstruck amazement on the face of the *doctor universalis*, as the past had called the celebrated Thomas.

A motorcyclist came up the empty street, thundering up the perspective bow-armed and bow-legged. His face had the solemn self-importance of a howling child. It reminded Ulrich of a photo he had seen a few days ago in a magazine of a famous woman tennis player poised on tiptoe, one leg exposed to above the garter, the other flung up toward her head as she reached for a high ball with her racket, on her face the expression of an English governess. In the same issue there was also a picture of a champion swimmer being massaged after a contest. Two women dressed in street clothes, one at the swimmer's feet, the other at her head, were solemnly looking down at her as she lay on a bed, naked on her back, one knee drawn up in a posture of sexual abandon, the masseur standing alongside resting his hands on it. He wore a doctor's gown and gazed out of the picture as though this female flesh had been skinned and hung on a meat hook. Such were the things people were beginning to see at the time, and somehow they had to be acknowledged, as one acknowledges the presence of skyscrapers and electricity. A man can't be angry at his own time without suffering some damage, Ulrich felt. Ulrich was also always ready to love all these manifestations of life. But he could never bring himself to love them wholeheartedly, as one's general sense of social well-being requires. For a long time now a hint of aversion had lain on everything he did and experienced, a shadow of impotence and loneliness, an all-encompassing distaste for which he could not find the complementary inclination. He felt at times as though he had been born with a talent for which there was at present no objective.

17

EFFECT OF A MAN WITHOUT QUALITIES
ON A MAN WITH QUALITIES

While Ulrich and Clarisse were talking, they did not notice that the music in the house behind them broke off now and again. At those moments Walter had gone to the window. He could not see them, but felt that they were just beyond his field of vision. Jealousy tormented him. The cheap intoxicant of sluggishly sensual music was luring him back to the piano. It lay behind him, open like a bed rumpled by a sleeper resisting consciousness in order to avoid facing reality. He was racked by the jealousy of a paralyzed man who can sense how the healthy walk, yet he could not bring himself to join them, for his anguish offered no possibility of defending himself against them.

When Walter got up in the morning and had to rush to the office, when he talked with people during the day and rode home among them in the afternoon, he felt he was an important person, called upon to do great things. He believed then that he saw things differently: he was moved where others passed by unresponsively, and where others reached for a thing without thinking, for him the very act of moving his own arm was fraught with spiritual adventure, or else it was paralyzed in loving contemplation of itself. He was sensitive, and his feelings were constantly agitated by brooding, depressions, billowing ups and downs; he was never indifferent, always seeing joy or misery in everything, so he always had something exciting to think about. Such people exercise an unusual attraction, because the moral flaw in which they incessantly live communicates itself to others. Everything in their conversation takes on a personal significance, and one feels free in their company to be constantly preoccupied with oneself, so that they provide a pleasure otherwise obtainable only from an analyst or therapist for a fee, with the further difference that with the psychiatrist one feels sick, while Walter helped a person to feel very important for reasons that had previously escaped one's attention. With this talent for encouraging self-preoccupation, he had in fact conquered Clarisse and in time driven all his rivals from the field. Since everything became for him an ethical movement, he could hold forth convincingly on the immorality of ornament, the hygiene of simple forms, and the beery fumes of Wagner's music, in accord with the new taste in the arts, terrorizing even his future father-in-law, whose painter's brain was like a peacock's tail unfurled. So there could be no question that Walter had his successes to look back on.

And yet, when he got home full of impressions and plans, ripe and new as perhaps never before, a demoralizing change took place in him. Merely putting a canvas on the easel or a sheet of paper on the table was the sign of a terrible flight from his heart. His head remained clear, and the plan inside it hovered as if in a very transparent and distinct atmosphere; indeed, the plan split and became two or more plans, all ready to compete for supremacy—but the connection between his head and the first movements needed to carry it out seemed severed. Walter could not even make up his mind to lift a finger. He simply did not get up from where he happened to be sitting, and his thoughts slid away from the task he had set himself like snow evaporating as it falls. He didn't know where the time went, but all of a sudden it was evening, and since after several such experiences he had learned to start dreading them on his way home, whole series of weeks began to slip, and passed away like a troubled half-sleep. Slowed down by a sense of hopelessness in all his decisions and movements, he suffered from bitter sadness, and his incapacity solidified into a pain that often sat like a nosebleed behind his forehead the moment he tried to make up his mind to do something. Walter was fearful, and the symptoms he recognized in himself not only hampered him in his work but also filled him with anxiety, for they were apparently so far beyond his control that they often gave him the impression of an incipient mental breakdown.

But as his condition had grown steadily worse in the course of the last year, he found a miraculous refuge in a thought he had never valued enough before. The idea was none other than that the Europe in which he was forced to live was hopelessly decadent. During ages in which things seem to be going well outwardly, while inwardly they undergo the kind of regression that may be the fate of all things, including cultural development—unless special efforts are made to keep them supplied with new ideas—the obvious question was, presumably, what one could do about it. But the tangle of clever, stupid, vulgar, and beautiful is at such times so particularly dense and intricate that many people obviously find it easier to believe that there is something occult at the root of things, and proclaim the fated fall of one thing or another that eludes precise definition and is portentously vague. It hardly matters whether the doomed thing is the human race, vegetarianism, or the soul; all that a healthy pessimism needs is merely something inescapable to hold on to. Even Walter, who in better days used to be able to laugh at such doctrines, soon discovered their advantages once he began to try them out. Instead of *his* feeling bad and unable to work, it was now the times that were sick, while he was fine. His life, which had come to nothing, was now, all at once, tremendously accounted for, justified on a world-historical scale that was worthy of him, so that picking up a pen or pencil and laying it down again virtually took on the aura of a great sacrifice.

With all this, however, Walter still had to struggle with himself, and Clarisse kept on tormenting him. She turned a deaf ear to his critical discussions of the times; with her it was genius or nothing.

What it was she did not know, but whenever the subject came up her whole body began to tremble and tense up. "You either feel it or you don't" was all the proof she could offer. For him she always remained the same cruel little fifteen-year-old girl. She had never quite understood his way of feeling, nor could he ever control her. But cold and hard as she was, and then again so spirited, with her ethereal, flaming will, she had a mysterious ability to influence him, as though shocks were coming through her from a direction that could not be fitted into the three dimensions of space. This influence sometimes bordered on the uncanny. He felt it most keenly when they played the piano together. Clarisse's playing was hard and colorless, prompted by stirrings in her that he did not share, and that frightened him as they reached him when their bodies glowed till the soul burned through. Something indefinable then tore itself loose inside her and threatened to fly away with her spirit. It came out of some secret hollow in her being that had to be anxiously kept shut up tight. He had no idea what made him feel this, or what it was, but it tortured him with an unutterable fear and the need to do something decisive against it, which he could not do because no one but him noticed anything.

As he stood at the window watching Clarisse coming back alone, he dimly knew that he would again not be able to resist the urge to make disparaging remarks about Ulrich. Ulrich had returned from abroad at a bad time. He was bad for Clarisse. He ruthlessly exacerbated something inside Clarisse that Walter dared not touch: the cavern of disaster, the pitiful, the sick, the fatal genius in her, the secret empty space where something was tearing at chains that might someday give way. Now she had entered and was standing bareheaded before him, sunhat in hand, and he looked at her. Her eyes were mocking, tender, clear—perhaps a little too clear. Sometimes he felt that she simply had a certain strength he lacked. Even when she was a child he had felt her as a thorn that would never let him find peace, and evidently he had never wanted her to be otherwise; perhaps this was the secret of his life, which the other two did not understand.

"How deeply we suffer," he thought. "I don't think it can happen often that two people love each other as deeply as we must."

And he began to speak without preamble: "I don't want to know what Ulo has been telling you, but I can tell you that the strength you marvel at in him is pure emptiness." Clarisse looked at the piano and smiled; he had involuntarily sat down again beside the open instrument. "It must be easy to feel heroic," he went on, "when one is naturally insensitive, and to think in miles when you've no idea what riches can be hidden in an inch!" They sometimes called him Ulo, his boyhood nickname, and he liked them for it, as one may keep a smiling respect for one's old nanny. "He's come to a dead end!" Walter added. "You don't see it, but don't imagine that I don't know him."

Clarisse had her doubts.

Walter said vehemently: "Today it's all decadence! A bottomless pit of intelligence! He is intelligent, I grant you that, but he knows nothing at all about the power of a soul in full possession of itself. What Goethe calls personality, what Goethe calls mobile order—those are things he doesn't have a clue about! 'This noble concept of power and restraint, of choice and law, of freedom and measure, mobile order . . .' " The poet's lines came in waves from his lips. Clarisse regarded these lips in amiable wonder, as though they had just let fly a pretty toy. Then she collected herself and interjected like a good little housewife: "Would you like a beer?" "Yes. Why not? Don't I always have one?" "Well, there is none in the house." "I wish you hadn't asked," Walter sighed. "I might never have thought of it."

And that was that, as far as Clarisse was concerned. But Walter had been thrown off the track and didn't know how to continue.

"Do you remember our conversation about the artist?" he asked tentatively.

"Which one?"

"The one we had a few days ago. I explained to you what a living principle of form in a person means. Don't you remember, I came to the conclusion that in the old days, instead of death and logical mechanization, blood and wisdom reigned?"

"No."

Walter was stymied; he groped, wavered. Suddenly he burst out: "He's a man without qualities!"

"What is that?" Clarisse asked, giggling.

"Nothing. That's just it, it's nothing."

But Clarisse found the phrase intriguing.

"There are millions of them nowadays," Walter declared. "It's the human type produced by our time!" He was pleased with the term he had hit upon so unexpectedly. As if he were starting a poem, he let the expression drive him on even before its meaning was clear to him. "Just look at him! What would you take him for? Does he look like a doctor, a businessman, a painter, or a diplomat?"

"He's none of those," Clarisse said dryly.

"Well, does he look like a mathematician?"

"I don't know—how should I know what a mathematician is supposed to look like?"

"You've hit the nail on the head! A mathematician looks like nothing at all—that is, he is likely to look intelligent in such a general way that there isn't a single specific thing to pin him down! Except for the Roman Catholic clergy, no one these days looks the way he should, because we use our heads even more impersonally than our hands. But mathematics is the absolute limit: it already knows as little about itself as future generations, feeding on energy pills instead of bread and meat, will be likely to know about meadows and young calves and chickens!"

Clarisse had meanwhile put their simple supper on the table, and Walter was already digging into it, which may have suggested the analogy to him. Clarisse was watching his lips. They reminded her of his late mother's. They were strong feminine lips that ate as if they were getting the housework done, and were topped off by a small clipped mustache. His eyes shone like freshly peeled chestnuts, even when he was merely looking for a piece of cheese on the platter. Although he was short, and flabby rather than delicate of build, he was a man of striking appearance, the kind who always seem to be standing in a good light. He now continued:

"His appearance gives no clue to what his profession might be, and yet he doesn't look like a man without a profession either. Consider what he's like: He always knows what to do. He knows how to gaze into a woman's eyes. He can put his mind to any question at any time. He can box. He is gifted, strong-willed, open-minded, fearless, tenacious, dashing, circumspect—why quibble, suppose we grant him all those qualities—yet he has none of them! They've made him what he is, they've set his course for him, and yet they don't belong to him. When he is angry, something in him laughs. When he is sad, he is up to something. When something moves him, he turns against it. He'll always see a good side to every bad action. What he thinks of any-thing will always depend on some possible context—nothing is, to him, what it is; everything is subject to change, in flux, part of a whole, of an infinite number of wholes presumably adding up to a superwhole that, however, he knows nothing about. So every answer he gives is only a partial answer, every feeling only an opinion, and he never cares *what* something is, only 'how' it is—some extraneous seasoning that somehow goes along with it, that's what interests him. I don't know whether I'm making myself clear—?"

"Quite clear," Clarisse said, "but I think that's all very nice of him."

Walter had unintentionally spoken with signs of growing dislike; his old boyhood sense of being weaker than his friend increased his jealousy. For although he was convinced that Ulrich had never really achieved anything beyond a few proofs of naked intellect and capac-ity, he could never shake off a secret sense of always having been Ulrich's physical inferior. The portrait he was sketching freed him, like bringing off a work of art, as if it were not his own doing at all but something that had begun as a mysterious inspiration, with word after word coming to him, while inwardly something dissolved with-out his being conscious of it. By the time he finished he had recog-nized that Ulrich stood for nothing but this state of dissolution that all present-day phenomena have.

"So you like it, do you?" he said, painfully surprised. "You can't be serious?"

Clarisse was chewing bread and soft cheese; she could only smile with her eyes.

"Oh well," Walter said, "I suppose we used to think that way our-selves, in the old days. But surely it can't be regarded as anything more than a preliminary phase? Such a man is not really a human being!"

Clarisse had swallowed her mouthful. "That's what he says him-self!" she affirmed.

"What does he say himself?"

"Oh, I don't know—that today everything is coming apart. Every-thing has come to a standstill, he says, not just him. But he doesn't take it as hard as you do. He once gave me a long talk about it: If you analyze a thousand people, you will find two dozen qualities, emotions, forms of development, types of structure and so on, which are what they all consist of. And if you do a chemical analysis of your body, all you get is water with a few dozen little heaps of matter swimming in it. The water rises inside us just as it does inside trees, and it forms the bodies of animals just as it forms the clouds. I think that's neatly put. But it doesn't help you to know what to say about yourself. Or what to do." Clarisse giggled. "So then I told him that you go fishing for days when you have time off, and lie around by the water."

"So what? I'd like to know if he could stand that for even ten minutes. But *human beings,*" Walter said firmly, "have been doing that for ten thousand years, staring up at the sky, feeling the warmth of the earth, without trying to analyze it any more than you'd analyze your own mother."

Clarisse couldn't help giggling again. "He says things have become more complicated meanwhile. Just as we swim in water, we also swim in a sea of fire, a storm of electricity, a firmament of magnetism, a swamp of warmth, and so on. It's just that we can't feel it. All that finally remains is formulas. What they mean in human terms is hard to say; that's all there is. I've forgotten whatever I learned about it at school, but I think that's what it amounts to. Anybody nowadays, says Ulrich, who wants to call the birds 'brothers,' like Saint Francis or you, can't do it so easily but must be prepared to be cast into a furnace, plunge into the earth through the wires of an electric trolley, or gurgle down the drain with the dishwater into the sewer."

"Oh sure, sure," Walter interrupted this report. "First, four elements are turned into several dozen, and finally we're left floating around on relationships, processes, on the dirty dishwater of processes and formulas, on something we can't even recognize as a thing, a process, a ghost of an idea, of a God-knows-what. Leaving no difference anymore between the sun and a kitchen match, or between your mouth at one end of the digestive tract and its other end either. Every thing has a hundred aspects, every aspect a hundred connections, and different feelings are attached to every one of them. The human brain has happily split things apart, but things have split the human heart too." He had leapt to his feet but remained standing behind the table.

"Clarisse," he said, "the man is a danger for you! Look, Clarisse,

what every one of us needs today more than anything else is simplicity, closeness to the earth, health—and yes, definitely, say what you
like, a child as well, because a child keeps us anchored to the ground.
Everything Ulo tells you is inhuman. I promise you I *have* the courage, when I come home, simply to have a cup of coffee with you,
listen to the birds, take a little walk, chat with a neighbor, and let the
day fade out quietly: that's human life!"

The tenderness of these sentiments had brought him slowly closer
to her. But the moment fatherish feelings could be detected raising
their gentle bass voice from afar, Clarisse balked. As he drew near,
her face became expressionless and tilted defensively.

When he had reached her side he radiated a gentle glow like a
good country stove. In this warm stream Clarisse wavered for a moment. Then she said: "Nothing doing, my dear!" She grabbed a
piece of bread and some cheese from the table and kissed him
quickly on the forehead. "I'm going out to see if there are any noctur-
nal butterflies."

"But Clarisse," Walter pleaded. "All the butterflies are gone this
time of year."

"Oh, you never can tell."

Nothing was left of her in the room but her laughter. With her
bread and cheese she roamed the meadows; it was a safe neighborhood and she needed no escort. Walter's tenderness collapsed like a
soufflé taken too soon from the oven. He heaved a deep sigh. Then
he hesitantly sat down again at the piano and struck a few keys. Willy-
nilly his playing turned into improvisations on themes from Wagner's
operas, and in the splashings of this dissolutely tumescent substance
he had refused in the days of his pride, his fingers cleared a path and
gurgled through the fields of sound. Let them hear it, far and wide!
The narcotic effect of this music paralyzed his spine and eased his
fate.

18

MOOSBRUGGER

The Moosbrugger case was currently much in the news. Moosbrugger was a carpenter, a big man with broad shoulders and no excess fat on him, a head of hair like brown lamb's wool, and good-natured strong paws. His face also expressed a good-natured strength and right-mindedness, qualities one would have smelled (had one not seen them) in the blunt, plain, dry workaday smell that belonged to this thirty-four-year-old man and came from the wood he worked with and a job that called as much for mindfulness as for exertion.

Anyone who came up against this face for the first time, a face blessed by God with every sign of goodness, would stop as if rooted to the spot, because Moosbrugger was usually flanked by two armed guards, his hands shackled with a small, strong steel chain, its grip held by one of his escorts.

When he noticed anyone staring at him a smile would pass over his broad, good-natured face with the unkempt hair and a mustache and the little chin tuft. He wore a short black jacket with light gray trousers, his bearing was military, and he planted his feet wide apart; but it was that smile that most fascinated the reporters in the courtroom. It might be an embarrassed smile or a cunning smile, an ironic, malicious, pained, mad, bloodthirsty, or terrifying smile: they were groping visibly for contradictory expressions and seemed to be searching desperately in that smile for something they obviously could find nowhere else in the man's entire upright appearance.

For Moosbrugger had killed a woman, a prostitute of the lowest type, in a horrifying manner. The reporters described in detail a knife wound in the throat from the larynx to the back of the neck, also the two stab wounds in the breast that penetrated the heart, and the two in the back on the left side, and how both breasts were sliced through so that they could almost be lifted off. The reporters had expressed their revulsion at this, but they did not stop until they had counted thirty-five stabs in the belly and explained the deep slash that reached from the navel to the sacrum, continuing up the back in numerous lesser cuts, while the throat showed marks of strangulation. From such horrors they could not find their way back to Moosbrugger's good-natured face, although they were themselves good-natured men who had nevertheless described what had happened in a factual, expert manner and, evidently, in breathless excitement. They hardly availed themselves of even the most obvious explanation, that the man before them was insane—for Moosbrugger had already been in various mental hospitals several times for similar crimes—even though a good reporter is very well informed on such questions these days; it looked as though they were still reluctant to give up the idea of the villain, to banish the incident from their own world into the world of the insane. Their attitude was matched by that of the psychiatrists, who had already declared him normal just as often as they had declared him not accountable for his actions. There was also the amazing fact that no sooner had they become known than Moosbrugger's pathological excesses were regarded as "finally something interesting for a change" by thousands of people who deplore the sensationalism of the press, from busy officeholders to fourteen-year-old sons to housewives befogged by their domestic cares. While these people of course sighed over such a monstrosity, they were nevertheless more deeply preoccupied with it than with their own life's work. Indeed, it might happen that a punctilious department head or bank manager would say to his sleepy wife at bedtime: "What would you do now if I were a Moosbrugger?"

When Ulrich first laid eyes on that face with its signs of being a child of God above handcuffs, he quickly turned around, slipped a few cigarettes to the sentry at the nearby court building, and asked him about the convoy that had apparently just left the gates; he was told . . . Well, anyway, this is how something of the sort must have happened in earlier times, since it is often reported this way, and Ulrich almost believed it himself; but the contemporary truth was that he had merely read all about it in the newspaper. It was to be a long time before he met Moosbrugger in person, and before that happened he caught sight of him only once during the trial. The probability of experiencing something unusual through the newspapers is much greater than that of experiencing it in person; in other words, the more important things take place today in the abstract, and the more trivial ones in real life.

What Ulrich learned of Moosbrugger's story in this fashion was more or less the following:

Moosbrugger had started out in life as a poor devil, an orphan shepherd boy in a hamlet so small that it did not even have a village street, and his poverty was such that he never dared speak to a girl. Girls were something he could always only look at, even later on when he became an apprentice and then when he was a traveling journeyman. One only need imagine what it must mean when something one craves as naturally as bread or water can only be looked at. After a while one desires it unnaturally. It walks past, skirts swaying around its calves. It climbs over a stile and is visible up to the knees. One looks into its eyes, and they turn opaque. One hears it laugh and turns around quickly, only to look into a face as immovably round as a hole in the ground into which a mouse has just slipped.

So it is understandable that Moosbrugger justified himself even after the first time he killed a girl by saying that he was constantly haunted by spirits calling to him day and night. They threw him out of bed when he slept and bothered him at his work. Then he heard them talking and quarreling with one another day and night. This was no insanity, and Moosbrugger could not bear being called insane, although he himself sometimes dressed up his story a little with bits of remembered sermons, or trimmed it in accordance with the advice on malingering one picks up in prison. But the material to work with was always there, even if it faded a little when his attention wandered.

It had been the same during his years as a journeyman. Work is not easy for a carpenter to find in winter, and Moosbrugger often had no roof over his head for weeks on end. He might have trudged along the road all day to reach a village, only to find no shelter. He would have to keep on marching late into the night. With no money for a meal, he drinks schnapps until two candles light up behind his eyes and the body keeps walking on its own. He would rather not ask for a cot at the shelter, regardless of the hot soup, partly because of the bedbugs and partly because of the offensive red tape; better to pick up a few pennies by begging and crawl into some farmer's haystack for the night. Without asking, of course; what's the point of spending a long time asking when you're only going to be insulted? In the morning, of course, there is often an argument and a charge of assault, vagrancy, and begging, and finally there is an ever-thickening file of such convictions. Each new magistrate opens this file with much pomposity, as if it explained Moosbrugger.

And who considers what it means to go for days and weeks without a proper bath? The skin gets so stiff that it allows only the clumsiest movements, even when one tries to be delicate; under such a crust the living soul itself hardens. The mind may be less affected, it goes on doing the needful after a fashion, burning like a small light in a huge walking lighthouse full of crushed earthworms and grasshoppers, with everything personal squashed inside, and only the fermenting organic matter stalking onward. As he wandered on through the villages, or even on the deserted roads, Moosbrugger would encounter whole processions of women, one now, and another one half an hour later, but even if they appeared at great intervals and had nothing to do with each other, on the whole they were still processions. They were on their way from one village to another, or had just slipped out of the house; they wore thick shawls or jackets that stood out in stiff, snaky lines around their hips; they stepped into warm rooms or drove their children ahead of them, or were on the road so alone that one could have thrown a stone at them like shying at a crow. Moosbrugger asserted that he could not possibly be a sex murderer, because these females had inspired only feelings of aversion in him. This is not implausible—we think we understand a cat, for instance, sitting in front of a cage staring up at a fat, fair canary hopping up and down, or batting a mouse, letting it go, then batting it again, just to see it run away once more; and what is a dog running after a bicycle, biting at it only in play—man's best friend? There is in this attitude toward the living, moving, silently rolling or flitting fellow creature enjoying its own existence something that suggests a deep innate aversion to it. And then what could one do when she started screaming? One could only come to one's senses, or else, if one simply couldn't do that, press her face to the ground and stuff earth into her mouth.

Moosbrugger was only a journeyman carpenter, a man utterly alone, and while he got on well enough with the other men wherever he worked, he never had a friend. Every now and then the most pow-

erful of instincts turned his inner being cruelly outward. But he may
have lacked only, as he said, the education and the opportunity to
make something different out of this impulse, an angel of mass destruction or a great anarchist, though not the anarchists who band
together in secret societies, whom he contemptuously called fakes.
He was clearly ill, but even if his obviously pathological nature provided the basis for his attitude, and this isolated him from other men,
it somehow seemed to him a stronger and higher sense of his own
self. His whole life was a comically and distressingly clumsy struggle
to gain by force a recognition of this sense of himself. Even as an
apprentice he had once broken the fingers of one master who tried to
beat him. He ran away from another with the master's money—in
simple justice, as he said. He never stayed anywhere for long. As long
as he could keep others at arm's length, as he always did at first,
working peacefully, with his big shoulders and few words, he stayed.
But as soon as they began to treat him familiarly and without respect,
as if they had caught on to him, he packed up and left, seized by an
uncanny feeling as though he were not firmly settled inside his skin.
Once, he had waited too long. Four bricklayers on a building site had
got together to show him who was boss—they would make the scaf-
folding around the top story give way under him. He could hear
them tittering behind his back as they came closer; he hurled himself
at them with all his boundless strength, threw one down two flights
of stairs, and cut all the tendons in the arms of two others. To be
punished for this, he said, had been a shock to his system. He emi-
grated to Turkey but came back again, because the world was in
league against him everywhere; no magic word and no kindness
could prevail against this conspiracy.

He had eagerly picked up such phrases in the mental wards and
prisons, with scraps of French and Latin stuck in the most unsuitable
places as he talked, ever since he had discovered that it was the possession of these languages that gave those in power the right to decide his fate with their "findings." For the same reason, he also did
his utmost during hearings to express himself in an exaggerated High
German, saying such things as "This must be regarded as the basis
for my brutality" or "I had imagined her to be even more vicious than
the others of her kind in my usual estimation of them." But when he
saw that this failed to make an impression he could rise to the heights

of a grand theatrical pose, declaring disdainfully that he was a "theoretical anarchist" whom the Social Democrats were ready to rescue at a moment's notice if he chose to accept a favor from those utterly pernicious Jewish exploiters of the ignorant working class. This would show them that he too had a "discipline," a field of his own where the learned presumption of his judges could not follow him.

Usually this kind of talk brought him high marks for "remarkable intelligence" in the court's judgment, respectful attention to his words during the proceedings, and tougher sentences; yet deep down, his flattered vanity regarded these hearings as the high points of his life. Which is why he hated no one as fervently as he hated the psychiatrists who imagined they could dismiss his whole complex personality with a few foreign words, as if it were for them an everyday affair. As always in such cases, the medical diagnoses of his mental condition fluctuated under the pressure of the superior world of juridical concepts, and Moosbrugger never missed a chance to demonstrate in open court his own superiority over the psychiatrists, unmasking them as puffed-up dupes and charlatans who knew nothing at all, and whom he could trick into placing him in a mental institution instead of sending him to prison, where he belonged. For he did not deny what he had done, but simply wanted his deeds understood as the mishaps of an important philosophy of life. It was those snickering women who were in the forefront of the conspiracy against him. They all had their skirt-chasers and turned up their noses at a real man's straight talk, if they didn't take it as a downright insult. He gave them a wide berth as long as he could, so as not to let them provoke him, but it was not possible all the time. There are days when a man feels confused and can't get hold of anything because his hands are sweating with restlessness. If one then has to give in, he can be sure that at the first step he takes there will be, far up the road like an advance patrol sent out by the others, one of those poisons on two feet crossing his path, a cheat who secretly laughs at the man while she saps his strength and puts on her act for him, if she doesn't do something much worse to him in her unscrupulousness!

And so the end of that night had come, a night of listless boozing, with lots of noise to keep down the inner restlessness. The world can be unsteady even when you aren't drunk. The street walls waver like stage sets behind which something is waiting for its cue. It gets quieter at the edge of town, where you come into the open fields lit by the moon. That was where Moosbrugger had to circle back to get home, and it was there, by the iron bridge, that the girl accosted him. She was one of those girls who hire themselves out to men in the fields, a jobless, runaway housemaid, a little thing of whom all you could see were two gleaming little mouse eyes under her kerchief. Moosbrugger turned her down and quickened his step, but she begged him to take her home with him. Moosbrugger walked: straight ahead, then around a corner, finally helplessly, this way and that; he took big strides, and she ran alongside him; he stopped, she stood there like a shadow. It was as if he were drawing her along behind him. He made one more attempt to drive her off: he suddenly turned around and spat twice in her face. It was no use; she was invulnerable.

This happened in the immense park, which they had to cross at its narrowest part. Moosbrugger began to feel sure that the girl had a protector nearby—how else would she have the nerve to keep after him despite his exasperation? He reached for the knife in his pants pocket; he wasn't anyone's fool! They might jump him together; behind those bitches the other man was always hiding to jeer at you. Come to think of it, didn't she look like a man in disguise? He saw shadows move and heard crackling in the bushes, while this schemer beside him repeated her plea again and again, at regular intervals like a gigantic pendulum. But he could see nothing to hurl his giant's strength at, and the uncanny way nothing at all was happening began to frighten him.

By the time they turned into the first, still very dark street, there were beads of sweat on his forehead, and he was trembling. He kept his eyes straight ahead and walked into the first café that was still open. He gulped down a black coffee and three brandies and could sit there in peace, for fifteen minutes or so; but when he paid his check the worry was there again: what would he do if she was waiting for him outside? There are such thoughts, like string winding in endless snares around arms and legs. He had hardly taken a few steps on the dark street when he felt the girl at his side. Now she was no longer humble but cocky and self-confident; nor did she plead anymore but merely kept silent. Then he realized that he would never get rid of her, because it was he himself who was drawing her after him. His throat filled up with tearful disgust. He kept walking, and that creature, trailing him, was himself again. It was just the same as when he was always meeting those processions of women in the road. Once, he had cut a big wooden splinter out of his own leg because he was too impatient to wait for the doctor; in the same way, he now felt his knife lying long and hard in his pocket.

But by a superhuman exertion of his moral sense, Moosbrugger hit upon one more way out. Behind the board fence along which the road now led was a playing field; one couldn't be seen there, and so he went in. He lay down in the cramped ticket booth and pushed his head into the corner where it was darkest; the soft, accursed second self lay down beside him. So he pretended to fall asleep right away, in order to be able to sneak out later on. But when he started to creep out softly, feet first, there it was again, winding its arms around his neck. Then he felt something hard, in her pocket or his. He tugged it out. He couldn't say whether it was a scissors or a knife; he stabbed her with it. He had claimed it was only a pair of scissors, but it was his own knife. She fell with her head inside the booth. He dragged her partway outside, onto the soft ground, and kept on stabbing her until he had completely separated her from himself. Then he stood there beside her for maybe another quarter of an hour, looking down at her, while the night grew calmer again and wonderfully smooth. Now she could never again insult a man and trail after him. He finally carried the corpse across the street and laid it down in front of a bush so that it could be more easily found and buried, as he stated, because now it was no longer her fault.

During his trial Moosbrugger created the most unpredictable problems for his lawyer. He sat relaxed on his bench, like a spectator, and called out "Bravo!" every time the prosecutor made a point of what a public menace the defendant was, which Moosbrugger regarded as worthy of him, and gave out good marks to witnesses who declared that they had never noticed anything about him to indicate that he could not be held responsible for his actions.

"You're quite a character," the presiding judge flattered him from time to time, humoring him along as he conscientiously tightened tɫ noose the accused had put around his own neck. At such moments Moosbrugger looked astonished, like a harried bull in the arena, let his eyes wander, and noticed in the faces around him, though he could not understand it, that he had again worked himself one level deeper into his guilt.

Ulrich was especially taken with the fact that Moosbrugger's defense was evidently based on some dimly discernible principle. He had not gone out with intent to kill, nor did his dignity permit him to plead insanity. There could be no question of lust as a motive—he had felt only disgust and contempt. The act could accordingly only be called manslaughter, to which he had been induced by the suspicious conduct of "this caricature of a woman," as he put it. If one understood him rightly, he even wanted the killing to be regarded as a political crime, and he sometimes gave the impression that he was fighting not for himself but for this view of the legal issue. The judge's tactics against him were based on the usual assumption that he was dealing with a murderer's obvious, cunning efforts to evade responsibility.

"Why did you wipe the blood off your hands? Why did you throw the knife away? Why did you change into fresh underwear and clean clothes afterward? Because it was Sunday? Not because you were covered with blood? Why did you go out looking for entertainment? So the crime didn't prevent you from doing so? Did you feel any remorse at all?" Ulrich well understood the deep resignation with which Moosbrugger at such moments lamented his lack of an education, which left him helpless to undo the knots in this net woven of incomprehension. The judge translated this into an emphatic reproof: "You always find a way to shift the blame to others!"

This judge added it all up, starting with the police record and the vagrancy, and presented it as Moosbrugger's guilt, while to Moosbrugger it was a series of completely separate incidents having nothing to do with one another, each of which had a different cause that lay outside Moosbrugger somewhere in the world as a whole. In the judge's eyes, Moosbrugger was the source of his acts; in Moosbrugger's eyes they had perched on him like birds that had flown in from somewhere or other. To the judge, Moosbrugger was a special case; for himself he was a universe, and it was very hard to say something convincing about a universe. Two strategies were here locked in combat, two integral positions, two sets of logical consistency. But Moosbrugger had the less favorable position; even a much cleverer man could not have expressed the strange, shadowy reasonings of his mind. They rose directly out of the confused isolation of his life, and while all other lives exist in hundreds of ways—perceived the same way by those who lead them and by all others, who confirm them—his own true life existed only for him. It was a vapor, always losing and changing shape. He might, of course, have asked his judges whether their lives were essentially different. But he thought no such thing. Standing before the court, everything that had happened so naturally in sequence was now senselessly jumbled up inside him, and he made the greatest efforts to make such sense of it as would be no less worthy than the arguments of his distinguished opponents. The judge seemed almost kindly as he lent support to this effort, offering a helpful word or idea, even if these turned out later to have the most terrible consequences for Moosbrugger.

It was like the struggle of a shadow with a wall, and in the end Moosbrugger's shadow was reduced to a lurid flickering. Ulrich was present on the last day of the trial. When the presiding judge read out the psychiatrists' findings that the accused was responsible for his actions, Moosbrugger rose to his feet and announced to the court: "I am satisfied with this opinion and have achieved my purpose." The response of scornful incredulity in the eyes around him made him add angrily: "Since it is I who forced the indictment, I declare myself satisfied with the conduct of the case." The presiding judge, who had now become all strictness and retribution, reprimanded him with the remark that the court was not concerned with giving him satisfaction. Then he read him the death sentence, exactly as if it were now time to answer seriously the nonsense Moosbrugger had been spouting throughout the trial, to the amusement of the spectators. Moosbrugger said nothing to this, so that he would not appear to be frightened. Then the proceedings were concluded and it was all over. His mind reeled; he fell back, helpless against the arrogance of those who failed to understand. Even as the guards were leading him out, he turned around, struggling for words, raised his hands in the air, and cried out, in a voice that shook him free of his guards' grip: "I am satisfied, even though I must confess to you that you have condemned a madman."

That was a non sequitur, but Ulrich sat there breathless. This was clearly madness, and just as clearly it was no more than a distortion of our own elements of being. Cracked and obscure it was; it somehow occurred to Ulrich that if mankind could dream as a whole, that dream would be Moosbrugger. Ulrich came back to reality only when "that miserable clown of a lawyer," as Moosbrugger ungratefully referred to him during the trial, announced that he would appeal to have the verdict set aside on grounds of some detail or other, while his towering client was led away.

19

A LETTER OF ADMONITION AND A CHANCE TO ACQUIRE QUALITIES. RIVALRY OF TWO ACCESSIONS TO THE THRONE

So the time passed, until one day Ulrich received a letter from his father.

"My dear son, once again several months have gone by without my being able to deduce from your scanty communications that you have taken the slightest step forward in your career or have made any preparations to do so.

"I will joyfully acknowledge that in the course of the last few years the satisfaction has been vouchsafed me of hearing your achievements praised in various esteemed quarters, with predictions on that basis of a promising future for you. But on the one hand, the tendency you have inherited, though not from me, to make enthusiastic first strides in some new endeavor that attracts you, only to forget soon afterward, so to speak, what you owe yourself and those who have rested their hopes on you, and on the other hand, my inability to detect in your communications the slightest sign of a plan for your future, fill me with grave concern.

"It is not only that at your age other men have already secured a solid position in life, but also that I may die at any time, and the property I shall bequeath in equal shares to you and your sister, though not negligible, is not sufficiently ample, under present circumstances, to secure unaided that social position which you will now, at last, have to establish for yourself. What fills me with grave concern is the thought that ever since you took your degree, you have only vaguely talked of plans to be realized in various fields, and which you, in your usual way, may considerably overestimate, but that you never write of taking any interest in a university appointment, nor of any preliminary approach to one or another university with regard to such plans, nor of making any other contact with influential circles. No one can possibly suspect me of denigrating a scholar's need for independence, considering that it was I who was the first, forty-seven years ago, to break with the other schools of criminal jurisprudence on that point in my book on Samuel Pufendorf's *Theory of the Responsibility for Moral Actions and Its Relation to Modern Jurisprudence,* which you know and which is now going into its twelfth edition, where I brought the true context of the problem to light. Just as little can I accept, after the experiences of a hardworking life, that a man rely on himself alone and neglect the academic and social connections that provide the support by means of which alone the individual's work prospers as part of a fruitful and beneficial whole.

"I therefore hope and trust that I shall be hearing from you at your earliest convenience, and that the expenditures I have made on behalf of your advancement will be rewarded by your taking up such connections, now that you have returned home, and by your ceasing to neglect them. I have also written in this vein to my old and trusted friend and patron, the former President of the Treasury and present Chairman of the Imperial Family Court Division, Office of the Court Chamberlain, His Excellency Count Stallburg, asking him to give his beneficent attention to the request you will in due course soon present to him. My highly placed friend has already been so kind as to reply by return mail. It is your good fortune that he will not only see you but expresses a warm interest in your personal progress as depicted by myself. This means that your future is assured, insofar as it is in my power and estimation to do so, assuming that you understand how to make a favorable impression on His Excellency, while also strengthening the esteem in which you are held by the leading academic circles.

"As regards the request I am certain you will be glad to lay before

His Excellency, as soon as you know what it is about, its object is the following:

"There will take place in Germany in 1918, specifically on or about the 15th of June, a great celebration marking the jubilee of Emperor Wilhelm II's thirtieth year upon the throne, to impress upon the world Germany's greatness and power. Although that is still several years away, a reliable source informs us that preparations are already being made, though for the time being quite unofficially, of course. Now you are certainly aware that in the same year our own revered Emperor Franz Josef will be celebrating the seventieth jubilee of his accession and that this date falls on December 2nd. Given the modesty which we Austrians display far too much in all questions concerning our own fatherland, there is reason to fear, I must say, that we will experience another Sadowa, meaning that the Germans, with their trained methodical aim for effect, will anticipate us, just as they did in that campaign, when they introduced the needle gun and took us by surprise.

"Fortunately, the anxiety I have just expressed has already been anticipated by other patriotic personages with good connections, and I can tell you confidentially that there is a campaign under way in Vienna to forestall the eventuality of such a coup and to bring to bear the full weight of a seventy-year reign, so rich in blessings and sorrows, against a jubilee of a mere thirty years. Inasmuch as December 2nd cannot of course possibly be moved ahead of June 15th, someone came up with the splendid idea of declaring the entire year of 1918 as a jubilee year for our Emperor of Peace. I am, however, only insofar apprised of this as the institutions of which I am a member have had occasion to express their views on this proposal. You will learn the details as soon as you present yourself to Count Stallburg, who intends to place you on the Planning Committee in a position of considerable distinction for so young a man as yourself.

"Let me also prevail upon you not to continue neglecting—as, to my acute embarrassment, you have—the relations I have so long recommended to you with Section Chief Tuzzi of the Imperial Foreign Office, but to call at once upon his wife, who, as you know, is the daughter of a cousin of my late brother's widow, and hence your cousin. I am told she occupies a prominent position in the project I have just described. My revered friend Count Stallburg has already had the extraordinary kindness to inform her of your intended visit to her, which is why you must not delay it a moment longer.

"As regards myself, there is nothing much to report; other than my lectures, work on the new edition of my aforementioned book takes up all of my time, as well as the remainder of energy one still has at one's disposal in old age. One has to make good use of one's time, for it is short.

"From your sister I hear only that she is in good health. She has a fine, capable husband, although she will never admit that she is satisfied with her lot and feels happy in it.

"With my blessing, your loving

Father."

PART II

PSEUDOREALITY PREVAILS

20

A TOUCH OF REALITY. IN SPITE OF THE
ABSENCE OF QUALITIES, ULRICH TAKES
RESOLUTE AND SPIRITED ACTION

That Ulrich actually decided to call on Count Stallburg was
prompted not least, though not only, by curiosity.

Count Stallburg had his office in that Imperial and Royal citadel
the Hofburg, and the Emperor and King of Kakania was a legendary
old gentleman. A great many books have of course been written
about him since, and exactly what he did, prevented, or left undone
is now known, but then, in the last decade of his and Kakania's life,
the younger people who kept abreast of the arts and sciences sometimes wondered whether he actually existed. The number of his portraits one saw was almost as large as the number of his kingdom's
inhabitants; on his birthday as much food and drink was consumed as
on that of the Savior, bonfires blazed on the mountains, and the
voices of millions vowed that they loved him as a father; an anthem in
his honor was the only work of poetry or music of which every
Kakanian knew at least a line. But this popularity and publicity was so
superconvincing that believing in his existence was rather like believing in stars that one sees though they ceased to exist thousands of
years ago.

The first thing that happened when Ulrich arrived in his cab at the
Imperial Hofburg was that the cabbie stopped in the outer courtyard
and asked to be paid, claiming that although he was allowed to drive
through the inner courtyard, he was not permitted to stop there. Ulrich was annoyed at the cabbie, whom he took for a cheat or a coward, but his protests were powerless against the man's timid refusal,
which suddenly made him sense the aura of a power mightier than
he. When he walked into the inner courtyard he was much impressed with the numerous red, blue, white, and yellow coats, trousers, and helmet plumes that stood there stiffly in the sun like birds

on a sandbank. Up to that moment he had considered "His Majesty" one of those meaningless terms which had stayed in use, as one may be an atheist and still say "Thank God." But now his gaze wandered up high walls and he saw an island—gray, self-contained, and armed—lying there while the city's speed rushed blindly past it.

After he had presented himself he was led up stairways and along corridors, through rooms large and small. Although he was very well dressed, he felt that his exact measure was being taken by every eye he encountered. It would apparently occur to no one here to confuse intellectual aristocracy with the real thing, and against this Ulrich had no recourse but ironic protest and bourgeois criticism. He ascertained that he was walking through a vast shell with little content; the great public rooms were almost unfurnished, but this empty taste lacked the bitterness of a great style. He passed a casual sequence of individual guardsmen and servants, who formed a guard more haphazard than magnificent; a half dozen well-trained and well-paid private detectives might have served far more effectively. One kind of servant, in a gray uniform and cap like a bank messenger's, shuttling between the lackeys and the guardsmen, made him think of a lawyer or dentist who does not keep his office and his living quarters sufficiently separate. "One feels clearly through all this how it must have awed the Biedermeier generation with its splendor," Ulrich thought, "but today it can't even compete with the attractiveness and comfort of a hotel, so it continues to fall back on being all noble restraint and stiffness."

But when he entered Count Stallburg's presence, Ulrich was received by His Excellency inside a great hollow prism of the best proportions, in the center of which this unpretentious, bald-headed, somewhat stooped man, his knees bent like an orangutan's, stood facing Ulrich in a manner that could not possibly be the way an eminent Imperial Court functionary of noble birth would naturally look—it had to be an imitation of something. His Excellency's shoulders were bowed, his underlip drooped, he resembled an aged beagle or a worthy accountant. Suddenly there could be no doubt as to whom he reminded one of; Count Stallburg became transparent, and Ulrich realized that a man who has been for seventy years the All-Highest Center of supreme power must find a certain satisfaction in retreating behind himself and looking like the most subservient of his subjects. Consequently it simply became good manners and a natural form of discretion for those in the vicinity of this All-Highest personage not to look more personal than he did. This seems to be why kings so often like to call themselves the first servants of their country, and a quick glance confirmed for Ulrich that His Excellency indeed wore those short, ice-gray muttonchop whiskers framing a clean-shaven chin that were sported by every clerk and railway porter in Kakania. The belief was that they were emulating the appearance of their Emperor and King, but the deeper need in such cases is reciprocity.

Ulrich had time for such reflections because he had to wait awhile for His Excellency to speak. The theatrical instinct for disguise and transformation, one of life's pleasures, could here be seen in all its purity, without the least taint or awareness of a performance; so strongly did it manifest itself here in this unconscious, perennial art of self-representation that by comparison the middle-class custom of building theaters and staging plays as an art that can be rented by the hour struck him as something quite unnatural, decadent, and schizoid. And when His Excellency finally parted his lips and said to him: "Your dear father . . . ," only to come to a halt, there was something in his voice that made one notice his remarkably beautiful yellowish hands and something like an aura of finely tuned morality surrounding the whole figure, which charmed Ulrich into forgetting himself, as intellectuals are apt to do. For His Excellency now asked him what he did, and when Ulrich said "Mathematics" responded with "Indeed, how interesting, at which school?" When Ulrich assured him that he had nothing to do with schools, His Excellency said, "Indeed, how interesting, I see, research, university." This seemed to Ulrich so natural and precise, just the way one imagines a fine piece of conversation, that he inadvertently took to behaving as though he were at home here and followed his thoughts instead of the protocol demanded by the situation. He suddenly thought of Moosbrugger. Here was the Power of Clemency close at hand; nothing seemed to him simpler than to make a stab at using it.

"Your Excellency," he said, "may I take this favorable opportunity to appeal to you on behalf of a man who has been unjustly condemned to death?"

The question made Count Stallburg's eyes open wide.

"A sex murderer, to be sure," Ulrich conceded, though he realized at once that he was entirely out of order. "The man's insane, of course," he hastily added to save the situation, and was about to add "Your Excellency must be aware that our penal code, dating from the middle of the last century, is outdated on this point," but he had to swallow and got stuck. It was a blunder to impose on this man a discussion of a kind that people used to intellectual activity engage in, often quite without purpose. Just a few words, adroitly planted, can be as fruitful as rich garden loam, but in this place their effect was closer to that of a little clump of dirt one has inadvertently brought into the room on the sole of one's shoe. But now Count Stallburg, noticing Ulrich's embarrassment, showed him his truly great benevolence.

"Yes, yes, I remember," he said with a slight effort after Ulrich had given him the man's name, "and so you say he is insane, and you would like to help him?"

"He can't be held responsible for what he does."

"Quite so, those are always especially unpleasant cases."

Count Stallburg seemed much distressed by the difficulties involved. Looking bleakly at Ulrich, he asked, as if nothing else were to be expected, whether Moosbrugger's sentence was final. Ulrich had to admit that it was not.

"Ah, in that case," he went on, sounding relieved, "there's still time," and he began to speak of Ulrich's "papa," leaving the Moosbrugger case in amiable ambiguity.

Ulrich's slip had momentarily made him lose his presence of mind, but oddly enough his mistake seemed not to have made a bad impression on Count Stallburg. His Excellency had been nearly speechless at first, as though someone had taken off his jacket in his presence, but then such spontaneity from a man so well recommended came to seem to him refreshingly resolute and high-spirited. He was pleased to have found these two words, intent as he was on forming a favorable impression. He wrote them immediately ("We hope that we have found a resolute and high-spirited helper") in his letter of introduction to the chairman of the great patriotic campaign. When Ulrich received this document a few moments later, he felt like a child who is dismissed with a piece of chocolate pressed into its little hand. He now held something between his fingers and received instructions to come again, in a manner that left him uncertain whether it was an order or an invitation, but without giving him an opportunity to protest. "There must be some misunderstanding—I really had no intention whatever . . . ," he would have liked to say, but by this time he was already on his way out, back along the great corridors and through the vast salons. He suddenly came to a stop, thinking, "That picked me up like a cork and set me down somewhere I never meant to go!" He scrutinized the insidious simplicity of the décor with curiosity, and felt quite certain in deciding that even now he was still unimpressed by it. This was simply a world that had not yet been cleared away. But still, what was that strong, peculiar quality it had made him feel? Damn it all, there was hardly any other way to put it: it was simply amazingly real.

21

THE REAL INVENTION OF THE PARALLEL CAMPAIGN BY COUNT LEINSDORF

The real driving force behind the great patriotic campaign—to be known henceforth as the Parallel Campaign, both for the sake of abbreviation and because it was supposed to "bring to bear the full weight of a seventy-year reign, so rich in blessings and sorrows, against a jubilee of a mere thirty years"—was not, however, Count Stallburg, but his friend His Grace the Imperial Liege-Count Leinsdorf.

At the time Ulrich was making his visit in the Hofburg, Count Leinsdorf's secretary was standing in that great nobleman's beautiful, tall-windowed study, amid multiple layers of tranquillity, devotion, gold braid, and the solemnity of fame, with a book in his hand from which he was reading aloud to His Grace a passage he had been directed to find. This time it was something out of Johann Gottlieb Fichte that he had dug up in the *Addresses to the German Nation* and considered most appropriate:

To be freed from the original sin of sloth [he read] and the cowardice and duplicity that follow in its wake, men need models, such as the founders of the great religions actually were, to prefigure for them the enigma of freedom. The necessary teaching of moral conviction is the task of the Church, whose symbols must be regarded not as homilies but only as the means of instruction for the proclamation of the eternal verities.

He stressed the words "sloth," "prefigure," and "Church." His Grace listened benevolently, had the book shown to him, but then shook his head.

"No," said the Imperial Count, "the book may be all right, but this Protestant bit about the Church won't do."

The secretary looked frustrated, like a minor official whose fifth draft of a memo has been returned to him by the head of his department, and cautiously demurred: "But wouldn't Fichte make an excellent impression on nationalistic circles?"

"I think," His Grace replied, "we had better do without him for the present." As he clapped the book shut his face clapped shut too, and at this wordless command the secretary clapped shut with a deep bow and took back his Fichte, as if removing a dish from the table, which he would file away again on the shelf with all the other philosophic systems of the world. One does not do one's own cooking but has it taken care of by the servants.

"So, for the time being," Count Leinsdorf said, "we keep to our four points: Emperor of Peace, European Milestone, True Austria, Property and Culture. You will draw up the circular letter along those lines."

Just then a political thought had struck His Grace, which translated into words came to, more or less, "They'll come along of their own accord." He meant those sectors of his Fatherland who felt they belonged less to Austria than to the greater German nation. He regarded them with disfavor. Had his secretary found a more acceptable quotation with which to flatter their sensibilities—hence the choice of J. G. Fichte—he might have let him write it down. But the moment that offensive note about the Church gave him a pretext to drop it, he did so with a sigh of relief.

His Grace was the originator of the great patriotic campaign. When the disturbing news reached him from Germany, it was he who had come up with the slogan "Emperor of Peace." This phrase instantly evoked the image of an eighty-eight-year-old sovereign—a true father of his people—and an uninterrupted reign of seventy years. The image naturally bore the familiar features of his Imperial Master, but its halo was not that of majesty but of the proud fact that his Fatherland possessed the oldest sovereign with the longest reign in the world. Foolish people might be tempted to see in this merely his pleasure in a rarity—as if Count Leinsdorf, had, for instance, rated the possession of the far rarer horizontally striped "Sahara" stamp with watermark and one missing perforation over the possession of an El Greco, as in fact he did, even though he owned both and was not unmindful of his family's celebrated collection of paintings—but this is simply because these people don't understand what enriching power a symbol has, even beyond that of the greatest wealth.

For Count Leinsdorf, his allegory of the aged ruler held the thought both of his Fatherland, which he loved, and of the world to which it should be a model. Count Leinsdorf was stirred by great and aching hopes. He could not have said what moved him more, grief at not seeing his country established in quite the place of honor among the family of nations which was her due, or jealousy of Prussia, which had thrust Austria down from that place of eminence (in 1866, by a stab in the back!), or else whether he was simply filled with pride in the nobility of a venerable state and the desire to show the world just how exemplary it was. In his view, the nations of Europe were helplessly adrift in the whirlpool of materialistic democracy. What hovered before him was an inspiring symbol that would serve both as a warning and as a sign to return to the fold. It was clear to him that something had to be done to put Austria in the vanguard, so that this "splendorous rally of the Austrian spirit" would prove a "milestone" for the whole world and enable it to find its own true being again; and all of this was connected with the possession of an eighty-eight-year-old Emperor of Peace.

Anything more, or more specific, Count Leinsdorf did not yet know. But he was certain that he was in the grip of a great idea. Not only did it kindle his passion—which should have put him on his guard, as a Christian of strict and responsible upbringing—but with dazzling conclusiveness this idea flowed directly into such sublime and radiant conceptions as that of the Sovereign, the Fatherland, and the Happiness of Mankind. Whatever obscurity still clung to his vision could not upset His Grace. He was well acquainted with the theological doctrine of the *contemplatio in caligine divina*, the contemplation in divine darkness, which is infinitely clear in itself but a dazzling darkness to the human intellect. Besides, he had always believed that a man who does something truly great usually doesn't know why. As Cromwell had said: "A man never gets as far as when he does not know where he is going!" So Count Leinsdorf serenely indulged himself in enjoying his symbol, whose uncertainty aroused him far more powerfully than any certainties.

Symbols apart, his political views were of an extraordinary solidity and had that freedom of great character such as is made possible only by a total absence of doubts. As the heir to a feudal estate he was a member of the Upper House, but he was not politically active, nor did he hold a post at Court or in the government. He was "nothing but a patriot." But precisely because of this, and because of his independent wealth, he had become the focus for all other patriots who followed with concern the development of the Empire and of mankind. The ethical obligation not to remain a passive onlooker but to "offer a helping hand from above" permeated his life. He was convinced that "the people" were "good." Since not only his many officials, employees, and servants but countless others depended on him for their economic security, he had never known "the people" in any other respect, except on Sundays and holidays, when they poured out from behind the scenery as a cheerful, colorful throng, like an opera chorus. Anything that did not fit in with this image he attributed to "subversive elements," the work of irresponsible, callow, sensation-seeking individuals. Brought up in a religious and feudal spirit, never exposed to contradiction through having to deal with middle-class people, not unread, but as an aftereffect of the clerical instruction of his sheltered youth prevented for the rest of his life from recognizing in a book anything other than agreement with or mistaken divergence from his own principles, he knew the outlook of more up-to-date people only from the controversies in Parliament or in the newspapers. And since he knew enough to recognize the many superficialities there, he was daily confirmed in his prejudice that the true bourgeois world, more deeply understood, was basically nothing other than what he himself conceived it to be. In general, "the true" prefixed to political convictions was one of his aids for finding his way in a world that although created by God too often denied Him. He was firmly convinced that even true socialism fitted in with his view of things. He had had from the beginning, in fact, a deeply personal notion, which he had never fully acknowledged even to himself, to build a bridge across which the socialists were to come marching into his own camp. It is obvious that helping the poor is a proper chivalric task, and that for the true high nobility there was really no very great difference between a middle-class factory owner and his workers. "We're all socialists at heart" was one of his pet sayings, meaning no more and no less than that there were no social distinctions in the hereafter. In this world, however, he considered them necessary facts of life, and expected the working class, after due attention to its material welfare, to resist the unreasonable slogans imported by foreign agitators and to accept the natural order of things in a world where everyone finds duty and prosperity in his allotted place. The true aristocrat accordingly seemed as important to him as the true artisan, and the solution of political and economic questions was subsumed for him in a harmonious vision he called "Fatherland."

His Grace could not have said how much of all this had run through his mind in the quarter of an hour since his secretary had left the room. All of it, perhaps. The medium-tall man, some sixty years old, sat motionless at his desk, his hands clasped in his lap, and did not know that he was smiling. He wore a low collar because of a tendency to goiter, and a handlebar mustache, either for the same reason or because it gave him a look slightly reminiscent of certain portraits of Bohemian noblemen of the Wallenstein era. A high-ceilinged room stood around him, and this in turn was surrounded by the huge empty spaces of the anteroom and the library, around which, shell upon shell, further rooms, quiet, deference, solemnity, and the wreath of two sweeping stone staircases arranged themselves. Where the staircases led to the entrance gate, a tall doorkeeper stood in a heavy braided coat, his staff in his hand, gazing through the hole of the archway into the bright fluidity of the day, where pedestrians floated past like goldfish in a bowl. On the border between these two worlds rose the playful tendrils of a rococo façade, famed among art historians not only for its beauty but because its height exceeded its width. It is now considered the first attempt to draw the skin of an expensive, comfortable country manor over the skeleton of a town house, grown tall because of the middle-class urban constriction of its ground plan, and represents one of the most important examples of the transition from feudal landed splendor to the style of middle-class democracy. It was here that the existence of the Leinsdorfs, art-historically certified, made the transition into the spirit of the age. But whoever did not know that saw as little of it as a drop of water shooting by sees of its sewer wall; all he would notice was the mellow grayish hole made by the archway breaking the otherwise solid façade of the street, a surprising, almost exciting recess in whose cavernous depth gleamed the gold of the braid and the large knob on the doorkeeper's staff. In fine weather, this man stood in front of the entrance like a flashing jewel visible from afar, intermingled with a row of housefronts that no one noticed, even though it was just these walls that imposed the order of a street upon the countless, nameless, passing throngs. It is a safe bet that most of the common people over whose order Count Leinsdorf kept anxious and ceaseless vigil linked his name, when it came up, with nothing but their recollection of this doorkeeper.

His Grace would not have felt pushed into the background; he would rather have been inclined to consider the possession of such a doorkeeper as the "true selflessness" that best becomes a nobleman.

22

THE PARALLEL CAMPAIGN, IN THE FORM OF AN INFLUENTIAL LADY OF INEFFABLE SPIRITUAL GRACE, STANDS READY TO DEVOUR ULRICH

It was this Count Leinsdorf whom Ulrich should have gone to see next, as Count Stallburg wished, but he had decided to visit instead the "great cousin" recommended by his father, because he was curious to see her with his own eyes. He had never met her but had taken a special dislike to her ever since all the well-meaning people who knew they were related had begun saying: "There's a woman you must get to know." It was always said with that marked emphasis on the "you" intended to single out the person addressed as exceptionally well placed to appreciate such a jewel, and which can be a sincere compliment or a cloak for the conviction that he was just the sort of fool for such an acquaintance. Ulrich's frequent requests for a detailed description of this lady's qualities never brought satisfying replies. It was either "She has such an ineffable spiritual grace" or "She is our loveliest and cleverest woman" or, as many would say, simply, "She's an ideal woman." "How old is she?" Ulrich would ask, but nobody knew her age and the person thus asked was usually amazed that it had never occurred to him to give it a thought. "Well then, who is her lover?" "An affair?" The not inexperienced young man he asked this of looked at him in wonder: "You're quite right. No one would ever suspect her of such a thing."

"I see—a high-minded beauty," Ulrich concluded, "a second Diotima." And from that day forth that was what he called her in his thoughts, after the celebrated female teacher of love.

But in reality her name was Ermelinda Tuzzi, and in truth it was just plain Hermine. Now, Ermelinda is, to be sure, not even a translation of Hermine, but she had earned the right to this beautiful name one day through a flash of intuition, when it suddenly stood before her spiritual ear as a higher form of truth, even though her husband went on being called Hans, and not Giovanni. Despite his surname he had first learned Italian at the consular school. Ulrich was no less prejudiced against this Section Chief Tuzzi than against his wife. He was the only commoner in a position of authority in the Imperial Ministry of Foreign Affairs, which was even more feudal than the other government departments. There Tuzzi was the head of the most influential section, was considered the right hand—even the brains, it was rumored—of his Minister, and was one of the few men who could influence the fate of Europe. But when a commoner rises to such a position in such exalted surroundings, he may reasonably be supposed to possess qualities favorably combining personal indispensability with a knack for keeping modestly in the background. Ulrich was close to imagining this influential section chief as a kind of upright regimental sergeant major in the cavalry obliged to drill one-year conscripts from the high nobility. The fitting complement, Ulrich thought, would be a spouse who, despite the extolling of her beauty, was ambitious, no longer young, and encased in a middle-class corset of culture.

But Ulrich was mightily surprised when he made his visit. Diotima received him with the indulgent smile of an eminent lady who knows that she is also beautiful and has to forgive men, superficial creatures that they are, for always thinking of her beauty first.

"I've been expecting you," she said, leaving Ulrich uncertain whether she meant this as a kindness or a rebuke. The hand she gave him was plump and weightless.

He held it a moment too long, his thoughts unable to let go of this hand at once. It rested in his own like a fleshy petal; its pointed nails, like beetle wings, seemed poised to fly off with her at any moment into the improbable. He was overwhelmed by the exaltation of this female hand, basically a rather shameless human organ that, like a dog's muzzle, will touch anything and yet is publicly considered the seat of fidelity, nobility, and tenderness. During these few seconds, he noted that there were several rolls of fat on Diotima's neck, covered with the finest skin; her hair was wound into a Grecian knot, which stood out stiffly and in its perfection resembled a wasp's nest.

Ulrich felt a hostile impulse, an urge to offend this smiling woman, and yet he could not quite resist her beauty.

Diotima, for her part, also gave him a long and almost searching gaze. She had heard things about this cousin that to her ear had a slight tinge of the scandalous, and besides, he was related to her. Ulrich noticed that she, too, could not quite resist the impression of his physical appearance. He was used to this. He was clean-shaven, tall, well-built, and supplely muscular; his face was bright but impenetrable; in a word, he sometimes regarded himself as the preconceived idea most women have of an impressive and still young man; he simply did not always have the energy to disabuse them. Diotima resisted this impression by deciding to feel compassion for him. Ulrich could see that she was constantly studying his appearance and, obviously not moved by unfavorable feelings, was probably telling herself that the noble qualities he so palpably seemed to possess must be suffocated by a vicious life and could be saved. Although she was not much younger than Ulrich and physically in full open bloom, her appearance emanated something withheld and virginal that formed a strange contrast to her self-confidence. So they went on surveying each other even after they had begun to talk.

Diotima began by calling the Parallel Campaign a unique, never-to-recur opportunity to bring into existence what must be regarded as the greatest and most important thing in the world. "We must and will bring to life a truly great idea. We have the opportunity, and we must not fail to use it."

"Do you have something specific in mind?" Ulrich asked naïvely.

No, Diotima did not have anything specific in mind. How could she? No one who speaks of the greatest and most important thing in the world means anything that really exists. What peculiar quality of the world would it be equivalent to? It all amounts to one thing being greater and more important, or more beautiful and sadder, than another; in other words, the existence of a hierarchy of values and the comparative mode, which surely implies an end point and a superlative? But if you point this out to someone who happens at that very moment to be speaking of the greatest and most important thing in the world, that person will suspect that she is dealing with an individual devoid of feelings and ideals. This was Diotima's reaction, and so had Ulrich spoken.

As a woman admired for her intellect, Diotima found Ulrich's objection irreverent. After a moment she smiled and replied: "There is so much that is great and good that has not yet been realized that the choice will not be easy. But we will set up committees from all sectors of the population, which will help us in our work. Or don't you think, Herr von ——, that it is an incredible privilege to be in a position to call on a whole nation—indeed, on the whole world—on such an occasion, to awaken it in the midst of its materialistic preoccupations to the life of the spirit? You must not assume that we have in mind something 'patriotic' in the long-outdated sense."

Ulrich was humorously evasive.

Diotima did not laugh, but barely smiled. She was accustomed to witty men, but they were all something else besides. Paradox for the sake of paradox struck her as immature, and aroused the need to remind her cousin of the seriousness of the reality that lent to this great national undertaking dignity as well as responsibility. In a tone of finality, she made a fresh start. Ulrich involuntarily sought between her words those black-and-yellow tapes that are used for interleaving and fastening official papers in Austrian government offices; but what came from Diotima's lips were by no means only bureaucratic formulas but also such cultural code words as "soulless age, dominated only by logic and psychology" or "the present and eternity," and suddenly there was mention of Berlin, too, and the "treasure of feeling" Austria had still preserved, in contrast to Prussia.

Ulrich attempted several times to interrupt these ex cathedra pronouncements, but the vestry incense of high bureaucracy instantly clouded over the interruption, gently veiling its tactlessness. Ulrich was astonished. He rose. His first visit was clearly at an end.

During these moments of his retreat Diotima treated him with that bland courtesy, carefully and pointedly a little overdone, which she had learned by imitating her husband. He used it in his dealings with young aristocrats who were his subordinates but might one day be his ministers. There was, in her manner of inviting him to come again, a touch of that supercilious uneasiness of the intellectual when faced with a ruder vitality. When he held her gentle, weightless hand in his own once more, they looked into each other's eyes. Ulrich had the distinct impression that they were destined to cause each other considerable annoyance through love.

"Truly," he thought, "a hydra of a beauty." He had meant to let the great patriotic campaign wait for him in vain, but it seemed to have become incarnate in the person of Diotima and stood ready to swallow him up. It was a semi-comical feeling: despite his maturity and experience, he felt like a destructive little worm being eyed attentively by a large chicken. "For heaven's sake," he thought, "I can't let myself be provoked to petty derelictions by this giantess of the soul!" He had had enough of his affair with Bonadea, and he committed himself to exercise the utmost restraint.

As he was leaving the apartment, he was cheered by a pleasant impression he had already had on his arrival. A little chambermaid with dreamy eyes showed him out. In the darkness of the entrance hall her eyes, fluttering up to his for the first time, had been like black butterflies; now, as he left, they floated down through the darkness like black snowflakes. There was something Arabian or Algerian-Jewish about the little girl, something so unobtrusively sweet that Ulrich again forgot to take a good look at her. It was only when he was out in the street again that he felt what an uncommonly alive and refreshing sight the little maid was after Diotima's presence.

23

A GREAT MAN'S INITIAL INTERVENTION

Ulrich's departure had left both Diotima and her maid in a state of vague excitement. But while the little black lizard always felt as though she had been allowed to flit up a high, shimmering wall whenever she saw a distinguished visitor to the door, Diotima handled her impression of Ulrich with the conscientiousness of a woman who doesn't really mind feeling touched though she should because she has the ability to keep herself gently in check. Ulrich did not know that on that same day another man had entered her life to lift her up like a giant mountain offering a tremendous view.

Dr. Paul Arnheim had called on her soon after arriving in town.

He was immeasurably rich. His father was the mightiest mogul of "Iron Germany," that is, Bismarck's Germany, to which even Section Chief Tuzzi had condescended. Tuzzi was laconic on principle. He felt that puns and the like, even if one could not do entirely without them in witty conversation, had better not be too good, because that would be middle-class. He had advised his wife to treat this visitor with marked distinction, for even if his kind were not yet on top in the German Reich, and their influence at Court was not to be compared with that of the Krupps, they might, in his opinion, be on top tomorrow. He also passed on to her a confidential rumor that the son—a man well into his forties, incidentally—was aiming not merely at his father's position but was preparing himself, based on the trend of the times and his international connections, to become a Reichsminister someday. Tuzzi of course regarded this as completely out of the question, unless a world cataclysm were to pave the way.

He had no idea what a tempest his words unleashed in his wife's imagination. In her circle it was a matter of principle not to think too highly of "men in trade," but like every person of bourgeois outlook, she admired wealth in those depths of the heart that are quite immune to convictions, and the prospect of actually meeting so incredibly rich a man made her feel as if golden angel's wings had come down to her from on high. Ever since her husband's rise, Ermelinda Tuzzi was not entirely unaccustomed to consorting with fame and riches. But fame based on intellectual achievements melts away with surprising speed as one becomes socially involved with its bearers, and feudal wealth manifests itself either in the foolish debts of young attachés or is constrained by a traditional style of living without ever attaining the brimming profusion of freely piled-up mountains of money and the brilliant cascading showers of gold with which the great banks and industrial combines fuel their business. All Diotima knew of banks was that even their middle-echelon executives traveled first-class on business, while she always had to go second-class unless accompanied by her husband. This was the standard by which she imagined the luxury that must surround the top despots of financial operations on so oriental a scale.

Her little maid, Rachel—it goes without saying that Diotima pronounced it in the French style—had heard fantastic things. The least she had to report was that the nabob had arrived in his own private train, had reserved an entire hotel, and had brought a little black slave with him. The truth was considerably more modest, if only because Paul Arnheim never acted conspicuously. Only the little blackamoor was real. Some years ago, on a trip in southernmost Italy, Arnheim had picked him out of a traveling dance troupe, partly for show and partly from an impulse to raise a fellow creature from the depths and carry out God's work by opening up the life of the mind to him. He soon enough lost interest and used the now sixteen-year-old boy only as a servant, even though before the boy was fourteen Arnheim had been giving him Stendhal and Dumas to read.

But even though the rumors her maid brought home were so childish in their extravagance that Diotima had to smile, she made her repeat them word for word, because she found it charming and unspoiled, as was only possible in this one great city, which was "rife with culture to the point of innocence." And the little black boy surprisingly caught even her imagination.

Diotima was the eldest of three daughters of a secondary-school teacher without private means, so that Tuzzi had been considered a good catch for her even before he had been anything but an as yet unknown middle-class vice-consul. In her girlhood she had had nothing but her pride, and since her pride had nothing to be proud about, it was only a rolled-up propriety bristling with feelers of sensitivity. But even such a posture may conceal ambition and daydreams, and can be an unpredictable force.

If Diotima had at first been lured by the prospect of distant entanglements in distant lands, she was soon disappointed. After a few years her experience served only as a discreetly exploited advantage over women friends who envied her her slight aura of the exotic, and it could not ward off the realization that at such foreign posts life remains, by and large, the life one has brought along with the rest of one's baggage. For a long time, Diotima's ambitions had been close to ending up in the genteel hopelessness of the fifth service grade, until by chance her husband's career took a sudden upward turn when a benevolent minister of a "progressive" cast of mind took this bourgeois into the central office of the ministry itself. In this position, Tuzzi was now approached by many people who wanted something from him, and from this moment something came alive in Diotima, almost to her own amazement, a treasure of memories of "spiritual beauty and grandeur" ostensibly gathered in a cultured home and the great world centers, but which in fact she had probably acquired in a girls' private school as a model student, and this she began turning cautiously to account. Her husband's sober but uncommonly dependable intelligence inevitably attracted attention to her as well, and as soon as she noticed that her cultural advantages were being appreciated, she joyfully began to slip little "highminded" ideas into the conversation in the right places, as completely guileless as a damp little sponge releasing the moisture it had previously soaked up for no particular purpose. And gradually, as her husband rose further in rank, more and more people were drawn into association with him, and her home became a "salon" which enjoyed a reputation as a place where "society and intellect" met. Now that she was seeing persons of consequence in many fields, Diotima began as well to seriously discover herself. Her feeling for what was correct, still on the alert as it had been in school, still adept at remembering its lessons and at bringing things together into an amiable unity, simply by extension, turned into a form of intellect in itself, and the Tuzzi house won a recognized position.

24

CAPITAL AND CULTURE. DIOTIMA'S FRIENDSHIP WITH COUNT LEINSDORF, AND THE OFFICE OF BRINGING DISTINGUISHED VISITORS INTO ACCORD WITH THE SOUL

But it took Diotima's friendship with Count Leinsdorf to make her salon an institution.

Among the parts of the body after which friends are named, Count

Leinsdorf's was so situated between the head and the heart that Diotima would have to be considered a bosom friend, if such a term were still in use. His Grace revered Diotima's mind and beauty without permitting himself any unseemly intentions. His patronage not only gave Diotima's salon an unassailable position but conferred on it—as he liked to say—an official status.

For his own person, His Grace the Imperial Liege-Count Leinsdorf was "nothing but a patriot." But the state does not consist only of the Crown and the people, with the administrative machinery in between; there is something else besides: thought, morality, principle! Devout as His Grace was, as a man permeated with a sense of responsibility who, incidentally, also ran factories on his estates, he never closed his mind to the realization that the human mind these days has in many respects freed itself from the tutelage of the Church. He could not imagine how a factory, for example, or a stock-exchange deal in wheat or sugar could be conducted on religious principles; nor was there any conceivable way to run a modern, large-scale landed estate rationally without the stock exchange and industry. When His Grace's business manager showed him how a certain deal could be made more profitably with a group of foreign speculators than in partnership with the local landed nobility, in most cases His Grace had to choose the former, because objective conditions have a rationale of their own, and this cannot be defied for sentimental reasons by the head of a huge economic enterprise who bears the responsibility not only for himself but for countless other lives as well. There is such a thing as a professional conscience that in some cases contradicts the religious conscience, and Count Leinsdorf was convinced that in such a case even the Cardinal Archbishop would not act differently than he. Of course, Count Leinsdorf was always willing to deplore this state of affairs at public sessions of the Upper House and to express the hope that life would find its way back to the simplicity, naturalness, supernaturalness, soundness, and necessity of Christian principles. Whenever he opened his mouth to make such pronouncements, it was as though an electric contact had been opened, and he flowed in a different circuit. The same thing happens to most people, in fact, when they express themselves in public, and if anyone had reproached Count Leinsdorf with doing in private what he denounced in public, he would, with saintly conviction, have branded it the demagogic babble of subversives who lacked even a clue about the extent of life's responsibilities. Nevertheless, he realized the prime importance of establishing a connection between the eternal verities and the world of business, which is so much more complicated than the lovely simplicity of tradition, and he also recognized that such a connection could not be found anywhere but in the profundities of middle-class culture. With its great ideas and ideals in the spheres of law, duty, morality, and beauty, it reached even the common everyday struggles and contradictions of life, and seemed to him like a bridge made of tangled living plants. It did not, of course, offer as firm and secure a foothold as the dogmas of the Church, but it was no less necessary and responsible, which is why Count Leinsdorf was not only a religious idealist but also a passionate civilian idealist.

These convictions of His Grace's corresponded to the composition of Diotima's salons. These gatherings were celebrated for the fact that on her "great days" one ran into people one could not exchange a single word with because they were too well known in some special field or other for small talk, while in many cases one had never even heard the name of the specialty for which they were world-famous. There were Kenzinists and Canisians, a grammarian of Bo might come up against a partigen researcher, a tokontologist against a quantum physicist, not to mention the representatives of new movements in arts and literature that changed their labels every year, all permitted to circulate in limited numbers along with their better-recognized colleagues. In general, things were so arranged that a random mixture blended harmoniously, except for the young intellectuals, whom Diotima usually kept apart by means of special invitations, and those rare or special guests whom she had a way of unobtrusively singling out and providing with a special setting. What distinguished Diotima's gatherings from all similar affairs was, incidentally, if one may say so, the lay element; people from the world of applied ideas, the kind who—in Diotima's words—had once spread out around a core of theological studies as a flock of faithful doers, really an entire community of lay brothers and sisters—in short, the element of *action*. But now that theology has been displaced by economics and physics, and Diotima's list of administrators of the spirit on earth who were to be invited had grown with time to resemble the

Catalogue of Scientific Papers of the Royal Society, the new lay brothers and sisters were correspondingly a collection of bank directors, technicians, politicians, high officials, and ladies and gentlemen of society with their hangers-on.

Diotíma made a particular point of cultivating the women, although she gave preference to the "ladies" over the "intellectuals" among them. "Life is much too overburdened with knowledge these days," she was accustomed to say, "for us to be able to do without the 'unfragmented woman.' " She was convinced that only the unfragmented woman still possessed the fated power to embrace the intellect with those vital forces that, in her opinion, it obviously sorely needed for its salvation. This concept of the entwining woman and the power of Being, incidentally, redounded greatly to her credit among the young male nobility who attended regularly because it was considered the thing to do and because Tuzzi was not unpopular; for the unfragmented Being is something the nobility really takes to, and more specifically, at the Tuzzis' couples could become deeply absorbed in conversation without attracting attention; so that for tender rendezvous and long heart-to-heart talks, her house—though Diotima had no inkling of this—was even more popular than a church.

His Grace the Liege-Count Leinsdorf summed up these two social elements, so various in themselves, which mingled at Diotima's—when he did not simply call them "the true elite"—as "capital and culture." But he liked best of all to think of them in terms of "official public service," a concept that had pride of place in his thinking. He regarded every accomplishment, that of the factory worker or the concert singer as well as that of the civil servant, as a form of official service.

"Every person," he would say, "performs an office within the state; the worker, the prince, the artisan, are all civil servants." This was an emanation of his always and under all circumstances impartial way of thinking, ignorant of bias, and in his eyes even the ladies and gentlemen of the highest society performed a significant if not readily definable office when they chatted with learned experts on the Bogazköy inscriptions or the question of lamellibranchiate mollusks, while eyeing the wives of prominent financiers. This concept of official public service was his version of what Diotima referred to as the religious unity, lost since the Middle Ages, of all human activity.

All enforced sociability, such as that at the Tuzzis', beyond a certain naïve and crude level, springs basically from the need to simulate a unity that could govern all of humanity's highly varied activities and that is never there. This simulation was what Diotima called culture, usually, with special amplification, "our Old Austrian culture." As her ambition had expanded to embrace intellect, she had learned to use this term more and more often. She understood by it: the great paintings of Velázquez and Rubens hanging in the Imperial Museum; the fact that Beethoven was, so to speak, an Austrian; Mozart, Haydn, St. Stephen's Cathedral, the Burgtheater; the weighty traditional ceremonials at the Imperial Court; Vienna's central district, where the smartest dress and lingerie shops of an empire with fifty million inhabitants were crowded together; the discreet manners of high officials; Viennese cuisine; the aristocracy, which considered itself second to none except the English, and their ancient palaces; high society's tone of sometimes genuine, mostly sham, aestheticism. She also understood by it the fact that in this country so eminent a gentleman as Count Leinsdorf had taken her under his wing and made her house the center of his own cultural endeavors. She did not know that His Grace was also moved by the consideration that it was not quite the thing to open his own noble house to innovations that might easily get out of hand. Count Leinsdorf was often secretly horrified by the freedom and indulgence with which his beautiful friend spoke of human passions and the turmoil they cause, or of revolutionary ideas. But Diotima did not notice this. She drew a line, as it were, between public immodesty and private modesty, like a female physician or a social worker. She was acutely sensitive to any word that touched her too personally, but impersonally she would talk freely about anything, and could only feel that Count Leinsdorf found the mixture most appealing.

Nothing in life is built, however, without the stones having to be broken out from somewhere else. To Diotima's painful surprise some tiny, dreamy-sweet almond kernel of imagination, once the core of her existence when there was nothing else in it, and which had still been there when she decided to marry Vice-Consul Tuzzi, who looked like a leather steamer trunk with two dark eyes, had vanished in the years of success. She realized that much of what she understood by "our Old Austrian culture," like Haydn or the

Habsburgs, had once been only a boring school lesson, while to be actually living in the midst of it all now seemed enchanting and quite as heroic as the midsummer humming of bees. In time, however, it became not only monotonous but also a strain on her, and even hopeless. Diotima's experience with her famous guests was no different from that of Count Leinsdorf with his banking connections; however much one might try to get them into accord with one's soul, it did not succeed. One can talk about cars and X rays, of course, with a certain amount of feeling, but what else can one do about the countless other inventions and discoveries that nowadays every single day brings forth, other than to marvel at human inventiveness in general, which in the long run gets to be too tiresome!

His Grace would drop in occasionally, and spoke with a political figure or had himself introduced to a new guest. It was easy for him to enthuse about the profound reaches of culture, but when you were as closely involved with it as Diotima, the insoluble problem was not its depths but its breadth! Even questions of such immediate concern as the noble simplicity of Greece or the meaning of the Prophets dissolved, in conversation with specialists, into an incalculable multiplicity of doubts and possibilities. Diotima found that even the celebrities always talked in twos, because the time had already come when a person could talk sensibly and to the point with at most one other person—and she herself could not really find anyone at all. At this point Diotima had discovered in herself the well-known suffering caused by that familiar malady of contemporary man known as civilization. It is a frustrating condition, full of soap, radio frequencies, the arrogant sign language of mathematical and chemical formulas, economics, experimental research, and the inability of human beings to live together simply but on a high plane. And even the relationship of her own innate nobility of mind to the social nobility, whom she had to handle with great care and who brought her, with all her successes, many a disappointment, gradually came to seem to her more and more typical of an age not of culture but merely of civilization.

Civilization, then, meant everything that her mind could not control. Including, for a long time now, and first of all, her husband.

25

SUFFERINGS OF A MARRIED SOUL

In her misery she read a great deal, and discovered that she had lost something she had previously not really known she had: a soul.

What's that? It is easy to define negatively: It is simply that which sneaks off at the mention of algebraic series.

But positively? It seems successfully to elude every effort to pin it down. There may once have been in Diotima something fresh and natural, an intuitive sensibility wrapped in the propriety she wore like a cloak threadbare from too much brushing, something she now called her soul and rediscovered in Maeterlinck's batik-wrapped metaphysics, or in Novalis, but most of all in the ineffable wave of anemic romanticism and yearning for God that, for a while, the machine age squirted out as an expression of its spiritual and artistic misgivings about itself. It might also be that this original freshness in Diotima could be defined more precisely as a blend of quiet, tenderness, devotion, and kindness that had never found a proper path and in the foundry in which Fate casts our forms had happened to pour itself into the comical mold of her idealism. Perhaps it was imagination; perhaps an intuition of the instinctive vegetative processes at work every day beneath the covering of the body, above which the soulful expression of a beautiful woman gazes at us. Possibly it was only the coming of certain indefinable hours when she felt warm and expansive, when her sensations were keener than usual, when ambition and will were becalmed and she was seized by a hushed rapture and fullness of life while her thoughts, even the slightest ones, turned away from the surface and toward the inward depths, leaving the world's events far away, like noise beyond a garden wall. At such times Diotima felt as if she had a direct vision of the truth within herself without having to strain for it; tender experiences that as yet bore no name raised their veils, and she felt—to cite only a few of the many descriptions of it she had found in the literature on the subject—harmonious, humane, religious, and close to that primal source that sanctifies everything arising from it and leaves sinful everything that does not. But even though it was all quite lovely to think about, Diotima could never get beyond such hints and intimations of this peculiar condition; nor did the prophetic books she relied on for help, which spoke of the same thing in the same mysterious and imprecise language. Diotima was reduced to blaming this, too, on a period of civilization that had simply filled up with rubble the access to the soul.

What she called "soul" was probably nothing more than a small amount of capital in love she had possessed at the time of her marriage. Section Chief Tuzzi was not the right business opportunity to invest in. His advantage over Diotima, at first and for a long time, was that of the older man; to this was later added the advantage of the successful man in a mysterious position, who gives his wife little insight into himself even as he looks on indulgently at the trivia that keep her busy. And apart from the tendernesses of courtship, Tuzzi had always been a practical man of common sense who never lost his balance. Even so, the well-cut assurance of his actions and his suits, the—one could say—urbanely grave aroma of his body and his beard, the guardedly firm baritone in which he spoke, all gave him an aura that excited the soul of the girl Diotima as the nearness of his master excites the retriever who lays his muzzle on the master's knees. And just as the dog trots along behind, his feelings safe and fenced in, so Diotima, too, under such serious-minded, matter-of-fact guidance, entered upon the infinite landscape of love.

Here Section Chief Tuzzi preferred the straight paths. His daily habits were those of an ambitious worker. He rose early, either to ride or, preferably, to take an hour's walk, which not only preserves the body's elasticity but also represents the kind of pedantic, simple routine that, strictly adhered to, consorts perfectly with an image of responsible achievement. It also goes without saying that on those evenings when they were not invited out and had no guests he immediately withdrew to his study; for he was forced to maintain his great stock of expert information at the high level that constituted his advantage over his aristocratic colleagues and superiors. Such a life sets firm restraints, and ranges love with the other activities. Like all those whose imagination is not consumed by the erotic, Tuzzi in his bachelor days—apart from having to show himself occasionally be-

cause of his diplomatic profession in the company of friends taking
out little chorus girls—had been a quiet visitor at one brothel or another, and carried the regular rhythm of this habit over into his marriage. Thus Diotima learned to know love as something violent,
assaultive, and brusque that was released only once every week by an
even greater power. This change in the nature of two people, which
always began promptly on time, to be followed, a few minutes later,
by a short exchange on those events of the day that had not come up
before and then a sound sleep, and which was never mentioned in
the times between, except perhaps in hints and allusions—like making a diplomatic joke about the *"partie honteuse"* of the body—nevertheless had unexpected and paradoxical consequences for her.

On the one hand, it was the cause of that extravagantly swollen
ideality—that officious, outwardly-oriented personality—whose
power of love, whose spiritual longing, reached out for all things
great and noble that turned up in her environment, and that so intensely spread itself and bound itself to these that Diotima evoked
the impression, so confusing to males, of a mightily blazing yet Platonic sun of love, the description of which had made Ulrich curious
to meet her. On the other hand, however, this broad rhythm of marital contact had developed, purely physiologically, into a habit that
asserted itself quite independently and without connection to the
loftier parts of her being, like the hunger of a farmhand whose meals
are infrequent but heavy. With time, as tiny hairs began to sprout on
Diotima's upper lip and the masculine independence of the mature
female woman mingled with the traits of the girl, she became aware
of this split as something horrible. She loved her husband, but this
was mingled with a growing revulsion, a dreadful affront to her soul,
which could only be compared to what Archimedes, deeply absorbed
in his mathematical problems, might have felt if the enemy soldier
had not killed him but made sexual demands on him. And since her
husband was not aware of this—nor would he have thought about it
if he had been—and since her body always ended up betraying her to
him against her will, she felt enslaved; it was a slavery that might not
be considered unvirtuous but was just as tormenting as she imagined
the appearance of a nervous tic or the inescapability of a vice to be.
Now, this might perhaps have made Diotima slightly melancholy and

even more idealistic, but unfortunately it happened just at the time that her salon began to cause her some spiritual difficulties.

Section Chief Tuzzi encouraged his wife's intellectual endeavors because he was not slow to see how they might serve to bolster his own position, but he had never taken part in them, and it is safe to say that he did not take them seriously. For the only things this experienced man took seriously were power, duty, high social status, and, at a certain remove, reason. He even warned Diotima repeatedly against being too ambitious in her aesthetic affairs of state, because even if culture is, so to speak, the spice in the food of life, the best people did not go in for an oversalted diet. He said this quite without irony, as it was what he believed, but Diotima felt belittled. She constantly felt that her husband followed her idealistic endeavors with a hovering smile; and whether he was at home or not, and whether this smile—if indeed he did smile; she could never be quite sure—was for her personally or merely part of the facial expression of a man who for professional reasons always had to look superior, as time went on it became increasingly unbearable to her, yet she could not shake off its infamous appearance of being in the right. At times, Diotima would try to blame a materialistic age that had turned the world into an evil, purposeless game in which atheism, socialism, and positivism left no freedom for a person with a rich inner life to rise to true being; but even this was not often of much use.

Such was the situation in the Tuzzi household when the great patriotic campaign quickened the pace of events. Ever since Count Leinsdorf had established his campaign headquarters in Diotima's house so as not to involve the aristocracy, an unspoken sense of responsibility had reigned there, for Diotima had made up her mind to prove to her husband, now or never, that her salon was no plaything. His Grace had confided in her that the great patriotic campaign needed a crowning idea, and it was her burning ambition to find it. The thought of creating something with the resources of an empire and before the attentive eyes of the world, an embodiment of culture at its greatest or, more modestly circumscribed, perhaps something that would reveal the innermost being of Austrian culture—this thought moved Diotima as if the door to her salon had suddenly sprung open and the boundless ocean were lapping at her threshold like an extension of the floor.

There is no denying that her first reaction to this vision was the sense of the momentary gaping of an illimitable void.

First impressions are so often right! Diotima felt sure that something incomparable was going to happen, and she summoned up her many ideals; she mobilized all the pathos of her schoolgirl history lessons, through which she had learned to think in terms of empires and centuries; she did absolutely everything one has to do in such a situation. But after a few weeks had passed in this fashion, she had to face the fact that no inspiration whatsoever had come her way. What Diotima felt toward her husband at this point would have been hatred, had she been at all capable of hatred—such a base impulse! Instead, she became depressed, and began to feel a "resentment against everything" such as she had never known before.

It was at this point that Dr. Arnheim arrived, accompanied by his little black servant, and shortly thereafter paid his momentous call on Diotima.

26

THE UNION OF SOUL AND ECONOMICS. THE MAN WHO CAN ACCOMPLISH THIS WANTS TO ENJOY THE BAROQUE CHARM OF OLD AUSTRIAN CULTURE. AND SO AN IDEA FOR THE PARALLEL CAMPAIGN IS BORN

Diotima never had an improper thought, but on this day there must have been all sorts of goings-on in her mind as it dwelled on the innocent little black boy, after she had sent "Rachelle" out of the room. She had willingly listened once again to the maid's story after Ulrich had left the house of his "great cousin," and the beautiful, ripe woman was feeling young and as if she were playing with a tinkling toy. There had once been a time when the aristocracy had kept black servants—delightful images of sleigh rides with gaily caparisoned horses, plumed lackeys, and frost-powdered trees passed through her mind—but all this picturesque aspect of high life had perished long ago. "The soul has gone out of society these days," she thought. Something in her heart sided with the dashing outsider who still dared keep a blackamoor, this improperly aristocratic bourgeois, this intruder who put to shame the propertied heirs of tradition, as the learned Greek slave had once shamed his Roman masters. Cramped as her self-confidence was by all sorts of considerations, it took wing and gladly deserted to his colors as a sister spirit, and this feeling, so natural compared with her other feelings, even made her overlook that Dr. Arnheim—the rumors were still contradictory, nothing was yet known for certain—was presumed to be of Jewish descent; at least on his father's side, it was reported with certainty. His mother had been dead so long that it would take some time for the facts to be established. It might even have been possible that a certain cruel Weltschmerz in Diotima's heart was not at all interested in a denial.

She had cautiously permitted her thoughts to stray from the black-amoor and approach his master. Dr. Paul Arnheim was not only a rich man but also a man of notable intellect. His fame went beyond the fact that he was heir to world-spanning business interests; the books he had written in his leisure hours were regarded in advanced circles as extraordinary. The people who form such purely intellec-tual groups are above social and financial considerations, but one must not forget that precisely for that reason they are especially fas-cinated by a rich man who joins their ranks; furthermore, Arnheim's pamphlets and books proclaimed nothing less than the merger of soul and economics, or of ideas and power. The sensitive minds of the time, those with the finest antennae for what was in the wind, spread the report that he combined these normally opposite poles in his own person, and they encouraged the rumor that here was a man for the times, who might be called on one day to guide for the better the destinies of the German Reich and perhaps—who could tell?—even the world. For there had long been a widespread feeling that the principles and methods of old-style politics and diplomacy were steering Europe right into the ditch, and besides, the period of turn-ing away from specialists had already begun.

Diotima's condition, too, could have been expressed as rebellion against the thinking of the older school of diplomacy, which is why she instantly grasped the marvelous similarity between her own position and that of this brilliant outsider. Besides, the famous man had called on her at the first possible moment; her house was the first by far to receive this mark of distinction, and his letter of introduction from a mutual woman friend mentioned the venerable culture of the Habsburg capital and its people, which this hardworking man hoped to enjoy between unavoidable business engagements. Diotima felt singled out like a writer who is being translated into the language of a foreign country for the first time, when she learned from the letter that this renowned foreigner knew the reputation of her intellect. She noted that he did not look in the least Jewish but was a noble-looking, reserved man of the classic-Phoenician type. Arnheim, too, was delighted to find in Diotima not only a woman who had read his books but who, as a classical beauty on the plump side, corresponded to his Hellenic ideal of beauty, with a bit more flesh on her, perhaps, to soften those strict classical lines. It could not long remain concealed from Diotima that the impression she was able to make in a twenty-minute conversation on a man of real worldwide connections was enough to completely dispel all those doubts through which her own husband, caught up as he was in his rather dated diplomatic ways, had insulted her importance.

She took quiet satisfaction in repeating that conversation to herself. It had barely begun when Arnheim was already saying that he had come to this ancient city only to recuperate a little, under the baroque spell of the Old Austrian culture, from the calculations, materialism, and bleak rationalism in which a civilized man's busy working life was spent nowadays.

There is such a blithe soulfulness in this city, Diotima had answered, as she was pleased to recall.

"Yes," he had said, "we no longer have any inner voices. We know too much these days; reason tyrannizes our lives."

To which she had replied: "I like the company of women. They don't know anything and are unfragmented."

And Arnheim had said: "Nevertheless, a beautiful woman understands far more than a man, who, for all his logic and psychology, knows nothing at all of life."

At which point she had told him that a problem similar to that of freeing the soul from civilization, only on a monumental and national scale, was occupying influential circles here.

"We must—" she had said, and Arnheim interrupted with "That is quite wonderful!"—"bring new ideas, or rather, if I may be permitted to say so"—here he gave a faint sigh—"bring ideas for the very first time into the domains of power." And she had gone on: Committees drawn from all sectors of the population were to be set up in order to ascertain what these ideas should be.

But just at this point Arnheim had said something most important, and in such a tone of warm friendship and respect that the warning left a deep mark on Diotima's mind.

It would not be easy, he had explained, to accomplish anything significant in this way. No democracy of committees but only strong individual personalities, with experience in both reality and the realm of ideas, would be able to direct such a campaign!

Up to this point, Diotima had gone over the conversation in her mind word for word, but here it dissolved into splendor—she could no longer remember what she had answered. A vague, thrilling feeling of joy and expectancy had been lifting her higher and higher all this time; now her mind resembled a small, brightly colored child's balloon that had broken loose and, shining gloriously, was floating upward toward the sun. And in the next instant it burst.

Thus was an idea it had lacked hitherto born to the great Parallel Campaign.

27

NATURE AND SUBSTANCE OF A GREAT IDEA

It would be easy to say what this idea consisted of, but no one could possibly describe its significance. For what distinguishes a great, stirring idea from an ordinary one, possibly even from an incredibly ordinary and mistaken one, is that it exists in a kind of molten state through which the self enters an infinite expanse and, inversely, the expanse of the universe enters the self, so that it becomes impossible to differentiate between what belongs to the self and what belongs to the infinite. This is why great, stirring ideas consist of a body, which like the human body is compact yet frail, and of an immortal soul, which constitutes its meaning but is not compact; on the contrary, it dissolves into thin air at every attempt to grab hold of it in cold words.

After this preamble it must be said that Diotima's great idea amounted to nothing more than that the Prussian, Arnheim, was the man to assume the spiritual leadership of the great Austrian patriotic endeavor, even though this Parallel Campaign contained a barb of jealousy aimed at Prussia-Germany. But this was only the dead verbal body of the idea, and whoever finds it incomprehensible or absurd is kicking a corpse. As concerns the soul of this idea, it was chaste and proper, and in any case her decision contained, so to speak, a codicil for Ulrich. She did not know that her cousin had also made an impression on her, although on a far deeper level than Arnheim, and overshadowed by the impression Arnheim had made; had she realized this, she would probably have despised herself for it. But she had instinctively guarded herself against such knowledge by declaring before her conscious mind that Ulrich was "immature," even though he was older than she was. She took the position that she felt sorry for him, which facilitated her conviction that it was a duty to choose Arnheim instead of Ulrich for the responsibilities of leading the campaign. On the other hand, after she had given birth to this resolution, feminine logic dictated that the slighted party now needed and deserved her help. If he felt shortchanged somehow, there was no better way to make up for it than by taking part in the great campaign, where he would have occasion to be much in her and Arnheim's company. So Diotima decided on that, too, but only as one tucks in a loose end.

28

A CHAPTER THAT MAY BE SKIPPED BY ANYONE
NOT PARTICULARLY IMPRESSED BY THINKING
AS AN OCCUPATION

Ulrich, meanwhile, was at home, sitting at his desk, working. He had got out the research paper he had interrupted in the middle weeks ago when he had decided to return from abroad; he did not intend to finish it, but it diverted him to see that he could still do that sort of thing. The weather was fine, but in the last few days he had gone out only on brief errands; he had not even set foot in the garden. He had drawn the curtains and was working in the subdued light like an acrobat in a dimly lit circus arena rehearsing dangerous new somersaults for a panel of experts before the public has been let in. The precision, vigor, and sureness of this mode of thinking, which has no equal anywhere in life, filled him with something like melancholy.

He now pushed back the sheets of paper covered with symbols and formulas, the last thing he had written down being an equation for the state of water as a physical example to illustrate the application of a new mathematical process; but his thoughts must have strayed a while before.

"Wasn't I telling Clarisse something about water?" he mused, but could not recall the particulars. But it didn't really matter, and his thoughts roamed idly.

Unfortunately, nothing is so hard to achieve as a literary representation of a man thinking. When someone asked a great scientist how he managed to come up with so much that was new, he replied: "Because I never stop thinking about it." And it is surely safe to say that unexpected insights turn up for no other reason than that they are expected. They are in no small part a success of character, emotional stability, unflagging ambition, and unremitting work. What a bore such constancy must be! Looking at it another way, the solution of an intellectual problem comes about not very differently from a dog with a stick in his mouth trying to get through a narrow door; he will turn his head left and right until the stick slips through. We do much the same thing, but with the difference that we don't make indiscriminate attempts but already know from experience approximately how it's done. And if a clever fellow naturally has far more skill and experience with these twistings and turnings than a dim one, the slipping-through takes the clever fellow just as much by surprise; it is suddenly there, and one perceptibly feels slightly disconcerted because one's ideas seem to have come of their own accord instead of waiting for their creator. This disconcerted feeling is nowadays called intuition by many people who would formerly, believing that it must be regarded as something suprapersonal, have called it inspiration; but it is only something impersonal, namely the affinity and coherence of the things themselves, meeting inside a head.

The better the head, the less evident its presence in this process. As long as the process of thinking is in motion it is a quite wretched state, as if all the brain's convolutions were suffering from colic; and when it is finished it no longer has the form of the thinking process as one experiences it but already that of what has been thought, which is regrettably impersonal, for the thought then faces outward and is dressed for communication to the world. When a man is in the process of thinking, there is no way to catch the moment between the personal and the impersonal, and this is manifestly why thinking is such an embarrassment for writers that they gladly avoid it.

But the man without qualities was now thinking. One may draw the conclusion from this that it was, at least in part, not a personal affair. But then what is it? World in, and world out; aspects of world falling into place inside a head. Nothing of any importance had occurred to him; after he had thought about water as an example, nothing had occurred to him except that water is something three times the size of the land, even counting only what everyone recognizes as water: rivers, seas, lakes, springs. It was long thought to be akin to air. The great Newton thought so, and yet most of his other ideas are still as up-to-date as if they had been thought today. The Greeks thought that the world and life had arisen from water. It was a god: Okeanos. Later, water sprites, elves, mermaids, and nymphs were invented. Temples and oracles were built by the water's edge. The cathedrals of Hildesheim, Paderborn, and Bremen were all built over springs, and behold, are these cathedrals not still standing today? And isn't water still used for baptism? And aren't there devotees of water and apostles of natural healing, whose souls are in such oddly sepulchral health? So there was a place in the world like a blurred spot or grass trodden flat. And of course the man without qualities also had modern scientific concepts in his head, whether he happened to be thinking of them or not. According to them water is a colorless liquid, blue only in thick layers, odorless and tasteless, as you recited over and over in school until you can never forget it, although physiologically it also contains bacteria, vegetable matter, air, iron, calcium sulfate, and calcium bicarbonate, and although physically this archetype of liquids is not basically a liquid at all but, depending on circumstances, a solid, a liquid, or a gas. Ultimately it all dissolves into systems of formulas, all somehow interlinked, and there were only a few dozen people in the whole wide world who thought alike about even so simple a thing as water; all the rest talk about it in languages that belong somewhere between today and some thousands of years ago. So one must say that as soon as a man begins to reflect even a little, he falls into disorderly company!

Now Ulrich remembered that he had, in fact, told all this to Clarisse, who was no better educated than a little animal; but notwithstanding the superstitions she was made of, one had a vague feeling of oneness with her. The thought pricked him like a hot needle.

He was annoyed with himself.

The well-known ability of thought as recognized by doctors to dissolve and dispel those deep-raging, morbidly tangled and matted conflicts generated in the dank regions of the self apparently rests on nothing other than its social and worldly nature, which links the individual creature to other people and objects. But unfortunately the healing power of thought seems to be the same faculty that diminishes the personal sense of experience. A casual reference to a hair on a nose weighs more than the most important concept, and acts, feelings, and sensations, when reported in words, can make one feel one has been present at a more or less notable personal event, however ordinary and impersonal the acts, feelings, and sensations may be.

"It's idiotic," Ulrich thought, "but that's how it is." It made him think of that dumb but deep, exciting sensation, touching immediately on the self, when one sniffs one's own skin. He stood up and pulled the curtains back from the window.

The bark of the trees was still moist from the morning. On the street outside a violet haze of gasoline fumes hovered. The sun shone through it, and people were moving along briskly. It was an asphalt spring, a seasonless spring day in autumn such as only cities can conjure up.

29

EXPLANATION AND DISRUPTIONS OF A NORMAL STATE OF AWARENESS

Ulrich and Bonadea had agreed on a signal to let her know that he was at home alone. He was always alone, but he gave no signal. He must have expected for some time that Bonadea, hatted and veiled, would show up unbidden. For Bonadea was madly jealous. When she came to see a man—even if it was only to tell him how much she despised him—she always arrived full of inner weakness, what with the impressions of the street and the glances of the men she passed on the way still rocking in her like a faint seasickness. But when the man sensed her weakness and made straight for her body, even though he had callously neglected her for so long, she was hurt, picked a quarrel, delayed with reproachful remarks what she herself could hardly bear to wait for any longer, and had the air of a duck shot through the wings that has fallen into the sea of love and is trying to save itself by swimming.

And all of a sudden she really was sitting here, crying and feeling mistreated.

At such moments when she was angry at her lover, she passionately begged her husband's forgiveness for her lapses. In accordance with a good old rule of unfaithful women, which they apply so as not to betray themselves by an untimely slip of the tongue, she had told her husband about the interesting scholar she sometimes ran into on her visits to a woman friend, although she was not inviting him over because he was too spoiled socially to come from his house to hers and she did not find him interesting enough to invite anyway. The half-truth in this story made it an easier lie, and the other half she used as a grievance against her lover.

How was she supposed to explain to her husband, she asked Ulrich, why she was suddenly visiting her friend less and less? How could she make him understand such fluctuations in her feelings? She cared about the truth because she cared about all ideals, but Ulrich was dishonoring her by forcing her to deviate further from them than was necessary!

She put on a passionate scene, and when it was over, reproaches, avowals, and kisses flooded the ensuing vacuum. When these, too, were over, nothing had happened; the chitchat gushed back to fill the void, and time blew little bubbles like a glass of stale water.

"How much more beautiful she is when she goes wild," Ulrich thought, "but how mechanically it all finished again." The sight of her had excited him and enticed him to make love to her, but now that it was done he felt again how little it had to do with him personally. Another abundantly clear demonstration of how a healthy man can be turned with incredible speed into a frothing lunatic. But this erotic transformation of the consciousness seemed only a special instance of something much more general: for an evening at the theater, a concert, a church service, all such manifestations of the inner life today are similar, quickly dissolving islands of a second state of consciousness that is sometimes interpolated into the ordinary one.

"Only a little while ago," he thought, "I was still working, and before that I was on the street and bought some paper. I said hello to a man I know from the Physics Society, a man with whom I had a serious talk not so long ago. And now, if only Bonadea would hurry up a little, I could look something up in those books I can see from here through the crack in the door. Yet in between we flew through a cloud of insanity, and it is just as uncanny how solid experiences close over this vanishing gap again and assert themselves in all their tenacity."

But Bonadea did not hurry up, and Ulrich was forced to think of something else. His boyhood friend Walter, little Clarisse's husband,

who had become so odd, had once said of him: "Ulrich always puts
tremendous energy into doing only whatever he considers unnecessary." He happened to remember it at this moment and thought,
"The same thing could be said about all of us nowadays." He remembered quite well! A wooden balcony ran all around the country
house; Ulrich was the guest of Clarisse's parents; it was a few days
before the wedding, and Walter was jealous of him. It was amazing
how jealous Walter could be. Ulrich was standing outside in the sunshine when Clarisse and Walter came into the room that lay behind
the balcony. He overheard their conversation without trying to keep
out of sight. All he remembered of it now was that one sentence. And
the scene: the shadowy depths of the room hung like a wrinkled,
slightly open pouch on the sunny glare of the outside wall. In the
folds of this pouch Walter and Clarisse appeared. Walter's face was
painfully drawn and looked as if it had long yellow teeth. Or one
could also say that a pair of long yellow teeth lay in a jeweler's box
lined with black velvet and that these two people stood spookily by.
The jealousy was nonsense, of course; Ulrich did not desire his
friends' wives. But Walter had always had a quite special ability to
experience intensely. He never got what he was after because he was
so swamped by his feelings. He seemed to have a built-in, highly me-
lodious amplifier of the minor joys and miseries of life. He was always paying out emotional small change in gold and silver, while
Ulrich operated on a larger scale, with, so to speak, intellectual
checks made out for vast sums—but it was only paper, after all.
When Ulrich visualized Walter at his most characteristic, he saw him
reclining at a forest's edge. He was wearing shorts and, oddly
enough, black socks. Walter did not have a man's legs, neither the
strong muscular kind nor the skinny sinewy kind, but the legs of a
girl; a not particularly attractive girl with soft, plain legs. With his
hands behind his head he gazed at the landscape, and heaven forbid
he should be disturbed. Ulrich did not remember actually having
seen Walter like this on any specified occasion which stamped itself
on his mind; it was more of an image that slowly hardened over a
decade and a half, like a great seal. And the memory that Walter had
been jealous of him at that time was somehow pleasantly stimulating.
It had all happened at that time of life when one still takes delight in
oneself. It occurred to Ulrich that he had now been to see them sev-

eral times, "and Walter hasn't been to see me once. But what of it? I might just go out there again this evening."

He planned, after Bonadea at last finished dressing and left, to send them word of his coming. It was not advisable to do that sort of thing in her presence because of the tedious cross-examination that would inevitably follow.

And since thoughts come and go quickly and Bonadea was far from finished, he had yet another idea. This time it was a little theory, simple, illuminating, and time-killing. "A young man with an active mind," Ulrich reflected, probably still thinking of his boyhood friend Walter, "is constantly sending out ideas in every direction. But only those that find a resonance in his environment will be reflected back to him and consolidate, while all the other dispatches are scattered in space and lost!" Ulrich took it as a matter of course that a man who has intellect has all kinds of intellect, so that intellect is more original than qualities. He himself was a man of many contradictions and supposed that all the qualities that have ever manifested themselves in human beings lie close together in every man's mind, if he has a mind at all. This may not be quite right, but what we know about the origin of good and evil suggests that while everyone has a mind of a certain size, he can still probably wear a great variety of clothing in that size, if fate so determines. And so Ulrich felt that what he had just thought was not entirely without significance. For if, in the course of time, commonplace and impersonal ideas are automatically reinforced while unusual ideas fade away, so that almost everyone, with a mechanical certainty, is bound to become increasingly mediocre, this explains why, despite the thousandfold possibilities available to everyone, the average human being is in fact average. And it also explains why even among those privileged persons who make a place for themselves and achieve recognition there will be found a certain mixture of about 51 percent depth and 49 percent shallowness, which is the most successful of all. Ulrich had perceived this for a long time as so intricately senseless and unbearably sad that he would have gladly gone on thinking about it.

He was put off by Bonadea's still giving no sign that she was done. Peering cautiously through the half-open door to the bedroom, he saw that she had stopped dressing. She felt it was indelicate of him to be so absentminded when they should be savoring the last drops of

their precious time together; hurt by his silence, she was waiting to
see what he would do. She had picked up a book that had in it, luckily, beautiful pictures from the history of art.

Ulrich was irritated by her waiting and pursued his meditations in
a state of vague impatience.

30

ULRICH HEARS VOICES

Suddenly his thoughts focused, and as though he were looking
through a chink between them, he saw Christian Moosbrugger, the
carpenter, and his judges.

In a manner that was painfully ridiculous to anyone not of his
mind, the judge spoke:

"Why did you wipe the blood off your hands?—Why did you
throw the knife away?—Why did you change into a clean suit and
underwear and clean clothes afterward?—Because it was Sunday?
Not because they were bloodstained?—How could you go to a dance
that same evening? What you had done did not prevent you from
going out for a good time? Did you feel no remorse whatsoever?"

Something flickers in Moosbrugger's mind—old prison wisdom:
Feign remorse. The flicker gives a twist to his mouth and he says: "Of
course I did!"

"But at the police station you said: 'I feel no remorse at all, only
such hate and rage I could explode!' " the judge caught him out.

"That may be so," Moosbrugger says, recovering himself and his
dignity, "it may be that I had no other feelings then."

"You are a big, strong man," the prosecutor cuts in, "how could
you possibly have been afraid of a girl like Hedwig?"

"Your Honor," Moosbrugger answers with a smile, "she was making up to me. She threatened to be even more treacherous than I
usually expected women of her sort to be. I may look strong, and I
am—"

"Well then," the presiding judge growls, leafing through his files.

"But in certain situations," Moosbrugger says loudly, "I am very shy, even cowardly."

The judge's eyes dart up from the file; like two birds taking off from a branch, they abandon the sentence they had just been perching on.

"But the time you picked that fight with the men on the building site you weren't at all cowardly!" the judge says. "You threw one of them down two floors, you pulled a knife on the others—"

"Your Honor," Moosbrugger cries out in a threatening voice, "I still stand today on the standpoint—"

The presiding judge waves this away.

"Injustice," Moosbrugger says, "must be the basis of my brutality. I have stood before the court, a simple man, and thought Your Honors must know everything anyway. But you have let me down!"

The judge's face had long been buried again in the file.

The prosecutor smiles and says in a kindly tone: "But surely Hedwig was a perfectly harmless girl?"

"Not to me she wasn't!" Moosbrugger says, still indignant.

"It seems to *me*," the presiding judge says emphatically, "that you always manage to put the blame on someone else."

"Now tell me, why did you start stabbing her?" the prosecutor gently begins at the beginning again.

31

WHOSE SIDE ARE YOU ON?

Was it something he had heard at the session of the trial he attended, or had he just picked it up from the reports he had read? He remembered it all so vividly now, as though he could actually hear these voices. He had never in his life "heard voices"—by God, he was not like that. But if one does hear them, then something descends like the quiet peace of a snowfall. Suddenly walls are there, from the earth to the sky; where before there was air, one strides through thick soft walls, and all the voices that hopped from one place to another in the cage of the air now move about freely within the white walls that have fused together down to their inmost essence.

He was probably overstimulated from work and boredom; such things happen sometimes; anyway, he didn't find it half bad, hearing voices. Suddenly he was saying under his breath, "We have a second home, where everything we do is innocent."

Bonadea was lacing up a string. She had meanwhile come into his room. She was displeased with their conversation; she found it in poor taste. She had long since forgotten the name of the man who had killed that girl, the case the papers had been so full of, and it all came back to mind only reluctantly when Ulrich began to speak of him.

"But if Moosbrugger can evoke this disturbing impression of innocence," he said after a while, "how much more innocent that poor, ragged, shivering creature was, with those mouse eyes under that kerchief, that Hedwig, who begged him for a night's shelter in his room and got herself killed for it."

"Must you?" Bonadea offered and shrugged her white shoulders. For when Ulrich gave this turn to the conversation, it came at the maliciously chosen moment when the clothes his offended friend had half put on when she came into his room, thirsting for reconciliation, were once more heaped on the carpet, forming a small, charmingly mythological crater of foam like the one that had given birth to Aphrodite. Bonadea was therefore ready to detest Moosbrugger, and to pass over the fate of his victim with a fleeting shudder. But Ulrich would not let it go at that, and insisted on vividly depicting for her Moosbrugger's impending fate.

"Two men who have no bad feelings against him at all will put the noose around his neck, only because that is what they are paid for. Perhaps a hundred people will be watching, some because it is their job, others because everyone wants to have seen an execution once in his life. A solemn gentleman in a top hat, frock coat, and black gloves will then tighten the noose, while at the same moment his helpers grab hold of Moosbrugger's legs and pull, to break his neck. Then the man with the black gloves plays doctor, and lays a hand on Moosbrugger's heart to check whether it is still beating—because if it is, the whole procedure has to be gone through once again, more impatiently and with less solemnity. Now, are you really for Moosbrugger or against him?" Ulrich asked.

Slowly and painfully, like a person awakened at the wrong time, Bonadea had lost "the mood," as she was accustomed to calling her fits of adultery. Now, after her hands had irresolutely held her slipping clothes and open corset for a while, she had to sit down. Like every woman in a similar situation, she had firm confidence in an established public order of such a degree of justice that one could go about one's private affairs without having to think about it. But now, reminded of the opposite, compassionate partisanship for Moosbrugger as victim took hold of her, sweeping aside any thought of Moosbrugger the criminal.

"Then you are always for the victim," Ulrich insisted, "and against the act?"

Bonadea expressed the obvious feeling that such a conversation in such a situation was not appropriate.

"But if your judgment is so consistent in condemning the act," Ulrich replied, instead of instantly apologizing, "then how can you justify your adulteries, Bonadea?"

It was the plural that was in such especially bad taste! Bonadea said nothing but sat down, with a disdainful look, in one of the luxurious armchairs and stared up, insulted, at the dividing line between wall and ceiling.

32

THE FORGOTTEN, HIGHLY RELEVANT STORY
OF THE MAJOR'S WIFE

It is not advisable to feel kinship with an obvious lunatic, nor did Ulrich do so. And yet why did one expert maintain that Moosbrugger was a lunatic and the other that he was not? Where had the reporters got their slickly factual account of the work of Moosbrugger's knife? And by what qualities did Moosbrugger arouse that excitement and horror that made half of the two million people who lived in this city react to him as if he were a family quarrel or a broken engagement, something so personally exciting that it stirred normally dormant areas of the soul, while his story was a more indifferent novelty in the country towns and meant nothing at all in Berlin or Breslau, where from time to time they had their own Moosbruggers, the Moosbruggers in their own families, to think about. The awful way society had of toying with its victims preoccupied Ulrich. He felt an echo of it in himself too. No impulse stirred in him either to free Moosbrugger or to assist justice, and his feelings stood on end like a cat's fur. For some unknown reason Moosbrugger concerned him more deeply than the life he himself was leading. Moosbrugger seized him like an obscure poem in which everything is slightly distorted and displaced, and reveals a drifting meaning fragmented in the depths of the mind.

"Thrill-seeking!" He pulled himself up short. To be fascinated with the gruesome or the taboo, in the admissible form of dreams and neuroses, seemed quite in character for the people of the bourgeois age. "Either/or!" he thought. "Either I like you or I don't. Either I defend you, freakishness and all, or I ought to punch myself in the jaw for playing around with this monstrosity!" And finally, a cool but energetic compassion would also be appropriate here. There was a lot that could be done in this day and age to prevent such events and such characters from happening, if only society would make half the moral effort it demands of such victims. But then it turned out that there was yet another angle from which the matter could be considered, and strange memories rose up in Ulrich's mind.

We never judge an act by that aspect of it which is pleasing or displeasing to God. It was Luther, oddly enough, who had said that, probably under the influence of one of the mystics with whom he was friends for a while. It could certainly have been said by many another religious. They were, in the bourgeois sense, all immoralists. They distinguished between the sins and the soul, which can remain immaculate despite the sins, almost as Machiavelli distinguished the ends from the means. The "human heart" had been "taken from them." "In Christ too there was an outer and an inner man, and everything he did with regard to outward things he did as the outer man, while his inner man stood by in immovable solitude," says Eckhart. Such saints and believers would in the end have been capable of acquitting even Moosbrugger! Mankind has certainly made progress since then, but even though it will kill Moosbrugger, it still has the weakness to venerate those men who might—who knows?—have acquitted him.

And now Ulrich remembered a sentence, which was preceded by a wave of uneasiness: "The soul of the Sodomite might pass through the throng without misgiving, and with a child's limpid smile in its eyes; for everything depends on an invisible principle." This was not so very different from the other sayings, yet in its slight exaggeration it had the sweet, sickly breath of corruption. And as it turned out, a space belonged to this saying, a room with yellow French paperbacks on the tables and glass-bead curtains instead of doors; and a feeling stirred in his chest as when a hand reaches inside the split carcass of a chicken to pull out the heart: It was Diotima who had uttered that sentence the last time he saw her. It came, moreover, from a contemporary author Ulrich had loved in his youth but whom he had since learned to regard as a parlor philosopher, and aphorisms like this taste like bread doused with perfume, so that for decades one doesn't want to have anything to do with any of it.

Yet however strong the distaste that this aroused in Ulrich, he thought it disgraceful that he had let it keep him all his life from returning to the other, authentic statements of that mysterious language. For he had a special, instinctive understanding for them, which might rather be called a familiarity that leapt over the understanding, although he could never make up his mind to embrace them wholeheartedly as tenets of faith. They lay—such statements, which spoke to him with a fraternal sound, with a gentle, dark inwardness that was the opposite of the hectoring tones of mathematical or scientific language, though otherwise indefinable—like islands scattered among his preoccupations, without connection and rarely visited; yet, when he surveyed them, to the extent that he had come to know them, it seemed to him that he could feel their coherence, as if these islands, only a little separated from each other, were the outposts of a coast hidden behind them, or represented the remains of a continent that had perished primordial eras ago.

He felt the softness of sea, mist, and low black ridges of land asleep in a yellowish-gray light. He remembered a little sea voyage, an escape along the lines of "A trip will do you good!" or "Try a change of scene!" and he knew precisely what a strange, absurdly magical experience had superimposed itself by its deterrent force once and for all, on all others of its kind. For an instant the heart of a twenty-year-old beat in his breast, whose hairy skin had thickened and coarsened with the years. The beating of a twenty-year-old heart inside his thirty-two-year-old chest felt like an improper kiss given by a boy to a man. Nevertheless, this time he did not shrink from the memory. It was the memory of a passion that had come to a strange end, a passion he had felt at twenty for a woman considerably older than he, not only in years but by virtue of her settled domestic state.

Characteristically, he remembered only imprecisely what she looked like. A stilted photograph and his memory of the hours he had spent alone thinking of her took the place of live impressions of the face, clothes, voice, and movements of this woman. He had in the meantime become so estranged from her world that the fact of her having been the wife of an army major struck him as so incredible, it was funny. By this time, he thought, she will long have been a retired colonel's wife. According to the regimental scuttlebutt she was a trained artist, a virtuoso pianist who had never performed publicly out of deference to the wishes of her family; later on, in any case, her marriage made such a career impossible. She did, in fact, play the piano beautifully at regimental parties, with all the radiance of a well-gilded sun floating above chasms of feelings, and from the first Ulrich had fallen in love not so much with this woman's sensual presence as with what she stood for. The lieutenant who at that time had borne his name was not shy; his eye had already practiced on female small game and even espied the faintly beaten poacher's path leading to this or that respectable woman. But for such twenty-year-old officers a "grand passion," if they thought of such a thing at all, was something else entirely; it was a concept, something that lay outside their range of activity and was as devoid of experienced content, hence as luminously vacuous, as only a really grand concept can be. So when for the first time in his life Ulrich saw in himself the possibility of applying this concept, it was as good as done; the part played in this by the major's wife was no more than that of the last contributory cause that triggers the outbreak of a disease. Ulrich became lovesick. And since true lovesickness is not a desire for possession but the world's gentle self-unveiling, for the sake of which one willingly renounces possession of the beloved, the lieutenant proceeded to explain the world to the major's wife in an unaccustomed and persistent manner such as she had never heard before. Constellations, bacteria, Balzac, and Nietzsche whirled around in a vortex of ideas the point of which, as she sensed with growing clarity, was directed at certain differences—not considered a proper subject of conversation in those days—between her own body and that of the lieutenant. She was bewildered by his insistence on linking love with subjects that, as far as she knew, had never had anything to do with love. One day, when they had gone out riding, as they walked beside their horses she left her hand in his for a moment and was appalled to find that her hand stayed there as if in a swoon. In the next second flames ran through them from their wrists to their knees and a bolt of lightning felled both of them so that they almost tumbled by the wayside, where they found themselves sitting on the moss, wildly kissing and then overcome with embarrassment, because love was so great and out of the ordinary that, to their surprise, they could find nothing to say or do other than what people usually do in such embraces. The horses, growing restive, at last released the lovers from this predicament.

The love between the major's wife and this too-young lieutenant remained short and unreal throughout its course. They both marveled at it; they held each other close a few more times, both sensing that something was wrong and would not let them come fully together, body to body in their embraces, even if they shed all obstacles of clothing and morality. The major's wife did not want to deny herself a passion she felt to be beyond her power to judge, but she was throbbing with secret reproaches on account of her husband and the difference in age. When Ulrich told her one day, on some threadbare pretext, that he had to take a long furlough, the officer's lady breathed a tearful sigh of relief. By this time Ulrich was so far gone in love that he had no more pressing need than to get away as quickly and as far as possible from the vicinity of the cause of this love. He traveled blindly at random, until a coast put an end to the railroad tracks, took a boat to the nearest island, and there, in some place he had never heard of, minimally provided with bed and board, he wrote that first night the first of a series of long letters to his beloved, which he never mailed.

These letters, written in the dead of night after filling his thoughts all day, were later lost—as they were probably meant to be. At first he had still had much to say about his love for her and all sorts of thoughts she inspired in him, but all that was soon and increasingly displaced by the scenery. Mornings the sun raised him from his sleep, and when the fishermen were out on the water, the women and children near their houses, he and a donkey who was grazing among the shrubs and hillocks between the island's two little villages seemed to be the only higher forms of life on this adventurous outpost of the world. Ulrich followed his companion's example and climbed up on a hillock or lay down on the island's rim in the company of sea, rock, and sky. He had no sense of presuming, because the difference in size did not seem to matter, nor did the difference between mind and nature, animate and inanimate; this communion diminished all kinds of differences. To put it quite soberly, these differences were neither lost nor lessened, but their meaning fell away; one was no longer "subject to those divisions that afflict mankind" as described by those religious seized by the mysticism of love, of whom the young cavalry lieutenant at that time knew absolutely nothing. Nor did he reflect on these phenomena—as a hunter on the track of wild game might track down an observation and follow it up—indeed, he hardly noticed them, but he took them into himself. He sank into the landscape, although it was just as much an inexpressible being borne up by it, and when the world surpassed his eyes, its meaning lapped against him from within in soundless waves. He had penetrated the heart of the world; from it to his far off love was no farther than the nearest tree. In-feeling linked living beings without space, as in a dream two beings can pass through each other without mingling, and altered all their relations. Other than this, however, his state of mind had nothing in common with dreaming. It was clear, and brimful of clear thoughts; however, nothing in him was moved by cause, purpose, or physical desire, but everything went rippling out in circle after ever-renewed circle, as when an infinite jet falls on a basin's surface. This was what he also described in his letters, and nothing else.

Life's very shape was completely altered. Not placed in the focus of ordinary attention but freed from sharpness. Seen this way, everything seemed a little scattered and blurred, and being infused all the while with a delicate clarity and certainty from other centers. All of life's questions and occurrences took on an incomparable mildness, gentleness, and serenity, while their meaning was utterly transformed. If in this state of being a beetle, for instance, should run past the hand of a man deep in thought, it was not an approach, a passing by, a moving off, nor was it beetle and man, but a happening that ineffably touched the heart, and not even a happening but, although it was happening, a condition. And with the help of such tranquil experiences everything that usually makes up an ordinary life was endowed with a radical new meaning for Ulrich at every turn.

In this condition even his love for the major's wife quickly took on its predestined form. Thinking of her incessantly, he sometimes tried to visualize her doing whatever she might be doing at that very moment, aided by his thorough knowledge of her circumstances. But as soon as he succeeded in seeing his beloved as if she were physically present, his feeling for her, which had grown so infinitely clairvoyant, became blind, and he had to quickly reduce her image to that blissful certainty of her-being-there-for-him-somewhere proper to a Great Love. It was not very long before she had turned entirely into that impersonal center of energy, the underground dynamo that kept his lights going, and he wrote her a final letter, setting forth that the great ideal of living for love actually had nothing to do with physical possession and the wish "Be mine!" that came from the sphere of thrift, appropriation, and gluttony. This was the only letter he mailed, and approximately the high point of his lovesickness, from which it soon declined and suddenly ended.

33

BREAKING WITH BONADEA

Meanwhile Bonadea, who could not go on staring continually at the ceiling, had stretched out on her back on the divan, her tender maternal belly in white batiste free to breathe unhampered by whalebone and laces. She called this position "thinking." It flashed through her mind that her husband was not only a judge but also a hunter, whose eyes sometimes sparkled when he spoke of the beasts that preyed on game; she felt there might be something in this to help both Moosbrugger and his judges. Yet she did not want her husband put in the wrong by her lover, except *as* a lover; her family feeling demanded that the head of her household be seen as dignified and respected. So she came to no decision. And while this conflict was drowsily darkening her horizon like two banks of clouds amorphously merging with each other, Ulrich enjoyed being free to follow his thoughts. But this had lasted for quite a while, and as nothing had occurred to Bonadea that would have given matters a new turn, she reverted to feeling aggrieved that Ulrich had negligently insulted her, and the time he was letting pass without making it up to her began to weigh on her as a provocation.

"So you think I am doing wrong in coming here to see you?" she finally asked him, with grave emphasis, sadly, but ready for battle.

Ulrich gave no answer but shrugged his shoulders. He had long since forgotten what she was talking about, but he simply couldn't stand her at this moment.

"So you are really capable of blaming *me* for our passion?"

"Every such question has as many answers hanging on it as there are bees in a hive," Ulrich replied. "All human spiritual disorder, with its never-resolved problems, hangs on every single one of them in some disgusting way."

He was only saying aloud what he had been thinking, off and on, all day. But Bonadea took "spiritual disorder" as referring to herself and decided that this was too much. She would have liked to draw the curtains again and so do away with this quarrel, but she would just as gladly have howled with grief. All at once she understood that Ulrich had grown tired of her. Given her temperament, she had hitherto never lost her lovers except as one mislays something and forgets it when attracted to something new, or in that other easy-come, easy-go fashion that, no matter how personally irritating sometimes, still had something of the air of the workings of a higher power. And so her first reaction to Ulrich's quiet resistance was the feeling that she had grown old. She was humiliated by her helpless and obscene position, half-naked on a sofa, an easy target for insults. Without stopping to think, she got up and grabbed her clothes. But the rustling and swishing of the silken chalices into which she was slipping back did not move Ulrich to remorse. Right above her eyes, Bonadea felt the stabbing pain of helplessness. "He's a brute," she said to herself over and over. "He said it on purpose to hurt me! He's not lifting a finger!" With every ribbon she tied and every hook she fastened, she sank deeper into that abysmally black well of a long-forgotten childish anguish at being abandoned. Darkness welled up around her; Ulrich's face was visible as if in the waning light, set hard and brutal against the dark of her misery. "How could I ever have loved that face?" Bonadea asked herself, but at the same moment the words "Lost forever!" tightened her whole chest in a spasm.

Ulrich, who guessed that she had made up her mind never to come back, did nothing to stop her. In front of the mirror, Bonadea firmly smoothed her hair put on her hat, and tied her veil. Now that the veil was fastened in front of her face it was all over; it was as solemn as a death sentence, or when the lock snaps shut on a suitcase. He was to have no last kiss, nor even to realize that he was missing his last chance ever to kiss her again!

At this thought she almost threw her arms around his neck in pity, and could have cried her eyes out on his chest.

34

A HOT FLASH AND CHILLED WALLS

After Ulrich had escorted Bonadea out and was alone again, he no longer had any desire to go on working. He went out to the street with the intention of sending a message to Walter and Clarisse that he would come to see them this evening. As he was crossing the small foyer, he noticed a pair of antlers on the wall; somehow they reminded him of Bonadea's movements when she had tied her veil before the mirror, except that here there was no resigned smile. He looked around, contemplating his environment. All these circular lines, intersecting lines, straight lines, curves and wreaths of which a domestic interior is composed and that had piled up around him were neither nature nor inner necessity but bristled, to the last detail, with baroque overabundance. The current and heartbeat that constantly flows through all the things in our surroundings had stopped for a moment. "I'm only fortuitous," Necessity leered. "Observed without prejudice, my face doesn't look much different from a leper's," Beauty confessed. Actually, it did not take much to produce this effect: a varnish had come off, a power of suggestion had lost its hold, a chain of habit, expectation, and tension had snapped; a fluid, mysterious equilibrium between feeling and world was upset for the space of a second. Everything we feel and do is somehow oriented "lifeward," and the least deviation away from this direction toward something beyond is difficult or alarming. This is true even of the simple act of walking: one lifts one's center of gravity, pushes it forward, and lets it drop again—and the slightest change, the merest hint of shrinking from this letting-oneself-drop-into-the-future, or even of stopping to wonder at it—and one can no longer stand upright! Stopping to think is dangerous. It occurred to Ulrich that every decisive point in his life had left behind a similar feeling.

He found a messenger and sent him off with his note. It was about four in the afternoon, and he decided to walk there, taking his time. It was a deliciously late-spring kind of fall day. There was a ferment in the air. People's faces were like spindrift. After the monotonous tension of his thoughts in the last few days he felt as if he were exchanging a prison for a warm bath. He made a point of walking in an amiable, relaxed manner. A gymnastically well trained body holds so much readiness to move and fight that today it gave him an unpleasant feeling, like the face of an old clown, full of oft-repeated false passions. In the same way, his truth-seeking had filled his being with capacities for mental agility, divided into troops of thoughts exercising each other, and given him that—strictly speaking—false clown expression that everything, even sincerity itself, assumes when it becomes a habit. So Ulrich thought. He flowed like a wave among its fellow waves, if one may say so, and why not, when a man who has been wearing himself out with lonely work at last rejoins the community and delights in flowing along with it?

At such a moment nothing may seem so remote as the thought that people are not much concerned, inwardly, with the life they lead and are led by. And yet we all know this as long as we are young. Ulrich remembered how such a day had looked to him in these same streets ten or fifteen years ago. It had all been twice as glorious then, and yet there had quite definitely been in all that seething desire an aching sense of being taken captive; an uneasy feeling that "Everything I think I am attaining is attaining me," a gnawing surmise that in this world the untrue, uncaring, personally indifferent statements will echo more strongly than the most personal and authentic ones. "This beauty," one thought, "is all well and good, but is it mine? And is the truth I am learning *my* truth? The goals, the voices, the reality, all this seductiveness that lures and leads us on, that we pursue and plunge into—is this reality itself or is it no more than a breath of the real, resting intangibly on the surface of the reality the world offers us? What sharpens our suspicions are all those prefabricated compartments and forms of life, semblances of reality, the molds set by earlier generations, the ready-made language not only of the tongue but also of sensations and feelings."

Ulrich had stopped in front of a church. Good heavens, if a gigantic matron were to have been sitting here in the shade, with a huge belly terraced like a flight of steps, her back resting against the houses behind her, and above, in thousands of wrinkles, warts, and pimples, the sunset in her face, couldn't he have found *that* beautiful too? Lord, yes, it was beautiful! He didn't want to weasel out of this by claiming he was put on earth with the obligation to admire this sort of thing; however, there was nothing to prevent him from finding these broad, serenely drooping forms and the filigree of wrinkles on a venerable matron beautiful—it is merely simpler to say that she is old. And this transition from finding the world old to finding it beautiful is about the same as that from a young person's outlook to the higher moral viewpoint of the mature adult, which remains absurdly didactic until one suddenly espouses it oneself. It was only seconds that Ulrich stood outside the church, but they rooted in him and compressed his heart with all the resistance of primal instinct against this world petrified into millions of tons of stone, against this frozen moonscape of feeling where, involuntarily, he had been set down.

It may be a convenience and a comfort for most people to find the world ready-made, apart from a few minor personal details, and there is no disputing that whatever endures is not only conservative but also the foundation of all advances and revolutions; but it must be said that this casts a feeling of deep, shadowy unease on those who live according to their own lights. It flashed on Ulrich with surprising suddenness, as he appreciated the architectural fine points of the sacred edifice, that one could just as easily devour people as build such monuments or allow them to stand. The houses beside it, the firmament above, the indescribable harmony of all the lines and spaces that caught and guided the eye, the look and expression of the people passing below, their books, their morals, the trees along the street . . . it all seems at times as stiff as folding screens, as hard as a printer's die stamp, complete—there is no other way of putting it— so complete and finished that one is mere superfluous mist beside it, a small, exhaled breath God has no time for anymore.

At this moment he wished he were a man without qualities. But it is probably not so very different for anyone. Few people in mid-life really know how they got to be what they are, how they came by their pastimes, their outlook, their wife, their character, profession, and successes, but they have the feeling that from this point on nothing much can change. It might even be fair to say that they were tricked, since nowhere is a sufficient reason to be found why everything should have turned out the way it did; it could just as well have

turned out differently; whatever happened was least of all their own
doing but depended mostly on all sorts of circumstances, on moods,
the life and death of quite different people; these events converged
on one, so to speak, only at a given point in time. In their youth, life
lay ahead of them like an inexhaustible morning, full of possibilities
and emptiness on all sides, but already by noon something is suddenly there that may claim to be their own life yet whose appearing is
as surprising, all in all, as if a person had suddenly materialized with
whom one had been corresponding for some twenty years without
meeting and whom one had imagined quite differently. What is even
more peculiar is that most people do not even notice it; they adopt
the man who has come to them, whose life has merged with their
own, whose experiences now seem to be the expression of their own
qualities, and whose fate is their own reward or misfortune. Something has done to them what flypaper does to a fly, catching it now by
a tiny hair, now hampering a movement, gradually enveloping it until
it is covered by a thick coating that only remotely suggests its original
shape. They then have only vague recollections of their youth, when
there was still an opposing power in them. This opposing power tugs
and spins, will not settle anywhere and blows up a storm of aimless
struggles to escape; the mockery of the young, their revolt against
institutions, their readiness for everything that is heroic, for martyrdom or crime, their fiery earnestness, their instability—all this
means nothing more than their struggles to escape. Basically, these
struggles merely indicate that nothing a young person does is done
from an unequivocal inner necessity, even though they behave as if
whatever they are intent upon at the moment must be done, and
without delay. Someone comes up with a splendid new gesture, an
outward or inward—how shall we translate it?—vital pose? A form
into which inner meaning streams like helium into a balloon? An expression of impression? A technique of being? It can be a new mustache or a new idea. It is playacting, but like all playacting it tries to
say something, of course—and like the sparrows off the rooftops
when someone scatters crumbs on the ground, young souls instantly
pounce on it. Imagine, if you will, what it is to have a heavy world
weighing on tongue, hands, and eyes, a chilled moon of earth,
houses, mores, pictures, and books, and inside nothing but an unstable, shifting mist; what a joy it must be whenever someone brings out

a slogan in which one thinks one can recognize oneself. What is more natural than that every person of intense feeling get hold of this new form before the common run of people does? It offers that moment of self-realization, of balance between inner and outer, between being crushed and exploding.

There is no other basis, Ulrich thought—and all this, of course, touched him personally as well—as he stood with his hands in his pockets, his face looking as peaceful and contentedly asleep as if he were dying in the sun's rays that whirled about him, a gentle death in snow—no other basis, he thought, for that everlasting phenomenon variously called the new generation, fathers and sons, intellectual revolution, change of style, evolution, fashion, and revival. What makes this craving for the renovation of life into a *perpetuum mobile* is nothing but the discomfort at the intrusion, between one's own misty self and the alien and already petrified carapace of the self of one's predecessors, of a pseudoself, a loosely fitting group soul. With a little attention, one can probably always detect in the latest Future signs of the coming Old Times. The new ideas will then be a mere thirty years older but contented and with a little extra fat on their bones or past their prime, much as one glimpses alongside a girl's shining features the extinguished face of the mother; or they have had no success, and are down to skin and bones, shrunken to a re-form proposed by some old fool who is called the Great So-and-so by his fifty admirers.

He came to a halt again, this time in a square where he recognized some of the houses and remembered the public controversies and intellectual ferment that had accompanied their construction. He thought of the friends of his youth; they had all been the friends of his youth, whether he knew them personally or only by name, whether they were the same age as he or older, all the rebels who wanted to bring new things and new people into the world, whether here or scattered over all the places he had ever known. Now these houses stood in the late, already fading afternoon light, like kindly aunts in outmoded hats, quite proper and irrelevant and anything but exciting. He was tempted to a little smile. But the people who had left these unassuming relics behind had meanwhile become professors, celebrities, names, recognized participants in the recognized development of progress; they had made it by a more or less direct path from the mist to the petrifact, and for that reason history may report of them someday, in giving its account of the century: "Among those present were . . ."

35

BANK DIRECTOR LEO FISCHEL AND THE PRINCIPLE OF INSUFFICIENT CAUSE

At this moment Ulrich was interrupted by an acquaintance addressing him out of nowhere. Before leaving home that morning this acquaintance had had the unpleasant surprise of finding in a side pocket of his briefcase a circular from Count Leinsdorf, which he had received some time ago and forgotten to answer because his sound business sense disinclined him from having anything to do with patriotic movements originating in high social circles. "Rotten business," he doubtless said to himself at the time, though that was not at all what he would have wanted to say publicly; but, as memory will, his had played a dirty trick on him by taking orders from this first, unofficial reaction of his feelings and letting the matter drop, instead of waiting for a considered decision. When he opened the form letter this time, he saw something he had previously overlooked and that now caused him acute embarrassment; it was really only a phrase, two little words that turned up in all sorts of places throughout the text, but these two words had cost the portly man several minutes of indecision as he stood, briefcase in hand, before leaving his house. They were: "the true."

Bank Director Fischel—for that is what he was called, Director Leo Fischel of the Lloyd Bank, though he was only a manager with the title of director—(Ulrich, though much younger, could regard himself as a friend from earlier days; he had been quite close to

Fischel's daughter, Gerda, the last time he had stayed in the city, though he had called on her only once since his return)—Director Fischel knew Count Leinsdorf as a man who made his money work for him and kept up with modern methods; in fact, running his mind over the account (Count Leinsdorf used Lloyd's, among other banks, for his dealings on the stock exchange), he recognized Count Leinsdorf for a man of consequence, as they say in business. Therefore Leo Fischel could not understand how he could have been so careless about so important an invitation, in which His Grace appealed to a select circle to take part in a great and communal undertaking. Fischel himself had been included in this circle only because of some very special circumstances, to be gone into later, and all this was the reason he had rushed up to Ulrich the moment he caught sight of him. He had heard that Ulrich had something to do with the affair, was indeed in a "prominent position"—one of those inexplicable but not uncommon rumors that anticipate the facts—and fired off three questions at him like a three-barreled pistol:

"What is really meant by 'the true patriotism,' 'the true progress,' and 'the true Austria'?"

Startled out of his mood but continuing its spirit, Ulrich replied in the manner he always fell into in his conversations with Fischel: "The P.I.C."

"The what?" Director Fischel innocently spelled the letters out after him, this time not suspecting a joke, because such abbreviations, while not so numerous then as they are now, were familiar from cartels and trusts, and radiated confidence. But then he said: "Please, no jokes just now, I'm in a hurry and late for a meeting."

"The Principle of Insufficient Cause," Ulrich elucidated. "You are a philosopher yourself and know about the Principle of Sufficient Cause. The only exception we make is in our own individual cases: in our real, I mean our personal, lives, and in our public-historical lives, everything that happens happens for no good or sufficient reason."

Leo Fischel wavered between disputing this and letting it pass. Director Leo Fischel of the Lloyd Bank loved to philosophize (there still are such people in the practical professions) but he actually was in a hurry, so he said: "You are dodging the issue. I know what progress is, I know what Austria is, and I probably know what it is to love my country too, but I'm not quite sure what true patriotism is, or what the true Austria, or true progress may be, and that's what I'm asking you."

"All right. Do you know what an enzyme is? Or a catalyst?"

Leo Fischel only raised a hand defensively.

"It doesn't contribute anything materially, but it sets processes in motion. You must know from history that there has never been such a thing as the true faith, the true morality, and the true philosophy. But the wars, the viciousness, and the hatreds unleashed in their name have transformed the world in a fruitful way."

"Some other time!" Fischel implored him, and then tried another tack: cards on the table. "Look, I have to cope with this on the Exchange, and I really would like to know what Count Leinsdorf actually has in mind: just what does he mean by that additional 'true' of his?"

"I give you my solemn word," Ulrich said gravely, "that neither I nor anyone else knows what 'the true' anything is, but I can assure you that it is on the point of realization."

"You're a cynic!" Director Fischel declared as he dashed off, but after the first step he turned back and amended himself: "Quite recently I was saying to Gerda that you would have made a first-rate diplomat. I hope you'll come see us again soon."

36

THANKS TO THE ABOVE-MENTIONED PRINCIPLE THE PARALLEL CAMPAIGN BECOMES A TANGIBLE REALITY BEFORE ANYONE KNOWS WHAT IT IS

Director Leo Fischel of the Lloyd Bank, like all bank directors before the war, believed in progress. As a capable man in his field he knew, of course, that only where one has a thorough knowledge of the facts can one have a conviction on which one would be willing to stake one's own money. The immense expansion of activities does not allow for such competence outside one's own field. Accordingly, efficient, hardworking people have no convictions beyond the limits of their own narrow specialties; none, that is, they will not instantly abandon under pressure from the outside. One might go so far as to say that conscientiousness forces them to act differently from the way they think. Director Fischel, for instance, could form no concept at all of true patriotism or the true Austria, but he did have his own opinion of true progress, which was certainly different from Count Leinsdorf's opinion. Exhausted by stocks and bonds or whatever it was he had to deal with, his only recreation an evening at the opera once a week, he believed in a progress of the whole that must somehow resemble his bank's progressively increasing profitability. But now that Count Leinsdorf claimed to know better even in this respect, and thus began to put pressure on Leo Fischel's conscience, Fischel felt that "you can never know, after all" (except, of course, with stocks and bonds), and since one might not know but on the other hand would rather not miss out on anything, he decided to informally sound out his general manager on the matter.

When he did, the general manager had for quite similar reasons already had a talk with the chief executive of the National Bank and knew all about it. For not only the general manager of the Lloyd Bank but, it goes without saying, the chief executive of the National Bank had also received an invitation from Count Leinsdorf. Leo Fischel, who was only a head of department, owed his invitation entirely to his wife's family connections: she came from the upper reaches of the government/bureaucracy and never forgot it, either in her social relations or in her domestic quarrels with Leo. He therefore contented himself, as he and his superior talked about the Parallel Campaign, with wagging his head significantly, as if to say "big proposition," though it might in other circumstances have meant "rotten business"—either way it couldn't hurt, but on account of his wife Fischel would probably have been happier if it had turned out to be a "rotten business."

So far, however, von Meier-Ballot, the chief executive who had been consulted by the general manager, had himself formed an excellent impression of the undertaking. When he received Count Leinsdorf's "suggestion," he went over to the mirror—naturally, though not for that reason—and there he saw, above the tailcoat and the little gold chain of his order, the composed face of a middle-class government minister, in which the hardness of money was at most barely visible somewhere far back in the eyes. His fingers hung down like flags in a calm, as though they had never in their life had to carry out the hasty movements with which an apprentice bank teller counts his cash. This bureaucratically overbred high financier who had hardly a thing in common any longer with the hungry, roaming wild dogs of the stock-exchange game, saw vague but pleasingly modulated possibilities ahead, an outlook he had an opportunity of confirming that same evening in conversation with the former Ministers of State von Holtzkopf and Baron Wisnieczky at the Industrialists' Club.

These two gentlemen were well-informed, distinguished, and discreet persons in some kind of high positions into which they had been shunted after the brief caretaker government between two political crises in which they had participated had become superfluous. They were men who had spent their lives in the service of the State and the Crown, with no taste for the limelight unless ordered into it by His Majesty himself. They had heard the rumor that the great campaign was to have a subtle barb aimed at Germany. They were still convinced, as they had been before the failure of their mission, that the lamentable manifestations that had even then been making the political life of the Dual Monarchy a focus of infection for Europe were extraordinarily complicated. But just as they had felt duty-bound to regard these problems as solvable when they received the order to solve them, so they would declare that it was not outside the realm of possibility that something might be achieved by the means Count Leinsdorf was suggesting. Specifically, they felt that "a landmark," "a splendid show of vitality," "a commanding role on the world stage that would have a bracing effect on the situation here at home," were goals so well formulated by Count Leinsdorf that one could no more refuse them than refuse a call for every man who desired the Good to step forward.

It is of course possible that von Holtzkopf and Wisnieczky, as men informed and experienced in public affairs, felt some qualms, especially as they might assume that they themselves would be expected to play a part in the further development of this campaign. But it is easy for people who live on the ground floor to be choosy and turn down whatever does not suit them. One whose gondola in life is nine thousand feet up in the air, however, can't simply step outside, even if one is not in accord with everything going on. And since persons in such high circles really are loyal and—as opposed to the previously mentioned bourgeois dither—do not like to act otherwise than they think, they must in many cases avoid giving too much careful thought to an issue. The banker von Meier-Ballot accordingly found his own favorable impression of the affair confirmed by what the two other gentlemen had to say about it; while he personally and professionally was given to caution, he had heard enough to decide that this was an affair to which he would lend his presence in any case, but without committing himself.

At this time the Parallel Campaign was not yet in existence, and not even Count Leinsdorf had any idea what form it would take. It can be said with certainty that at the moment, the only definite thing that had occurred to him was a list of names.

But even this is a great deal. It meant that even at this stage, without anyone needing to have a clear conception of anything, a network of readiness that covered a great many connections was in place; and one can certainly maintain that this is the proper sequence. For first it was necessary to invent knife and fork, and *then* mankind learned to eat properly. This was how Count Leinsdorf explained it.

37

By launching the slogan "Year of Austria," a journalist makes a lot of trouble for Count Leinsdorf, who issues a frantic call for Ulrich

Although Count Leinsdorf had sent out invitations in many directions "to start people thinking," he might not have made headway so quickly had not an influential journalist who had heard that something was in the wind quickly published two long articles in his paper offering as his own ideas everything he had guessed to be in the works. He did not know much—where, indeed, could he have found out?—but no one noticed; indeed, this was just what made it possible for his articles to be so irresistibly effective. He was really the inventor of the idea of the "Year of Austria" that he wrote about in his columns, without himself knowing what he meant by it but writing sentence after sentence in which this phrase combined with others as in a dream and took on new forms and unleashed storms of enthusiasm. Count Leinsdorf was horrified at first, but he was wrong. The phrase "Year of Austria" showed what it means to be a journalistic genius, for it was a triumph of true instinct. It caused vibrations to sound that would have remained dumb at the mention of an "Austrian Century"; the call to bring about such an era would have struck sensible people as impossible to take seriously. Why this is so would be hard to say. Perhaps a certain vagueness, a metaphorical quality that lessens realistic perceptions, lent wings to the feelings of more people than just Count Leinsdorf. For vagueness has an elevating and magnifying power.

It seems that the bona fide, practical realist just doesn't love reality or take it seriously. As a child he crawls under the table when his parents are out, converting their living room by this simple yet inspired trick into an adventure. As a boy he longs for a watch; as a young man with a gold watch, for a wife to go with it; as a man with watch and wife, for a promotion; and yet, when he has happily achieved this little circle of desires and should be peacefully swinging back and forth in it like a pendulum, his supply of unsatisfied yearnings does not seem to have diminished at all. For if he wants to elevate himself above the daily rut, he resorts to figures of speech. Since to him snow is evidently unpleasant at times, he compares it to a woman's shimmering bosom, and as soon as he begins to tire of his wife's breasts, he likens them to shimmering snow. He would be horrified if the beaks of his wife's nipples actually turned to coral, or their billing and cooing turned out to come from the horny beak of a real dove, but poetically it excites him. He is capable of turning everything into something else—snow to skin, skin to flower petals, petals to sugar, sugar to powder, powder to drifting snow again—as long as he can make it out to be something it is not, which may be taken to prove that he cannot bear to stay in the same place for long, no matter where he may find himself. Most of all, no true Kakanian could, in his soul, bear Kakania for long. To ask of him an "Austrian Century" would be tantamount to asking him to sentence himself and the world to the punishments of hell by an absurdly voluntary effort. An Austrian Year, on the other hand, was quite something else. It meant: Let's show them, for once, who we could be!—but, so to speak, only until further notice, and for a year at most. One could understand by it whatever one liked, it wasn't for eternity, and this somehow touched the heart. It stirred to life the deepest love of one's country.

And so Count Leinsdorf had an undreamed-of success. After all, his original idea had also come to him as such a figure of speech, but a number of names had occurred to him as well, and his moral nature aspired to something beyond such intangibles. He had a well-defined concept of the way the imagination of the common people or, as he now put it to a faithful journalist, the imagination of the public, must be directed to a goal that was clear, sound, reasonable, and in harmony with the true aims of mankind and their own country. This journalist, spurred on by his colleague's success, wrote all this down immediately, and as he had the advantage of having it from "an authentic source," it was part of the technique of his profession to draw attention to this by attributing his information in large type to "influential circles." This was precisely what Count Leinsdorf had expected of him, for His Grace attached great importance to being no ideologue but an experienced practical statesman, and he wanted a fine line drawn between a "Year of Austria" as the brainchild of a clever member of the press and the circumspection of responsible circles. To this end he borrowed the technique of someone he would not normally have liked to regard as a model—Bismarck—to let newsmen serve as the mouthpiece for his actual intentions so as to be able to acknowledge or disavow them as circumstances might dictate.

But while Count Leinsdorf acted with such shrewdness, he overlooked something. For it was not only a man like himself who saw the Truth we so much need; innumerable other people saw themselves as possessing it as well. It may be defined as a calcification of the previously described state of mind, in which one still makes metaphors. Sooner or later even the desire for these metaphors disappears, and many of the people who still retain a supply of definitively unfulfilled dreams create for themselves a point at which they stare in secret, as though it marks the beginning of a world that life still owes them. In almost no time after he had sent out his statement to the press, His Grace had intimations that all those who have no money harbor inside them an unpleasant crank. This opinionated man-within-the-man goes with him to the office every morning and has absolutely no way to air his protest against the way things are done in the world; so instead he keeps his eyes glued to a lifelong secret point of his own that everyone else refuses to see, although it is obviously the source of all the misery in a world that will not recognize its savior. Such fixed points, where the center of a person's equilibrium coincides with the world's center of equilibrium, may be, for instance, a spittoon that can be shut with a simple latch; or the abolition of open salt cellars in restaurants, the kind people poke their knives into, so as to stop at one stroke the spread of that scourge of mankind, tuberculosis; or the adoption of Oehl's system of shorthand, so effective a time-saver it can solve the problems of society once and for all; or conversion to a natural mode of living that would halt the present random destruction of the environment; not to mention a metaphysical theory of the motions of celestial bodies, simplification of the administrative apparatus, and a reform of sex life. In the right circumstances a man can help himself by writing a book about his point, or a pamphlet, or at least a letter to the editor, thereby putting his protest on the historical record, which is marvelously comforting even if nobody ever reads it. Usually, however, it can be counted on to attract the attention of a few readers who assure the author that he is a new Copernicus, whereupon they introduce themselves as unrecognized Newtons. This custom of picking the points out of each other's fur is widespread and a great comfort, but it is without lasting effect because the participants soon fall to quarreling and find themselves isolated again. However, it can also happen that a small circle of admirers gathers around one prophet or another, and with united energy accuses heaven of being remiss in not sufficiently supporting its anointed son. And if a ray of hope should suddenly fall from on high upon such little piles of points, as it did when Count Leinsdorf issued a public statement that a "Year of Austria"— if it should materialize, which was still not yet settled—would in any case have to be in accord with the true aims of existence, they receive it like saints vouchsafed a divine vision.

Count Leinsdorf had aimed at bringing about a powerful demonstration arising spontaneously out of the midst of the people themselves, meaning the universities, the clergy, certain names never absent from the rosters of charity affairs, and even the press. He was counting on the patriotic parties, the "sound sense" of the middle class, which hung out flags on the Emperor's birthday, and the support of leading financiers; he even included the politicians, because he hoped in his heart that his great work would render politics superfluous by bringing it all down to the common denominator of "our fatherland," from which he subsequently intended to subtract the "land," leaving the fatherly ruler as the only remainder. But the one thing His Grace had not reckoned with and that surprised him was the widespread need to improve the world, which was hatched out by the warmth of a great occasion as insect eggs are hatched by a fire. His Grace had not counted on this; he had expected a great amount of patriotism but was not prepared for inventions, theories, schemes for world unity, and people demanding that he release them from intellectual prisons. They besieged his palace, hailed the Parallel Campaign as a chance to help make the truth prevail at last, and Count Leinsdorf did not know what to do with them. In awareness of his social position he could not, after all, sit down at table with all these people, yet, given a mind filled with intense morality, he did not want to avoid meeting them, either; but since his education had been in politics and philosophy to the exclusion of science and technology, he had no way of telling whether there was anything to their proposals or not.

In this situation he felt an increasingly desperate need for Ulrich, who had been recommended to him as the very man for the occasion; obviously, his secretary or any ordinary secretary could not cope with such exigencies. Once, when he had been very annoyed with his secretary, he had even prayed to God—though he was ashamed of it the next day—for Ulrich to come. And when this did not happen, he personally took systematic steps to find him. He ordered the directory to be checked, but Ulrich was not yet in it. He then went to his friend Diotima, who could usually be counted on for advice, and it turned out that the admirable woman had actually seen Ulrich already, but she had forgotten to ask for his address, or pretended she had in order to use the opportunity to propose a new and far better candidate for secretary of the great campaign. But Count Leinsdorf was quite agitated and declared most positively that he had already grown used to Ulrich, that a Prussian was out of the question, even a reformed Prussian, and that he wanted to hear nothing at all about still further complications. Dismayed to see that he had apparently hurt his friend's feelings, he came up with an idea of his own—he told her that he would drive straight to his friend the Commissioner of Police, who should certainly be able to dig up the address of any citizen whatever.

38

CLARISSE AND HER DEMONS

When Ulrich's note arrived Walter and Clarisse were again playing the piano so violently that the spindly reproduction furniture rattled and the Dante Gabriel Rossetti prints on the walls trembled. The aged messenger who had found house and doors open without being challenged was met by a full blast of thunder in the face as he fought his way into the sitting room, and the holy uproar he had wandered into left him nailed to the wall with awe. It was Clarisse who finally discharged the onrushing musical excitement with two powerful crashes and set him free. While she read the note, the interrupted outpouring still writhed under Walter's hands; a melody ran along jerkily like a stork and then spread its wings. Clarisse kept a mistrustful ear on this while she deciphered Ulrich's handwriting.

When she announced their friend's impending arrival, Walter said: "Too bad!"

She sat down again beside him on her little revolving piano stool, and a smile that for some reason struck Walter as cruel parted her lips, which looked sensual. It was that moment when the players rein in their blood in order to be able to release it in the same rhythm, eyes blazing out of their heads in four long parallel axes while their buttocks tense and grip the little stools that keep trying to wobble on the long necks of their wooden screws.

The next instant, Clarisse and Walter were off like two locomotives racing side by side. The piece they were playing came rushing at their eyes like flashing rails, vanished under the thundering engine, and spread out behind them as a ringing, resonant, marvelously present landscape. In the course of this ride these two people's separate feelings were compressed into a single entity; hearing, blood, muscles, were all swept along irresistibly by the same experience; shimmering, bending, curving walls of sound forced their bodies onto the same track, bent them as one, and expanded and contracted their chests in the same breath. In a fraction of a second, gaiety, sadness, anger, and fear, love and hatred, desire and satiety, passed through Walter and Clarisse. They became one, just as in a great panic hundreds of people who a moment before had been distinct in every way suddenly make the same flailing movements of flight, utter the same senseless screams, their gaping mouths and staring eyes the same, all swept backward and forward, left and right, by the same aimless force, howling, twitching, tangling, trembling. But this union did not have the same dull, overwhelming force as life itself, where this kind of thing does not happen so easily, although it blots out everything personal when it does. The anger, love, joy, gaiety, and sadness that Clarisse and Walter felt in their flight were not full emotions but little more than physical shells of feelings that had been worked up into a frenzy. They sat stiffly in a trance on their little stools, angry, in love, or sad, at nothing, with nothing, about nothing, or each of them at, with, about something else, thinking and meaning different things of their own; the dictate of music united them in highest passion, yet at the same time it left them with something absent, as in the compulsive sleep of hypnosis.

Each of these two people felt it in his own way. Walter was happy and excited. Like most musical people, he considered these billowing surges and emotional stirrings, all this cloudy, churned-up, somatic sediment of the soul, to be the simple language of the eternal that binds all mankind together. It delighted him to press Clarisse to himself with the powerful arm of primal emotion. On this day, he had come home earlier than usual from the office, where he had been cataloging works of art that still bore the imprint of great, unfragmented times and emitted a mysterious strength of will. Clarisse had given him a friendly welcome, and now in the awesome world of music she was firmly bound to him. It was a day of mysterious successes, a soundless march as if gods were approaching. "Perhaps today is the day?" Walter thought. He wanted to bring Clarisse back, but not by force; the realization would have to rise up from her innermost self and incline her gently to him.

The piano was hammering glinting note heads into a wall of air. Although the origin of this process was entirely real, the walls of the room soon disappeared, and there arose in their place golden partitions of music, that mysterious space in which self and world, perception and feeling, inside and outside, plunge into one another in the most indefinable way, while the space itself consists entirely of sensation, certainty, precision, a whole hierarchy of ordered detail of glory. It was to these sensual details that the threads of feeling were fastened, spun from the billowing haze of their souls, and this haze was mirrored in the precision of these walls of sound and appeared clear to itself. The two players' souls hung like cocoons in these threads and rays. The more tightly they became enwrapped and the farther their beams were spread, the cozier Walter felt; his dreams were assuming so much of the shape of a small child that he was beginning here and there to strike the notes with a false and too sentimental emphasis.

But before it came to the point of making a spark of ordinary feeling strike through the golden mist and bring them back to an earthly relationship to each other, Clarisse's thoughts had diverged as far from Walter's as is possible for two people who are storming along side by side with twinned gestures of desperation and rapture. In fluttering mists, images sprang up, overlapped, fused, faded—that was Clarisse's thinking. She had her own way of thinking; sometimes several ideas were intertwined simultaneously, sometimes none at all, but then one could feel the thoughts lurking like demons behind the stage. The temporal sequence of events that gives such real support to most people became in Clarisse a veil that threw its folds one over the other, only to dissolve them into a barely visible puff of air.

This time, three people were around Clarisse: Walter, Ulrich, and the woman-killer Moosbrugger.

Ulrich had told her about Moosbrugger.

Attraction and repulsion blended into a peculiar spell.

Clarisse was gnawing at the root of love. It is a forked root, with kisses and bites, glances clinging and a tormented last-minute aversion of the gaze. "Does getting along well together lead to hate?" she wondered. "Does a decent life crave brutality? Does peacefulness need cruelty? Does orderliness long to be torn apart?" Such were, and were not, the thoughts provoked by Moosbrugger. Beneath the thunder of the music a world was suspended around her, a conflagration on the verge of breaking out, inwardly eating away at the timbers. But it was also like a metaphor, where the things compared are the same yet on the other hand quite different, and from the dissimilarity of the similar as from the similarity of the dissimilar two columns of smoke drift upward with the magical scent of baked apples and pine twigs strewn on the fire.

"We should never have to stop playing," she said to herself, and flicking the pages back she started again at the beginning when they reached the end. Walter smiled self-consciously and joined in.

"What is Ulrich actually doing with his mathematics?" she asked him.

Walter shrugged his shoulders while playing, as if he were at the wheel of a racing car.

"One would have to go on and on playing, till the very end," Clarisse thought. "If one could go on playing uninterruptedly to the end of one's life, what would Moosbrugger be then? A horror? An idiot? A black bird in the sky?" She did not know.

She knew nothing at all. One fine day—she could have calculated to the day when it happened—she had awakened from the sleep of childhood and found the conviction ready-made that she was called upon to accomplish something, to play a special role, perhaps even chosen for some great purpose. At the time, she knew nothing of the world. Nor did she believe what she was told about it—by her parents, her older brothers; their chattering was all well and good, but one could not assimilate what they said, one simply couldn't, any more than a chemical substance can absorb another that does not "fit" it. Then came Walter; that was the day; from that day on everything "fit." Walter wore a little mustache, a toothbrush on his upper lip; he called her "Fräulein," and all at once the world was no longer a barren, chaotic, parched plain but a gleaming circle, with Walter at the center, herself at the center, two centers coinciding in one. Earth, buildings, fallen leaves not swept away, aching lines of perspective (she remembered the moment as one of the most tormenting of her childhood, when she stood with her father looking at a scenic view, and her father, the painter, went into endless raptures over it, while for her, gazing into the world along those long aerial lines of perspective only hurt, as if she had to run her finger along the sharp edge of a ruler)—these were the things that had made up life before. Now, all at once, it had become hers, flesh of her flesh.

She knew then that she would do something gigantic, though what it would be she did not yet know. Meanwhile she felt it most powerfully with music, and hoped then that Walter would become an even greater genius than Nietzsche, to say nothing of Ulrich, who arrived on the scene later and who had merely given her Nietzsche's works as a present.

From then on things had progressed. How fast, it was now impossible to say. How badly she had played the piano before; how little she had known about music! Now she played better than Walter. And all the books she had read! Where had they all come from? She saw it all before her like swarms of black birds fluttering around a little girl standing in the snow. But somewhat later she saw a black wall with white spots in it; black stood for all she didn't know, and while the white ran together to form little, and sometimes larger, islands, the black remained unchangingly infinite. This blackness emitted fear and agitation. "Is this the devil?" she thought. "Has the devil turned into Moosbrugger?" Between the white spots she now noticed thin gray tracks; on these she had moved from one thing to the next in her life; they were events: departures, arrivals, excited discussions, battling with her parents, the marriage, the house, the incredible struggle with Walter. The thin gray tracks coiled like snakes. "Snakes!" Clarisse thought. "Snakes!" These events entangled her, trapped her, kept her from getting where she wanted to go, were slippery, and made her aim at a target she did not want.

Snakes, snares, slippery; that was life's way. Her thoughts began to race like life. Her fingertips dipped into the torrent of music. In the streambed of music snakes and snares came slithering down. Then the prison where they kept Moosbrugger hidden opened like the refuge of a quiet bay. Clarisse's thoughts entered his cell with a shudder. "One must make music to the end," she repeated to herself for encouragement, but her heart was trembling violently. When it had calmed down the entire cell was filled with her self. It was as gentle a feeling as salve on a wound, but when she tried to hang on to it forever it began to open and spread apart like a fairy tale or a dream. Moosbrugger sat with his head in his hand, and she freed him from his fetters. As her fingers moved, and as if at their summons, strength, courage, virtue, kindness, beauty, and riches entered the cell like a breeze from many meadows. "It doesn't matter at all why I am doing this, it doesn't matter why I feel like doing this," Clarisse felt, "what counts is that now I am doing it." She laid her hands, a part of her own body, on his eyes, and when she withdrew her fingers Moosbrugger had turned into a handsome youth and she stood beside him as an incredibly beautiful woman with a body as sweet and soft as a southern wine, not at all recalcitrant, as little Clarisse's body usually was. "This is the form of our innocence," she noted in some deep-down thinking layer of consciousness.

But why couldn't Walter be like this? Emerging from the depths of her music fantasy, she remembered what a child she still had been, already in love with Walter at fifteen, and prepared to save him by her courage, strength, and kindness from all the dangers that threatened his genius. And how beautiful it had been when Walter glimpsed those deep spiritual pitfalls everywhere. She wondered whether it had all been mere childishness. Their marriage had irradiated it with a disturbing light. Somehow their marriage was suddenly creating a great embarrassment for their love. Not that things hadn't also been wonderful of late, perhaps even richer in meaning and substance than formerly; still, that huge conflagration, those flames everywhere flickering across the sky, had dwindled to the difficulties of a fire of the hearth that is reluctant to burn. Clarisse was not quite sure whether her struggles with Walter still mattered. Meanwhile life was racing by like this music that was vanishing under her hands. In a wink it would be over! She was gradually overcome by hopeless terror. At this moment she noticed that Walter's playing was becoming unsure. His feelings were splashing like big raindrops on the keys. She instantly guessed what he was thinking of: the child. She knew that he wanted to bind her to himself with a child. They argued about it day in, day out. And the music did not stop for a second. The music knew no denial. Like a net whose entangling meshes she had not noticed, it was pulling shut with lightning speed.

Clarisse leapt up in mid-chord and banged the piano shut; Walter barely managed to save his fingers.

Oh, how that hurt! Still shocked, he understood everything. It was Ulrich's coming, the mere news of which was enough to throw her mind into a frenzy! Ulrich was bad for Clarisse in that he callously roused in her something that Walter himself hardly dared touch, that wretched streak of genius in Clarisse. The secret cavern where something calamitous was tearing at chains that might one day give way.

He did not stir, but only gave Clarisse a dumbfounded stare.

And Clarisse offered no explanations, stood there, and breathed hard.

She was definitely not at all in love with Ulrich, she assured Walter after he had spoken. If she were in love with him, she would say so at once. But she did feel kindled by him, like a light. She felt she shone more herself, amounted to more, when he was near; Walter on the other hand always wanted only to close the shutters. Besides, her feelings were nobody else's business, not Ulrich's and not Walter's!

Yet Walter thought that between the fury and indignation that breathed from her words he could scent a narcotic, deadly kernel of something that was not fury.

Dusk had fallen. The room was black. The piano was black. The silhouettes of two people who loved each other were black. Clarisse's eyes gleamed in the dark, kindled like a light, and in Walter's mouth, restless with pain, the enamel on a tooth shone like ivory. Regardless of the greatest affairs of state occurring in the world outside, and despite its vexations, this seemed to be one of those moments for which God had created the earth.

39

A MAN WITHOUT QUALITIES CONSISTS OF QUALITIES WITHOUT A MAN

But Ulrich did not come that evening. After Director Fischel had left him in such haste, he fell to mulling over the question of his youth: why the world so uncannily favored inauthentic and—in a higher sense—untrue statements. "One always gets one step ahead precisely when one lies," he thought. "That's another thing I should have told him."

Ulrich was a passionate man, but not in the sense of passions as commonly understood. There must indeed have been something that drove him again and again into this state, and it was perhaps passion, but when he was actually excited or behaving in an excited manner, his attitude was both passionate and detached at the same time. He had run the gamut of experience, more or less, and felt that he might still now at any time plunge into something that need not mean anything to him personally so long as it stimulated his urge to action. So without much exaggeration he was able to say of his life that everything in it had fulfilled itself as if it belonged together more than it belonged to him. *B* had always followed *A*, whether in battle or in love. Therefore he had to suppose that the personal qualities he had achieved in this way had more to do with one another than with him; that every one of them, in fact, looked at closely, was no more intimately bound up with him than with anyone else who also happened to possess them.

Nevertheless, one is undoubtedly conditioned by one's qualities and is made up of them, even if one is not identical with them, and so one can sometimes seem just as much a stranger to oneself at rest as in motion. If Ulrich had been asked to say what he was really like he would have been at a loss, for like so many people he had never tested himself other than by a task and his relation to it. His self-confidence had not been damaged, nor was it coddled and vain; it never needed that overhauling and lubrication that is called probing one's conscience. Was he a strong person? He didn't know; on that point he was perhaps fatefully mistaken. But he had surely always been a person with faith in his own strength. Even now he did not doubt that the differences between identifying with one's own experiences and qualities and distancing oneself from them was only a difference in attitude, in a sense a deliberate decision or a choice of the degree to which one saw one's life as a general manifestation or an individual one. Put simply, one can take what one does or what happens to one either personally or impersonally. One can feel a blow as an insult as well as a pain, in which case it becomes unbearably intensified; but one can also take it in a sporting sense, as a setback by which one should not let oneself be either intimidated or enraged, and then, often enough, one never even notices it. But in this second case, all that has happened is that the blow has been put in a general context, that of combat, so that it is seen to depend on the purpose it is meant to serve. And it is just this—that an experience derives its meaning, even its content, only from its position in a chain of logically consistent events—which is apparent when a man sees his experience not only as a personal event but as a challenge to his spiritual powers. He will also be less emotionally affected by what he does. But oddly enough, what we consider a sign of superior intelligence in a boxer is judged to be cold and callous in people who can't box but incline to an intellectual way of life. Whether we apply and demand a general or a personal attitude in a given situation is governed by all sorts of distinctions. A murderer who goes coolly about his business is likely to be judged particularly vicious; a professor who continues to work out a problem in the arms of his wife is seen as a dry-as-dust pedant; a politician who climbs to high office over the bodies of those he has destroyed will be called a monster or a hero, depending on his success; but soldiers, hangmen, or surgeons, on the other hand, are expected to behave with the same impassivity that is condemned in others. Without going further into the morality of these examples, we cannot overlook the uncertainty that leads in every case to a compromise between the objectively and the subjectively proper attitude.

This uncertainty gave Ulrich's personal problem a broader context. In earlier times, one had an easier conscience about being a person than one does today. People were like cornstalks in a field, probably more violently tossed back and forth by God, hail, fire, pestilence, and war than they are today, but as a whole, as a city, a region, a field, and as to what personal movement was left to the individual stalk—all this was clearly defined and could be answered for. But today responsibility's center of gravity is not in people but in circumstances. Have we not noticed that experiences have made themselves independent of people? They have gone on the stage, into books, into the reports of research institutes and explorers, into ideological or religious communities, which foster certain kinds of experience at the expense of others as if they are conducting a kind of social experiment, and insofar as experiences are not actually being developed, they are simply left dangling in the air. Who can say nowadays that his anger is really his own anger when so many people talk about it and claim to know more about it than he does? A world of qualities without a man has arisen, of experiences without the person who experiences them, and it almost looks as though ideally private experience is a thing of the past, and that the friendly burden of personal responsibility is to dissolve into a system of formulas of possible meanings. Probably the dissolution of the anthropocentric point of view, which for such a long time considered man to be at the center of the universe but which has been fading away for centuries, has finally arrived at the "I" itself, for the belief that the most important thing about experience is the experiencing, or of action the doing, is beginning to strike most people as naïve. There are probably people who still lead personal lives, who say "We saw the So-and-sos yesterday" or "We'll do this or that today" and enjoy it without its needing to have any content or significance. They like everything that comes in contact with their fingers, and are purely private persons insofar as this is at all possible. In contact with such people, the world becomes a private world and shines like a rainbow. They may be very happy, but this kind of people usually seems absurd to the others, although it is still not at all clear why.

And suddenly, in view of these reflections, Ulrich had to smile and admit to himself that he was, after all, a character, even without having one.

40

A MAN WITH ALL THE QUALITIES, BUT HE IS INDIFFERENT TO THEM. A PRINCE OF INTELLECT IS ARRESTED, AND THE PARALLEL CAMPAIGN GETS ITS HONORARY SECRETARY

It is not difficult to describe the basic traits of this thirty-two-year-old man Ulrich, even though all he knows about himself is that he is as close to as he is far from all qualities, and that they are all, whether or not he has made them his own, in a curious fashion indifferent to him. With a suppleness of mind, owing simply to his being gifted in various directions, he combines a certain aggressiveness. His is a masculine mind. He is not sensitive toward other people and rarely puts himself in their place, except to get to know them for his own purposes. He is no respecter of rights unless he respects the person whose rights they are, which is not very often. With the passage of time, a certain inclination toward the negative has developed in him, a flexible dialectic of feeling that easily leads him to discover a flaw in something widely approved or, conversely, to defend the forbidden and to refuse responsibilities with a resentment that springs from the desire to create his own responsibilities. Despite this need, however, and apart from certain self-indulgences, he lets himself be guided morally by the chivalrous code that is followed by almost all men as long as they live in secure circumstances in middle-class society, and so, with all the arrogance, ruthlessness, and negligence of a man called to his vocation, he leads the life of another man who has made of his inclinations and abilities more or less ordinary, practical and social use. He was accustomed, instinctively and without vanity, to regard himself as the instrument of a not unimportant purpose, which he intended to discover in good time; even now, early in this year of groping unrest, after he realized how his life had been drifting, the feeling that he was on his way somewhere was soon restored, and he made no special effort with his plans. It is none too easy to recognize in such a temperament the passion that drives it; ambiguously formed by predisposition and circumstances, its fate has not yet been laid bare by any really tough counterpressure. But the main thing is that the missing element needed in order to crystallize a decision is still unknown. Ulrich was a man forced somehow to live against himself, though outwardly he appeared to be indulging his inclinations without constraint.

Comparing the world to a laboratory had rekindled an old idea in his mind. Formerly he had thought of the kind of life that would appeal to him as a vast experimental station for trying out the best ways of being a man and discovering new ones. That the great existing laboratory was functioning rather haphazardly, lacking visible directors or theoreticians at the top, was another matter. It might even be said that he himself would have wanted to become something like a philosopher king; who wouldn't? It is so natural to regard the mind as the highest power, the supreme ruler of everything. That is what we are taught. Anybody who can dresses up in intellect, decks himself out in it. Mind and spirit, in combination with a numinous other something, is the most ubiquitous thing there is. The spirit of loyalty, the spirit of love, a masculine mind, a cultivated mind, the greatest living mind, keeping up the spirit of one cause or another, acting in the spirit of this or that movement: how solid and unexceptionable it sounds, right down to its lowest levels. Beside it everything else, be it humdrum crime or the hot pursuit of profits, seems inadmissible, the dirt God removes from His toenails.

But what of "spirit" standing by itself, a naked noun, bare as a ghost to whom one would like to lend a sheet? One can read the poets, study the philosophers, buy paintings, hold all-night discussions—does all this bestow spirit on us?* If it does, do we then possess it? And even if we should, this spirit is so firmly bound up with the accidental form in which it happens to manifest itself! It passes right through the person who wants to absorb it, leaving only a small tremor behind. What can we do with all this spirit? It is constantly being spewed out in truly astronomical quantities on masses of paper, stone, and canvas, and just as ceaselessly consumed at a tremendous cost in nervous energy. But what becomes of it then? Does it vanish like a mirage? Does it dissolve into particles? Does it evade the earthly law of conservation? The motes of dust that sink and slowly settle down to rest inside us bear no relation to all that expense. Where has it gone, where and what is it? If we knew more about it there might be an awkward silence around this noun, "spirit."

Evening had come; buildings as if broken out of pure space, asphalt, steel rails, formed the cooling shell that was the city. The mother shell, full of childlike, joyful, angry human movement. Where every drop begins as a droplet sprayed or squirted; a tiny explosion caught by the walls, cooling, calming, and slowing down, hanging quietly, tenderly, on the slope of the mother shell, hardening at last into a little grain on its wall.

"Why," Ulrich thought suddenly, "didn't I become a pilgrim?" A

---

*The German word *Geist* is variously rendered in this chapter as "mind," "spirit," and "intellect." A powerful concept in German culture, *Geist* embraces all three. —ED.

pure, uncontingent way of life, as piercingly fresh as ozone, presented itself to his senses; whoever cannot say "Yes" to life should at least utter the "No" of the saint. And yet it was simply impossible to consider this seriously. Nor could he see himself becoming an adventurer, though it might feel rather like an everlasting honeymoon, and appealed to his limbs and his temperament. He had not been able to become a poet or one of those disillusioned souls who believe only in money and power, although he had the makings of either. He forgot his age, he imagined he was twenty, but even so, something inside him was just as certain that he could become none of those things; every possibility beckoned him, but something stronger kept him from yielding to the attraction. Why was he living in this dim and undecided fashion? Obviously, he said to himself, what was keeping him spellbound in this aloof and nameless way of life was nothing other than the compulsion to that loosening and binding of the world that is known by a word we do not care to encounter by itself: spirit, or mind. Without knowing why, Ulrich suddenly felt sad, and thought: "I simply don't love myself." Within the frozen, petrified body of the city he felt his heart beating in its innermost depths. There was something in him that had never wanted to remain anywhere, had groped its way along the walls of the world, thinking: There are still millions of other walls; it was this slowly cooling, absurd drop "I" that refused to give up its fire, its tiny glowing core.

The mind has learned that beauty makes things or people good, bad, stupid, or enchanting. It dissects a sheep and a penitent and finds humility and patience in both. It analyzes a substance and notes that it is a poison in large quantities, a stimulant in smaller ones. It knows that the mucous membrane of the lips is related to the mucous membrane of the intestine, but also knows that the humility of those lips is related to the humility of all that is saintly. It jumbles things up, sorts them out, and forms new combinations. To the mind, good and evil, above and below, are not skeptical, relative concepts, but terms of a function, values that depend on the context they find themselves in. The centuries have taught it that vices can turn into virtues and virtues into vices, so the mind concludes that basically only ineptitude prevents the transformation of a criminal into a useful person within the space of a lifetime. It does not accept anything as permissible or impermissible, since everything may have some quality that may someday make it part of a great new context. It secretly detests everything with pretensions to permanence, all the great ideals and laws and their little fossilized imprint, the well-adjusted character. It regards nothing as fixed, no personality, no order of things; because our knowledge may change from day to day, it regards nothing as binding; everything has the value it has only until the next act of creation, as a face changes with the words we are speaking to it.

And so the mind or spirit is the great opportunist, itself impossible to pin down, take hold of, anywhere; one is tempted to believe that of all its influence nothing is left but decay. Every advance is a gain in particular and a separation in general; it is an increase in power leading only to a progressive increase in impotence, but there is no way to quit. Ulrich thought of that body of facts and discoveries, growing almost by the hour, out of which the mind must peer today if it wishes to scrutinize any given problem closely. This body grows away from its inner life. Countless views, opinions, systems of ideas from every age and latitude, from all sorts of sick and sound, waking and dreaming brains run through it like thousands of small sensitive nerve strands, but the central nodal point tying them all together is missing. Man feels dangerously close to repeating the fate of those gigantic primeval species that perished because of their size; but he cannot stop himself.

This reminded Ulrich of that rather dubious notion in which he had long believed and even now had not quite uprooted from himself: that the world would be best governed by a senate of the wisest, the most advanced. It is after all very natural to think that man, who calls in professionally trained doctors rather than shepherds to treat him when sick, has no reason, when well, to let public affairs be conducted by windbags no better qualified than shepherds. This is why the young, who care about the essentials in life, begin by regarding everything in the world that is neither true nor good nor beautiful, such as the Internal Revenue Service or a debate in the legislature, as irrelevant; at least they used to. Nowadays, thanks to their education in politics and economics, they are said to be different. But even at that time, as one got older and on longer acquaintance with the smokehouse of the mind, in which the world cures the bacon of its daily affairs, one learned to adapt oneself to reality, and a person with a trained mind would finally end up limiting himself to his specialty and spend the rest of his life convinced that the whole of life should perhaps be different, but there was no point in thinking about it. This is more or less how people who follow intellectual pursuits maintain their equilibrium. Suddenly Ulrich saw the whole thing in the comical light of the question whether, given that there was certainly an abundance of mind around, the only thing wrong was that mind itself was devoid of mind.

He felt like laughing. He was himself, after all, one of those specialists who had renounced responsibility for the larger questions. But disappointed, still-burning ambition went through him like a sword. At this moment there were two Ulrichs, walking side by side. One took in the scene with a smile and thought: So this is the stage on which I once hoped to play a part. One day I woke up, no longer snug in mother's crib, but with the firm conviction that there was something I had to accomplish. They gave me cues, but I felt they had nothing to do with me. Like a kind of feverish stagefright, everything in those days was filled with my own plans and expectations. Meanwhile the stage has continued revolving unobtrusively, I am somewhat farther along on my way, and I may already be standing near the exit. Soon I shall be turned out, and the only lines of my great part that I will have uttered are "The horses are saddled! The devil take all of you!"

But while the Ulrich smiling at these reflections walked on through the hovering evening, the other had his fists clenched in pain and rage. He was the less visible of the two and was searching for a magic formula, a possible handle to grasp, the real mind of the mind, the missing piece, perhaps only a small one, that would close the broken circle. This second Ulrich had no words at his disposal. Words leap like monkeys from tree to tree, but in that dark place where a man has his roots he is deprived of their kind mediation. The ground streamed away under his feet. He could hardly open his eyes. Can a feeling rage like a storm and yet not be a stormy feeling at all? By a storm of feeling we mean something that makes our trunk groan and our branches flail to the verge of breaking. But this storm left the surface quite undisturbed. It was almost a state of conversion, of turning back. There was no flicker of change in his facial expression, yet inside him not an atom seemed to stay in place. Ulrich's senses were unclouded, and yet each person he passed was perceived in some out-of-the-ordinary way by his eye, each sound differently by his ear. He could not have said more sharply, nor more deeply either, nor more softly, nor more naturally or unnaturally. Ulrich could not say anything at all, but at this moment he thought of that curious experience, "spirit," as he would of a beloved who had deceived him all his life without his loving her less, and it bound him to everything that came his way. For in love everything is love, even pain and revulsion. The tiny twig on the tree and the pale windowpane in the evening light became an experience deeply embedded in his own nature, barely expressible in words. Things seemed to consist not of wood and stone but of some grandiose and infinitely tender immorality that, the moment it came in contact with him, turned into a deep moral shock.

All this lasted no longer than a smile, and just as Ulrich was thinking, "Now for once I shall remain wherever it has carried me," he had the misfortune to run into an obstacle that shattered this tension.

What happened now came out of a wholly different world than the one in which Ulrich had just been experiencing trees and stones as a sensitive extension of his own body.

A left-wing tabloid had slavered its venomous spittle all over the Great Idea, as Count Leinsdorf might have put it, calling it just another sensation for the ruling class in the wake of the latest sex murder, and this caused an honest workingman who had been drinking to lose his temper. He had brushed up against two solid citizens pleased with their day's business who, convinced that a contented frame of mind could express itself anywhere, were rather loudly airing their approval of the great patriotic campaign they had read about in *their* paper. Words were exchanged, and as the proximity of a policeman encouraged the citizens as much as it provoked their attacker, the scene became increasingly impassioned. The policeman began by watching it over his shoulder, subsequently turning to face it and then coming closer; he attended as an observer, like a protruding offshoot of the iron machinery of the state, which ends in buttons and other metal trim. There is always something ghostly about living constantly in a well-ordered state. You cannot step into the street or drink a glass of water or get on a streetcar without touching the balanced levers of a gigantic apparatus of laws and interrelations, setting them in motion or letting them maintain you in your peaceful existence; one knows hardly any of these levers, which reach deep into the inner workings and, coming out the other side, lose themselves in a network whose structure has never yet been unraveled by anyone. So one denies their existence, just as the average citizen denies the air, maintaining that it is empty space. But all these things that one denied, these colorless, odorless, tasteless, weightless, and morally indefinable things such as water, air, space, money, and the passing of time, turn out in truth to be the most important things of all, and this gives life a certain spooky quality. Sometimes a man may be seized by panic, helpless as in a dream, thrashing about wildly like an animal that has blundered into the incomprehensible mechanism of a net. Such was the effect of the policeman's buttons on the workingman, and it was at this moment that the arm of the state, feeling that it was not being respected in the proper manner, proceeded to make an arrest.

It was not made without resistance and repeated pronouncements of rebellious sentiments. Flattered by the sensation he was creating, the drunk unleashed a previously hidden, total antipathy toward his fellowman. An impassioned struggle for self-assertion began. A heightened sense of self had to contend in him with the uncanny feeling that he was not settled inside his own skin. The world, too, was unsettled; it was a wavering mist continually losing and changing shape. Buildings stood slanted, broken out of space; between them people were ridiculous, swarming, yet fraternal ninnies. I have been called to straighten things out here, the staggering drunk felt. The whole scene was filled with something shimmering, and some piece of what was happening was clearly getting through to him, but then the walls started spinning again. His eyes were popping out of his head like stalks, while the soles of his feet still clung to the ground. An amazing stream had begun to pour from his mouth; words came from somewhere deep inside; there was no comprehending how they had ever got in there in the first place; possibly they were abusive. It was hard to tell. Outside and inside were all tangled up together. The anger was not an inner anger, but only the physical shell of anger roused to frenzy, and the face of a policeman came very slowly forward to meet a clenched fist until it bled.

But the policeman, too, had meanwhile turned into three policemen. With the other policemen a crowd had come running; the drunk had thrown himself to the ground and was resisting arrest. Ulrich now did something rash. He had picked up the words "offense against the Crown" and remarked that the man was in no condition to be held responsible for insulting anyone and should be sent home to sleep it off. He said it casually enough, but to the wrong people. The fellow now shouted that Ulrich was welcome to join His Majesty in kissing his————! and a policeman who obviously blamed this relapse on Ulrich's interference barked at him to clear out. But Ulrich was unaccustomed to regarding the state as other than a hotel in which one was entitled to polite service, and objected to being addressed in such a tone; whereupon the police unexpectedly decided that one drunk did not justify the presence of three policemen and arrested Ulrich as well.

The hand of a uniformed man now clutched his arm. Ulrich's arm was considerably stronger than this offensive grip, but he did not dare break it; it would have meant letting himself in for a hopeless boxing match with the armed power of the state, so he had no other recourse than a polite request that they let him go along voluntarily. The station was in the district headquarters, and as he entered, Ulrich was reminded by the floor and walls of an army barracks. They were filled with the same grim struggle between relentlessly dragged-in dirt and crude detergents. The next thing he noticed was the appointed symbol of civil authority, two writing desks—writing crates, really—topped by a balustrade with several of its little columns missing, and covered with torn and scorched cloth and resting on very low, ball-shaped feet with only the last peeling traces of brownish-yellow varnish clinging to the wood it had once coated, back in the reign of the Emperor Ferdinand. Third, the place was filled with a heavy intimation that here one was expected to wait, without asking any questions. His policeman, after stating the grounds of the arrest, stood beside Ulrich like a column. Ulrich immediately tried to give some sort of explanation. The sergeant in command of this fortress raised an eye from the form he had been filling in when the convoy arrived, looked Ulrich up and down, then dropped his eye again and without a word went on filling in his form. Ulrich had a sense of infinity. Then the sergeant pushed the form aside, took a volume from the shelf, made an entry, sprinkled sand on it, put the book back, took down another, made an entry, sprinkled sand, pulled a file out of a bundle of similar files, and continued as before. Ulrich felt a second infinity unfolding during which the constellations moved in their predetermined orbits and he did not exist.

From this office an open door led into a corridor lined with cells. Ulrich's protégé had been taken there immediately on arrival, and as nothing more was heard from him, his intoxication had probably blessed him with sleep. But there was a sense of ominous other things going on. The corridor with the cells must have had a second entrance; Ulrich kept hearing heavy-footed comings and goings, doors slamming, muffled voices, and suddenly, as someone else was brought in, one of those voices rose in a desperate plea: "If you have a spark of human feeling, don't arrest me!" The voice broke, and there was something curiously out of place, almost ridiculous, in this appeal to a functionary's feelings, since functions are only carried out impersonally. The sergeant raised his head for a moment, without entirely abandoning his file. Ulrich heard the determined shuffle of many feet, whose bodies were presumably mutely pushing a resistant body along. Then came the sound of two feet alone, stumbling as after a shove. A door slammed shut loudly, a bolt clicked, the uniformed man at the desk had bent his head again, and in the air lay the silence of a full stop set in its proper place at the end of a sentence.

Ulrich seemed to have been mistaken, however, in assuming that he himself did not yet exist in the cosmos of the police, for the next time the sergeant raised his head he looked straight at Ulrich; the last lines he had written gleamed damply, unblotted with sand, and Ulrich's case suddenly appeared to have been officially in this bureaucratic existence for some time. Name? Age? Occupation? Address? Ulrich was being questioned.

He felt as though he had been sucked into a machine that was dismembering him into impersonal, general components before the question of his guilt or innocence came up at all. His name, the most intellectually meaningless yet most emotionally charged words in the language for him, meant nothing here. His works, which had secured his reputation in the scientific world, a world ordinarily of such solid standing, here did not exist; he was not asked about them even once. His face counted only as an aggregate of officially describable features—it seemed to him that he had never before pondered the fact that his eyes were gray eyes, one of the four officially recognized kinds of eyes, one pair among millions; his hair was blond, his build tall, his face oval, and his distinguishing marks none, although he had his own opinion on that point. His own feeling was that he was tall and broad-shouldered, with a chest curving like a filled sail on the mast, and joints fastening his muscles like small links of steel whenever he was angry or fighting or when Bonadea was clinging to him; but that he was slender, fine-boned, dark, and as soft as a jellyfish floating in the water whenever he was reading a book that moved him or felt touched by a breath of that great homeless love whose presence in the world he had never been able to understand. So he could, even at such a moment as this, himself appreciate this statistical demystification of his person and feel inspired by the quantitative and descriptive procedures applied to him by the police apparatus as if it were a love lyric invented by Satan. The most amazing thing about it was that the police could not only dismantle a man so that nothing was left of him, they could also put him together again, recognizably and unmistakably, out of the same worthless components. All this achievement takes is that something imponderable be added, which they call "suspicion."

All at once, Ulrich realized that it would take the coolest wit he could muster to extricate himself from the fix his foolishness had got him into. The questioning continued. He tried to imagine their reaction if he were to answer that his address was that of a stranger. Or if he replied, in answer to the question why he had done what he had done, that he always did something other than what he was really interested in doing? But outwardly he gave the proper answers as to street and house number, and tried to make up an acceptable version of his conduct. The feebleness of his mind's inward authority vis-à-vis the police sergeant's outward authority was acutely embarrassing; nevertheless, he finally glimpsed a chance of saving the situation. Even as he responded to the query "Occupation?" with "Independent"—he could not have brought himself to say "Engaged in independent research"—he saw, in the eye that was fixed on him, the same lackluster expression as if he had said "homeless," but then, when in the list of particulars his father's status came up and it appeared that his father was a member of the Upper House, the look changed. It was still mistrustful, but something in it immediately gave Ulrich the feeling of a swimmer, tossed this way and that by huge waves, who suddenly feels his big toe scraping solid ground.

With quickening presence of mind he seized his advantage. He instantly qualified everything he had so far admitted; he confronted this authority of ears bound by their oath of office with the express demand to be heard by the Commissioner himself, and when this merely evoked a smile he lied—quite casually, with a happily recovered naturalness, prepared to talk himself out of it if threatened with a noose of demands for precise details—and said that he was a friend of Count Leinsdorf's and secretary of the great patriotic campaign one read so much about in the newspapers. He could see immediately that this had the effect, previously unaroused, of causing him to be taken seriously as a person, and he pressed his advantage.

The result was that the sergeant now eyed him indignantly, because he did not want to take the responsibility either of detaining this catch or of letting it go. As there was no higher official in the building at this hour he resorted to an expedient that showed, to the simple sergeant's credit, how much he had learned from his superiors about handling awkward cases. He made a solemn face and expressed grave misgivings that Ulrich apparently not only had been guilty of insulting an officer of the law and interfering with the execution of his duty but, considering the position he claimed to hold, also came under suspicion of being involved in obscure, possibly political, machinations and would therefore have to submit to being transferred to the political division at central police headquarters.

So a few minutes later Ulrich was on his way through the night, in a cab he had been permitted to hire, at his side a plainclothesman not much inclined to conversation. As they approached police headquarters the prisoner saw the brightly lit windows on the second floor, where at this late hour an important conference was still going on in the Chief Commissioner's office. This building was no gloomy hole but rather more like a Ministry, and Ulrich was already breathing a more familiar air. He soon noticed, too, that the officer on night duty quickly recognized what an absurd blunder the exasperated peripheral apparatus had made in arresting Ulrich; still, it was quite inadvisable to release from the clutches of the law someone so reckless as to run into them uninvited. The next-higher official at headquarters also had an iron machine for a face and insisted that the prisoner's own rashness made it extremely difficult for the police to take responsibility for his release. Ulrich had already twice gone over all the points that had worked so well with the sergeant, but with no effect on this higher official, and he was about to give up hope when suddenly his judge's face underwent a remarkable, almost happy, change. Reading the charge again with care, he asked Ulrich to repeat his name, made sure of his address, politely asked him to wait a moment, and left the room. After ten minutes he came back, looking like a man who had remembered something that pleased him, and with striking courtesy invited the arrested gentleman to follow him. At the door of one of the well-lit rooms on the upper floor he said only: "The Chief Commissioner would like to speak with you personally," and the next moment Ulrich found himself facing a gentleman with the muttonchop whiskers he knew so well by now, who had just come from the conference room next door.

He was about to explain, in a tone of gentle reproach, his presence as the consequence of an error at the local police office but was anticipated by the Chief Commissioner, who greeted him with the words: "An unfortunate misunderstanding, my dear Herr Doktor, the Inspector has already told me all about it. All the same, a slight penalty is in order, in view of . . . ," and he looked at Ulrich roguishly (if such a word may be used at all of the highest police official), as though giving him a chance to guess the answer himself.

Ulrich was totally stumped by the riddle.

"His Grace!" the Commissioner offered by way of assistance.

"His Grace Count Leinsdorf," he went on, "asked me most urgently for your whereabouts, just a few hours ago."

Ulrich still did not quite follow.

"You are not in the directory, my dear sir," the Commissioner explained in a tone of mock reproach, and as though this were Ulrich's only crime.

Ulrich bowed, with a formal smile.

"I gather that you are expected to call on His Grace tomorrow on a matter of great public importance, and I cannot bring myself to prevent you from doing so by locking you up," the master of the iron machine concluded his little joke.

It may be assumed that the Chief Commissioner would have regarded Ulrich's arrest as unwarranted in any case, since the Inspector who had happened to recall Ulrich's name coming up the first time at central police headquarters a few hours before had represented the incident to the Chief Commissioner in such a way as to make the conclusion inevitable that no one had actually interfered with the law arbitrarily. His Grace, incidentally, never heard how Ulrich had been tracked down. Ulrich felt obliged to pay his call the day following this evening of lèse-majesté, and during this visit was immediately appointed Honorary Secretary to the great patriotic campaign. Count Leinsdorf, had he known how it had all come about, would not have been able to say otherwise than that it was like a miracle.

41

RACHEL AND DIOTIMA

Shortly afterward the first session of the great patriotic campaign was held at Diotima's.

The dining room had been transformed into a conference room. The dining table, fully extended and covered with green baize, occupied the center of the room. Sheets of bone-white ministry paper with pencils of varying degrees of hardness were laid at each place. The sideboard had been removed. The corners of the room were empty and austere. The walls were reverently bare but for a portrait of His Majesty hung by Diotima and that of a wasp-waisted lady which Tuzzi in his consular days had brought home from somewhere and which might pass for an ancestral portrait. Diotima would have loved to put a crucifix at the head of the table, but Tuzzi had laughed her out of it before tactfully absenting himself from his house for the day.

For the Parallel Campaign was to be inaugurated quite privately. No government ministers or official bigwigs appeared, nor any politicians. The intention was to start with a small, select group of none but selfless servants of the Idea: The head of the International Bank, Herr von Holtzkopf and Baron Wisnieczky, a few ladies of the high nobility, some well-known figures associated with the city's great charities, and, in accord with Count Leinsdorf's principle of "capital and culture," representatives of the great universities, the art academies, industry, the landowning families, and the Church were expected. The government was represented by a few unobtrusive young ministry officials who fitted into this social circle and enjoyed their chiefs' confidence. This mixture was in keeping with the wishes of Count Leinsdorf, who had dreamed of a spontaneous manifestation arising from the midst of the people but who found it a great relief, after his experience with their reformist zeal, to know with whom one was dealing.

The little maid Rachel (somewhat freely translated by her mistress into a French "Rachelle") had been up and about since six o'clock that morning. She had extended the big dining table, pushed two card tables up to it, covered the whole with green baize, and dusted with special care, carrying out all these burdensome tasks in great excitement. Diotima had said to her the previous evening: "Tomorrow we may be making world history here!" and Rachel's whole body was aglow with happiness at being part of a household where such an event could take place—a great compliment to the event, since Rachel's body, beneath its black uniform, was as exquisite as Meissen porcelain.

Rachel was nineteen and believed in miracles. She had been born in a squalid shack in Poland, where a mezuzah hung on the doorpost and the soil came up through the cracks in the floorboards. She had been cursed and driven out of the door, her mother standing by with a helpless look on her face, her brothers and sisters grinning with fear. She had pleaded for mercy on her knees, her heart strangled with shame, but to no avail. An unscrupulous young fellow had seduced her; she no longer knew how; she had had to give birth to her child in the house of strangers and then had left the country. Rachel had traveled; despair rolled along with her under the filthy cart in which she rode until, wept out, she saw the capital city, toward which some instinct had driven her, as some great wall of fire into which she wanted to hurl herself to die. But—oh true miracle—this wall parted and took her in. Since then, Rachel had always felt as though she were living in the interior of a golden flame. Chance had brought her to Diotima's house, and Diotima regarded running away from home in Galicia as quite natural, if it led to her. After they had got to know each other well, Diotima sometimes told the little girl about the famous and important people who regularly visited the house where "Rachelle" had the privilege of serving; she had even told her a few things about the Parallel Campaign for the pleasure of seeing Rachel's eyes light up like a pair of golden mirrors radiantly reflecting her mistress's image.

For even if she had been cursed by her father because of some unscrupulous fellow, Rachel was an honorable girl and loved simply everything about Diotima: her soft dark hair, which Rachel was allowed to brush mornings and evenings; the dresses she helped her into; the Chinese lacquerwork and the little carved Indian tables; the books in foreign languages lying about, of which she understood not a word; she also loved Herr Tuzzi and, most recently, the nabob who had paid a call on her mistress the second day after his arrival in town—she made it out to be the first day. Rachel had stared at him in the hall with a rapture worthy of the Christian Savior descending from his golden shrine, and the only thing that vexed her was that he had not brought along his Soliman to pay his respects to her mistress.

But today, with so historic an event in the offing, she felt confident that something wonderful would happen to her too, and she supposed that this time Soliman would probably be in attendance, as the solemnity of the occasion demanded. Not that everything hinged on this expectation, but it was a necessary flourish, part of the plot of amorous intrigue present in every novel Rachel read to improve her mind. For Rachel was allowed to read the novels Diotima had put aside, just as she was allowed to cut down and alter for herself Diotima's discarded lingerie. Rachel sewed well and read fluently— that was her Jewish heritage—but when she was reading a novel Diotima had recommended as a great work of art (these were her favorites) she understood what was happening in it only as one perceives a lively event from a distance, or in a strange country; she was engrossed and moved by goings-on she did not understand and that she could not influence, and this she enjoyed enormously. She enjoyed in the same way, when sent out on an errand or when distinguished visitors came to the house, the imposing and exciting demeanor of an imperial city, its superabundance of brilliant detail, surpassing her understanding, in which she shared simply by being in a privileged place in its midst. She was not at all interested in understanding it better; she had forgotten, in her anger, the basic teachings of her Jewish home, the wise maxims heard there, and felt as little need for them as a flower needs a spoon and fork in order to nourish itself with the juices of earth and air.

So now she collected all the pencils once more and carefully slipped their shiny points into the little machine affixed to the corner of the table, which peeled off the wood so perfectly when you turned the handle that, when you repeated the process, not the tiniest chip fell off. Then she put the pencils back beside the velvety sheets of paper, three different kinds in each place, reflecting that this perfect machine she was allowed to use had been brought over yesterday evening with the pencils and the paper from the Foreign Ministry and the Imperial household by a uniformed messenger. It was now seven o'clock. Rachel quickly cast a general's glance over all the details of the arrangement and hurried out of the room to waken Diotima, for the meeting was set for a quarter past ten, and Diotima had stayed in bed awhile after the master had left the house.

These mornings with Diotima were a special treat for Rachel. The word "love" does not fit the case; the word "veneration" is closer, if one pictures it in its full meaning, in which the honor conferred so completely penetrates a person that it fills his inmost being and pushes him, so to speak, out of his own place within himself. From her adventure back home Rachel had a little daughter, now eighteen months old, whom she saw when she regularly took a large portion of her wages to the foster mother on the first Sunday of every month. But although she did not neglect her duty as a mother, she saw in it only a punishment incurred in the past, and her feelings had again become those of a girl whose chaste body had not yet been opened by love.

She approached Diotima's bed, and her gaze, adoring as that of a mountain climber catching sight of the snowy peak rising out of the morning darkness into the first blue of dawn, glided over Diotima's shoulder before she touched the tender mother-of-pearl warmth of her mistress's skin with her fingers. Then she savored the subtly mingled scent of the hand that came sleepily out from under the covers to be kissed, smelling of the previous day's colognes but also of the faint steaminess of the night's rest. Rachel held the slipper for the groping, naked foot and received the awakening glance. But the sensual contact with that magnificent female body would not have been so thrilling by far had it not been wholly irradiated by Diotima's moral significance.

"Did you remember to place the chair with the armrests for His Grace? And the little silver bell for me? Did you put out twelve sheets of paper for the secretary? And six pencils, Rachelle, six, not just three, for him?" was what Diotima said on this occasion. At each of these questions, Rachel inwardly ticked off on her fingers all she had done, with a frightened thrill of ambition, as though her life were at stake. Her mistress had thrown on a dressing gown and went into the conference room. Her way of training "Rachelle" involved reminding her that it was not enough to regard everything done or undone as one's personal concern, but to consider its general import. If Rachel broke a glass, "Rachelle" was told that the damage in itself signified nothing but that the transparent glass was a symbol of the daily little duties the eye barely perceived because it gladly dwelled on higher things, which was all the more reason that one had to pay the most particular attention to these duties. To find herself treated with such ministerial courtesy could bring remorse and happiness to Rachel's eyes as she swept up the fragments. Her cooks, from whom Diotima expected right thinking and recognition of errors they had committed, had come and gone often enough since Rachel had entered her service, but Rachel loved Diotima's sublime phrases with all her heart, just as she loved the Emperor, the state funerals, and the flaming candles in the darkness of the Catholic churches. She might fib a little to get out of a scrape, but she was thoroughly ashamed of herself afterward. Perhaps she even took a perverse pleasure in her little lies because they made her feel how really bad she was, compared with Diotima; but she usually indulged herself in this only when she hoped to be able to turn the falsehood, secretly and quickly, into a truth.

When one human being looks up to another so much in every way, it happens that his body is, so to speak, taken away from him and plunges like a little meteorite into the sun of the other body. Diotima had no fault to find with Rachel's performance and kindly patted her little maid on the shoulder. Then they both went into the bathroom to dress Diotima for the great day. When Rachel tempered the bathwater, lathered the soap, and was permitted to rub Diotima's body down with the bath towel as boldly as though it were her own, it gave her much more pleasure than if it really were merely her own, which seemed of no account, inspired no confidence; she was far from thinking of it even for comparison, but felt, in touching Diotima's statuesque abundance, rather like an oaf of a recruit who belonged to a dazzling regiment.

So was Diotima girded for the great day.

42

THE GREAT SESSION

On the minute of the appointed hour, Count Leinsdorf appeared, accompanied by Ulrich. Rachel, already aglow from admitting an uninterrupted stream of guests for whom she had to open the door and help with their coats, recognized Ulrich at once and noted with satisfaction that he, too, had been no casual visitor but a man brought to her mistress's house by a significant chain of events, as was now demonstrated by his arrival in the company of His Grace. She fluttered to the door, which she opened ceremoniously, and then crouched down at the keyhole to see what would now happen inside. It was a large keyhole, and she saw the banker's clean-shaven chin and the prelate Niedomansky's violet neckband, as well as the golden sword knot of General Stumm von Bordwehr, who had been sent by the War Ministry although it really had not been invited; the Ministry had declared, in a letter to Count Leinsdorf, that it did not wish to be absent on "so highly patriotic" an occasion, though not directly involved in bringing it about or in the foreseeable course it would take. Diotima had forgotten to mention this to Rachel, who was quite excited by the presence of a general at this gathering but could make out nothing more, for the present, about what was going on.

Diotima, meanwhile, had welcomed His Grace, not paying much attention to Ulrich, as she was introducing other guests to the Count, beginning with Dr. Paul Arnheim. She explained to His Grace that a lucky chance had brought this distinguished friend of her house, and even though as a non-Austrian he could not expect to take a formal part in their conference, she hoped he would be permitted to stay as her personal adviser, because—here she appended a gentle threat— his great experience and connections in the field of international culture and its relations with economic questions were an invaluable support to her, considering that she had so far been obliged to take sole responsibility for covering these areas and could not soon be replaced even in the future, although she was only too aware of her inadequacy.

Count Leinsdorf found himself ambushed; it was the first time since he had known her that his middle-class friend had surprised him by committing an indiscretion. Arnheim, too, felt taken aback, like a sovereign whose entrance has not been staged with the proper fanfare; he had of course been certain that Count Leinsdorf had known and approved of his being invited. But Diotima, with an obstinate look on her flushed face, did not give an inch; like all women with too clear a conscience in the matter of marital fidelity, she could develop an insufferable feminine persistence in a good cause.

She was at that time already in love with Arnheim, who had by this time called on her more than once, but in her inexperience she had no inkling of the nature of her feeling. They talked about what it is that moves the soul, that ennobles the flesh between the sole of the foot and the crown of the head and transforms the confused impressions of civilized life into harmonious spiritual vibrations. But even this was a great deal, and because Diotima was inclined to caution and always on guard against compromising herself, this intimacy struck her as too sudden, and she had to mobilize truly great emotions, the very greatest, in fact, and where were they most likely to be found? Where everyone has shifted them, to the drama of history. For Diotima and Arnheim, the Parallel Campaign was, so to speak, a safety island in the swelling traffic of their souls. They regarded it as clearly fated that they should have been brought together at such an important moment, and they could not agree more that the great patriotic enterprise was an immense opportunity and responsibility for intellectual people. Arnheim said so too, though he never forgot to add that it depended primarily upon people with strong personalities who had experience in economics as well as the world of ideas, and only secondarily on the scope of the organization. So in Diotima the Parallel Campaign had become inextricably bound up with Arnheim; the void it had presented to her imagination at the beginning had given way to a copious abundance. Her hope that the great treasures of feeling embodied in the Austrian heritage could be strengthened by Prussian intellectual discipline was now most happily justified, and these impressions were so strong that this normally very correct woman had not realized what a breach of protocol she had committed in undertaking to invite Arnheim to the inaugural conference. Now there was no retreat; anyway, Arnheim, who sensed how it had happened, found it essentially disarming, however annoyed he was at finding himself in a false position; and His Grace was basically too fond of his friend Diotima to show his surprise beyond his first, involuntary, recoil. He met Diotima's explanation with silence and after an awkward little pause amiably held out his hand to Arnheim, assuring him in the most civil and complimentary terms that he was welcome, as in fact he was. Most of the others present had probably noticed the little scene and wondered about Arnheim's presence insofar as they knew who he was; but among well-bred people it is generally assumed that there is a sufficient reason for everything, and it is considered poor taste to ask too many prying questions.

Diotima had meanwhile recovered her statuesque impassivity. After a few moments she called the meeting to order and asked His Grace to honor her house by taking a chair.

His Grace made a speech. He had been preparing it for days, and his cast of mind was much too fixed to let him change anything at the last minute; he could only just manage to tone down the most outspoken allusions to the Prussian needle gun, which (an underhanded trick) had got the better of the Austrian muzzle-loaders in '66.

"What has brought us together," Count Leinsdorf said, "is the shared conviction that a great testimonial arising from the midst of the people themselves must not be left to chance but needs guidance by an influence that sees far into the future from a place with a broad perspective—in other words, from the top. His Majesty, our beloved Emperor and Sovereign, will in the year 1918 celebrate the almost unique jubilee of the seventieth year since his richly blessed ascent to the throne with all the strength and vigor, please God, we have always been accustomed to admire in him. We are certain that this occasion will be celebrated by the grateful people of Austria in a manner to show the world not only our deep love for him, but also that the Austro-Hungarian Monarchy stands together, grouped firm as a rock around its Sovereign."

At this point Count Leinsdorf wavered, wondering whether to mention anything about the signs of decay to which this rock, even at a unified celebration of its Emperor and King, was exposed; resistance by Hungary, which recognized only a King, had to be reckoned with. This was why His Grace had originally meant to speak of two firm rocks. But somehow this also failed to do justice to his sense of the Austro-Hungarian state.

This sense of the Austro-Hungarian state was so oddly put together that it must seem almost hopeless to explain it to anyone who has not experienced it himself. It did not consist of an Austrian part and a Hungarian part that, as one might expect, complemented each other, but of a whole and a part; that is, of a Hungarian and an Austro-Hungarian sense of statehood, the latter to be found in Austria, which in a sense left the Austrian sense of statehood with no country of its own. The Austrian existed only in Hungary, and there as an object of dislike; at home he called himself a national of the kingdoms and lands of the Austro-Hungarian Monarchy as represented in the Imperial Council, meaning that he was an Austrian plus a Hungarian minus that Hungarian; and he did this not with enthusiasm but only for the sake of a concept that was repugnant to him, because he could bear the Hungarians as little as they could bear him, which added still another complication to the whole combination. This led many people to simply call themselves Czechs, Poles, Slovenes, or Germans, and this was the beginning of that further decay and those well-known "unpleasant phenomena of an internal political kind," as Count Leinsdorf called them, which according to him were "the work of irresponsible, callow, sensation-seeking elements" not kept sufficiently in check by the politically unenlightened mass of inhabitants. As the subject here touched upon has since been dealt with in many well-informed and clever books, the reader will be glad to be reassured that neither at this point nor later will any serious attempt be made to paint a historical canvas and enter into competition with reality. It is fully sufficient to note that the mysteries of this Dualism (the technical term for it) were at the very least as recondite as those of the Trinity, for the historical process nearly everywhere resembles a juridical one, with hundreds of clauses, appendices, compromises, and protests, and it is only to this that attention should be drawn. The common man lives and dies among these complications all unsuspecting, which is just as well for him, because if he were to realize in what sort of a trial, with what lawyers, costs, and conflicting motives, he was entangled, he might be seized by paranoia no matter what country he lived in. Understanding reality is exclusively a matter for the philosopher of political history. For him the present period follows upon the Battle of Mohács or Lietzen as the roast the soup; he knows all the proceedings and has at every moment the sense of necessity arising out of lawful process. If he is, moreover, like Count Leinsdorf an aristocratic philosopher trained in political history, whose forebears, wielding sword or spindle, had personally played their parts in the preliminaries, he can survey the result as a smoothly ascending line.

And so His Grace Count Leinsdorf had said to himself before the conference: "We must not forget that His Majesty's noble and generous resolve to let the people take part in the conduct of their own affairs, up to a point, has not been in effect long enough to have produced everywhere the kind of political maturity in every respect worthy of the confidence so magnanimously placed in the people by His Majesty. So we will not discern, as does the grudging world beyond our frontiers, signs of senile decay in such execrable demonstrations as we are now unfortunately experiencing, but rather signs of a still immature, hence inexhaustible, youthful strength of the Austrian people."

He had meant to bring all this up at the meeting, but because Arnheim was present he did not say everything he had thought out beforehand but contented himself with hinting at the ignorance abroad of true conditions in Austria, leading to exaggeration where certain unpleasant phenomena were concerned. "For," His Grace concluded, "if we wish to give unmistakable proof of our strength and unity, we do so entirely in the interests of the wider world, since a happy relationship among the European family of nations is based upon mutual esteem and respect for one another's power." He then repeated only once more that such a forceful, blunt display of strength must truly come from the midst of the people and hence be directed from above, the purpose of this meeting being to find ways and means of so doing. Considering that only a short time ago Count Leinsdorf had thought of nothing more than a list of names, to which only the suggestion of a "Year of Austria" had been added from outside, this could be characterized as great progress, even though His Grace had not even expressed everything in his mind.

After this speech, Diotima took the floor to clarify the chairman's objectives. The great patriotic campaign, she explained, must find a great aim that would emerge, as His Grace had said, from the midst of the people. "We who are gathered here today for the first time do not feel called upon to define this aim as of now, but we are assembled to create first of all an organization to prepare the way for the framing of suggestions leading toward this aim." With these words she opened the discussion.

At first there was silence. Shut birds of different species and song patterns, none of whom have any idea what is going to happen to them, together in a cage, and they will initially be silent exactly the same way.

Finally, a professor asked for permission to speak. Ulrich did not know him. His Grace had presumably got his secretary to invite this gentleman at the last moment. He spoke of the path of history. When we look ahead, he said, we see an impenetrable wall. If we look left and right, we see an overwhelming mass of important events without recognizable direction. To cite just a few instances: the present conflict with Montenegro, the Spanish ordeals in battle in Morocco, the obstructionism of the Ukrainians in the Austrian Imperial Council. But looking back, everything, as if by a miracle, has become order and purpose. . . . Therefore, if he might say so, we experience at every moment the mystery of a miraculous guidance. So he wanted to welcome as a great idea opening the eyes of a nation, as it were, to this, to let it look consciously into the ways of Providence by calling upon it on a definite occasion of rare sublimity. . . . This was all he had wanted to say. It was much like modern methods of teaching, letting the pupil work out the answers together with the teacher, rather than imposing on him ready-made results.

The assembled company stared stonily, but with a pleasant expression, at the green tablecloth; even the prelate representing the Archbishop reacted to this clerical performance by a layman with the same polite reserve as the gentlemen from the ministries, without allowing his face to betray a hint of cordial agreement. It was like the way people feel when someone on the street suddenly begins to address all and sundry at the top of his voice; everyone, even those who had been thinking of nothing at all, feels suddenly that he is out on serious business, or that someone is making improper use of the street. As he spoke, the professor had been struggling with a sense of embarrassment, squeezing out his words with jerky constraint, as if a strong wind were snatching away his breath; he waited for an answering echo, then slowly withdrew the expectant look from his face, not without dignity.

It was a relief to all when the representative of the Imperial Privy Purse came to the rescue by quickly giving them a list of foundations and endowments to be expected, in that jubilee year, from His Majesty's private funds. It began with the donation of a sum for the building of a pilgrims' church, a foundation for the support of deacons without private means, gifts to the Archduke Karl and Field Marshal Radetzky Veterans' Clubs, to the soldiers' widows and orphans from the campaigns of '66 and '78, followed by funds for pensioned noncommissioned officers, for the Academy of Sciences, and so it went, on and on. There was nothing exciting about these lists; they simply had their place and took their course as a public expression of Imperial benevolence. The moment they had all been read off a Frau Weghuber, a manufacturer's wife with an impressive record of charitable works, rose promptly to her feet, quite impervious to any idea that there might be something more pressing than the objects of her concern. She advanced a proposal for a Greater Austrian Franz Josef Soup Kitchen, which was received sympathetically. However, the delegate from the Ministry of Public Worship and Education pointed out that his own department had received a somewhat similar suggestion, namely, the publication of a monumental work, *Emperor Franz Josef I and His Time*. But after this happy start silence again prevailed, and most of those present felt trapped in an awkward situation.

Had they been asked on their way to this meeting whether they knew what historical events or great events or things of that sort were, they would certainly have replied in the affirmative; but confronted with the weighty imperative of making up such an event on the spot, they slowly began to feel faint, and something like rumblings of a very natural kind stirred inside them.

At this dangerous moment the ever-tactful Diotima, who had prepared refreshments, interrupted the meeting.

43

ULRICH MEETS THE GREAT MAN FOR THE FIRST TIME. NOTHING IRRATIONAL HAPPENS IN WORLD HISTORY, BUT DIOTIMA CLAIMS THAT THE TRUE AUSTRIA IS THE WHOLE WORLD

During the pause for refreshments, Arnheim observed that the more all-inclusive the organization, the further the various proposals would diverge from one another. This was a characteristic symptom of its present state of development, based, as it was, only on reason. Yet it was just this that made it a tremendous undertaking, to force a whole people into awareness of the will, inspiration, and all that was basic, which lay far deeper than reason.

Ulrich replied by asking him whether he really believed that anything would come of this campaign.

"No doubt about it," Arnheim said, "great events are always the expression of a general situation." The mere fact that a meeting such as this had been possible anywhere was proof of its profound necessity.

And yet discrimination in such matters seems difficult, Ulrich said. Suppose, for instance, that the composer of the latest worldwide musical hit happened to be a political schemer and managed to become president of the world—which was certainly conceivable, given his enormous popularity—would this be a leap forward in history or an expression of the cultural situation?

"That's quite impossible!" Arnheim said seriously "Such a composer couldn't possibly be either a schemer or a politician—otherwise, his genius for musical comedy would be inexplicable, and nothing absurd happens in world history."

"But so much that's absurd happens in the world, surely?"

"In world history, never!"

Arnheim was visibly on edge. Diotima and Count Leinsdorf stood nearby in lively, low-voiced conversation. His Grace had, after all, expressed to his friend his amazement at meeting a Prussian on this markedly Austrian occasion. For reasons of discretion, if nothing else, he regarded it as wholly out of the question to let an alien play a leading part in the Parallel Campaign, although Diotima pointed out the splendid and confidence-inspiring impression such freedom from political egotism would inevitably make abroad. She then changed her tactics, giving her plan a surprising new dimension. She spoke of a woman's tact, an intuitive certainty deeply immune to society's prejudices. If His Grace would only listen, just this once, to that voice. Arnheim was a European, an intellectual force known throughout Europe; precisely because he was not an Austrian, his participation would prove that the intellect as such was at home in Austria. Suddenly she came out with the pronouncement that the True Austria was the whole world. The world, she explained, would find no peace until its nations learned to live together on a higher plane, like the Austrian peoples in their Fatherland. A Greater Austria, a Global Austria—that was the idea His Grace had inspired in her at this happy moment—the crowning idea the Parallel Campaign had been missing all along!

Irresistible, commanding her pacifist zeal, the beautiful Diotima stood before her noble friend. Count Leinsdorf could not yet make up his mind to surrender his objections, but he again admired this woman's fiery idealism and breadth of vision, and pondered whether it might not be more advantageous to sound out Arnheim first rather than deal on the spot with suggestions of such weighty consequence.

Arnheim was restless, sensing the nature of this conversation yet unable to influence it. He and Ulrich were surrounded by the curious, drawn by the presence of this Croesus, and Ulrich was just saying:

"There are several thousand occupations in which people lose themselves, where they invest all their wits. But if you are looking for the universal human element, for what they all have in common, there are really only three possibilities left: stupidity, money, or, at most, some leftover memory of religion."

"Quite right, religion!" Arnheim broke in emphatically, and asked Ulrich whether he really believed that it had all died out, down to the roots. He had stressed the word "religion" so loudly that Count Leinsdorf was bound to hear.

His Grace seemed to have come to terms, meanwhile, with Diotima, for led by her he now approached the group, which tactfully made way, and addressed Arnheim.

Ulrich suddenly found himself alone, and bit his lip.

He began, for some reason—perhaps to kill time or not to stand there so awkwardly—to think of the drive to this meeting. As a man who moved with the times, Count Leinsdorf, who had brought him along, owned several cars, but inasmuch as he also clung to tradition, he occasionally used a pair of superb chestnut horses that he kept, together with a coachman and a light carriage; so when his majordomo had come for his instructions, His Grace had decided that it would be fitting to drive these two beautiful, almost historical creatures to the inaugural meeting of the Parallel Campaign.

"This one is Pepi, and that one is Hans," Count Leinsdorf had explained on the way, as they watched the dancing brown hillocks of the horses' cruppers and now and then one of the nodding heads moving rhythmically sideways so that the foam flew from its mouth. It was hard to comprehend what was going on inside the animals; it was a beautiful morning and they moved at a fast trot. Perhaps fodder and speed were the only passions left to horses, since Pepi and Hans were geldings and knew nothing of love as a tangible desire, but only as a breath and a haze that sometimes veiled their vision of the world with thin, lucent clouds. The passion for fodder was preserved in a marble manger full of delicious oats, a hayrack full of fresh hay, the sound of the stable halter rubbing on its ring, and, concentrated in the warm, steamy stable smell, a spicy, steady aroma needled with the ammonia-charged strong sense of self: Here are horses! Speed was something else again. In this, the poor soul is still bound to the herd, where motion suddenly takes possession of the lead stallion, or all of them together, and the lot of them goes galloping off into the wind and the sun; for when the animal is alone and free to charge off to all four points of the compass, often a mad shudder will run through its skull and it will go storming off aimlessly, plunging into a terrible freedom as empty in one direction as another, until it comes to a bewildered halt and can be lured back with a bucket of oats. Pepi and Hans were well-trained horses, used to running in harness; they moved forward eagerly, their hooves beating the sunny street fenced in by houses. People were gray swarms for them, causing them neither joy nor fear; the bright window displays, the women parading in their colorful finery—patches of meadow no good for grazing; hats, neckties, books, diamonds along the street: a desert. Only the two dream-islands of stable and trotting rose up, and sometimes, as though in a dream or in play, Hans and Pepi shied at a shadow, pressed against the shafts, were revived by a flick of the whip, and leaned gratefully into the reins.

Suddenly Count Leinsdorf had sat up straight in the cushions and asked Ulrich: "Stallburg tells me, Herr Doktor, that you are taking an interest in someone?" Ulrich was so taken by surprise that he did not immediately grasp the connection, and Leinsdorf went on: "Very good of you. I know all about it. I'm afraid there's not much to be done—such a terrible fellow. But that intangible personal something in need of grace, which every Christian has in him, often shows itself in just such an individual. And when a man sets out to do something great, he should think most humbly of the helpless. Perhaps this fellow can be given another physical examination."

After Count Leinsdorf had delivered himself of this long speech, sitting upright in the jolting carriage, he let himself drop back into the upholstery and added: "But we cannot forget that at this moment we owe all our energies to the realization of a historic event!"

Ulrich really felt a liking for this naïve old aristocrat, who was standing there still talking with Diotima and Arnheim, and felt almost a twinge of jealousy. For the conversation seemed to be quite lively; Diotima was smiling; Count Leinsdorf's eyes were popping with alarm as he tried to follow Arnheim, who was holding forth with noble composure. Ulrich caught the phrase "bringing ideas into the spheres of power." He could not stand Arnheim, simply as a model of existence, on principle. This combination of intellect, business, good living, and learning was absolutely insufferable. He was convinced that Arnheim had organized everything the previous evening so that he would be neither the first nor the last to arrive at the session this morning; and yet he had certainly not looked at his watch before he left home but had probably done so for the last time before sitting down to breakfast and receiving the report of his secretary, who had handed him the mail; then he had transformed the time at his disposal into the precise amount of mental activity he intended to do before he had to leave, and when he dispassionately gave himself up to that activity, he was certain it would fill up the time exactly; for the right thing and the time it takes are mysteriously connected, like a sculpture and the space it inhabits, or a javelin thrower and the target he hits without looking at it. Ulrich had already heard a great deal about Arnheim and had read some of his works. In one of them, Arnheim had written that a man who inspects his suit in the mirror is incapable of fearless conduct, because the mirror, originally created to give pleasure—as Arnheim explained it—had become an instrument of anxiety, like the clock, which is a substitute for the fact that our activities no longer follow a natural sequence.

Ulrich had to force himself to look away in order not to be seen staring rudely at the nearby group, and his eyes came to rest on the little maid who was moving about among the chatting groups, offering refreshments with respectful glances. But little Rachel did not notice him; she had forgotten him and even neglected to bring her tray over to him. She was approaching Arnheim and presenting her refreshments to him as to a god; she longed to kiss the short, masterful hand that reached out for the lemonade and held the glass absentmindedly, without the nabob's taking a sip. Once this high point was passed she continued on her rounds like a dazed little robot and made her way as quickly as she could out of this world-historical room, where everything was filled with legs and talk, back into the hall again.

44

CONTINUATION AND CONCLUSION OF THE
GREAT SESSION. ULRICH TAKES A LIKING TO
RACHEL, AND RACHEL TO SOLIMAN. THE
PARALLEL CAMPAIGN GETS ORGANIZED

Ulrich liked girls like this: ambitious, well-behaved, in their well-trained timidity like little fruit trees whose sweet ripe fruit is destined to fall one day into the mouth of some young knight of Cockaigne as soon as he deigns to open his lips. "They have to be brave and tough," he thought, "like Stone Age women who shared their hunter's bed by night and carried his weapons and household gear on marches by day," although he himself had never gone on such an expedition except in the distant prehistoric age of his awakening manhood. With a sigh he sat down again, for the session had resumed. In remembering, he was struck that the black-and-white vestments one put on these maids were the same colors as nuns' habits; this had never occurred to him before, and he wondered at it. But the divine Diotima was speaking again, saying that the Parallel Campaign must culminate in a great symbol. That meant that it would not do to have just any sort of goal, no matter how widely visible, no matter how patriotic. This goal would have to seize the heart of the world. It could not be just practical, it also had to be a poem. It had to be a landmark. It had to be a mirror in which the world would see itself and blush. And not just blush but, as in a fairy tale, see its own true countenance and never again be able to forget it. His Grace had suggested for this symbol "Emperor of Peace."

This being the premise, there could be no mistaking that the suggestions considered thus far had been wide of the mark, Diotima went on. When she spoke of symbols earlier in the meeting, she had naturally meant not soup kitchens but that nothing less was at stake than the need to recover that unity of mankind that had been lost because the disparity of interests in society had grown so great. The question arises whether at the present time the peoples of today are still at all capable of such great, unifying ideas? All the suggestions made so far were splendid, of course, but they diverged so widely, which already showed that none of them had unifying power.

As she spoke, Ulrich was watching Arnheim. His dislike did not attach itself to any particular details of that physiognomy but quite simply to the totality. Not that the individual features—the industrial baron's hard Phoenician skull, the sharp face that seemed to be formed of too little material, so that it had a certain flatness, the lordly, English-tailor repose of the figure, and, at the second place where a man peeks out of his suit, the rather too-short-fingered hands—were not in themselves sufficiently noteworthy. What irritated Ulrich was the harmony in which all of this coexisted. Arnheim's books also had the same kind of self-assurance; the world was in order, as soon as Arnheim had given it his due consideration. As he sat watching Arnheim being so dramatically attentive to the foolishness they were having to sit through, Ulrich suddenly felt a slum kid's impulse to throw rocks or mud at this man who had grown up in all that wealth and perfection. Arnheim was drinking it all in like a connoisseur whose face says: Without going overboard, I must say this is a noble vintage!

Diotima had now come to the end of her speech. Right after the intermission, when they had all sat down again, everyone had looked confident that something conclusive was about to occur. Nobody had given it any real thought, but they all had that look of waiting for something important to happen. And now Diotima concluded: So when the question imposed itself whether the present time and the peoples of today's world were at all capable of such great, unifying ideas, it was necessary and proper to add: The idea of the power to redeem. For it was a question of redemption, of a redeeming upsurge. In short: even if we could not yet imagine it in any detail. It must come out of the total community, or it would not come at all. And so she would take it upon herself, after having consulted with His Grace, to conclude today's meeting with the following proposal: As His Grace had rightly observed, the august ministerial departments already represented a division of the world in accordance with its main aspects, such as religion and education, commerce, industry, law, and so on. If those present would therefore agree to set up committees, each headed by a delegate from a government department, with representatives of the respective institutions and sectors of the population at his side, the resulting organization would already embody the major moral forces of the world in their proper order and would serve as an instrument through which these forces could flow in and be filtered. The final determination would be made by an executive committee, and the entire structure would then need only several special committees and subcommittees, such as a publicity committee, a fund-raising committee, and the like, while she would like to reserve to herself personally the forming of a special committee for the further elaboration of the campaign's fundamental ideas, of course in constant cooperation with all the other committees.

Again there was a general silence, but this time of palpable relief. Count Leinsdorf nodded his head several times. Someone asked as a point of further clarification how the specifically Austrian note would come into the campaign as thus conceived.

In response to this question, General Stumm von Bordwehr rose to speak, even though all the preceding speakers had remained seated. He was well aware, he said, that the soldier's role in the council chamber was a modest one. If he spoke nevertheless, it was not to inject his own opinion into the unsurpassable critical remarks and suggestions already made, all of them excellent, but only to offer one more idea at the end, for everyone's indulgent consideration. The planned demonstration was intended to impress the outside world. But what impressed the outside world was the power of a people. And in view of the present situation in the European family of nations, as His Grace had said, a demonstration of this kind would certainly not be pointless. The idea of the state was, after all, the idea of power; as Treitschke said, the state is the power of self-preservation in the struggle for national survival. The general was only touching on a well-known sore spot in mentioning the condition of our artillery and our navy, both in unsatisfactory condition owing to the apathy of Parliament. Which is why he hoped they would consider, in case no other goal should be found, which was still an open question, that a broadly based popular concern with the problems of the army and its equipment would be a decidedly worthy aim. *Si vis pacem, para bellum!* Strength in peace wards off war, or at least shortens its span. He could therefore confidently maintain that steps taken in that direction would have a conciliatory effect on other nations and would make for an impressive demonstration of peaceable intentions.

At this moment there was a curious feeling in the room. Most of those present had at first felt that this speech was not in keeping with the meeting's real purpose, but as the General became more dominant acoustically, the effect on his listeners was like the reassuring tramp of well-ordered battalions. The original impulse of the Parallel Campaign, "Better than Prussia," shyly raised its head, as though some distant regimental band were trumpeting the march about Prince Eugène riding against the Turks, or the anthem "God Save the Emperor," . . . though of course if His Grace had now stood up to propose—as he was far from intending to do—that they should put their Prussian brother Arnheim at the head of the regimental band, they might have believed, in the state of vague exaltation in which they found themselves, that they were hearing the Prussian anthem instead, and would hardly have been able to object.

At the keyhole, "Rachelle" reported: "Now they're talking about war."

Her quick return to the hall at the end of the intermission owed a little to the fact that this time Arnheim had actually brought Soliman in his wake. As bad weather was threatening, the little African boy had followed his master, carrying an overcoat. When Rachel opened the door he had made an impudent face, since he was a spoiled young Berliner who was used to women fussing over him in a way he had not yet learned to take advantage of. But Rachel had assumed that he must be spoken to in his native African language; it simply never occurred to her to try German. Since she absolutely had to make herself understood, she had put her arm around the sixteen-year-old's shoulder and pointed the way to the kitchen, where she gave him a chair and pushed in front of him whatever cakes and drinks were within reach. She had never done this sort of thing in her life, and when she straightened up from the table her heart was pounding like sugar being pulverized in a mortar.

"What's your name?" Soliman asked; so he spoke German!

"Rachelle, Rachel," she said, and ran off.

In the kitchen, Soliman made the most of the cake, wine, and hors d'oeuvres, lit a cigarette, and started a conversation with the cook.

Seeing this when she came back from waiting on the guests gave Rachel a stab.

"In there," she said, "they'll be talking about something very important again any minute now."

But Soliman was not impressed, and the cook, an older woman, laughed.

"It might even mean war!" Rachel added excitedly—and was able to cap this a little later with her news from the keyhole that it had almost reached that point.

Soliman pricked up his ears. "Are there any Austrian generals in there?" he asked.

"See for yourself," Rachel said. "There's one, at least." And they went together to the keyhole.

Their glance fell now on some white paper, then on a nose; a big shadow passed by, a ring flashed. Life broke up into bright details. Green baize stretching away like a lawn; a white hand at rest somewhere, without a context, pale as in a waxworks; peering in slantwise, one could see the golden tassel of the General's sword gleaming in a corner. Even the pampered Soliman showed some excitement. Seen through the crack of a door and an imagination, life swelled to weird and fairy-tale dimensions. The stooping position made the blood buzz in one's ears, and the voices behind the door now rumbled like falling rocks, now glided as on greased planks. Rachel slowly straightened up. The floor seemed to heave under her feet; she was enveloped by the spirit of the occasion as though she had put her head under one of those black cloths used by conjurors and photographers. Soliman stood up too, and the blood drained fluttering from their heads. The little black boy smiled, and behind his bluish lips his scarlet gums shimmered.

While this instant in the hall, among the hanging overcoats of influential personages, faded slowly like a bugle call, a resolution was being passed in the conference room after Count Leinsdorf had thanked the General for his important and valuable suggestions, though the time had not yet come for examining proposals on their merits, as the organizational groundwork must be laid first. To this end, all that was needed now—apart from suiting the plan to the realities as represented by the ministries—was a final resolution to the effect that those present had unanimously agreed to submit the wishes of the people, as soon as these could be determined by the Parallel Campaign, to His Majesty, with the most humble petition to be allowed to dispose freely of the means for their material fulfillment (which would have to be raised by then) if such were His Majesty's most gracious pleasure.

This had the advantage that the people would be placed in the position of setting the worthiest possible aim for themselves, but through the agency of the Sovereign's most gracious will. The resolution was passed at His Grace's special request; for although it was only a matter of form, he considered it important that the people not take action on their own and without the consent of constitutional authority—not even to honor it.

The other participants would not have made such a point of this, but by the same token they had no objection to it. And it was in order, too, that the meeting should end with the passing of a resolution. For whether one sets a final period to a brawl with a knife, or ends a musical piece by crashing all ten fingers simultaneously down on the keyboard a few times, or whether the dancer bows to his lady, or whether one passes a resolution, it would be an uncanny world if events simply slunk off, if there were not a final ceremony to assure that they had indeed taken place. And that is why it is done.

45

SILENT ENCOUNTER OF TWO
MOUNTAIN PEAKS

When the session was over, Arnheim had quietly maneuvered, at a hint from Diotima, to be left behind, alone. Section Chief Tuzzi was observing a respectful margin of time to be sure of not returning home before the end of the session.

In these minutes between the departure of the guests and the settling down of the house, as her passage from room to room was interrupted by brief, sometimes conflicting, orders, considerations, and the general unrest that a fading great event leaves behind, Arnheim smiled as his eyes followed Diotima's movements. She felt that her domicile was in a state of tremulous movement; all the things that had had to abandon their customary places because of the great event returned piece by piece, like a big wave ebbing from the sand in countless little hollows and runnels. While Arnheim waited in urbane silence until she and the commotion around her settled down again, it struck Diotima that no matter how many people had gone in and out of her house, no man—other than Section Chief Tuzzi—had ever been so domestically alone with her that one palpably felt the mute life of the empty apartment. And suddenly her chaste mind was troubled by a bizarre notion: her empty apartment, in the absence of even her husband, seemed like a pair of trousers Arnheim had just slipped into. There are such moments, when chastity itself may be visited by such abortive flashes from the pit of darkness, and so the wonderful dream of a love in which body and soul are entirely one bloomed in Diotima.

Arnheim had no inkling of this. His trousers made an impeccably perpendicular line to the gleaming parquet; his morningcoat, his cravat, his serenely smiling patrician head, said nothing, so perfect were they. Actually, he had intended to complain to Diotima about the incident on his arrival, to make sure that no such thing happened in future. But there was at this moment something that made this man, who hobnobbed with American money magnates as an equal, who had been received by emperors and kings, this nabob who could offer any woman her weight in platinum, something that made him, instead of complaining, stare entranced at Diotima, whose name was really Ermelinda, or actually only Hermine Tuzzi, the mere wife of a ranking official. For this something it is here once again necessary to resort to the word "soul."

The word has already turned up more than once, though not in the clearest contexts; as, for instance, something lost in our time, or incompatible with civilization; as something at odds with physical urges and connubial habits; something that is moved, and not only to repugnance, by a murderer; something that was to be liberated by the Parallel Campaign; as a subject for religious meditations and *contemplatio in caligine divina* by Count Leinsdorf; as, with many people, a love of metaphor; and so on. The most peculiar of all the peculiarities of the word "soul," however, is that young people cannot pronounce it without laughing. Even Diotima and Arnheim were shy of using it without a modifier, for it is still possible to speak of having a great, noble, craven, daring, or debased soul, but to come right out with "my soul" is something one simply cannot bring oneself to do. It is distinctly an older person's word, and this can only be understood by assuming that in the course of life people become more and more aware of something for which they urgently need a name they cannot find until they finally resort, reluctantly, to the name they had originally despised.

How to describe it, then? Whether one is at rest or in motion, what matters is not what lies ahead, what one sees, hears, wants, takes, masters. It forms a horizon, a semicircle before one, but the ends of this semicircle are joined by a string, and the plane of this string goes right through the middle of the world. In front, the face and hands look out of it; sensations and strivings run ahead of it, and no one doubts that whatever one does is always reasonable, or at least passionate. In other words, outer circumstances call for us to act in a way everyone can understand; and if, in the toils of passion, we do something incomprehensible, that too is, in its own way, understandable. Yet however understandable and self-contained everything seems, this is accompanied by an obscure feeling that it is only half the story. Something is not quite in balance, and a person presses forward, like a tightrope walker, in order not to sway and fall. And as he presses on through life and leaves lived life behind, the life ahead and the life already lived form a wall, and his path in the end resembles the path of a woodworm: no matter how it corkscrews forward or even backward, it always leaves an empty space behind it. And this horrible feeling of a blind, cutoff space behind the fullness of everything, this half that is always missing even when everything is a whole, this is what eventually makes one perceive what one calls the soul.

We always include it, of course, in our thoughts, intuitions, feelings, in all sorts of surrogate ways and according to our individual temperament. In youth it manifests itself as a distinct feeling of insecurity about whether everything one does is really the right thing, after all; in old age as a sense of wonder at how little one has done of all one had really meant to do. In between, one takes comfort in the thought that one is a hell of a good, capable fellow, even if every little thing can't be justified; or that the world is not the way it ought to be either, so that one's failures come to represent a fair enough compromise. Then there are always some people who think beyond all this of a God who has their missing piece in His pocket. Only love has a special position in this; in this exceptional case the missing half grows back: the beloved seems to stand where ordinarily something was always missing. The souls unite "dos-à-dos," as it were, making themselves superfluous in the process. This is why most people, after the one great love in their youth is over, no longer feel the absence of their soul, so that this so-called foolishness fulfills a useful social function.

Neither Diotima nor Arnheim had ever loved. We already know this about Diotima, but the great financier also had, in a wider sense, a chaste soul. He had always been afraid that the feelings he aroused in women might not be for himself but for his money, and so he lived only with women to whom he also gave, not love, but money. He had never had a friend for fear of being used; he had only business friends, even if the business happened to be an intellectual exchange. This shrewd man, although imbued with experience of life, was still untouched and in danger of being permanently alone when he met Diotima, whom destiny had intended for him. The mysterious forces within them converged. It could be compared only with the movement of the trade winds, the Gulf Stream, the volcanic tremors of the earth's crust; forces vastly superior to those of man, akin to the stars, were set in motion from one to the other, overriding such barriers as hours and days, measureless currents. At such moments the actual words spoken are supremely unimportant. Rising from the vertical creases of his trousers, Arnheim's body seemed to stand there in the godlike solitude of a towering mountain. United with him through the valley between them, Diotima rose on its other side, luminous with solitude, in her fashionable dress of the period with its puffed sleeves on the upper arms, the artful pleats over the bosom widening above the stomach, the skirt narrowing again below the knees to cling to her calves. The glass-bead curtains at the doors cast moving reflections like ponds, the javelins and arrows on the walls trembled with their feathered and deadly passions, and the yellow volumes of Calman-Lévy on the tables were as silent as lemon groves. We will reverently pass over the first words spoken.

46

IDEALS AND MORALITY ARE THE BEST MEANS FOR FILLING THAT BIG HOLE CALLED SOUL

Arnheim was the first to shake off the spell. To linger in such a state was, to his way of thinking, impossible, without either sinking into a dull, vacuous, lethargic brooding or else foisting on one's devotion a solid framework of ideas and convictions that could not but distort its nature.

This method, which admittedly kills the soul but then, so to speak, preserves it for general consumption by canning it in small quantities, has always been its bridge to rational thought, convictions, and practical action, in their successful conduct of all moralities, philosophies, and religions. God knows, as we have already said, what a soul is anyway. There can be no doubt whatsoever that the burning desire to obey only the call of one's soul leaves infinite scope for action, a true state of anarchy, and there are cases of chemically pure souls actually committing crimes. But the minute a soul has morals, religion, philosophy, a well-grounded middle-class education, ideals in the spheres of duty and beauty, it has been equipped with a system of rules, conditions, and directives that it must obey before it can think of being a respectable soul, and its heat, like that of a blast furnace, is directed into orderly rectangles of sand. All that remains are only logical problems of interpretation, such as whether an action falls under this or that commandment, and the soul presents the tranquil panorama of a battlefield after the fact, where the dead lie still and one can see at once where a scrap of life still moves or groans. Which is why we cross that bridge as quickly as we can. If a person is plagued by religious doubts, as many are in their youth, he takes to persecuting unbelievers; if troubled by love, he turns it into marriage; and when overcome by some other enthusiasm, he takes refuge from the impossibility of living constantly *in* its fire by beginning to live *for* that fire. That is, he fills the many moments of his day, each of which needs a content and an impetus, not with his ideal state but with the many ways of achieving it by overcoming obstacles and incidents— which guarantees that he will never need to attain it. For only fools, fanatics, and mental cases can stand living at the highest pitch of soul; a sane person must be content with declaring that life would not be worth living without a spark of that mysterious fire.

Arnheim's life was filled to the brim with activity. He was a realist and had listened with an indulgent smile and not without appreciation for the good form shown by these representatives of the old Austrian tradition in the session he witnessed as they spoke of an Imperial Franz-Josef Soup Kitchen and the link between duty and military marches. He was far from making fun of it, as Ulrich had done, for he was convinced that it took far less courage and superiority to pursue great ideas than to recognize the touching kernel of idealism in such average, slightly absurd people of good appearance.

But when in the midst of all this, Diotima, this classical beauty with a Viennese plus, uttered her term "Global Austria," a phrase as hot and almost as incomprehensible to the human mind as a flame, something had seized his heart.

There was a story told about him that he had in his Berlin house a splendid room full of Baroque and Gothic sculptures. As it happens, the Catholic Church (for which Arnheim had a great love) depicts its saints and standard-bearers of Goodness mostly in poses of joy, even ecstasy. Here were saints dying in all kinds of postures, with the soul wringing out the body as if it were squeezing water out of a piece of laundry. All those gestures of arms crossed like sabers, of twisted necks, taken from their original surroundings and brought together in an alien space, gave the impression of a catatonics' ward in a lunatic asylum.

This collection was highly esteemed and brought many art historians to Arnheim, with whom he conversed knowledgeably; but often he sat alone and lonely in his gallery, with a quite different feeling, a kind of horrified amazement, as though he were looking at a half-demented world. He felt how morality had once glowed with an ineffable fire, but now even a mind like his own could do no more than stare into the burned-out clinkers. This dark vision of what all religions and myths express in the tale of commandments given originally to men by the gods, this intuition of a pristine state of the soul, somewhat uncanny and yet presumably pleasing to the gods, formed a strange fringe of uneasiness around the otherwise complacent expanse of his thoughts. Arnheim also had an assistant gardener, a simple but deep man, as Arnheim put it, with whom he often talked about the life of the flowers because one can learn more from such a man than from the experts. Until one day Arnheim discovered that this gardener's helper was stealing from him. It seems that he made off with everything he could lay his hands on, in a kind of desperation, saving the proceeds to set up on his own; this was the one idea that obsessed him day and night. But one day a small sculpture disappeared, and the police who were called in exposed the whole operation. The evening Arnheim was informed of this, he sent for the man and reproached him all night long for having allowed his passionate acquisitiveness to lead him astray. It was said that he was extremely upset himself and at times came close to weeping in a dark adjoining room. For he envied this man, for reasons he could not explain to himself. The next morning, he had the police take him away.

This story was confirmed by close friends of Arnheim's. Now, standing alone with Diotima in this room, he felt rather as he had felt then, sensing something like the soundless flames of the world leaping all around them along its four walls.

47

WHAT ALL OTHERS ARE SEPARATELY,
ARNHEIM IS ROLLED INTO ONE

In the following weeks Diotima's salon experienced a tremendous upsurge. People came to hear the latest news of the Parallel Campaign and to see the new man Diotima was reported to have prescribed for herself: variously, a German nabob, a rich Jew, and an eccentric who wrote poetry, dictated the price of coal, and was the German Kaiser's personal friend. It was not only the highborn ladies and gentlemen from Count Leinsdorf's world and diplomatic circles who came; the upper-middle-class figures who controlled the economy and led the world of culture seemed also increasingly attracted. And so specialists in the Ewe language and composers who had never heard a note of one another's music ran into one another here, shooting box met confessional box, and people to whom the word "course" meant the race course, the course of the stock exchange, or a university course.

And now something unheard of came to pass: there was a man who could speak with everyone in their own language, and that man was Arnheim.

After the embarrassment he had suffered at the beginning of the first meeting he held himself aloof from the official sessions, nor did he attend all the social gatherings, as he was often out of town. There was, of course, no further mention of the secretarial post; he had himself explained to Diotima that this idea could not be acceptable to the other side, and she yielded to Arnheim's judgment, although she could never look at Ulrich without regarding him as a usurper. Arnheim came and went. Three or five days would pass in a flash, he would be back from Paris, Rome, Berlin; what was going on at Diotima's was only a small slice of his life. But he favored it, and took part in it with all his energy.

That he could discuss industry with industrial giants and the economy with bankers was to be expected, but he could also chat just as freely about molecular physics, mysticism, and pigeon shooting. He was an extraordinary talker; once he was off, he never stopped, like a book one cannot close until everything in it demanding utterance has been said. But he had a quietly dignified, fluent manner of speaking, with a touch of sadness about it like a stream overhung by dark bushes, and this gave the flow of his words an air of necessity. His reading and his memory were of truly extraordinary compass; he could give experts the subtlest cues in their own fields, but he also knew every person of note in the English, French, and Japanese nobility, and was at home at racetracks and golf links not only in Europe but in Australia and America as well. So even the chamois hunters, champion horsemen, and holders of boxes at the Imperial Theater, who had come to see a crazy rich Jew (something a little different, as they put it), left Diotima's house shaking their heads with respect.

His Grace once took Ulrich aside and said to him:

"You know, our ducal houses have had bad luck with their tutors these last hundred years. They used to get the kind of people many of whom would later get into the encyclopedia, and these tutors would bring along music masters and drawing masters who showed their appreciation by creating things we now refer to as our old culture. But ever since we have had the new, universal education, and people from my own circles—forgive me—go in for academic degrees, our tutors have somehow fallen off. Our sons are quite right, of course, to shoot pheasant and boar, ride, and chase pretty girls—there's little to be said against that if one is young. But in the old days, it was the tutors who channeled part of that youthful energy into the necessity of cultivating the mind and the arts as well as the pheasants, and this no longer happens."

It was only an idea that just crossed His Grace's mind, as such things did from time to time; suddenly he turned to face Ulrich and concluded: "You see, it was that fateful year 1848 that drove a wedge between the middle class and the aristocracy, to the loss of both sides." He looked at the assembled company with concern. He was irked every time the opposition speakers in Parliament boasted of culture as middle class; he would have liked true middle-class culture to be found in the aristocracy, but the poor aristocracy could see nothing in it; it was a weapon invisible to them with which they were being trounced, and since they had been increasingly losing power all along, there was finally nothing left for them to do but come to Diotima's and see the thing for themselves. Count Leinsdorf sometimes felt this way with a heavy heart as he observed the hubbub, wishing that the high office this house had been given the opportunity to serve were taken more seriously.

"Excellency, the middle class is having exactly the same experience with the intellectuals now as the high nobility had with its tutors then," Ulrich tried to comfort him. "They don't know what to make of them. Just look at all these people gaping at Dr. Arnheim."

But all along Count Leinsdorf had only been looking at Arnheim anyway.

"That's no longer intellect," Ulrich said, explaining the general amazement, "it is a phenomenon like a rainbow with a foot you can take hold of and actually feel. He talks about love and economics, chemistry and trips in kayaks; he is a scholar, a landowner, and a stockbroker; in short, what the rest of us are separately, he is rolled into one; of course we're amazed. You shake your head, Excellency? But I'm convinced the cloud of so-called temporal progress, into which no one of us can see, has set him down on the parquet in our midst."

"I was not shaking my head over you," His Grace elucidated. "I was thinking of Dr. Arnheim. All in all, one has to admit he's an interesting figure."

48

THE THREE CAUSES OF ARNHEIM'S FAME AND THE MYSTERY OF THE WHOLE

But that was simply the way Arnheim usually affected people.

He was a man of stature.

His activity spread over terrestrial continents and continents of knowledge. He knew everything: philosophers, economics, music, the world, sports. He expressed himself fluently in five languages. The world's most famous artists were his friends, and he bought the art of tomorrow when it was still green on the vine, at prices that were not yet inflated. He was received at the Imperial Court and knew how to talk with workers. He owned a villa in the latest style, which appeared in photographs in all the publications on contemporary architecture, and also, somewhere in the sandiest wastes of Prussia, a ramshackle old castle that actually looked like the decomposed cradle of Prussian chauvinism.

Such expansiveness and receptivity are seldom accompanied by personal achievement; but in this respect, too, Arnheim was an exception. Once or twice a year he secluded himself on his country estate and there wrote down the experiences of his intellectual life. These books and articles, by now quite an imposing number of them, were widely read, enjoyed large printings, and were translated into many languages. A sick physician inspires no confidence, but when a man who has known how to do so well for himself speaks, there must be something in it. This was the first source of Arnheim's fame.

The second had its origin in the nature of science and scholarship. We hold knowledge in high esteem, and rightly so. But though a man's life may be completely filled by research into the functioning of the kidneys, there will be moments, humanistic moments, so to speak, when he may ponder the relationship between the kidneys and his country. This is why Goethe is so widely quoted in Germany. But when a scholar wants to show expressly that he is not only a man of learning but also possesses a lively mind with an interest in the future, he will do well to show himself acquainted with works it not only does him credit to know but promises to bring even more credit in the future—like a stock appreciating in value with time—and in such cases quotations from Paul Arnheim were enjoying increasing popularity. His excursions into scientific areas for support of his general views did not, it is true, always satisfy the strictest criteria; while they showed an easy command of the literature, the specialist would invariably find in them those little slips and misconceptions that betray the dilettante, just as surely as the stitching of a single seam betrays the homemade dress as compared with the product of the couturier's studio. But one should by no means think that this prevented the specialists from admiring Arnheim. They smiled complacently; he impressed them as a true product of the new age, a man whose name was in all the newspapers, an economic king, a man whose intellectual achievements, at least compared with those of earlier kings, were astonishing; and if they might be allowed to note that in their own sphere they represented something considerably different from him, they nevertheless showed their appreciation by calling him a brilliant man, a man of genius, or, quite simply, a universal man, which among specialists amounts to the same thing as when men say to each other of a woman that she is a woman's idea of a beauty.

The third source of Arnheim's fame was economics. He managed not at all badly with the old salts, the seasoned captains of industry; in a big deal, he could outsmart the craftiest of them. They did not regard him as much of a businessman, in any case, and called him the "Crown Prince," to distinguish him from his father, whose short, thick tongue was not so adroit in conversation but made up for it by picking up the flavor of a good business deal at whatever distance and by the subtlest chemistry. Him they feared, and revered, but when they heard of the philosophical demands the Crown Prince made on the business class, which he would weave even into the most matter-of-fact discussions, they smiled. He was notorious for quoting poets at board meetings, and for insisting that the economy could not be separated from other human activities and could be dealt with only within the larger context of all vital problems, national, intellectual, and even spiritual.

But even while they smiled at this sort of thing, they could not quite overlook that precisely by adding such frills to business, Arnheim junior was cutting an increasingly important figure in public opinion. News of him would turn up now in the financial, now in the political, now in the literary and art columns of leading newspapers throughout the world, whether it was a review of a work from his pen, the report of a notable speech he had given somewhere, or notice of his reception by some ruler or art association, until there was no man in the circle of industrial movers and shakers, who operate in silence and behind double-locked doors, as much talked about outside that circle as he was. All these presidents, board chairmen, directors, top managers, heads of banks, corporations, mine works, shipping companies, are by no means, in their hearts, the evil manipulators they are often represented to be. Apart from their highly developed sense of family, the inner rationale of their lives is that of money, and that is a rationale with very sound teeth and a healthy appetite. They were all convinced that the world would be much better off if left to the free play of supply and demand rather than to armored warships, bayonets, potentates, and diplomats ignorant of economics. But the world being what it is, with its ingrained prejudice against a life dedicated primarily to its own self-interest and only secondarily to the public good, and its preference for chivalry, public-spiritedness, and public missions above private enterprise, these magnates were the last people in the world to leave this out of their calculations, and they energetically made use of the advantages offered to the public good through customs negotiations backed by armed force, or the use of the military against strikers. On this road, however, business leads directly to philosophy, for nowadays only criminals dare to harm others without philosophy, and so they accustomed themselves to regarding Arnheim junior as a kind of papal legate for their affairs. Despite the irony with which they were always ready to regard his tendencies, they were pleased to have in him a man who could take their case as readily before a conclave of bishops as to a sociological conference; ultimately he won influence over them like a beautiful and cultivated wife who regards her husband's everlasting office work as a bore but is useful to the business because everyone admires her. Now, beyond this one need only imagine the effect of Maeterlinckian or Bergsonian philosophy applied to questions about the price of coal or to cartel politics, to estimate how depressing Arnheim junior's presence could be to industrialists' conferences and directors' meetings in Paris or St. Petersburg or Cape Town when he turned up as his father's ambassador and had to be heard out from beginning to end. His resulting successes in business were as impressive as they were mysterious, and out of all this grew the well-known report of the man's towering stature and his lucky hand.

A good deal more could be said about Arnheim's successes. With diplomats, for instance, who handled the important but alien field of economics with the circumspection of men charged with the care of an unpredictable elephant, while Arnheim treated it with the nonchalance of a native keeper. With artists, for whom he hardly ever did anything, which did not prevent them from seeing him as a Maecenas. And lastly with journalists, who should in all fairness have been the first to be mentioned, because it was they who through their admiration had first created Arnheim's image as a great man, though they did not realize how much he was their own creation; for someone had whispered in their ear and they consequently believed they could hear the grass of history growing. The basic pattern of his success was everywhere the same: Surrounded by the magic aura of his wealth and the legend of his importance, he always had to deal with people who towered over him in their own fields but who liked him as an outsider with a surprising knowledge of their subject and were daunted by his personally representing a link between their world and other worlds of which they had no idea. So it had come to seem quite natural for him to appear in a world of specialists as a whole man, and to have the effect of a harmonious entity. At times he dreamed of a new Weimar or Florentine renaissance of industry and trade, a new prosperity under the leadership of strong personalities, each of whom would have to be capable of combining individual achievements in technology, science, and the arts, and able to guide them from the highest standpoint. He felt he had this capacity. He possessed the gift of never being superior in any specific, provable respect but, owing to some fluid, perpetually self-renewing equilibrium, of still coming out on top in every situation. It was probably the fundamental talent of a politician, but Arnheim was also convinced that it was a profound mystery. He called it "the Mystery of the Whole." For even the beauty of a person consists of almost nothing demonstrable, or any specific feature, but rather that magical something that makes even small defects useful, just as the profound goodness and love, the dignity and greatness, of a person are almost independent of what he does, are indeed capable of ennobling everything he does. In this life, in some mysterious fashion, the whole always takes precedence over its parts. While ordinary people may indeed be the sum of their virtues and faults, the great man is he who first bestows rank on his qualities. And if the secret of his success is that it cannot quite be explained as the result of his achievements and his qualities, then the presence of a force greater than its manifestations is the mystery upon which all greatness in life rests. This is how Arnheim had phrased it in one of his books, and as he set down these words he almost felt that he had touched the hem of the supernatural, and this, too, he allowed to shine through in the text.

49

ANTAGONISM SPROUTS BETWEEN THE OLD AND THE NEW DIPLOMACY

His association with persons whose specialty was to have been born to the hereditary nobility constituted no exception. Arnheim so muted his own high distinction, so modestly laid claim only to a certain intellectual nobility, which knows its own merits and limits, that beside him the bearers of the most venerable noble names seemed after a while to be bowed down under their burden like gnarled laborers. It was Diotima who appreciated this most keenly. She recognized the Mystery of the Whole with the eye of an artist who sees the dream of his life realized in an unsurpassable way.

She was now wholly reconciled to her salon again. Arnheim warned her against putting too much emphasis on formal organization; crude material interests would take over, stifling the original pure intention; he preferred keeping the salon as it was.

Section Chief Tuzzi, on the other hand, expressed his misgivings that this would never get them beyond endless floods of talk.

He had crossed one leg over the other and clasped one knee with his heavily veined, lean, dark hands. Next to Arnheim, who sat upright in a flawlessly cut suit of some soft fabric, Tuzzi, with his trim little beard and southern eyes, looked like a Levantine pickpocket beside a Hanseatic merchant prince. It was an encounter between two kinds of distinction, and the Austrian, a mosaic of highly cultivated cosmopolitanism, with its casual dash, certainly did not regard itself as the lesser. Section Chief Tuzzi had an engaging manner of asking how the Parallel Campaign was coming along, as though he was not supposed to know at first hand what was going on in his own house.

"We would love to know as soon as possible what your plans are," he said with an amiable smile at his wife and Arnheim, as if to say that he was of course only an outsider in this matter. Then he explained that this joint enterprise of his wife's and Count Leinsdorf's was already causing grave concern in official quarters. At his most recent briefing session with His Majesty, the Minister of Foreign Affairs had taken soundings as to what kind of public demonstrations in honor of the jubilee might be acceptable to His Majesty, namely, up to what point His Majesty might be graciously willing to countenance a plan anticipating the trend of the times by taking a lead in an international peace program. Which was the only way, Tuzzi pointed out, to translate into political terms the idea of a Global Austria that had come up in His Grace's speech. But His Gracious Majesty, with his world-famous punctiliousness and reserve, Tuzzi went on, had instantly waved the suggestion aside, saying firmly: "Oh, I don't like being pushed into the limelight," and now no one could say whether this meant His Majesty was definitely opposed to the idea or not.

Such was Tuzzi's discreet way of being indiscreet about the little secrets of his profession, as only a man who knows how to keep the big secrets can be. He ended by saying that it was now up to the various embassies to sound out their respective courts abroad, as we were not sure of our own ground but had to find some solid point of departure somewhere. Technically, after all, there were all sorts of given possibilities, from calling a general peace conference, to a summit meeting for twenty sovereigns, all the way down to decorating the Peace Palace at The Hague with frescoes by Austrian artists, or a foundation for the benefit of the children and orphans of The Hague's domestic staff. At this point he asked Arnheim what they were thinking about the jubilee year at the Prussian court. Arnheim disclaimed having any information in this regard. He was repelled by this Austrian cynicism. He, who knew how to chat so elegantly, froze up in Tuzzi's company like a man who wants it clearly understood that affairs of state must be discussed with the utmost gravity and coolness. In this fashion two contrasting kinds of urbanity, two national- and two life-styles, not without a touch of sexual rivalry, presented themselves to Diotima. But place a greyhound beside a pug, a willow beside a poplar, a glass of wine on a freshly plowed field, a portrait in a sailboat instead of in an art gallery—in short, place side by side two highbred and distinct forms of life, and a void will come into being between them; they will cancel each other out, with the effect of a quite malicious, bottomless absurdity. Diotima felt this with her eyes and ears without understanding it, but she was sufficiently alarmed to give a turn to the conversation by telling her husband firmly that she intended to achieve something spiritually great with the Parallel Campaign, and would allow only the needs of truly modern minds to influence its leadership.

Arnheim was grateful to her for restoring the dignity of the concept, especially because he had to be on his guard, at times, against going under; he could no more afford to be facetious about the events that so nobly justified his being with Diotima than a drowning man can be about his life jacket. Yet he surprised himself by asking Diotima, his voice betraying some uncertainty, whom she would include, in that case, in the intellectual spearhead of the Parallel Campaign.

Diotima was of course quite unprepared to give a clear answer to this question. The days she spent with Arnheim had given her such an abundance of suggestions and ideas that she had not yet got around to sorting them out, and while he had repeated to her more than once that the democracy of the committees mattered far less than strong personalities with a comprehensive view of things, all it meant to her was simply "You and I"—though she was still far from deciding anything, or even from having the necessary insight. It was probably just this of which she was reminded by the pessimism in Arnheim's voice, because she answered: "Do we have anything at all nowadays that we can regard as truly important and great, something worth working for with all our might?"

"It is the mark of a time that has lost the inner certainty of healthier times," Arnheim responded, "that it is hard for something to crystallize as the greatest and most important thing of all."

Section Chief Tuzzi had lowered his eyes to a speck of dust on his trousers, so that one might interpret his smile as a sign of agreement.

"And indeed, what should it be?" Arnheim went on tentatively. "Religion?"

Section Chief Tuzzi now directed his smile upward; Arnheim had pronounced the word this time not quite so emphatically and unskeptically as before in His Grace's presence, but with sonorous gravity nonetheless.

Diotima, defending herself against her husband's smile, threw in: "Why not? Religion too!"

"Of course. But since we must come to a practical decision: Have you ever thought of appointing a bishop to the committee, who should come up with a modern goal for the campaign? God is profoundly unmodern: we simply cannot imagine him in tails, clean-shaven, with neatly parted hair; our image of him is still patriarchal. And what is there apart from religion? The nation? The state?"

Diotima was pleased at this, because Tuzzi regarded the state as a masculine subject one did not discuss with women. But now he was silent, only his eyes still hinting that there might be something further to be said on that score.

"Science?" Arnheim went on. "Culture? That leaves art. Truly, it is art that should first reflect the unity of existence and its inner order. But we know the picture art presents today. Fragmentation everywhere; extremes without connections. Stendhal, Balzac, and Flaubert have already created the epic of the new mechanized social and inner life, while the demonic substrata of our lives have been laid bare by Dostoyevsky, Strindberg, and Freud. We who live today have a deep sense that there is nothing left for us to do."

Here Section Chief Tuzzi interjected that when he wanted to read something solid, he took down his Homer, or Peter Rosegger.

Arnheim took up the suggestion: "You should include the Bible. With the Bible, Homer, and Rosegger or Reuter, one can manage. And this takes us right to the heart of the problem. What if a new Homer should come along, would we, frankly, be at all capable of listening to him? I believe the answer is no. We don't have him because we don't need him!" Arnheim was now in the saddle and riding high. "If we needed him, we would have him! For in the final analysis, nothing negative happens in world history. What can it mean that we place everything that is truly great and essential in the past? Homer and Christ have never again been equaled, to say nothing of being surpassed; there is nothing more beautiful than the Song of Songs. The Gothic age and the Renaissance stand before modern times like mountain ranges at the entrance to a great plain, and where, today, are the great rulers? How short-winded even the deeds of Napoleon look beside those of the pharaohs, the work of Kant beside that of the Buddha, that of Goethe beside Homer! But here we are, and we must live for something. What does it all add up to? Nothing but—" But here Arnheim broke off and confessed that he was reluctant to put it into words, because he was forced to conclude that all we regard as great and important in life has nothing to do with the innermost force of our lives.

"And that would be?" Tuzzi inquired. He had hardly any objection to the implication that most things were taken far too seriously.

"No one today knows the answer," Arnheim replied. "The problem of civilization can be solved only by the heart. By the appearance of a new type of man. By an inner vision and a pure will. The intellect has achieved nothing but watering down the great past into liberalism. But perhaps we do not see far enough, perhaps we reckon on too small a scale; every moment may be that of a great historic turning point!"

Diotima had been on the point of objecting that this would leave nothing for the Parallel Campaign to do. But in some peculiar way she found herself enthralled by Arnheim's somber visions. Perhaps there was a residue of "too much homework" in her that burdened her when she always had to read the newest books and talk about the newest pictures; pessimism toward art liberated her from all sorts of beauty she had not really liked at all, just as a pessimistic view of science eased her anxiety in the face of culture, the overabundance of the knowable and the influential. Thus Arnheim's despairing judgment of the times came, as she suddenly realized, as a release. And the thought flitted pleasantly through her heart that Arnheim's melancholy somehow had something to do with herself.

50

FURTHER DEVELOPMENTS.
SECTION CHIEF TUZZI DECIDES TO INFORM
HIMSELF ABOUT ARNHEIM

Diotima had guessed right. From the moment Arnheim had noticed that the bosom of this enchanting woman who had read his books on the soul was lifted and moved by a force of an unmistakable kind, he had suffered a loss of nerve otherwise foreign to him. Putting it briefly and in his own terms, it was the faintheartedness of the moralist who suddenly and unexpectedly meets heaven on earth. To empathize with him, one need only imagine how it would be if we were surrounded by nothing but this quiet blue puddle with soft white wads of feathers floating in it.

The moral person as such is ridiculous and unpleasant, as we know by the odor of those poor, resigned people who have nothing they can call their own but their morality. Morality needs great tasks from which to derive its significance, which is why Arnheim had always striven to complement his nature, which inclined to moralizing, by drawing on world events and history, and saturating his activities with ideology. That was his favorite concept: carrying ideas into the spheres of power and talking business only in connection with cultural questions. He liked to draw analogies from history in order to fill it with new life; the role of present-day finance seemed to him similar to that of the Catholic Church: a great influence behind the scenes; unyielding yet yielding in its dealings with the ruling powers; and he sometimes saw himself functioning like a cardinal.

But on this occasion he had come to Austria more on a whim, and even though he never traveled wholly without a purpose, even on a whim, he could not quite remember how the plan—incidentally, a plan of some scope—had originally entered his mind. The inspiration for this trip seemed to have come out of the blue, an instant resolve, and it may have been this small circumstance of freedom about it that a trip to Bombay would hardly have made a less exotic impression on him than this out-of-the-way German-language metropolis in which he had landed. The thought, inconceivable in Prussia, of playing a leading role in the Parallel Campaign had done the rest and made him feel illogically fantastic, like a dream, whose absurdity his practical good sense recognized but whose spell he was powerless to break. He could probably have accomplished the business purpose of his trip far more simply and directly, but he regarded it as a holiday from reason to keep coming back here, and for these excursions into fairyland he was punished by his business sense in that he smudged the black good-conduct mark he should have given himself into a gray blur over everything.

There was no repetition, at least, of that far-reaching contemplation in the dark as had happened in Tuzzi's presence, if only because Section Chief Tuzzi turned up only in passing, and Arnheim had to parcel out his words to all sorts of persons whom he found amazingly receptive in this beautiful country. In His Grace's presence he called criticism sterile and the present age godless, once more letting it be understood that redemption from so negative an existence could come only through the heart; for Diotima's sake he added that the German spirit, and perhaps the world as well, could be freed from the excesses of rationalism and petty bookkeeping only by the rich culture of its southern lands. Encircled by ladies, he spoke of the need to organize the inner resources of human tenderness, in order to save mankind from arms races and soullessness. To a circle of active professionals he expounded Hölderlin's saying that there were no longer human beings in Germany but only professionals, winding up with: "And no one can achieve anything in his profession without a sense of some overarching purpose, least of all the financier!"

People listened to him gladly because it was so nice that a man with so many ideas also had money, and the circumstance that all those who spoke with him came away with the impression that an undertaking like the Parallel Campaign was a most dubious affair, riddled with the most explosive intellectual contradictions, also reinforced in everyone the notion that no one else was as obviously cut out as he was for taking the helm in this adventure.

However, Section Chief Tuzzi would not have been, in his quiet way, one of his country's leading diplomats had he noticed nothing of

Arnheim's pervasive presence in his house; he simply could not make head or tail of it. He did not let on, because a diplomat never shows what he is thinking. Personally, and also in principle, so to speak, he found this outsider most irritating, and that he had blatantly chosen the salon of Tuzzi's wife as the scene of operations for some secret objective Tuzzi regarded as a challenge. Not for an instant did he believe Diotima's assurances that the nabob visited the Imperial City on the Danube so often because his mind felt most at home in its ancient culture. Tuzzi's problem was that he had no clue to help him solve this mystery, because in all his official experience he had never come across a person like Arnheim.

And since Diotima had announced that she intended to give Arnheim a leading position in the Parallel Campaign, and had complained about His Grace's resistance to this idea, Tuzzi was seriously concerned. He did not think much of either the Parallel Campaign or Count Leinsdorf, but he regarded his wife's idea as politically so amazingly tactless that he was overcome with the feeling that all these years of patient husbandly training such as he flattered himself to have given her had collapsed like a house of cards. He had in fact used exactly this figure of speech in thinking about it, even though Section Chief Tuzzi never indulged himself in figures of speech because they are too literary and, socially, smell of poor taste; but this time he felt quite shaken by it.

However, Diotima strengthened her position again as things went on by her stubbornness. She had become gently aggressive and spoke of a new kind of person who could no longer passively leave the spiritual responsibility for the course of world events to the professional leaders. Then she spoke of feminine tact that could sometimes be a visionary gift perhaps capable of penetrating distances beyond the daily routine of professionals. Finally, she said that Arnheim was a European, a thinker known throughout Europe, that the conduct of affairs of state in Europe was not sufficiently European, not spiritual enough, and that the world would find no peace until it was as permeated by a universally Austrian spirit as the ancient Austrian culture that embraced all the peoples, with their different languages, within the borders of the monarchy.

She had never before dared to stand up so resolutely against her husband's authority, but Section Chief Tuzzi was temporarily reassured by it, because he had never regarded his wife's strivings as higher in significance than problems with her dressmaker, was delighted when she was admired by others, and could now take a less alarming view of her current goings-on, much as if a woman who loved color had for once chosen too gaudy a ribbon. So he confined himself to going over again, with grave courtesy, all the reasons why in a man's world decisions on Austrian affairs could not be publicly entrusted to a Prussian, even though he could see that there might be some advantage in being on friendly terms with a man in so unique a position. He assured Diotima that she would be misunderstanding his scruples if she inferred from them that he was not pleased to see Arnheim in her company as often as possible. Privately he hoped that this would give him the opportunity, sooner or later, to set a trap for the outsider.

Only when Tuzzi had to stand by and see Arnheim sweeping from success to success everywhere did he come back to the idea that she seemed overinvolved with this man—only to find again that she did not respect his wishes as of old but argued with him and declared his misgivings chimerical. He decided as a man not to struggle against the dialectics of a woman but to bide his time and wait for circumstances to prove him right in the end. But then something happened to give him a powerful incentive.

One night, something like the sound of very distant weeping aroused him from his sleep. It barely disturbed him at first; he simply did not understand what it was. But from time to time the spiritual distance lessened by a jump, until suddenly the menacing disturbance was quite close to his ears, and he started so violently out of his sleep that he sat bolt upright in bed. Diotima lay on her side facing away from him and gave no sign of being awake, but something made him feel that she was. He whispered her name once, then again, and tenderly tried to turn her white shoulder to him. But as he turned her around and her face rose above her shoulder in the dark, it looked at him angrily, expressed defiance, and had been crying. Unfortunately, Tuzzi's sound sleep was reclaiming him and dragging him relentlessly back into his pillows, while Diotima's face hovered above him as a painfully bright distortion he could make no sense of. "Whatsamatter?" he muttered in the soft bass of returning unconsciousness, and received a clear, irritable, unwelcome answer that stamped itself on his ear, fell into his drowsiness, and lay there like a sparkling coin in the water.

"You toss about so much in your sleep, no one can sleep next to you!" Diotima had said harshly and distinctly; his ear had taken it in, but he had already slipped back into sleep without being able to utter a word in his own defense.

He merely felt that he was the victim of a grave injustice. Quiet, restful sleep was in his opinion one of a diplomat's chief virtues, for it was a condition of all success. It was a point on which he was acutely sensitive, and Diotima's remark was a serious challenge to his very existence. He realized that something in her had changed. While it never occurred to him even in his sleep to suspect his wife of any tangible infidelity, he never doubted for a moment that the personal discomfort inflicted on him must be connected with Arnheim. He slept on angrily, as it were, till morning and awakened with the firm resolve to find out all he could about this disturbing person.

51

THE HOUSE OF FISCHEL

Director Fischel of the Lloyd Bank was that bank director, or, more properly, manager with the title of director, who had somehow unaccountably forgotten to acknowledge Count Leinsdorf's invitation and had thereafter not been invited again. And even that first invitation he had owed only to the connections of his wife, Clementine. Clementine Fischel's family were old civil service. Her father had been Accountant General, her grandfather had been a senior official in the finance department, and three of her brothers held high positions in various ministries. Twenty-four years ago she had married Leo Fischel, for two reasons: first, because families high in the civil service sometimes have more children than means; but second, for a romantic reason, because compared with the relentlessly thrifty tightness of her parental home, banking seemed a liberal-minded, modern profession, and in the nineteenth century a cultivated person did not judge another person's value according to whether he was a Jew or a Catholic; indeed, as matters stood then, she almost felt there was something particularly refined in rising above the crude anti-Semitic prejudice of the common people.

Later the poor woman was destined to see a nationalist spirit welling up all over Europe, and with it a surge of Jew-baiting, transforming her husband in her very arms, as it were, from a respected free spirit into a corrosive spawn of an alien race. In the beginning she had resisted this transformation with all the indignation of a "magnanimous heart," but as the years passed she was worn down by the naïvely cruel and steadily growing hostility and intimidated by the general prejudice. In time, as the differences between herself and her husband gradually became acrimonious—when, for reasons he would never quite go into, he never rose above the rank of manager and lost all prospects of ever being appointed a bank director—she came to justify to herself, with a shrug, many things that wounded her by remembering that Leo's character was, after all, alien to her own, though toward outsiders she never abandoned the principles of her youth.

Their differences, however, were basically nothing more than a lack of understanding; as in many marriages, a natural misfortune, as it were, surfaced as soon as the couple ceased to be rapturously happy. Ever since Leo's career had hesitantly ground to a halt at what was in effect a stockbroker's desk, Clementine was no longer able to excuse certain of his peculiarities by taking into account that he was not ensconced in the glassy calm of a ministerial office but was sitting at the "roaring loom of time"—and who knows whether she had not married him just on account of this quotation from Goethe? His side-whiskers, which, with the pince-nez riding the middle of his nose, had once reminded her of an English lord with muttonchops, now suggested a stockbroker, and some of his mannerisms of gesture and turns of phrase became positively insufferable to her. At first Clementine tried to improve her husband, but she ran into terrible snags as it became apparent that nowhere in the world was there a standard by which to judge whether muttonchop whiskers rightly suggested a lord or a broker, or at what point on the nose a pince-nez, combined with a wave of the hand, expressed enthusiasm or cynicism. Besides, Leo Fischel was simply not the man to let himself be improved. He dismissed as social tomfoolery the faultfinding that tried to turn him into the Christian-Teutonic beau ideal of a high ministry official, and rejected her arguments as unworthy of a reasonable man; for the more his wife took offense at certain details, the more he stressed the great guidelines of reason. And so the Fischel household was gradually transformed into the battleground of two contending philosophies of life.

Director Fischel of the Lloyd Bank enjoyed philosophizing, but only for ten minutes a day. He enjoyed thinking that human life had a solid rational basis and that it paid off intellectually; he imagined this on the pattern of the harmonious hierarchy of a great bank and noted with satisfaction the daily signs of progress he read about in the papers.

This faith in the immutable guidelines of reason and progress had for a long time enabled him to dismiss his wife's carpings with a shrug or a cutting retort. But since misfortune had decreed that in the course of this marriage the mood of the times would shift away from the old principles of liberalism that had favored Leo Fischel—the great guiding ideals of tolerance, the dignity of man, and free trade—and reason and progress in the Western world would be displaced by racial theories and street slogans, he could not remain untouched by it either. He started by flatly denying the existence of these changes, just as Count Leinsdorf was accustomed to deny the existence of certain "unpleasant political manifestations" and waited for them to disappear of their own accord. Such waiting is the first, almost imperceptible degree of the torture of exasperation that life inflicts on men of principle. The second degree is usually called, and was therefore also called by Fischel, "poison." This poison is the appearance, drop by drop, of new views on morals, art, politics, the family, newspapers, books, and social life, already accompanied by the helpless feeling that there is no turning back and by indignant denials, which cannot avoid a certain acknowledgment of the thing denied. Nor was Director Fischel spared the third and final degree, when the isolated showers and sprinklings of the New turn into a steady, drenching rain. In time this becomes one of the most horrible torments that a man who has only ten minutes a day to spare for philosophy can experience.

Leo came to know on how many points people can have differences of opinion. The drive to be right, a need almost synonymous with human dignity, began to celebrate excesses in the Fischel household. For millennia this drive has produced thousands of admirable philosophies, works of art, books, deeds, and partisan alliances, and when this admirable, but also fanatical and monstrous, innate human drive has to make do with ten minutes on practical philosophy or a debate on the basic principles of the household, it cannot fail to burst, like a drop of molten lead, into innumerable sharp splinters that inflict the most painful wounds. It burst over the question of whether a maid was to be given notice or not, and whether toothpicks belonged on the table or not; but whatever made it burst, it had the capacity to reconstitute itself immediately into two infinitely detailed opposing views of the world.

This was all very well by day, since Director Fischel was in his office then, but at night he was only human, and this gravely worsened the relations between him and Clementine. Things today are so complicated that a person can really keep fully informed only in one field, basically, which in his case was stocks and bonds, and so he was inclined at night to be of a generally yielding disposition. Clementine, on the contrary, remained sharp and unyielding, raised as she had been in a strict civil-service household with its constant emphasis on duty. Besides, her class consciousness would not permit them separate bedrooms, which would have made their already inadequate apartment even smaller. But a shared bedroom, with the lights out, puts a man in the situation of an actor having to play before an invisible house the rewarding but by now worn-out role of a hero impersonating a growling lion. For years now, Leo's dark auditorium had not let slip the faintest hint of applause, nor yet the smallest sign of disapproval, and this was surely enough to shatter the strongest nerves. In the morning at breakfast, which the couple took together in accordance with time-honored tradition, Clementine was stiff as a frozen corpse and Leo twitchy with nerves. Even their daughter, Gerda, noticed something of this every time and had come to imagine married life with dread and bitter loathing, as a catfight in the dark of night.

Gerda was twenty-three, and the favorite bone of contention of both her progenitors. Leo Fischel thought it was time to start thinking of a good match for her. But Gerda said, "You're old-fashioned, Papa," and had chosen her friends in a swarm of Christian nationalists her own age, none of whom offered the slightest prospect of being able to support a wife; instead, they despised capitalism and maintained that no Jew had yet proved capable of serving as a great symbol of humanity. Leo Fischel called them anti-Semitic louts and would have forbidden them the house, but Gerda said, "You don't understand, Papa, they only mean it symbolically"; and nervous and anemic as she was, Gerda immediately got upset if she was not handled with care. So Fischel suffered her friends' society, as once Odysseus had had to suffer Penelope's suitors in his house, for Gerda was the ray of sunshine in his life. But he did not suffer in silence, because that was not in his nature. He thought he knew all about morality and great ideas himself, and held forth on them at every opportunity in order to exert a good influence on Gerda. Every time he did so Gerda answered: "Yes, Papa, you would be absolutely right if the whole thing did not have to be looked at from a wholly different point of view from the one you still cling to!"

What did Clementine do when Gerda talked like this? Not a thing. She made a resigned face and kept her own counsel, but Leo could be sure that behind his back she would be on Gerda's side—as if she knew what symbols were! Leo Fischel had always had every reason to assume that his good Jewish head was superior to his wife's, and nothing outraged him so much as to observe that she was using Gerda's craziness to her own advantage. Why should he, of all people, suddenly no longer be capable of keeping up with the times? They were in this together! Then he remembered last night. This was no longer sniping at a man's self-esteem, it was digging it up by the roots! At night a man has only his nightshirt on, and right underneath that is his character. No expertise, no professional shrewdness, can protect him. Here a man stakes his whole life, nothing less. So what did it mean that Clementine, whenever the conversation turned to Christian-Germanic ideas, made a face as if he were fresh from the jungle?

Now, man is a being who can stand mistrust as little as tissue paper can the rain. Since Clementine had ceased to find Leo attractive she found him unbearable, and since Leo began to feel that Clementine doubted him he saw at every turn a conspiracy in his own house. At the same time Clementine and Leo deluded themselves, like everyone whose mind has been formed by the prevailing customs and literature, that their passions, characters, destinies, and actions made them dependent on each other. In truth, of course, more than half of life consists not of actions but of formulas, of opinions we make our own, of on-the-one-hands and on-the-other-hands, and of all the piled-up impersonality of everything one has heard and knows. The fate of this husband and wife depended mostly on a murky, persistent, confused structuring of ideas that were not even their own but belonged to public opinion and shifted with it, without their being able to defend themselves against it. Compared with this dependence their personal dependence on each other represented only a tiny fraction, a wildly overestimated residue. And while they deluded themselves that they had their own private lives, and questioned each other's character and will, the agonizing difficulty lay in the unreality of their conflict, which they covered with every possible peevishness.

It was Leo Fischel's bad luck that he neither played cards nor found pleasure in taking out pretty girls, but, worn out by his work, suffered from a marked craving for family life, whereas his wife, who had nothing to do day or night but be the bosom of the family, was no longer subject to any romantic illusions about that. There were times when Leo Fischel felt he was suffocating, attacked by nothing he could put his finger on from all sides at once. He was a hardworking small cell in the body politic, doing its duty with a will, but receiving from all sides poisoned juices. And so, though it far exceeded his need for philosophy, the aging man, left in the lurch by his life-partner and seeing no grounds for abandoning the rational fashion of his youth, began to sense the profound emptiness of emotional life, its formlessness which is eternally changing its forms, its slow but relentless overturning that pulls everything with it.

It was on one such morning, his head occupied with family problems, that Fischel had forgotten to answer His Grace's invitation, and on many subsequent mornings he had to listen to accounts of what was going on in Section Chief Tuzzi's wife's circle, which made it appear most regrettable not to have seized such a chance for Gerda to enter the best society. Fischel's conscience was none too clear, since his own general manager and the chief executive of the National Bank attended those gatherings, but as everyone knows, a man will defend himself most violently against reproaches the more strongly he is torn between guilt and innocence. But every time Fischel tried, with all the superiority of a practical man, to make fun of these patriotic goings-on, he was advised that a financier who was abreast of the times, such as Paul Arnheim, evidently thought otherwise. It was amazing how much Clementine, and even Gerda—who normally, of course, took the opposite line from her mother's—had found out about this man, and as the stock exchange, too, was buzzing with all sorts of stories about him, Fischel felt driven onto the defensive, unable to keep up with them or to come out and say about so eminent a businessman that he was not to be taken seriously.

But when Fischel was on the defensive he adopted a suitably bearish stance, in this instance keeping up an impenetrable silence in the face of all allusions to the Tuzzi household, Arnheim, the Parallel Campaign, and his own failure. He tried to find out where and how long Arnheim was staying in town, and furtively hoped for an event that would at one blow expose the hollow pretense of it all and bring down his family's high rating of those stocks with a crash.

52

SECTION CHIEF TUZZI FINDS A BLIND SPOT IN THE WORKINGS OF HIS MINISTRY

After he had decided to find out all about Arnheim, Section Chief Tuzzi soon made the satisfying discovery of a large blind spot in the workings of the Ministry of Foreign Affairs and of the Imperial House, which were his special concern: it had not been designed to deal with persons like Arnheim. Other than memoirs, Tuzzi read no literary works but the Bible, Homer, and Rosegger, priding himself that this saved him from dissipating his mental forces. But that not a single man was to be found in the whole Foreign Ministry who had read a book of Arnheim's he recognized as an error.

Section Chief Tuzzi had the right to summon the heads of other departments to his own office, but on the morning after that night disturbed by tears, he had gone himself to see the chief of the press department, impelled by a feeling that the occasion which led him to seek a discussion did not warrant full official status. The chief of the press department admired Section Chief Tuzzi for knowing so many personal details about Arnheim, admitted that he, too, had frequently heard the name mentioned, but promptly warded off any intimation that the man could possibly be found in any of his departmental files, since Arnheim had not, as far as he recalled, ever been the object of official consideration and since the processing of news material could not, of course, be extended to cover the public expressions of private individuals. Tuzzi conceded that this was as it should be, but pointed out that these days the borderline between the official and the private status of persons and events was not always clearly definable, which the chief of the press department found a most acute observation, whereupon the two section chiefs agreed that they had before them a most intriguing flaw in the system.

It was clearly a morning on which Europe was enjoying a little peace and quiet, because the two officials sent for the head clerk and instructed him to start a file headed *Arnheim, Dr. Paul,* though there was as yet nothing in it. After the head clerk came the chief file clerk and the clerk in charge of news clippings, both of whom were able to state on the spot, all aglow with efficiency, that no Arnheim was to be found in their files. Finally the press secretaries were called in, whose job it was to go through the newspapers every day and lay their clippings before the various chiefs. When asked about Arnheim they all made serious faces, and testified that he was indeed mentioned often and most favorably in the papers they read, but that they could not say what his writings were about because his activities—as they could immediately affirm—were not included within the sphere of their official concern with the news. Thus the flawless functioning of the Foreign Ministry's apparatus was demonstrated whenever one touched a button, and all these officials left the room with the sense of having made the best show of their reliability.

"It's exactly as I told you," the chief of the press department said to Tuzzi with satisfaction. "Nobody knows a thing."

The two section chiefs had listened to the reports with smiling dignity, sitting—as if embalmed forever by their surroundings, like flies in amber—in luxurious leather armchairs, on the deep-pile red carpet, framed by the tall windows draped in dark red in that white-and-gold room dating from the time of Maria Theresa, and acknowledged that the blind spot in the system, which they now had at least spotted, would be hard to cure.

"In this department," its chief said with satisfaction, "we deal with every public utterance, but a borderline must be drawn somewhere around the term 'public.' I can guarantee that every 'Hear, hear' shouted by some deputy at one of this year's regional council meetings can be located in our files within ten minutes, and every such interjection made in the last ten years, as far as it concerns foreign affairs, within half an hour at most. The same applies to every political newspaper article; my men do painstaking work. But those are tangible, so to speak responsible, utterances, in connection with well-defined conditions, powers, and concepts. However, if I have to decide, from a purely professional point of view, under which heading the clerk who compiles the excerpts or the catalog is to file some personal effusion by—let's see, whom could we use as an example?"

Tuzzi helpfully gave him the name of one of the latest writers to frequent Diotima's salon. The chief of the press department glanced up at him uneasily, as if he were hard of hearing.

"All right, him, let's say—but where do we draw the line between what to note and what to pass over? We've even had political poems. Does this mean that every versifier—or perhaps only authors who write for our Burgtheater . . . ?"

Both laughed.

"How is one to deduce what these people mean, even if they were Schiller and Goethe? Of course there's always a higher meaning in it, but for all practical purposes they contradict themselves with every second word they say."

By this time the two men had become aware that they were running the risk of becoming involved in something "impossible," a word with the added nuance of something socially ridiculous, to which diplomats are so keenly sensitive.

"Of course we can't bring a whole staff of literary and drama critics into the ministry," Tuzzi said with a smile, "but on the other hand, once we've become aware of it, there's no denying that such people are not without influence on world opinion and consequently do affect politics."

"It isn't done in any Foreign Office in the world," the press chief said helpfully.

"Agreed. But drop after drop will hollow out stone." Tuzzi found that this proverb served nicely to express a certain danger. "Shouldn't we try to set up a way of handling this?"

"I don't know. I have qualms," the other section chief said.

"So do I, of course!" Tuzzi replied. As the conversation neared its end he felt ill at ease, as if his tongue were coated, uncertain whether he had been talking nonsense or whether it would turn out after all to be another instance of that perspicacity for which he was celebrated. The press chief was equally undecided, and so they ended by assuring each other that they would have another talk on the subject later.

The press chief issued instructions to order Arnheim's complete works for the ministry library, by way of concluding the matter, and Tuzzi went to a political department, where he requested a detailed report on the man Arnheim from the Austrian Embassy in Berlin. This was the only thing left for him to do at the moment, and until the report arrived his only source of information about Arnheim was his wife, a source he now felt strongly disinclined to use. He recalled Voltaire's saying that people use words only to hide their thoughts and use thoughts only to justify the wrongs they have done. Certainly, that is what diplomacy had always been. But that a person spoke and wrote as much as Arnheim did, to hide his real intentions behind words, was something new; it made Tuzzi uneasy, and he would have to get to the bottom of it.

53

MOOSBRUGGER IS MOVED TO ANOTHER PRISON

The killer of a prostitute, Christian Moosbrugger, had been forgotten a few days after the newspapers stopped printing the reports of his trial, and the public had turned to other things for excitement. Only a circle of experts still took an interest in him. His lawyer had entered a plea to have the trial invalidated, demanded a new psychiatric examination, and taken other steps as well: the execution was indefinitely postponed and Moosbrugger moved to another prison.

The precautions with which this was done flattered him: loaded guns, many people, arms and legs in irons. They were paying attention to him, they were afraid of him, and Moosbrugger loved it. When he climbed into the prison van, he glanced around for admiration and tried to catch the surprised gaze of the passersby. Cold wind, blowing down the street, played with his curly hair; the air drained him. Two seconds; then a guard shoved his behind into the van.

Moosbrugger was vain. He did not like to be pushed like that; he was afraid that the guards would punch him, shout or laugh at him. The fettered giant did not dare to look at any of his escort and slid to the front of the van of his own accord.

But he was not afraid of death. Life is full of things that must be endured, and that certainly hurt more than being hanged, and whether a man has a few years more or less to live really doesn't matter. The passive pride of a man who has been locked up for long stretches would not let him fear his punishment; but in any case, he did not cling to life. What was there in life that he should love? Surely not the spring breeze, or the open road, or the sun? They only make a man tired, hot, and dusty. No one loves life who really knows it. "If I could say to someone," Moosbrugger thought, " 'Yesterday I had some terrific roast pork at the corner restaurant!' that might be something." But one could do without even that. What would have pleased him was something that could satisfy his ambition, which had always come up against nothing but stupid insults.

An uneven jolting ran from the wheels through the bench into his body. Behind the bars in the door the cobblestones were running backward; heavy wagons were left behind; at times, men, women, or children stumbled diagonally across the bars; a distant cab was gaining on them, growing, coming closer, beginning to spray out life as an anvil throws off sparks; the horses' heads seemed to be about to push through the door; then the clatter of hooves and the soft sound of rubber-tired wheels ran on past behind the wall of the van. Moosbrugger slowly turned his head back to stare again at the ceiling where it met the van's side in front of him. The noises outside roared, blared, were stretched like a canvas over which now and then flitted the shadow of something happening. Moosbrugger took the ride as a change, without paying much attention to its meaning. Between two dark, inert stretches in prison a quarter of an hour's opaque, white, foaming time was shooting by. This was how he had always experienced his freedom. Not really pretty. "That business about the last meal," he thought, "the prison chaplain, the hangmen, the quarter hour before it's all over, won't be too different. It will bounce along on wheels too; I'll be kept busy all the time, like now, trying to keep from sliding off this bench at every jolt, and I won't be seeing or hearing much of anything with all those people hopping around me. It's the best thing that can happen: finally I'll get some peace."

A man who has liberated himself from wanting to live feels immensely superior. Moosbrugger remembered the superintendent who had been his first interrogator at the police station. A real gent, who spoke in a low voice.

"Look here, Mr. Moosbrugger," he had said, "I beseech you: grant me success!" And Moosbrugger had replied, "Well, if success means that much to you, let's draw up a statement."

The judge, later on, was skeptical, but the superintendent had confirmed it in court. "Even if you don't care about relieving your conscience on your own account, please give me the personal satisfaction that you are doing it for my sake." The superintendent had repeated this before the whole court, even the presiding judge had looked pleased, and Moosbrugger had risen to his feet:

"My deep respect to His Honor the superintendent for making

this statement!" he had loudly proclaimed, then added, with a grace-ful bow: "Although the superintendent's last words to me were 'We will probably never see each other again,' it is an honor and a privi-lege to see you, the superintendent, again today."

A smile of self-approval transformed Moosbrugger's face, and he forgot the guards sitting opposite him, flung to and fro like himself by the jolting van.

54

IN CONVERSATION WITH WALTER AND CLARISSE, ULRICH TURNS OUT TO BE REACTIONARY

Clarisse said to Ulrich: "Something must be done for Moosbrugger; this murderer is musical!"

Ulrich had finally, on a free afternoon, paid them a visit to make up for the one so fatefully prevented by his arrest.

Clarisse was clutching at his lapel; Walter stood beside her with a look on his face that was not quite sincere.

"What do you mean, musical?" Ulrich asked with a smile.

Clarisse looked merrily shamefaced. Unintentionally. As if she had to clap a tight comic grin on her face to hold back the embarrassment oozing from every pore. She let go of his lapel.

"Oh, nothing special," she said. "You seem to have become an in-fluential man!" It was not always easy to make her out.

Walter had already made a start, and then stopped again. Here, outside the city, there was still some snow on the ground; white fields and between them, like dark water, black earth. The sun washed over everything equitably. Clarisse wore an orange jacket and a blue wool cap. The three of them were out for a walk, and Ulrich, in the midst of nature's desolate disarray, had to explain Arnheim's writings to her. These dealt with algebraic series, benzol rings, the materialist as well as the universalist philosophy of history, bridge supports, the evolution of music, the essence of the automobile, Hata 606, the theory of relativity, Bohr's atomic theory, autogeneous welding, the flora of the Himalayas, psychoanalysis, individual psychology, experimental psychology, physiological psychology, social psychology, and all the other achievements that prevent a time so greatly enriched by them from turning out good, wholesome, integral human beings. However, Arnheim dealt with all these subjects in his writing in the most soothing fashion, assuring his readers that whatever they did not understand represented only an excess of sterile intellect, while the truth was always simplicity itself, like human dignity and that instinct for transcendent realities within reach of everyone who lived simply and was in league with the stars.

"Plenty of people are saying this kind of thing nowadays," Ulrich explained, "but Arnheim is the one whom people believe because they see him as a big, rich man who really knows whatever it is he is talking about, who has actually been to the Himalayas, owns automobiles, and can wear as many benzol rings as he likes."

Clarisse, prompted by a vague notion of carnelian rings, wanted to know what benzol rings looked like.

"You're a dear girl, Clarisse, all the same!" Ulrich said.

Walter came to her defense. "Thank heaven she doesn't have to understand all that chemical gobbledygook." But then he proceeded to defend the works of Arnheim, which he had read. He would not claim that Arnheim was the best one could imagine, but he was still the best the present age had produced; this was a new spirit! Scientifically sound, yet also capable of going beyond technical knowledge.

Thus their walk came to an end. The result for all of them was wet feet, an irritated brain—as though the thin, bare branches on the trees, sparkling in the winter sun, had turned to splinters stuck in the retina—a vulgar craving for hot coffee, and the feeling of human forlornness.

Steaming snow rose from their shoes; Clarisse enjoyed the mess they were making on the floor, and Walter kept his femininely sensuous lips pursed the whole time, because he was itching to start an argument. Ulrich told them about the Parallel Campaign. When Arnheim's name cropped up again the argument began.

"I'll tell you what I hold against him," Ulrich persisted. "Scientific man is an entirely inescapable thing these days; we can't not want to know! And at no time has the difference between the expert's experience and that of the layman been as great as it is now. Everyone can see this in the ability of a masseur or a pianist. No one would send a horse to the races these days without special preparation. It is only on the problems of being human that everyone feels called upon to pronounce judgment, and there's an ancient prejudice to the effect that one is born and dies a human being. But even if I know that five thousand years ago women wrote the same love letters, word for word, that they write today, I can't read such letters any longer without wondering whether it isn't ever going to change!"

Clarisse seemed inclined to agree. Walter, however, smiled like a fakir preparing not to bat an eyelash while someone runs a hatpin through his cheeks.

"Meaning only, presumably, that until further notice you refuse to be a human being?" he broke in

"More or less. It has an unpleasant feeling of dilettantism about it."

"But I'll grant you something quite different," Ulrich went on after some thought. "The experts never finish anything. Not only are they not finished today, but they are incapable of conceiving an end to their activities. Even incapable, perhaps, of wishing for one. Can you imagine that man will still have a soul, for instance, once he has learned to understand it and control it biologically and psychologically? Yet this is precisely the condition we are aiming for! That's the trouble. Knowledge is a mode of conduct, a passion. At bottom, an impermissible mode of conduct: like dipsomania, sex mania, homicidal mania, the compulsion to know forms its own character that is off-balance. It is simply not so that the researcher pursues the truth; it pursues him. He suffers it. What is true is true, and a fact is real, without concerning itself about him: he's the one who has a passion for it, a dipsomania for the factual, which marks his character, and he doesn't give a damn whether his findings will lead to something human, perfect, or anything at all. Such a man is full of contradictions and misery, and yet he is a monster of energy!"

"And—?" Walter asked.

"What do you mean, 'And—?' "

"Surely you're not suggesting that we can leave it at that?"

"I would like to leave it at that," Ulrich said calmly. "Our conception of our environment, and also of ourselves, changes every day. We live in a time of passage. It may go on like this until the end of the planet if we don't learn to tackle our deepest problems better than we have so far. Even so, when one is placed in the dark, one should not begin to sing out of fear, like a child. And it is mere singing in the dark to act as though we knew how we are supposed to conduct ourselves down here; you can shout your head off, it's still nothing but terror. All I know for sure is: we're galloping! We're still a long way from our goals, they're not getting any closer, we can't even see them, we're likely to go on taking wrong turns, and we'll have to change horses; but one day—the day after tomorrow, or two thousand years from now—the horizon will begin to flow and come roaring toward us!"

Dusk had fallen. "No one can see my face now," Ulrich thought. "I don't even know myself whether I'm lying." He spoke as one does when making an uncertain snap judgment about the results of decades of certainty. It occurred to him that this youthful dream he had just unfurled for Walter had long since turned hollow. He didn't want to go on talking.

"Meaning," Walter said sharply, "that we should give up trying to make any sense of life?"

Ulrich asked him why he needed to make sense of it. It seemed to be doing nicely without that, it seemed to him.

Clarisse giggled. She didn't mean to mock Walter; Ulrich's question had struck her as funny.

Walter turned on the light, as he saw no reason why Ulrich should exploit the advantage, with Clarisse, of being the dark man. An irritating glare enveloped the three of them.

Ulrich stubbornly expanded on his point: "What one needs in life is merely the conviction that one's business is doing better than one's neighbor's. Your pictures, my mathematics, somebody else's wife and children—everything that can assure a person that he is in no way unusual but that in this way of being in no way unusual he will not so easily find his equal!"

Walter had not yet sat down again. He was full of unrest. Triumph.

"Do you realize what you're talking about?" he shouted. "Muddling through! You're simply an Austrian, and you're expounding the Austrian national philosophy of muddling through!"

"That may not be as bad as you think," Ulrich replied. "A passionate longing for keenness and precision, or beauty, may very well bring one to prefer muddling through to all those exertions in the modern spirit. I congratulate you on having discovered Austria's world mission."

Walter wanted to make some retort. But it turned out that the unrest that had kept him on his feet was not only a sense of triumph but—how to put it?—also the need to leave the room. He hesitated between the two impulses, but they were irreconcilable, and his gaze slid away from Ulrich's eyes toward the door.

When they were alone, Clarisse said: "This murderer is musical. I mean . . ." She paused, then went on mysteriously: "I can't explain it, but you must do something for him."

"But what can I do?"

"Set him free."

"You must be dreaming."

"You can't mean all those things you say to Walter?" Clarisse asked, and her eyes seemed to be urging him to an answer whose content he could not guess.

"I don't know what you want," he said.

Clarisse kept her eyes stubbornly on his lips; then she came back to her point: "You ought to do what I said, anyway; you would be transformed."

Ulrich observed her, trying to understand. He must have missed something—an analogy, or some "as if" that might have given a meaning to what she was saying. It sounded strange to hear her speaking so naturally without making sense, as though referring to some commonplace experience she had had.

But Walter was back. "I'm prepared to admit—" he began. The interruption had taken the edge off the argument.

He perched on his piano stool again and noticed with satisfaction some soil clinging to his shoes. "Why is there no dirt on Ulrich's shoes?" he thought. "It's the last hope of salvation for European man."

But Ulrich was looking above Walter's shoes at his legs, sheathed in black cotton, with their unlovely shape of the soft legs of young girls.

"A man today who still aspires to integrity deserves a lot of credit," Walter said.

"There's no such thing anymore," Ulrich countered. "You only have to look in a newspaper. It's filled with an immeasurable opacity. So many things are being talked about, it would surpass the intellectual capacity of a Leibniz. But we don't even notice; we have changed. There's no longer a whole man confronting a whole world, only a human something moving about in a general culture-medium."

"Quite so," Walter shot back. "There is in fact no complete education anymore, in Goethe's sense. Which is why today every idea has its opposite. Every action and its opposite are accompanied by the subtlest arguments, which can be defended or attacked with equal ease. How on earth can you champion such a state of affairs?"

Ulrich shrugged.

"One has to withdraw completely," Walter said softly.

"Or just go along," his friend replied. "Perhaps we're on our way to the termite state, or some other un-Christian division of labor." Ulrich thought privately that it would be just as easy to agree as to argue. Contempt showed as clearly through the politeness as a tidbit in aspic. He knew that Walter would again be annoyed with what he had just said, but he was beginning to long for a conversation with someone with whom he could agree completely, for once. There had been a time when he and Walter had had such conversations: the words are drawn from the breast by some mysterious power, and not one word misses its mark. But when one talks with antipathy the words rise like fog from an icy plain. He looked at Walter without resentment, certain that Walter also felt that the further this conversation went the more it was deforming his inner convictions, but that he was blaming Ulrich for it. "Everything we think is either sympathy or antipathy!" Ulrich thought. At this moment he was so vividly struck by the truth of this that he felt it as a physical pressure, like the bodily contact of people swaying in unison when they are jammed together. He looked around for Clarisse.

But Clarisse seemed to have stopped listening some time ago; at some point she had picked up the newspaper that had lain in front of her on the table and had begun asking herself why she found this so pleasurable. She felt herself looking at the boundless opacity Ulrich had spoken of before, with the paper between her hands. Her arms unfolded the darkness and opened out. Her arms formed two cross-beams with the trunk of her body, with the newspaper hanging between them. That was the pleasure, but the words to describe it were nowhere within her. She knew only that she was looking at the paper without reading it, and that it seemed to her there must be some savage mystery inside Ulrich, a power akin to her own, though she could not pin it down. Her lips had opened as if she were about to smile, but it was unconscious, a loosening of a still-frozen tension.

Walter continued in a low voice: "You're right when you say there's nothing serious, rational, or even intelligible left; but why can't you see that it is precisely this growing rationality, infecting everything like a disease, that is to blame? Everyone's brain is seized with this craving to become more and more rational, to rationalize and compartmentalize life more than ever, but unable to imagine what's to become of us when we know everything and have it all analyzed, classified, mechanized, standardized. It can't go on like this."

"Well," Ulrich said with composure, "when the monks were in charge, a Christian had to be a believer, even though the only heaven he could conceive of, with its clouds and harps, was rather boring; and now we are confronted with the Heaven of Reason, which reminds us of our school days with its rulers, hard benches, and horrible chalk figures."

"I have the feeling there will be a reaction of an unbridled excess of fantasy," Walter added thoughtfully. There was a hint of cowardice and cunning in this remark. He was thinking of Clarisse's mysterious irrationality, and as he spoke of reason threatening to drive the irrational to excess he was thinking of Ulrich. The two others did not catch on, which made him feel, in triumph and pain, that they did not understand him. He would have loved to ask Ulrich not to set foot in this house so long as he stayed in town, if only he could have done so without provoking Clarisse to mutiny.

The two men watched Clarisse in silence.

Clarisse suddenly noticed that they were no longer arguing, rubbed her eyes, and blinked amiably at Ulrich and Walter, who sat in the rays of yellow light against the dusky blue of the windowpanes like exhibits in a glass case.

55

SOLIMAN AND ARNHEIM

Meanwhile Christian Moosbrugger, the murderer of the young woman, had acquired yet another female admirer. The question of his guilt or his affliction had captured her heart a few weeks before as vividly as it had those of many others, and she had her own view of the case, which diverged somewhat from that of the court. The name "Christian Moosbrugger" appealed to her, evoking a tall, lonely man sitting by a mill overgrown with moss, listening to the roar of the water. She firmly believed that the accusations against him would be cleared up in some entirely unexpected way. As she sat in the kitchen or the dining room with her needlework, a Moosbrugger who had somehow shaken off his chains would appear beside her—and wild fantasies spun themselves out. It was far from impossible that Christian, had he only met Rachel in time, would have given up his career as a killer of girls and revealed himself as a robber chieftain with an immense future.

The poor man in his prison never dreamed of the heart that was beating for him as it bent over the mending of Diotima's underwear. It was no great distance from the apartment of Section Chief Tuzzi to the court building. From one roof to the other an eagle would have needed only a few wingbeats, but for the modern soul, which playfully spans oceans and continents, nothing is as impossible as finding its way to souls who live just around the corner.

And so the magnetic currents had dissipated again, and for some time Rachel had loved the Parallel Campaign instead of Moosbrugger. Even if things were not going as well as they might inside the reception rooms, a great deal was going on in the antechambers. Rachel, who had always managed to read the newspapers that passed from her employer's quarters to the kitchen, no longer had the time, since she was standing from dawn to dusk as a small guard post in front of the Parallel Campaign. She loved Diotima, Section Chief Tuzzi, His Grace Count Leinsdorf, the nabob, and, once she had noticed that he was beginning to play a role in the household, even Ulrich, as a dog loves his master's friends with a single love, though excitingly varied by their different smells. But Rachel was intelligent. In Ulrich's case, for instance, she was well aware that he was always somewhat at variance with the others, and her imagination started trying to think up some special, unexplained part he must play in the Parallel Campaign. He always looked at her in a friendly fashion, and little Rachel noticed that he kept on looking at her most particularly when he thought she was not aware of it. She felt sure that he wanted something from her; well, she had nothing against it; her little white pelt twitched with expectation, and a tiny golden dart would shoot at him out of her fine black eyes from time to time. Ulrich, without being able to figure it out, sensed the sparks flying from this little person as she flitted around the furniture and the stately visitors, and it offered him some distraction.

He owed his place in Rachel's attention not least to certain secret talks in the antechamber, which tended to undermine Arnheim's dominant position. That dazzling figure was quite unaware that he had a third enemy, besides Ulrich and Tuzzi, in the person of his little page Soliman. This small black fellow was the glittering buckle on the magic belt with which the Parallel Campaign had engirdled Rachel. A funny little creature, who had followed his master from magic climes to the street where Rachel worked, he was simply appropriated by her as that part of the fairy tale intended for her, in accordance with the social law that made the nabob the sun who belonged to Diotima, while Soliman, an enchanting colorful fragment of stained glass sparkling in that sun, was Rachel's booty. The boy, however, saw things somewhat differently. Although physically small he was sixteen going on seventeen, a creature full of romantic notions, malice, and personal pretension. Arnheim had plucked him out of a traveling dance troupe in southern Italy and taken him into his household. The strangely restless little fellow with the mournful monkey's eyes had touched his heart, and the rich man decided to open higher vistas to him. It was a longing for a close, faithful companionship, such as not infrequently overcame the solitary man—a weakness he usually hid behind increased activity. And so Arnheim treated Soliman, until his fourteenth year, on more or less those same terms of equality as rich families once casually brought up their wet nurse's offspring side by side with their own, letting them share the games and fun, until the moment when it appears that the same milk is of a lower grade when it is a mother's milk compared with that of a wet nurse. Soliman used to crouch day and night at his master's desk or at his feet, behind his back or on his knees, during Arnheim's long hours of conversation with famous visitors. He had read Scott, Shakespeare, and Dumas when Scott, Shakespeare, and Dumas had happened to be lying around on the tables, and had learned to spell from the *Handbook on the Humanities.* He ate his master's sweets, and when no one was looking soon took to smoking his cigarettes as well. A private tutor came and gave him—though somewhat erratically, because of all the traveling they did—an elementary education. It was all terribly boring to Soliman, who loved nothing more than serving as a valet, which he was also allowed to do, and which was serious, grown-up work, satisfying his need for action. But one day— not so long ago either—his master had called him in and told him, in a friendly way, that he had not quite fulfilled the hopes set on him. Now he was no longer a child, and Arnheim, his master, was responsible for seeing that Soliman, the little servant, turned into a decent citizen; which is why he had decided to treat him henceforth as exactly what he would have to be, so that he could learn to get used to it. Many successful men, Arnheim added, had begun as bootblacks and dishwashers; this beginning had indeed been the source of their strength, because the most important thing in life was to do whatever one does with all one's heart.

That hour, when he was promoted from the undefined status of a pet kept in luxury to that of a servant with free board and lodging and a small wage, ravaged Soliman's heart to a degree of which Arnheim had no notion at all. Arnheim's statements had gone clear over Soliman's head, but Soliman's feelings made him guess what they meant, and he had hated his master ever since the change had been imposed on him. Not that he stopped helping himself to books, sweets, and cigarettes, but while he had formerly taken merely what gave him pleasure, he now deliberately stole from Arnheim, with so insatiable a vengefulness that he sometimes simply broke things, or hid them, or threw them away—things Arnheim obscurely thought he remembered, puzzled that they never turned up again. While Soliman was revenging himself like a goblin, he pulled himself together remarkably in carrying out his duties and presenting a pleasing appearance. He continued to be a sensation with all the cooks, housemaids, hotel staff, and female visitors; was spoiled by their glances and smiles, gaped at by jeering ragamuffins on the street; and generally felt like a fascinating and important personage, even when oppressed. His master, too, occasionally favored him with a pleased or complacent glance, or with a kind, wise word. Everyone praised Soliman as a handy, obliging boy, and if it happened that such praise came just after he had got something especially awful on his conscience he grinned obsequiously, enjoying his triumph as if he had swallowed a searingly cold lump of ice.

Rachel had won this boy's trust the moment she told him that what was going on in the house might be preparations for war; ever since, she had been subjected by him to the most scandalous revelations about her idol, Arnheim. Despite Soliman's blasé airs, his imagination was like a pincushion bristling with swords and daggers, and the tales he poured into Rachel's ear about Arnheim were full of thundering horses' hooves and swaying torches and rope ladders. He revealed that his name was not really Soliman, rattling off a long exotic name with such speed that she could never catch it. He later imparted the secret that he was the son of an African prince, kidnapped as a baby from his father, whose warriors, cattle, slaves, and jewels numbered in the thousands. Arnheim had bought him only in order to sell him back to his father for a staggering sum, but Soliman was going to run away, and would have done it sooner were his father not so far away.

Rachel was not fooled by these stories, but she believed them because nothing connected with the Parallel Campaign could be incredible enough. She would also have liked to forbid Soliman such talk about Arnheim, but had to stop short of regarding his presumption with horrified mistrust because his assurance that his master was not to be trusted promised, for all her doubts, a tremendous imminent, thrilling complication for the Parallel Campaign.

Such were the storm clouds behind which the tall man brooding by the moss-grown millrace disappeared, and a pallid light gathered in the wrinkled grimaces of Soliman's little monkey face.

56

THE PARALLEL CAMPAIGN COMMITTEES SEETHE WITH ACTIVITY. CLARISSE WRITES TO HIS GRACE PROPOSING A NIETZSCHE YEAR

At about this time Ulrich had to report to His Grace two or three times a week. A high-ceilinged, shapely room, delightful in its very proportions, had been set aside for him. At the window stood a large Maria Theresa desk. On the wall hung a dark picture, mutely glowing with patches of red, blue, and yellow, of some horsemen or other driving their lances into the bellies of other, fallen horsemen. On the opposite wall hung the portrait of a solitary lady whose vulnerable body was carefully armored in a gold-embroidered, wasp-waisted corset. There seemed no reason why she had been banished all by herself to this wall, as she was obviously a Leinsdorf; her young, powdered face resembled the Liege-Count's as closely as a footprint in dry snow matches one in wet loam. Ulrich, incidentally, had little opportunity to study Count Leinsdorf's face. Since the last meeting, the Parallel Campaign had received such a boost that His Grace never found leisure to devote to the great ideas anymore but had to spend his time reading correspondence, receiving people, discussions, and expeditions. He had already had a consultation with the Prime Minister, a talk with the Archbishop, a conference at the Chamberlain's office, and had more than once sounded out a number of the high aristocracy and the ennobled commoners in the

Upper House. Ulrich had not been invited to these discussions and gathered only that all sides expected strong political resistance from the opposition, so they all declared they would be able to support the Parallel Campaign the more vigorously the less their names were linked with it, and for the time being only sent observers to represent them at the committee meetings.

The good news was that these committees were making great strides from week to week. As agreed at the inaugural sessions, they had divided up the world according to the major aspects of religion, education, commerce, agriculture, and so on; every committee already contained a representative of the corresponding ministry, and all committees were already devoting themselves to their task, to wit, that every committee in accord with all the other committees was waiting for the representatives of the respective organizations and sectors of the population to present their wishes, suggestions, and petitions, which would be screened and passed on to the executive committee. In this fashion it was hoped that a steady stream of the country's principal moral forces could be channeled, in an ordered and concentrated way, to the executive committee, an expectation already gratified by the swelling tide of written communications. Very shortly the flood of memoranda from the various committees to the executive committee were able to refer to their own earlier memoranda, previously transmitted to the executive committee, so that they took to beginning with a sentence that gained in importance from one instance to the next and started with the words: "With reference to our mem. no. so-and-so, ref. to no. such-and-such/XYZ, no. this-and-that"; all these numbers grew larger with each communication. This in itself was already a sign of healthy growth. In addition, even the embassies began to report through semi-official channels on the impression being made abroad by this vigorous display of Austrian patriotism; the foreign ambassadors were already sending out cautious feelers for information; alerted deputies were asking questions in Parliament; and private enterprise manifested itself by way of inquiries from business firms that took the liberty of making suggestions or seeking a way in which they could link their firms with patriotism. The apparatus was set up, and because it was there it had to function, and once it was functioning, it began to accelerate; once a car starts rolling in an open field, even if no one is at the wheel, it will always take a definite, even a very impressive and remarkable course of its own.

And so a great force had been set in motion, and Count Leinsdorf began to feel it. He put on his pince-nez and read all the incoming mail with great seriousness from beginning to end. It was no longer the proposals and desires of unknown, passionate individuals, such as had inundated him at the outset, before things had been set on a regular course, and even though these applications or inquiries still came from the heart of the people, they were now signed by the chairmen of alpine clubs, leagues for free thought, girls' welfare associations, workingmen's organizations, social groups, citizens' clubs, and other such nondescript clusterings that run ahead of the transition from individualism to collectivism like little heaps of street sweepings before a stiff breeze. And even if His Grace was not in sympathy with everything they asked for, he felt that, all in all, important progress had been made. He took off his pince-nez, handed the communication back to the official who had presented it to him, and nodded his satisfaction without saying a word; he felt that the Parallel Campaign was in good order and clearly on its way, and in due time would find its proper form.

The ministry official who took the letter back usually placed it on a pile of other letters, and when the last one of the day lay on top, he read for His Grace's eyes. Then His Grace's mouth would speak: "Excellent, but we can't say yes and we can't say no as long as we have no really firm idea what our central goal is." But this was just what the official had read in His Grace's eyes after every previous letter, and it was precisely what he thought himself, and he had his gold-plated pocket pencil ready to write what he had already written at the bottom of every previous letter, the magic formula: "Fi." This magic formula, widely used in the Kakanian civil service, stood for "Filed for later decision," and was a model of that circumspection that loses sight of nothing, and rushes into nothing. "Fi," for instance, took care of a minor civil servant's application for an emergency grant-in-aid to pay for his wife's impending confinement by filing it away until the child was grown and old enough to earn a living, simply because the matter might be in the process of being dealt with by pending legislation, and in the meantime the senior official did not have the heart to turn down his subordinate's petition out of hand. The same treatment would also be accorded an application from an influential personage or a government bureau that one could not afford to offend by a refusal, even though one knew some other influential quarter was opposed to this application. And basically, everything that came to the department's attention for the first time was kept on file on principle, until a similar case came up to serve as a precedent.

But it would be quite wrong to make fun of this administrative custom, since a great deal more is filed for later decision in the world outside government offices. How little it means that monarchs on their accession still take an oath to make war on Turks or other infidels, considering that in all the history of mankind no sentence has ever been completely crossed out or quite completed, which at times gives rise to that bewildering tempo of progress exactly resembling a flying ox. In government offices, at least, a few things get lost, but nothing ever gets lost in the world. "Fi" is indeed one of the basic formulas of the structure of our life. When, however, something struck His Grace as particularly urgent, he had to choose another method. He would then send the proposal to Court, to his friend Count Stallburg, with the query whether it might be regarded as "tentatively definitive," as he put it. After some time he would receive a reply, always to the effect that His Majesty's wishes on this point could not as of now be conveyed, but in the meantime it seemed desirable to begin by letting public opinion follow its own direction and then to reconsider the proposal in due course, depending on how it had been received and on any other contingencies that might arise in the meantime. This reply caused the proposal to become a duly constituted file, and as such it was passed on to the proper ministerial department, whence it returned with the note that the department did not consider itself authorized to arrive at an independent decision in the matter, and when this happened Count Leinsdorf made a note to propose at one of the next meetings of the executive committee that an interdepartmental subcommittee be set up to study the problem.

In only one case was His Grace's mind inexorably made up, that of a letter not signed by the chairman of any society or any officially recognized religious, scientific, or artistic body. Such a letter had come recently from Clarisse, using Ulrich's name as a reference, and proposing the proclamation of an Austrian Nietzsche Year, in conjunction with which something would have to be done for the murderer of women, Moosbrugger. She wrote that, as a woman, she felt called upon to make this suggestion, and also because of the significant coincidence that Nietzsche had been a mental case and so was Moosbrugger. Ulrich barely managed a joke to conceal his annoyance when Count Leinsdorf showed him this letter, which he had already recognized by its oddly immature handwriting crisscrossed with heavy horizontal T-bar strokes and underlinings. Count Leinsdorf, however, sensing his embarrassment, said seriously and kindly: "This is not without interest. One might say that it shows ardor and energy, but I'm afraid we must shelve all such personal suggestions, or we shall never get anywhere. As you know the writer personally, perhaps you would like to pass this letter on to your cousin?"

57

GREAT UPSURGE. DIOTIMA DISCOVERS THE STRANGE WAYS OF GREAT IDEAS

Ulrich slipped the letter into his pocket to make it disappear, but in any case it would not have been easy to take it up with Diotima. Ever since the newspaper article about the "Year of Austria" had appeared, she had been swept along by a rising tide of incoherent activity. Not only did Ulrich hand over to her, preferably unread, all the files he received from Count Leinsdorf, but every day the mail brought heaps of letters and press clippings, and masses of books on approval came from booksellers; her house swelled with people as the sea swells when moon and wind tug at it together, and the telephone never stopped ringing. Had little Rachel not taken charge of it with seraphic zeal, and given most of the information herself because she said she could not bother her mistress incessantly, Diotima would have collapsed under the burden.

Yet this nervous breakdown that never happened, even as it kept quivering and pulsating in her body, brought Diotima a kind of happiness she had never known before. It was a shudder, a being endlessly showered with significance, a crackling like that of the pressure in the capstone of the world arch, a prickling like the awareness of nothingness when one stands on the summit of the highest mountain peak for miles around. It was, in short, a sense of position that was awakening in this daughter of a modest secondary-school teacher and this young wife of a middle-class vice-consul, which she had remained in the freshness of her heart despite her rise in society. Such a sense of position belongs to the unnoticed but essential conditions of life, like not noticing the revolutions of the earth or the part our personality plays in directing our perceptions. Since man is taught not to bear vanity in his heart, he keeps most of it underfoot, in that he walks on the soil of a great fatherland, religion, or income-tax bracket; or else, lacking such a vantage point, he makes do with a place anyone can have, on the momentarily highest point reached by the pillar of time as it rises out of the void; in other words, we take pride in living in and for the present moment, when all our predecessors have turned to dust and no successors have yet appeared. But if for some reason this vanity, of which we are usually unconscious, suddenly mounts from the feet to the head, it can cause a mild craziness, like that of those virgins who imagine they are pregnant with the globe of the earth itself.

Even Section Chief Tuzzi now paid Diotima the tribute of inquiring how things were going, sometimes even asking her to oversee one minor matter or another; at such times the smile with which he usually referred to her salon was replaced by a dignified seriousness. It was still not known to what extent the idea of finding himself placed in the forefront of an international pacifist movement would be agreeable to His Gracious Majesty, but on this point Tuzzi repeatedly asked Diotima not to take the slightest step into the field of foreign affairs without first consulting him. He even suggested on the spot that if ever any serious move should be made toward an international peace campaign, every precaution first immediately be taken against any possible political complications that might ensue. Such a noble idea should in no way be rejected, he explained to his wife, not even if there might be some possibility of realizing it, but it was abso-

lutely necessary to keep open one's options for going ahead or retreating from the very beginning. He then laid out for Diotima the
differences between disarmament, a peace conference, a summit
meeting, and so on, all the way down to the already mentioned foundation for decorating the Peace Palace at The Hague with murals by
Austrian artists; he had never before spoken with his wife in this factual manner. Sometimes he would even come back to the bedroom
with his briefcase to supplement his remarks, in case he had forgotten to add, for instance, that he personally could regard everything
having to do with a Global Austria as conceivable only, of course, as
part of a pacifist or humanitarian undertaking of some kind; anything
else could only make one look dangerously irresponsible, or some
such thing.

Diotima answered with a patient smile: "I shall do my best to do as
you wish, but you should not exaggerate the importance of foreign
affairs for us. There is a tremendous upsurge, an inner sense of redemption, coming from the anonymous depths of the people; you
can't imagine the floods of petitions and suggestions that overwhelm
me every day."

She was admirable, for she gave no hint of the enormous difficulties she actually had to contend with. In the deliberations of the great
central committee, which was organized under the headings of Religion, Justice, Agriculture, Education, and so forth, all idealistic
suggestions met with that icy and timorous reserve so familiar to Diotima from her husband in the days before he had become so attentive. There were times when she felt quite discouraged from sheer
impatience, when she could not conceal from herself that this iner-
tial resistance of the world would be hard to break. However clearly
she herself could see the Year of Austria as the Year of a Global
Austria, and the Austrian nations as the model for the nations of the
world—all it took was to prove that Austria was the true home of
the human spirit everywhere—it was equally clear that for the slow-
witted this concept would have to be fleshed out with a particular
content and supplemented by some inspired symbol, something less
abstract, with more sense-appeal, to help them understand. Diotima
pored for hours over many books, searching for the right image, and
it would have to be a uniquely Austrian symbolic image, of course.

But now Diotima was having strange experiences with the nature of great ideas.

It appeared that she was living in a great age, since the age was full of great ideas. But one would not believe how hard it was to translate the greatest and most important of them into reality, considering that all the conditions for doing so existed except one: knowing which of them was the greatest and most important. Every time Diotima had almost opted in favor of some idea, she could not help noticing that its opposite was equally great and equally worthy of realization. That's the way it is, after all, and she couldn't help it. Ideals have curious properties, and one of them is that they turn into their opposites when one tries to live up to them. Take Tolstoy, for instance, and Bertha Suttner, two writers whose ideas were about equally discussed at the time—but how, Diotima thought, can mankind even have roast chicken without violence? And if one should not kill, as these two writers demanded, what was to be done with the soldiers? They would be unemployed, poor devils, and the criminals would see the dawn of a golden age. Such proposals had actually been made, and signatures were said to be in the process of being collected. Diotima could never have imagined a life without eternal verities, but now she found to her amazement that there are two, or more, of every eternal verity. Which is why every reasonable person—Section Chief Tuzzi, in this case, who was to that extent vindicated—has a deeply rooted mistrust of eternal verities. Of course he will never deny that they are indispensable, but he is convinced that people who take them literally must be mad. According to his way of thinking—which he helpfully offered to his wife—ideals make excessive demands on human nature, with ruinous consequences, unless one refuses at the outset to take them quite seriously. The best proof of this that Tuzzi could offer was that such words as "ideal" and "eternal verity" never occur at all in government offices, which deal with serious matters. A civil servant who would think of using such an expression in an official communication would instantly be advised to see a doctor to request a medical leave. But even if Diotima listened to him sadly, she always drew new strength from such moments of weakness, and plunged back into her researches.

Even Count Leinsdorf marveled at her mental energy when he

finally found the time to come for a consultation with her. His Grace
wanted a spontaneous testimonial arising from the midst of the people. He sincerely wanted to find out the will of the people and to
refine it by cautiously influencing it from above, for he hoped one
day to submit it to His Majesty, not as a ritual offering from a Byzan-
tine monarchy but as a sign of true self-awareness achieved by nations adrift in the vortex of democracy. Diotima knew that His Grace
still clung to the "Emperor of Peace" concept and that of a splendid
testimonial demonstration of the True Austria, even though he did
not in principle reject the idea of a Global Austria, but only so long as
it properly expressed the sense of a family of nations gathered
around their patriarch. From this political family His Grace covertly
and tacitly excluded Prussia, even though he had nothing against Dr.
Arnheim personally and even made a point of referring to him as "an
interesting person."

"We certainly don't want anything patriotic in the outworn sense
of the word," he offered. "We must shake up the nation, the world. A
Year of Austria is a fine idea, it seems to me, and I have in fact already told the fellows from the press myself that the public imagination should be steered in that direction. But once we've agreed on
that, what do we do in this Austrian Year—have you thought of that,
my dear? That, you see, is the problem! That's what we really need to
know. Unless we help things along a little from above, the immature
elements will gain the upper hand. And I simply haven't the time to
think of anything!"

Diotima thought His Grace seemed worried, and said vivaciously:
"The campaign is no good at all unless it culminates in a great symbol. That much is certain. It must seize the heart of the world, but it
also needs some influence from above; there is no denying that. An
Austrian Year is a brilliant suggestion, but in my opinion a World
Year would be still finer, a World-Austrian Year, in which Europe
could recognize Austria as its true spiritual home."

"Not so fast! Not so fast!" warned Count Leinsdorf, who had often
been startled by his friend's spiritual audacity. "Aren't your ideas always perhaps a little excessive, Diotima? This is not the first time
you've brought this up, but one can't be too careful. What have you
come up with to do in this World Year?"

With this question, however, Count Leinsdorf, led by the bluntness that made his thinking so full of character, had touched Diotima at precisely her most vulnerable point. "Count," she said after some hesitation, "that is the hardest question in the world to answer. I intend as soon as possible to invite a circle of the most distinguished men, poets and philosophers, and I will wait to hear what this group has to say before I say anything."

"Good!" His Grace exclaimed, instantly won over for a postponement. "How right you are! One can never be careful enough. If you only knew what I have to listen to day in and day out!"

58

QUALMS ABOUT THE PARALLEL CAMPAIGN. BUT IN THE HISTORY OF MANKIND THERE IS NO VOLUNTARY TURNING BACK

On one occasion His Grace also had time to go into it more deeply with Ulrich.

"I can't say I care too much for this Dr. Arnheim," he said confidentially. "A brilliant man, of course; no wonder your cousin is impressed with him. But he is, after all, a Prussian. He has a way of looking on. You know, when I was a little boy, in '65 it was, my sainted father had a shooting party at Chrudim Castle and one of the guests had the same way of looking on, and a year later it turned out that no one had the remotest idea who had brought him along and that he was a major on the Prussian general staff! Not, of course, that I'm suggesting anything, but I don't altogether like this fellow Arnheim knowing all about us."

"Your Grace," Ulrich said, "I'm glad you offer me a chance to speak my mind on the subject. It's time something was done; things are going on that make me wonder and that aren't suitable for a foreign observer to see. After all, the Parallel Campaign is supposed to raise everyone's spirits, isn't it? Surely that is what Your Grace intended?"

"Well of course, naturally."

"But the opposite is happening!" Ulrich exclaimed. "I have the impression it's making all the best people look unusually concerned, even downhearted!"

His Grace shook his head and twiddled his thumbs, as he always did when his mood darkened. He had, in fact, made similar observations himself.

"Ever since it got around that I have some connection with the Parallel Campaign," Ulrich went on, "whenever I get into conversation with someone it doesn't take three minutes before he says to me: 'What is it you're really after with this Parallel Campaign? There's no such thing nowadays as great achievements or great men!' "

"Well, themselves excepted, of course," Count Leinsdorf interjected. "I know all about that; I hear it all the time too. The big industrialists grumble that the politicians don't give them enough protective tariffs, and the politicians grumble about industry for not coming up with enough money for their election campaigns."

"Quite so!" Ulrich proceeded with his exposition. "The surgeons clearly believe that surgery has made progress since the days of Billroth, but they say that medicine as a whole, and science in general, are doing too little for surgery. I would even go so far, if you will permit me, as to suppose that the theologians believe theology has made advances since the time of Christ—"

Count Leinsdorf raised a hand in mild protest.

"Excuse me if I said something inappropriate, especially as it was quite unnecessary; my point is a quite general one. The surgeons, as I said, claim that scientific research is not fulfilling its promise, but if you talk to a research scientist about the present, he will complain that, much as he would like to broaden his outlook a bit, the theater bores him and he can't find a novel that entertains and stimulates him. Talk to a poet, and he'll tell you that there is no faith. Talk to a painter—since I want to leave the theologians out of it—and he'll be pretty sure to tell you that painters can't give their best in a period that has such miserable literature and philosophy. Of course the sequence in which they blame one another is not always the same, but it always reminds one a bit of musical chairs, if you know what I mean, sir, or Puss in the Corner, and I've no idea what the law or the rule is at the bottom of it. I'm afraid it looks as though each individual may still be satisfied with himself, more or less, but collectively, for some universal reason, mankind seems ill at ease inside its own skin, and the Parallel Campaign seems destined to bring this condition to light."

"Good heavens," His Grace said in response to this analysis, without its being quite clear what he meant by it, "nothing but ingratitude!"

"I have already, incidentally," Ulrich continued, "two folders full of general proposals, which I've had no previous opportunity to return to Your Grace. One of them I've headed: *Back to—!* It's amazing how many people tell us that the world was better off in earlier times and want the Parallel Campaign to take us back there. Without counting the understandable slogan, Back to Religion!, we still have a Back to the Baroque, Back to Gothic, Back to Nature, Back to Goethe, to Ancient Germanic Law, to Moral Purity, and quite a few more."

"Hmm, yes. But perhaps there is a real idea in there somewhere, which it would be a mistake to discourage?" Count Leinsdorf offered.

"That's possible, but how should one deal with it? 'After careful consideration of your esteemed letter of such-and-such a date, we regret that we do not regard the present moment as suitable . . .'? Or 'We have read your letter with interest, please supply details on how restoration of the world as it was in the Baroque, the Gothic, et cetera, et cetera, is to be effected . . . and so on'?"

Ulrich was smiling, but Count Leinsdorf felt he was treating the situation with a little too much levity, and twiddled his thumbs with renewed vigor to ward it off. His face, with its handlebar mustache, assumed a hardness reminiscent of the Wallenstein era, and then he came out with a most noteworthy statement:

"Dear Doctor," he said, "in the history of mankind there is no voluntary turning back!"

This statement surprised no one more than Count Leinsdorf himself, who had actually intended to say something quite different. As a conservative, he had been annoyed with Ulrich, and had wanted to point out to him that the middle classes had spurned the universal spirit of the Catholic Church and were now suffering the consequences. He was also on the point of praising the times of absolute

252 · THE MAN WITHOUT QUALITIES

centralism, when the world was still led by persons aware of their responsibilities in accordance with fixed principles. But while he was still groping for words, it suddenly occurred to him what a nasty surprise it would be to wake up one morning without a hot bath and trains, with an Imperial town crier riding through the streets instead of the morning papers. And so Count Leinsdorf thought: "Things can never again be what they were, the way they were," and as he thought this he was quite astonished. For one assumed that if there was indeed no voluntary going back in history, then mankind was like a man driven along by some inexplicable wanderlust, a man who could neither go back nor arrive anywhere, and this was a quite remarkable condition.

Now, while His Grace had an extraordinary knack for keeping apart two ideas that might contradict each other so that they never came together in his consciousness, he should have firmly rejected this particular idea, which was inimical to all his principles. However, he had taken rather a liking to Ulrich, and as far as time permitted, he enjoyed explaining political matters on a strictly logical basis to this intellectually alert young man who had come to him so well recommended, whose only drawback was his middle-class status, which made him something of an outsider when it came to the really great issues. But once one begins with logic, where one idea follows from the immediately preceding one, one never knows where it may all come out at the end. And so Count Leinsdorf did not retract his statement but merely gazed at Ulrich in intense silence.

Ulrich picked up a second folder and took advantage of the pause to hand both files to His Grace.

"I had to head the second one *Forward to—!*" he began to explain, but His Grace started to his feet and found that his time was up. He urged Ulrich to leave the continuation of their talk for another time, when there would be more leisure to give it some thought.

"By the way," he said, already on his feet, "your cousin is going to have a gathering of our most distinguished thinkers to discuss all these problems. Do go; please be sure to go; I don't know whether I shall be permitted to be there."

Ulrich put back his folders, and Count Leinsdorf, in the shadow of

the open door, turned around once more. "A great experiment naturally makes everyone nervous. But we'll shake them up!" His sense of
propriety would not let him leave Ulrich behind without some word
of comfort.

59

MOOSBRUGGER REFLECTS

Moosbrugger had meanwhile settled down in his new prison as best
he could. The gate had hardly shut behind him when he was bel-
lowed at. He had been threatened with a beating when he protested,
if he remembered rightly. He had been put in solitary. For his walk
in the yard he was handcuffed, and the guards' eyes were glued to
him. They had shaved his head, even though his sentence was under
appeal and not yet legally in force, because, they said, they had to
take his measurements. They had lathered him all over with a stink-
ing soft soap, on the pretext of disinfecting him. As an old hand, he
knew that all this was against regulations, but behind that iron gate it
is not so easy to maintain one's dignity. They did as they pleased with
him. He demanded to see the warden, and complained. The warden
had to admit that some things were not in accordance with regulations, but it was not a punishment, he said, only a precaution. Moosbrugger complained to the prison chaplain, but the chaplain was a
kindly old man whose amiable ministry was anachronistically flawed
by his inability to cope with sexual crimes. He abhorred them with
the lack of understanding of a body that had never even touched the
periphery of such feelings, and was even dismayed that Moosbrugger's honest appearance moved him to the weakness of feeling personally sorry for him. He sent Moosbrugger to the prison doctor, and
for his own part, as in all such cases, sent up to the Creator an omni-
bus prayer that did not go into detail but dealt in such general terms

with man's proneness to error that Moosbrugger was included in the moment of prayer along with the freethinkers and atheists. The prison doctor told Moosbrugger that he was making a mountain out of a molehill, gave him a friendly slap on the back, and absolutely refused to pay any attention to his complaints, on the grounds that— if Moosbrugger understood him right—it was all beside the point as long as the question of whether he was insane or only malingering had not been settled by the medical authorities. Infuriated, Moosbrugger suspected that all these people spoke to suit themselves, and that it was this trick with words that gave them the power to do as they pleased with him. He had the feeling of simple people that the educated ought to have their tongues cut out. He looked at the doctor's face with its dueling scars; at the priest's face, withered from the inside; at the austerely tidy office face of the warden; saw each face looking back at him in its own way, and saw in all of them something beyond his reach that they had in common, which had been his life-long enemy. The constricting pressure that in the outside world forces every person, with all his self-conceit, to wedge himself with effort among all that other flesh, was somewhat eased—despite all the discipline—under the roof of the prison, where everything lived for waiting, and the interaction of the inmates, even when it was coarse and violent, was undermined by a shadow of unreality. Moosbrugger reacted with his whole powerful body to the slackening of tension after the trial. He felt like a loose tooth. His skin itched. He felt miserable, as if he had caught an infection. It was a self-pitying, tenderly nervous hypersensitivity that came over him sometimes: the woman who lay underground and who had got him into this mess seemed to him a crude, nasty bitch contrasted with a child, if he compared her to himself.

Just the same, Moosbrugger was not altogether dissatisfied. He could tell in many ways that he was a person of some importance here, and it flattered him. Even the attention given to all convicts alike gave him satisfaction. The state had to feed them, bathe them, clothe them, and concern itself with their work, their health, their books, and their songs from the moment they had broken the law; it had never done these things before. Moosbrugger enjoyed this attention, even if it was strict, like a child who has succeeded in forcing its mother to notice it with anger. But he did not want it to continue much longer. The idea that his sentence might be commuted to life in prison or in a lunatic asylum sparked in him the resistance we feel when every effort to escape from our circumstances only leads us back to them, time and again. He knew that his lawyer was trying to get the case reopened, that he was to be interrogated all over again, but he made up his mind to oppose that as soon as he could and insist that they kill him.

Above all, he had to make a dignified exit, for his life had been a battle for his rights. In solitary, Moosbrugger considered what his rights were. He couldn't say. But they were everything he had been cheated of all his life. The moment he thought of that he swelled with emotion. His tongue arched and started to move like a Lippizaner stallion in his zeal to pronounce the word nobly enough. "My right," he thought, drawing the word out as long as he could, to realize this concept, and thought, as if he were speaking to someone: "It's when you haven't done anything wrong, or something like that, isn't it?" Suddenly he had it: "Right is justice." That was it. His right was his justice! He looked at his wood-plank bed in order to sit on it, turned awkwardly around to tug at it—in vain, as it was screwed to the floor—then slowly sat down.

He had been cheated of his justice! He remembered his master's wife, when he was sixteen. He had dreamed that something cold was blowing on his belly, then it had disappeared inside his body; he had yelled and fallen out of bed, and the next morning felt as if he had been beaten black-and-blue. Other apprentices had once told him that you could always get a woman by showing her your fist with the thumb sticking out between the middle and the forefinger. He didn't know what to make of it; they all said they had tried it, but when he thought about it the ground gave way under him, or his head seemed to be screwed on wrong; in short, something was going on inside him that separated him by a hairbreadth from the natural order and was not quite steady. "Missus," he said, "I'd like to do something nice to you. . . ." They were alone; she looked into his eyes and must have seen something there; she said: "You just clear out of this kitchen!" He then held up his fist with the thumb sticking out. But the magic worked only halfway: her face turned dark red and she hit him with the wooden ladle in her hand, too fast for him to dodge the blow, right across the face; he realized it only when the blood began to trickle over his lips. But he remembered that instant vividly now, for the blood suddenly turned and flowed upward, up above his eyes, and he threw himself on the strapping woman who had so viciously insulted him; the master came in; and what happened then, until the moment he stood in the street with his legs buckling and his things thrown after him, was like a big red cloth being ripped to shreds. That was how they made a mockery and a shambles of his right, and he took to the road again. Can a man find his rights on the road? All the women were already somebody else's right, and so were all the apples and all the beds. And the police and the judges were worse than the dogs.

But what it really was that always gave people a hold on him, and why they were always throwing him in jails or madhouses, Moosbrugger could never really figure out. He stared long and hard at the floor, at the corners of his cell; he felt like a man who has dropped a key on the floor. But he couldn't find it; the floor and the corners turned day-gray and ordinary again, though just a while ago they had been a dreamscape where a thing or a person springs up at the drop of a word.

Moosbrugger mustered all his logic. He could only remember distinctly all the places it began. He could have ticked them off on his fingers and described them. Once, it had been in Linz, another time in Braila. Years had passed between. And the last time it was here in the city. He could see every stone so sharply outlined, as stones usually aren't. He also remembered the rotten feeling that always went with it, as if he had poison instead of blood in his veins, or something like that. For instance, he was working outdoors and women passed by; he didn't want to look at them, because they bothered him, but new ones kept constantly passing by, so finally his eyes would follow them with loathing, and that slow turning of his eyes this way and that felt as if his eyes were stirring in tar or in setting cement inside him. Then he noticed that his thoughts were growing heavy. He thought slowly anyway, the words gave him trouble, he never had enough words, and sometimes, when he was talking to someone, the other man would look at him in surprise: he wouldn't understand how much was being said in the one word Moosbrugger was uttering so slowly. He envied all those people who had learned to talk easily when they were young. His own words seemed to stick to his gums to spite him just when he needed them most, and it sometimes took forever to tear out the next syllable so he could go on from there. There was no getting around it: this couldn't be due to natural causes. But when he said in court that it was the Freemasons or the Jesuits or the Socialists who were torturing him this way, nobody understood what he was talking about. Those lawyers and judges could outtalk him, all right, and had all sorts of things to say against him, but none of them had a clue to what was really going on.

When this sort of thing had continued for some time, Moosbrugger got frightened. Just try standing in the street with your hands tied, waiting to see what people will do! He knew that his tongue, or something deep inside him, was glued down, and it made him miserably unsure of himself, a feeling he had to struggle for days to hide. But then there came a sharp, one could almost say soundless, boundary. Suddenly a cold breeze was there. Or else a big balloon rose up in the air right in front of him and flew into his chest. At the same instant he felt something in his eyes, his lips, the muscles of his face; everything around him seemed to fade, to turn black, and while the houses lay down on the trees, some cats quickly leapt from the bushes and scurried away. This lasted only for an instant, then it was over.

This was the real beginning of the time they all wanted to know about and never stopped talking about. They pestered him with the most pointless questions; unfortunately, he could remember his experiences only dimly, through what they meant to him. Because these periods were all meaning! They sometimes lasted for minutes, sometimes for days on end, and sometimes they changed into other, similar experiences that could last for months. To begin with the latter, because they are simpler, and in Moosbrugger's opinion even a judge could understand then: Moosbrugger heard voices or music or a wind, or a blowing and humming, a whizzing and rattling, or shots, thunder, laughing, shouts, speaking, or whispering. It came at him from every direction; the sounds were in the walls, in the air, in his clothes, in his body. He had the impression he was carrying it in his body as long as it was silent; once it was out, it hid somewhere in his surroundings, but never very far from him. When he was working, the voices would speak at him mostly in random words or short phrases, insulting and nagging him, and when he thought of something they came out with it before he could, or spitefully said the opposite of what he meant. It was ridiculous to be declared insane on this account; Moosbrugger regarded these voices and visions as mere monkeyshines. It entertained him to hear and see what they did; that was ever so much better than the hard, heavy thoughts he had himself. But of course he got very angry when they really annoyed him, that was only natural. Moosbrugger knew, because he always paid close attention to all the expressions that were applied to him, that this was called hallucinating, and he was pleased that he had this knack for hallucination that others lacked; it enabled him to see all sorts of things others didn't, such as lovely landscapes and hellish monsters. But he found that they always made far too much of it, and when the stays in mental hospitals became too unpleasant, he maintained outright that he was only pretending. The know-it-alls would ask him how loud the sounds were; a senseless question, because of course what he heard was sometimes as loud as a thunderclap, and sometimes the merest whisper. Even the physical pains that sometimes plagued him could be unbearable or slight enough to be imaginary. That wasn't the important thing. Often he could not have described exactly what he saw, heard, and felt, but he knew what it was. It could be very blurred; the visions came from outside, but a shimmer of observation told him at the same time that they were really something inside himself. The important thing was that it is not at all important whether something is inside or outside; in his condition, it was like clear water on both sides of a transparent sheet of glass.

When he was feeling on top of things Moosbrugger paid no attention at all to his voices and visions but spent his time in thinking. He called it thinking because he had always been impressed with the word. He thought better than other people because he thought both inside and outside. Thinking went on inside him against his will. He said that thoughts were planted in him. He was hypersensitive to the merest trifles, as a woman is when her breasts are tight with milk, but this did not interfere with his slow, manly reflectiveness. At such times his thoughts flowed like a stream running through a lush meadow swelled by hundreds of leaping brooks.

Now Moosbrugger had let his head drop and was looking down at the wood between his fingers. "A squirrel in these parts is called a tree kitten," it occurred to him, "but just let somebody try to talk about a tree cat with a straight face! Everyone would prick up their ears as if a real shot had gone off among the farting sound of blanks on maneuvers. In Hesse, on the other hand, it's called a tree fox. Any man who's traveled around knows such things."

But oh, how curious the psychiatrists got when they showed him a picture of a squirrel and he said: "That's a fox, I guess, or it could be a hare, or maybe a cat or something." They'd always shoot a question right back at him then: "How much is fourteen plus fourteen?" and he would say in his deliberate way, "Oh, about twenty-eight to forty." This "about" gave them trouble, which made Moosbrugger grin. It was really so simple. He knew perfectly well that you get twenty-eight when you go on from fourteen to another fourteen; but who says you have to stop there? Moosbrugger's gaze would always range a little farther ahead, like that of a man who has reached the top of a ridge outlined against the sky and finds that behind it there are other, similar ridges. And if a tree kitten is no cat and no fox, and has teeth like a hare's, and the fox eats the hare, you don't have to be so particular about what you call it; you just know it's somehow sewn together out of all those things and goes scampering over the trees. Moosbrugger's experience and conviction were that no thing could be singled out by itself, because things hang together. It had happened that he said to a girl, "Your sweet rose lips," but suddenly the words gave way at their seams and something upsetting happened: her face went gray, like earth veiled in a mist, there was a rose sticking out of it on a long stem, and the temptation to take a knife and cut it off, or punch it back into the face, was overwhelming. Of course, Moosbrugger did not always go for his knife; he only did that when he couldn't get rid of the temptation any other way. Usually he used all his enormous strength to hold the world together.

In a good mood, he could look a man in the face and see in it his own face, as it might gaze back at him from among the minnows and bright pebbles of a shallow stream; in a bad mood, he could tell by a fleeting glance at a man's face that here was the same man who always gave him trouble, everywhere, no matter how differently he disguised himself each time. How can anyone object to this? We all have trouble with the same man almost every time. If we were to investigate who the people are we get so idiotically fixated on, it is bound to turn out to be the one with the lock to which we have the key. And in love? How many people look at the same beloved face day in, day out, yet when they shut their eyes can't say what it looks like? Or even aside from love and hate; how incessantly things are subject to change, depending on habit, mood, point of view! How often joy burns out and an indestructible core of sadness emerges! How often a man calmly beats up another, whom he might as easily leave in peace. Life forms a surface that acts as if it could not be otherwise, but under its skin things are pounding and pulsing. Moosbrugger always kept his legs solidly planted on real earth, holding them together, sensibly trying to avoid whatever might confuse him. But sometimes a word burst in his mouth, and what a revolution, what a dream of things then welled up out of such a cold, burned-out double word as tree kitten or rose lips!

Sitting on that plank in his cell that was both his bed and his table, he deplored his education, which had not taught him to express himself properly. The little creature with her mouse eyes who was still making so much trouble for him, even though she'd been underground for some time, made him angry. They were all on her side. He lumbered to his feet. He felt fragile, like charred wood. He was hungry again; the prison fare fell far short of satisfying a huge man like him, and he had no money for better. In such a state it was impossible for him to think of everything they wanted to know. One of these changes had come on, for days and weeks, the way March comes, or April, and then this business had happened. He knew nothing more about it than the police already had in their files; he didn't even know how it had got into their files. The reasons, the considerations he could remember, he had already stated in court anyway. But what had really happened seemed to him as if he had suddenly said fluently in a foreign language something that made him feel good but that he could no longer repeat.

"I just want it over and done with as soon as possible!" Moosbrugger thought.

60

EXCURSION INTO THE REALM OF LOGIC
AND MORALS

Legally, Moosbrugger's case could be summed up in a sentence. He was one of those borderline cases in law and forensic medicine known even to the layman as a case of diminished responsibility.

These unfortunates typically suffer not only substandard health but also have a substandard disease. Nature has a peculiar preference for producing such people in droves. *Natura non fecit saltus*, she makes no jumps but prefers gradual transitions; even on the grand scale she keeps the world in a transitional state between imbecility and sanity. But the law takes no notice of this. It says: *Non datur tertium sive medium inter duo contradictoria*, or in plain language, a person is either capable or not capable of breaking the law; between two contraries there is no third or middle state. It is this ability to choose that makes a person liable to punishment. His liability to punishment makes him legally a person, and as a person in the legal sense he shares in the suprapersonal benefaction of the law. Anyone who cannot grasp this right away should think of the cavalry. A horse that goes berserk every time someone attempts to mount it is treated with special care, given the softest bandages, the best riders, the choicest fodder, and the most patient handling. But if a cavalryman is guilty of some lapse, he is put in irons, locked in a flea-ridden cage, and deprived of his rations. The reasoning behind this difference is that the horse belongs merely to the empirical animal kingdom, while the dragoon belongs to the logical and moral kingdom. So understood, a person is distinguished from the animals—and, one may add, from the insane—in that he is capable, according to his intellectual and moral faculties, of acting against the law and of committing a crime. Since a person's liability to punishment is the quality that elevates him to the status of a moral being in the first place, it is understandable that the pillars of the law grimly hang on to it.

There is also the unfortunate complication that court psychiatrists, who would be called upon to oppose this situation, are usually far more timid professionally than the jurists. They certify as really insane only those persons they cannot cure—which is a modest exaggeration, since they cannot cure the others either. They distinguish between incurable mental diseases, the kind that with God's help will improve after a while of their own accord, and the kind that the doctor cannot cure either but that the patient could have avoided, assuming of course that the right influences and considerations had providentially been brought to bear on him in time. These second and third groups supply those lesser patients whom the angel of medicine treats as sick people when they come to him in his private practice, but whom he shyly leaves to the angel of law when he encounters them in his forensic practice.

Such a case was Moosbrugger. In the course of his life, respectable enough except when interrupted by those unaccountable fits of bloodthirstiness, he had as often been confined in mental institutions as he had been let go, and had been variously diagnosed as a paralytic, paranoiac, epileptic, and manic-depressive psychotic, until at his recent trial two particularly conscientious forensic psychiatrists had restored his sanity to him. Of course, there was not a single person in that vast crowded courtroom, the doctors included, who was not convinced that Moosbrugger was insane, one way or another; but it was not a way that corresponded to the conditions of insanity laid down by the law, so this insanity could not be acknowledged by conscientious minds. For if one is partly insane, one is also, juridically, partly sane, and if one is partly sane one is at least partly responsible for one's actions, and if one is partly responsible one is wholly responsible; for responsibility is, as they say, that state in which the individual has the power to devote himself to a specific purpose of his own free will, independently of any compelling necessity, and one cannot simultaneously possess and lack such self-determination.

Not that this excludes the existence of persons whose circumstances and predispositions make it hard for them to "resist immoral impulses" and "opt for the good," as the lawyers put it, and Moosbrugger was such a person, in whom circumstances that would have no effect at all on others were enough to trigger the "intent" to commit an offense. First, however, his powers of reasoning and judgment were sufficiently intact, in the view of the court, so that an effort on his part could just as well have left the crime uncommitted, and there was no reason to exclude him from the moral estate of responsibility. Second, a well-ordered judicial system demands that every culpable act that is wittingly and willingly performed be punished. And third, judicial logic assumes that in all insane persons—with the exception of the most unfortunate, who when asked to multiply 7 times 7 stick out their tongue, or answer "Me" when asked to name His Imperial and Royal Majesty—there is still present a minimal power of discrimination and self-control and that it would only have taken a special effort of intelligence and willpower to recognize the criminal nature of the deed and to resist the criminal impulses. It is surely the least one has a right to expect from such dangerous persons!

Law courts resemble wine cellars in which the wisdom of our forefathers lies in bottles. One opens them and could weep at how unpalatable the highest, most effervescent, degree of the human striving for precision can be before it reaches perfection. And yet it seems to intoxicate the insufficiently seasoned mind. It is a well-known phenomenon that the angel of medicine, if he has listened too long to lawyers' arguments, too often forgets his own mission. He then folds his wings with a clatter and conducts himself in court like a reserve angel of law.

61

The ideal of the three treatises,
or the utopia of exact living

This is how Moosbrugger had come by his death sentence. It was only thanks to the influence of Count Leinsdorf and His Grace's friendship for Ulrich that there was now a chance to review Moosbrugger's mental condition one more time. Ulrich actually had no intention of taking any further interest in Moosbrugger's fate, then or later. The depressing mixture of brutality and suffering that is the nature of such people was as distasteful to him as the blend of precision and sloppiness that characterized the judgments usually pronounced upon them. He knew precisely what he had to think of Moosbrugger, if he took a sober view of the case, and what measures one might try with such people who belong neither in prison nor in freedom and for whom the mental hospitals were not the answer either. He also realized that thousands of other people knew this, too, and were constantly discussing every such problem from the aspects that each of them was interested in; he also knew that the state would eventually kill Moosbrugger because in the present state of incompleteness this was simply the cleanest, cheapest, and safest solution. It may be callous to resign oneself to this; but then, our speeding traffic claims more victims than all the tigers of India, yet the ruthless, unscrupulous, and casual state of mind in which we put up with it is what also enables us to achieve our undeniable successes.

This state of mind, so perceptive in detail and so blind to the total picture, finds its most telling expression in a certain ideal that might be called the ideal of a life's work and that consists of no more than three treatises. There are intellectual activities where it is not the big books but the short monographs or articles that constitute a man's proud achievement. If someone were to discover, for instance, that under hitherto unobserved circumstances stones were able to speak, it would take only a few pages to describe and explain so earth-shattering a phenomenon. On the other hand, one can always write yet another book about positive thinking, and this is far from being of only academic interest, since it involves a method that makes it impossible ever to arrive at a clear resolution of life's most important questions. Human activities might be graded by the quantity of words required: the more words, the worse their character. All the knowledge that has led our species from wearing animal skins to people flying, complete with proofs, would fill a handful of reference books, but a bookcase the size of the earth would not suffice to hold all the rest, quite apart from the vast discussions that are conducted not with the pen but with the sword and chains. The thought suggests itself that we carry on our human business in a most irrational manner when we do not use those methods by which the exact sciences have forged ahead in such exemplary fashion.

Such had in fact been the mood and the tendency of a period—a number of years, hardly of decades—of which Ulrich was just old enough to have known something. At that time people were thinking—"people" is a deliberately vague way of putting it, as no one could say who and how many thought that way; let us say it was in the air—that perhaps life could be lived with precision. Today one wonders what they could have meant by that. The answer would possibly be that a life's work can as easily be imagined as consisting of three poems or three actions as of three treatises, in which the individual's capacity for achievement is intensified to its highest degree. It would more or less come down to keeping silent when one has nothing to say, doing only the necessary where one has nothing special to do, and, most important, remaining indifferent unless one has that ineffable sense of spreading one's arms wide, borne aloft on a wave of creation. One will observe that this would be the end of most of our inner life, but that might not be such a painful loss. The thesis that the huge quantities of soap sold testify to our great cleanliness need not apply to the moral life, where the more recent principle seems more accurate, that a strong compulsion to wash suggests a dubious state of inner hygiene. It would be a useful experiment to try to cut down to the minimum the moral expenditure (of whatever kind) that accompanies all our actions, to satisfy ourselves with being moral only in those exceptional cases where it really counts, but otherwise not to think differently from the way we do about standardizing pencils or screws. Perhaps not much good would be done that way, but some things would be done better; there would be no talent left, only genius; the washed-out prints that develop from the pallid resemblance of actions to virtues would disappear from the image of life; in their place we would have these virtues' intoxicating fusion in holiness. In short, from every ton of morality a milligram of an essence would be left over, a millionth part of which is enough to yield an enchanting joy.

But the objection will be raised that this is a utopia. Of course it is. Utopias are much the same as possibilities; that a possibility is not a reality means nothing more than that the circumstances in which it is for the moment entangled prevent it from being realized—otherwise it would be only an impossibility. If this possibility is disentangled from its restraints and allowed to develop, a utopia arises. It is like what happens when a scientist observes the change of an element within a compound and draws his conclusions. Utopia is the experiment in which the possible change of an element may be observed, along with the effects of such a change on the compound phenomenon we call life. If the element under observation is precision itself, one isolates it and allows it to develop, considering it as an intellectual habit and way of life, allowed to exert its exemplary influence on everything it touches. The logical outcome of this should be a human being full of the paradoxical interplay of exactitude and indefiniteness. He is incorruptibly, deliberately cold, as required by the temperament of precision; but beyond this quality, everything else in him is indefinite. The stable internal conditions guaranteed by a system of morality have little value for a man whose imagination is geared to change. Ultimately, when the demand for the greatest and most exact fulfillment is transferred from the intellectual realm to that of the passions, it becomes evident—as already indicated—that the passions disappear and that in their place arises something like a primordial fire of goodness.

Such is the utopia of precision. One doesn't know how such a man will spend the day, since he cannot continually be poised in the act of creation and will have sacrificed the domestic hearth fire of limited sensations to some imaginary conflagration. But this man of precision exists already! He is the inner man who inhabits not only the scientist but the businessman, the administrator, the sportsman, and the technician, though for the present only during those daytime hours they call not their life but their profession. This man, given to taking everything seriously and without bias, is biased to the point of abhorrence against the idea of taking himself seriously, and there is, alas, no doubt that he would regard the utopia of himself as an immoral experiment on persons engaged in serious business.

Which is why Ulrich, in his concern with the question of whether everything else should be subordinated to the most powerful forms of inner achievement—in other words, whether a goal and a meaning can be found for what is happening and has happened to us—had always, all his life, been quite alone.

62

THE EARTH TOO, BUT ESPECIALLY ULRICH, PAYS HOMAGE TO THE UTOPIA OF ESSAYISM

Precision, as a human attitude, demands precise action and precise being. It makes maximal demands on the doer and on life. But here a distinction must be made.

In reality, as we all know, there is not only an imaginary precision (not yet present in reality at all) but also a pedantic kind, the difference being that the imaginary kind sticks to the facts and the pedantic kind to imaginary constructs. The precision, for instance, with which Moosbrugger's peculiar mentality was fitted into a two-thousand-year-old system of legal concepts resembled a madman's pedantic insistence on trying to spear a free-flying bird with a pin; this precision was concerned not at all with the facts but only with the imaginary concept of cumulative law. But with respect to the big question of whether Moosbrugger could be legally condemned to death, the psychiatrists were absolutely precise: they did not dare say more than that Moosbrugger's clinical picture did not exactly correspond to any hitherto observed syndrome, and left any further conclusions entirely to the jurists.

The courtroom on that occasion offered an image of life itself, in that all those energetic up-to-the-minute characters who wouldn't dream of driving a car more than five years old, or letting a disease be treated by methods that had been the best ten years ago, and who further give all their time, willy-nilly, to promoting the latest inventions and fervently believe in rationalizing everything in their domain . . . these people nevertheless abandon questions of beauty, justice, love, and faith—that is, all the questions of humanity—as long as their business interests are not involved, preferably to their wives or, where their wives are not quite up to it, to a subspecies of men given to intoning thousand-year-old phrases about the chalice and sword of life, to whom they listen casually, irritably, and skeptically, without believing any of it but also without considering the possibility that it might be done some other way. Thus there are really two kinds of outlook, which not only conflict with each other but, which is worse, usually coexist side by side in total noncommunication except to assure each other that they are both needed, each in its place. The one is satisfied to be precise and stick to the facts, while the other is not, but always looks at the whole picture and derives its insights from so-called great and eternal truths. The first achieves success, the other scope and prestige. Clearly, a pessimist could say that the results in the first case are worth nothing and in the second case are not true. For what use will it be on the Day of Judgment, when all human achievements are weighed, to offer up three articles on formic acid, or even thirty? On the other hand, what do we know of the Day of Judgment if we do not even know what may have become of formic acid by then?

It was between these two poles of Neither and Nor that the pendulum of evolution was swinging when mankind first learned, more than eighteen but not quite twenty centuries ago, that there would be such a spiritual court at the end of the world. It corresponds to the experience that a swing in one direction is always followed by a swing in the opposite direction. And while it might be conceivable and desirable for such a revolution to proceed as a spiral, which climbs higher with every change of direction, for unknown reasons evolution seldom gains more than it loses through detours and destruction. So Dr. Paul Arnheim was quite right when he told Ulrich that world history never allows the negative to prevail; world history is optimistic, it always decides enthusiastically for the one, and only afterward for its opposite! And so, too, the pioneer dreams of precision were followed by no attempt whatever to realize them but were abandoned to the unwinged uses of engineers and scientists, while everyone else reverted to a more worthy and far-reaching frame of mind.

Ulrich could still remember quite well how uncertainty had made its comeback. Complaints were heard in ever greater number from people who followed a somewhat uncertain calling—writers, critics, women, and those practicing the profession of being the new generation—all protesting that pure knowledge tore apart every sublime achievement of mankind without ever being able to put it back together, and they demanded a new humane faith, a return to inner primal values, a spiritual revival, and all sorts of things of that kind. At first Ulrich had naïvely assumed that the outcries came from hard-riding people who had dismounted, limping, screaming to have their sores rubbed with soul; but he gradually realized that these repetitive calls for a new dispensation, which had struck him as so comical at first, were being echoed far and wide. Science had begun to be out-dated, and the unfocused type of person that dominates the present had begun to assert itself.

Ulrich had refused to take this seriously and went on developing his intellectual bent in his own way.

From the earliest youthful stirrings of self-confidence, which are often so touching, even moving, to look back upon in later years, all sorts of once-cherished notions lingered in his memory even now, among them the expression "living hypothetically." It still expressed the courage and the inescapable ignorance of life that makes every step an act of daring without experience; it showed the desire for grand connections and the aura of revocability a young man feels as he hesitantly ventures into life. Ulrich felt that none of this really needed to be taken back. A thrilling sense of having been chosen for something is the best and the only certain thing in one whose glance surveys the world for the first time. If he monitors his feelings, he finds nothing he can accept without reservation. He seeks a possible beloved but can't tell whether it's the right one; he is capable of kill-ing without being sure that he will have to. The drive of his own na-ture to keep developing prevents him from believing that anything is final and complete, yet everything he encounters behaves as though it were final and complete. He suspects that the given order of things is not as solid as it pretends to be; no thing, no self, no form, no prin-ciple, is safe, everything is undergoing an invisible but ceaseless transformation, the unsettled holds more of the future than the set-tled, and the present is nothing but a hypothesis that has not yet been surmounted. What better can he do than hold himself apart from the world, in the good sense exemplified by the scientist's guarded atti-tude toward facts that might be tempting him to premature conclu-sions? Hence he hesitates in trying to make something of himself; a character, a profession, a fixed mode of being, are for him concepts that already shadow forth the outlines of the skeleton, which is all that will be left of him in the end. He seeks to understand himself differently, as someone inclined and open to everything that may enrich him inwardly, even if it should be morally or intellectually taboo; he feels like a stride, free to move in any direction, from equilibrium to equilibrium, but always forward. And when he sometimes thinks he has found the right idea, he perceives that a drop of indescribable incandescence has fallen into the world, with a glow that makes the whole earth look different.

Later, when Ulrich's intellectual capacity was more highly developed, this became an idea no longer connected with the vague word "hypothesis" but with a concept he oddly termed, for certain reasons, "essay." It was more or less in the way an essay, in the sequence of its paragraphs, explores a thing from many sides without wholly encompassing it—for a thing wholly encompassed suddenly loses its scope and melts down to a concept—that he believed he could most rightly survey and handle the world and his own life. The value of an action or a quality, and indeed its meaning and nature, seemed to him to depend on its surrounding circumstances, on the aims it served; in short, on the whole—constituted now one way, now another—to which it belonged. This is only a simple description of the fact that a murder can appear to us as a crime or a heroic act, and making love as a feather that has fallen from the wing of an angel or that of a goose. But Ulrich generalized this: all moral events take place in a field of energy whose constellation charges them with meaning. They contain good and evil the way an atom contains the possibilities of certain chemical combinations. They are what they will become, so to speak; and just as the word "hard" denotes four entirely different essences, depending on whether it is connected with love, brutality, zeal, or discipline, the significance of all moral events seemed to him to be the function of other events on which they depended. In this way an open-ended system of relationships arises, in which independent meanings, such as are ascribed to actions and qualities by way of a rough first approximation in ordinary life, no longer exist at all. What is seemingly solid in this system becomes a porous pretext for many possible meanings; the event occurring becomes a symbol of something that perhaps may not be happening but makes itself felt through the symbol; and man as the quintessence of his possibilities, potential man, the unwritten poem of his existence, confronts man as recorded fact, as reality, as character. Accordingly, Ulrich felt that he was basically capable of every virtue and every baseness; the fact that in a balanced social order virtues as well as vices are tacitly regarded as equally burdensome attested for him to what happens in nature generally, that every play of forces tends in time toward an average value and average condition, toward compromise and inertia. Ulrich regarded morality as it is commonly understood as nothing more than the senile form of a system of energies that cannot be confused with what it originally was without losing ethical force.

It is possible that these views also reflected some uncertainty about life, but uncertainty is sometimes nothing more than mistrust of the usual certainties, and anyway, it is good to remember that even so experienced a person as mankind itself seems to act on quite similar principles. In the long run it revokes everything it has done, to replace it with something else; what it used to regard as a crime it regards as a virtue, and vice versa; it builds up impressive frameworks of meaningful connections among events, only to allow them to collapse after a few generations. However, all this happens in succession instead of as a single, homogeneous experience, and the chain of mankind's experiments shows no upward trend. By contrast, a conscious human essayism would face the task of transforming the world's haphazard awareness into a will. And many individual lines of development indicate that this could indeed happen soon. The hospital aide clothed in lily-white, who, with the help of acids, thins out a patient's stool in a white china dish in order to obtain a purple smear, rubbing it until the right hue rewards her attention, is already living, whether she knows it or not, in a world more open to change than is the young lady who shudders at the sight of the same stuff in the street. The criminal, caught up in the moral magnetic field of his act, can only move like a swimmer who has to go with the current that sweeps him along, as every mother knows whose child has ever suffered this fate, though no one would believe her, because there was no place for such a belief. Psychiatry calls great elation "a hypomanic disturbance," which is like calling it a hilarious distress, and regards all heightened states, whether of chastity or sensuality, scrupulosity or carelessness, cruelty or compassion, as pathologically suspect—how little would a healthy life mean if its only goal were a middle condition between two extremes! How drab it would be if its ideal were really no more than the denial of the exaggeration of its ideals! To recognize this is to see the moral norm no longer as a set of rigid commandments but rather as a mobile equilibrium that at every moment requires continual efforts at renewal. We are beginning to regard as too limiting the tendency to ascribe involuntarily acquired habits of repetitiveness to a man as his character, and then to make his character responsible for the repetitions. We are learning to recognize the interplay between inner and outer, and it is precisely our understanding of the impersonal elements in man that has given us new clues to the personal ones, to certain simple patterns of behavior, to an ego-building instinct that, like the nest-building instinct of birds, uses a few techniques to build an ego out of many various materials. We are already so close to knowing how to use certain influences to contain all sorts of pathological conditions, as we can a wild mountain stream, and it will soon be a mere lapse of social responsibility or a lingering clumsiness if we fail to transform criminals into archangels at the right time. And there is so much more one could add, scattered manifestations of things that have not yet coalesced to act together, the general effect of which is to make us tired of the crude approximations of simpler times, gradually to make us experience the necessity of altering the basic forms and foundations of a moral order that over two thousand years has adjusted only piecemeal to evolving tastes and exchanging it for a new morality capable of fitting more closely the mobility of facts.

Ulrich was convinced that the only thing missing was the right formula, the expression that the goal of a movement must find in some happy moment before it is achieved, in order that the last lap can be accomplished. Such an expression is always risky, not yet justified by the prevailing state of affairs, a combination of exact and inexact, of precision and passion. But it was in just those years that should have spurred him on that something peculiar happened to Ulrich. He was no philosopher. Philosophers are despots who have no armies to command, so they subject the world to their tyranny by locking it up in a system of thought. This apparently also accounts for the presence of great philosophers in times of great tyrants, while epochs of progressive civilization and democracy fail to bring forth a convincing philosophy, at least to judge by the disappointment one hears so widely expressed on the subject. Hence today we have a terrifying amount of philosophizing in brief bursts, so that shops are the only places where one can still get something without Weltanschauung, while philosophy in large chunks is viewed with decided mistrust. It is simply regarded as impossible, and even Ulrich was by no means innocent of this prejudice; indeed, in the light of his scientific background, he took a somewhat ironic view of philosophy. This put him in a position where he was always being provoked to think about what he was observing, and yet at the same time was burdened with a certain shyness about thinking too hard.

But what finally determined his attitude was still another factor. There was something in Ulrich's nature that in a haphazard, paralyzing, disarming way resisted all logical systematizing, the single-minded will, the specifically directed drives of ambition; it was also connected with his chosen term, "essayism," even though it contained the very elements he had gradually and with unconscious care eliminated from that concept. The accepted translation of "essay" as "attempt" contains only vaguely the essential allusion to the literary model, for an essay is not a provisional or incidental expression of a conviction capable of being elevated to a truth under more favorable circumstances or of being exposed as an error (the only ones of that kind are those articles or treatises, chips from the scholar's workbench, with which the learned entertain their special public); an essay is rather the unique and unalterable form assumed by a man's inner life in a decisive thought. Nothing is more foreign to it than the irresponsible and half-baked quality of thought known as subjectivism. Terms like true and false, wise and unwise, are equally inapplicable, and yet the essay is subject to laws that are no less strict for appearing to be delicate and ineffable. There have been more than a few such essayists, masters of the inner hovering life, but there would be no point in naming them. Their domain lies between religion and knowledge, between example and doctrine, between *amor intellectualis* and poetry; they are saints with and without religion, and sometimes they are also simply men on an adventure who have gone astray.

Nothing is more revealing, by the way, than one's involuntary experience of learned and sensible efforts to interpret such essayists, to turn their living wisdom into knowledge to live by and thus extract some "content" from the motion of those who were moved: but about as much remains of this as of the delicately opalescent body of a jellyfish when one lifts it out of the water and lays it on the sand. The rationality of the uninspired will make the teachings of the inspired crumble into dust, contradiction, and nonsense, and yet one has no right to call them frail and unviable unless one would also call an elephant too frail to survive in an airless environment unsuited to its needs. It would be regrettable if these descriptions were to evoke an impression of mystery, or of a kind of music in which harp notes and sighing glissandi predominate. The opposite is the case, and the underlying problem presented itself to Ulrich not at all intuitively but quite soberly, in the following form: A man who wants the truth becomes a scholar; a man who wants to give free play to his subjectivity may become a writer; but what should a man do who wants something in between? Examples of what lies in between can be found in every moral precept, such as the well-known and simple: Thou shalt not kill. One sees right off that that is neither a fact nor a subjective experience. We know that we adhere to it strictly in some respects, while allowing for a great many, if sharply defined, exceptions; but in a very large number of cases of a third kind, involving imagination, desires, drama, or the enjoyment of a news story, we vacillate erratically between aversion and attraction. What we cannot classify as either a fact or a subjective experience we sometimes call an imperative. We have attached such imperatives to the dogmas of religion and the law and thereby give them the status of deduced truth. But the novelists tell us about the exceptions, from Abraham's sacrifice of Isaac to the most recent beauty who shot her lover, and dissolve it again into something subjective. We can cling to one of these poles or let ourselves be swept back and forth between them by the tide—but with what feelings? The feeling of most people for this precept is a mixture of wooden obedience (including that of the "wholesome type" that flinches from even thinking of such a thing but, only slightly disoriented by alcohol or passion, promptly does it) and a mindless paddling about in a wave of possibilities. Is there really no other approach to this precept? Ulrich felt that as things stood, a man longing to do something with all his heart does not know whether he should do it or leave it undone. And yet he suspected that it could be done, or not done, wholeheartedly. In themselves, an impulse to act and a taboo were equally meaningless to him. Linking them to a law from above or within aroused his critical intelligence; more than that, the need to ennoble a self-sufficient moment by giving it a noble pedigree diminished its value. All this left his heart silent, while only his head spoke; but he felt that there might be another way to make his choice coincide with his happiness. He might be happy because he didn't kill, or happy because he killed, but he could never be the indifferent fulfiller of an imperative demanded of him. What he felt at this moment was not a commandment; it was a region he had entered. Here, he realized, everything was already decided, and soothed the mind like mother's milk. But what gave him this insight was no longer thinking, nor was it feeling in the usual incoherent way: it was a "total insight" and yet again only a message carried to him from far away by the wind, and it seemed to him neither true nor false, neither rational nor irrational; it seized him like a faint, blissful hyperbole dropped into his heart.

And as little as one can make a truth out of the genuine elements of an essay can one gain a conviction from such a condition—at least not without abandoning the condition, as a lover has to abandon love in order to describe it. The boundless emotion that sometimes stirred Ulrich without activating him contradicted his urge to act, which insisted on limits and forms. Now, it may be only right and natural to want to *know* before letting one's feelings speak; he involuntarily imagined that what he wanted to find and someday would, even if it should not be truth, would be no less firm than truth. But in his special case, this made him rather like a man busily getting equipment together while losing interest in what it is meant for. If someone had asked him at any point while he was writing treatises on mathematical problems or mathematical logic, or engaged in some scientific project, what it was he hoped to achieve, he would have answered that there was only one question worth thinking about, the question of the right way to live. But if one holds up an imperative for a long time without anything happening, the brain goes to sleep, just as the arm does that has held something up for too long; our thoughts cannot be expected to stand at attention indefinitely any more than soldiers on parade in summer; standing too long, they will simply fall down in a faint. As Ulrich had settled on his view of life around his twenty-sixth year, it no longer seemed quite genuine in his thirty-second. He had not elaborated his ideas any further, and apart from a vague, tense feeling such as one has when waiting for something with one's eyes closed, there was not much sign of personal emotion in him, since the days of his tremulous earliest revelations had gone. Yet it was probably an underground movement of this kind that gradually slowed him down in his scientific work and kept him from giving it all he had. This generated a curious conflict in him. One must not forget that basically the scientific cast of mind is more God-oriented than the aesthetic mind, ready to submit to "Him" the moment "He" deigns to show Himself under the conditions it prescribes for recognizing Him, while our aesthetes, confronted with His manifestation, would find only that His talent was not original and that His view of the world was not sufficiently intelligible to rank Him with really God-given talents. Ulrich could not abandon himself to vague intimations as readily as anyone of that species could, but neither could he conceal from himself that in all those years of scientific scrupulosity he had merely been living against his grain. He wished something unforeseen would happen to him, for when he took what he somewhat wryly called his "holiday from life" he had nothing, in one direction or the other, that gave him peace.

Perhaps one could say on his behalf that at a certain age life begins to run away with incredible speed. But the day when one must begin to live out one's final will, before leaving the rest behind, lies far ahead and cannot be postponed. This had become menacingly clear to him now that almost six months had gone by and nothing had changed. He was waiting: all the time, he was letting himself be pushed this way and that in the insignificant and silly activity he had taken on, talking, gladly talking too much, living with the desperate tenacity of a fisherman casting his nets into an empty river, while he was doing nothing that had anything to do with the person he after all signified; deliberately doing nothing: he was waiting. He waited hiding behind his person, insofar as this word characterizes that part of a human being formed by the world and the course of life, and his quiet desperation, dammed up behind that façade, rose higher every day. He felt himself to be in the worst crisis of his life and despised himself for what he had left undone. Are great ordeals the privilege of great human beings? He would have liked to believe it, but it isn't so, since even the dullest neurotics have their crises. So all he really had left in the midst of his deep perturbation was that residue of imperturbability possessed by all heroes and criminals—it isn't courage, willpower, or confidence, but simply a furious tenacity, as hard to drive out as it is to drive life out of a cat even after it has been completely mangled by dogs.

If one wants to imagine how such a man lives when he is alone, the most that can be said is that at night his lighted windows afford a view of his room, where his used thoughts sit around like clients in the waiting room of a lawyer with whom they are dissatisfied. Or one could perhaps say that Ulrich once, on such a night, opened the window and looked out at the snake-smooth trunks of the trees, so black and sleekly twisted between the blankets of snow covering their tops and the ground, and suddenly felt an urge to go down into the garden just as he was, in his pajamas; he wanted to feel the cold in his hair. Downstairs he turned out the light, so as not to stand framed in the lighted doorway; a canopy of light projected into the shadow only from his study. A path led to the iron gate fronting the street; a second crossed it, darkly outlined. Ulrich walked slowly toward it. And then the darkness towering up between the treetops suddenly, fantastically, reminded him of the huge form of Moosbrugger, and the naked trees looked strangely corporeal, ugly and wet like worms and yet somehow inviting him to embrace them and sink down with them in tears. But he didn't do it. The sentimentality of the impulse revolted him at the very moment it touched him. Just then some late passersby walked through the milky foam of the mist outside the garden railing, and he may have looked like a lunatic to them, as his figure in red pajamas between black tree trunks now detached itself from the trees. But he stepped firmly onto the path and went back into his house fairly content, feeling that whatever was in store for him would have to be something quite different.

63

BONADEA HAS A VISION

When Ulrich got up on the morning following this night, late and feeling as if he had been badly beaten up, he was told that Bonadea had come to call; it was the first time since their quarrel that they would see each other.

During the period of their separation, Bonadea had shed many tears. She often felt in this time that she had been ill-treated. She had often resounded like a muffled drum. She had had many adventures and many disappointments. And although the memory of Ulrich sank into a deep well with every adventure, after every disappointment it emerged again, helpless and reproachful as the desolate pain in a child's face. In her heart, Bonadea had already asked her friend a hundred times to forgive her jealousy, "castigating her wicked pride," as she put it, until at last she decided to sue for peace.

She sat before him, charming, melancholy, and beautiful, and feeling sick to her stomach. He stood in front of her "like a youth," his skin polished like marble from the great events and high diplomacy she believed him engaged in. She had never before noticed how strong and determined his face looked. She would gladly have surrendered herself to him entirely, but she dared not go so far, and he showed no disposition to encourage her. This coldness saddened her beyond words, but had the grandeur of a statue. Unexpectedly, Bonadea seized his dangling hand and kissed it. Ulrich stroked her hair pensively. Her legs turned to water in the most feminine way in the world, and she was about to fall to her knees. But Ulrich gently pushed her back in her chair, brought whiskey and soda, and lit a cigarette.

"A lady does not drink whiskey in the morning!" Bonadea protested. For an instant she regained enough energy to be offended, and her heart rose to her head with the suspicion that the matter-of-fact offer of such a strong and, as she thought, licentious drink contained a heartless implication.

But Ulrich said kindly: "It will do you good. All the women who have played a major role in politics have drunk whiskey." For in order to justify her visit, Bonadea had said how impressed she was with the great patriotic campaign, and that she would like to lend a hand in it.

That was her plan. She always believed several things at the same time, and half-truths made it easier for her to lie.

The whiskey was pale gold and warming like the sun in May.

Bonadea felt like a seventy-year-old woman sitting on a garden bench outside her house. She was getting old. Her children were growing up. The eldest was already twelve. It was certainly disgraceful to follow a man one didn't even know very well into his house, just because he had eyes that looked at one like a man behind a window. One notices, she thought, little details about this man one doesn't like and that could be a warning. One could, in fact—if only there were something to hold one back at such times!—break it off, flushed with shame and perhaps even flaming with anger; but because this doesn't happen, this man grows more and more passionately into his role. And one feels oneself very clearly like a stage set in the glare of artificial light; what one has before one is stage eyes, a stage mustache, the buttons of a costume being unbuttoned, and the whole scene from the first entrance into the room to the first horrible moment of being sober again all takes place inside a consciousness that has stepped outside one's head and papered the walls with pure hallucination. Bonadea did not use precisely these words—her thought was only partly verbal anyway—but even as she was trying to visualize it she felt herself at the mercy of this change in consciousness. "Whoever could describe it would be a great artist—no, a pornographer!" she thought, looking at Ulrich. She never for an instant lost her good intentions, her determination to hold on to decency, even in this condition; only then they stood outside and waited but had absolutely nothing to say in a world transformed by desire. When Bonadea's reason returned, this was her worst anguish. The change of consciousness during sexual arousal, which people pass over as something natural, was in her so overpowering in the depth and suddenness not only of her ecstasy but also of her remorse that it frightened her in retrospect as soon as she had returned to the peace of her family circle. She thought she must be going mad. She hardly dared look at her children, for fear of harming them with her corrupt glance. And she winced whenever her husband looked at her with more than his usual warmth, but was afraid of freedom from constraint in being alone. All this led her, in the weeks of separation, to plan that henceforth she would have no other lover beside Ulrich; he would be her mainstay and would save her from excesses with strangers.

"How could I have allowed myself to find fault with him?" she now thought as she sat facing him for the first time in so long. "He is so much more complete than I am." She gave him credit for her having been a much improved person during their embraces, and was probably also thinking that he would have to introduce her to his new social circle at the next charity affair. Bonadea inwardly swore an oath of allegiance, and tears of emotion came to her eyes as she turned all this over in her mind.

Ulrich meanwhile was finishing his whiskey with the deliberateness of a man who has to act on a hard decision. For the time being, he told her, it was not yet possible to introduce her to Diotima.

Bonadea naturally wanted to know exactly why it was not possible; and then she wanted to know exactly when it would be possible.

Ulrich had to point out to her that she was not a person of prominence in the arts, nor in the sciences, nor in organized charity, so that it would take a very long time before he could convince Diotima of the need for Bonadea's assistance.

Bonadea had in the meantime been filled with curious feelings toward Diotima. She had heard enough about Diotima's virtues not to be jealous; rather, she envied and admired this woman, who could hold the interest of Bonadea's beloved without making improper concessions to him. She ascribed the statuesque serenity she thought she saw in Ulrich to this influence. Her term for herself was "passionate," by which she understood both her dishonorable state and an honorable excuse for it. But she admired cool women with much the same feeling with which unfortunate owners of perpetually damp hands put their hands in a hand that is particularly dry and lovely. "It is her doing!" she thought. "It is she who has changed Ulrich so much!" A hard drill in her heart, a sweet drill in her knees: these two drills whirring simultaneously and in opposite directions made Bonadea feel almost ready to faint as she came up against Ulrich's resistance. So she played her trump card: Moosbrugger.

She had realized on agonizing reflection that Ulrich must have a strange liking for this horrible character. She herself simply felt revolted by "the brutal sensuality," as she saw it, expressed in Moosbrugger's acts of violence. In this respect her feeling was much the same—though of course she did not know this—as that of the prostitutes who quite single-mindedly, untainted by bourgeois romanticism, see in the sex murderer simply a hazard of their profession. But what she needed, including her unavoidable lapses, was a tidy and credible world, and Moosbrugger would help her to restore it. Since Ulrich had a weakness for him, and she had a husband who was a judge and could supply useful information, the thought had ripened of its own accord in her forlorn state that she might link her weakness to Ulrich's weakness by way of her husband; this yearning image had the comforting power of sensuality sanctioned by a feeling of justice. But when she approached her spouse on the subject, he was astounded at her juridical fervor, although he knew how easily she got carried away by everything great and good in human nature. But since he was not only a judge but a hunter too, he put her off good-humoredly by saying that the only way to deal with such vermin was to exterminate them wherever one came across them without a lot of sentimental fuss, and he did not respond to further inquiries. On her second try, some time later, all Bonadea could get out of him was the supplementary opinion that childbearing was a woman's affair while killing was a job for men, and as she did not want to stir up any suspicions by being overzealous on this dangerous subject she was debarred, for the time being, from the path of the law. This left mercy as the only way of pleasing Ulrich by doing something for Moosbrugger, and this way led her—one can hardly call this a surprise, more a kind of attraction—to Diotima.

In her mind she could see herself as Diotima's friend, and she granted herself her own wish to be forced to make her admired rival's acquaintance for the sake of the cause, which brooked no delay, although of course she was too proud to seek it for herself. She was going to win Diotima over to Moosbrugger's cause—something Ulrich had clearly not succeeded in doing, as she had instantly guessed—and her imagination painted the situation in beautiful scenes. The tall, marmoreal Diotima would put her arm around Bonadea's warm shoulders, bowed down by sins, and Bonadea expected that her own role would more or less be to anoint that divinely untouched heart with a drop of mortal fallibility. This was the stratagem she proposed to her lost friend.

But today Ulrich was impervious to any suggestion of saving Moosbrugger. He knew Bonadea's noble sentiments and knew how easily the flaring up of a single worthy impulse could turn into a raging fire consuming her whole body. He made it clear that he did not have the slightest intention of meddling in the Moosbrugger case.

Bonadea looked up at him with hurt, beautiful eyes in which the water rose above the ice like the borderline between winter and spring.

Ulrich had never entirely lost a certain gratitude for the childlike beauty of their first meeting, that night he lay senseless on the pavement with Bonadea crouching by his head, and the wavering, romantic vagueness of the world, of youth, of emotion, came trickling into his returning consciousness from this young woman's eyes. So he tried to soften his offending refusal, to dissipate it in talk.

"Imagine yourself walking across a big park at night," he suggested, "and two ruffians come at you. Would your first thought be to feel pity for them and that their brutality is society's fault?"

"But I never walk through a park at night," Bonadea promptly parried.

"But suppose a policeman came along: wouldn't you ask him to arrest them?"

"I would ask him to protect me."

"Which means that he would arrest them."

"I don't know what he would do with them. Anyway, Moosbrugger is not a ruffian."

"All right, then, let's assume he is working as a carpenter in your house. You're alone with him in the place, and his eyes start to slither from side to side."

Bonadea protested: "What an awful thing you're making me do!"

"Of course," Ulrich said, "but I'm only trying to show you how extremely unpleasant the kind of people are who lose their balance so easily. One can only indulge in an impartial attitude toward them when someone else takes the beating. In that case, I grant you, as the victims of society or fate they bring out our tenderest feelings. You must admit that no one can be blamed for his faults, as seen through his own eyes; from his point of view they are, at worst, mistakes or bad qualities in a whole person who is no less good because of them, and of course he's perfectly right."

Bonadea had to adjust her stocking and felt compelled as she did so to look up at Ulrich with her head slightly tilted back, so that— unguarded by her eye—a richly contrasting life of lacy frills, smooth stocking, tensed fingers, and the gentle pearly gleam of skin emerged around her knee.

Ulrich hastily lit a cigarette and went on:

"Man is not good, but he is always good; that's a tremendous difference, don't you see? We find a sophistry of self-love amusing, but we ought to conclude from it that a human being can really do no wrong; what is wrong can only be an effect of something he does. This insight could be the right starting point for a social morality."

With a sigh, Bonadea smoothed her skirt back in place, straightened, and sought to calm herself with a sip of the pale golden fire.

"And now let me explain to you," Ulrich went on with a smile, "why it is possible to have all sorts of feeling for Moosbrugger but not to do anything for him. Basically, all these cases are like the loose end of a thread—if you pull at it, the whole fabric of society starts to unravel. I can illustrate this, for a start, by some purely rational problems."

Somehow or other, Bonadea lost a shoe. Ulrich bent down for it, and the foot with its warm toes came up to meet the shoe in his hand like a small child. "Don't bother, don't, I'll do it myself," Bonadea said, holding out her foot to him.

"There are, to begin with, the psychiatric-juridical questions," Ulrich continued relentlessly, even as the whiff of diminished responsibility rose from her leg to his nostrils. "We know that medicine has already practically reached the point of being able to prevent most such crimes if only we were prepared to spend the necessary amounts of money. So now it's only a social question."

"Oh please, not that again!" Bonadea pleaded, now that he had said "social" for the second time. "When they get started on that at home, I leave the room; it bores me to death."

"All right," Ulrich conceded, "I meant to say that just as we already have the technology to make useful things out of corpses, sewage, scrap, and toxins, we almost have the psychological techniques too. But the world is taking its time in solving these questions. The government squanders money on every kind of foolishness but hasn't a penny to spare for solving the most pressing moral problems. That's in its nature, since the state is the stupidest and most malicious person there is."

He spoke with conviction. But Bonadea tried to lead him back to the heart of the matter.

"Dearest," she said longingly, "isn't it the best thing for Moosbrugger that he's not responsible?"

Ulrich fought her off: "It would probably be more important to execute several responsible people than to save one irresponsible person from execution!"

He was now pacing the floor in front of her. Bonadea found him revolutionary and inflaming. She managed to catch his hand, and laid it on her bosom.

"Fine," he said. "I shall now explain to you the emotional questions."

Bonadea opened his fingers and spread his hand over her breast. The accompanying glance would have melted a heart of stone. For the next few moments Ulrich felt as if he had two hearts in his breast, like the confusion of clocks ticking in a watchmaker's shop. Mustering all his willpower, he restored order in his breast and said gently: "No, Bonadea."

Bonadea was now on the brink of tears, and Ulrich spoke to her: "Isn't it contradictory that you get yourself worked up about this one affair just because I happened to tell you about it, whereas you don't even notice the millions of equally unjust things that happen every day?"

"What difference does that make?" Bonadea protested. "The point is, I do happen to know about this one, and I would be a bad person if I stayed calm!"

Ulrich said that one had to keep calm; absolutely, passionately calm, he added. He had repossessed his hand and sat down some distance from Bonadea. "Nowadays everything is done 'meanwhile' and 'for the time being,' " he observed. "It can't be helped. We are driven by the scrupulousness of our reason into an atrocious un-scrupulousness of our hearts." He poured another whiskey for him-self, too, and put his feet up on the sofa. He was beginning to feel tired.

"Everyone starts out wanting to understand life as a whole," he said, "but the more accurately one thinks about it, the more it nar-rows down. When he's mature, a person knows more about one par-ticular square millimeter than all but at most two dozen other people in the world; he knows what nonsense people talk who know less about it, but he doesn't dare move because if he shifts even a mi-cromillimeter from his spot he will be talking nonsense too."

His weariness was now the same transparent gold as his drink on the table. I've been talking nonsense for the last half hour too, he thought. But this diminished state was comfortable enough. The only thing he feared was that it might occur to Bonadea to come and sit down next to him. There was only one way to forestall this: keep talk-ing. He had propped up his head on his hands and lay stretched at full length like the effigies on the tombs in the Medici Chapel. He suddenly became aware of this, and as he assumed his pose he actu-ally felt a certain grandeur flowing through his body, a hovering in their serenity, and he felt more powerful than he was. For the first time he thought he distantly understood these works of art, which he had previously only looked at as foreign objects. Instead of saying anything, he fell silent. Even Bonadea felt something. It was a "mo-ment," as one calls it, that defies characterization. Some dramatic ex-altation united the two of them, and left them mute.

"What is left of me?" Ulrich thought bitterly. "Possibly someone who has courage and is not for sale, and likes to think that for the sake of his inner freedom he respects only a few external laws. But this inner freedom consists of being able to think whatever one likes; it means knowing, in every human situation, why one doesn't need to be bound by it, but never knowing what one wants to be bound by!" In this far from happy moment, when the curious little wave of feel-ing that had held him for an instant ebbed away again, he would have been ready to admit that he had nothing but an ability to see two sides to everything—that moral ambivalence that marked almost all his contemporaries and was the disposition of his generation, or per-haps their fate. His connections to the world had become pale, shadowy, and negative. What right did he have to treat Bonadea badly? It was always the same frustrating talk they had, over and over again; it arose from the inner acoustics of emptiness, where a shot resounds twice as loudly and echoes on and on. It burdened him that he could no longer speak to her except like this. For the special misery this caused them both, he came up with an almost witty, appealing name: Baroque of the Void. He sat up to say something nice to her.

"It just struck me," he said to Bonadea, who had kept her seat and dignified position. "It's a funny thing. A remarkable difference: a person able to be responsible for what he does can always do something different, but a person who isn't *never* can."

Bonadea responded with something quite profound: "Oh, Ulrich!" she said. That was the only interruption, and silence closed around them once more.

When Ulrich spoke in generalities in her presence, she did not like it at all. She felt quite rightly that despite her many lapses, she lived surrounded by people like herself, and she had a sound instinct for the unsociable, eccentric, and solipsistic way he had of treating her with ideas instead of feelings. Still, crime, love, and sadness had linked themselves in her mind, a highly dangerous mixture. Ulrich now seemed to her not nearly as intimidating, as much of a paragon, as he had at the beginning of their meeting; by way of compensation she now saw in him a boyish quality that aroused her idealism, the air of a child not daring to run past some obstacle in order to throw itself into its mother's arms. She had felt for the longest time a free-floating, almost uncontrollable tenderness for him. But after Ulrich had checked her first hint of this, she forced herself with great effort to hold back. The memory of how she had lain undressed and powerless on his sofa on her previous visit still rankled, and she was resolved to sit, if she had to, on that chair in her hat and veil to the very end in order to teach him that he had before him a person who knew how to control herself as much as her rival, Diotima. Bonadea always missed the great idea that was supposed to go along with the great excitement she felt through the nearness of a lover. Unfortunately, this can, of course, be said of life itself, which contains a lot of excitement and little sense, but Bonadea did not know this, and she tried to express some great idea. Ulrich's thoughts lacked the dignity she needed, to her way of thinking, and she was probably searching for something finer, more deeply felt. But refined hesitancy and vulgar attraction, attraction and a terrible dread of being attracted prematurely, all became part of the stimulus of the silence in which the suppressed actions twitched, and mingled, too, with the memory of the great peace that had so united her with her lover for a second. It was, in the end, like when rain hangs in the air but cannot fall; a numbness that spread over her whole skin and terrified her with the idea that she might lose her self-control without noticing it.

Suddenly a physical illusion sprang from all this: a flea. Bonadea could not tell whether it was reality or imagination. She felt a shudder in her brain, a dubious impression as if an idea had detached itself from the shadowy bondage of all the rest but was still only a fantasy—and at the same time she felt an undeniable, quite realistic shudder on her skin. She held her breath. When one hears something coming, pit-a-pat, up the stairs, knowing there is no one there but quite distinctly hearing pit-a-pat—that's how it is. Bonadea realized in a flash that this was an involuntary continuation of the lost shoe. A desperate expedient for a lady. But just as she was trying to banish the spook, she felt a sharp sting. She gave a little shriek, her cheeks flushed a bright red, and she called upon Ulrich to help her look for it. A flea favors the same regions as a lover; her stocking was searched down to the shoe; her blouse had to be unbuttoned in front. Bonadea declared that she must have picked it up in the streetcar or from Ulrich. But it was not to be found, and had left no traces behind.

"I can't imagine what it could have been!" Bonadea said.

Ulrich smiled with unexpected friendliness.

Bonadea burst into tears, like a little girl who has misbehaved.

64

GENERAL STUMM VON BORDWEHR
VISITS DIOTIMA

General Stumm von Bordwehr had paid his first call on Diotima. He was the army officer sent by the War Ministry as their observer to the great inaugural meeting, where he made an impressive speech, which, however, could not prevent the War Ministry from being passed over—for obvious reasons—when the committees for the great peace campaign were set up, one for each ministry.

He was a not very imposing general, with his little paunch and the little toothbrush on his upper lip in place of a real mustache. His face was round and expressed something of the family man with no money beyond the funds for the statutory bond required when an officer wanted to marry. He said to Diotima that a soldier could expect to play only a modest role in the council chamber. Besides, it went without saying that for political reasons the Ministry of War could not be included in the roster of committees. Nevertheless, he dared maintain that the proposed campaign should have an effect abroad, and what had an influence abroad was the might of a people. He repeated the celebrated philosopher Treitschke's observation that the state is the power to survive in the struggle of nations. Power displayed in peace kept war at bay, or at least shortened its cruelty. He went on like this for another quarter of an hour, slipping in classical quotations he fondly remembered from his school days; maintained that those years of humanistic studies had been the happiest of his life; tried to make Diotima feel that he admired her and was delighted with the way she had conducted the great conference; wanted only to repeat once again that, rightly understood, the building up of the armed forces that lagged far behind those of the other great powers could be the most impressive demonstration of peaceful intentions; and for the rest declared his confident expectation that a widespread popular concern for the country's military problems was bound to arise of its own accord.

This amiable general gave Diotima the fright of her life. There were in those days in Kakania families whose houses were frequented socially by army officers because their daughters married army officers, and then there were families whose daughters did not marry army officers, either because there was no money for the mandatory security bond or on principle, so they did not receive army officers socially. Diotima's family had belonged to the second sort for both reasons, with the consequence that this conscientiously beautiful woman had gone out into life with a concept of the military that was something like an image of Death decked out in motley.

She replied that there was so much that was great and good in the world that the choice was not easy. It was a great privilege to be allowed to give a great sign in the midst of the world's materialistic bustle, but also a grave responsibility. And the demonstration was meant, after all, to arise spontaneously from the midst of the people themselves, for which reason she had to keep her own wishes a little in the background. She placed her words with care, as though stitching them together with threads in the national colors, and burned the mild incense of high bureaucratic phraseology upon her lips.

But when the General had left, the sublime woman suffered an inner breakdown. Had she been capable of so vulgar a sentiment as hatred she would have hated the pudgy little man with his waggling eyes and the gold buttons on his belly, but since this was impossible she felt vaguely insulted but could not say why. Despite the wintry cold she opened the windows and paced the room several times, her silks rustling. When she shut the windows again there were tears in her eyes. She was quite amazed. This was now the second time she was weeping without reason. She remembered the night when, in bed at her husband's side, she had shed tears without being able to explain them. This time the purely nervous character of the process, unrelated to any tangible cause, was even more evident; this fat general caused tears to gush from her eyes like an onion, without any sensible feeling being involved. She had good cause to be worried; a shadowy fear told her that a wolf was prowling round her flocks and that it was high time to exorcise it by the power of the Idea. This is how it happened that after the General's visit Diotima made up her mind to organize with the greatest speed the planned gathering of great minds who would help her define the proper content of the patriotic campaign.

65

FROM THE CONVERSATIONS BETWEEN ARNHEIM AND DIOTIMA

It greatly eased Diotima's heart that Arnheim had just returned from a trip and was at her disposal.

"Your cousin and I were talking about generals just a few days ago," he instantly responded, with the air of a man alluding to a suspicious coincidence without wanting to be specific. Diotima received the impression that her contradictory cousin, with his unenthusiastic view of the great campaign, also favored the vague menaces emanating from the General.

"I wouldn't like to expose this to ridicule in the presence of your cousin," Arnheim went on, changing the subject, "but I would like to be able to make you feel something you would hardly come upon by yourself, far away as you are from such things: the connection between business and poetry. Of course, I mean business in the largest sense, the world's business, such as I have been fated to conduct by the position to which I was born; it is related to poetry, it has irrational, even mystical aspects. I might even say that business is quite particularly endowed with those aspects. You see, money is an extraordinarily intolerant power."

"There is probably a certain intolerance in everything people stake their lives on," Diotima said hesitantly, her mind still on the unfinished first part of the conversation.

"Especially with money!" Arnheim quickly said. "Foolish people imagine it's a pleasure to have money. It is in fact a terrible responsibility. I won't speak of the countless lives dependent on me, for whom I represent a sort of fate; let me just mention that my grandfather started by picking up garbage in a middle-sized town in the Rhineland."

At these words Diotima actually felt a sudden shiver of what she thought was economic imperialism, but this was an error; since she was not quite without the prejudice of her social circle, she associated garbage removal with what was called in her regional dialect the dungman, and so her friend's courageous confession made her blush.

"With this refining process for waste," he continued his confession, "my grandfather laid the groundwork for the influence of the Arnheims. But even my father was a self-made man, if you consider that it was he who in forty years expanded the firm into a worldwide concern. Two years at a trade school was all he had, but he can see through the most tangled world affairs at a glance, and knows everything he needs to know before anyone else does. I myself studied economics and every conceivable branch of science, all quite beyond his ken, and no one has any idea how he does it, but he never misses a detail. That is the mystery of a vigorous, simple, great, and healthy life!"

Arnheim's voice, as he spoke of his father, took on a special, reverential tone, as though its magisterial calm had a small crack somewhere. It struck Diotima all the more because Ulrich had told her that old Arnheim was supposed to be a short, broad-shouldered fellow with a bony face and a button nose, who always wore a gaping swallowtail coat and handled his investments with the dogged circumspection of a chess player moving his pawns. Without waiting for her response, Arnheim continued after a brief pause:

"Once a business has expanded to the degree reached only by the very few I speak of, there is hardly anything in life it is not somehow involved with. It is a little cosmos. You would be amazed if you knew what seemingly quite uncommercial problems—artistic, moral, political—I sometimes have to bring up in conferring with my managing director. But the firm is no longer mushrooming the way it did in its early days, which I'd like to call its heroic days. No matter how prosperous a business firm may be, there is a mysterious limit to its growth, as there is with everything organic. Have you ever asked yourself why no animal in our time grows bigger than an elephant? You'll find the same mystery in the history of art and in the strange relationships of the life of peoples, cultures, and epochs."

Diotima was now ashamed of herself for having shrunk from the refining process for waste disposal, and felt confused.

"Life is full of such mysteries. There is something that defies all reason. My father is in league with it. But a man like your cousin,"

Arnheim said, "an activist with a head full of ideas how things could be done differently and better, has no feeling for it."

Diotima responded to this second reference to Ulrich with a smile suggesting that a man like her cousin had no claim to exert any influence on her. Arnheim's even, somewhat sallow skin, which in his face was as smooth as a pear, had flushed over the cheekbones. He had succumbed to a curious urge Diotima had been arousing in him for some time now to let down his guard and confide in her totally, down to the last hidden detail. Now he locked himself up again, picked up a book from the table, read its title without taking it in, impatiently laid it down again, and said in his usual voice—it moved Diotima as deeply at this moment as the gesture of a man who, in gathering up his clothes, reveals that he has been naked—"I have wandered from the point. What I have to say to you about the General is that you could do nothing better than to realize your plan as quickly as possible and raise the level of our campaign with the help of humanistic ideas and their recognized representatives. But there's no need to turn the General away on principle. Personally he may be a man of goodwill, and you know my principle of not missing any opportunity to bring the life of the spirit into a sphere of mere power."

Diotima seized his hand and summed up the conversation in her good-bye: "Thank you for being so frank with me."

Arnheim irresolutely let that gentle hand rest in his own for a moment, staring down at it thoughtfully as though there were something he had forgotten to say.

66

ALL IS NOT WELL BETWEEN ULRICH AND ARNHEIM

Her cousin often took pleasure, at that time, in reporting to Diotima his experiences as His Grace's aide-de-camp, and always made a special point of showing her the files with all the proposals that kept pouring into Count Leinsdorf's office.

"Almighty cousin," he reported, with a fat folder in his hand, "I can no longer handle this alone. The whole world seems to expect improvements from us. Half of them begin with the words 'No more of . . .' and the other half with 'Forward to . . .' Here is a batch of demands starting with 'No more Rome!' and going all the way to 'Forward to kitchen gardens!' What would you want to choose?"

It was not easy to sort out all the petitions the world was addressing to Count Leinsdorf, but two kinds surpassed all the rest in volume. One blamed the troubles of the times on one particular detail and demanded its abolition; such details were nothing less than the Jews or the Church of Rome, socialism or capitalism, mechanistic thinking or the neglect of technical possibilities, miscegenation or segregation, big landed estates or big cities, overemphasis on intellect or inadequate popular education. The second group, on the other hand, pointed to a goal just ahead that, when reached, would suffice to take care of everything. These desirable goals of the second persuasion differed from the specific evils denounced by the first mostly by nothing more than the emotional plus or minus signs attached, obviously because the world is made up of both critical and affirming temperaments. So there were letters of the second category that joyfully took the negative line that it was high time to break with the ridiculous cult of the arts, because life was a far greater poet than all the scribblers. These letters demanded courtroom reports and travel books for general use; while letters on the same subject from the first category would be joyfully positive in maintaining that the mountaineer's ecstasy upon reaching the summit outdid all the sublimities of art, philosophy, and religion, so instead of these one should support mountain-climbing clubs. In this double-jointed fashion the public demanded a slowing down of the tempo of the times just as much as a competition for the best short essay, because life was unbearably/exquisitely short, and there was a desperate need for the liberation of mankind from/by garden apartments, the emancipation of women, dancing, sports, interior decoration, and from any number of other burdens by any number of other panaceas.

Ulrich closed his folder and spoke privately.

"Mighty cousin," he said, "it is amazing that half of them seek salvation in the future and the other half in the past. I don't know what we are to make of that. His Grace would say that the present is without salvation."

"Is His Grace thinking in terms of the Church?" Diotima asked.

"He has only just come up with the discovery that in the history of mankind there is no turning back voluntarily. What makes it difficult is that going forward is not much use either. Permit me to say that we're in a very peculiar situation, unable to move either forward or backward, while the present moment is felt to be unbearable too."

When Ulrich talked like this Diotima barricaded herself in her tall body as in a tower marked with three stars in Baedeker.

"Do you believe, dear lady, that anyone fighting for or against a cause today," Ulrich asked, "who tomorrow by some miracle were to become the all-powerful ruler of the world, would instantly do what he had been clamoring for all his life? I am convinced he would grant himself a few days' delay."

Ulrich paused. Diotima suddenly turned to him without responding and asked him sternly:

"Why did you encourage the General about our campaign?"

"What general?"

"General von Stumm!"

"Do you mean that round little general from the first big meeting? Me? I haven't even seen him since, let alone encouraged him!"

Ulrich's astonishment was convincing and called for an explanation on her part. Since it was impossible that a man like Arnheim should be guilty of a falsehood, there had to be a misunderstanding somewhere, and Diotima gave him the reason for her assumption.

"So I am supposed to have spoken with Arnheim about General

von Stumm? I never did that either," Ulrich assured her. "I did talk with Arnheim—just a moment . . ." He searched his memory, then broke into a laugh. "It would be very flattering if Arnheim attached so much importance to every word I say. We have had several discussions lately—if that's the word for our differences—and I did once say something about a general, but not any particular one, only incidentally to illustrate a point. I maintained that a general who for strategic reasons sends his battalions to certain doom is a murderer, if you think of them as thousands of mothers' sons, but that he immediately becomes something else seen from some other perspective, such as, for example, the necessity of sacrifice, or the insignificance of life's short span. I used a lot of other examples. But here you must allow me to digress. For quite obvious reasons, every generation treats the life into which it is born as firmly established, except for those few things it is interested in changing. This is practical, but it's wrong. The world can be changed in all directions at any moment, or at least in any direction it chooses; it's in the world's nature. Wouldn't it be more original to try to live, not as a definite person in a definite world where only a few buttons need adjusting—what we call evolution—but rather to behave from the start as someone born to change surrounded by a world created to change, roughly like a drop of water inside a cloud? Are you annoyed with me for being so obscure again?"

"I'm not annoyed with you, but I can't understand you." Diotima commanded: "Do tell me the whole conversation!"

"Well, Arnheim started it. He stopped me and formally challenged me to a conversation," Ulrich began. " 'We businessmen,' he said to me with a rather puckish smile, quite in contrast to his usual quiet pose, but still very majestic, 'we businessmen are not as calculating as you might think. Actually, we—I mean the leading men, of course; the small fry may spend all their time calculating—we come to regard our really successful ideas as something that defies all calculation, like the personal success of a politician, and, in the last analysis, like the artist's too.' Then he asked me to judge what he was going to say next with the indulgence we grant the irrational: from the first day he saw me, he confided, he'd had certain ideas about me—and it seems, gracious cousin, that you also told him many things about me, which he assured me he had not needed to hear to form his opinion, which was that strangely enough I had made a mistake in choosing a purely abstract, conceptual profession, because no matter how gifted I was in that direction, I was basically a scientist, and no matter how surprised I might be to hear it, my real talent lay in the field of action and personal effectiveness!"

"Oh really?" Diotima said.

"I quite agree with you," Ulrich hastened to say. "There is nothing I am less fit for than being myself."

"You are always making fun of things instead of devoting yourself to life," Diotima said, still annoyed with him over the files.

"Arnheim maintains the opposite. I am under a compulsion to think my way to excessively thorough conclusions about life—he says."

"You're always sardonic and negative, always leaping into the impossible and avoiding every real decision," Diotima maintained.

"It is simply my conviction," Ulrich replied, "that thinking is a world of its own, and real life is another. The difference between their respective levels of development at the present time is too great. Our brain is some thousands of years old, but if it had worked out only half of everything and forgotten the other half, its true image would be our reality. All one can do is refuse intellectual participation in it."

"Aren't you making things much too easy for yourself?" Diotima asked, without any offensive intention, rather like a mountain looking down on a little brook at its foot. "Arnheim enjoys theorizing too, but I think he lets hardly anything pass without examining all its aspects. Don't you feel that the point of thinking is to be a concentrated capacity for applying—"

"No," Ulrich said.

"I'd like to hear what answer Arnheim gave you."

"He told me that the intellect today is the helpless spectator of real developments because it is dodging the great tasks of life. He asked me to look at what subjects the arts treat, at what trivia the churches concern themselves with, at how narrow even the perspective of the scholars is—and I should consider that all the while, the earth is being literally carved up! Then he said that this was precisely what he wanted to talk with me about."

"And what was your answer?" Diotima asked eagerly, supposing that Arnheim had been trying to appeal to her cousin's conscience about his indifferent attitude to the problems of the Parallel Campaign.

"I told him that realizing a potential always attracts me less than the unrealized, and I mean not only the future but also the past and missed opportunities. It seems to me our history has been that every time we have fulfilled some small part of an idea, we are so pleased that we leave the much greater remainder unfinished. Magnificent institutions are usually the bungled drafts of their ideas; so, incidentally, are magnificent personalities. That's what I answered. A difference in the angle of perspective, so to speak."

"How argumentative of you!" said Diotima, with a sense of injury.

"He retaliated by telling me his impression of me when I resist the active life because of some unfulfilled intellectual element in the general scheme. Would you like to hear it? Like a man who lies down on the ground beside a bed that has been prepared for him. A squandering of energy, something physically immoral, is what he called it, to make sure I didn't miss the point. He kept at me to make me see that great goals can be reached only by using the existing economic, political, and, not least, intellectual structure of power. For his own part, he considers it more ethical to make use of it than to neglect it. He really hammered away at me. He called me a man of action in a defensive stance, a cramped defensive stance. I think he has some sinister reason for wanting to gain my respect."

"He wants to be helpful!" Diotima cried out in reproof.

"Oh no," Ulrich said. "I may be only a little pebble, and he is a splendid, puffed-out glass ball. But I have the impression he's afraid of me."

Diotima made no answer. What Ulrich had said might be presumptuous, but it had occurred to her that the conversation he had just recounted was not at all what it should have been according to the impression she had got from Arnheim. It even worried her a bit. Although she thought Arnheim quite incapable of intrigue, Ulrich was gaining her confidence, and so she asked him what she should do about the case of General Stumm.

"Keep him off!" was Ulrich's answer, and Diotima could not spare herself the reproach that she was well pleased with it.

67

DIOTIMA AND ULRICH

Diotima's relationship to Ulrich had much improved, now that they had formed the habit of getting together regularly. They often had to drive out together to call on people, and he came to see her several times a week, often unannounced and at unconventional hours. In the circumstances, their being related was convenient for a domestic relaxation of the strict social code. Diotima did not always receive him in the drawing room armored in full panoply from chignon to skirt hem, but sometimes in slight domestic disarray, even if only a very cautious disarray. A kind of fellowship had grown up between them that lay mainly in the form of their association, but forms have their inward effects, and the emotions that create them can also be awakened by them.

Ulrich sometimes felt with great intensity that Diotima was very beautiful. On these occasions he saw her as a young, tall, plump heifer of good stock, surefooted and studying with a deep gaze the dry grasses she was feeding on. In other words, even then he did not look on her without the malice and irony that revenged themselves on her spiritual nobility by drawing on images from the animal kingdom and that arose from a deep annoyance less against this foolish paragon than against the school where her performances were a success. "How likable she could be," he thought, "if she were uneducated and careless and as good-natured as a big warm female body always is when it doesn't flatter itself that it has any special ideas!" The celebrated wife of the much-whispered-about Section Chief Tuzzi evaporated from her body, leaving it behind like a dream that, together with pillows, bed, and dreamer, turned into a white cloud all alone in the world with its tenderness.

But when Ulrich came back to earth from such a flight of the imagination, what he found before him was an ambitious middle-class mind eager to associate with aristocratic ideas. Physical kinship together with a strong difference in temperament, incidentally, is disturbing; sometimes the mere idea of kinship is enough, the consciousness of self; siblings often cannot bear each other in a way that goes far beyond anything that might be justified; it derives merely from the existence of the one throwing into doubt the existence of the other, from the slightly distorted mirror image they have of each other. Sometimes Diotima's being about the same height as Ulrich was enough to remind him that they were related and made him feel repugnance for her body. He had transferred to her, with some differences, a function usually reserved for his boyhood friend Walter—that of humbling and irritating his pride, much as seeing ourselves again in certain unpleasant old photographs has the power to humiliate us and at the same time challenge our pride. It followed that even in the mistrust Ulrich felt for Diotima there had to be something of a bond and a drawing together, in short a touch of genuine affection, just as his old warm allegiance with Walter still survived in the form of mistrust. But since he did not like Diotima, this baffled him for a long time without his being able to get to the bottom of it. They sometimes set off on little expeditions together. With Tuzzi's encouragement they took advantage of the fine weather, despite the unfavorable time of year, to show Arnheim "the lovely sights around Vienna"—Diotima never used any other expression but this cliché—and Ulrich always felt that he was being taken along in the role of an elderly female relation serving as chaperone because Section Chief Tuzzi could not spare the time. Later it happened that Ulrich also drove out alone with Diotima when Arnheim was out of town. For such expeditions, as well as for the immediate purposes of the campaign, Arnheim had made available as many automobiles as might be needed, since His Grace's carriage, ornate with its coat of arms, was too well known about town and too conspicuous. These cars, incidentally, were not necessarily Arnheim's own; the rich always can find others who are only too pleased to oblige.

Such excursions served not merely for diversion but also served the purpose of winning support for the campaign from influential or wealthy persons, so they took place more often within the city limits than in the countryside. The cousins saw many beautiful things together: Maria Theresa furniture, Baroque palaces, people still borne through life on the hands of their many servants, modern houses with great suites of rooms, palatial banks, and the blend of Spanish austerity and middle-class domestic habits in the homes of high-ranking civil servants. All in all, it was, for the aristocracy, what was left of the grand manner with no running water, repeated in paler imitation in the houses and conference rooms of the wealthy middle class with improved hygiene and, on the whole, better taste. A ruling caste always remains slightly barbaric. In the castles of the nobility, cinders and leftovers not burned away by the slow smoldering of time were still lying where they had fallen. Close beside magnificent staircases one stepped on boards of soft wood, and hideous new furniture stood carelessly alongside magnificent old pieces. The new rich, on the other hand, in love with the imposing and grandiose moments of their predecessors, had instinctively made a fastidious and refined selection. Wherever a castle had passed into middle-class hands, was it not merely seen to be provided with modern comfort, like an heirloom chandelier through which electric wiring had been threaded, but the inferior furnishings had also been cleared out and valuable pieces brought in, chosen either by the owner or according to the unassailable recommendation of experts. It was not, incidentally, in the castles where this refinement showed itself most impressively but in the town houses that, in keeping with the times, had been furnished with all the impersonal luxury of an ocean liner and yet had preserved, in this country of subtly refined social ambition, through some ineffable breath, some hardly perceptible widening of the space between the pieces of furniture or the dominant position of a painting on a wall, the tender, clear echo of a great sound that had faded away.

Diotima was enchanted by so much "culture." She had always known that her native country harbored such treasures, but even she was amazed at their abundance. They would be invited together to visit in the country, and Ulrich noticed, among other things, that the fruit here was not infrequently picked up in the fingers and eaten unpeeled, whereas in the houses of the upper bourgeoisie the ceremonial of knife and fork was strictly observed. The same could also be said about conversation, which tended to be flawlessly distinguished only in the middle-class homes, while among the nobility the well-known, relaxed idiom reminiscent of cabdrivers prevailed. Diotima presented her cousin with an enthusiastic defense of all this. She conceded that the bourgeois estates had better plumbing and showed more intelligence in their appointments, while at the nobility's country seats one froze in winter, there were often narrow, worn stairs, stuffy, low-ceilinged bedrooms were the behind-the-scenes counterpart of magnificent public rooms, and there were no dumbwaiters or bathrooms for the servants. But that was just what made it all, in a sense, more heroic, this feeling for tradition and this splendid nonchalance! she wound up ecstatically.

Ulrich used these excursions to examine the feeling that bound him to Diotima. But there were so many digressions along the way that it is necessary to follow them awhile before coming to the point.

At that time, women were encased in clothes from throat to ankle. Men's clothes today are like what they were then, but they used to be more appropriate because they still represented an organic outward sign of the flawless cohesion and strict reserve that marked a man of the world. In those days, even a person of few prejudices, unhampered by shame in appreciating the undraped human body, would have regarded a display of nudity as a relapse into the animal state, not because of the nakedness but because of the loss of the civilized aphrodisiac of clothing. Actually, it would then have been considered below the animal state, for a three-year-old Thoroughbred and a playing greyhound are far more expressive in their nakedness than a human body can ever be. But animals can't wear clothes; they have only the one skin, while human beings in those days had many skins. In full dress, with frills, puffs, bell skirts, cascading draperies, laces, and gathered pleats, they had created a surface five times the size of the original one, forming a many-petaled chalice heavy with an erotic charge, difficult of access, and hiding at its core the slim white animal that had to be searched out and that made itself terribly desirable. It was the prescribed process Nature herself uses when she bids her creatures fluff out their plumage or spray out clouds of ink, so that desire and terror raised to a degree of unearthly frenzy will mask the matter-of-fact proceedings that are the heart of the matter.

For the first time in her life Diotima felt herself more than superficially affected by this game, though in the most decorous way. Coquetry was not wholly unknown to her, since it was one of the social accomplishments a lady had to master. Nor had she ever failed to notice when a young man looked at her with a glance that expressed something besides respect; in fact she rather liked it, because it made her feel the gentle power of feminine reproof when she forced the eyes of a man, intent on her like the horns of a bull, to turn away by uttering high-minded sentiments. But Ulrich, in the security of their kinship and his selfless services to the Parallel Campaign, and protected, too, by the codicil established in his favor, permitted himself liberties that pierced straight through the tangled weavings of her idealism. On one occasion, for instance, as they were driving through the countryside, they passed some delightful valleys where hillsides covered with dark pine woods sloped down toward the road, and Diotima pointed to them with the lines "Who planted you, O lovely woods, so high up there above?" She of course quoted these lines as poetry, without any hint of the tune that went along with them; she would have considered that old hat and inane. Ulrich was quick to answer: "The Landbank of Lower Austria. Don't you know, cousin, that all the forests hereabouts belong to the Landbank? The master you are about to praise in the next line is a forester on the bank's payroll. Nature in these parts is a planned product of the forestry industry, a storehouse of serried ranks of cellulose for the manufacturers, as you can see at a glance."

His answers were quite often like that. When she spoke of beauty, he spoke of the fatty tissue supporting the epidermis. When she mentioned love, he responded with the statistical curve that indicates the automatic rise and fall in the annual birthrate. When she spoke of the great figures in art, he traced the chain of borrowings that links these figures to one another. Somehow it always began with Diotima talking as if on the sixth day of Creation God had placed man as a pearl in the shell of the world, whereupon Ulrich reminded her that mankind was a tiny pile of dots on the outermost crust of a dwarf globe. She was not quite sure what Ulrich was up to, though it was obviously an attack on that sphere of greatness with which Diotima felt allied, and most of all she felt that he was rudely showing off. She found it hard to take that her cousin, whom she regarded as an intellectual enfant terrible, imagined he knew more than she did, and his materialistic arguments, which meant nothing to her, drawn as they were from the lower culture of facts and figures, annoyed her mightily.

"Thank heaven," she once came back at him sharply, "there are still people capable of believing in simple things, no matter how great their experience!"

"Your husband, for instance," Ulrich said. "I've been meaning to tell you for a long time that I much prefer him to Arnheim."

They had got into the habit of exchanging ideas by speaking about Arnheim. For like all people in love, Diotima derived pleasure from talking about the object of her love without, at least so she believed, betraying herself; and since Ulrich found this insufferable, as does any man who has no ulterior motive in yielding the stage to another, it often happened on such occasions that he lashed out against Arnheim. Between Arnheim and himself a relationship of a peculiar kind had developed. When Arnheim was not traveling, they met almost every day. Ulrich knew that Section Chief Tuzzi regarded the Prussian with suspicion, as he did himself from observing Arnheim's effect on Diotima since the very beginning. Not that there was yet anything improper between them, so far as could be judged by a third party who was confirmed in this judgment by the revolting excess of propriety between these lovers, who were evidently emulating the loftiest examples of a Platonic union of souls. Yet Arnheim showed a striking inclination to draw his friend's cousin (or was she his lover after all?, Ulrich wondered, but considered it most probably something like lover plus friend divided by two) into this intimate relationship. He often addressed Ulrich in the manner of an older friend, a tone made permissible by the difference in age between them but that became unpleasantly tainted with condescension because of the difference in their position. Ulrich's response was almost always standoffish in a rather challenging way: he made a point of not seeming in the least impressed by speaking with a man who might just as easily have been speaking with kings and chancellors instead. Annoyed with himself because of his lack of propriety, he contradicted Arnheim with impolite frequency and unseemly irony, as a substitute for which he would have done better to enjoy himself as a silent observer. He was astonished that Arnheim irritated him so violently. Ulrich saw in him, fattened by favorable circumstances, the model example of an intellectual development he hated. For this celebrated writer was shrewd enough to grasp the questionable situation man had got himself into ever since he ceased looking for his image in the mirror of a stream, and sought it instead in the sharp, broken surfaces of his intelligence; but this writing iron magnate blamed the predicament on intelligence itself and not on its imperfections. There was a con game in this union between the soul and the price of coal, a union that at the same time purposefully served to keep apart what Arnheim did with his eyes wide open and what he said and wrote in his cloud of intuition. Added to this, to exacerbate Ulrich's uneasiness, was something new to him, the combination of intellect and wealth. When Arnheim talked about some particular subject almost like a specialist and then suddenly, with a casual wave of his hand, made all the details disappear in the light of a "great thought," he might be acting on some not unjustified need of his own, but at the same time this manner of freely disposing of things in two directions at once was too suggestive of the rich man who can afford the best and most expensive of everything. He had a wealth of ideas that was always slightly reminiscent of the ways of real wealth. But perhaps it was not even this that most provoked Ulrich into creating difficulties for the celebrated man; perhaps it was rather the inclination of Arnheim's mind toward a dignified mode of holding court and keeping house that of itself led to an association with the best brands of the traditional as well as of the unusual. For in the mirror of this Epicurean connoisseurship Ulrich saw the affected grimace that is the face of the times, if one subtracts the few really strong lines of passion and thought in it; all this left him with hardly a chance to reach a better understanding of the man, who could probably be credited with all sorts of merits as well. It was, of course, an utterly senseless battle he was waging, in an environment predisposed in Arnheim's favor, and in a cause that had no importance at all; the most that could be said for it was that this senselessness gave the sense of the total expenditure of his own energies. It was also a quite hopeless struggle, for if Ulrich actually once managed to wound his opponent, he had to recognize that he had hit the wrong Arnheim; if Arnheim the thinker lay defeated on the ground, Arnheim the master of reality rose like a winged being with an indulgent smile, and hastened from the idle games of such conversations to Baghdad or Madrid.

This invulnerability made it possible for him to counter the younger man's bad manners with that amiable camaraderie the source of which Ulrich could never quite pinpoint. Besides, Ulrich was himself concerned not to go too far in tearing Arnheim down, because he was determined not to slip again into one of those half-baked and demeaning adventures in which his past had been far too rich; and the progress he observed between Arnheim and Diotima served as an effective insurance against weakening. So he generally directed the points of his attacks like the points of a foil, which yield on impact and are shielded with a friendly little rubber button to soften the blow. It was Diotima who had come up with this comparison. She found herself mystified by this cousin of hers. His candid face with the clear brow, his quietly breathing chest, the ease in all his movements, all clearly indicated to her that no malicious, spiteful, sadistic-libidinous impulses could dwell in such a body. Nor was she quite without pride in so personable a member of her family; she had made up her mind from the beginning of their acquaintance to take him under her wing. Had he had black hair, a crooked shoulder, a muddy skin, or a low forehead, she would have said that his views accorded with his looks. But as it was, she was struck by a certain discrepancy between his looks and his ideas that made itself felt as an inexplicable uneasiness. The antennae of her famed intuition groped in vain for the cause, but she enjoyed the groping at the other end of the antennae. In a sense, though not of course seriously, she sometimes even preferred Ulrich's company to Arnheim's. Her need to feel superior was more gratified by him, she felt more sure of herself, and to regard him as frivolous, eccentric, or immature gave her a certain satisfaction that balanced the idealism, becoming increasingly dangerous from day to day, that she saw taking on incalculable dimensions in her feelings for Arnheim. Soul is a terribly grave affair, and materialism by contrast is lighthearted. The conduct of her relationship with Arnheim was sometimes as much of a strain as her salon, and her contempt for Ulrich made her life easier. She did not understand herself, but she noticed this effect, and this enabled her whenever she was annoyed with her cousin over one of his remarks to give him a sideways look that was only a tiny smile in the corner of her eye, while the eye itself, idealistically untouched and indeed even slightly disdainful, gazed straight ahead.

Anyway, whatever their reasons may have been, Diotima and Arnheim behaved toward Ulrich like two fighters clinging to a third person whom in their alternating fear they shove back and forth between themselves; a situation not without its dangers for Ulrich, for through Diotima the question arose: Must people be in accord with their bodies or not?

68

A DIGRESSION: MUST PEOPLE BE IN ACCORD WITH THEIR BODIES?

Independently of what their faces were talking about, the motion of the car on those long drives rocked the two cousins so that their clothes touched, overlapped a bit, and moved apart again. One could only see this from their shoulders, because the rest of them was enveloped by a shared blanket, but the bodies felt this contact, muffled by their clothing, as delicately indistinct as things seen in moonlight. Ulrich was not unreceptive to this kind of flirting, without taking it too seriously. The overrefined transmission of desire from the body to the clothes, from the embrace to the obstacles, or, in short, from the goal to the approach, answered to his nature, whose sensuality drove him toward the woman; but its critical faculties held him back from the alien, uncongenial person it suddenly, with relentless lucidity, perceived her to be, and this made for a lively tug-of-war between inclination and aversion. But this meant that the body's sublime beauty, its human beauty, the moment when the spirit's song rises from nature's instrument, or that other moment when the body is like a goblet filling up with a mystic potion, was something he had never known, leaving aside those dreams of the major's wife that had for the longest time put an end to such inclinations in him.

All his relationships with women, since then, had somehow not been right. With a certain amount of goodwill on both sides that happens, unfortunately, all too easily. From the moment they first began to think about it, a man and a woman find a ready-made matrix of feelings, acts, and complications waiting to take them in charge, and beneath this matrix the process takes its course in reverse; the stream no longer flows from the spring; the last things to happen push their way to the front of consciousness, the pure pleasure two people have in each other, this simplest and deepest of all feelings in love, and the natural source of all the rest, disappears completely in this psychic reversal.

So on his trips with Diotima, Ulrich not infrequently remembered their leave-taking after his first visit. He had taken her mild hand, an artfully and nobly perfected weightless hand, in his own as they gazed into each other's eyes. They both undoubtedly felt some aversion, and yet it occurred to them that they might nevertheless fuse to the point of extinction. Something of this vision had remained between them. Thus two heads above cast a horrible chill on each other while the bodies below helplessly melt together at white heat. There is in this something nastily mythical, as in a two-headed god or the devil's cloven hoof, and it had often led Ulrich astray in his youth, when he had experienced it fairly often; but with the years it had proved to be no more than a very bourgeois aphrodisiac, in exactly the same way that the unclothed body substitutes for the nude. Nothing so inflames the middle-class lover as the flattering discovery of the power to drive another person into an ecstasy so wild that to be the cause of such changes by any other means one would have to become a murderer.

And truly, that there can be such changes in civilized people, that we actually can produce such effects!—isn't this the question and the amazement in the bold, glazed eyes of all those who dock at the lonely island of lust, where they are murderer, destiny, and God, and experience the maximum irrationality and adventurousness in the greatest comfort?

The repugnance he came to acquire with time against this kind of love eventually extended to his own body too, which had always encouraged these misbegotten affairs by giving women the illusion of a reliable virility, for which Ulrich was too cerebral and too conflicted. At times he was as downright jealous of his own appearance as if it were a rival using cheap tricks against him—in which a contradiction emerged that is also present in others who are not aware of it. For he was the one who kept his body trim by exercising it, giving it the shape, expression, and readiness for action that influence the mind no less than an ever-smiling or an ever-solemn face can. Oddly enough, the majority of people have either a neglected body, formed and deformed by chance circumstances, which seems to have almost no relation at all to their mind and character, or else a body disguised by the mask of sports, giving it the look of those hours when it is on vacation from itself. Those are the hours when a person spins out the daydream of his appearance, casually picked up from the magazines of the smart, great world. All those bronzed and muscular tennis players, horsemen, and race-car drivers, who look like world-record holders though usually they are merely competent; those ladies all dressed up or all undressed; they are all daydreamers, differing from common daydreamers only in that their dream doesn't stay in their brain but comes out into the open air as a projection of the mass soul—physically, dramatically, and (as one might say in the idiom of more-than-dubious occult phenomena) ideoplastically. But in common with the usual spinners of fantasies they have a certain shallowness of the dream, both as to its content and its nearness to the waking state. The problem of the integral physiognomy still eludes us, even though we have learned to draw conclusions about man's nature, sometimes even amazingly correct conclusions, from his handwriting, voice, sleeping position, and God knows what else; yet for the body as a whole we have only the fashionable models on which it forms itself, or at most a kind of nature-cure philosophy.

But is this the body of our mind, our ideas, intimations, plans, or—the pretty ones included—the body of our follies? That Ulrich had loved those follies and still to some extent had them did not prevent him from feeling not at home in the body they had created.

69

DIOTIMA AND ULRICH, CONTINUED

And it was above all Diotima who confirmed in a new way his sense that the surface and depths of his person were not one and the same. This came through clearly for him on these trips with her, which sometimes felt like drives through moonlight, when the young woman's beauty detached itself from her person altogether and momentarily veiled his eyes like gossamer spun by a dream. He knew, of course, that Diotima compared everything he said with the conventional wisdom on the subject—the higher conventional wisdom, to be sure—and was pleased that she found it "immature," so that he constantly sat there as if he were before the wrong end of a telescope trained on him. He became smaller and smaller, and believed when he spoke with her (or at least was not far from believing) in his role of devil's advocate and materialist that he could hear in his own words conversations from his last terms at school, when he and his classmates had idolized all the villains and monsters of world history because the teachers had presented them in tones of idealistic abhorrence. And when Diotima looked at him indignantly he grew smaller still, regressing from the morality of heroism and the drive for expansion to the defiant lies, callousness, and wavering excesses of adolescence—only quite figuratively, of course, as one can detect in a gesture or a word some distant similarity with gestures and words one has long since discarded, or only dreamed, or seen and disliked in others. In any event, this all resonated in his delight in shocking Diotima. The mind of this woman, who would have been so beautiful without her mind, aroused an inhuman feeling in him, perhaps a fear of mind itself, an aversion for all great things, a feeling that was quite faint, hardly detectable—and perhaps feeling was a much too pretentious expression for something that was but a mere breath. But if one magnified it into words, they would have gone something like this: at times he saw not only this woman's idealism but all the idealism in the world, in all its extent and ramifications, appear bodily in the form of an image hovering just above that Grecian head—it only just missed being the horns of the Devil! Then Ulrich grew even smaller still and—again figuratively speaking—regressed to the first hotly moral state of childhood, in whose eyes temptation and terror lie as in the stare of a gazelle. The tender emotions of that age can in a single moment of yielding cause the whole, still-tiny world to burst into flames, since they have neither an aim nor the ability to make anything happen, but are a completely boundless fire. It was quite unlike him, and yet in Diotima's company Ulrich ended up longing for these childhood feelings, though he could barely imagine them because they have so little in common with the conditions under which an adult lives.

At one point he very nearly confessed it to her. On one of their trips they had left the car to walk into a small valley that was like a river delta of meadows with steep forested banks and that formed a crooked triangle with a winding brook in its center stilled by a light frost. The slopes had been partly cleared of timber, with a few trees left standing like feather dusters stuck in the bare hillsides and hilltops. This scene had tempted them to take a walk. It was one of those wistful, snowless days that seem in the middle of winter like a faded, no-longer-fashionable summer gown. Diotima abruptly asked her cousin: "Why does Arnheim call you an activist? He says that you're always full of ideas how to do things differently and better." She had suddenly remembered that her talk with Arnheim about Ulrich and the General had ended inconclusively.

"I don't understand," she went on. "It always seems to me that you hardly ever mean anything seriously. But I must ask you, because we are involved together in such a responsible task. Do you remember our last conversation? There was something you said: you maintained that nobody, if he had the necessary power, would do what he wants to do. Now I would like to know what you meant by that. Wasn't it a horrible idea?"

Ulrich did not reply at once. And during this silence, after she had spoken as impudently as possible, she realized how much she had been preoccupied with the forbidden question of whether Arnheim and she would do what each of them secretly wanted. She suddenly thought she had given herself away to Ulrich. She blushed, tried to stop herself, blushed even more, and did her best to gaze out over the valley, away from him, with the most unconcerned expression she could muster.

Ulrich had observed the process. "I'm very much afraid that the only reason Arnheim, as you say, calls me an activist is that he over-estimates my influence with the Tuzzi family," he answered. "You know yourself how little attention you pay to what I say. But now that you have asked me, I realize what my influence on you ought to be. May I tell you without your instantly criticizing me again?"

Diotima nodded silently as a sign of assent and tried to pull herself together behind an appearance of absentmindedness.

"So I said," Ulrich began, "that nobody would turn his dreams into realities even if he could. You remember our file folders full of suggestions? And now I ask you: Is there anyone who would not be embarrassed if something he had passionately demanded all his life were suddenly to come true? If, for instance, the Kingdom of God were suddenly to burst on the Catholics, or the classless society of the future on the socialists? But perhaps this doesn't prove anything. We get used to demanding things and aren't quite ready to have our wishes realized; it's only natural, many people would say. Let me go on: Music must be the most important thing in the world to a musi-cian, and painting to a painter, and probably even the building of cement houses to a cement specialist. Do you think that this will in-duce him to imagine God as a specialist in reinforced concrete and that the others will prefer a painted world, or a world blown on the bugle, to the real one? You'll call it a silly question, but what makes it serious is that we are expected to insist on just this kind of silliness!

"Now please don't think," he said, turning to her in all seriousness, "that all I mean by this is that everyone wants what is hard to get, and despises the attainable. What I mean is this: Within reality there is a senseless craving for unreality."

He had inconsiderately led Diotima a long way into the little val-ley; the snow trickling down the slopes was perhaps what made the ground wetter the higher they went, and they had to hop from one small clump of grass to the next, which punctuated their talk and forced Ulrich to go on with it by fits and starts. There were, as a re-sult, so many obvious objections to what he was saying that Diotima did not know where to begin. She had got her feet wet and stood still on a grassy mound, led astray and anxious, clutching at her skirts.

Ulrich turned back and laughed. "You've started something exceedingly dangerous, great cousin. People are vastly relieved to be left in a position where they can't put their ideas into practice."

"And what would *you* do," Diotima asked irritably, "if you could rule the world for a day?"

"I suppose I would have no choice but to abolish reality."

"I'd love to know how you'd go about it."

"I don't know either. I hardly know what I mean by it. We wildly overestimate the present, the sense of the present, the here and now; like you and me being here in this valley, as if we'd been put in a basket and the lid of the present had fallen on it. We make too much of it. We'll remember it. Even a year from now we may be able to describe how we were standing here. But what really moves us—me anyway—is always—putting it cautiously; I don't want to look for an explanation or a name for it—opposed in a sense to this way of experiencing things. It is displaced by so much here and now, so much Present. So it can't become the present in its turn."

In the narrow valley Ulrich's words sounded loud and confused. Diotima suddenly felt uneasy and moved to get back to the car. But Ulrich made her stay and look at the landscape.

"Some thousands of years ago this was a glacier," he explained. "Even the earth isn't altogether what it's pretending to be for the moment. This well-rounded character is a hysteric. Today it is acting the good middle-class mother feeding her children. Back then the world was frigid and icy, like a spiteful girl. Several thousand years before that it luxuriated in hot fern forests, sultry swamps, and demonic beasts. We can't say that it has evolved toward perfection, nor what its true condition is. And the same goes for its daughter, mankind. Imagine the clothes in which people have stood here through the ages, right where we are standing now. Expressed in terms of the madhouse, it suggests long-standing obsessions with suddenly erupting manic ideas; after these run their course, a new concept of life is there. So you see, reality does away with itself!

"There's something else I'd like to tell you"—Ulrich made a fresh start after a while. "That sense of having firm ground underfoot and a firm skin all around, which appears so natural to most people, is not very strongly developed in me. Think back to how you were as a child; all gentle glow. And then a teenager, lips burning with longing. Something in me rebels against the idea that so-called mature adulthood is the peak of such a development. In a sense it is, and in a sense it isn't. If I were a myrmeleonina, the ant predator that resembles a dragonfly, I'd be horrified to think that the year before I had been the squat gray myrmeleon, the ant lion, running backward and living at the edge of the forest, dug in at the bottom of a funnel-shaped hole in the sand, catching ants by the waist with invisible pincers after first exhausting them by somehow bombarding them with grains of sand. There are times when the thought of my youth horrifies me in quite the same way, even though I may have been a dragonfly then and may be a monster now."

He did not really know what he was aiming at. With his myrmeleon and myrmeleonina he had only been aping Arnheim's cultured omniscience a little. But he had it on the tip of his tongue to say: "Please, won't you make love to me, just to be nice? We are kindred, not wholly separate, certainly not one; in any case, the polar opposite of a dignified and formal relationship."

But Ulrich was mistaken. Diotima was the kind of person who is satisfied with herself and therefore regards each age she passes through as a step on a stairway leading upward from below. She had no way of understanding what Ulrich was talking about, especially as she did not know what he had left unsaid. But they had meanwhile returned to the car, so she felt serene again, taking in what he was saying as his usual kind of chatter, somewhere between amusing and irritating, commanding no more of her attention than at most the corner of an eye. At this moment he really had no influence whatsoever on her except that of bringing her down to earth. A filmy cloud of shyness, risen from some hidden corner of her heart, had dissipated in a dry void. For the first time, perhaps, she had a hard, clear glimpse of the fact that her relations with Arnheim would force her, sooner or later, to make a choice that could change her whole life. One could not say that she was happy about this just now, but it had the weighty presence of a real mountain range. A weak moment had passed. That "not to do what one wants to do" had had for an instant an absurd glow she no longer understood.

"Arnheim is altogether the opposite of me. He is always overestimating the happiness with which time and space rendezvous with him to form the present moment," Ulrich sighed with a smile, moved to bring what he had been saying to an orderly conclusion. But he said nothing further about childhood, so it never came to the point where Diotima would have found out that he had a tender side.

70

CLARISSE VISITS ULRICH TO
TELL HIM A STORY

Redecorating old castles was the specialty of the well-known painter van Helmond, whose masterpiece was his daughter Clarisse, and one day she unexpectedly walked in on Ulrich.

"Papa sends me," she informed him, "to find out whether you couldn't use your splendid aristocratic connections just a little for him too." She eyed the room with interest, threw herself into one chair and her hat onto another. Then she held out her hand to Ulrich.

"Your Papa overestimates me," he started to say, but she cut him short.

"Nonsense. You know perfectly well the old man always needs money. Business simply isn't what it used to be!" She laughed. "Elegant place you've got here. Nice!" She scrutinized her surroundings again and then looked at Ulrich. Her whole bearing had something of the endearing shyness of a pet dog whose bad conscience makes its skin twitch.

"Anyway, if you can do it, you will. If not, then you won't. Of course, I promised him you would. But I came for another reason. His asking me to see you put an idea into my head. It's about a certain problem in my family. I'd like to hear what you think." Her mouth and eyes hesitated and flickered for an instant; then she took her leap over the initial hurdle. "Would the term 'beauty doctor' suggest anything to you? A painter is a beauty doctor."

Ulrich understood; he knew her parents' house.

"Dark, distinguished, splendid, luxurious, upholstered, pennanted, and tasseled," she went on. "Papa is a painter, a painter is a kind of beauty doctor, and visiting our house has always been regarded as quite the thing socially, like going to the newest spa. You understand what I'm talking about. And one of Papa's main sources of income has always been decorating palaces and big country houses. Do you know the Pachhofens?"

Ulrich was not acquainted with this patrician family except for a Fräulein Pachhofen he had met once, years ago, in Clarisse's company.

"She was my friend," Clarisse said. "She was seventeen, and I was fifteen. Papa was supposed to renovate the castle and do the interiors. The Pachhofen place, of course. We were all invited. Walter too; it was the first time he came along with us. And Meingast."

"Meingast?" Ulrich did not know who Meingast was.

"But of course you know him; Meingast, who went to Switzerland later on. He wasn't yet a philosopher in those days, but a rooster in every family with daughters."

"I've never met him," Ulrich said. "But now I do know who he is."

"All right, then." Clarisse did some strenuous mental arithmetic. "Just a minute! Walter was then twenty-three and Meingast somewhat older. Walter was a great secret admirer of Papa's, and it was the first time he'd ever been invited to stay at a castle. Papa often had an air of wearing inner royal robes. I think at first Walter was more in love with Papa than with me. And Lucy—"

"Slow down, Clarisse, for heaven's sake!" Ulrich pleaded. "I seem to have lost the connection."

"Lucy," Clarisse said, "is Lucy Pachhofen, of course, the daughter of the Pachhofens with whom we were staying. Now do you understand? All right, then, you understand. Papa wrapped Lucy in velvet or brocade with a long train and posed her on one of her horses; she imagined he must be a Titian or Tintoretto. They were absolutely mad about each other."

"Papa about Lucy, and Walter about Papa?"

"Give me a chance, will you? At that time, there was Impressionism. Papa was still painting old-fashioned/musical, the way he still does today, brown gravy and peacocks' tails. But Walter was all for open air, the clean lines of English functionalism, the new and sincere. In his heart, Papa found him as insufferable as a Protestant sermon; he couldn't stand Meingast either, but he had two daughters to marry off; he had always spent more than he made, so he was long-suffering with the souls of the two young men. Walter, for his part, secretly loved Papa, as I said, but publicly he had to criticize him because of the new art movements, and Lucy never understood anything about art at all, but she was afraid of making a fool of herself in front of Walter, and she was afraid that Walter might turn out to be right, in which case Papa would only be a ridiculous old man. Do you get the picture?"

Before committing himself, Ulrich wanted to know where Mama had been.

"Mama was there too, of course. They quarreled every day as always, no more and no less. You can see that in these circumstances Walter enjoyed a favorable position. Everthing converged on Walter: Papa feared him, Mama egged him on, and I was beginning to fall in love with him. But Lucy played up to him. So Walter had a certain power over Papa, which he was beginning to savor in a cautiously lascivious way. I mean, it was then that Walter began to have a sense of his own importance; without Papa and me he would have been nothing. Do you see how it all hangs together?"

Ulrich felt it was safe to say he did.

"But I wanted to tell you something else!" Clarisse exclaimed. She took some time to think before she said: "Listen. Let's just start with me and Lucy: that was complicated in an exciting way. I was naturally worried about Papa, whose infatuation was on the point of ruining the whole family. But I was also curious about how this kind of thing happens. They were both out of their minds. Lucy's friendship for me was of course mixed up with the feeling that she had a man for a lover whom I still obediently called 'Papa.' She was more than a little proud, but at the same time it made her terribly ashamed to face me. I don't think the old castle had sheltered such complications under its roof since it was built. All day long Lucy hung around Papa whenever she could, and then at night she came to me in the tower to confess. I slept in the tower, and we had the lights on almost all night long."

"How far did Lucy actually go with your father?"

"That was the only thing I could never find out. But just think of those summer nights! The owls whimpering, the night moaning, and when it all got too spooky we both got into my bed so we could go on talking. We couldn't see how a man in the grip of so fatal a passion could do anything but shoot himself. We were really waiting for it to happen from one day to the next—"

"It strikes me," Ulrich interrupted, "that nothing much had really happened between them."

"That's what I think too—not everything. Yet things did happen. You'll see in a minute. All of a sudden, Lucy had to leave because her father arrived unexpectedly and took her off on a trip to Spain. You should have seen Papa then, when he was left on his own. I think there were times he came awfully close to strangling Mama. He was off on horseback from dawn to dusk, with a folding easel strapped behind his saddle, but he never painted a stroke, and he never touched a brush at home either. The point is, he usually paints like a robot, but in those days I'd find him sitting in one of those huge, empty rooms with a book he hadn't even opened. He would sometimes brood like this for hours, then he'd get up and do the same thing in some other room or in the garden, sometimes all day long. Well, he was an old man, and youth had left him in the lurch; it's understandable, isn't it? And I suppose the image of Lucy and me, seeing us all the time as two girlfriends with their arms around each other's waists, chatting confidentially, must have sprouted in him then—like some wild seed. Perhaps he knew that Lucy always used to join me in the tower. So one night, around eleven, all the lights in the castle were out, and there he was. That was quite something!" Clarisse was carried away with the import of her own story. "You hear this tapping and scraping on the stairs, and don't know what to make of it; then you hear the clumsy fiddling with the door handle, and the door opening spookily—"

"Why didn't you call out for help?"

"That's what was so peculiar about it. I knew from the first sound who it was. He must have stood still in the doorway, because I didn't hear anything for quite a while. He was probably frightened too. Then he slowly, carefully shut the door and whispered my name. I was absolutely stunned. I had no intention of answering him, but this weird thing happened: from somewhere deep inside me, as though I were a deep space, came a sound like a whimper. Have you ever heard of such a thing?"

"No. Go on!"

"Well, that's all; the next instant he was clutching at me with infinite despair; he almost fell on my bed, and his head was lying on the pillow beside mine."

"Tears?"

"Dry spasms. An old body, abandoned. I understood that at once. Oh, I tell you, if it were possible to tell afterward all one felt at such a moment, it would be something really enormous. I think he was beside himself with fury against the whole world of propriety, because of what it had made him miss. Suddenly I sense that he is himself again, and I know right away, although it's pitch-dark, that he's absolutely convulsed with a ruthless hunger for me. I know there is not going to be any mercy or consideration for me; there hasn't been a sound since that moan of mine; my body was blazing dry and his was like a piece of paper one sets at the edge of a fire. He became incredibly light. I felt his arm snaking down my body, away from my shoulder. And now there's something I want to ask you. It's why I came. . . ."

Clarisse broke off.

"What? You haven't asked anything!" Ulrich prompted her after a short pause.

"No. There's something else I have to say first: The idea that he must be taking my keeping so still as a sign of consent made me loathe myself. Yet I lay there, my mind a blank, petrified with fear. What do you make of that?"

"I don't know what to say."

"With one hand he kept stroking my face; the other wandered around. Trembling, pretending it wasn't up to anything, passing over my breast like a kiss, then, as if waiting, listening for some response. Then finally it moved—well, you know, and at the same time his face sought mine. But at that point I pulled myself away with all my strength and turned on my side; and again that sound came out of my chest, a sound I didn't know, something halfway between pleading and moaning. You see, I have a birthmark, a black medallion—"

"And what did your father do?" Ulrich interrupted coolly.

But Clarisse refused to be interrupted. "Right here," she said with a tense smile, pointing through her dress to a spot inward from her hip. "This is how far he got, to the medallion. This medallion has a magic power, or anyway, there's something special about it."

Suddenly the blood rushed to her face. Ulrich's silence had sobered her and dissipated the idea that had kept her under its spell. With an embarrassed smile she quickly finished:

"My father? He instantly sat up. I couldn't see what was going on in his face; embarrassment, I suppose. Maybe gratitude. After all, I had saved him at the last moment. You must understand: an old man, and a young girl has the strength to do that! He must have thought I was strange somehow, because he pressed my hand quite tenderly, and stroked my head twice with his other hand. Then he went away, without a word. So I hope you'll do what you can for him? After all, I had to tell you, so you'd understand."

Trim and correct, in a tailored dress she wore only when she came into town, she stood there, ready to leave, and held out her hand to say good-bye.

71

THE COMMITTEE TO DRAFT GUIDELINES FOR HIS MAJESTY'S SEVENTIETH JUBILEE CELEBRATION OPENS ITS FIRST SESSION

About her letter to Count Leinsdorf and her request that Ulrich save Moosbrugger, Clarisse had not said a word; she seemed to have forgotten all that. But for Ulrich, too, some time had to pass before he remembered it. For Diotima had at last come to the point in her preparations where, within the framework of the "Enquiry to Draft Guidelines and Ascertain the Wishes of All Sectors of the Population in Connection with His Majesty's Seventieth Jubilee Celebration," a meeting of the special "Committee to Draft Guidelines in Connection with His Majesty's Seventieth Jubilee Celebration" could be

called, whose leadership Diotima had personally reserved for herself. His Grace had composed the invitation himself, Tuzzi had edited it, and Arnheim had been shown Tuzzi's suggestions before it
was finally approved. In spite of all that, it contained everything that
weighed on His Grace's mind.

"What brings us together in this meeting," it read, "is our mutual
understanding that a powerful demonstration arising from the midst
of the people must not be left to chance, but calls for a farsighted
influence from a quarter commanding a broad, panoramic view, that
is, an influence from above." This was followed by "the extremely
rare occasion of this seventieth anniversary of an accession to the
throne so richly blessed," the "grateful throng of peoples," the Emperor of Peace, the lack of political maturity, the Global Year of
Austria, and finally the appeal to "Property and Culture" to fashion
all this into a glorious manifestation of the True Austrian spirit, but
only after giving it the most painstaking consideration.

From Diotima's lists, the groups for Art, Literature, and Science
were chosen and with great care and effort augmented, while, on the
other hand, of those who might be allowed to attend although not
expected to take an active part, only a very small number had remained after the most thorough sifting. But the number of invited
guests was still so large that there could be no question of a regular
sit-down dinner at the green baize table; the only alternative was an
informal evening reception with a cold buffet. The guests sat or stood
however it could be arranged, and Diotima's rooms resembled the
encampment of a spiritual army, supplied with sandwiches, pastries,
wines, liqueurs, and tea in such quantities as could only have been
made possible by special budgeting concessions Tuzzi granted to his
wife—with, it must be added, not a word of protest, from which it
may be inferred that he proposed to make use of new, intellectual
methods of diplomacy.

The handling of such a throng made great demands on Diotima as
a hostess, and she might perhaps have taken exception to many
things had her head not resembled a superb fruit bowl with words
constantly falling over the edge of its superabundance; words with
which the lady of the house welcomed each arriving guest, enchanting him with detailed knowledge of his latest work. Her preparations
for this had been extraordinary and could only have been accom-

plished with Arnheim's help; he had placed his private secretary at her disposal to arrange the material and make extracts of the most important texts. The splendid slag left behind by this volcanic endeavor was a large library bought with funds Count Leinsdorf had provided to start the Parallel Campaign, and together with Diotima's own books they had been set up as the only decoration in the last of the emptied rooms. The flowered wallpaper, or what could still be seen of it, betrayed the boudoir, a stimulus to flattering reflections about its occupant. This library turned out to have other advantages as well: every one of the invitees, after having been graciously greeted by Diotima, wandered aimlessly through the rooms and was drawn without fail to the wall of books at the far end as soon as he caught sight of it. A cluster of scrutinizing backs constantly rose and sank before it, like bees in front of a flowering hedge, and even if the cause was only the noble curiosity every creative person feels for book collections, delicious contentment seeped into the marrow of his bones when the viewer finally discovered his own works, and the patriotic campaign benefited from it.

Diotima at first allowed the assembly to drift, intellectually, at its own sweet will, though she made a point of assuring the poets in particular that all life, even the world of business, rested on an inner poetry if one "regarded it magnanimously." This surprised no one, but it turned out that most of those singled out for such confidences had come on the assumption that they were expected to launch the Parallel Campaign with some brief words of advice—somewhere between five and forty-five minutes' worth—which, if heeded, would guarantee its success, even if subsequent speakers squandered time with pointless and misguided suggestions. This almost drove Diotima to tears at first, and it was only with great effort that she kept her unruffled look, for she realized that each one of them was saying something different and she would never be able to pull it all together. She was still inexperienced in coping with such high concentrations of superior minds, and since so universal a gathering of great men would not come about again so easily, it could only be assimilated laboriously and methodically, step by step. There are many things in the world, incidentally, that taken singly mean something quite different to people from what they mean in the mass. Water, for instance, is less of a pleasure in excessive than in small doses, by exactly the difference between drowning and drinking, and the same can be said of poisons, amusements, leisure, piano playing, ideals, indeed probably everything, so that what something is depends on its degree of density and other circumstances. It is only necessary to add that even genius is no exception, lest the following impressions appear to suggest some sort of denigration of the eminent personages who had placed themselves so selflessly at Diotima's disposal.

For even at this first gathering one could receive the impression that every great mind feels extremely insecure as soon as it leaves the refuge of its treetop aerie and has to make itself understood on common ground. The extraordinary language that passed over Diotima's head like some movement in the skies as long as she conversed alone with one of the powerful turned, as soon as they were joined by a third or a fourth person and several lines of discourse got entangled in contradiction, into a distressing inability to arrive at any kind of order. Whoever does not shrink from such similes might try to visualize a swan that, after its proud flight, waddles along on the ground. But on longer acquaintance this, too, becomes quite understandable. The lives of great minds today are founded on a certain "no one knows what for." They enjoy great veneration, expressed on their fiftieth to their hundredth birthdays, or on the tenth anniversary of some agricultural college that garlands itself with honorary doctorates, or on various other occasions when speeches must be made about the country's cultural treasures. We have a history of great men, and we regard it as an institution that belongs to us, just like prisons or the army; having it means we have to have people to put into it. And so, with a certain automatism inherent in such social needs, we always pick the next in line and shower him with the honors ripe to be handed out. But this veneration is not quite sincere; at its base lies the gaping, generally accepted conviction that there is really not a single person who deserves it, and it is hard to tell whether the mouth opens to acclaim someone or to yawn. To call a man a genius nowadays, with the unspoken gloss that there is really no longer any such thing, smacks of some cult of the dead, something like hysterical love making a great to-do for no other reason than that there is no real feeling present.

For sensitive people this is of course not a pleasant situation, and they try to get rid of it in various ways. Some are driven in their despair to get rich by learning to exploit the demand not only for great minds but also for wild men, profound novelists, puffed-up lovers, and leaders of the new generation; others wear an invisible royal crown on their heads that they will not remove under any circumstances, prepared with embittered modesty not to expect the value of their creation to be seen in its true light before two to ten centuries have passed. They all feel that it is a terrible tragedy for the nation that its truly great men can never become a part of its living culture because they are too far ahead of it.

It must be emphasized, however, that the minds under consideration so far have been those of an aesthetic bent, since there is a considerable difference in the ways the mind relates to the world. While the aesthetic mind wants the same sort of admiration accorded to Goethe and Michelangelo, Napoleon and Luther, hardly anyone today knows the name of the man who gave humanity the untold blessing of anesthesia; nobody searches the lives of Gauss, Euler, or Maxwell for an Immortal Beloved, and hardly anyone cares where Lavoisier and Cardanus were born and died. Instead, we learn how their ideas and inventions were further developed by the ideas and inventions of other, equally uninteresting people, and continually concentrate on their achievements, which live on through others long after the brief flame of the individual has burned out. One is amazed at first to see how sharp the distinction is between two kinds of human endeavor, but soon enough counterexamples come to mind, and it begins to look like the most natural of differentiations. Familiar custom assures us it is the difference between person and work, between the greatness of a human being and that of a cause, between culture and knowledge, humanity and nature. Work and outstanding productivity do not increase moral stature, nor being a man in the eyes of heaven, nor those unanalyzable lessons of life that are handed down only by the example of statesmen, heroes, saints, singers, and, one must admit, movie actors—in short, that great irrational power in which the poet, too, feels he has a part, as long as he believes in what he says and holds fast to his belief that whatever his circumstances, his voice is the voice of the inner life, the blood, the heart, the nation, Europe, or all mankind. It is the mysterious whole of which he feels himself to be the medium, while the others are merely rummaging around in the comprehensible—and this is a mission one must believe in before one can learn to see it! What assures us of this is a voice of truth, certainly, but isn't there something odd about this truth? For where one looks less at the person than at the cause, there is, remarkably, always a fresh person to carry on the cause, while on the other hand, wherever the emphasis is on the person, there is always the feeling after a certain level has been reached that there is no longer anyone who measures up anymore, and that true greatness lies in the past.

Each and every one of the men gathered at Diotima's that night was a vessel of the whole, and that was a lot all at once. Writing and thinking, activities as natural to man as swimming is to a duckling, was something they practiced as a profession, and they were, in fact, really better at it than most. But what was it all for? What they did was beautiful, it was great, it was unique, but so much uniqueness bore the collective breath of mortality and the graveyard, having no evident meaning or purpose, ancestors or progeny. Countless remembered experiences, myriads of crisscrossing vibrations of the spirit, were gathered in these heads, which were stuck like a carpet weaver's needles in a carpet extending without seams or edges all around them in every direction and somewhere, at some random place, creating a pattern that seemed to repeat itself elsewhere but was actually a little different. But is this the proper use of oneself, to set such a little patch on eternity?

It would probably be saying far too much to say that Diotima had grasped all this, but she felt the wind of the grave over the fields of the spirit, and the nearer this first day drew to its close, the deeper she slipped into discouragement. Luckily, it brought to her mind a certain hopelessness Arnheim had expressed on another occasion, when they had spoken of such things, though at the time she had not quite grasped his meaning; now her friend was away on a trip, but she remembered how he had warned her not to place too great hopes in this gathering. So it was actually Arnheim's melancholy into which she was drifting, which made it ultimately an almost sensuously pensive and flattering pleasure. Musing on his prophetic words, she wondered: "Isn't it, deep down, the pessimism people of action are always bound to feel when they come in contact with those who traffic in words?"

72

SCIENCE SMILING INTO ITS BEARD, OR A FIRST FULL-DRESS ENCOUNTER WITH EVIL

Now for a few necessary words about a smile, specifically a man's smile, and about a beard, created for the male act of smiling into one's beard; the smile of the scholars who had accepted Diotima's invitation and were listening to the famous artists. Although they were smiling, they were absolutely not to be suspected of doing so ironically. On the contrary, it was their way of expressing deference and incompetence, as has already been explained. But this, too, should fool no one. They were sincere in this, consciously; but subconsciously, to use a fashionable term, or, better still, in the sum of their being, they were people in whom a propensity for Evil crackled like a fire under a caldron.

This has a paradoxical ring, of course, and any of our university professors in whose presence one attempted to assert it would probably counter that he was a humble servant of truth and progress and otherwise knew nothing about anything. That is his professional ideology. But high-mindedness is the mark of every professional ideology. Hunters, for instance, would never dream of calling themselves the butchers of wild game; they prefer to call themselves the duly licensed friends of nature and animals; just as businessmen uphold the principle of an honorable profit, while the businessman's god, Mercury, that distinguished promoter of international relations, is also the god of thieves. So the image of a profession in the minds of its practitioners is not too reliable.

If we ask ourselves dispassionately how science has arrived at its present state—an important question in itself, considering how entirely we are in its power and how not even an illiterate is safe from its domination, since he has to learn to live with countless things born of science—we get a different picture. Credible received wisdom indicates that it all began in the sixteenth century, a time of the greatest spiritual turbulence, when people ceased trying to penetrate the deep mysteries of nature as they had done through two millennia of religious and philosophical speculation, but were instead satisfied with exploring the surface of nature in a manner that can only be called superficial. For instance the great Galileo Galilei, always the first to be mentioned in this connection, eliminated the question of what were nature's deep intrinsic reasons for abhorring a vacuum and consequently letting a falling body penetrate space after space until it finally comes to rest on solid ground, and settled for something more common: he simply established how quickly such a body falls, the course it takes, the time it takes, and what is its rate of downward acceleration. The Catholic Church made a grave error in threatening this man with death and forcing him to recant instead of summarily executing him without much ceremony, since it was from his way of looking at things, and that of others of like mind, that afterward—in next to no time, in the scale of history—there arose railway timetables, industrial machines, physiological psychology, and our era's moral decay against which the Church no longer stands a chance. The Church probably erred in being overprudent, because Galileo was not only the discoverer of the law of falling bodies and the motion of the earth, but also an inventor in whom, as we would say today, major capital took an interest; besides, he was not the only one in his time who was seized by the new spirit. On the contrary, historical accounts show that the matter-of-factness that inspired him raged and spread like an infection. However disconcerting it may sound nowadays to speak of someone as inspired by matter-of-factness, believing as we do that we have far too much of it, in Galileo's day the awakening from metaphysics to the hard observation of reality must have been, judging by all sorts of evidence, a veritable orgy and conflagration of matter-of-factness! But should one ask what mankind was thinking of when it made this change, the answer is that it did no more than what every sensible child does after trying to walk too soon; it sat down on the ground, contacting the earth with a most dependable if not very noble part of its anatomy, in short, that part on which one sits. The amazing thing is that the earth showed itself to be uncommonly receptive, and ever since that moment of contact has allowed men to entice inventions, conveniences, and discoveries out of it in quantities bordering on the miraculous.

Such preliminaries might lead one to think, with some justice, that it is the miracle of the Antichrist we now find ourselves in the midst of; for the metaphor of "contact" used here is to be interpreted not only in the sense of dependability, but also just as much in the sense of the unseemly and disreputable And in truth, before intellectuals discovered their pleasure in "facts," facts were the sole preserve of soldiers, hunters, and traders—people by nature full of violence and cunning. The struggle for existence makes no allowance for sentimental considerations; it knows only the desire to kill one's opponent in the quickest, most factual way; here everyone is a positivist. Nor is it a virtue in business to let oneself be taken in instead of going for the solid facts, since a profit is ultimately a psychological overpowering of your opponent arising from the circumstances. If, on the other hand, one looks at the qualities that lead to the making of discoveries, one finds freedom from traditional considerations and inhibitions, courage, as much initiative as ruthlessness, the exclusion of moral considerations, patience in haggling for the smallest advantage, dogged endurance on the way to the goal, if necessary, and a veneration for measure and number that expresses the keenest mistrust of all uncertainty. In other words, we find just those ancient vices of soldiers, hunters, and traders, here merely translated into intellectual terms and interpreted as virtues. This raises them above the pursuit of personal and relatively vulgar advantage, but even in this transformation the element of primal evil is not lost; it is seemingly indestructible and everlasting, at least as everlasting as everything humanly sublime, since it consists of nothing less and nothing else than the urge to trip up that sublimity and watch it fall on its face. Who has never felt a nasty itch, looking at a beautifully glazed, luxuriantly curved vase, at the thought of smashing it to bits with a single blow of one's stick? This temptation, raised to its full heroic bitterness—that nothing in life can be relied on unless it is firmly nailed down—is a basic feeling embedded in the sobriety of science; and though we are too respectable to call it the Devil, a whiff of burned horsehair still clings to it.

We can begin at once with the peculiar predilection of scientific thinking for mechanical, statistical, and physical explanations that have, as it were, the heart cut out of them. The scientific mind sees kindness only as a special form of egotism; brings emotions into line with glandular secretions; notes that eight or nine tenths of a human being consists of water; explains our celebrated moral freedom as an automatic mental by-product of free trade; reduces beauty to good digestion and the proper distribution of fatty tissue; graphs the annual statistical curves of births and suicides to show that our most intimate personal decisions are programmed behavior; sees a connection between ecstasy and mental disease; equates the anus and the mouth as the rectal and the oral openings at either end of the same tube—such ideas, which expose the trick, as it were, behind the magic of human illusions, can always count on a kind of prejudice in their favor as being impeccably scientific. Certainly they demonstrate the love of truth. But surrounding this clear, shining love is a predilection for disillusionment, compulsiveness, ruthlessness, cold intimidation, and dry rebuke, a spiteful predilection, or at least an involuntary emanation of such a kind.

To put it differently, the voice of truth is accompanied by a suspicious static noise to which those most closely involved turn a deaf ear. Well, contemporary psychology knows many such repressed phenomena and is ready with advice to haul them out and make them as clear as possible to oneself, to prevent their having harmful effects. How about putting it to the test, then, and trying to make an open display of that ambiguous taste for the truth, with its malicious undertones of human spitefulness, its hound-of-hell attitude, letting it take its chances in life, as it were? What might come of this is, more or less, that lack of idealism already discussed under the heading of a utopia of exact living, an attitude of experiment and revocation, but subject to the iron laws of warfare involved in all intellectual conquests. This approach to shaping life is of course in no way nurturing or appeasing. It would regard everything worthy of life not with simple veneration but rather as a line of demarcation being constantly redrawn in the battle for inner truth. It would question the sanctity of the world's momentary condition, not from skepticism but rather in the conviction of the climber that the foot with the firmer hold is always the lower one. In the fire of such a Church Militant, which hates doctrine for the sake of revelation yet to come and sets aside law and values in the name of an exacting love for their imminent new configurations, the Devil would find his way back to God or, more simply, truth would again be the sister of virtue and would no

longer have to play tricks on goodness behind its back, like a young
niece with an old maiden aunt.

All that sort of thing is absorbed more or less consciously by a
young man in the lecture halls of learning, along with the basics of a
great, constructive way of thinking capable of bringing together with
ease such disparate phenomena as a falling stone and an orbiting
star, and of analyzing something as seemingly whole and indivisible
as the origin of a simple act within the depths of consciousness into
currents whose inner sources lie thousands of years apart. But should
anyone presume to use such an approach outside the limits of specific professional problems, he would quickly be given to understand
that the needs of life are different from the requirements of thought.
What happens in life is more or less the opposite of whatever the
trained mind is accustomed to. Life places a very high value on natural distinctions and congenialities; whatever exists, no matter what it
is, is regarded up to a point as the natural thing, and not to be lightly
tampered with; changes that become necessary proceed reluctantly
and in a kind of two-steps-forward, one-step-back rhythm. If someone of purely vegetarian convictions, say, were to address a cow as
"Ma'am"—on the perfectly reasonable assumption that one is likely
to behave more brutally toward someone addressed with "Hey
there!"—he would be called a conceited ass or even a crackpot, but
not because of his vegetarian convictions or his respect for animals,
which are regarded as most humane, but because he was acting them
out directly in the real world. In short, what we think and what we do
coexist in an intricate compromise whereby the claims of the intellect are paid off at the rate of no more than 50 percent of every thousand, while to make up for the rest it is adorned with the title of
honorary creditor.

But if the human mind, in the imposing shape that is its most recent manifestation, is indeed, as we have suggested, a very masculine
saint with warlike and hunterlike ancillary vices, one might conclude
from the circumstances described above that the mind's inherent
tendency toward depravity, grandiose as it is, can neither reveal itself
nor find any occasion to purge itself through contact with reality,
with the result that it is likely to turn up on all sorts of quite strange,
unsupervised paths by which it evades its sterile captivity. Whether

everything up to this point has been merely a play of conceits is an open question, but there is no denying that this last surmise has its own peculiar confirmation. There is a nameless mood abroad in the world today, a feeling in the blood of more than a few people, an expectation of worse things to come, a readiness to riot, a mistrust of everything one reveres. There are those who deplore the lack of idealism in the young but who, the moment they must act themselves, automatically behave no differently from someone with a healthy mistrust of ideas who backs up his gentle persuasiveness with the effect of some kind of blackjack. Is there, in other words, any pious intent that does not have to equip itself with a little bit of corruption and reliance on the lower human qualities in order to be taken in this world as serious and seriously meant? Terms like "bind," "force," "put the screws on," "don't be afraid to smash windows," "take strong measures," all have the pleasant ring of dependability. Propositions of the kind that the greatest philosopher, after a week in barracks, will learn to spring to attention at the drill sergeant's voice, or that a lieutenant and eight men are enough to arrest any parliament in the world, achieved their classic form only somewhat later, in the discovery that a few spoonfuls of castor oil poured down the throat of an idealist can make the sternest convictions look ridiculous; but long before that, and although they were disclaimed with indignation, such ideas had the savage buoyancy of sinister dreams.

It just so happens that the second thought, at the very least, of every person today confronted by an overwhelming phenomenon, even if it should be its beauty that so overwhelms him, is "You can't fool me! I'll cut you down to size!" And this mania for cutting things down to size, typical of an era that not only flees with the fox but also pursues with the hounds, has hardly anything to do any longer with life's natural separation of the raw from the sublime; it is, rather, much more a self-tormenting bent of mind, an inadmissible lust at the spectacle of the good being humiliated and too easily destroyed altogether. It is not dissimilar from some passionate desire to give the lie to oneself, and perhaps there are bleaker prospects than believing in a time that has come into the world coccyx-first and merely needs the Creator's hands to turn it around.

Much of this sort of thing may be expressed by a man's smile, even when the man is not himself aware of it or it has never even gone through his consciousness at all, and this was the sort of smile with which most of the invited celebrated experts lent themselves to Diotima's praiseworthy efforts. It began as a prickling sensation moving up the legs, which did not quite know in which direction they should turn, and finally landed as a look of benevolent amazement on the face. With relief one spotted an acquaintance or a colleague one could speak to. One had the feeling that going home, outside the gate, one would have to stamp firmly a few times to test the ground. Still, it was a very pleasant occasion. Such general undertakings never find a proper content, of course, like all universal and elevated concepts. One cannot even imagine the concept "dog"; the word is only a reference to particular dogs and canine qualities, and this is even more the case with "patriotism" or the loftiest patriotic ideas. But even if it has no content, it certainly has a meaning, and it is surely desirable from time to time to bring that meaning to life! This was what most of those present were communicating to one another, although mostly within the silence of the unconscious. But Diotima, still standing in the main reception room and favoring stragglers with her little speeches of welcome, was astonished to hear what appeared to be lively conversations starting up on such subjects as the difference between Bohemian and Bavarian beer, or publishers' royalties.

It was too bad that she could not watch her reception from the street. From out there it looked marvelous. The light shone brightly through the curtains of the tall windows along the façade of the house, heightened by the additional glow of authority and distinction emanating from the waiting cars, as well as by the gaping passersby who stopped to look up for a while without quite knowing why. Diotima would have been pleased by the sight. There were people constantly standing in the half-light the festivity cast on the street; behind their backs, the great darkness began that within a short distance quickly became impenetrable.

73

LEO FISCHEL'S DAUGHTER GERDA

In all this hubbub, Ulrich kept putting off fulfilling his promise to Fischel that he would pay the family a visit. He actually never did get around to it until something unexpected happened: Fischel's wife, Clementine, came to see him.

She had phoned to announce her visit, and Ulrich awaited her not without apprehension. It had been three years since he had regularly come to their house, during a stay of some months in town; since his return he had been there only once, not wanting to stir up a past flirtation and dreading having to deal with a mother's disappointment. But Clementine Fischel was a woman of "magnanimous spirit," with so little opportunity to exercise it in her daily petty struggles with her husband, Leo, that for special occasions, regrettably so rare in her life, she had reserves of truly heroic high-mindedness to draw upon. Even so, this thin woman with her austere, rather careworn face felt a bit embarrassed when she found herself face-to-face with Ulrich, saying she needed to speak to him privately, even though they were alone as it was. But he was the only person Gerda would still listen to, she said, adding that she hoped he would not misunderstand her request.

Ulrich was aware of the Fischel family's situation. Not only were the father and mother constantly at war, but their daughter, Gerda, already twenty-three, had surrounded herself with a swarm of odd young people who had somehow co-opted Papa Leo, who ground his teeth, as a most grudging Maecenas and backer of their "new movement" because his house was the most convenient for their get-togethers. Gerda was so nervous and anemic, and got so terribly upset every time anyone tried to make her see less of these friends— Clementine reported—who were, after all, just silly boys without real breeding; still, the way they insisted on parading their mystical anti-Semitism was not only in poor taste, it revealed an inner brutality. Not that she had come to complain about anti-Semitism, she added, which was a sign of the times, one simply had to resign oneself to it—she was even prepared to admit that in some respects there might be something in it. Clementine paused and would have dried a tear with her handkerchief had she not worn a veil; but as it was she refrained from dropping the tear, contenting herself with merely pulling her white handkerchief out of her little handbag.

"You know what Gerda's like," she said, "a beautiful and gifted girl but—"

"A bit rebellious." Ulrich finished it for her.

"Yes, Heaven help us, always going to extremes."

"So she's still a German Nationalist?"

Clementine spoke of the parents' feelings. "A mother's errand of mercy" was what she somewhat pathetically called her visit, which had as its secondary aim to entice Ulrich back as a regular visitor to their family circle, now that he was known to have risen to such eminence in the Parallel Campaign. "I hate myself," she went on, "for the way I encouraged Gerda's friendship with these boys in recent years, against Leo's will. I thought nothing of it; these youngsters are idealists in their way, and an open-minded person can let the occasional offensive word pass. . . . But Leo—you know how he is—is upset by anti-Semitism, whether it's merely mystical or symbolic or not."

"And Gerda, in her free-spirited, Germanic, blond fashion, won't recognize the problem?" Ulrich rounded it out.

"She's the same as I was at her age in this respect. Do you think, by the way, that Hans Sepp has any prospects?"

"Is Gerda engaged to him?" Ulrich asked cautiously.

"That boy has no means whatever of providing for her," Clementine sighed. "How can you talk of an engagement? But when Leo ordered him out of the house Gerda ate so little for three weeks running that she turned to skin and bone." All at once, she broke out angrily: "You know, it seems to me like hypnosis, like some sort of spiritual infection! That boy incessantly expounds his philosophy under our roof, and Gerda never notices the continual insult to her parents in it, even though she's always been a good and affectionate child otherwise. But whenever I say anything, she answers: 'You're so old-fashioned, Mama.' So I thought—you're the only man who counts for something with her, and Leo thinks the world of you!—couldn't you come over and try to open Gerda's eyes to the callowness of Hans and his cronies?'"

For such a model of propriety as Clementine to resort to so aggressive a tactic could only mean that she was seriously worried. Whatever their conflicts, she was inclined to a certain solidarity with her husband in this situation. Ulrich raised his eyebrows in concern.

"I'm afraid Gerda will call me old-fashioned too. These new young people pay no attention to us elders on such matters of principle."

"It occurred to me that the easiest way to distract Gerda might be your finding something for her to do in that patriotic campaign of yours everyone is talking about," Clementine offered, and Ulrich hastened to promise her a visit, even while assuring her that the Parallel Campaign was far from being ready for such uses.

When Gerda saw him coming through the door a few days afterward, two circular red spots appeared on her cheeks, but she energetically shook his hand. She was one of those charmingly purposeful young women of our time who would instantly become bus drivers if some higher purpose called for it.

Ulrich had not been mistaken in the assumption that he would find her alone; it was the hour when Mama was out shopping and Papa was still at the office. Ulrich had hardly taken his first steps into the room when he was overcome with a sense of déjà vu, everything so reminded him of a particular day during their earlier times together. It had been a few weeks later in the year then, still spring but one of those piercingly hot days that sometimes precede the summer like burning embers, hard for the still unseasoned body to bear. Gerda's face had looked haggard and thin. She was dressed in white and smelled white, like linen dried on meadow grass. The blinds were down in all the rooms, and the whole apartment was full of rebellious half-lights and arrows of heat whose points were broken off from piercing through the sack-gray barrier. Ulrich felt that Gerda's body was made up entirely of the same freshly washed linen hangings as her dress. He felt this quite without emotion and could have calmly peeled layer after layer off her, without needing the least erotic stimulus to egg him on. He had the very same feeling again this time. Theirs seemed to be a perfectly natural but pointless intimacy, and they both feared it.

"Why did it take you so long to come see us?" Gerda asked.

Ulrich told her straight out that her parents would surely not wish them to be so close unless they intended to marry.

"Oh, Mama," Gerda said. "Mama's absurd. So we're not supposed to be friends if we don't instantly think about that! But Papa wants you to come often; you're said to be quite somebody in that big affair."

She came out with this quite openly, this foolishness of the old folk, secure in her assumption that she and Ulrich were naturally in league against it.

"I'll come," Ulrich replied, "but now tell me, Gerda, where does that leave us?"

The point was, they did not love each other. They had played a lot of tennis together, met at social functions, gone out together, taken an interest in each other, and thus unawares had crossed the borderline that separates an intimate friend whom we allow to see us in all our inward disorder from those for whom we cultivate our appearance. They had unexpectedly become as close as two people who have loved each other for a long time, who in fact almost no longer love each other, without actually going through love. They were always arguing, so it looked as if they did not care for each other, but it was both an obstacle and a bond between them. They knew that with all this it would only take one spark to start a big fire. Had there been less of a difference in their ages, or had Gerda been a married woman, then "opportunity would probably have created the thief," and the theft might have led, at least afterward, to passion, since we talk ourselves into love as we talk ourselves into a rage, by making the proper gestures. But just because they knew all this, they did not do it. Gerda had remained a virgin, and furiously resented it.

Instead of answering Ulrich's question, she had busied herself about the room, when suddenly he stood beside her. That was reckless of him, because one can't stand so close to a girl at such a moment and just start talking about something. They followed the path of least resistance, like a brook that, avoiding obstacles, flows down a meadow, and Ulrich put his arm around Gerda's hip so that his fingertips reached the precipitate downward line of the inside elastic that follows from garter belt to stocking. He turned up Gerda's face, with its confused and slightly sweaty look, and kissed her on the lips. Then they stood still, unable to let go or come together. His finger-tips connected with the broad elastic of her garter belt and let it snap gently against her thigh a few times. Then he tore himself away and with a shrug asked her again:

"Where do we go from here, Gerda?"

Gerda fought down her excitement and said: "Is this how it has to be?"

She rang for refreshments; she set the household in motion.

"Tell me something about Hans," Ulrich asked her gently, when they had sat down and had to begin the conversation again. Gerda, who had not quite regained her poise, did not answer at first, but after a while she said: "You're so pleased with yourself, you'll never understand younger people like us."

"Sticks and stones . . . ," Ulrich said evasively. "I think, Gerda, that I'm done with science now. Which means that I am making common cause with the younger generation. Is it enough to swear to you that knowledge is akin to greed? That it is a shabby form of thriftiness? A supercilious kind of spiritual capitalism? There is more feeling in me than you think. But I want to spare you the kind of talk that amounts to nothing but words."

"You must get to know Hans better," Gerda replied weakly, then she erupted again: "Anyway, you'd never understand that it's possi-ble to fuse with others into a community, without any thought of yourself!"

"Does Hans still come so often?" Ulrich asked warily. Gerda shrugged her shoulders.

Her shrewd parents had refrained from forbidding Hans Sepp the house altogether; he was allowed to come a few days every month. In turn Hans Sepp, the student who was nothing and had as yet no pros-pect of becoming something, had to promise not to make Gerda do anything she shouldn't, and to suspend his propagandizing for some mystical, Germanic action. In this way they hoped to rob him of the charm of forbidden fruit. And Hans Sepp in his chastity (only the sensual man wants to possess, but then sensuality is a Jewish-capital-istic trait) had calmly given his word as requested, without, however, taking it to mean that he would give up his frequent secret comings and goings, making incendiary speeches, hotly pressing Gerda's hands or even kissing her, all of which still comes naturally to soul-mates, but only that he would refrain from advocating sexual union without benefit of clergy or civic authority, which he had been ad-vocating, but on a purely theoretical plane. He had pledged his word all the more readily as he did not feel that he and Gerda were spiritu-ally mature enough as yet to turn his principles into action; setting up a barrier to the temptations of the baser instincts was quite in line with his way of thinking.

But the two young people naturally suffered under these restraints imposed on them before they had found their own inner discipline. Gerda especially would not have put up with such interference from her parents, had it not been for her own uncertainties; this made her resentment all the greater. She did not really love her young friend all that much; it was more a matter of translating her opposition to her parents into an attachment to him. Had Gerda been born some years later than she was, her papa would have been one of the richest men in town, even if not too highly regarded as a result, and her mother would have admired him again, before Gerda could have been of an age to experience the bickerings of her progenitors as a conflict within herself. She would then probably have taken pride in being of "racially mixed" parentage; but as things stood, she rebelled against her parents and their problems, did not want to be genetically tainted by them, and was blond, free, Germanic, and forceful, as if she had nothing at all to do with them. This solution, as good as it looked, had the disadvantage that she had never got around to bring-ing the worm that was gnawing at her inwardly out into the light of day. In her home, nationalism and racism were treated as nonexis-tent, even though they were convulsing half of Europe with hysteri-cal ideas and everything in the Fischel household in particular turned on nothing else. Whatever Gerda knew of it had come to her from the outside, in the dark form of rumors, suggestion, and exag-geration. The paradox of her parents—who normally reacted strongly to anything talked about by many people—making so nota-ble an exception in this case had made a deep impression early in her life, and since she attached no definite, objective meaning to this ghostly presence, she tended to connect with it everything disagree-able and peculiar in her home life, especially during her adolescence.

One day she met the Christian-Germanic circle of young people to which Hans Sepp belonged, and suddenly felt she had found her true home. It would be hard to say what these young people actually believed in; they formed one of those innumerable undefined "free-spirited" little sects that have infested German youth ever since the breakdown of the humanistic ideal. They were not racial anti-Semites but opponents of "the Jewish mind," by which they meant capitalism and socialism, science, reason, parental authority and parental arrogance, calculation, psychology, and skepticism. Their basic doctrinal device was the "symbol"; as far as Ulrich could make out, and he had, after all, some understanding of such things, what they meant by "symbol" was the great images of grace, which made everything that is confused and dwarfed in life, as Hans Sepp put it, clear and great, images that suppress the noise of the senses and dip the forehead in streams of transcendence. Such symbols were the Isenheim Altar, the Egyptian pyramids, and Novalis; Beethoven and Stefan George were acceptable approximations. But they did not state, in so many words, what a symbol was: first, because a symbol cannot be expressed in so many words; second, because Aryans do not deal in dry formulas, which is why they achieved only approximations of symbols during the last century; and third, because some centuries only rarely produce the transcendent moment of grace in the transcendent human being.

Gerda, who was no fool, secretly felt not a little distrust toward these overblown sentiments, but she also distrusted her distrust, in which she thought she detected the legacy of her parents' rationalism. Behind her façade of independence she was anxiously at pains to disobey her parents, in dread that her bloodlines might hinder her from following Hans's ideas. She felt deeply mutinous against the taboos girding the morals of her so-called good family and against the arrogant parental rights of intrusion that threatened to suffocate her personality, while Hans, who had "no family at all," as her mother put it, suffered much less than she did; he had emerged from her circle of companions as Gerda's "spiritual guide," passionately harangued the girl, who was as old as he was, trying to transport her, with his tirades accompanied by kisses, into the "region of the Unconditional," though in practice he was quite adept at coming to terms with the conditioned state of the Fischel household, as long as he was permitted to reject it "on principle," which of course always led to rows with Papa Leo.

"My dear Gerda," Ulrich said after a while, "your friends torment you about your father—they really are the worst kind of blackmailers!"

Gerda turned pale, then red. "You are no longer young yourself," she replied. "You think differently from us." She knew that she had stung Ulrich's vanity, and added in a conciliatory tone: "I don't expect much from love anyway. Maybe I am wasting my time with Hans, as you say; maybe I have to resign myself altogether to the idea that I'll never love anyone enough to open every crevice of my soul to him: my thoughts and feelings, work and dreams; I don't even think that would be so very awful."

"How wise beyond your years you sound, Gerda, when you talk like your friends," Ulrich broke in.

Gerda was annoyed. "When I talk with my friends," she said, "our thoughts flow from one to the other, and we know that we live and speak as one with our people—do you have any idea what this means? We stand with countless others of our own kind, we feel their presence, in a sensory, physical way I'm sure you've never . . . In fact, you can't even imagine such a thing, can you? Your desire has always been for a *single* person; you think like a beast of prey!"

Why a beast of prey? Her words hung in midair, giving her away; she realized their senselessness and felt ashamed of her eyes, wide with fear, which were staring at Ulrich.

"Let's not go into that," Ulrich said gently. "Let me tell you a story instead. Do you know"—he drew her closer with his hand, inside which her wrist disappeared like a child among high crags—"the sensational story of the capture of the moon? You know, of course, that long ago our earth had several moons. And there's a very popular theory that such moons are not what we take them for, cosmic bodies that have cooled like the earth itself, but great globes of ice rushing through space that have come too close to the earth and are held fast by it. Our moon is said to be the last of them. Come and have a look at it!"

Gerda had followed him to the window and looked for the pale moon in the sunny sky.

"Doesn't it look like a disk of ice?" Ulrich asked. "That's no source of light. Have you ever wondered why the man in the moon always faces us the same way? Our last moon is no longer turning on its axis, that's why; it's already fixed in place! You see, once the moon has come into the earth's power it doesn't merely revolve around the earth but is drawn steadily closer. We don't notice it because it takes thousands of years or even longer for the screw to tighten. But there's no getting away from it, and there must have been thousands of years in the history of the earth during which the previous moons were drawn very close and went on racing in orbit with incredible speed. And just as our present moon pulls a tide from three to six feet high after it, an earlier one would have dragged in its wake whole mountain ranges of water and mud, tumbling all over the globe. We can hardly imagine the terror in which generation after generation must have lived on such a crazy earth for thousands upon thousands of years."

"But were there human beings on earth already?" Gerda asked.

"Certainly. In the end, such an ice moon cracks up, comes crashing down like giant hailstones, and the mountainous flood it has been dragging along in its orbit collapses and covers the whole globe with one vast tidal wave before it settles down again: That's none other than the great biblical Flood, meaning a great universal inundation! How else could all the myths be in such agreement, if mankind hadn't experienced it all? And since we have one moon left, such ages are bound to come once more. It's a strange thought. . . ."

Gerda gazed breathlessly out of the window and up at the moon; her hand was still resting in his, the moon was a pale, ugly stain on the sky, and it was precisely this unassuming presence that made this fantastic cosmic adventure—of which she somehow saw herself as the victim—look like an ordinary, everyday reality.

"But there's no truth at all to this story," Ulrich said. "The experts call it a crackpot theory, and the moon isn't really coming any closer to the earth; it is, in fact, thirty-two kilometers farther from us than it should be, according to our calculations, if I remember it right."

"Then why did you tell me this story?" Gerda asked, and tried to extricate her hand from his. But her defiance had quite run out of steam, as it always did when she spoke with this man, who was certainly not Hans's intellectual inferior and yet managed to keep from going to extremes in his views, to keep his fingernails clean and his

hair combed. Ulrich noticed the fine black down growing like a contradiction on Gerda's fair skin; the tiny hairs sprouting from her body
seemed to bespeak the variously composite nature of poor modern
mankind.

"I don't really know," he replied. "Shall I come and see you
again?"

Gerda took out the excitement of her liberated hand on various
small objects, which she pushed this way and that, without saying
anything.

"See you soon, then," Ulrich promised, although this had not been
his intention before he came.

74

THE FOURTH CENTURY B.C. VERSUS THE YEAR 1797. ULRICH RECEIVES ANOTHER LETTER FROM HIS FATHER

The rumor had quickly spread that the meetings at Diotima's were
an extraordinary success. And now Ulrich received an unusually long
letter from his father, stuffed with enclosed pamphlets and offprints.
The letter read more or less like this:

My dear son:
Your extended silence . . .
However, I have had the pleasure of hearing from another
source that my efforts on your behalf . . . my kind friend Count
Stallburg . . . His Grace Count Leinsdorf . . . our kinswoman the
wife of Section Chief Tuzzi . . . And now I must ask you, if you
will, to use all your influence in your new circle in the following
matter:
The world would come apart if everything held to be true were
indeed to be accepted as such and every will could have its way

as long as it seems to itself legitimate. All of us are therefore duty-bound to determine the one truth and the proper aim; then, insofar as we have succeeded in so doing, to take care, with an unflinching sense of our duty, that it is set down in the clear form of scientific thought. You may gather from this what it means when I tell you that in lay circles, but also, sad to say, in scientific circles susceptible to the promptings of a confused age, an extremely dangerous movement has been afoot for a long time to bring about certain presumed reforms and ameliorations in the proposed revision of the penal code. To fill you in, a committee of noted experts has been in existence for a number of years, appointed by the Minister of Justice to draw up such a proposed revision, to which committee I have the honor to belong, as does my university colleague Professor Schwung, whom you may remember from earlier days before I had seen through him, so that for many years he could pass as my best friend. As regards the liberalizations mentioned above, a rumor has reached me—unfortunately only too likely to be true!—that in the approaching jubilee year of our revered and merciful sovereign, exploiting, as it were, all inclinations to magnanimity, special efforts are likely to be made to pave the way for just such a disastrous emasculation of our legal system. It goes without saying that Professor Schwung and I are equally resolved to forestall this.

I realize that you are not versed in legal matters, but the chances are you know that the method of breaching our fortifications most favored by the present tendency to legal obfuscation, which falsely dubs itself humanitarianism, consists in the effort to extend the concept of mental impairment, for which punishment is not in order, in the vague form of diminished responsibility, even to those numerous individuals who are neither insane nor morally normal: that army of inferior persons the morally feebleminded, which sadly enough constitutes one of the ever-growing diseases of our civilization. You will see for yourself that this concept of diminished responsibility—if you can call it a concept, which I contest—is most intimately connected with the manner in which we interpret the concepts of full responsibility, or irresponsibility, as the case may be, and this brings me to the point of this letter:

Proceeding from already existing formulations of the law, and in view of the circumstances cited, I have proposed to the previously mentioned planning committee the following version of Paragraph 318 of our future penal code:

"No criminal act has been committed if the perpetrator was in a state of unconsciousness or pathological disturbance of his mind at the time he was engaged in the act under consideration, so that—" and Professor Schwung submitted a proposal beginning with exactly the same words.

But then *he* continued as follows: "so that he could not exercise his free will," while mine was to read: "so that he did not have the capacity to perceive the wrongfulness of his act." I must admit that I did not at first realize the malicious intent of this contradiction. My personal view has always been this, that as the intellect and reasoning power develops, the will comes to dominate desires or instincts by way of considered thoughts and the decisions springing from them. Any willed act is accordingly always the result of prior thought and not purely instinctive. Man is free insofar as he has the power of choice in the exercise of his will; when under the influence of human cravings, that is to say, cravings prompted by his sensual nature which interfere with his ability to think clearly, then he is not free. Volition is simply not a matter of chance but an act of self-determination arising necessarily from within the person, and so the will is determined by thought, and when the thought process is disturbed, the will is no longer the will, as the man's action is prompted only by his natural cravings. I am of course aware that the opposite view is also represented in the literature, i.e., that thought is regarded as being determined by the will. This is a view, however, that has its adherents among modern jurists only since 1797, while the one I hold has stood up to all attacks since the fourth century B.C. But to show that I was willing to meet my colleague halfway, I put forward a formulation that would join both proposals, as follows:

"No criminal act shall have been committed if the offender was at the time of his act in a state of unconsciousness or a morbid disturbance of his mental activity, so that he did not have the capacity to perceive the wrongfulness of his act and could not exercise his free will."

But here Professor Schwung revealed himself in his true colors! Showing no appreciation whatsoever of my willingness to meet him halfway, he arrogantly insisted that the "and" in my statement had to be replaced with an "or." You see the point? What differentiates the thinker from the layman is precisely this fine distinction of an "or" where the layman simply puts an "and," and Schwung was trying to stigmatize me as a superficial thinker by exposing my readiness to find a compromise, using the "and" to unite both formulations, exposing it to the suspicion that I had failed to grasp the full magnitude of the difference to be bridged, with all its implications!

It goes without saying that from that moment on I have rigorously opposed him on every point.

I immediately withdrew my compromise proposal and have had to insist on the acceptance of my first version without any compromise whatsoever; since when, however, Schwung has been making trouble for me with a most perfidious ingenuity. He claims, for instance, that under my proposed version, which is based on the capacity to recognize a wrongful act as such, a person who suffers from special delusions but is otherwise normal, as sometimes happens, could be exonerated on grounds of mental illness only if it could be proved that this person had assumed, because of his delusions, the existence of circumstances under which his act would be justified or not punishable under the law, so that he would have been acting correctly, although within a false concept of reality. This objection has no merit at all, however, for while empirical logic recognizes the existence of persons who are partly insane and partly sane, the logic of the law must never admit such a mixture of juridical states; before the law, a person is either responsible for his actions or not responsible, and we may assume that even in persons suffering from special kinds of delusions, a general capacity to know right from wrong still exists. If this is blurred by delusions in a specific instance, it needs only a special effort of the intelligence to bring it into harmony with the rest of the personality, and there is no reason to see any special problem in that.

And so I immediately pointed out to Professor Schwung that if the state of being responsible and that of not being responsible for one's actions cannot logically exist simultaneously, these states must be assumed to follow each other in rapid alternation, giving rise to the problem, especially where his theory is concerned, from which of these alternating states has the act in question resulted? To determine this, you would have to cite all the influences to which the accused has been subjected since his birth, and everything that may have influenced the actions of all his forebears, from whom his good and bad traits are inherited.

You will hardly believe this, but Schwung actually had the cheek to retort that this was quite so, as the logic of the law must never admit a mixture of two juridical states with respect to one and the same act, so that it is necessary to decide even with regard to each specific act of volition whether it was possible for the accused, in the light of his psychological history, to control his will or not. He chooses to claim that we are far more clearly aware of our free will than of the fact that everything that happens has a cause, and as long as we are basically free, we are also free with respect to specific causes, so that we must assume that in such a case it only requires a special effort of the will to resist the causally determined criminal impulses.

At this point Ulrich desisted from further exploration of his father's plans and pensively hefted in his hand the many enclosures cited in the letter's margin. Casting one more hasty glance at the letter's conclusion, he learned that his father expected him to use his "objective influence" on Counts Leinsdorf and Stallburg, and strongly advised him to warn the appropriate committees of the Parallel Campaign in good time of the dangers to the spiritual foundation of the entire government should so important a problem be wrongly formulated and resolved in the Year of the Jubilee.

75

GENERAL STUMM VON BORDWEHR CONSIDERS VISITS TO DIOTIMA AS A DELIGHTFUL CHANGE FROM HIS USUAL RUN OF DUTY

The tubby little General had paid Diotima another visit. Although the soldier has but a modest part to play in the council chamber, he began by saying, he would take it upon himself to predict that the state is the power to hold one's own in the struggle among nations, and that the military strength displayed in peacetime wards off war. But Diotima had instantly pulled him up short.

"General," she said, quivering with indignation, "all of life depends upon the forces of peace; even the life of business, rightly regarded, is a form of poetry."

The little General stared at her for a moment, dumbfounded, but soon regained his seat in the saddle.

"Your Excellency . . . ," he hastened to agree. In order to understand this form of address, we must remember that Diotima's husband was a ministerial section chief, and that in Kakania a section chief held the same rank as divisional commanders, who alone were entitled to be addressed as Excellency and only when on duty, at that; but since the soldier's profession is a knightly one, no soldier could expect to advance his career without so addressing them even when off duty, and in the spirit of chivalrous striving one also addressed their wives as Excellency, without wasting much thought on the question of when *they* were on duty. Such intricate considerations flashed through the little General's mind and enabled him to reassure Diotima instantly, with his first words, of his unqualified agreement and humble devotion, as he said, "Your Excellency takes the words out of my mouth. It goes without saying that, for political reasons, the War Ministry could not have been considered when the committees were set up, but we heard that the great movement is to be pacifist in its aims—an international peace campaign, they say, or perhaps the donation of Austrian murals to the Peace Palace at The Hague—and I can assure Your Excellency of our entire sympathy with such an aim. People generally tend to have certain misconception tions about the military; of course I won't deny that a young lieutenant is likely to yearn for a war, but all responsible quarters are most deeply convinced that the sphere of force, which we unfortunately do represent, must be linked with the blessings of the human spirit, precisely as Your Excellency has just put it."

He now dug a little brush out of his trouser pocket and went over his little mustache with it a number of times; it was a bad habit dating back to his time as a cadet, a phase during which the mustache still stands for life's impatiently awaited great hope, and he was totally unaware of it. His big brown eyes were fixed on Diotima's face, trying to read the effect of his words. Diotima seemed mollified, though in his presence she never quite was, and deigned to fill him in on what had been going on since the first meeting. The general showed enthusiasm, especially for the Great Council, expressed his admiration for Arnheim, and declared his conviction that such a gathering was bound to bear splendid fruit.

"There are so many people, after all, who don't realize how little order there is in the world of the mind," he explained. "I am even convinced, if Your Excellency will permit me to say so, that most people suppose they are seeing some progress in the order of things every day. They see order everywhere: in the factories, the offices, the railway timetables, the schools—here I may also mention proudly our own barracks, which in their modest way positively recall the discipline of a good orchestra—and no matter where you look, you will see order of some kind, rules and regulations for pedestrians, drivers, taxation, churches, business, social protocol, etiquette, morality, and so on. I'm sure that almost everyone considers our era the best-ordered of all time. Don't you have this feeling too, deep down, Your Excellency? I certainly do. If I'm not very careful, I let myself be overcome by the feeling that the modern spirit rests precisely on such a greater order, and that the great empires of Nineveh and Rome fell only because somehow they let things slide. That's what I think most people feel; they go on the unspoken assumption that the past is dead and gone as a punishment for something that got out of order. But of course that's a delusion that people who know their history shouldn't succumb to. It's why, unfortunately, we can't do without power and the soldier's profession."

It was deeply gratifying to the General to chat like this with this brilliant young woman; what a delightful change from the usual run of his official duties. But Diotima had no idea how to answer him, so she fell back on repeating herself:

"We really do hope to bring the most distinguished minds to bear on it, though our task even then will be a hard one. You can't imagine what a great variety of suggestions keep pouring in, and we do want to make the best choices. But you were speaking of order, General. We will never reach our goal through order, by a sober weighing of pros and cons, comparisons and tests. Our solution must come as a flash of lightning, a fire, an intuition, a synthesis! Looking at the history of mankind, we see no logical development; what it does suggest, with its sudden flashes of inspiration, the meaning of which emerges only later on, is a great poem!"

"If I may say so, Your Excellency," the General replied, "a soldier knows very little about poetry; but if anyone can breathe lightning and fire into a movement, it is Your Excellency; that much an old army officer can understand."

76

COUNT LEINSDORF HAS HIS DOUBTS

So far the tubby little General had been quite urbane, even though he had come uninvited to see her, and Diotima had confided more to him than she had intended. What made her fear him nonetheless, so that she afterward regretted again her amiability to him, was not really his doing but, as Diotima told herself, her old friend Count Leinsdorf's. Could His Grace be jealous? And if so, of whom? Although he always put in a brief appearance at meetings, Leinsdorf did not seem as favorably inclined to the Council as Diotima had expected. His Grace was decidedly averse to what he called mere literature. It stood for something he associated with Jews, newspapers, sensation-hungry booksellers, and the liberal, hopelessly garrulous paid hirelings of the bourgeoisie; the expression "mere literature" had positively become his new signature phrase. Every time Ulrich offered to read him the latest proposals that had come in the mail, including all the suggestions for moving the world forward or backward, he would cut him off with the words everyone uses when in addition to his own plans he hears about those everyone else has:

"No, no, I'm busy today, and all that is mere literature anyway."

What he was thinking of, in contrast to mere literature, was fields, the men who worked them, little country churches, and that great order of things which God had bound as firmly together as the sheaves on a mown field, an order at once comely, sound, and rewarding, even if it did sometimes tolerate distilleries on country estates because one had to keep pace with the times. Given this tranquil breadth of outlook, gun clubs and dairy cooperatives, no matter how far from the great centers they were to be found, must appear as part and parcel of that solid order and community; and if they should be moved to make a claim on general philosophical principles, that claim must enjoy the priority of a duly registered spiritual property, as it were, over any spiritual claims put forward by private individuals. This is why, every time Diotima wanted to speak with him seriously about something she had gleaned from her Great Minds, Count Leinsdorf was usually holding in his hand, or pulling out of his pocket, some petition from a club of five simpletons, saying that this paper weighed more in the world of real problems than the bright ideas of some genius.

This attitude resembled the one praised by Section Chief Tuzzi, as embodied in his ministerial archives, which withheld their official recognition of the Council's existence while taking every fleabite from the most insignificant provincial news sheet in deadly earnest; and Diotima, when beset by such problems, had no one she could confide in except Arnheim. But Arnheim, of all people, took His Grace's part in the matter. It was he who explained to her about that grandseigneur's tranquil breadth of outlook, when she complained to him about Count Leinsdorf's predilection for crack shots and co-op dairies.

"His Grace believes that we must take our direction from the land and the times," he explained gravely. "Believe me, it comes naturally of owning land. The soil uncomplicates life, just as it purifies water. Even I feel its effect every time I stay on my own very modest country estate. Real life makes everything simple." And after a slight hesitation he added: "The grand scale on which His Grace's life takes place also makes him extremely tolerant, not to say recklessly indulgent. . . ."

This side of her noble patron was new to Diotima, so she looked up expectantly.

"I wouldn't wish to state as a certainty," Arnheim went on with a vague emphasis, "that Count Leinsdorf is aware how very much your cousin, as his secretary, abuses his confidence—in principle only, I hasten to add—by his skepticism toward lofty schemes, by his sarcasm as a form of sabotage. I would be inclined to fear that his influence on His Grace was not a wholesome one, if this true peer were not so firmly entrenched in the great traditional feelings and ideas that support real life, so that he can probably afford to risk this confidence."

These were strong words, and Ulrich had deserved them. But Diotima did not pay as much attention to them as she might have, because she was so impressed with the other aspect of Arnheim's outlook, his owning landed estates not as a landowner but rather as a kind of spiritual massage; she thought it was magnificent, and mused on what it might be like to find oneself the lady of such a manor.

"I sometimes marvel," she said, "at the generosity with which you yourself judge His Grace. All of that is surely part of a vanishing chapter of history?"

"And so it is," Arnheim replied, "but the simple virtues of courage, chivalry, and self-discipline, which his caste developed to such an exemplary degree, will always keep their value. In a word, the ideal of the Master! I have learned to value the principle of the Master more and more in my business life as well."

"Then the ideal of the Master would, in the end, amount to almost the same thing as that of the Poem?" Diotima asked pensively.

"That's a wonderful way of putting it!" her friend agreed. "It's the secret of a vigorous life. Reason alone is not enough for a moral or a political life. Reason has its limits; what really matters always takes place above and beyond it. Great men have always loved music, poetry, form, discipline, religion, and chivalry. I would go so far as to say, in fact, that they and only they can succeed! Those are the so-called imponderables that make the master, make the man, and there is something, some obscure residue of this, in what the populace admires in the actor. But to return to your cousin: Of course it isn't simply a matter of turning conservative when we begin to prefer our comforts to sowing wild oats. But even if we were all born as revolutionaries, there comes a day when we notice that a simple, good person, regardless of what we think of his intelligence—a dependable, cheerful, brave, loyal human being, in other words—is not only a rare delight but also the true soil from which all life springs. Such wisdom is as old as the hills, but it denotes a change in taste, which in our youth naturally favors the exotic, to that of the mature man. I admire your cousin in many respects, or if this is saying too much, because there is little he says that is defensible, I could almost say that I love him, for something that is extraordinarily free and independent in his nature, together with much that is inwardly rigid and eccentric; it is just this mixture of freedom and mental rigidity that may account for his special charm, by the way. But he is a dangerous man, with his infantile moral exoticism and his highly developed intelligence that is always on the lookout for some adventure without knowing what, exactly, is egging him on."

77

ARNHEIM AS THE DARLING OF THE PRESS

Diotima repeatedly had occasion to contemplate the imponderables of Arnheim's attitude.

It was on his advice, for instance, that the representatives of the leading newspapers were sometimes invited to the sessions of the Council (as Section Chief Tuzzi had somewhat sarcastically dubbed the Committee to Draft a Guiding Resolution with Regard to the Seventieth Jubilee of His Majesty's Reign), and Arnheim, who was only a guest without any official status, enjoyed a degree of attention from them that put all other celebrities in the shade. For some reason newspapers are not the laboratories and experimental stations of the mind that they could be, to the public's great benefit, but usually only its warehouses and stock exchanges. If he were alive today, Plato—to take him as an example, because along with a dozen others he is regarded as the greatest thinker who ever lived—would certainly be ecstatic about a news industry capable of creating, exchanging, refining a new idea every day; where information keeps pouring in from the ends of the earth with a speediness he never knew in his own lifetime, while a staff of demiurges is on hand to check it all out instantaneously for its content of reason and reality. He would have supposed a newspaper office to be that *topos uranios*, that heavenly realm of ideas, which he has described so impressively that to this day all the better class of people are still idealists when talking to their children or employees. And of course if Plato were to walk suddenly into a news editor's office today and prove himself to be indeed that great author who died over two thousand years ago, he would be a tremendous sensation and would instantly be showered with the most lucrative offers. If he were then capable of writing a volume of philosophical travel pieces in three weeks, and a few thousand of his well-known short stories, perhaps even turn one or the other of his older works into a film, he could undoubtedly do very well for himself for a considerable period of time. The moment his return had ceased to be news, however, and Mr. Plato tried to put into practice one of his well-known ideas, which had never quite come into their own, the editor in chief would ask him to submit only a nice little column on the subject now and then for the Life and Leisure section (but in the easiest and most lively style possible, not heavy: remember the readers), and the features editor would add that he was sorry, but he could use such a contribution only once a month or so, because there were so many other good writers to be considered. And both of these gentlemen would end up feeling that they had done quite a lot for a man who might indeed be the Nestor of European publicists but still was a bit outdated, and certainly not in a class for current newsworthiness with a man like, for instance, Paul Arnheim.

Arnheim himself would of course never concur in this, because his reverence for all greatness would be offended by it, yet in many respects he was bound to find it understandable. These days, with everything in the world being talked about helter-skelter, when prophets and charlatans rely on the same phrases, except for certain subtle differences no busy man has the time to keep track of, and editors are constantly pestered with alarms that someone or other may be a genius, it is very hard to recognize the true value of a man or an idea; all one can do is keep an ear cocked for the moment when all the murmurs and whispers and shufflings at the editor's door grow loud enough to be admitted as the voice of the people. From that moment on, however, genius does enter a new state. It ceases to be a windy business of book or drama reviews, with all their contradictions, which the paper's ideal reader will take no more seriously than the babble of children, but has achieved the status of a fact, with all the consequences that entails.

Fools who keep inveighing against such realities overlook the desperate need for idealism behind all this. The world of those who write and have to write is chockablock with big terms and concepts that have lost their referent. The attributes of great men and great causes tend to outlive whatever it was that gave rise to them, and so a great many attributes are left over. They had once been coined by a distinguished man for another distinguished man, but these men are long dead, and the surviving concepts must be put to some use. Writers are in consequence always searching for the right man for the words. Shakespeare's "powerful imagination," Goethe's "universality," Dostoyevsky's "psychological depth," and all the other legacies of a long literary history hang like endless laundry in the heads of writers, and the resulting mental overstock reduces these people to calling every tennis player a profound strategist and every fashionable writer a great man of letters. Obviously they will always be grateful for a chance to use up their surplus without reducing its value. But it must always be applied to a man whose distinction is already an established fact, so that everyone understands that the words can be pinned on him, and it hardly matters where. And such a man was Arnheim, because Arnheim was Arnheim, whose very birth as the heir of his father was already an event, and there could be no doubt about the news value of anything he said. All he had to do was to take just enough trouble to say something that, with a little goodwill, could be regarded as significant. Arnheim himself formulated it as a principle: "Much of a man's real importance," he used to say, "lies in his ability to make himself understood by his contemporaries."

So now once again he got along beautifully, as always, with the papers, which fastened on him. He could afford to smile at those ambitious financiers or politicians who stand ready to buy up whole forests of newspapers. Such an effort to influence public opinion seemed to him as uncouth and timid as offering to pay for a woman's love when it could be had so much more cheaply just by stimulating her imagination. He had told the reporters who asked him about the Council that the very fact of its convocation proved its profound necessity, because nothing in world history happened without a rational cause; a sentiment that so fully corresponded to their professional outlook that it was quoted appreciatively in several newspapers. It was in fact, on closer scrutiny, a good statement. For the kind of people who take everything that happens seriously would feel nauseated if they could assume that not every event has a good cause; on the other hand, they would also rather bite their tongues, as we know, than take anything too seriously, even significance itself. The pinch of pessimism in Arnheim's statement greatly contributed to the solid dignity of their professional endeavors, and even the fact that he was a foreigner could be read as a sign that the whole world was concerning itself with these enormously interesting movements in Austria.

The other celebrities in attendance did not have the same instinctive flair for pleasing the press, but they noticed its effect; and since celebrities in general know little about each other and in that train to immortality in which they are traveling together usually set eyes on each other only in the dining car, the special public recognition Arnheim enjoyed had its unexamined effect on them too; and even though he continued to stay away from all official committee meetings, in the Council itself he came quite automatically to play the role of a central figure. The further this meeting of minds progressed, the clearer it became that he was the really sensational element in it, although he basically did nothing to create that effect other than, possibly, by expressing in conversation with its famous members his judgment, which could be interpreted as an openhearted pessimism, that the Council could hardly be expected to accomplish much of anything, but that, on the other hand, so noble a task merited all the trustful devotion one could muster. So subtle a pessimism inspires confidence even in great minds, for the idea that the intellect nowadays cannot really accomplish much is, for some reason, more congenial than the possibility that the intellect of some colleague might succeed in accomplishing something, and Arnheim's reserved judgment about the Council could be taken as leaning toward the more acceptable negative chance.

78

DIOTIMA'S METAMORPHOSES

Diotima's feelings did not develop in quite the same straight ascending line as Arnheim's success.

It sometimes happened, in the midst of a social gathering in her transformed apartment, with its rooms stripped of their usual furnishings, that she felt as though she were awakening in some dreamland. She would be standing there, surrounded by space and people, the light of the chandelier flowing over her hair and on down her shoulders and hips so that she seemed to feel its bright flood, and she was all statue, like some figure on a fountain, at the epicenter of the world, drenched in sublime spiritual grace. She saw it as a once-in-a-lifetime chance to bring about everything that she had always held to be most important and supremely great, and she no longer cared particularly that she had no very clear idea what this might be. The whole apartment, the presence of the people in it, the whole evening, enveloped her like a dress lined in yellow silk; she felt it on her skin, though she did not see it. From time to time she turned her gaze to Arnheim, who was usually standing somewhere in a group of men, talking; but then she realized that her gaze had been resting on him all along, and it was only her awakening that now followed her eyes. Even when she was not looking at him, the outermost wingtips of her soul, so to speak, always rested on his face and told her what was going on in it.

And as long as we're on the subject of feathers, one might add that there was also something dreamlike in his appearance, something of a businessman with golden angel's wings who had descended into the midst of this gathering. The rattle of express and luxury trains, the humming of limousines, the peace of hunting lodges, the flapping of sails on a yacht, were all in these invisible, folded plumes that rustled softly whenever he raised his arm in a gesture, in these wings with which her feelings had dressed him. Arnheim was often away on his trips, as always, and this gave his presence a permanent air of reaching out beyond the present moment and local events, important as they were for Diotima. She knew that while he was in town a secret coming and going of telegrams, visitors, and emissaries in charge of his business affairs was constantly afoot. She had gradually formed an idea, perhaps even an exaggerated one, of the importance of a firm with global interests and its involvement in world affairs on the highest level. Arnheim sometimes told breathtaking stories about the ramifications of international finance, overseas trade, and their connection with politics; quite new horizons, indeed first-ever horizons, opened up for Diotima; all it took was to hear him once on the subject of Franco-German confrontation, of which Diotima knew not much more than that almost everyone she knew felt slightly anti-German while acknowledging a certain burdensome fraternal duty. In Arnheim's presentation it became a Gallo-Celtic–East European–Transalpine complex interlinked with the problems of the coal mines of Lorraine and the oil fields of Mexico as well as the antagonism between Anglo- and Latin America. Of such ramifications Section Chief Tuzzi had no idea, or showed none. He confined himself to pointing out to Diotima yet again, from time to time, that in his opinion Arnheim's presence and marked preference for their home was definitely inexplicable without ulterior motives, but he did not say what these might be, and did not know himself.

And so his wife was deeply impressed with the superiority of a new breed of men over the methods of an obsolete diplomacy. She had not forgotten the moment of her decision to make Arnheim the head of the Parallel Campaign. It had been the first great idea of her life, accompanied by the most amazing sensations of dreaming and melting all at once, and as the idea broadened out into marvelous distances, everything that had made up Diotima's life hitherto melted toward it. What little part of this state of mind could be put into words did not amount to much: a glittering, a flickering, a strange emptiness and flight of ideas; nor did she mind admitting—Diotima thought—that its nucleus, the thought of placing Arnheim at the head of the unprecedented patriotic campaign, would be impossible. Arnheim was a foreigner in Austria, there was no getting around it. To put him in charge from the start, as she had presented it to her husband and Count Leinsdorf, was simply not feasible. Nevertheless, everything had turned out as, in her spellbound state, she had known it would. For all her other efforts to inject a truly inspiring content into the campaign had remained fruitless so far; the great first session, all the committee work, even this special council, against which Arnheim, by some strange irony of fate, had actually warned her himself, had so far led to nothing other than . . . Arnheim, whom people were always crowding around, who had to keep talking endlessly, who formed the secret focus of all their hopes. He was the New Man, destined to take over the helm of history from the old powers. She could flatter herself that it was she who had discovered him on sight, talked with him about the entrance of the New Man into the spheres of power, and helped him against all resistance to follow his path here. Even if Arnheim did have ulterior motives, as Tuzzi suspected, Diotima would in any case have felt almost justified in supporting him all the way; at such a fateful moment one cannot stop to split hairs, and Diotima felt with absolute certainty that her life had reached a pinnacle.

Apart from the born losers and the lucky devils of this world, one human being is about as badly off as the next, but they lead their lives on different levels. For the man of today, who has on the whole not much perspective on the meaning of his life, the confident sense of his own level is a most desirable second best. In exceptional cases this confidence can rise to an ecstasy of height or power, just as there are those who turn giddy when they know themselves to be high up in a building, even though they are standing in the middle of a room with the windows shut. When Diotima reflected that one of the most influential men in Europe was working together with her to infuse ideas into the strongholds of power, and how destiny itself must have

brought them together, and what was going on, even if on this particular day nothing special was actually happening on this high floor
of a World-Austrian humanitarian undertaking: when she reflected
on it, her tangled thoughts soon resembled knots that had slackened
into loops; they came more easily and were soon racing along,
accompanied by an unusual sense of joy and success, as though
streaming toward her and bringing flashes of amazing insights. Her
self-confidence rose; successes she would never have dreamed of lay
within reach; she felt more cheerful than was her habit, sometimes
even a daring joke would occur to her, and something she had never
known in all her life, waves of gaiety, even of exuberance, coursed
through her. She felt as though she were high up in a turret, in a
room with many windows. But it was also a queer, scary feeling. She
felt plagued by an indefinable, general, indescribable sense of well-
being that made her want to do things, do something, anything,
though she couldn't imagine what. It was as if she had suddenly
become aware of the globe turning under her feet and could not
shake this awareness off; or as if all this excitement without tangible
cause were as inhibiting as a dog leaping about at one's feet, though
how it had got there no one could say. And so Diotima sometimes
worried about the change she had undergone without her own express permission, and her condition, all in all, most resembled that
bright, nervous gray, the color of the faint, weightless sky at the hour
of utter hopelessness, when the heat is at its worst.

At this point Diotima's striving toward the ideal underwent a significant change. This striving had never been clearly distinguishable
from the proper admiration for all greatness; it was a noble idealism,
a decorous high-mindedness, a disciplined exaltation, and since, in
these more robust times of ours, we hardly recognize any of this anymore, perhaps it should be laid out briefly once more. This idealism
had nothing to do with realities, because reality always involves working at something, which means getting your hands dirty. It was more
like the flower paintings done by archduchesses, for whom flowers
were the only seemly choice of life study, and quite typical of this
idealism was the term "culture"; it regarded itself as the vessel of
culture. But this idealism could also be described as harmonious, because it detested everything unbalanced and saw the task of education as reconciling all the crude antagonisms sadly so prevalent in the

world; in short, it was not perhaps so very different from what we still mean—though of course only wherever the great middle-class traditions are still upheld—by a sound and pure idealism, the kind that distinguishes most carefully between conflicts worthy of its concern and those that aren't, and which, because of its faith in a higher humanity, does not share the conviction of the saints (along with doctors and engineers) that even moral garbage may contain unused heavenly fuels. Formerly, had Diotima been roused from her sleep and asked what she wanted, she would have said, without having to think, that a living soul's powers of love felt the need to share itself with all the world; but after being awake for a while she would have modified this by noting that in our present world, with its overgrowth of civilization and intellect, it would perhaps be safer to speak more cautiously, even in cases of the highest sensibilities, of a force analogous to the power of love. And she would really have meant it. Even today there are still thousands of people who are like atomizers, spraying the power of love around like a perfume.

When Diotima sat down to read her books she brushed her lovely hair back from her forehead, which gave her a logical air, and proceeded to read responsibly, with a view to extracting from what she called culture whatever might help her in the none too easy social situation in which she found herself; and this was how she lived, distributing herself in tiny droplets of rarefied love among all the things that deserved it, condensing as a cloudy breath upon them at some distance from herself, so that she was actually left with nothing but the empty bottle of her body, one of the household effects of Section Chief Tuzzi. Before Arnheim appeared on the scene this had finally led to moods of deep depression, when Diotima was still alone between her husband and that most incandescent event of her life, the Parallel Campaign; since then, however, her energies had quite naturally regrouped. The power of love had firmly pulled itself together and had reentered her body, as it were, and the "analogous" force had become something very selfish and unmistakable. The feeling her cousin had been the first to evoke, that she was about to take some kind of action and that something she could not yet bring herself to imagine was about to happen between herself and Arnheim, had now grown so much more intense than anything she had ever known that she felt exactly as if she had passed from dreaming to waking. A void, typical of the first stage of that transition, had opened up in Diotima, and she seemed to remember descriptions she had read that suggested it might herald the beginning of a great passion. She thought she could understand in that light much of what Arnheim had been saying to her recently. Everything he told her about his position, the qualities needed and the duties laid upon him by his life, was in preparation for something inexorable, and Diotima, surveying everything that had been her ideal hitherto, felt the pessimism that casts its shadow on every act, just as, with one's trunks all packed, one casts a last look around the rooms that have been home for years and are now seen with the life nearly gone out of them. The unexpected effect was that Diotima's soul, temporarily unsupervised by the higher faculties, behaved like a truant schoolboy boisterously careening around until he is overcome by the sadness of his pointless liberty; and owing to this curious situation something briefly entered into her relations with her husband, despite the increasing distance between them, that bore a strange resemblance, if not to a late springtime of love, then at least to a potpourri of all love's seasons.

The little Section Chief, with his pleasant aroma of tanned dry skin, was baffled by what was happening. He had noticed several times that his wife, when guests were present, seemed strangely dreamy, withdrawn, remote, and highly nervous, truly nervous and yet far away at the same time; still, when they were alone again and he approached her, somewhat intimidated and disconcerted, to ask her about it, she would suddenly throw her arms around him with inexplicable exuberance, and the pair of lips she pressed on his forehead were so hot they reminded him of the barber's curling irons on his mustache when they got too close to his skin. Such unscheduled affection was not to his taste, and he stealthily wiped away its traces when Diotima was not looking. But whenever he felt like taking her in his arms, or had actually done so, which made it even worse, she hotly accused him of never having loved her, of only pouncing on her like an animal. Now, from the days of his youth, a certain degree of touchiness and moodiness had of course formed part of his image of a desirable woman who would complement a man's nature, and the ineffable grace with which Diotima proffered a cup of tea, picked up a new book, or passed judgment on a problem that, in his opinion, she could not possibly understand, had always delighted him with its formal perfection. It all affected him like perfect background music by which to dine, something he dearly loved; but then, Tuzzi was also sure that the detachment of music from dining (or from church services) and the endeavor to cultivate it for its own sake was a sign of middle-class presumption, even though he knew that one should never say so; anyway, it was not the sort of thing he ever seriously concerned himself with. But what was he to do when Diotima hugged him one minute and the next denounced him as a man beside whom a person with a soul of her own could never be free to fulfill herself? What could a man say in answer to exhortations that he give more thought to the oceanic depths of beauty within, instead of fastening on her body? All of a sudden he was supposed to see the difference between Eros, the free spirit of love unburdened by lust, and mechanical sex. It was all, of course, stuff she had read somewhere, and comical at that, but when a woman lectures a man in this fashion as she is undressing in front of him!—Tuzzi thought—it becomes downright insulting. For he could not fail to notice that Diotima's underwear had evolved in the direction of a certain worldly frivolity. She had always dressed with care and deliberation, since her social position required her to be smart without dressing above her station. But within the gradations from respectable durability to filmy, frilly provocation she was now making concessions to beauty she would once have called unworthy of an intelligent woman. However, when Giovanni (Tuzzi's name was really Hans, but he had been stylishly rechristened in keeping with his surname) noticed, she blushed down to her shoulders and brought up Frau von Stein, who had made no concessions even to a Goethe! So now Section Chief Tuzzi was no longer free, when *he* felt that the time had come, to escape from those weighty concerns of state beyond the private sphere and find release in the very lap of his own household; he found himself instead at Diotima's mercy; instead of the former clear line between mental exertion at the office and physical relaxation at home, he was faced with a virtual return to the strenuous and slightly ridiculous union of mind and body appropriate to courtship, to carrying on like a cock pheasant or some lovesick, versifying youth.

It is hardly too much to say that he found this utterly revolting at times, and that because of it his wife's public success at this time caused him physical pain. Diotima had public opinion on her side, something Section Chief Tuzzi respected so unconditionally that he shied away from asserting his authority or meeting her incomprehensible moods with sarcasm, lest he seem unappreciative. It began to dawn on him that being the husband of a distinguished woman was a painful affliction that had to be carefully hidden from the world, much like an accidental castration. He took great pains to show nothing of what he felt, came and went inconspicuously, always in a cloud of amiable official impenetrability, whenever Diotima had visitors or meetings, dropping the occasional politely helpful suggestion or comforting ironic remark, and seemed to lead his life in a separate but friendly adjoining world, always in accord with Diotima, even entrusting her with a little mission now and then when they were alone, publicly encouraging Arnheim's visits to his home; in whatever spare time he had from the weighty cares of office, he studied Arnheim's publications, and hated men who published their writings as the cause of his troubles.

For this was the question to which the main question—why was Arnheim frequenting his house?—sometimes reduced itself: Why did Arnheim write? Writing is a particular form of chatter, and Tuzzi couldn't stand men who chatter. They made him want to clench his jaws and spit through his teeth like a sailor. There were exceptions, of course; that he granted. He knew some high-ranking civil servants who had written their memoirs after they retired, and others who sometimes wrote for the newspapers. As Tuzzi saw it, a civil servant wrote only when he was dissatisfied or when he was a Jew, because Tuzzi held that Jews were ambitious and dissatisfied. Then there were also men of achievement who had written books about their experiences, but only in their old age and in America or, at most, in England. Besides, Tuzzi was of course versed in literature and, like all diplomats, had a preference for memoirs, from which one could pick up witty remarks and insights into the workings of men's minds. Still, that such works were no longer being written must signify something, so perhaps his was an old-fashioned taste, not in keeping with an age of functionalism. Finally, people wrote because it was their profession. Tuzzi could accept this without reservation, so long as it brought in enough money, or fell into the after all recognized category of "poet." He even felt quite honored to receive the leading men in this profession, in which he had hitherto included those writ-

ers supported by the Foreign Office's Save the Reptile Fund, but
without giving it much thought he would also have counted the *Iliad*
and the Sermon on the Mount, both of which he certainly revered,
among those achievements we owe to a profession that may either be
practiced independently or have to be subsidized. But why a man
like Arnheim, who had no need whatsoever to write at all, should
write so much was a problem behind which Tuzzi, now more than
ever, suspected something that persisted in eluding him.

79

SOLIMAN IN LOVE

Soliman, the little black slave or African prince, as the case may be,
had meanwhile managed to convince Rachel, Diotima's little maid
or, alternatively, confidante, that they would have to keep a sharp eye
on what went on in the house, in order to forestall a sinister plan of
Arnheim's when the time came. Not that she was entirely convinced,
but the two of them kept watch like conspirators, and always eaves-
dropped when there were visitors. Soliman talked endlessly about
couriers coming and going and mysterious visitors to his master at
the hotel, and said he was prepared to give his oath as an African
prince that he would get to the bottom of it. The African princely
oath entailed Rachel's slipping her hand between the buttons of his
jacket and shirt so she could lay it on his bare chest while he recited
the vow, and his hand doing the same to her; this Rachel declined.
All the same, little Rachel, who dressed and undressed her mistress
and took her telephone calls, and through whose hands Diotima's
black hair flowed every morning and evening while golden words
from her mistress's lips flowed through her ears: this ambitious little
creature who had been living as though posed atop a pillar ever since
the Parallel Campaign had started, trembling with adoration that
flowed upward from her eyes to the goddess she served day after day,

had for some time taken pleasure in spying on her, plain and simple.

Through open doors from neighboring rooms or the crack of a slowly closing door or simply while lingering over some small task nearby, she tried to overhear everything said by Diotima and Arnheim, Tuzzi and Ulrich, and picked up glances, sighs, hand-kissings, words, laughter, gestures, like scraps of a torn-up document she could not fit together again. But most of all it was the little keyhole that opened up vistas which curiously, somehow, reminded Rachel of the long-forgotten time when she lost her virtue. That tiny opening let her gaze slip deep inside the room's interior, where people broken up into sections flat as cardboard moved about, their voices no longer held within the fine borders of words but proliferating into meaningless sound; the awe, reverence, and admiration that bound Rachel to these people then came wildly undone, dissolving in excitement as when a lover suddenly penetrates, with all his being, so deeply into the beloved that everything grows dark before her eyes, and behind the drawn curtain of her skin the light flares up. Little Rachel crouched at the keyhole, her black dress tight over her knees, throat, and shoulders; Soliman cowered beside her in his livery, like hot chocolate in a dark-green cup; when he happened to lose his balance he would steady himself against Rachel's shoulder, knee, or skirt with a quick movement of his hand, letting it rest there for an instant till he let go until only his fingertips still touched her; then these, too, were slowly, caressingly, withdrawn. He couldn't help giggling, and then Rachel would lay her soft fingers on the swelling bolsters of his lips.

Unlike Rachel, Soliman was not interested in the Council, and whenever he could dodged the chore of helping her serve the guests. He preferred coming along on Arnheim's private visits to Diotima. This meant waiting in the kitchen for Rachel to be free again, to the annoyance of the cook, who had so enjoyed his first visit, because he had since then apparently lost his tongue. But Rachel never had time to sit in the kitchen for long, and when she was gone again the cook, a single woman in her thirties, paid him little motherly attentions. He put up with that for a while, with an extremely haughty look on his chocolate face; then he would get up, like someone who has forgotten something or is looking for something, his eyes rolled up to the ceiling, his back to the door, walking backward as if to see the ceiling

better. The cook already knew this clumsy act was coming, as soon as
he stood up and rolled his eyes, showing the whites; but she was too
annoyed and jealous to let on that she noticed, until Soliman finally
ceased bothering about his act, now reduced to a formula that took
him to the threshold of the brightly lit kitchen, where he would hesitate with a most ingenuous expression on his face. The cook then
made a point of not looking in his direction. Soliman glided backward into the dark foyer, like a dark image in dark water, listening for
another second, quite unnecessarily, and then suddenly took to pursuing Rachel with fantastic leaps throughout the strange house.

Section Chief Tuzzi was never at home, and Soliman was not worried about Arnheim and Diotima, knowing that they had ears only for
each other. He had even tested this now and then, by knocking
something over, without being noticed. He lorded it throughout the
rooms like a stag in the forest. His blood pressed upward through his
head like antlers with eighteen dagger points. The tips of these antlers brushed walls and ceilings. The blinds were usually drawn in all
the rooms not in use, to save the colors of the furnishings from being
faded by the sunlight, and so Soliman rowed through this twilit world
with wide movements of his arms, as if through leafy undergrowth.
He enjoyed making a dramatic dance of it. He was intent on violence. This youngster, whom women tended to spoil out of curiosity,
had never actually had intercourse with a woman but only picked up
all the vices of European boys, and his cravings were as yet so unappeased by experience, so unbridled and flaring in every direction,
that his lust did not know whether it was supposed to be quenched
by Rachel's blood or her kisses, or else by a freezing up of all the
veins in his body the moment he set eyes on his beloved.

Wherever Rachel might be hiding, he suddenly turned up, with a
smile of triumph at his own cleverness. He would bar her way, re-
specting the sanctity of neither the master's study nor Diotima's bedroom; he popped up from behind curtains, desk, closets, beds,
making Rachel's heart stand still every time, in horror at such impudence, such a tempting of fate, whenever the dimness somewhere
condensed into a black face in which two white rows of teeth
gleamed. But the moment Soliman found himself face-to-face with
Rachel in the flesh, he was instantly recalled to propriety. This girl
was so much older than he, and so beautiful, like a fine shirt of his

master's one couldn't bring oneself to soil the very first moment it came fresh from the laundry, and anyway she was so real that all his fantasies paled in her presence. She scolded him for carrying on like a little savage, and tried to teach him some respect for Diotima, Arnheim, and the great honor of having a share in the Parallel Campaign; Soliman, for his part, always had little presents for her, whether it was a flower plucked from his master's bouquet for Diotima, a cigarette stolen at the hotel, or a handful of bonbons he had scooped up in passing from a bowl; he only pressed Rachel's fingers and, as he gave her his gift, laid her hand on his heart, which was flaming inside his black body like a red torch in a dark night.

There was also the time Soliman had made his way right into Rachel's room, where she had been banished with her sewing on strict orders from Diotima, who had been disturbed the previous day by some scuffling in the hall while Arnheim was with her. Before entering on her house arrest she had quickly looked around for him without finding him, but when she stepped sadly into her little room, there he was, seated on her bed with a radiant expression on his face. Rachel hesitated before shutting the door, but Soliman leapt up and did it for her. Then he rummaged in his pockets, pulled something out, blew on it to clean it off, and approached the girl like a hot flatiron.

"Hold out your hand!" he ordered.

Rachel held it out to him. He had some twinkling shirt studs in his hand and tried to fit them into her cuff. Rachel thought they were glass.

"Diamonds!" he explained proudly.

The girl, sensing that something was wrong, hastily pulled her arm back. Not that she had any definite suspicion; the son of an African prince, even if he had been kidnapped, might still have a few gemstones sewed secretly into his shirt; one never knew. Yet some instinct made her afraid of these buttons, as if Soliman were offering her poison, and suddenly all the flowers and candies he had already given her took on in retrospect a sinister air. She pressed her hands to her body and looked at him aghast. It was time to speak to him seriously; she was older than he and in service with a kind mistress. But all she could think of was old saws like "Honesty is the best policy" or "Give the Devil your little finger and he'll take your whole hand." She turned pale; such sayings were not enough. It was the wisdom she had been raised on at home; it was upright, proper, and simple as old pots and pans, but there was not much you could do with it; such a saying was usually just one sentence, with a period at the end. At this moment she felt ashamed of parading such child-hood maxims, as one feels ashamed of old, threadbare clothes. That the ancient clothes chest from some poor man's attic turns up, a hun-dred years later, as a decorative item in the salons of the rich was beyond her ken; like all respectable simple people, she admired a new chair made of wickerwork. She tried hard to come up with something she had learned in her new life, but of all the thrilling scenes of love and terror she remembered from the books Diotima had given her, none fitted the present case; all those fine words and feelings were tied to their contexts and would be as much use here as a key in the wrong lock. It was the same with the great pronounce-ments and admonitions she had from Diotima. Rachel felt a red mist swirling around her and was close to tears. At length she said hotly: "I don't steal from *my* mistress!"

"Why not?" Soliman flashed his teeth at her.

"I just don't."

"I didn't either. This is mine!" Soliman shouted.

A good mistress takes care of the likes of us, Rachel felt. Love was what she felt for Diotima. Boundless respect for Arnheim. Deep loathing for those mischievous and mutinous types who are called subversive elements by the good police. But she could not find the words for all this; like a huge farm wagon overloaded with hay and fruit, with its brakes out of order, this huge ballast of feelings went rolling out of control inside her.

"It's mine! Take it!" Soliman repeated, grabbing for Rachel's hand again. She snatched her arm away, and as he tried to hang on to it, with his anger mounting as he sensed he would have to let go be-cause his boyish strength was no match for Rachel's resistance—she was pulling away from his grasp with the whole weight of her body—he lost his head, bent over, and bit her ferociously in the arm.

Rachel gave a scream, but had to stifle it, and hit Soliman in the face.

But by this time his eyes were brimming with tears; he threw himself to his knees, pressed his lips to Rachel's dress, and cried so hard that Rachel felt the hot wetness coming through to her thighs.

There she stood, helpless in the clutch of the kneeling boy who had taken hold of her skirt and was digging his head into her body. She had never in her life known such a feeling, and gently stroked the soft wiry mop of his hair with her fingers.

80

GETTING TO KNOW GENERAL STUMM, WHO TURNS UP UNACCOUNTABLY AT THE COUNCIL

Meanwhile the Council had been enriched by a remarkable addition: despite the rigorous weeding out of those asked to attend, the General had turned up one evening, thanking Diotima effusively for the honor of her invitation. A soldier had only a modest part to play in the council chamber, he averred, but to be allowed to be present at so eminent a gathering, even if only as a silent bystander, was a dream he had cherished since his youth. Diotima gazed around over his head in silence, looking for the guilty party: Arnheim was talking, as one statesman to another, with His Grace; Ulrich, looking unutterably bored, stared at the buffet as though he were counting the cakes on it; the familiar scene presented a solid front without the slightest opening for the intrusion of such an unusual suspicion. Yet there was nothing Diotima was so sure of as that she herself had not invited the General, unless she had taken to walking in her sleep or having fits of amnesia. It was an awkward moment. Here stood the little General, undoubtedly with an invitation in the breast pocket of his forget-me-not-blue uniform tunic, for a man in his position could not possibly be suspected of so outrageous a gamble as coming without being asked; on the other hand, there in the library stood Diotima's graceful desk, with all the leftover printed invitations in a locked drawer to which Diotima almost alone had access. Tuzzi? she briefly wondered, but this, too, was unlikely. How the invitation and the General had come together remained something of a spiritualistic conundrum, and since Diotima was inclined to believe in the supernatural where she personally was concerned, she felt a shiver go through her from head to foot. But she had no choice, in any case, other than to bid the General welcome.

He had wondered a little at the invitation himself, incidentally, late as it was in coming, since Diotima had regrettably given him not the slightest sign of such an intention on his two visits, and he had noticed that the address, obviously written by an underling, showed inaccuracies as to his rank and the style of salutation not to be expected from a lady of Diotima's social position. But the General was an easygoing man, not inclined to suspect anything out of the ordinary, let alone anything out of this world. He assumed that there had been some little slip-up, which was not going to stop him from enjoying his success.

For Major General Stumm von Bordwehr, Chief of the War Ministry's Department for Military Education and Cultural Affairs, was sincerely pleased with the official mission that had come his way. On the eve of the great inaugural meeting of the Parallel Campaign, the Chief of Administration had sent for him and said: "Stumm, old man, you're the scholarly type. We're going to write you a letter of introduction, and off you go. Just give it the once-over and tell us what they're up to." No amount of protesting afterward did any good; the fact that he had not succeeded in gaining a foothold in the Parallel Campaign was a mark against him in his file, which he had tried in vain to erase by his visits to Diotima. So he had hotfooted it to Administration when the invitation arrived after all, and daintily setting one foot before the other under his paunch, with a touch of nonchalant impudence, but a little out of breath, he reported that his carefully planned initiatives had led to the expected result, after all.

"There you are, then," Lieutenant General Frost von Aufbruch said. "I always knew you'd make it." He offered Stumm a chair and a cigarette, switched on the electric sign over the door that said "In Conference, No Admittance," then briefed Stumm on his mission, mainly a matter of reconnaissance and reporting back. "There's really nothing special we're after, you see, so long as you just show up there as often as you can and let them see we're in the picture; not being on any of the committees is probably in order, at this point, but there's no reason we shouldn't be in on any plans to honor our Supreme Commander and Sovereign with some spiritual sort of present on his birthday. That's why I picked you, personally, and proposed you to His Excellency the Minister for this detail; nobody can have any objection. So good luck to you, old man, and do a good job." Lieutenant General Frost von Aufbruch dismissed him with a friendly nod, and General Stumm von Bordwehr forgot that a soldier is supposed to show no emotion, clicked his heels from the bottom of his heart, so to speak, and said, snapping to attention: "At your service, Excellency, and thanks!"

If there are civilians of warlike temperament, why can't there be military men who love the arts of peace? Kakania had them in quantity. They painted, collected insects, started stamp albums, or studied world history. Their isolation in all those tiny garrisons, and the fact that regulations did not permit officers to publish their intellectual findings except with the approval of their superiors, tended to give their efforts the appearance of something peculiarly personal. General Stumm, too, had gone in for such hobbies in his earlier years. He had originally served with the cavalry, but his small hands and short legs were ill-suited to clutching and controlling so unreasonable a beast as a horse, and he so conspicuously lacked the qualities needed for giving military orders that his superiors used to say that if a squadron were positioned on the barracks square with their horses' heads rather than their tails, as usual, toward the stable wall, he would be incapable of getting them out through the gates. In revenge, little Stumm grew a beard, dark brown and rounded; he was the only officer in the Emperor's cavalry with a full beard, but regulations did not specifically forbid it. And he took to collecting pocketknives, in a scientific spirit. On his pay he could not afford a collection of weapons, but of knives, classified according to their make, possession of corkscrew and nail file, grade of steel, place of origin, the casing material and so on, he soon had a large number; in his room stood tall cabinets with many shallow drawers, all neatly labeled, which brought him a reputation for learning. He could also make verses, and even as a cadet at the military academy he had always got the best grades in religion and composition; and so one day the colonel called him into the office.

"You'll never make a passable cavalry officer," he said. "If I stuck a suckling babe on a horse and sent it to the front, he'd put up about as much of a show as you do. But it's a long time since the regiment has had anyone at staff college. Why don't you apply, Stumm?"

So Stumm had two glorious years at the staff college in the capital. While he again failed to show the intellectual keenness needed to ride a horse, he attended every military concert, visited the museums, and collected theater programs. He decided to switch to a civilian career but did not know how to go about it. In the end, he was found neither suited nor definitely unfit for service on the general staff; he was regarded as clumsy and unambitious, but something of a philosopher, so for the next two years he was tentatively assigned to the general staff in command of an infantry division, which ended in his belonging, as a captain of cavalry, to the large number of those who, as the general staff's auxiliary reserve, never get away from the line unless something unusual happens. Captain Stumm now served with another regiment, where he passed for an expert in military theory as well. But it did not take his new superiors long to catch on that in practical matters he was a babe-in-the-saddle. His career was a martyrdom, all the way up to lieutenant colonel; but even as a major he no longer dreamed of anything but a long furlough on half pay until he could be put on the retired list as an acting colonel, with the title and the uniform but not the pension of a colonel. He was through with giving any thought to promotion, which in line regiments went by seniority, in excruciating slow motion; through with those mornings when, with the sun still rising, a man comes in from the barracks quadrangle, chewed out from head to foot, in dusty boots, and goes into the mess hall to add some empty wine bottles to the long emptiness of the day ahead; through with the so-called social life, the regimental stories, and those regimental amazons who spend their lives at their uniformed husbands' sides, echoing their progress up the ladder of rank on a social scale of silvery precision, tones so inexorably refined as to be only just within range of the human ear. And he was through with those nights when dust, wine, boredom, the expanses of fields crossed on horseback, and the tyranny of the endless talk about horses drove every officer, married and unmarried alike, to those parties behind drawn curtains where women were stood on their heads to have champagne poured into their petticoats, and they got the inevitable Jew of those godforsaken little Galician garrison towns, who was a one-man institution like some small weather-beaten country store, where you could get everything from love to saddle soap on credit, with interest—to procure girls trembling with awe, fear, and curiosity. His only self-indulgence in those days was the studious enrichment of his collection of knives and corkscrews, many of them brought personally to the crackbrained lieutenant colonel by the same Jew, who polished them on his sleeve before he placed them on the table, with a reverent look on his face as though they were prehistoric relics.

The unexpected breakthrough came when a fellow alumnus from the staff college remembered Stumm and proposed his transfer to the War Office, where the Department of Education was looking for an assistant to its chief; they wanted someone with an outstanding grasp of the civilian world. Two years later Stumm, by now advanced to colonel, had been entrusted with running the department. Now that he was mounted on a desk chair instead of the beast sacred to the cavalry, he was a different man. He made major general and could be fairly certain of making it to lieutenant general. He had of course shaved off his beard long ago, but now, with advancing age, he was growing a forehead, and his tendency to tubbiness gave him the look of a well-rounded man in every sense of the term. He even became happy, and happiness can do wonders for a man's latent possibilities. He had been meant for a life at the top, and it showed in every way. Be it the sight of a stylishly dressed woman, the showy bad taste of the latest Viennese architecture, the outspread colors of a great produce market, be it the grayish-brown asphalt air of the streets, that mild atmospheric asphalt full of miasmas, smells, and fragrances, or the noise that broke apart for a few seconds to let out one specific sound, be it the endless variety of the civilian world, even those little white restaurant tables that are so incredibly individual although they undeniably all look alike: he took a delight in them all that was like the jingling of spurs in his head. His was a happiness such as civilians find only in taking a train ride into the country, knowing that they will pass a day green, happy, and overarched by something or other. This feeling included a sense of his own significance, that of the War Office, of culture, of the meaningfulness of everyone else, and was so intense that Stumm had not once, since his arrival, thought of visiting the museums or going to the theater again. It was the sort of feeling of which one is hardly ever fully aware, though it permeates everything, from the general's gold braid to the voices of the carillons, and is itself a kind of music without which the dance of life would instantly come to a dead stop.

What the devil, he had certainly made his way! So Stumm thought as he now stood here, his cup brimming over, in these rooms, a part of this brilliant assemblage of great minds. Here he was, at last! The only uniform, where all else was steeped in intellect! And there was something more to fill him with amazement. Imagine the sky-blue sphere of the earth, slightly brightened by the forget-me-not blue of Stumm's military tunic, filled to bursting with happiness, with significance, with the mysterious brain-phosphorus of inward illumination, and at the very center of this sphere the General's heart, upon which was poised, like the Virgin Mary upon the serpent's head, a goddess of a woman whose smile is interwoven with everything and is in fact the mysterious magnetic center of all things: then you have, more or less, the impression Diotima made on Stumm von Bordwehr from the moment her image first filled his widening eyes. Actually, General Stumm cared as little for women as he did for horses. His rather short, plump legs had never felt quite at home on horseback, and when he'd had to talk horses too, even when off duty, he used to dream of nights that he had ridden himself sore, down to the bone, and couldn't dismount; in the same fashion his comfort-loving nature had always disposed him against sexual athleticism, and the daily grind of his duties was sufficiently fatiguing to leave him with no need for letting off excess steam at night. Not that he had been a spoilsport in his day, but when he had to spend his evenings not with his knife collection but with his fellow officers, he usually resorted to a wise expedient; his sense of bodily harmony had soon taught him to drink himself through the riotous state into the sleepy one, which suited him far better than the risks and disappointments of love. It was only later on, after he had married and soon had two children as well as their ambitious mother to support, that he fully appreciated how sensible his habits had been before he succumbed to the temptation to marry, lured into it no doubt by the somewhat unmilitary aura attaching to the notion of a married warrior. Since then he had developed a vivid ideal of woman outside marriage, something that had evidently been germinating in his unconscious long before and consisted in a mild infatuation with the kind of woman by whom he felt intimidated, so that there was no question of having to exert himself in any form of courtship. When he looked over the pictures of women he had clipped from popular periodicals in his bachelor days—never more than a sideline among his activities as a collector—they all had in common that daunting quality, though he had not realized it at the time; and he had never known such overwhelming adoration until his first meeting with Diotima. Quite apart from the impact of her beauty, he had looked up her name in his encyclopedia as soon as he heard that she was a second Diotima, and though he still did not quite understand what a Diotima might be, he gathered it had something to do with that great sphere of civilian culture of which he still knew far too little, sad to say, despite his official position, and the world's intellectual superiority fused with this woman's physical grace. Nowadays, when relations between the sexes have become so simplified, it is probably necessary to point out that this is likely to be the most sublime experience a man can have. General Stumm felt that his arms were too short to embrace Diotima's lofty voluptuousness, while at the same time his mind felt the same about the world and its culture, so that he experienced everything that came his way in a state of gently pervasive infatuation, just as his rounded body took on something of the suspended roundness of the globe itself.

It was this infatuation that brought Stumm von Bordwehr, soon after Diotima had dismissed him from her presence, irresistibly back to her. He planted himself close to the object of his admiration, especially as he knew no one else among those present, and listened in on her conversations with the other guests. He would have loved to take notes, for he would hardly have believed the sovereign ease with which she handled such intellectual riches, like someone toying with a string of priceless pearls, had his own ears not borne witness to her skill as she welcomed, one after another, such a variety of celebrities. It was only when she had given him a look after ungraciously turning away from him several times, that he realized the unseemliness of a general's eavesdropping on his hostess in that fashion, and backed away. He made a few lonely tours of the overcrowded premises, drank a glass of wine, and was just about to find a decorative place to stand against a wall when he noticed Ulrich, whom he had seen once before, at the first meeting, and his memory lit up; Ulrich had been a bright, restless lieutenant in one of the two squadrons General Stumm had once gently led as a lieutenant colonel.

"A man of my own sort," Stumm thought. "And to think how young he still is, to have made it to so high a position!" He made a beeline for Ulrich, and after they had shaken hands and compared notes for a while, Stumm indicated the assembled company and said: "An incredible opportunity for me to learn about the most important problems in the civilian world."

"You'll be amazed, General," Ulrich said.

The General, who needed an ally, warmly shook his hand. "You were a lieutenant in the Ninth Uhlans," he said significantly, "and someday that will turn out to have been a great honor for us, even if the others don't yet realize it as I do."

81

COUNT LEINSDORF'S VIEWS OF *REALPOLITIK*.
ULRICH FOSTERS ORGANIZATIONS

While the Council did not yet give the slightest sign of coming up with any answers, the Parallel Campaign was making great strides at the Palais Leinsdorf: it was there that the threads of reality meshed. Ulrich came twice a week.

He had never dreamed that such numbers of organizations existed. Organizations for field sports and water sports, temperance clubs and drinking clubs, were heard from—in short, organizations and counterorganizations of every kind. They worked to promote the interests of their members and to hamper those of the others. Everyone in the world seemed to belong to at least one organization. Ulrich in his amazement said:

"Your Grace, this goes far beyond what we, in our innocence, have always regarded as natural manifestations of the social instinct. We're faced with the monstrous fact that in the kind of state we have invented, with its law and order, everybody is also a member of a gang. . . ."

But Count Leinsdorf was in favor of organizations. "Remember," he said, "that no good has ever come of ideological politics; we must go in for practical politics. I won't deny that I even regard the far too intellectual concerns of your cousin's circle as potentially dangerous!"

"Could you give me some guidelines, sir?" Ulrich asked.

Count Leinsdorf looked at him, wondering whether the inexperienced young man was ready for so daring a disclosure. But then he decided to risk it.

"Well now, you see," he began cautiously, "I'll tell you something that may be new to you, because you are young: *realpolitik* means *not* doing the very thing you would love to do; however, you can win people over by letting them have their way in little things!"

His listener's eyes popped; Count Leinsdorf smiled complacently.

"So you see," he explained, "all I am saying is that in practice, politics must be guided not by the power of an idea but always by some actual need. Of course everyone would like to make the great ideas come true, that goes without saying. So one should never do what one would like to do. Kant was the first to say so."

"Really!" Ulrich exclaimed in amazement. "But one must aim at something, surely?"

"Aim? Bismarck wanted to make the King of Prussia great; that was his aim. He didn't know from the start that to achieve it, he would have to make war on Austria and France, and that he would found the German Empire."

"Is Your Grace suggesting that we should aim at a great and powerful Austria and nothing else?"

"We still have four years to go. In four years all sorts of things can happen. You can put a people on its feet, but it must do its own walking. Do you see what I mean? Put it on its feet—that's what we must do. But a people's feet are its firm institutions, its political parties, its organizations, and so on, and not a lot of talk."

"Your Grace! Even if it doesn't exactly sound like it, you have just uttered a truly democratic idea!"

"Well, it may be aristocratic too, even though my fellow peers don't see eye-to-eye with me on this. Old Hennenstein and Türckheim told me they expected nothing but a filthy mess to come of all this. So we must watch our step. We must start building on a small scale, so be very nice to the people who come to us."

Consequently Ulrich for some time after this turned no one away. One man who came to him talked a great deal about stamp collecting. To begin with, he said, it made for international understanding; second, it satisfied the need for property and position on which society was unquestionably based; third, it not only called for considerable knowledge but also required decisions on a level that it was not too much to call artistic. Ulrich looked the man over, with his careworn and rather shabby appearance; but the man caught the question in Ulrich's glance and countered it by saying that stamps were also commercially valuable, a factor not to be underrated; millions were made in trading them; the great stamp auctions attracted dealers and collectors from all over the world. It was one way to get rich. But as for himself, he was an idealist; he was putting together a special collection for which there was no commercial interest as yet. All he asked was that a great stamp exhibition be held in the Jubilee Year, when he could be depended upon to bring his specialty to public attention.

After him came a man with the following story: On his walks through the streets—though it was even more exciting when one rode a trolley—he had for years been in the habit of counting the number of straight strokes in the big block letters of the shop signs (there were three strokes in an *A*, for instance, and four in an *M*) and dividing the sum total by the number of letters counted. His average so far had been consistently two and a half strokes to a letter, but this was obviously not invariable, since it could change with every new street. Now, deviations from the norm could be quite distressing, while there was great satisfaction every time the numbers came out right—an effect quite like the catharsis said to be achieved while watching classical tragedy on the stage. If you considered the letters themselves, however—anyone could check this out—divisibility by three was a rare bit of luck, which is why most inscriptions tended to leave you with a noticeable sense of frustration, except for those consisting of several letters each composed of four strokes, as in M, E, W, for instance, which could be depended upon to leave one feeling remarkably happy. So what to do? the visitor asked. Simply this, an order issued by the Public Health Office favoring four-stroke letter series in shop signs and discouraging as far as possible the use of one-stroke letters, such as O, S, I, C, which lead to poor and therefore depressing results.

Ulrich looked the man over and took care to keep a distance between them; yet he did not really look like a mental case, but was a well-dressed person in his thirties with an intelligent and amiable expression. He went on calmly explaining that mental arithmetic was an indispensable skill in every line of work, that to teach by means of games was in keeping with modern educational methods, that statistics had often revealed deep connections between things long before these could be explained, that everyone knew the damage done by an education based on book learning alone, and, in conclusion, that the excitement his findings had aroused in all those who had chosen to repeat his experiments spoke for itself. If the Public Health Office could be induced to adopt his discovery, other countries would soon follow suit, and the Jubilee Year could turn out to be a blessing for all mankind.

Ulrich advised all these people to organize: "You still have almost four years' time, and if you succeed, His Grace will be sure to use all his influence on your behalf."

Most of them, however, were already organized, which of course changed matters. It was relatively simple when a soccer club wanted an honorary professorship for its outside right, to demonstrate the importance of modern physical culture; one could always promise to take the matter under consideration. But it was hard in such cases as the following: A man in his fifties presented himself as a senior executive in a government department; his forehead shone with the light of martyrdom when he identified himself as the founder and president of the Oehl Shorthand Association, hoping to draw the attention of the great patriotic campaign's Secretary to the Oehl short-hand system.

Oehl shorthand was an Austrian system, he went on to explain, which was all you needed to know to understand why it was not widely adopted or encouraged. Was the Secretary himself a practicing stenographer, by any chance? No? Then he was perhaps not aware of the advantages of any stenographic system: the saving in time, in mental energy. Did he have any idea what a tremendous waste of mental effort was entailed by all those curlicues and prolixities, the imprecision and the bewildering repetition of similar parts, and the confusion that arose between truly expressive, significant graphic components and merely ritualistic and arbitrarily idiosyncratic flourishes of the pen?

Ulrich was amazed to meet a man so implacably determined to stamp out ordinary, presumably harmless, handwriting. When it came to saving mental effort, shorthand was a vital necessity for a rapidly growing world that had to get things done quickly. But even from a moral standpoint the question of Short or Long was crucial. The long-eared script, as the senior official bitterly termed it because of the senseless loops it was full of, encouraged tendencies to imprecision, arbitrariness, and wastefulness, especially the waste of time, while shorthand inculcated precision, willpower, manliness. Shorthand, he said, taught people to do what was necessary and to avoid what was unnecessary and irrelevant. Surely there was a lesson in practical morality here, of the greatest possible significance especially for any Austrian. And then there was the aesthetic side of it. Wasn't prolixity rightly considered an ugly quality? Had not the great classical authors rightly declared economy of means to be an essential element of beauty? But even regarding it from the public-health angle, the senior executive official went on, it was most important to shorten the time spent sitting hunched over one's desk. After having in this fashion illuminated the subject of shorthand from various other scientific-scholarly angles as well, to his listener's edification, the visitor finally began to dilate upon the Oehl system's immense superiority over all other systems of shorthand. He showed that from every one of the points of view under consideration, all other systems of shorthand were a mere betrayal of the very principle of shorthand.

He then unfolded the story of his own personal martyrdom to the cause. There were all the older, more powerful systems, which had had time to ally themselves with all sorts of vested interests. All the trade schools were teaching the Vogelbauch system and stood pat against any change, backed up, in accordance with the laws of inertia, by the business community. The newspapers, which obviously profit enormously from the advertisements of the trade schools, would not hear of any proposals for reform. And the Education Office? What a sad joke that was, according to Herr Oehl. Five years ago, when shorthand was first made a required subject in the secondary schools, the Office of Education had set up a committee of advisers on the system to be chosen; the committee was naturally packed with representatives of the trade schools and the business community and with government stenographers, who were of course hand in glove with the press, and that was that! It was all too obvious that the Vogelbauch system was slated to win! The Oehl Shorthand Association had issued a warning and a protest against such criminal indifference to the public interest. But its delegates could no longer get anyone at the Education Office to see them!

Ulrich took cases of this kind to His Grace. "Oehl?" Count Leinsdorf said. "An official, you say?" His Grace rubbed his nose for a long time but came to no decision. "Perhaps you should see his head of department and find out if there's anything to what he says," he mused after a while, but he was feeling creative and canceled this suggestion. "No, I'll tell you what we'll do: we'll draw up a memorandum. Let's find out what they have to say for themselves." And he added confidentially, to give Ulrich an insight into the deeper workings of things: "With any of these things, you can never tell whether they are nonsense or not," he said. "But you see, my dear fellow, you can always depend on something important coming of the fact that somebody attaches importance to it. Take the case of Dr. Arnheim, that darling of all the newspapers. The newspapers could just as easily pursue some other hare. But given that they pursue him, that makes Arnheim important. You said, didn't you, that this man Oehl has an organization behind him? Not that it proves anything, of course, but on the other hand, as I said, we must keep up with the times, and when a good many people are for something, the chances are that something will come of it."

82

CLARISSE CALLS FOR AN ULRICH YEAR

There was really no reason for Ulrich to pay Clarisse a visit other than his having to give her a good talking-to about the letter she had written to Count Leinsdorf; when she had come to see him a few days earlier, he had forgotten all about it. On his way there, however, it occurred to him that Walter was definitely jealous of him and would be upset about the visit when he heard of it. But there was nothing Walter could do about it. The majority of men find themselves in this funny situation if they happen to be jealous: they cannot keep an eye on their women until after office hours.

The time of day Ulrich had chosen to go there made it unlikely that he would find Walter at home. It was quite early in the afternoon. He had phoned to say he was coming. The snowy whiteness of the landscape outside shone so intensely into the room that it was as though there were no curtains at all on the windows. In this merciless light that glittered off every object stood Clarisse, greeting Ulrich with a laugh from the center of the room. On the side toward the window, the minimal curvature of her boyish body flashed in vivid colors, while the side in shadow was a bluish-brown mist from which her forehead, nose, and chin jutted out like snowy ridges whose edges are blurred by wind and sun. The impression she gave was less that of a human being than of the meeting of ice and light in the spectral solitude of an Alpine winter. Ulrich caught some of the spell she must cast on Walter at times, and his mixed feelings for his boyhood friend briefly gave way to an insight into the image two people presented to each other, whose life he perhaps knew hardly at all.

"I don't know whether you told Walter anything about the letter you wrote to Count Leinsdorf," he began, "but I've come to speak to you alone, and to warn you never to do that kind of thing again."

Clarisse pushed two chairs together and made him sit down.

"Don't tell Walter," she asked him, "but tell me what you have against it. You mean the Nietzsche Year? What did your Count say to that?"

"What do you suppose he could have said? The way you tied it in with Moosbrugger was utterly crazy. And even without that he'd probably have thrown your letter away."

"Oh, really?" Clarisse was very disappointed. Then she said: "Luckily, you have some say in it too!"

"But don't you see, you're simply out of your mind!"

Clarisse smiled, accepting this as a compliment. She laid her hand on his arm and asked him: "But an Austrian Year is nonsense, isn't it?"

"Of course it is."

"But a Nietzsche Year would be a fine thing. Why should it be wrong to want something just because we happen to like the idea ourselves?"

"And what exactly is your idea of a Nietzsche Year?"

"That's your affair."

"Very funny."

"Not at all. Why does it seem funny to you to try to put into practice something you take seriously as an intellectual matter? Tell me that."

"I'll be glad to," Ulrich said, freeing his arm from her hand. "After all, Nietzsche isn't the issue; it could just as well be Christ or Buddha."

"Or you. Why not get to work on an Ulrich Year!" She said this with the same casual air as when she had urged him to free Moosbrugger. This time, however, his attention had not strayed, and he was looking at her face while he listened to her words. All he saw was Clarisse's usual smile, that funny little grimace that was the unintended result of the mental effort she was making.

"Oh well," he thought, "she doesn't mean any harm."

But Clarisse drew closer to him again. "Why don't you make it You Year? You might just be in a position to do it now. Only don't say anything to Walter about it—I've told you that already—nor about my Moosbrugger letter. Not a word, ever, that I've talked to you about it. But I assure you, this murderer is musical, even though he can't actually compose. Haven't you ever noticed that every human being is the center of a cosmic sphere? When the person moves, the sphere moves with him. That's the way to make music, without thinking about it, simple as the cosmic sphere around you. . . ."

"And you feel that I should work on something of that sort for a year of my own, do you?"

"No," Clarisse answered, playing it safe. Her fine lips seemed about to say something but held their peace, and the flame blazed silently from her eyes. It was hard to say what it was that emanated from her at such moments. One felt scorched, as if one had come too close to something red hot. Now she smiled, but it was a smile that curled on her lips like an ash left behind in the wake of the burned-out flare from her eyes.

"Still, that is the sort of thing I could do, if I had to," Ulrich went on, "but I'm afraid you think I should make a coup d'état?"

Clarisse thought it over. "Let's say a Buddha Year, then," she said evasively. "I don't know what Buddha stood for, or only vaguely, but let's accept it, and if we think it matters, then we should do something about it. It either deserves our faith in it or it doesn't!"

"Fine. Now . . . a Nietzsche Year was what you said. But what was it Nietzsche actually wanted?"

Clarisse reconsidered. "Well, of course I don't mean a Nietzsche monument or a Nietzsche street," she said in some embarrassment. "But people should try to live as he—"

"As he wanted?" he interrupted her. "But what did he want?"

Clarisse started to answer, hesitated, and finally said: "Oh come on, you know all that yourself. . . ."

"I don't know a thing," he teased her. "But I can tell you this: You can set up a Kaiser Franz Josef Soup Kitchen, and you can meet the needs of a Society for the Protection of the House Cat, but you cannot turn great ideas into reality any more than you can do it with music. Why is that? I don't know. But that's how it is."

He had finally found refuge on the little sofa behind the little table; it was a position easier to defend than the chair. In the open space in the middle of the room, on the far bank, as it were, of an illusory prolongation of the shining tabletop, Clarisse was still standing and talking. Her whole slender body was involved; she actually felt everything she wanted to say with her whole body first of all, and was always needing to do something with it. Ulrich had always thought of her body as hard and boyish, but now, as it gently swayed on legs pressed close together, he saw Clarisse as a Javanese dancer. Suddenly it occurred to him that he would not be surprised if she fell into a trance. Or was he in a trance himself? He launched into a long speech:

"You want to organize your life around an idea," he began. "And you'd like to know how to do that. But an idea is the most paradoxical thing in the world. The flesh in the grip of an idea is like a fetish. Bonded to an idea, it becomes magical. An ordinary slap in the face, bound up with ideas of honor, or of punishment and the like, can kill a man. And yet ideas can never maintain themselves in the state in which they are most powerful; they're like the kind of substance that, exposed to the air, instantly changes into some other, more lasting, but corrupted form. You've been through this often yourself. Because an idea is what *you* are: an idea in a particular state. You are touched by a breath of something, and it's like a note suddenly emerging from the humming of strings; in front of you there is something like a mirage; out of the confusion of your soul an endless parade is taking shape, with all the world's beauty looking on from the roadside. All this can be the effect of a single idea. But after a while it comes to resemble all your previous ideas, it takes its place among them, becomes part of your outlook and your character, your principles or your moods; in the act of taking shape it has lost its wings and its mystery."

Clarisse answered: "Walter is jealous of you. Not on my account, I'm sure. It's because you look as though you could do what he wishes he could do. Do you see what I mean? There is something about you that cuts him down. I wish I knew how to put it." She scrutinized him.

Their two speeches intertwined.

Walter had always been life's special pet, always held on its lap. He transformed everything that happened to him and gave it a tender vitality. Walter had always been the one whose life had been the richer in experiences. "But having more of a life is one of the earliest and subtlest signs of mediocrity," Ulrich thought. "Seen in context, an experience loses its personal venom or sweetness." That was how it was, more or less. Even the assertion that this was the case established a context, and one got no kiss of welcome or good-bye for it.

And despite all that, Walter was jealous of him? He was glad to hear it.

"I told him he ought to kill you," Clarisse reported.

"What?"

"Exterminate him! I said. Suppose you're not really all you think you are, and suppose Walter is the better man and has no other way to gain his peace of mind: it would make sense, wouldn't it? Besides, you can always fight back."

"No half measures for you, I see," Ulrich said, somewhat shaken.

"Well, we were only talking. How do you feel about it, by the way? Walter says it's wrong even to think such things."

"Oh no, thinking is quite in order," he replied hesitantly, taking a good look at Clarisse. She had a peculiar charm all her own. Was it as though she were somehow standing side by side with herself? She was not quite there, yet all there, both in close proximity.

"Bah, thinking!" she cut in. Her words were addressed to the wall behind him, as though her eyes were fixed on a point somewhere between. "You're every bit as passive as Walter." These words, too, fell somewhere midway between them, keeping their distance like an insult, yet sounding conciliatory, because of the confidential closeness they implied. "What *I* say is, if you can think something, you should be able to do it too," she insisted dryly.

Then she moved off, walked to the window, and stood there with her hands clasped behind her back.

Ulrich stood up quickly, went over to her, and placed an arm around her shoulders.

"Dear little Clarisse," he said, "you're being a bit strange today, aren't you? But I must put in a good word for myself; you're not really concerned with me anyway, are you?"

Clarisse was staring out the window. But now her gaze sharpened; she was focusing on something specific out there, for support. She felt as if her thoughts had strayed outside and had only just returned. This feeling of being like a room, with the sense of the door just having shut, was nothing new to her. On and off she had days, even weeks, when everything around her was brighter and lighter than usual, as though it would take hardly any effort to slip out of herself and go traipsing about the world unencumbered; then again there were the bad times, when she felt imprisoned, and though these times usually passed quickly, she dreaded them like a punishment, because everything closed in on her and was so sad. Just now she was aware of a lucid, sober peacefulness, and it worried her a little; she was not sure what it was she had wanted just a while ago, and this sense of leaden clarity and quiet control was often a prelude to the time of punishment. She pulled herself together with the feeling that if she could keep this conversation going with conviction, she would be back on safe ground.

"Don't say 'dear little' to me," she said, pouting, "or I might end up killing you myself." It came out like a joke, so she felt she had made one. She stole a cautious look at him, to see how he was taking it. "Of course, it was only a way of putting it, but you must realize that I'm serious. Where were we? You said it wasn't possible to live by an idea. There's no real energy in you, neither you nor Walter!"

"You horrified me by calling me a passivist! But there are two kinds. There's a passive passivism, like Walter's and then there's the active kind!"

"What is active passivism?" Clarisse was intrigued.

"A prisoner waiting for his chance to break out!"

"Bah!" said Clarisse. "Excuses."

"Well, yes," he conceded. "Maybe."

Clarisse still held her hands clasped behind her back and stood with her legs wide apart, as though in riding boots.

"You know what Nietzsche says? Wanting to know for sure is like wanting to know where the ground is for your next step, mere cowardice. One has to start somewhere to act on one's intentions, not just talk about it. And I've always expected you of all people to do something special someday!"

Suddenly she had taken hold of a button on his vest and started twisting it, her face lifted up to his. Instinctively he laid his hand on hers to save the button.

"I've been thinking for a long time," she went on shyly, "that the really rotten, vile things that go on happen not because someone is doing them but because we are letting them happen. They expand to fill a void!" After this coup she looked at him expectantly. Then she burst out: "Letting things happen is ten times more dangerous than doing them, don't you see?" She struggled inwardly for a more exact formulation, but then she only added: "You know exactly what I mean, don't you? Even though you are always saying that we have to let things go their own way. But I understand what you're saying. It's occurred to me more than once that you're the Devil himself!" These words had slipped out of Clarisse's mouth like a lizard. They frightened her. All she had been thinking of at the outset was Walter's begging her to have a child by him. Ulrich caught a flicker in her eyes; she wanted him. Her upturned face was suffused with something—nothing at all lovely, something ugly but touching. Something like a violent outbreak of sweat blurring the features. But it was disembodied, purely imaginary. He felt infected by it against his will and overcome by a slight absentmindedness. He was losing his power to hold out against her craziness, and so he grabbed her hand to make her sit down on the sofa, and sat down beside her.

"Let me tell you now why I do nothing," he began, and fell silent.

Clarisse, who had become herself again the moment she felt his touch, urged him on.

"There's nothing a man can do, because . . . but I can't really expect you to understand this," he began, then he extracted a cigarette and devoted himself to lighting it.

"Go on," Clarisse prompted him. "What are you trying to say?"

But he kept silent. She pushed her arm behind his back and shook him, like a boy showing how strong he can be. With her, there was no need to say anything; the mere suggestion of something out of the ordinary was enough to set her imagination going. "You're really evil!" she said, and tried in vain to hurt him. But at this moment they were unpleasantly interrupted by Walter's return.

83

PSEUDOREALITY PREVAILS; OR, WHY DON'T WE MAKE HISTORY UP AS WE GO ALONG?

What could Ulrich have said to Clarisse anyway?

He had kept it to himself because she had somehow brought him to the verge of actually saying "God." He had been about to say, more or less: God does not really mean the world literally; it is a metaphor, an analogy, a figure of speech that He has to resort to for some reason or other, and it never satisfies Him, of course. We are not supposed to take Him at his word, it is we ourselves who must come up with the answer for the riddle He sets us. He wondered whether Clarisse would have agreed to regard the whole thing as a game of Cowboys and Indians or Cops and Robbers. Of course she would. Whoever took the first step, she would stick by him like a she-wolf and keep a sharp lookout.

But there was something else he had also had on the tip of his tongue, something about mathematical problems that do not admit of a general solution but do allow for particular solutions, which one could combine to come nearer to a general solution. He might have added that he regarded the problem of human life as that kind of problem. What we call an age—without specifying whether we mean centuries, millennia, or the time span between schoolchild and grandparent—that broad unregulated flow of conditions would come to mean a more or less chaotic succession of unsatisfactory and, in themselves, false answers out of which there might emerge the right and whole solution only when mankind had learned to put all the pieces together.

On his way home in the streetcar, it all came back to him, but he was rather ashamed of such thoughts in the presence of the other passengers riding into town with him. One could tell by looking at them that they were on their way home from definite occupations or setting out toward definite entertainments; even just by looking at their clothes one could tell where they had come from or were going.

He studied the woman next to him; clearly a wife and mother, forty-ish, probably the wife of an academic, and she had small opera glasses on her lap. Sitting beside her, toying with those ideas, he felt like a little boy at play, and playing something slightly improper, at that.

For to think without pursuing some practical purpose is surely an improper, furtive occupation; especially those thoughts that take huge strides on stilts, touching experience only with tiny soles, are automatically suspect of having disreputable origins. There was a time when people talked of their thoughts taking wing; in Schiller's time such intellectual highfliers would have been widely esteemed, but in our own day such a person seems to have something the matter with him, unless it happens to be his profession and source of income. There has obviously been a shift in our priorities. Certain concerns have been taken out of people's hearts. For high-flown thoughts a kind of poultry farm has been set up, called philosophy, theology, or literature, where they proliferate in their own way beyond anyone's ability to keep track of them, which is just as well, because in the face of such expansion no one need feel guilty about not bothering with them personally. With his respect for professionalism and expertise, Ulrich was basically determined to go along with any such division of labor. Nevertheless, he still indulged in thinking for himself, even though he was no professional philosopher, and at the moment he could see that to do otherwise was to take the road leading to the beehive state. The queen would lay her eggs, the drones would devote themselves to lust and the life of the mind, and the specialists would toil. It was quite possible to imagine the world so organized; total productivity might even go up as a result. For the present, every human being is still a microcosm of all humanity, as it were, but this has clearly become too much to bear and it no longer works, so that the humane element has become a transparent fraud. For the new division of labor to succeed, it might be necessary to arrange for at least one set of workers to evolve an intellectual synthesis. After all, without mind . . . What Ulrich meant was that it would give him nothing to look forward to. But this was of course a prejudice. No one really knows what life depends on. He shifted in his seat and studied the reflection of his face in the windowpane opposite, looking for something else to think about. But there was his head floating along in the fluid glass, midway between the inside and the outside, becoming remarkably compelling after a while in its insistence on some kind of completion.

Was there a war actually going on in the Balkans or not? Some sort of intervention was undoubtedly going on, but whether it was war was hard to tell. So much was astir in the world. There was another new record for high-altitude flight; something to be proud of. If he was not mistaken, the record now stood at 3,700 meters and the man's name was Jouhoux. A black boxer had beaten the white champion; the new holder of the world title was Johnson. The President of France was going to Russia; there was talk of world peace being at stake. A newly discovered tenor was garnering fees in South America that had never been equaled even in North America. A terrible earthquake had devastated Japan—the poor Japanese. In short, much was happening, there was great excitement everywhere around the turn of 1913–1914. But two years or five years earlier there had also been much excitement, every day had had its sensations, and yet it was hard, not to say impossible, to remember what it was that had actually happened. A possible synopsis: The new cure for syphilis was making . . . Research into plant metabolism was moving . . . The conquest of the South Pole seemed . . . Professor Steinach's experiments with monkey glands were arousing . . . Half the details could easily be left out without making much difference. What a strange business history was! We could safely say of this or that event that it had already found its place in history, or certainly would find it; but whether this event had actually taken place was not so sure! Because for anything to happen, it has to happen at a certain date and not at some other date or even not at all; also, the thing itself has to happen and not by chance something merely approximating it or something related. But this is precisely what no one can say of history, unless he happens to have written it down at the time, as the newspapers do, or it's a matter of one's professional or financial affairs, since it is of course important to know how many years one has to go till retirement or when one will come into a certain sum of money or when one will have spent it, and in such a context even wars can become memorable occurrences. Examined close up, our history looks rather vague and messy, like a morass only partially made safe for pedestrian traffic, though oddly enough in the end there does seem to be a path across it, that very "path of history" of which nobody knows the starting point. This business of serving as "the stuff of history" infuriated Ulrich. The luminous, swaying box in which he was riding seemed to be a machine in which several hundred kilos of people were being rattled around, by way of being processed into "the future." A hundred years earlier they had sat in a mail coach with the same look on their faces, and a hundred years hence, whatever was going on, they would be sitting as new people in exactly the same way in their updated transport machines—he was revolted by this lethargic acceptance of changes and conditions, this helpless contemporaneity, this mindlessly submissive, truly demeaning stringing along with the centuries, just as if he were suddenly rebelling against the hat, curious enough in shape, that was sitting on his head.

Instinctively he got to his feet and made the rest of his way on foot. In the more generous human confines of the city, in which he now found himself, his uneasiness gave way to good humor again. What a crazy notion of little Clarisse's, to want a year of the mind. He concentrated his attention on this point. What made it so senseless? One might just as well ask why Diotima's patriotic campaign was senseless.

Answer Number One: Because world history undoubtedly comes into being like all the other stories. Authors can never think of anything new, and they all copy from each other. This is why all politicians study history instead of biology or whatever. So much for authors.

Answer Number Two: For the most part, however, history is made without authors. It evolves not from some inner center but from the periphery. Set in motion by trifling causes. It probably doesn't take nearly as much as one would think to turn Gothic man or the ancient Greek into modern civilized man. Human nature is as capable of cannibalism as it is of the *Critique of Pure Reason;* the same convictions and qualities will serve to turn out either one, depending on circumstances, and very great external differences in the results correspond to very slight internal ones.

Digression One: Ulrich recalled a similar experience dating from his army days. The squadron rides in double file, and "Passing on orders" is the drill; each man in turn whispers the given order to the next man. So if the order given up front is: "Sergeant major move to the head of the column," it comes out the other end as "Eight troopers to be shot at once," or something like that. And this is just how world history is made.

Answer Number Three: If, therefore, we were to transplant a generation of present-day Europeans at a tender age into the Egypt of 5000 B.C., world history would begin afresh in the year 5000 B.C., repeat itself for a while, and then, for reasons nobody could fathom, gradually begin to deviate from its established course.

Digression Two: The law of world history—it now occurred to him—was none other than the fundamental principle of government in old Kakania: "muddling through." Kakania was an incredibly clever state.

Digression Three or Answer Number Four: The course of history was therefore not that of a billiard ball—which, once it is hit, takes a definite line—but resembles the movement of clouds, or the path of a man sauntering through the streets, turned aside by a shadow here, a crowd there, an unusual architectural outcrop, until at last he arrives at a place he never knew or meant to go to. Inherent in the course of history is a certain going off course. The present is always like the last house of a town, which somehow no longer counts as a house in town. Each generation wonders "Who am I, and what were my forebears?" It would make more sense to ask "Where am I?" and to assume that one's predecessors were not different in kind but merely in a different place; that would be a move in the right direction, he thought.

He had been numbering his own answers and digressions as he went along, while glancing now into some passing face, now into a shop window, to keep his thoughts from running away with him entirely, but had nevertheless gone slightly astray and had to stop for a moment to see where he was and find the best way home. Before taking this route, he tried once more to get his question straight in his mind. Crazy little Clarisse was quite right in saying that we should make history, make it up, even though he had argued against it with her. But why didn't we?

All that occurred to him in answer at the moment was Director Fischel of Lloyd's Bank, his friend Leo Fischel, with whom years ago he had sometimes sat outside a café in the summer. For if Ulrich had been talking to Fischel instead of to himself, Fischel would typically have said: "I should only have your worries!" Ulrich appreciated this refreshing answer Fischel would have given. "My dear Fischel," he immediately replied in his mind, "it's not that simple. When I say history, I mean, if you recall, our life. And I did admit from the start that it's in very bad taste for me to ask: Why don't people create history—that is, why do they attack history like so many beasts only when they are wounded, when their shirttails are on fire, in short, only in an emergency? So why is this question in such bad taste? What do we have against it, when all it means is that people shouldn't let their lives drift as they do?"

"Everybody knows the answer," Director Fischel would retort. "We're lucky when the politicians and the clergy and the big shots with nothing to do, and everybody else who runs around with all the answers, keep their hands off our daily lives. Besides which, we're a civilized people. If only so many people nowadays weren't so uncivilized!" And of course Director Fischel was right. A man is lucky if he knows his way around stocks and bonds, and other people refrain from dabbling so much in history just because they think they know how it works. We couldn't live without ideas, God forbid, but we have to aim at a certain equilibrium among them, a balance of power, an armed truce of ideas, so that none of the contending parties can get too much done. Fischel's sedative was civilization. It was the fundamental sentiment of civilization, in fact. And yet there is also the contrary sentiment, asserting itself more and more, that the times of heroic-political history, made by chance and its champions, have become largely obsolete and must be replaced by a planned solution to all problems, a solution in which all those concerned must participate.

At this point the Ulrich Year came to an end with Ulrich's arrival on his own doorstep.

84

ASSERTION THAT ORDINARY LIFE, TOO, IS UTOPIAN

At home he found the usual stack of mail forwarded from Count Leinsdorf's. An industrialist was offering an outsize cash award for the best results in the military training of young civilians. The archbishopric opposed the founding of a great orphanage, on the grounds that it had to be on guard against creeping interdenominationalism. The Committee on Public Worship and Education reported on the progress of the definitive suggestion, tentatively announced, to erect a great Emperor of Peace and Austrian Peoples Monument near the Imperial Residence; after consultation with the Imperial and Royal Office for Public Worship and Education, and after sounding out the leading art, engineering, and architectural associations, the Committee had found the differences of opinion such that it saw itself constrained—without prejudice to eventual future requirements and subject to the Central Executive Committee's consent—to announce a competition for the best plan for a competition with regard to such an eventual monument. The Chamberlain's Office, having taken due cognizance of the proposals submitted three weeks earlier, was returning them to the Central Executive Committee with regrets that no decision thereon by His Most Gracious Majesty could be passed on at this time, but that it was in any case desirable for the time being to let public opinion continue to crystallize on these as well as other points. The Imperial and Royal Office for Public Worship and Education stated in response to the Committee's communication ref. no. so-and-so that it was not in a position to favor any special action in support of the Oehl Shorthand Association. The Block Letter Society for Mental Health announced its foundation and applied for a grant.

And so it went. Ulrich pushed aside this packet of "realities" and brooded on it for a while. Suddenly he got to his feet, called for his hat and coat, left word that he would be back in an hour or so, phoned for a cab, and returned to Clarisse.

Darkness had fallen. A little light fell onto the road from only one window of her house; footprints in the snow had frozen, making holes to stumble over; the outer door was locked and the visitor unexpected, so that his shouts, knocking, and hand clapping went unheard for the longest time. When at last Ulrich was back inside, it did not seem to be the same room he had left such a short time ago but seemed another world, surprised to see him, with a table laid for a simple private meal for two, every chair occupied by something that had settled down on it, and walls that offered the intruder a certain resistance.

Clarisse was wearing a plain woolen bathrobe and laughing. Walter, who had let the latecomer in, blinked his eyes and slipped the huge house key into a table drawer. Without beating about the bush, Ulrich said, "I'm back because I owe Clarisse an answer." Then he resumed talking at the point where Walter's arrival had interrupted their conversation. After a while, the room, the house, and all sense of time had vanished, and the conversation was hanging somewhere up in the blue of space, in the net of the stars.

Ulrich presented them with his scheme for living the history of ideas instead of the history of the world. The difference, he said to begin with, would have less to do with what was happening than with the interpretation one gave it, with the purpose it was meant to serve, with the system of which the individual events were a part. The prevailing system was that of reality, and it was just like a bad play. It's not for nothing that we speak of a "theater of world events"—the same roles, complications, and plots keep turning up in life. People make love because there is love to be made, and they do it in the prevailing mode; people are proud as the Noble Savage, or as a Spaniard, a virgin, or a lion; in ninety out of a hundred cases even murder is committed only because it is perceived as tragic or grandiose. Apart from the truly notable exceptions, the successful political molders of the world in particular have a lot in common with the hacks who write for the commercial theater; the lively scenes they create bore us by their lack of ideas and novelty, but by the same token they lull us into that sleepy state of lowered resistance in which we acquiesce in everything put before us. Seen in this light, history arises out of routine ideas, out of indifference to ideas, so that reality comes primarily of nothing being done for ideas. This might be briefly summed up, he claimed, by saying that we care too little about what is happening and too much about to whom, when, and where it is happening, so that it is not the essence of what happens that matters to us but only the plot; not the opening up of some new experience of life but only the pattern of what we already know, corresponding precisely to the difference between good plays and merely successful plays. Which means that we must do the opposite of what we do, and first of all give up being possessive about our experiences. We should look upon our experiences less as something personal and real and more as something general and abstract, or with the detachment with which we look at a painting or listen to a song. They should not be turned in upon ourselves but upward and outward. And if this was true on the personal plane, something more would have to be done on the collective plane, something that Ulrich could not quite pin down and that he called a pressing of the grapes, cellaring the wine, concentrating the spiritual juices, and without all of which the individual could not feel other than helpless, of course, abandoned to his own resources. As he talked on in this vein, he remembered the moment when he had told Diotima that reality ought to be done away with.

Almost as a matter of course, Walter began by declaring all this to be an obvious commonplace. As if the whole world, literature, art, science, religion, were not already a "pressing and cellaring" in any case! As if any literate person denied the value of ideas or failed to pay homage to the spirit, to beauty and goodness! As if education were anything other than an initiation into the world of the human spirit!

Ulrich clarified his position by suggesting that education was merely an initiation into the contemporary and prevalent modes and manners, which are random creations, so that those who seek to acquire a mind of their own must first of all realize that they have none as yet. An entirely open mind, poetically creative and morally experimental on a grand scale, was what he called it.

Now Walter said that Ulrich was being impossible. "You paint a charming picture," he said, "as though we had any choice between living our ideas or living our lives. But you may remember the lines

I am no syllogism nor a fiction—
I am a man, with all his contradiction!

Why not go a step further? Why not demand that we get rid of the belly to make space for the mind? But I say to you: A man is made of common clay! That we stretch out an arm and draw it back again, that we have to decide whether to turn right or left, that we are made of habits, prejudices, and earth, and nevertheless make our way as best we can—that is what makes us fully human. What you are saying, tested even slightly against reality, shows it up as being, at best, mere literature."

"If you will let me include all the other arts under that heading too," Ulrich conceded, "all the teachings on how to live, the religions, and so on, then I do mean something like that: namely, that our existence should consist wholly of literature."

"Really? You call the Savior's mercy or the life of Napoleon *literature?*" Walter exclaimed. But then he had a better idea, and he turned to his friend with all the aplomb of the man holding trumps and said: "You are the kind of man who regards canned vegetables us the raison d'être of fresh greens."

"You're absolutely right. And you could also say that I am one of those who will only cook with salt," Ulrich coolly admitted. He was tired of talking about it.

At this point Clarisse joined in, turning to Walter:

"Why do you contradict him? Aren't you the one who always says, whenever something special happens: Here is something we should be able to put on the stage, for everyone to see and understand?" And turning to Ulrich in agreement, she said: "What we really ought to do is sing! We ought to sing ourselves!"

She had stood up and entered the little circle formed by the chairs. She held herself with a certain awkwardness, as though about to demonstrate her idea by going into a dance. Ulrich, who found such displays of naked emotion distasteful, remembered at this point that most people or, bluntly speaking, the average sort, whose minds are stimulated without their being able to create, long to act out their own selves. These are of course the same people who are so likely to find, going on inside them, something "unutterable"—truly a word that says it all for them and that is the clouded screen upon which whatever they say appears vaguely magnified, so that they can never tell its real value. To put a stop to this, he said: "This was not what I meant, but Clarisse is right; the theater proves that intense personal feelings may serve an impersonal purpose, a complex of meaning and metaphor that makes them more or less transcend the merely personal."

"I know exactly what Ulrich means," Clarisse chimed in again. "I can't remember ever getting a special pleasure out of something because it was happening to *me*. It was *happening*, that was the thing! Like music, for instance," she said, turning to her husband. "You don't want to own it; the joy of it is that it's there! We absorb our experiences and expand them into something beyond ourselves in a single movement; we seek to realize ourselves, yes, but not the way a shopkeeper realizes a profit!"

Walter clutched his head, but for Clarisse's sake he switched to another argument. He did his best to make his words come with the force of a steady, cold jet. "If you value an experience only to the degree that it generates spiritual energy," he said to Ulrich, "then let me ask you this: Doesn't that presuppose a life that has no other aim than to produce spiritual energy and power?"

"It is the life that all existing societies claim as their goal," Ulrich replied.

"In such a world the people would presumably lead their lives under the influence of great passions and ideas, philosophies and novels," Walter continued. "Let me take it a step further: Would they live so as to make great philosophy and poetry possible, or would their lives *be* philosophy and poetry in the flesh, as it were? I'm sure I know which you mean, since the first case would be exactly what we mean by a civilization in the first place. But if you mean the second, aren't you overlooking the fact that such a life-as-art, or whatever you'd call it, unimaginable as it is to begin with, would make philosophy and art quite superfluous; it means one thing only, the end of art!" He flashed this trump card for Clarisse's benefit.

It took the trick. Even Ulrich needed a while to marshal his forces. Then he laughed and said: "Don't you know that every perfect life would be the end of art? It seems to me that you yourself are on the way to perfecting your life at the expense of your art."

He had intended no sarcasm, but Clarisse pricked up her ears.

Ulrich went on: "Every great book breathes this spirit of love for the fate of individuals at odds with the forms the community tries to impose on them. It leads to decisions that cannot be decided; there is nothing to be done but to give a true account of their lives. Extract the meaning out of all literature, and what you will get is a denial, however incomplete, but nonetheless an endless series of individual examples all based on experience, which refute all the accepted rules, principles, and prescriptions underpinning the very society that loves these works of art! In the end, a poem, with its mystery, cuts through to the point where the meaning of the world is tied to thousands of words in constant use, severs all these strings, and turns it into a balloon floating off into space. If this is what we call beauty, as we usually do, then beauty is an indescribably more ruthless and cruel upheaval than any political revolution ever was."

Walter had turned pale to the lips. He hated this view of art as a negation of life, of art against life. He regarded it as offensively bohemian, the dregs of an outdated impulse to shock the conventional mind. He caught the irony of the self-evident fact that in a perfect world there would be no more beauty because it would be superfluous, but he did not hear his friend's unspoken question. For Ulrich was aware of having oversimplified his case. He could just as easily have said the opposite, that art is subversive because art is love; it beautifies its object by loving it, and there may be no other way in this world to beautify a thing or a creature than by loving it. And it is only because even our love consists of mere fragments that beauty works by intensification and contrast. And it is only in the sea of love that the concept of perfection, beyond all intensification, fuses with the concept of beauty, which depends on intensification. Once again Ulrich's thoughts had brushed against "the realm," and he stopped short, annoyed with himself. Walter had meanwhile pulled himself together, and after having rejected his friend's suggestion that people should live more or less as they read, as a commonplace idea as well as an impossible one, he proceeded to prove it evil and vulgar too.

"If a man," he began in the same artfully controlled fashion as before, "were to live his life as you suggest, he would have to accept—not to mention other impossible implications—everything that gave him a good idea, in fact everything even capable of doing so. This would of course mean universal decadence, but since you don't mind that side of it, presumably—unless you are thinking of those vague general arrangements about which you haven't gone into detail—let me ask you only about the personal consequences. It seems to me that such a man is bound to be, in every case in which he doesn't happen to be the poet of his own life, worse off than an animal; if he couldn't come up with an idea, then he couldn't come to any decision either, so that for a great part of his life he would simply be at the mercy of all his impulses, moods, the usual banal passions— in short, at the mercy of all the most impersonal elements of which a man consists, and for as long as the channel leading upward remained blocked, he would have to let himself be the toy of everything that came into his head!"

"Then he would have to refuse to do anything," Clarisse answered in Ulrich's stead. "This is the active passivism of which a person must be capable in some circumstances."

Walter could not make himself look at her. Her capacity for refusal was, after all, a major factor in their life together; Clarisse, looking like a little angel in the long nightgown that covered her feet, had stood on her bed declaiming Nietzschean sentiments, with her teeth flashing: "I toss my question like a plumb line into your soul! You want a child and marriage, but I ask you: Are you the man to have a child? Are you the victorious master of his own powers? Or is it merely the voice of the animal in you, the slave of nature, speaking?" In the twilight of the bedroom this had made a rather gruesome spectacle, while Walter had tried in vain to coax her back down under the bedclothes. And now here she was, armed for the future with a new slogan: active passivism, of which a person had to be capable if need be—a phrase that clearly smacked of a man without qualities. Had she been confiding in Ulrich? Was he encouraging her in her eccentricities? These questions were writhing like worms in Walter's heart, so that he almost felt sick to his stomach. His face turned ashen and all the tension went out of it, leaving it a mass of helpless wrinkles.

Ulrich saw this and asked him warmly if anything was wrong?

With an effort, Walter said no and brightly smiling, invited Ulrich to go on with his nonsense.

"Oh well," Ulrich conceded, "you're not so wrong there. But in a spirit of good sportsmanship we often tolerate actions that are harmful to ourselves, if our opponent performs them in an attractive way; the quality of the performance somehow contends with the quality of the damage done. Very often, too, we have an idea that takes us a step farther along, but all too soon habit, inertia, selfish promptings, and so on take its place, because that's the way things go. So I may have been describing a condition that can never be carried to its proper conclusion, but there's no denying that it is wholly the condition of the world in which we live."

Walter had regained his equanimity. "If you turn the truth upside down, you can always say something that is just as true as it is topsy-turvy," he said gently, without disguising his reluctance for any further argument. "It's just like you to call something impossible but real."

Clarisse, however, was rubbing her nose hard. "And yet it seems very important to me," she said, "that there's something impossible in every one of us. It explains so many things. While I was listening to you both, it seemed to me that if we could be cut open our entire life might look like a ring, just something that goes around something." She had already, earlier on, pulled off her wedding ring, and now she peered through it at the lamplit wall. "There's nothing inside, and yet it looks as though that were precisely what matters most. Ulrich can't be expected to express this perfectly the first time he tries."

And so this discussion ended after all, sad to say, with Walter getting hurt once again.

85

GENERAL STUMM TRIES TO BRING SOME ORDER INTO THE CIVILIAN MIND

Ulrich had probably been out an hour longer than he had indicated on leaving, and was told on his return that a military gentleman had been waiting for him for quite some time. Upstairs, to his surprise, he found General Stumm, who greeted him as an old comrade in arms.

"Do forgive me, old friend," the General called out to him in welcome, "for barging in on you so late, but I couldn't get off duty any sooner, so I've been sitting here for a good two hours, surrounded by your books—what terrifying heaps of them you've got!"

After an exchange of courtesies, it turned out that Stumm had come for help with an urgent problem. Sitting there with one leg flung jauntily over the other, not an easy posture for a man with his waistline, and holding out his arm with its little hand, he said: "Urgent? When one of my aides comes along with an urgent piece of business I usually tell him there's nothing urgent in this world except making it in time to a certain closet. But jokes aside, I had to come and see you about something most important. I've already told you that I regard your cousin's house as a special opportunity for me to learn more about the civilian world and its major concerns. Something nonmilitary, for a change, and I can assure you that I am enormously impressed. On the other hand, while we brass hats may have our weaknesses, we're not nearly as stupid as most people seem to think. I hope you'll agree that when we get something done, we make a good job of it. You do agree? I knew I could trust you to see that, which is why I can confess to you frankly that even so, I am ashamed of our army mentality. Ashamed, I say! Other than our Chaplain General, I seem to be the man in our army who has most to do with the spiritual and mental side of things. But I don't mind telling you that if you take a good look at the military mind, outstanding as it is, it seems to me like a morning roll call. You do remember what a morning roll call is like? The duty officer puts down on his report: So many men and horses present, so many men and horses absent, sick or whatever, Uhlan Leitomischl absent without leave, and so on. But *why* such and such numbers of men and horses are present or sick or whatever, that he never puts down. And it's precisely the sort of thing you need to know when dealing with a civilian administration. When a soldier has something to say, he keeps it short, simple, and to the point, but I often have to confer with those civilian types from the various ministries, and they always want to know, at every turn, the whys and wherefores of every proposal I make, with reference to considerations and interactions on a higher plane. So what I did—this is just between ourselves, you understand—I proposed to my chief, His Excellency General Frost von Aufbruch, or rather I hope to surprise him with it . . . anyhow, my idea is to use my opportunities at your cousin's to get the hang of it all, all these higher considerations and significations, and put them to use, if I may say so without blowing my own horn, to upgrade our military mentality. After all, the army has its doctors, vets, pharmacists, clergy, auditors, commissary officers, engineers, and bandmasters, but what it hasn't got yet is a Central Liaison for the civilian mind.

Only now did Ulrich notice that Stumm von Bordwehr had brought along a briefcase, which he had propped against the desk, one of those leather bags with a shoulder strap for carrying official files through the mazes of government corridors and from one government building to another. The General must have come with an orderly who was waiting for him downstairs, although Ulrich had not seen anyone, for it was costing Stumm quite an effort to pull the heavy bag onto his knees, so as to spring the little steel lock with its imposing air of battlefield technology.

"I haven't been wasting any time since I started attending your meetings"—he smiled, while the light-blue tunic of his uniform tightened around its gold buttons as he stooped—"but there are things, you see, I'm still not quite sure about." He fished out of the bag a number of sheets covered with odd-looking notes and lines.

"Your cousin," he elucidated, "your cousin and I had a quite exhaustive talk about it, and what she wants, understandably enough, is that her efforts to raise a spiritual monument to our Gracious Sovereign should lead to an idea, an idea outranking, as it were, all of the current ideas. But I've noticed already, much as I admire all these people she's invited to work on it, that it's a very tall order. The minute one man says something, another will come up with the opposite—haven't you noticed it?—but what strikes me, for one, as even worse is that the civilian mind seems to be what we call, speaking of a horse, a poor feeder. You remember, don't you? You can stuff that kind of beast with double rations, but it never gets any fatter! Or if it does," he qualified, in response to a mild objection from his host, "even if it does gain weight, its bones don't develop, and its coat stays dull; all it gets is a grass belly. I find that fascinating, you see, and I've made up my mind to look into it, to figure out why we can't get some order into this business."

Stumm smiled as he handed his former lieutenant the first of his papers. "They can say what they like about us," he said, "but we army men have always known how to get things in order. Here's my outline of the main ideas I got out of those fellows at your cousin's meetings. As you'll see, every one of them, when you ask him privately, places top priority on something different." Ulrich looked at the paper in astonishment. It was drawn up like a registration form or, in fact, a military list, divided by horizontal and vertical lines into sections, with entries in words that somehow resisted the format, for what he read here, written in military calligraphy, were the names of Jesus Christ; Buddha, Gautama, aka Siddhartha; Lao-tzu; Luther, Martin; Goethe, Wolfgang; Ganghofer, Ludwig; Chamberlain, and evidently many more, running on to another page. In a second column he read the words "Christianity," "Imperialism," "Century of Interchange," and so on, with yet more columns of words beyond.

"I might even call it a page from the Domesday Book of modern culture," Stumm commented, "because we have expanded it further, and it now contains the names of the ideas, plus their originators, that have moved us in the last twenty-five years. I had no idea what a job it would be!" When Ulrich asked him how he had got this inventory together, he was glad to explain his system.

"I had to commandeer a captain, two lieutenants, and five noncoms to get it done in such short order. If we'd been able to do it in a really up-to-date fashion, we'd simply have sent around a questionnaire to all the regiments: 'Who do you think is the greatest man?' The way it's done nowadays when the papers take a poll and all that, you know, together with an order to report the results in percentages. But of course you can't do that sort of thing in the army, because no unit would be allowed to report any answer other than 'His Majesty the Emperor.' So then I thought of going into which books are the most widely read and have the biggest printings, but there we soon found out that next to the Bible it's the Post Office New Year's booklet, with the new postal rates and the old jokes, which every 'occupant' gets free from his postman in return for his annual tip, which again made us realize what a tricky thing the civilian mind is, since those books that appeal to everyone are generally rated the best, or at least, as they tell me, an author in Germany must have an awful lot of like-minded readers before he can pass for an impressive thinker. So we couldn't take that route either, and how we finally did it I couldn't tell you right now; it was an idea of Corporal Hirsch's, together with Lieutenant Melichar, but we did it."

General Stumm put the sheet of paper aside and, with an expression eloquent with disappointment, pulled out another. After taking inventory of the Central European stock of ideas, he had not only discovered to his regret that it consisted of nothing but contradictions but also been amazed to find that these contradictions, on closer scrutiny, tended to merge into one another.

"By now I'm used to being told something different by each of the famous men at your cousin's when I ask them to enlighten me about something," he said, "but every time I've been talking to them for a while, they still seem to be saying the same thing—that's what I can't get into my head, and it could be that my army-issue brain isn't up to it." The problem that was worrying General Stumm was no trifle and actually should not have been left in the War Office's lap, even though it could be shown that it was intimately related to war. Our times rejoice in a number of great ideas, and by a special kindness of fate each idea is paired with its opposite, so that individualism and collectivism, nationalism and internationalism, socialism and capitalism, imperialism and pacifism, rationalism and superstition, are all equally at home in them, together with the unused remnants of countless opposites of an equal or lesser contemporary value. By now this seems as natural as day and night, hot and cold, love and hate, and, for every tensor muscle in the body, the presence of its opposing extensor muscle, nor would it have occurred to General Stumm—or anyone else—to see anything unusual in any of this, had his ambition not taken the plunge into this adventure because of his love for Diotima. Love cannot settle for a unity of Nature based upon opposites; its need for tenderness demands a unity without contradictions, and so the General had tried in every possible way to establish such a unity.

"Here I have," he told Ulrich as he showed him the relevant pages of his report, "a list I've made up of all the Commanders in Chief of Ideas, i.e., all the names in recent times that have led sizable battalions of ideas to victory. On this other page here you see the battle order; this one is a strategical plan; and this last one is an attempt to establish depots or ordnance bases from which to move further supplies of ideas up to the front. Now, I'm sure you can see—I've made certain that the drawing shows this clearly—when looking at any set of ideas in action, that it draws its supplies of additional troops and intellectual matériel not only from its own depots but also from those of its opponents; you see how it keeps shifting positions and how it suddenly turns unaccountably against its own backup forces; you can see ideas constantly crossing over to the other side and back again, so that you will find them now in one line of battle, now in the other. In short, there's no way to draw up a decent plan of communications or line of demarcation or anything else, and the whole thing is—though I can't actually believe what I'm saying!—what any one of our commanding officers would be bound to call one hell of a mess!"

Stumm slipped several dozen pages into Ulrich's hands. They were covered with strategic plans, railway lines, networks of roads, charts of range and firing power, symbols for different units and for brigade headquarters, circles, squares, crosshatched areas; just like a regular General Staff's plan of operations, it had red, green, yellow, and blue lines running this way and that, with all sorts of little flags, meaning a variety of things (such as were to become so popular the following year), painted in all over the place.

"It's no use," Stumm sighed. "I've tried doing it differently, by representing the problem from a military-geographical angle instead of a strategic one, in the hope of getting at least a clearly defined field of operations, but that didn't work either. Have a look at the oro- and hydrographic sketches." Ulrich saw symbols for mountain peaks branching out and massing together again elsewhere, and for springs, networks of streams, lakes. "I've experimented with all sorts of other ways of trying to pull the whole thing together," the General said, with a gleam of irritation or panic in his normally merry gaze. "But do you know what it's like? It's like traveling second class in Galicia and picking up crab lice. I've never felt so filthy helpless! When you spend a lot of time with ideas you end up itching all over, and you can scratch till you bleed, without getting any relief." His vivid description made Ulrich laugh.

"No, no, don't laugh!" the General pleaded. "I've been thinking that you, now that you've become a leading civilian, would understand this stuff and that you'd understand my problem too. So I've come to you for help. I have far too much respect for the world of the intellect to believe that I can be right about all this."

"You take thinking far too seriously, Colonel," Ulrich said to comfort him. The "Colonel" had just slipped out, and he apologized: "Sorry, General; for a minute you had me back in the days when you sometimes ordered me to join you in a philosophical chat in the corner of the mess hall. I can only repeat, a man shouldn't take the art of thinking as seriously as you are doing."

"Not take it seriously!" Stumm groaned. "But I can't go back to just getting along in the mindless way I used to live. Don't you see that? It makes me shudder to think how long I lived between the parade ground and the barracks, with nothing but my messmates' dirty jokes and their stories about their sexual exploits."

They sat down to supper. Ulrich was touched by the General's childlike ideas, on which he then acted with such manly courage, and by the inexhaustible youthfulness that comes from having lived in small garrison towns at the right time of life. He had invited his companion of those years long gone to share his evening meal, and the General was so obsessed by his desire to enter into Ulrich's arcane world that he picked up each slice of sausage with utmost concentration.

"Your cousin," he said, raising his wineglass, "is the most marvelous woman I know. They rightly call her a second Diotima; I've never known anyone like her. You know, my wife . . . you haven't met her. I've nothing to complain of, and then we have the children, but a woman like Diotima . . . well, there's no comparison! When she's receiving I sometimes position myself behind her—what majestic feminine curves!—while at the same time she's talking up front with some outstanding civilian on so high a level that I honestly wish I could take notes! And that Section Chief she's married to has absolutely no idea how lucky he is to have her! I'm sorry if this fellow Tuzzi happens to be someone you like, but I personally can't stand him! All he ever does is slink around with a smirk on his face as if he knew all the answers and won't tell. But I'm not buying that, because with all my respect for the civilian world, government officials are the lowest on my totem pole; they're nothing but a kind of civilian army that try to get the better of us every chance they have, with the outrageous politeness of a cat sitting high up in a tree and looking down at a dog. Your Dr. Arnheim now, that's a man of a different caliber entirely," Stumm went on, "though he may be a bit conceited too, but there's no denying his superiority." He had evidently been drinking too fast, after so much talking, because he was now warming up and growing confidential.

"I don't know what it is," he said. "Maybe the reason I don't understand is that a fellow's mind gets so complicated nowadays, but even though I admire your cousin myself as if—I must say, as if I had a great lump sticking in my throat—still, it's a relief to me that she's in love with Arnheim."

"What? Are you sure there's something going on between them?" Ulrich burst out, although it should not really have been any concern of his; Stumm goggled at him mistrustfully with his shortsighted eyes, still misty with emotion, and snapped on his pince-nez.

"I never said he'd had her," was his straight, soldierly retort. He put his pince-nez back in his pocket and added in quite unsoldierly fashion: "But I wouldn't mind if he had either; devil take me, I've told you already that a man's mind gets complicated in that company. I'm certainly no lover boy, but when I imagine the tenderness Diotima could offer this man I feel a tenderness for him myself, and vice versa, as if the kisses he gave her were my own."

"He gives her kisses?"

"How do I know? I don't go around spying on them. I only mean, if he did. I don't really know what I mean. But I did see him once catching her hand, when they thought nobody was looking, and then for a while they were so quiet together, the kind of stillness you get on the command 'All helmets off, kneel for prayer!' and then she whispered something, it sounded like an appeal, and he answered something. I remember what they said word for word, because it was so hard to understand; what she said was: 'If only we could find the right idea to save us,' and he said: 'Only a pure, unflawed idea of love can save us.' He seemed to have taken her words too personally, because she must have meant the saving idea she needs for her great campaign—What are you laughing at? But feel free to laugh; I've always had my own funny ways, I guess, and now I've made up my mind to help her. There must be something one can do; there are so many ideas floating around, one of them will have to be the saving idea in the end. But I'll need you to give me a hand!"

"My dear General," Ulrich said, "I can only tell you again that you take thinking too seriously. But since you care so much, I'll try to explain as best I can how the civilian mind works." By now they had lighted their cigars, and he began: "First of all, General, you're on the wrong track. The civilian world has no more of a monopoly on the spiritual life than the military has on the physical side, as you think. If anything, it's exactly the other way around. The mind stands for order, and where will you find more order than in the army, where every collar is exactly four centimeters high, the number of buttons on your tunic never varies, and even on nights made for dreams the beds are lined up straight along the wall? The deployment of a squadron in battle formation, the lining up of a regiment, the proper position of bridle and bit—if all these are not significant spiritual achievements, there is no such thing as spiritual achievement!"

"Go teach your grandmother to suck eggs," the General growled warily, uncertain whether to mistrust his ears or the wine.

"Just a minute," Ulrich persisted. "Science is possible only where situations repeat themselves, or where you have some control over them, and where do you have more repetition and control than in the army? A cube would not be a cube if it were not just as rectangular at nine o'clock as at seven. The same kind of rules work for keeping the planets in orbit as in ballistics. We'd have no way of understanding or judging anything if things flitted past us only once. Anything that has to be valid and have a name must be repeatable, it must be represented by many specimens, and if you had never seen the moon before, you'd think it was a flashlight. Incidentally, the reason God is such an embarrassment to science is that he was seen only once, at the Creation, before there were any trained observers around."

But Stumm von Bordwehr, whose entire life had been prescribed for him since his military-school days, from the shape of his cap to permission to marry, was hardly inclined to listen to such doctrines with an open mind.

"My dear fellow," he said craftily. "Maybe so, but what has that to do with me? Very witty of you to suggest that science was invented by us army men, but I wasn't speaking of science at all but, as your cousin says, of the soul, and when she speaks of the soul I feel like taking off all my clothes because the uniform clashes so with it!"

"Stumm, old man," Ulrich went on doggedly, "a great many people accuse science of being soulless and mechanical and of making everything it touches the same. Yet they don't notice that there's much more mechanical or predictable regularity in sentimental matters than in intellectual ones. For when is a feeling really natural and simple? When it can be automatically expected to manifest itself in everybody, given the same circumstances. How could we expect people to behave in a virtuous manner if a virtuous act were not repeatable at will? I could give you many more examples, and if you escape from this drab repetitiveness into the darkest recesses of your being, where the uncontrolled impulses live, those sticky animal depths that save us from evaporating under the glare of reason, what do you find? Stimuli and strings of reflexes, entrenched habits and skills, reiteration, fixation, imprints, series, monotony! That's the same as uniforms, barracks, and regulations, my dear Stumm; and the civilian soul shows an amazing kinship to the military. You might say that it desperately clings to this model, though it can never quite equal it. And where it can't do that, it feels like a child left entirely on its own. Take a woman's beauty, for instance: the beauty that takes you by surprise and bowls you over as if you were seeing it for the first time in your life is really something you have known and sought forever, an image your eyes have long since anticipated, which now comes into full daylight, as it were. But when it's really a case of love at first sight, a kind of beauty you have never perceived before, you simply don't know what to do about it. Nothing like it has ever come your way, you have no name for it, you are not prepared to respond to it, you're hopelessly bewildered, dazzled, reduced to a state of blind amazement, a kind of idiocy that seems to have very little to do with happiness. . . ."

The General could no longer contain his excitement. He had been listening with that expertise one acquired during military exercises when subjected to critical and edifying remarks by superior officers that one must be able to repeat at command but should not really take to heart, or else one might just as well ride home bareback on a porcupine. But now Ulrich had touched him to the quick, and he broke in: "I must say, what you're describing is amazingly on target! When I lose myself in admiration for your cousin, everything inside me seems just to dissolve! And when I do my utmost to pull myself together and come up with some useful idea, my mind turns into an agonizing blank again—'idiotic' may be too strong a word for it, but it's close enough. And so you're saying, as I understand it, that we army men do use our heads, that the civilian mind . . . of course I can't accept your suggestion that they model their thinking on ours; that's just one of your jokes . . . but that we have just as good a mind, well, that's what I sometimes think too. And everything that goes above and beyond thinking, as you say, all that stuff we soldiers regard as so notably civilian, such as the soul, virtue, deep feeling, sentiment—the kind of thing this fellow Arnheim handles with such flair—anyway, you're saying that it's of course part of the human spirit and in fact involves those so-called considerations of a higher sort we've been talking about, but you're also saying that it's quite stupefying, and I must say I totally agree with you, but when all's said and done, the civilian intellect is indisputably the superior one, and so I must ask you, how does it all add up?"

"What I said just now was, *first of all*—you forgot that—first of all, I said, the military life is intellectual by nature, and second, the civilian life is physical by nature. . . ."

"But that's nonsense, surely?" Stumm objected mistrustfully. The physical superiority of the military was a dogma, like the conviction that the officer caste stands nearest to the throne, and even though Stumm had never regarded himself as an athlete, the moment any doubt was cast upon his physical superiority he felt sure that a comparable civilian paunch had to be several degrees flabbier than his own.

"No more and no less nonsense than everything else," Ulrich defended himself. "But let me finish. About a hundred years ago, you see, the leading brains in German civilian life believed that a man using his head could deduce the world's laws while sitting at his desk, like so many geometric theorems about triangles. And the typical thinker was a man in homespun who tossed his long hair back from his forehead and hadn't even heard of the oil lamp, much less of electricity and the phonograph. Such arrogance has been purged out of our system since then; in these last hundred years we've become much better acquainted with ourselves and with nature and everything, but as a result, the better we understand things in detail, the less we understand the whole, as it were, so what we get is a great many more systems of order and much less order over all."

"That fits in with my own findings," Stumm agreed.

"Only most people aren't as keen as you are on making sense of it,"

Ulrich continued. "After so many struggles, we're on a downward slide now. Just think what's happening today: As soon as some leading thinker comes up with an idea it is immediately pulled apart by the sympathies and antipathies generated: first its admirers rip large chunks out of it to suit themselves, wrenching their masters' minds out of shape the way a fox savages his kill, and then his opponents destroy the weak links so that soon there's nothing left but a stock of aphorisms from which friend and foe alike help themselves at will. The result is a general ambiguity. There's no Yes without a No dangling from it. Whatever you do, you can find twenty of the finest ideas in support and another twenty against it. It's much like love or hatred or hunger, where tastes have to differ so that each can find his own."

"You've said it!" Stumm exclaimed, in wholehearted agreement again. "I myself have already put something like it to Diotima. But don't you think that all this confusion seems to justify the military position—though I'd be mortified to have to believe it even for a minute!"

"I'd advise you," Ulrich said, "to tip off Diotima that God, for reasons still unknown to us, seems to be leading us into an era of physical culture, for the only thing that gives ideas some sort of foothold is the body to which they belong—which gives you, as an army officer, something of an advantage."

The tubby little General winced. "On the plane of physical culture I look about as beautiful as a peeled peach," he said after a while, with bitter satisfaction. "And I'd better make it clear that I think of Diotima only in an honorable way, and hope to pass muster in her eyes in the same fashion."

"Too bad," Ulrich said. "Your aims would be worthy of a Napoleon, but you won't find this the right century for them."

The General swallowed this gentle gibe with the dignity of a man conscious of suffering for the lady of his heart, and only said, after a moment's thought: "Thank you, in any case, for your interesting advice."

86

THE INDUSTRIAL POTENTATE AND THE MERGER OF SOUL WITH BUSINESS. ALSO, ALL ROADS TO THE MIND START FROM THE SOUL, BUT NONE LEAD BACK AGAIN

At this time, when the General's love for Diotima took a back seat to his admiration for Diotima and Arnheim as a pair, Arnheim should long since have made up his mind never to come back. Instead, he made arrangements to prolong his stay; he kept his suite at the hotel, and the great mobility of his life seemed to have come to a standstill. It was a time when the world was being shaken up in various ways, and those who kept themselves well informed toward the end of the year 1913 lived on the edge of a seething volcano, although the peaceful processes of production everywhere suggested that it could never really erupt again. The power of this suggestion was not equally strong everywhere. The windows of the handsome old palace on the Ballhausplatz where Section Chief Tuzzi held sway often lit up the bare trees in the gardens across the way until late into the night, giving a thrill of awe to the better class of strollers who might be passing by in the darkness. For just as his sainthood permeates the figure of the humble carpenter Joseph, so the name Ballhausplatz permeated that palace with the aura of being one of a half-dozen mysterious kitchens where, behind drawn curtains, the fate of mankind was being dished up. Dr. Arnheim was quite well informed of what was going on. He received coded telegrams and, from time to time, a visit from one of his managers, bringing confidential information from company headquarters; the windows of his hotel suite, too, were often lit up till all hours, and an imaginative observer might easily have thought that a secondary or counter-government was here in nightly session, a modern, apocryphal battle station of economic diplomacy.

Nor did Arnheim for his part ever neglect to produce such an impression; without the power of suggestion in his appearance, a man is only a sweet watery fruit without a peel. Even at breakfast, which for this reason he never took in private but in the hotel restaurant, open to all, he dictated his orders for the day to his shorthand-scribbling secretary with the authoritative air of the experienced ruler and the courteous poise of a man who knows all eyes are upon him. Arnheim would have found none of the details inspiring in themselves, but since they not only combined to lay claim to his attention but also made room for the charms of breakfast, they produced a heightened sense of things. Human talent, he liked to think, probably needs to be somewhat restricted if it is to unfold to its best potential; the really fertile borderland between reckless freedom of thought and a dispirited blankness of mind is, as everyone who knows life is aware, a very narrow strip of territory. Besides, he never doubted that it made all the difference *who* had an idea. Everyone knows that new and important ideas seldom arise in only one mind at a time, while, on the other hand, the brain of a man who is accustomed to thinking is constantly breeding thoughts of unequal value, so that the end result, its final effective form, always comes to an idea from the outside, not merely from the thinker's mind but from the whole concatenation of his circumstances. A question from the secretary, a glance at a nearby table, a greeting from someone entering the room, or some such thing would always remind Arnheim, at just the right moment, that he must keep up an imposing presence, and this perfecting of his appearance carried over to his thinking as well. It all culminated in his conviction, suiting his needs, that the thinking man must always be simultaneously a man of action.

Nevertheless, he attached no great importance to his present occupation; even though it was designed to achieve something that might, under certain circumstances, be remarkably profitable, he still felt that he was overstaying his time here. He repeatedly reminded himself of that cold breath of ancient wisdom, *Divide et impera*, which applies to every transaction and calls for a certain subordination of each individual instance to the whole, for the secret of the successful approach to any undertaking is the same as that of the man who is loved by many women while himself careful to play no favorites. But it was no use. Fully mindful of the demands the world imposes on a man born to action on a grand scale, and no matter how often he took pains to search his soul, he could not close his eyes to the fact that he was in love. It was an awkward fix, because a heart turned fifty is a tough muscle, not so easily stretched as that of a twenty-year-old in love's springtime, and it caused him considerable vexation.

It troubled him, to begin with, that his interest in his far-flung international concerns was withering like a flower cut off at the root, while everyday trivia like a sparrow on his windowsill or a waiter's smile positively blossomed into significance for him. As to his moral concepts, normally a comprehensive system for being always in the right, without any loopholes, he saw them shrinking in scope while taking on a certain physical quality. It could be called devotion, but this again was a word that usually had a much wider and anyway a quite different meaning, for without devotion nothing can be achieved in any sphere: devotion to duty, to a superior or a leader, even devotion to life itself, in all its richness and variety, seen as a manly quality, had always seemed to him to be uprightness itself, which for all its openness had more to do with restraint than with a yielding up of the self. And the same might be said of faithfulness, which, confined to a woman, smacks of limitation, as was true of chivalry and gentleness, unselfishness and delicacy, all of them virtues usually thought of in association with her but losing their richest quality thereby, so that it is hard to say whether a man's experience of love only flows toward a woman as water tends to collect in the lowest, generally not the most acceptable spot, or whether the love of a woman is the volcanic center whose warmth sustains all life on earth. A supreme degree of male vanity therefore feels more at ease in male rather than female company, and when Arnheim compared the wealth of ideas he had brought to the spheres of power with the state of bliss he owed to Diotima, he could not shake off the sense of having slipped somehow.

At times he longed for embraces and kisses like a boy ready to fling himself passionately at the feet of the coldhearted beloved refusing him, or else he caught himself wanting to burst out sobbing, or hurl a challenge to the world and, finally, carry off the beloved in his arms. Now, we all know that the irresponsible margin of the conscious personality that breeds stories and poems is also the home base of all sorts of childish memories that surface on those rare occasions when the intoxication of fatigue, the release of alcohol, or some other disturbance brings them to light. Arnheim's bursts of feeling were no more substantial than these phantoms, so that he need not have been upset by them (thereby considerably increasing his original agitation), if these infantile regressions had not forced him to realize that his inner life was swarming with faded moral stereotypes. The stamp of general validity he was always at pains to give to his actions, as a man conscious of living with the eyes of all Europe upon him, suddenly showed itself as having nothing to do with his inner life. This may be quite natural for anything supposed to be valid for everyone, but what troubled him was the implication that if what is generally valid is not the inward truth, then contrariwise the inward man is not generally valid. And so Arnheim now felt haunted at every step not only by the urge to sound some deafening wrong note, or perform some foolishly illegitimate act, but also by the annoying thought that on some irrational level this would be the right thing to do. Ever since he had come to know again the fire that makes the tongue go dry in the mouth, he was overcome with the sense of having lost a path he had always followed, the feeling that the whole ideology of the great man he lived by was only an emergency substitute for something that was missing.

This naturally brought his childhood to mind. In his early portraits he had big, dark, round eyes, like the paintings of the boy Jesus disputing with the doctors in the Temple, and he saw all his governesses and tutors standing around him in a circle, marveling at his precocity, because he had been a clever boy who had always had clever teachers. He had also proved himself to be a warmhearted, sensitive child who would tolerate no unfairness; since his life was far too sheltered to let any unfairness come his way, he made the wrongs of others his own where he came across them, and got himself into fights on their account. This was quite an achievement, considering what obstacles were put in his way to prevent this very thing, so that it never took more than a minute for someone to come rushing up to pry him loose from his opponent. Because such fights lasted just long enough to give him a taste of some painful experience but were always interrupted in time to leave him with the impression of his own unflinching courage, Arnheim still remembered them with self-satisfaction; and this lordly quality of courage that would shrink from nothing passed later into his books and his principles, as becomes a man who needs to tell his contemporaries how to conduct themselves for self-respect and happiness.

This childhood state was still vividly present to his mind, while another condition, of a somewhat later period, that had succeeded and partly transformed it now appeared to be dormant or on the verge of petrifaction—if this is understood as turning not to stone, in the ordinary sense, but to diamonds. It was love, now startled into a new life by his contact with Diotima, and it was characteristic of Arnheim that his first youthful experience of love had nothing to do with women, or indeed any specific persons; this was a rather perplexing business he had never quite resolved for himself, even though in the course of time he had come to learn the most up-to-date explanations for it.

"What he meant was perhaps only the baffling manifestation of something still absent, like those rare expressions that appear on faces with which they have no connection, belonging rather to other, different faces suddenly intuited beyond the horizon of the visible; simple melodies in the midst of mere noise, feelings inside people, feelings he sensed inside himself, in fact, that were not yet real feelings when he tried to capture them in words, but only something inside him reaching outward, its tips already breaking the surface, getting wet, as things sometimes do reach out on fever-bright spring days when their shadows creep beyond them and come to rest so quietly, all flowing in one direction, like reflections in a stream."

This was how it was expressed, much later on and in other accents, by a poet Arnheim esteemed because to know of this reclusive man who avoided all notoriety made one an insider; not that Arnheim understood him, for he associated such allusions with the talk about the awakening of a new soul that had been in fashion during his youth, or with the then popular pictures of reedy girls, painted with a pair of lips that looked like fleshy flower buds.

At that time, around the year 1887—"good heavens, almost a generation ago!" Arnheim thought—he appeared in photographs as the "new man" of the period, in a high-buttoned black satin waistcoat with a wide, heavy silk cravat deriving from the Biedermeier style but meant to suggest the Baudelairean, with the help of an orchid (the latest thing) in his buttonhole, exerting a malevolent fascination on all who saw Arnheim junior on his way to dine and impress his youth-

ful person on some robust businessmen friends of his father's. Portraits of young Arnheim at work ran to a slide rule peeping decora-
tively from the breast pocket of a tweedy English sport jacket, worn
quite comically with a towering stiff collar, which nevertheless
heightened the effect of the head. That was how Arnheim had
looked, and he still could not keep from looking at his image with a
certain approval. He had played good tennis when it was still played
on lawns, with all the zeal of a passion as yet reserved for the few;
surprised his father by openly attending workers' meetings, after a
student year in Zurich where he had become unsuitably acquainted
with socialist ideas, which did not prevent him from galloping his
horse recklessly through a working-class quarter of town on another
day. In short, it had all been a whirl of contradictory but challenging
new experiences which gave him the enchanting illusion of having
been born at just the right time, an illusion so important to a young
man, even though he realizes later on that its value does not lie in its
rarity, exactly. As time went on and Arnheim came to think more and
more conservatively, he did wonder whether this ever-renewed feeling of being the last word wasn't part of nature's wastefulness; but he
never gave it up, because he never did like to give up anything that
had ever belonged to him, and his collector's nature had carefully
preserved within him all there was at the time. But today it seemed
to him, however rounded and various his life appeared to be, that he
had been most particularly moved and most lastingly influenced by
what had seemed at first the most unreal element of all: precisely
that romantically expectant state of mind whispering to him that he
belonged not only to the world of bustling activity but to yet another
world, suspended inside it, as if holding its breath.

This dreamy expectancy, restored to him in its full original freshness by Diotima's influence, becalmed all activity and busyness now;
the tumult of youthful conflict and hopeful, ever-changing vistas
gave way to a daydream in which all words, events, and needs were
basically the same deep down, away from their surface differences.
At such moments even ambition was hushed; the world was a distant
noise beyond the garden wall, as though his soul had overflowed its
banks and was truly present to him for the first time. It cannot be too
strongly emphasized that this was not a philosophy but as physical an
experience as seeing the moon, though overwhelmed by daylight,

hovering mutely in the morning sky. In such a state of mind even the young Paul Arnheim had calmly dined at select restaurants, dressed with care to attend all the social functions, done everything that had to be done but always, as it were, with no greater or lesser distance from one part of himself to the other than to or from the next person or object; somehow the outer world did not leave off at his skin, and his inner world did not merely shine out through the window of re-flection, but both blended into a single undivided state of separate-ness and presence, as mild, calm, and lofty as a dreamless sleep. Morally it felt like a truly great indifference, a sense of all values being equal; nothing was minor or major: a poem and a kiss on a woman's hand were the equal in significance of a scholarly work in several volumes or some great act of statesmanship, and just as ev-erything evil was meaningless, so, basically, everything good had become superfluous in this immersion in the tender primal kinship of all created things. Arnheim behaved quite normally, except that he was doing it in an intangible atmosphere of special significance, behind the tremulous flame of which the inner man stood motion-less, watching the outer man eating an apple or being measured for a new suit.

Was it illusion, then, or the shadow of a reality never to be quite understood? The only possible answer is that all religions, at certain stages of their development, have asserted the reality of this shadow, and so have all lovers, all romantics, all those with a hankering for the moon, for springtime, and the blissful dying of the days in early fall. Eventually it fades away, however, it evaporates and dries up, one cannot say which—until one day something else has taken its place and it is instantly forgotten as only unreal experiences, dreams, and illusions are forgotten. Since this primal and cosmic love experience is normally encountered the first time one falls in love, one usually thinks even later in life that one knows just what to make of it, re-garding it as part of the foolishness one may indulge in before one is old enough to vote. So this was how it was with him, but since for Arnheim it had never been associated with a woman, it could never quite leave his heart in the usual way, along with her; instead, it was overlaid by impressions received, after completing his schooling, when he entered his father's business. Since he did nothing by halves, he soon discovered here that the productive and well-balanced life is a poem greater by far than any hatched out by a poet in his garret, and a different sort of thing altogether.

Now for the first time he showed his talent for being an exemplary character. The poem of life has this advantage over all other poems, that it is set in all capital letters, as it were, no matter what its content may be. Even the youngest trainee in a firm of world rank has the whole world circling around him, with continents peering over his shoulder, so that nothing he does is without significance, while the lone writer in his seclusion has at most flies circling around him no matter how hard he tries to get something done. This is so obvious that many people, from the moment they begin to work in the medium of life itself, regard everything that used to move them before as "mere literature," meaning that the effect it has is at best weak and muddled, generally contradictory so that it cancels itself out, and anyway not in proportion to the fuss made over it. Arnheim was not quite like that, of course; he neither denied the noble influence of art nor was capable of regarding anything that had once strongly moved him as foolishness or a delusion. When he recognized the superiority of his adult responsibilities over the dreamy outlook of his youth he took steps, guided by his new mature insights, to effect a fusion of both kinds of experience. He did, in fact, what so many, certainly the majority of the professional classes, do after beginning their careers: far from wishing to turn their backs entirely on their former interests, they find themselves for the first time in a serene, mature relationship to the enthusiastic impulses of their younger years. Discovering the great poem of life, knowing their own part in it, restores to them the courage of the dilettante they had lost when they burned their own poems. Working on the poem of their own life, they can at last regard themselves as *born* experts and set about permeating their daily round with a sense of intellectual responsibility, feeling themselves faced with a thousand small decisions in making it moral and attractive, modeling themselves on their notion of how Goethe led his life and giving everyone to understand that without music, without the beauties of nature and the sight of animals and children at play, and without a good book, life would not be worth having. This soulful middle class is still, among Germans, the leading consumer of the arts and of all literature that is not too heavy; but its members understandably look down upon art and literature, which they once regarded as the ultimate fulfillment, as upon an earlier stage of development, even though it may have been more perfect in its way than what fate allotted to them; or else they regard it much as a manufacturer of sheet metal, say, might regard a sculptor of plaster statues if he were weak enough to see any beauty in that sort of product.

Now Arnheim resembled this cultural middle class as a glorious hothouse double carnation resembles a weedy little pink growing wild at the roadside. He never thought in terms of a cultural revolution or radical innovation, but thought only of the interweaving of the new into the traditional, a taking over, with gentle modifications and a moral reanimation, of the faded privileges of the powers that were. He was no snob, no worshiper of those who outranked him in society. Received at court and on terms with the high nobility and the leading government officialdom, he adjusted himself to this environment not at all as an imitator but only as an amateur of the conservative feudal manner, one who never forgets or seeks to make others forget his patrician, quasi-Goethean-Frankfurt, origins. But with this concession his capacity for resistance was exhausted, and any greater distancing of himself from greatness would have seemed to him untrue to life. He was deeply convinced that the creators of wealth—led by the businessmen who directed life and would be shaping a new era—were destined to take over at some point from the ruling powers, and this gave him a certain quiet arrogance, which had been proved valid enough by the subsequent course of events. But taking money's claim to power as a given, the question was still how the desired power was to be rightly used. The bank directors' and industrial magnates' predecessors had no problem; they were feudal knights who made literal mincemeat of their enemies, leaving the clergy to handle the morals. But while contemporary man has in money, as Arnheim saw it, the surest control of society, a means as tough and precise as the guillotine, it can also be as vulnerable as an arthritic—how painfully the money market limps and aches all over at the slightest draft!—and is most delicately involved with everything it controls. Because he understood this subtle interdependence of all the forms of life, which only the blind arrogance of the ideologue can overlook, Arnheim came to see the regal man of business as the synthesis of change and permanence, power and civility, sensible risk-

taking and strong-minded reliance on information, but essentially as
the symbolic figure of democracy-in-the-making. By the persistent
and disciplined honing of his own personality, by his intellectual
grasp of the economic and social complexes at hand, and by giving
thought to the leadership and structure of the state as a whole, he
hoped to help bring the new era to birth, that age where the social
forces made unequal by fate and nature would be properly and fruit-
fully organized and where the ideal would not be shattered by the
inevitable limitations of reality, but be purified and strengthened instead. Objectively put, he had brought about the fusion of interests
between business and the soul by working out the overall concept of
the Business King, and that feeling of love that had once taught him
the unity of all things now formed the nucleus of his conviction that
culture and all human interests formed a harmonious whole.

It was at about this time, too, that Arnheim began to publish his
writings, and in them surfaced the term "soul." He presumably resorted to it as a device, a flying start, a royal motto, since princes and
generals certainly have no souls, and as for financiers, he was the very
first to have one. It undoubtedly also played a part in his need to set
up defenses that could not be breached by the business mentality of
those forming his intimate circle, and more specifically by the imperious nature and greater business sense of his father, beside whom
he was beginning to assume the role of the aging crown prince. And
it is equally certain that his ambition to master all worthwhile knowledge—a taste for polyhistory so consuming that no single man could
have lived up to the goals he set himself—found in the soul a means
to rise above all that his intellect could not encompass. In this he was
a man of his time, which had recently developed a strong religious
bent, not because it had a call to religion but only, it seems, out of an
irritable feminine revolt against money, science, and calculation, to
all of which it succumbed with a passion. What was questionable and
uncertain, however, was whether Arnheim, in speaking of the soul,
believed in it; whether it was real to him, like his stock portfolio. He
used the word to express something for which he had no other term.
Driven by his need to use it in conversation—Arnheim was a talker
who did not easily let anyone else get a word in—and finding that he
made an impression, he came to use it more and more in his writings,
referring to it as though its existence were as assured as that of one's

own back, even though one never gets to see it. And so he wrote with real fervor of something vague and portentous that is interwoven with the all-too-factual world of business affairs as a profound silence is interwoven with vivid speech. He did not deny the usefulness of knowledge; quite the contrary, he was himself an impressively busy compiler of data, as only a man who has all the resources at his command can be, but once he had proved himself in that arena he would say that above and beyond this level of keenness and precision there was a higher realm of wisdom that was accessible only to the visionary. He spoke of the will by which nation-states and international business giants are founded, so as to let it be understood that with all his greatness he was nothing but an arm that could be moved only by a heart beating somewhere beyond the range of human vision. He held forth on technological advances or moral values in the most down-to-earth fashion, in terms familiar to the man in the street, only to add that such exploitation of nature and man's spiritual energies amounted to nothing more than a fatal ignorance if the sense was lacking that they were merely the surface ripples of an ocean the immense depths of which were hardly touched by them. He delivered such sentiments in the manner of the regent of an exiled queen who had received her personal instructions and orders the world accordingly.

This keeping the world in order was perhaps his truest and fiercest passion, a craving for power far surpassing everything even a man in his position could afford, which drove this man who was so powerful in the real world to withdraw at least once a year to his castle in East Prussia, where he dictated a whole book to his secretary. The strange sense of mission that had surfaced first and most vividly in his early days of youthful enthusiasm and still afflicted him from time to time, though with lessened intensity, had found this outlet for itself. In the thick of his global undertakings it came over him like a sweet trance, a longing for the cloister, murmuring to him that all the contradictions, all the great ideas, all worldly experience and effort, were a unity, not only as vaguely understood by what we call culture and humanity but also in a wildly literal and shimmeringly passive sense, as when on a morbidly lovely day one might gaze out over river and meadows, hands crossed in one's lap, unwilling to tear oneself away, evermore. In this sense, his writing was a compromise. And because there is only one soul, not within reach but in exile, from which it has only one way to make itself known to us in all its hazy ambiguity, while there are such countless, endless problems in the world to which its royal message can be applied, so, as the years went by, he found himself in that grave embarrassment suffered by all legitimists and prophets when it is all taking too long to happen. Arnheim had only to sit down alone to write for his pen to start leading him, with a truly uncanny flow of words, from the soul to the problems of the mind, the moral life, economics, and politics, all brilliantly lighted from some invisible source and appearing in a clear and magically unifying illumination. There was something intoxicating in this expansiveness, but it depended on that split consciousness which alone makes creative composition possible for so many writers, in that the mind shuts out and forgets whatever does not happen to fit into its scheme. Speaking to another person, whose presence was a link to the rest of the world, Arnheim would never have let himself go so recklessly; but bent over a sheet of paper that was ready to reflect his views, he joyfully abandoned himself to a metaphoric expression of his convictions, only a small portion of which had any basis in fact, while the greater part was a billowing cloud of words whose sole— and incidentally not inconsiderable—claim to reality was that it always arose spontaneously in the same places.

Anyone inclined to find fault should remember that having a split personality has long since ceased to be a trick reserved for lunatics; at the present-day tempo, our capacity for political insight, for writing a piece for the newspapers, for faith in the new movements in art and literature, and for countless other things, depends wholly on a knack for being, at times, convinced against our own convictions, splitting off a part of our mind and stretching it to form a brand-new wholehearted conviction. So it was another point in Arnheim's favor that he never quite honestly believed what he was saying. As a man in his prime he had already had his say on anything and everything; he had his convictions, which covered much ground, and saw no barriers to going on spinning new convictions smoothly out of the old ones, indefinitely. A man whose mind worked to such good effect and who could switch it in other states of consciousness to checking balance sheets and estimating profits to be made on his deals could not fail to notice that there was no shape or set course to his activity, though it continued to expand almost inexhaustibly in every direction; it was bounded only by the unity of his person, and although Arnheim could hold a large amount of self-esteem, this was not for him an intellectually satisfactory state of affairs. He tried blaming it on the residual element of irrationality that the informed observer can detect everywhere in life; he tried to shrug it off on the grounds that in our time everything tends to overflow its borders, and since no man can quite transcend the weaknesses of his century, he saw in this a welcome chance to practice that modesty typical of all great men by setting up above himself, quite unenviously, such figures as Homer and Buddha, because they had lived in more favorable eras. But as time went on and his literary success peaked without making any real difference to his crown-princely state, that element of irrationality, the absence of tangible results, and his troubling sense of having missed his target and lost his original resolve became more oppressive. He surveyed his work, and even though he saw that it was good, he felt as though all these ideas were setting up a barrier between some haunting primal home and himself, like a wall of diamonds growing daily more encrusted.

Something unpleasant of this sort had happened and left its mark on him just recently. He had made use of the leisure he currently indulged himself in more frequently than was his habit, to dictate to his secretary an essay on the essential accord between government architecture and the concept of the state, and he had broken off a sentence intended to run "Contemplating this edifice, we see the silence of the walls" after the word "silence," in order to linger for a moment over the image of the Cancelleria in Rome, which had just risen up unbidden before his inner eye. But as he looked at the typescript over his secretary's shoulder he noticed that, anticipating him as usual, the secretary had already written: ". . . we see the silence of the soul." That day Arnheim dictated no more, and on the following day he had the sentence deleted.

Compared with experiences that reached so far and so deep, what price the ordinary physical love for a woman? Sadly, Arnheim had to admit to himself that it mattered just as much as the realization, summing up his life, that all roads to the mind start in the soul, but none lead back there again. There were of course many women who had enjoyed close relations with him, but other than the parasitic species they tended to be professionally engaged, educated women or artists, for with these two kinds, the kept women and the self-sustaining types, it was possible to have a clear-cut understanding. His moral nature had always guided him into relationships where instinct and the consequent inevitable arrangements with women could somehow be dealt with rationally. But Diotima was the first woman to penetrate into his pre-moral, secret inner life, and this almost made him look at her askance. She was only the wife of a government official, after all, socially most presentable, of course, but without that supreme degree of cultivation that comes only with power, while Arnheim could marry a daughter of American high finance or of an English duke. He had moments of recoiling with a primitive nursery antagonism, the naïvely cruel arrogance and dismay of the well-bred child taken for the first time to a city school, so that his growing infatuation seemed to threaten him with disgrace. When at such moments he resumed his business activities with the icy superiority of a spirit that had died to the world and been reborn to it, then the cool rationality of money, immune to contamination, seemed an extraordinarily clean force compared with love.

But this only meant that for him the time had come when the prisoner wonders how he could have let himself be robbed of his freedom without putting up a life-and-death struggle. For when Diotima said: "What do the affairs of the world amount to? *Un peu de bruit autour de notre âme . . . ,*" he felt a tremor go through the edifice of his life.

87

MOOSBRUGGER DANCES

Meanwhile Moosbrugger was still sitting in a detention cell at the district courthouse while his case was under study. His counsel had got fresh wind in his sails and was using delaying tactics with the authorities to keep the case from coming to a final conclusion.

Moosbrugger smiled at all this. He smiled from boredom.

Boredom rocked his mind like a cradle. Ordinarily boredom blots out the mind, but his was rocked by it, this time anyway. He felt like an actor in his dressing room, waiting for his cue.

If Moosbrugger had had a big sword, he'd have drawn it and chopped the head off his chair. He would have chopped the head off the table and the window, the slop bucket, the door. Then he would have set his own head on everything, because in this cell there was only one head, his own, and that was as it should be. He could imagine his head sitting on top of things, with its broad skull, its hair like a fur cap pulled down over his forehead; he liked that.

If only the room were bigger and the food better!

He was quite glad not to see people. People were hard to take. They often had a way of spitting, or of hunching up a shoulder, that made a man feel down in the mouth and ready to drive a fist through their back, like punching a hole in the wall. Moosbrugger did not believe in God, only in what he could figure out for himself. His contemptuous terms for the eternal truths were: the cop, the bench, the preacher. He knew he could count on no one but himself to take care of things, and such a man sometimes feels that others are there only to get in his way. He saw what he had seen so often: the inkstands, the green baize, the pencils, the Emperor's portrait on the wall, the way they all sat there around him: a booby trap camouflaged, not with grass and green leaves, just with the feeling: That's how it is. Then remembered things would pop into his head—the way a bush stood at the river bend, the creak of a pump handle, bits of different landscapes all jumbled up, an endless stock of memories of things he hadn't realized he'd noticed at the time. "I bet I could tell them a thing or two," he thought. He was daydreaming like a youngster: a man they had locked up so often he never grew older. "Next time I'll have to take a closer look at it," Moosbrugger thought, "otherwise they'll never understand." Then he smiled sternly and spoke to the judges about himself, like a father saying about his son: "Just you lock him up, that good-for-nothing, he needs to be taught a lesson."

Sometimes he felt annoyed, of course, with the prison regulations. Or he was hurting somewhere. But then he could ask to see the prison doctor or the warden, and things fell into place again, like water closing over a dead rat that had fallen in. Not that he thought

of it quite in these terms, but he kept having the sense almost constantly these days, even if he did not have the words for it, that he was
like a great shining sheet of water, not to be disturbed by anything.

The words he did have were: hm-hm, uh-uh.

The table was Moosbrugger.

The chair was Moosbrugger.

The barred window and the bolted door were himself.

There was nothing at all crazy or out of the ordinary in what he
meant. It was just that the rubber bands were gone. Behind every
thing or creature, when it tries to get really close to another, is a rubber band, pulling. Otherwise, things might finally go right through
one another. Every movement is reined in by a rubber band that
won't let a person do quite what he wants. Now, suddenly, all those
rubber bands were gone. Or was it just the feeling of being held in
check, as if by rubber bands?

Maybe one just can't cut it so fine? "For instance, women keep
their stockings up with elastic. There it is!" Moosbrugger thought.
"They wear garters on their legs like amulets. Under their skirts. Just
like the rings they paint around fruit trees to stop the worms from
crawling up."

But we mention this only in passing. Lest anyone suppose that
Moosbrugger felt he had to stay on good terms with everything. It
wasn't really like that. It was only that he was both inside and outside.

He was the boss now, and he acted bossy. He was putting things in
order before they killed him off. The moment he thought of anything, anything he pleased, it obeyed him like a well-trained dog to
whom you say: "Down, boy!" Locked up though he was, he had a
tremendous sense of power.

On the dot, his soup was brought. On the dot, he was awakened
and taken out for his walk. Everything in his cell was on the mark,
strict and immovable. This sometimes seemed incredible to him. He
had the strangely topsy-turvy impression that all this order emanated
from him, even though he knew that it was being imposed on him.

Other people have this sort of experience when they are stretched
out in the summery shade of a hedge, the bees are buzzing, and the
sun rides small and hard in the milky sky: the world revolves around
them like a mechanical toy. Moosbrugger felt it when he merely
looked at the geometric scene presented by his cell.

At such times he noticed that he had a mad craving for good food; he dreamed of it, and by day the outlines of a good plate of roast pork kept rising up before his eyes with an uncanny persistence the moment his mind turned back from other preoccupations. "Two portions!" Moosbrugger then ordered. "No, make it three!" He thought this so hard, and heaped up his imaginary plate so greedily, that he instantly felt full to bursting, to the point of nausea; he gorged himself in his imagination. "Why," he wondered, wagging his head, "why do I feel so stuffed, so soon after wanting to eat? Between eating and bursting lie all the pleasures of this world! Hell, what a world! There are hundreds of examples to prove how little space it gives you. To take just one, for instance: a woman you don't have is like the moon at night climbing higher and higher, sucking and sucking at your heart; but once you've had her, you feel like trampling on her face with your boots. Why is it like that?" He remembered being asked about it lots of times. One could answer: Women are women *and* men too, because men chase after them. But it was only one more thing that the people who asked all the questions wouldn't really understand. So they asked him why he thought that people were in cahoots against him. As if even his own body wasn't in cahoots with them! This was quite obvious where women were concerned, of course, but even with men his body understood things better than he did himself. One word leads to another, you know what's what, you're in each other's pocket all day long, and then, in a flash, you've somehow crossed that narrow borderline where you get along with them without any trouble. But if his body had got him into this, it had better get him out of it again! All Moosbrugger could remember was that he'd been vexed or frightened, and his chest with its arms flailing had rushed at them like a big dog on command. That was all Moosbrugger could understand anyway; between getting along and being fed up there's only a thin line, that's all, and once something gets started it soon gets scary and tight.

Those people who were always using those foreign words and were always sitting in judgment on him would keep throwing this up to him: "But you don't go and kill a man just for that, surely!" Moosbrugger only shrugged. People have been done in for a few pennies, or for nothing at all, when someone happened to feel like it. But he had more self-respect than that, he wasn't one of that kind. In time the rebuke registered with him; he found himself wondering why he felt the world closing in on him, or whatever you might call it, time and again, so that he had to clear a space for himself by force, in order that the blood could drain out of his head again. He thought it over. But wasn't it just the same with thinking too? Whenever he felt in the right mood for doing some thinking, the pleasure of it made him want to smile. Then his thoughts stopped itching under the skull, and suddenly there was just one idea there. It was like the difference between an infant's toddling along and a fine figure of a woman dancing. It was like being under a spell. There's the sound of an accordion being played, a lamp stands on the table, butterflies come inside, out of the summer night—that was how his thoughts came fluttering into the light of the one idea, or else Moosbrugger grabbed them with his big fingers as they came and crushed them, looking for one breathtaking moment like little dragons caught there. A drop of Moosbrugger's blood had fallen into the world. You couldn't see it because it was dark, but he could feel what was going on out there. The tangled mess smoothed itself out. A soundless dance replaced the intolerable buzzing with which the world so often tormented him. Everything that happened was lovely now, just as a homely girl can be lovely when she no longer stands alone but is taken by the hand and whirled around in a dance, her face turned upward to a staircase from which others are looking down at her. It was a strange business. When Moosbrugger opened his eyes and looked at the people who happened to be nearby at such a moment, when everything was dancing to his tune, as it were, they, too, seemed lovely to him. They were no longer in league against him, they did not form a wall against him, and he realized that it was only the strain of getting the better of him that twisted the look of people and things like some crushing weight. At such times Moosbrugger danced for them. He danced with dignity and invisibly, he who never danced with anyone in real life, moved by a music that increasingly turned into self-communion and sleep, the womb of the Mother of God, and finally the peace of God himself, a wondrously incredible state of deathlike release; he danced for days, unseen by anyone, until it was all outside, all out of him, clinging to things around him like a cobweb stiffened and made useless by the frost.

How could anyone who had never been through all this judge the rest? After those days and weeks when Moosbrugger felt so light he could almost slip out of his skin, there always came those long stretches of imprisonment. The public prisons were nothing by comparison. Then when he tried to think, everything inside him shriveled up, bitter and empty. He hated the workingmen's study centers and the night schools where they tried to tell him how to think—after all, he knew the heady feeling of his thoughts taking off with long strides, as if on stilts! They made him feel as if he had to drag himself through the world on leaden feet, hoping to find some place where things might be different again.

Now he thought back to that hope with no more than a pitying smile. He had never managed to find a possible resting point midway between his two extremes. He was fed up. He smiled grandly at oncoming death.

He had, after all, seen quite a bit of the world. Bavaria and Austria, all the way to Turkey. And a great deal had happened during his lifetime that he had read about in the papers. An eventful time, on the whole. Deep down he was quite proud to have been a part of it all. Thinking it over bit by bit, he had to take it as a troubled and dreary business, but his own track did run right across it; looking back, you could see it clearly, from birth to death. Moosbrugger was far from feeling that he would actually be executed; he was executing himself, with the help of those other people, that was the way he looked at what was coming. It all added up to a whole, of sorts: the highways, the towns, the cops and the birds, the dead and his own death. It wasn't altogether clear to him, and the others understood it even less, though they could talk more glibly about it.

He spat and thought of the sky, which looks like a mousetrap covered in blue. "The kind they make in Slovakia, those round, high mousetraps," he thought.

88

ON BEING INVOLVED WITH MATTERS OF CONSEQUENCE

It is now high time to consider something previously touched upon in various connections, which might be formulated as: There is nothing so hazardous to the mind as its involvement with matters of great consequence.

A man wanders through a forest, climbs a mountain and sees the world spread out below him, stares at his infant just put into his arms for the first time, or enjoys the good fortune of holding a position in life envied by all. And we ask: What is it like for him? Surely, he thinks, this is all many-layered, deep, important; it's just that he doesn't have the presence of mind to take it at its word, so to speak. The marvel that is facing him and outside him, enclosing him like a magnetic casing, drains his mind and leaves it a blank. While his gaze is held fast by a thousand details, he secretly feels as if he had spent all his ammunition. Outwardly the soul-drenched, sun-drenched, deepened or heightened moment glazes the world with a galvanic silver coating, down to the tiniest leaflets and their capillaries, but here inside, at the world's personal end, a certain lack of inner substance makes itself felt, in the form of a big, vacuous, round O. This condition is the classic symptom of making contact with all that is eternal and great, like dwelling upon the peaks of humanity and nature. Those of us who prefer to live with greatness—first and foremost among whom will be found those great souls for whom little things simply don't exist—find their inward life drawn out of them involuntarily and stretched into an extended superficiality.

The danger of having to do with great things may therefore also be regarded as a law of the conservation of spiritual energy, and it seems to be more or less generally valid. The utterances of socially prominent persons of great influence are usually more vacuous than our own. Ideas closely involved with particularly estimable subjects usually look as though it is only their privileged status that saves them from being regarded as not up to snuff. The causes dearest to our hearts—the nation, peace, humanity, character, and similarly sacred objectives—sprout on their backs the cheapest flora of the mind. This would make ours a topsy-turvy world, unless we assume that the more significant the subject, the more inanely it may be discussed, in which case the world is turned right side up again.

This law, however, helpful as it was toward our understanding of European culture, is not always clearly in evidence, and in times of transition from one group of great causes to another, the mind that seeks to serve some great cause may even seem subversive, although it is only changing its uniform. A transition of this kind was already noticeable when the people we are speaking of were having their anxieties and triumphs. There were already, for instance—to start with a subject of special concern to Arnheim—books enjoying huge sales, though these were not yet the books most respected, even though great respect was reserved only for those books that had impressive sales. Football and lawn tennis had already become influential industries, but there was still some hesitation at the institutes of advanced technology when it came to setting up professorial chairs for teaching them. All in all, whether it was in fact the late lamented rakehell and admiral Drake who introduced the potato from America, heralding the end of recurrent famines throughout Europe, or the less lamented, highly cultivated, and equally pugnacious Admiral Raleigh, or some anonymous Spanish sailors, or even that worthy rascal and slave trader Hawkins, it was a long time before it occurred to anyone to consider these men more important, thanks to the potato, than, say, the physicist Al Shirazi, who is known only for his correct explanation of the rainbow. But with the bourgeois era a revaluation of such achievements began, which in Arnheim's time was far advanced and hindered only by some residual old-fashioned prejudices. The quantity of the effect, and the effect of quantity, as the new, self-evident object of veneration, still struggled against an aging, blind, aristocratic regard for quality, but in the popular imagination this struggle had already spawned fantastic hybrids, quite like the concept of the "great mind" itself, which, in the form we have come to know it in the last generation, is a blend of its significance-as-such and its potato-significance, for we lived in expectation of a man who would personify the solitary genius and yet be instantly understandable to all and sundry like a nightingale.

It was hard to tell what to expect along these lines, since the hazardousness of being involved with greatness is usually not perceived until such greatness is halfway past and gone. Nothing is easier than to look down on the flunky who visibly condescends to His Majesty's guests in His Majesty's name, but whether the man who treats Today respectfully in the name of Tomorrow is a flunky or not is usually not known until the day after Tomorrow. The hazard of being involved with great things includes the unpleasant certainty that while the things change, the hazard remains the same.

89

ONE MUST MOVE WITH THE TIMES

Dr. phil. Arnheim had received a scheduled visit from two top executives of his firm and had held a long conference with them; in the morning, all the papers and calculations still lay in disorder in his sitting room, for his secretary to deal with. Arnheim had decisions to make before his firm's emissaries left by the afternoon train, and he always enjoyed this sort of situation for the pleasurable tension it never failed to arouse. In ten years' time, he reflected, technology will have reached the point when our firm will have its own business planes, and I shall be able to direct my team long distance during a summer vacation in the Himalayas. As he had reached his decisions overnight and had only to go over them and confirm them in the light of day, he was at the moment free. He had ordered his breakfast sent up and was relaxing with his first cigar of the day, mulling over last night's gathering at Diotima's, which he had been obliged to leave rather early.

This time, it had been a most entertaining party, with a large number of the guests under thirty, few over thirty-five, almost still bohemians but already beginning to be famous and noticed in the newspapers: not only native talents but visitors from all over the world attracted by word that in Kakania a lady who moved in the highest circles was blazing a trail for the spirit to penetrate the world. It was, at times, like finding oneself in a literary café, and Arnheim had to smile at the thought of Diotima looking almost intimidated under her own roof; but it had been quite stimulating on the whole and in any case an extraordinary experiment, he felt. His friend Diotima, disappointed with the fruitless meetings of the very eminent, had made a determined effort to give the Parallel Campaign an infusion of the latest trends in thought and had made good use of Arnheim's contacts for the purpose. He merely shook his head when he remembered the conversations he had been obliged to listen to, crazy enough, in his opinion, but one must give way to youth, he told himself; to simply reject them puts one in an impossible position. So he felt as it were seriously amused by the whole thing, which had been a bit much all at once.

They had said to hell with . . . what was it, now? Oh yes, experience. That personal sensory experience the earthy warmth and immediacy of which the Impressionists had apostrophized fifteen years earlier, as though it were some miraculous flower. Flabby and mindless, was their verdict on Impressionism now. They wanted sensuality curbed and a spiritual synthesis.

Now, synthesis probably meant the opposite of skepticism, psychology, scientific study, and analysis, all the literary tendencies of their fathers' generation.

So far as could be gathered, theirs was not so much a philosophical stance as, rather, the craving of young bones and muscles to move freely, to leap and dance, unhampered by criticism. When they felt like it they would not hesitate to consign synthesis to the devil too, along with analysis and all reflection. Then they maintained that the mind needed the sap of immediate experience to make it grow. Usually it was members of some other group who took this position, of course, but sometimes in the heat of argument it could turn out to be the same people.

What fine slogans they came up with! They called for the intellectual temperament. And lightning thought, ready to leap at the world's throat! Cosmic man's sharply honed brain! And what else had he heard?

A new human race, restyled on the basis of an American world plan for production by mechanized power.

Lyricism allied to the most intense dramatism of life.

Technicism—a spirit worthy of the machine age.

Blériot—one of them had cried out—was at that very moment soaring over the English Channel at thirty-five miles an hour! If we could write this "Thirty-five Mile" poem we would be able to chuck all the rest of our moth-eaten literature into the garbage!

What was needed was accelerationism, the ultimate speeding up of experience based on the biomechanics learned in sports training and the circus acrobat's precision of movement!

Photogenic rejuvenation, by means of film . . .

Someone pointed out that a man was a mysterious innerspace, who should be helped to find his place in the cosmos by means of the cone, the sphere, the cylinder, and the cube. Whereupon an opposing voice made itself heard, to the effect that the individualistic view of art underlying that statement was on its way out and that a future humanity must be given a new sense of habitation by means of communal housing and settlements. While an individualistic faction and a socialistic one were forming along these lines, a third one began by voicing the opinion that only religious artists were truly socialminded. At this point a group of New Architects was heard from, claiming leadership on the grounds that religion was at the heart of architecture, besides which it promoted love of one's country and stability, attachment to the soil. The religious faction, reinforced by the geometric one, averred that art was not a peripheral but a central concern, a fulfillment of cosmic laws; but as the discussion went on, the religionists lost the cubists to the architects, whom they joined in insisting that man's relation to the cosmos was, after all, best expressed through spatial forms that gave validity and character to the individual element. The statement was made that one had to project oneself deep into the human soul and give it a fixed three-dimensional form. Then an angry voice dramatically asked all and sundry what they really thought: What was more important, ten thousand starving human beings or a work of art? Since almost all of them were artists of one kind or another, they did in fact believe that art alone could heal the soul of man; they had merely been unable to agree on the nature of this healing process, or on what claims for it should be put to the Parallel Campaign. But now the original social group came to the fore again, led by fresh voices: the question whether a work of art was more important than the misery of ten thousand people raised the question whether ten thousand works of art could make up for the misery of a single human being. Some rather robust artists proposed that artists should take themselves less seriously, become less narcissistic. Let the artist go hungry and develop some social concern! they demanded. Life was the greatest and the only work of art, someone said. A voice boomed out that it was not art but hunger that brought people together! A mediating voice reminded everyone that the best antidote to the overestimation of the self in art was a thorough grounding in craftsmanship. After this offer of a compromise, someone made use of the pause, born of fatigue and mutual revulsion, to ask serenely whether anyone present really supposed that anything at all could be done before the contact between man and space had even been defined? This became the signal for technologists, accelerationists, and the rest to take the floor again, and the debate flowed on, this way and that, for a good while longer. Eventually an accord was struck, however, because everyone wanted to go home, but not without reaching some kind of conclusion, so they all fell in with a statement to the general effect that while the present time was full of expectation, impatient, wayward, and miserable, the messiah for whom it was hoping and waiting was not yet in sight.

Arnheim reflected for a moment.

He had been the center of a circle throughout all this; whenever those on the outer fringe who could not hear or make themselves heard slipped away, others immediately took their place; he had clearly become the center of this gathering too, even when this was not always apparent during the somewhat unmannerly debate. After all, he had for a long time been well up on the subjects discussed. He knew all about the cube and its applications; he had built garden housing for his employees; he knew machines, what made them work, their tempo; he spoke effectively on gaining insight into the self; he had money invested in the burgeoning film industry. Reconstructing the drift of the discussion, he realized besides that it had by no means gone as smoothly as his memory had represented it. Such discussions move in odd ways, as though the contending parties had been assembled blindfolded in a polyhedron, each armed with a stick and ordered to go straight ahead. A confused and wearisome spectacle devoid of logic. But isn't this an image of the way things generally go in life? Here, too, control is gained not by the restraints and dictates of logic, which at most function like a police force, but only by the untamed dynamic forces of the mind. Such were Arnheim's reflections as he remembered the attention that had been paid to him, and he decided that the new style in thinking could be likened to the process of free association, when the conscious mind relaxed its controls, all undeniably very stimulating.

He made an exception and lit a second cigar, though he did not normally give in to such sensual self-indulgence. And even as he was still holding up the match and needed to contract his facial muscles to suck in the first smoke, he could not help smiling as he thought of the little General, who had started a conversation with him at the party the night before. Since the Arnheims owned a cannon and armor-plate works and were prepared to turn out vast quantities of munitions, if it came to that, Arnheim was ready to listen when the slightly funny but likable General (who sounded quite different from a Prussian general, far more unbuttoned in his speech but also, one might say, more expressive of an ancient culture—though, one would have to say, a declining culture) turned to him confidentially and—with such a sigh, downright philosophic!—commented on the discussion going on around them, which at least in part, one had to admit, was radically pacifist in tone.

The General, as the only military officer present, obviously felt a little out of place and bemoaned the fickleness of public opinion, because some comments on the sanctity of human life had just met with general approbation.

"I don't understand these people," were the words with which he turned to Arnheim, seeking enlightenment from a man of internationally recognized intellect. "I simply don't see why these new men in all their ignorance keep talking about generals drenched in blood! I think I understand quite well the older men who usually come here, even though they're rather unmilitary in their outlook as well. When, for instance, that famous poet—what's his name?—that tall older gentleman with the paunch, who's supposed to have written those verses about the Greek gods, the stars, and our timeless emotions: our hostess told me he's a real poet in an age that turns out nothing but intellectuals . . . well, as I was saying, I haven't read any of his works, but I'm sure I'd understand him, if it's true that he's noted mainly for not wasting his time on petty stuff, because that's what we in the army call a strategist. A sergeant—if I may resort to such a humble example—must of course concern himself with the welfare of every single man in his company; the strategist, on the other hand, deals with at least a thousand men at a time and must be prepared to sacrifice ten such units at once if a higher purpose demands it. I see no logic in calling this sort of thing a blood-drenched general in one case and a sense of timeless values in the other! I wish you'd help me understand this if you can."

Arnheim's peculiar position in this city and its society had stung him into a certain, otherwise carefully watched, impulse to mockery. He knew whom the little military gentleman meant, though he did not let on; besides, it didn't matter, since he himself could have mentioned several other varieties of such eminences who had unmistakably made a poor showing this evening.

Glumly thinking it over, Arnheim held back the smoke of his cigar between parted lips. His own situation in this circle had also been none too easy. Despite all his prominence, he had overheard quite a number of nasty remarks that could have been aimed at him personally, and what they condemned was often nothing less than what he had loved in his youth, just as these young men now cherished the pet ideas of their own generation. It was a strange feeling, almost spooky, to find himself revered by young men who, almost in the same breath, savagely ridiculed a past in which he had a secret share of his own; it gave him a sense of his own elasticity, adaptability, and enterprising spirit—almost, one might say, the reckless daring of a well-hidden bad conscience. He swiftly pondered what it was that differentiated him from this younger generation. These young men were at odds with one another on every single point at issue; all they unambiguously had in common was their joint assault on objectivity, intellectual responsibility, and the balanced personality.

There was one thing in particular that enabled Arnheim to take a kind of spiteful joy in this situation. The overestimation of certain of his contemporaries, in whom the personal element was especially conspicuous, had always irked him. To name names, even in his thoughts, was a self-indulgence that so distinguished an opponent as himself would never permit, of course, but he knew exactly whom he meant. "A sober and modest young fellow, lusting for illustrious delights," to quote Heine, whom Arnheim secretly cherished, and whom he recruited for the occasion. "One is bound to extol his aims and his dedication to his craft as a poet . . . his bitter toil, the indescribable doggedness, the grim exertions with which he shapes his verses. . . . The muses do not smile upon him, but he holds the genius of the language in his hand . . . the terrifying discipline to which he must subject himself, he calls a great deed in words." Arnheim had an excellent memory and could recite pages by heart. He let his thoughts wander. He marveled at Heine, who, in attacking a man of his own time, had anticipated phenomena that had only now come fully into their own, and it inspired him to emulate this achievement as he now turned his thoughts to the second representative of the great German idealistic outlook, the General's poet. This was now, after the lean, the fat intellectual kine. This poet's portentous idealism corresponded to those big deep brass instruments in the orchestra that resemble upended locomotive boilers and produce an unwieldy grunting and rumbling. With a single note they muffle a thousand possibilities. They huff and puff out huge bales of timeless emotions. Anyone capable of trumpeting poetry on such a scale— Arnheim thought, not without bitterness—is nowadays rated by us as a poet, as compared with a mere literary man. Then why not rate him as a general as well? Such people after all live on the best of terms with death and constantly need several thousand dead to make them enjoy their brief moment of life with dignity.

But just then someone had made the point that even the General's dog, howling at the moon some rose-scented night, might if challenged defend himself by saying: "So what, it's the moon, isn't it? I am expressing the timeless emotions of my race!" quite like one of those gentlemen so famous for doing the very same. The dog might even add that his emotion was unquestionably a powerful experience, his expression richly moving, and yet so simple that his public could understand him perfectly, and as for his ideas playing second fiddle to his feelings, that was entirely in keeping with prevailing standards and had never yet been regarded as a drawback in literature.

Arnheim, discomfited by this echoing of his thoughts, again held back the cigar smoke between lips that for a moment remained half open, as a token barrier between himself and his surroundings. He had praised some of these especially pure poets on every occasion, because it was the thing to do, and had sometimes even supported them with cash, though in fact, as he now realized, he could not stand them and their inflated verses. "These heraldic figures who can't even support themselves," he thought, "really belong in a game preserve, together with the last of the bison and eagles." And since, as this evening had proved, it was not in keeping with the times to support them, Arnheim's reflections ended not without some profit for himself.

90

DETHRONING THE IDEOCRACY

It probably makes sense that times dominated by the spirit of the marketplace see as their true counterpart those poets who have nothing at all to do with their time, who do not besmirch themselves with the topical concerns of their day but supply only pure poetry, as it were, addressing their faithful in obsolete idioms on great subjects, as though they were just passing through on earth, coming from eternity, where they live, like the man who went to America three years ago and is already speaking broken German on his first visit home. This is much the same as compensating for a big hole by setting a hollow dome on top of it, and since the higher hollowness only enlarges the ordinary one below, nothing is more natural, after all, than that such a period fostering the cult of personality should be followed by one that turns its back on all this fuss over responsibility and greatness.

Arnheim tried cautiously, experimentally, and with the cozy sense of being personally insured against damage, to feel his way into this conjectured future development. This was certainly no minor undertaking. He had to take into account everything he had seen in recent years in America and Europe: the new dance fanatics, whether they were jazzing up Beethoven or transposing the new sensualism into fresh rhythms; the new painters, who tried to express a maximum of meaning by a minimum of lines and colors; the art of the film, where a gesture universally understood, presented with a new little twist, took the world by storm; and finally he thought of the common man, who already, as a great believer in sports, was kicking like a furious baby in his efforts to take possession of Nature's bosom. What is so striking about all this is a certain tendency to allegory, if this is understood as an intellectual device to make everything mean more than it has any honest claim to mean. Just as the world of the Baroque saw in a helmet and a pair of crossed swords all the Greek gods and their myths, and it was not Count Harry who kissed Lady Harriet but a god of war kissing the goddess of chastity, so today, when Harry and Harriet are smooching, they are experiencing the temper of our times, or something out of our array of ten dozen contemporary myths, which of course no longer depict an Olympus floating above formal gardens but present the entire modern hodgepodge itself. On screen and on stage, on the dance floor and at concerts, in cars, on planes, on the water and in the sun, at the tailor's and in the business office, there is constantly in the making an immense new surface consisting of im- and expressions, of gestures, role-playing, and experiences. All these goings-on, each with its distinct outward forms, in the aggregate suggest a body in lively circular motion, with everything inside it thrusting out toward the surface, where it enters into combination with all the rest, while the interior goes on seething and heaving with amorphous life. Had Arnheim been able to see only a few years into the future, he would have seen that 1,920 years of Christian morality, millions of dead men in the wake of a shattering war, and a whole German forest of poetry rustling in homage to the modesty of Woman could not hold back the day when women's skirts and hair began to grow shorter and the young girls of Europe slipped off eons of taboos to emerge for a while naked, like peeled bananas. He would have seen other changes as well, which he would hardly have believed possible, nor does it matter which of those would last and which would disappear, if we consider what vast and probably wasted efforts would have been needed to effect such revolutions in the way people lived by the slow, responsible, evolutionary road traveled by philosophers, painters, and poets, instead of tailors, fashion, and chance; it enables us to judge just how much creative energy is generated by the surface of things, compared with the barren conceit of the brain.

Such is the dethronement of ideocracy, of the brain, the displacement of the mind to the periphery: the ultimate problem, Arnheim thought. This has always been life's way with man, of course, restructuring humankind from the surface inward; the only difference is that people used to feel that they in turn should contribute something from their inside to their outside. Even the General's dog, which Arnheim now kindly remembered, would never have understood any other line of development, for this loyal friend of man's character had still been formed by the stable, docile man of the previous century, in that man's image; but its cousin the prairie wolf, or the prairie rooster, would have understood readily enough. When that wild fowl, dancing for hours on end, plumes itself and claws the ground, there is probably more soul generated than by a scholar linking one thought to another at his desk. For in the last analysis, all thoughts come out of the joints, muscles, glands, eyes, and ears, and from the shadowy general impressions that the bag of skin to which they belong has of itself as a whole. Bygone centuries were probably sadly mistaken in attaching too much importance to reason and intelligence, convictions, concepts, and character; like regarding the record office and the archives as the most important part of a government department because they are housed at headquarters, although they are only subordinate functions taking orders from elsewhere.

All at once, Arnheim—stimulated perhaps by a certain dissolving of tensions under the influence of love—found his way to the redeeming idea that would put all these complications in perspective; it was somehow pleasantly associated with the concept of increased turnover. An increased turnover of ideas and experiences was undeniably characteristic of the new era, if only as the natural consequence of bypassing the time-consuming process of intellectual assimilation. He pictured the brain of the age replaced by the mechanism of supply and demand, the painstaking thinker replaced, as the regulating factor, by the businessman, and he could not help enjoying the moving vision of a vast production of experiences freely mingling and parting, a sort of pudding with a nervous life of its own, quivering all over with sensations; or a huge tom-tom booming with immense resonance at even the lightest tap. The fact that these images did not quite jell, as it were, was already owing to the state of reverie they had induced in Arnheim, who felt that it was just such a life that could be compared with a dream in which one finds oneself simultaneously outside, witnessing the strangest events, and quietly inside, at the very center of things, one's ego rarefied, a vacuum through which all the feelings glow like blue neon tubes. It is life that does the thinking all around us, forming with playful ease the connections our reason can only laboriously patch together piecemeal, and never to such kaleidoscopic effect. So it was that Arnheim mused as a man of business, while at the same time electrified to the twenty tips of his fingers and toes by his sense of the free-flowing psychophysical traffic of the dawning age. It seemed to him far from impossible that a great, superrational collectivity was coming to birth and that, abandoning an outworn individualism, we were on our way back, with all the superiority and ingenuity of the white race, to a Paradise Reformed, bringing a modern program, a rich variety of choices, to the rural backwardness of the Garden of Eden.

There was only one fly in the ointment. Just as in dreams we are able to inject an inexplicable feeling that cuts through the whole personality into some happening or other, we are able to do this while awake—but only at the age of fifteen or sixteen, while still in school. Even at that age, as we all know, we live through great storms of feeling, fierce urgencies, and all kinds of vague experiences; our feelings are powerfully alive but not yet well defined; love and anger, joy and scorn, all the general moral sentiments, in short, go jolting through us like electric impulses, now engulfing the whole world, then again shriveling into nothing; sadness, tenderness, nobility, and generosity of spirit form the vaulting empty skies above us. And then what happens? From outside us, out of the ordered world around us, there appears a ready-made form—a word, a verse, a demonic laugh, a Napoleon, Caesar, Christ, or perhaps only a tear shed at a father's grave—and the "work" springs into being like a bolt of lightning. This sophomore's "work" is, as we too easily overlook, line for line the complete expression of what he is feeling, the most precise match of intention and execution, and the perfect blending of a young man's experience with the life of the great Napoleon. It seems, however, that the movement from the great to the small is somehow not reversible. We experience it in dreams as well as in our youth: we have just given a great speech, with the last words still ringing in our ears as we awaken, when, unfortunately, they do not sound quite as marvelous as we thought they were. At this point we do not see ourself as quite the weightlessly shimmering phenomenon of that dancing prairie cock, but realize instead that we have merely been howling with much emotion at the moon, like the General's much-cited fox terrier.

So there was something not quite in order here, Arnheim thought, arousing himself from his trance— but in any case, a man must move with the times, he added, now fully alert; for what, after all, should come more naturally to him than to apply this tried-and-true principle of production to the fabrication of life as well?

91

SPECULATIONS ON THE INTELLECTUAL BULL AND BEAR MARKET

The gatherings at the Tuzzis now resumed their regular and crowded course.

At a meeting of the Council, Section Chief Tuzzi turned to the "cousin," saying: "Do you realize that all this has been done before?"

With a glance, he indicated the seething human contents of the home of which he was currently dispossessed.

"In the early days of Christianity, the centuries around the birth of Christ. In that Christian-Levantine-Hellenistic-Judaic melting pot

where innumerable sects crystallized." He launched on a list: "Ada-
mites, Cainites, Ebionites, Collyridians, Archontians, Euchites, Oph-
ites . . ." With a funny, hasty deliberateness of tempo that comes of
slowing the pace in order to conceal one's fluency on a subject, he
recited a long series of pre- and early-Christian sect names, as if he
were trying to give his wife's cousin to understand that he knew more
about what was going on in his house than, for reasons of his own, he
usually cared to show.

He then went on to specify that one of the sects named opposed
marriage because of the high value it placed on chastity, while another, also prizing chastity above all, had a funny way of attaining this
aim by means of ritual debauchery. One sect practiced self-mutilation because they regarded female flesh as an invention of the Devil,
while another made its men and women attend services stark naked.
There were those who, brooding on their creed and coming to the
conclusion that the Serpent who had seduced Eve was a divine person, went in for sodomy, while others tolerated no virgins among
their flock because their studies proved that the Mother of God had
borne other children besides Jesus, so that virginity was a dangerous
heresy. Some were always doing the opposite of what others were
doing, for more or less the same reasons and on the same principles.

Tuzzi delivered himself of all this with the gravity appropriate to a
historical disquisition, however peculiar the facts, yet with an under-
tone of what were then called smoking-room stories. They were
standing close to the wall; the Section Chief threw his cigarette stub
into an ashtray with a grim little smile, still absentmindedly eyeing
the throng of guests, as though he had meant to say only enough to
last the time it takes to finish a cigarette, and ended with: "It seems
to me that the differences of opinion and points of view in those days
show a state of affairs not too dissimilar to the controversies among
our intellectuals today. They'll be gone with the wind tomorrow. If
various historical circumstances had not given rise at the right moment to an ecclesiastical bureaucracy with the necessary political
powers, hardly a trace of the Christian faith would be left today. . . ."

Ulrich agreed. "Properly paid officials in charge of the faith can be
trusted to uphold the regulations with the necessary firmness. In
general I feel that we never do justice to the value of our vulgar
qualities; if they were not so dependable, no history would be made

at all, because our purely intellectual efforts are incurably controversial and shift with every breeze."

The Section Chief glanced up at him mistrustfully and then immediately shifted his gaze away again. That sort of comment was too unbuttoned for his taste. He nevertheless acted in a noticeably friendly and congenial fashion, even on such short acquaintance, toward this cousin of his wife's. He came and went and had the air, amid all that was going on in his house, of living in some other, closed world, the loftier significance of which he kept hidden from all eyes; yet there were always times when he could hold out no longer and had to reveal himself to somebody, if only indistinctly, for an instant, and then it was always this cousin with whom he struck up a conversation. It was the natural human consequence of feeling neglected by his wife, despite her occasional fits of tenderness for him. At such times Diotima kissed him like a little girl, a girl of perhaps fourteen, who out of heaven knows what affectation suddenly smothers an even littler boy with kisses. Tuzzi's upper lip, under its curled mustache, would then instinctively draw back in embarrassment. The new conditions in his household got him and his wife into impossible situations. He had certainly not forgotten Diotima's complaint about his snoring, and had also, meanwhile, read the works of Arnheim and was prepared to discuss them with her; they contained some things he could accept, a great deal that struck him as all wrong, and a certain amount he did not understand, though serene in the assumption that this was the author's problem rather than his own. But he had always been accustomed in such matters simply to state the authoritative opinion of a man experienced in these things, and the present likelihood of Diotima's contradicting him every time, of having to debate with her points he considered to be beneath him, struck him as so unfair a change in his private life that he could not bring himself to have it out with her; he even caught himself in vague fantasies of having it out in a duel with Arnheim instead.

Tuzzi suddenly narrowed his beautiful brown eyes in irritation and told himself that he must keep a sharper watch on his moods. The cousin beside him—not at all the sort of man Tuzzi would normally want to become too closely involved with—only reminded him of his wife through an association of ideas that hardly had any real content, the mere fact of their being blood relatives. He had also noticed for

some time that Arnheim seemed, rather cautiously, to be favoring
this young man, who for his own part did not conceal his marked
antipathy to Arnheim: two observations that did not really amount to
much, yet were enough to make Tuzzi aware of his own inexplicable
liking for Ulrich. He opened his eyes again and stared briefly like an
owl across the room, without really looking at anything.

His wife's cousin, incidentally, was staring straight ahead just as
Tuzzi was, bored but at ease with him, and had not even noticed the
pause in their exchange. Tuzzi felt obliged to say something, like a
man who fears that his silence might give away his inwardly troubled
condition.

"You like to take a cynical view," he said with a smile, as if Ulrich's
remark about the bureaucratic administration of religious faith had
only just been allowed to come to his attention, "and I daresay my
wife is not unjustified in fearing to count on your support, despite
her sympathies for you as a cousin. If I may say so, your views on your
fellowmen tend to be on the bearish side."

"What an excellent term for it!" Ulrich said, clearly pleased. "Even
though I'm afraid I don't quite live up to it. It's really history that has
always taken a bearish or a bullish line with all mankind—bearish
when it is using trickery or violence, and bullish more or less in your
wife's manner, by trying to have faith in the power of ideas. Dr. Arnheim, too, if you can believe what he says, is a bull. While you, as a
professional bear amid this choir of angels, must have feelings I
would be interested to hear about."

He regarded the Section Chief with a sympathetic expression.
Tuzzi drew his cigarette case from his pocket and shrugged his shoulders. "What makes you think that my outlook must be different from
that of my wife?" he countered. He had meant to discourage the personal turn the conversation had taken, but his retort had only reinforced it. Luckily, Ulrich had not noticed this, and went on: "We're
made of stuff that takes on the shape of every mold it gets into, one
way or another."

"That's over my head," Tuzzi replied evasively.

Ulrich was glad to hear it. Tuzzi's way was the opposite of his own,
and he took real pleasure in talking with a man who refused to be
goaded into an intellectual discussion and had no other defense, or
would use no other, than to interpose his whole person as a shield.

His original dislike of Tuzzi had long since reversed itself under the pressure of his far greater dislike of the doings under Tuzzi's roof; he simply couldn't understand why Tuzzi put up with it, and could only try to guess. He was getting to know him only very slowly, as one keeps an animal under observation, outwardly, without the ease of insight their words give us into people, who talk because they are clearly impelled to. What appealed to him at first was the dessicated look of the man, who was of just middle height, and the dark, intense eye, betraying much uneasy feeling, not at all the eye of a bureaucrat, nor did it seem to fit in with Tuzzi's present personality as revealed in conversation; unless one assumed something not altogether unusual, that it was a boy's eye peering out from among the man's features, like a window opening out of an unused, locked-up, and long-forgotten part of the interior. The next thing Ulrich had noticed was Tuzzi's body odor, something of china or dry wooden boxes or a mix of sun, sea, exotic landscapes, an obdurate hardness and a discreet whiff of the barbershop. This odor gave Ulrich pause; he had come across only two people with a distinct personal odor; the other one was Moosbrugger. When he called to mind Tuzzi's sharp yet subtle smell and also thought of Diotima, whose ample surface emanated a fine powdery scent that did not seem to mask anything, it came to contrasting kinds of passion that seemed to have nothing to do with the actual life this rather incongruous couple shared. Ulrich now had to make an effort to call his thoughts to order before he could respond to Tuzzi's cool disclaimer.

"It's presumptuous of me," he resumed, in that faintly bored but resolute tone in which one apologizes for having to be a bore in one's turn, because the situation leaves one no alternative, "it certainly is presumptuous of me to offer you my definition of diplomacy, but I do it in the hope that you will straighten me out. Let me put it this way: diplomacy assumes that a dependable social order can be achieved only by mendacity, cowardice, cannibalism, in short, the predictable baseness of human nature. It is based on a bearish idealism, to resort once more to your admirable expression. This is sad in a fascinating way, because it goes with the assumption that our higher faculties are so ambiguous in nature that they can lead us equally well to cannibalism as to the *Critique of Pure Reason.*"

"It really is too bad," the Section Chief protested, "that you have so romantic a view of diplomacy and, like so many others, you confuse politics with intrigue. There may have been something in what you say when diplomacy was still being conducted by highborn dilettantes, but it no longer applies in an age of responsible social leadership. We are not sad, we are optimistic. We must have faith in the future, or we could not live with our conscience, which is no different from everyone else's. If you must talk of cannibalism, then all I can say is that diplomacy can take credit for keeping the world from turning cannibalistic; but to do so, one has to believe in something higher."

"What do you believe in?" Ulrich demanded bluntly.

"Oh, come now," Tuzzi said. "I'm no longer a boy, who might answer such a question point-blank. All I meant was that the more a diplomat can identify himself with the spiritual currents of his time, the easier he will find his profession. And vice versa: we have learned in the course of a few generations that the more progress we make in every direction, the greater our need for diplomacy—but that's only natural, after all."

"Natural? But then you're saying just what I've said!" Ulrich exclaimed, with all the animation consistent with the image they wished to present, of two civilized men engaged in casual conversation. "I pointed out with regret that our spiritual and moral values cannot sustain themselves in the long run without support from what is material and evil, and you reply, more or less, that the more spiritual energy is at work, the more caution is needed. Let us say, then, that we can treat a man as a worm and by this means get him to do not quite everything, and we can appeal to what is best in him and by this means get him to do not quite everything. So we waver between these two approaches, we mix them, that's all there is to it. It seems to me that I may flatter myself on being in far greater accord with you than you're willing to admit."

Section Chief Tuzzi turned to his inquisitor; a tiny smile lifted his little mustache, and his gleaming eyes took on an ironically indulgent expression as he tried to find a way to end this conversation, which was as unsafe as an icy pavement underfoot, and as pointlessly childish as boys skidding on such a pavement. "You know," he answered, "I hope you don't regard this as too crude of me, but I must say that philosophizing should be left to the professors. Always excepting our official great philosophers, whom I hold in greatest esteem and all of whom I've read; they're what we've got to live with. And our professors, well, it's their job, there doesn't have to be any more to it than that; we have to have teachers, to keep things going. But other than that, the fine old Austrian principle that a good citizen shouldn't rack his brains over everything still holds water. It hardly ever does any good, and it is a touch presumptuous too."

The Section Chief rolled himself a cigarette and held his peace; he felt no further need to apologize for his "crudeness." Ulrich, watching his slender brown fingers at their work, was delighted with Tuzzi's half-witted effrontery.

"You have just stated the same, very modern principle that the churches have applied to their members for nearly two thousand years, and which the socialists have begun to follow too," he said politely.

Tuzzi shot him a glance to see what the cousin meant by this analogy; expecting Ulrich to expatiate on it further, he was already annoyed in anticipation of such interminable intellectual indiscretion. But the cousin contented himself with indulgently scrutinizing the man at his side with his pre-1848 mentality. Ulrich had long assumed that Tuzzi must have his reasons for tolerating his wife's relationship with Arnheim within certain limits, and would have liked to know what he hoped to gain by it. It still mystified him. Was Tuzzi acting on the same principle as the banks with respect to the Parallel Campaign (they were keeping as aloof from it as they could without quite giving up their chance to have a finger in the pie) and meanwhile being blind to Diotima's new springtide of love, which was becoming so obvious? Ulrich was inclined to doubt it. He took a certain pleasure in scrutinizing the deep furrows and seams in the man's face and watching the hard modeling of the jaw muscles when those teeth bit into the cigarette holder. Here was an image of pure masculinity. Ulrich was a bit fed up with talking to himself so much, and enjoyed trying to imagine what it must be like to be a man of few words. He supposed that even as a boy Tuzzi had disliked other boys who talked too much, the kind who grow up to be intellectuals, while the boys who would rather spit through their teeth than open their mouths turn into men who prefer not to waste their time, but seek to compensate in action or intrigue, in simple endurance and self-defense, for not indulging any more than they can help in those inescapable acts of feeling and thinking which they somehow find so profoundly embarrassing that they wish they could use thoughts and feelings only to mislead other people. Had anyone said such a thing to Tuzzi, he would naturally have denied it, just as he would deny anything too emotional, because he would not, on principle, tolerate exaggerations and eccentricities in any direction. It was simply out of order to speak to him about what he so admirably represented in person, just as it was to ask a musician, an actor, or a dancer what he was really getting at, and Ulrich was tempted at this point to pat the Section Chief on his shoulder or gently run a hand through his hair, some wordless pantomime or other for the sympathetic understanding between them.

The one thing that Ulrich did not take fully into account was that Tuzzi, not only as a boy but now, that very moment, felt the urge to spit between his teeth in a blast of masculinity. For he sensed something of that vague benevolence at his side, and he felt ill at ease with it. He realized that his remark about philosophy contained an admixture of elements it was not advisable to risk on an outsider, and he didn't know what had possessed him to let himself go so rashly with this cousin (for some reason this was what he always called Ulrich). He couldn't stand voluble men, and wondered with dismay whether he might unconsciously be trying to win this man over as an ally where his wife was concerned; the thought darkened his skin with shame, because such help was unacceptable, and he involuntarily took several steps away from Ulrich, masking his impulse with some awkward excuse.

But then he changed his mind, moved back, and asked: "Incidentally, have you wondered at all why Dr. Arnheim is staying with us so long?" He suddenly imagined that such a question would be the best proof that he regarded any connection between Arnheim's stay and his wife as out of the question.

The cousin gave him an outrageously dumbfounded stare. The answer was so obvious that it was hard to think what else to say. "Do you think," he said haltingly, "that there must be a special reason for it? If so, it would be business, surely?"

"I have nothing to go on," Tuzzi answered, feeling every inch the diplomat again. "But could there be another reason?"

"Of course there can't actually be any other reason," Ulrich conceded civilly. "How very observant of you. For my part I must admit that I never gave it any thought at all; I assumed that it had more or less to do with his literary bent. Wouldn't that be another possibility?"

The Section Chief favored this with no more than an absent smile. "In that case you would have to give me some notion why a man like Arnheim has literary interests in the first place," he said, to his instant regret, because he could see the cousin winding up for one of his lengthy answers.

"Have you never noticed," Ulrich began, "that an incredible lot of people can be seen these days talking to themselves on the street?"

Tuzzi gave a shrug.

"There's something the matter with people. It seems they're unable to take in their experiences or else to wholly enter into them, so they have to pass along what's left. An excessive need to write, it seems to me, comes from the same thing. You may not be able to spot this in the written product, which tends to turn into something far removed from its origin, depending on talent and experience, but it shows up quite unambiguously in the reading of it; hardly anyone reads anymore today; everyone just uses the writer to work off his own excess on him, in some perverse fashion, whether by agreeing or disagreeing."

"So you think there's something the matter with Arnheim's life?" Tuzzi asked, all attention again. "I've been reading his books lately, out of curiosity, because so many people seem to think he has great political prospects, but I must say I can't see what need they fill, or any purpose to them."

"Putting this question in more general terms," the cousin said, "when a man is so rich in money and influence that he can have anything he wants, why does he write at all? It boils down to the naïve question Why do professional storytellers write? They write about something that never happened as if it had actually happened, obviously. Does this mean that they admire life as a beggar admires the rich, whose indifference to him he never tires of describing? Or is it a form of chewing the cud? Or a way of stealing a little happiness by creating in imagination what cannot be attained or endured in reality?"

"Have you never written anything yourself?" Tuzzi broke in.

"Much as it troubles me, never. Since I am far from being so happy that I have no need of it, I am resolved that if I do not soon feel the urge to write, I shall kill myself for being constitutionally so totally abnormal."

He said this with such grave amiability that his little joke unintentionally rose up from the flow of the conversation like a flooded stone surfacing as the water recedes.

Tuzzi noticed, and tactfully covered it over. "All in all, then," he concluded, "you are only confirming my point that government officials begin to write only when they retire. But how does that apply to Arnheim?"

The cousin remained silent.

"Do you know that Arnheim's view of this undertaking to which he is sacrificing so much of his expensive time is totally pessimistic and not at all bullish?" Tuzzi suddenly said, lowering his voice. He had just remembered how Arnheim, in conversation with himself and his wife, had at the very outset expressed grave doubts about the prospects of the Parallel Campaign, and the fact that he happened to recall this at this particular moment, after so long a time, struck him somehow as a diplomatic coup on his own part, even though he had been able to find out virtually nothing, so far, about the reasons for Arnheim's prolonged stay.

The cousin's face actually registered astonishment.

Perhaps he was only accommodating Tuzzi with this look, because he preferred to go on saying nothing. In any case, both gentlemen, who were separated the next moment by guests coming up to them, were in this fashion left with the sense of having had a stimulating talk.

92

SOME OF THE RULES GOVERNING
THE LIVES OF THE RICH

Having so much attention and admiration lavished on him might have made any man other than Arnheim suspicious and unsure of himself, on the assumption that he owed it all to his money. But Arnheim regarded suspicion as the mark of an ignoble character, permissible to a man in his position only on the basis of unequivocal financial reports, and anyway he was convinced that being rich was a personal quality. Every rich man regards being rich as a personal quality. So does every poor man. There is a universal tacit understanding on the point. This general accord is troubled only slightly by the claims of logic that having money, while capable of conferring certain traits of character on whoever has it, is not in itself a human quality. Such an academic quibble need not detain us. Every human nose instantly smells the subtle scent of independence, the habit of command, the habit of always choosing the best of everything for oneself, the whiff of misanthropy, and the unwavering sense of responsibility that goes with power, that rises up, in short, from a large and secure income. Everyone can see at a glance that such a person is nourished and daily renewed by quintessential cosmic forces. Money circulates visibly just under his skin like the sap in a blossom. Here there is no such thing as conferred traits, acquired habits; nothing indirect or secondhand! Destroy his bank account and his credit, and the rich man has not merely lost his money but has become, on the very day he realizes what has happened, a withered flower. With the same immediacy with which his riches were once seen as one of his personal qualities, the indescribable quality of his nothingness is now perceived, smelling like a smoldering cloud of uncertainty, irresponsibility, incapacity, and poverty. Riches are simply a personal, primary quality that cannot be analyzed without being destroyed.

But the effect and the functions of this rare property are most complicated, and it takes great spiritual strength to control them.

Only people with no money imagine riches as a dream fulfilled; those who have it never tire of explaining to those who do not have it how much trouble it gives them. Arnheim, for instance, had often pondered the fact that every technical or administrative executive in his firm had a great deal more specialized knowledge than he did, and he had to reassure himself every time that, seen from a sufficiently lofty perspective, such things as ideas, knowledge, loyalty, talent, prudence, and the like can be bought because they are available in abundance, while the ability to make use of them presupposes qualities given only to the few who happen to have been born and bred on the heights.

Another equally burdensome problem of the rich is that everyone wants money from them. Money doesn't matter, of course, and a few thousands or tens of thousands more or less make hardly any difference to a rich man, and so rich people like to emphasize at every opportunity that money does not affect a human being's value one way or the other, meaning that they would be equally valuable even without their money, and their feelings are apt to be hurt when they feel misunderstood on this point. It is really too bad that such misunderstandings keep arising, particularly in their dealings with gifted people. Such people remarkably often have no money, just projects and talent, which does not lessen their sense of their own value, and nothing seems more natural to them than to ask a rich friend who doesn't care about money to put his surplus at the service of some good cause or other. They don't seem to understand that their rich friend would like to support them with his ideas, his abilities, his charisma. Besides, their expectations place him in a false position with respect to money, the nature of which demands increase, just as animal nature is set on procreation. Money can be put into bad investments, where it perishes on the monetary field of honor; it will buy a new car, even though the old one is still as good as new, or enable its owner to stay at the most expensive hotels in world-famous resorts, accompanied by his polo ponies, or to establish prizes for horse races or art, or to give a party for a hundred guests that costs enough in one evening to feed a hundred families for a year: with all this, one throws one's money out the window like a farmer casting out seed, so that it will come back with interest through the door. But to give it away quietly for purposes and people who are of no use to it is simply to commit murder most foul upon one's money. The purposes may be good, and the people incomparable, in which case they should be given every kind of help—except with money. This was a principle with Arnheim, and his consistent application of it had gained him a reputation for taking a creative and active part in the intellectual advancement of his time.

Arnheim could also claim that he thought like a socialist, and many rich people do think like socialists. They don't mind their capital being decreed to them by a natural law of society, and are firmly convinced that it is the man who confers value on property, not vice versa. They can calmly discuss a future when they will no longer be around, which will see the end of property, and are further confirmed in regarding themselves as social-minded by the frequency with which upright socialists prefer to await the inevitable revolution in the company of the rich rather than that of the poor. One could go on like this for a long time, describing all the functions of money Arnheim had mastered. Economic activity cannot really be separated from the other intellectual activities, and it was surely natural for him to give money as well as good advice to his intellectual and artistic friends when their need was urgent, but he did not always give it, and he never gave them much. They assured him that he was the only man in the whole world they could ask for money, because he alone had the necessary intellectual grasp of the matter, and he believed them, because he was convinced that the need for capital permeates all human functions much like the need for air to breathe, but he also met them halfway in their vision of money as a spiritual force by applying it only with the most tactful restraint.

Why is it, anyway, that a man is admired and loved? Isn't it an almost unfathomable mystery, rounded and fragile as an egg? Is a man more truly loved for his mustache than for his car? Is the love aroused by a sun-bronzed son of the South more personal than that aroused by a son of a leading industrial magnate? In a period when almost all well-dressed men were clean-shaven, Arnheim went on sporting a Vandyke beard and a clipped mustache; this small, extraneous, yet familiar presence on his face reminded him somehow, rather agreeably, whenever he was letting himself go a bit in talking to his always eager listeners, of his money.

93

EVEN THROUGH PHYSICAL CULTURE IT IS HARD TO GET A HOLD ON THE CIVILIAN MIND

For a long time the General had been sitting on one of the chairs that lined the walls around the intellectual arena, his "sponsor," as he liked to call Ulrich, occupying the next chair but one, while the free chair between them held refreshments in the form of two wine-glasses they had carried away from the buffet. The General's light-blue tunic had been creeping upward, until it now formed furrows over his paunch, like a worried forehead. They were absorbed in listening to a conversation going on just in front of them.

"Beaupré's game," somebody was saying, "is positively touched with genius; I watched him here this summer, and the previous winter on the Riviera. Even when he slips up, luck stays on his side and makes up for it. And he slips up fairly often, because the actual structure of his game negates a really sound tennis style—but then, he's a truly inspired player, which evidently exempts him from the normal laws of tennis."

"As for me, I prefer scientific tennis to the intuitive kind," someone objected. "Braddock, for instance. There may be no such thing as perfection, but Braddock comes close."

The first speaker: "Beaupré's genius, his dazzling unpredictability, is at its peak at the point where science fails."

A third voice: "Isn't calling it genius overdoing it a bit?"

"What would you call it? Genius is what inspires a man to return the ball just right at the most unlikely moment!"

"I'm bound to agree," the Braddockian said in support, "that a personality must make itself felt whether a man is holding a tennis racket or the fate of a nation in his hand."

"No, no, 'genius' is going too far," the third man protested.

The fourth man was a musician. He said: "You're quite wrong. You're overlooking the physical thinking involved in sport, because you're evidently still in the habit of overvaluing the logical, systematic kind of thinking. That's practically as out of date as the prejudice that music enriches the emotional life, and sport is a discipline of the will. But physical movement in itself is so magical that we can't stand it without some kind of buffer. You can see that in films when there's no music. Music is inward motion, it supports the kinetic imagination. Once you have grasped the sorcery in music, you can see the genius in sports without a second's hesitation. It's only science that's devoid of genius; it's mere mental acrobatics."

"So then I'm right," Beaupré's fan said, "when I say that Braddock's scientific game shows no genius."

"You're not taking into account that we would need to start by revitalizing the term 'science,'" the Braddock fan said defensively.

"Incidentally, which of them outranks the other one?" someone wondered.

No one knew the answer. Each of them had frequently beaten the other, but no one knew the exact figures.

"Let's ask Arnheim!" someone suggested.

The group dispersed. The silence in the area of the three chairs lingered on. At last General Stumm said pensively: "Well, I was listening to all that the whole time, you know, and it seems to me you could say the same thing about a victorious general, leaving out the music, perhaps. So why do they call it genius when it's a tennis player and barbarism when it's a general?"

Ever since his sponsor had suggested that he try getting through to Diotima by advocating physical culture as his particular cause, he had given considerable thought to the question of how he could best use this promising approach to the civilian mind, despite his personal aversion to the actual practice of it; but the difficulties, as he was forced to observe again and again, were inordinately large.

94

Diotima's nights

Diotima wondered how Arnheim could stand all these people, visibly enjoying himself, when her own feelings corresponded all too closely to what she had expressed a number of times in saying that the world's business was no more than *un peu de bruit autour de notre âme.*

There were times when she looked around and saw her house filled with the cream of society and culture—and felt bewildered. It reduced the story of her life to nothing but that extreme contrast between the depths and the heights, between the young girl's anxiety inside a tight middle-class world and now this blinding life at the summit. Already poised on a dizzily high narrow ledge, she felt the call to lift up her foot once more, toward an even greater height. The risk was seductive. She wrestled with the resolve to enter into a life where action, mind, soul, and dream are one. Basically she no longer fretted over the failure of a crowning idea for the Parallel Campaign to emerge; nor did her vision of a World Austria still matter quite so much; even her discovery that for every great projection of the human mind there was an equally valid opposite had lost its terrors for her. The really important movements of life have less to do with logic than with lightning and fire, and she had grown used to not trying to make sense of all the greatness by which she felt surrounded. She would gladly have dropped her campaign altogether and married Arnheim, as a little girl solves her problems by forgetting all about them and leaping into her father's arms. But the incredible ramification of her project had her trapped. She could take no time to think. The outer chain of events and the inward one ran on independently side by side, even as she tried in vain to link them up. Just like her marriage, outwardly appearing happier than ever, when in fact everything was inwardly dissolving.

Had Diotima been able to act in character, she would have spoken frankly with her husband; but there was nothing she could tell him. Was it love she felt for Arnheim? What they were to each other could be given so many names that even this trivial one occasionally surfaced among her thoughts. They had never even kissed, and an utmost intermingling of souls was something Tuzzi would not understand even if such a thing were confessed to him. Diotima herself sometimes wondered at the fact that nothing more reportable was going on between herself and Arnheim. But she had never dropped her good-girl's tendency to look up, ambitiously, to older men, and she could more easily have imagined something at least describable if not actually tangible going on between herself and her cousin, who seemed younger than herself and upon whom she looked down just a little, rather than with the man she loved and who seemed so to appreciate her ability to dissipate her feelings into general reflections on the loftiest plane. Diotima knew that one had to let oneself tumble headlong into radical changes in one's circumstances and wake up amid one's new four walls without quite knowing how one got there, but she felt exposed to influences that kept her wide awake. She was not entirely free from the distaste the typical Austrian of her period felt toward his German kin. In its classical form, which has become a rarity in our day, this distaste corresponded more or less to an image of the venerated heads of Goethe and Schiller planted guilelessly on bodies that had been fed on sticky puddings and gravies, and shared something of their nonhuman inwardness. And great as Arnheim's success was in her circle, it did not escape her that after the first surprise certain resistances made themselves felt, never taking on form or coming out into the open, yet by their whispering presence undermining her self-assurance and making her aware of the differences between her own bias and the reservations felt by many persons upon whom she had been accustomed to model her own conduct. Now, ethnic prejudice is usually nothing more than self-hatred, dredged up from the murky depths of one's own conflicts and projected onto some convenient victim, a traditional practice from time immemorial when the shaman used a stick, said to be the repository of the demon's power, to draw the sickness out of the afflicted. That her beloved was a Prussian troubled Diotima's heart with further terrors, of which she could form no clear image, so she was surely not quite unjustified in perceiving her wavering condition, so sharply different from the brute simplicity of her married state, as a passion.

Diotima suffered sleepless nights, during which she was torn between a Prussian industrial autocrat and an Austrian bureaucrat. In the state between trance and dream, Arnheim's great, luminous life passed in parade before her. She saw herself airborne at this adored man's side through a heaven of new honors, but it was a heaven of a distasteful Prussian blue. Meantime, in the black Austrian night, the yellow body of Section Chief Tuzzi still lay beside her own. She was only dimly aware of this, as of a black-and-yellow symbol of the old Kakanian culture, though he had little enough of that. It was backed by the Baroque façade of her noble friend Count Leinsdorf's great town residence, and the shades of Beethoven, Mozart, and Haydn, and of Prince Eugene of Savoy, Austria's liberator from the Turks, hovered over it, like homesickness anticipating actual exile. Diotima could not make up her mind to take such a step outside her own world, just like that, even though she almost hated her husband for being the obvious obstacle. Inside her beautiful big body, her soul felt helplessly trapped as in a vast landscape in full flower.

"I mustn't be unfair," Diotima thought. "The government official, the man given over to his work, may no longer be awake and open and receptive, but in his youth he might have been capable of it." She remembered certain moments when they were still engaged to be married, though even then Section Chief Tuzzi had been no longer exactly a youth. "He achieved his position and his personality by hard work and devotion to duty," she thought tolerantly, "and he has no suspicion that it has cost him his own personal life."

Ever since she had achieved her social triumph she thought more indulgently of her husband, and so she now made him yet another inward concession. "No one is a born rationalist and utilitarian," she reflected. "We all start out as a living soul. But ordinary, everyday existence silts us up, the usual human passions go through us like a firestorm, and the cold world brings out that coldness in us that freezes the soul." Perhaps she had been too reticent to force him into facing up to this. How sad it was. It seemed to her that she could never summon up the courage to involve Section Chief Tuzzi in the scandal of a divorce, such a shattering blow to anyone as wrapped up as he was in his public role.

"Even adultery is preferable!" she suddenly told herself.

Adultery was what Diotima had been considering for some time.

To do one's duty in one's appointed place is a sterile notion; quantities of energy are poured out to no purpose! The right course is to choose one's place and shape one's circumstances deliberately. If she was going to condemn herself to staying with her husband, there still remained a choice between a useless and a fruitful martyrdom, and it was her choice to make. So far Diotima had been hampered by the moral sleaziness and the unattractive air of irresponsibility that were inseparable from all the stories of adultery that had ever come her way. She simply couldn't imagine herself in such a situation. To touch the doorknob of a certain kind of hotel room seemed tantamount to diving into a cesspool. To slip, with rustling skirts, up some strange staircase—a certain moral complacency of her body resisted the thought. Hasty kisses went against her grain, as did clandestine words of love. Catastrophe was more in her line. Those last walks together, choked good-byes, torn between a mother's duty and love, were much more her style. But owing to her husband's thrifty disposition she had no children, and catastrophe was precisely the thing to be avoided. So she opted, if it should come to that, for a Renaissance model. A love that had to live with a dagger through the heart. While she could form no very clear image of this, there was something decidedly upright about it, with a background of classic ruins under fleeting clouds. Guilt and its transcendence, passion expiated by suffering, trembled in this image and filled Diotima with an unutterable intensity and awe. "Wherever a person finds her highest potential and the richest field for her energies is where she belongs," she thought, "because it is there that she can do the most to intensify life as a whole!"

She looked at her husband as best she could in the dark. Just as the eye does not register the ultraviolet rays of the spectrum, so this rationalist would never notice certain emotional realities of the inner life!

Section Chief Tuzzi was breathing evenly, suspecting nothing, cradled by the assumption that during his well-earned eight hours of mental absence nothing of importance could be happening in Europe. Such tranquillity did not fail to impress Diotima, and more than once she pondered the idea: Renunciation! good-bye to Arnheim! great, noble words of anguish, heaven-storming resignation, leave-taking on the scale of a Beethoven; the powerful muscle of her heart tensed up under these demands made on it. The future billowed with conversations full of a tremulous, autumnal brilliance, the poignancy of far-off blue mountain ranges. But could renunciation coexist with the double marriage bed? Diotima started up from her pillows, her black hair flying in wild ringlets. Section Chief Tuzzi's sleep was no longer the sleep of innocence but rather that of a serpent with a rabbit in its belly. She came dangerously close to waking him up and, in view of this new dilemma, shrieking in his face that she must, she must and would, leave him! Such a flight into hysteria in her conflicted situation would certainly have been understandable, but her body was too healthy for that; she felt that it simply did not react with the requisite horror to Tuzzi's proximity. She faced the absence of this horror with a dry shudder. No tears succeeded in running down her cheeks, but oddly enough it was the thought of Ulrich that gave her a certain comfort in this particular situation. These days she normally never gave him a thought, but his peculiar remarks about wanting to abolish reality, while Arnheim overestimated it, had a mysterious overtone, a hovering note Diotima had ignored at the time, only to have it surface in her mind during these night watches of hers. "All it means is that one shouldn't worry too much about what is going to happen," she told herself irritably. "It's the most commonplace idea in the world!" Yet even as she phrased this thought so badly and simplistically, she realized that it contained something she did not understand, the very thing that acted on her like a sedative, paralyzing her despair along with her consciousness. Time flitted away like a dark shadow line, as she comforted herself that somehow her inability to muster a lasting despair might also redound to her credit; but this consoling thought no longer took hold.

At night thoughts keep flowing through alternately bright and dark patches, like water in high mountains, and when they quietly reappeared after a while Diotima felt as though she had merely dreamed all that earlier frothing. The boiling little stream behind the dark mountain range was not the same as the quiet river she slid into at the end. Anger, loathing, courage, fear, all had drained away, there must be no such feelings, they didn't exist: In the soul's struggles with itself there is no one to blame! Ulrich, too, slipped back into oblivion. All that was left now were the ultimate mysteries, the soul's eternal longings. Their moral worth does not depend on what one does. It does not depend on the movements of consciousness or of passion. Even the passions are only *un peu de bruit autour de notre âme*. Kingdoms may be won or lost while the soul does not stir, and one can do nothing to attain one's destiny; in its own time it grows out of the depths of one's being, serene and everyday, like the music of the spheres. Then Diotima lay awake more than ever, but full of confidence. Such thoughts, with their final period somewhere out of sight, had the beauty of putting her to sleep very quickly, even on the most sleepless nights. Like a velvety vision, she felt her love fusing with the infinite darkness that reaches out beyond the stars, insepa rable from herself, inseparable from Paul Arnheim, immune to all schemes and set purposes. She hardly found the time to reach for the tumbler of sweetened water she kept on her little night table for her insomnia but used only at the very last moment of consciousness, because it always slipped her mind when she was agitated. The soft sound of her drinking purled, like lovers' whisperings behind a wall, beside her husband's sleep, unheard by him; then Diotima lay back reverently on her pillows and sank into the silence of unconscious being.

95

THE GREAT MAN OF LETTERS: REAR VIEW

It is almost too familiar a phenomenon to be worth mentioning: Once her celebrated guests had realized that the seriousness of her campaign did not call for any great effort on their part, they behaved like mere people, and Diotima, her house filled with noise and high ideas, was disappointed. High-minded as she was, she was ignorant of that law of circumspection which makes a man's conduct in private the opposite of his professional conduct. She did not know that politicians who had called each other liars and crooks in the assembly hall went amicably to lunch side by side in the dining hall. That judges who, in their juridical capacity, have just imposed a heavy fine on some unfortunate may press his hands in sympathy at the end of the proceedings she knew, but saw nothing out of the way in that. That female entertainers sometimes lead irreproachable domestic lives behind the scenes of their dubious public displays she had heard, and even found touching. She also saw a fine symbolism in princes laying aside their crowns on occasion to be simple human beings. But when she saw princes of the cultural realm enjoying themselves as if they were just anybody, she found it hard to make allowances for such a double standard. What is the underlying need, the psychological law behind this common tendency that makes men turn their backs on who they are in their professional lives? Every man is two people, and one hardly knows whether it is in the morning or in the evening that he reverts to his real self.

And so, however pleased she was to see her soul mate so popular with all the men of her circle, and in particular to see him singling out the younger men for his attention, it sometimes depressed her to see him so caught up in all this social activity. A truly great mind, she felt, should not care quite so much to mingle with the ordinary cultural elite, nor be so ready to traffic in the fluctuating marketplace of ideas.

The truth was that Arnheim was not a great mind but only a great man of letters.

In our cultural landscape, the great man of letters has replaced the great mind just as the plutocrats have replaced royalty in the political world. Just as the regal intellect and imagination had its place in the days of reigning princes, the great man of letters has his place in the days of great political campaigns and great department stores. The leading man of letters represents a special form of the connection between the mind and all large-scale operations. The least one may therefore expect of a great author is that he should drive a great car. He has to be a great traveler, be received by high officials, give lectures, and be a moral force not to be underestimated by the leaders of public opinion; he is the keeper of a nation's soul, the upholder of its humanitarian aspirations before the rest of the world; at home, he must receive notable visitors, and with all that, there is still his work to be done, which must be turned out with the agility of a circus performer who never shows the strain of doing his act. A great author is by no means the same thing as a writer who makes lots of money. He need not necessarily write the best-seller of the year or the book of the month himself, as long as he doesn't challenge this sort of evaluation, because it is he who sits on all the award committees, signs all the manifestos, writes all the introductions, delivers all the commencement addresses, pronounces on all the important events, and is called in whenever it is necessary to demonstrate what new heights of progress have just been achieved. For in all his activities, the literary eminence represents not his country as a whole but only its vanguard, its great elite, which already almost constitutes a majority, and so he lives within a magnetic field of chronic intellectual tension. It is of course our present forms of social life that make culture a mega-industry, just as for its part our mega-industrial complex aims to control culture, politics, and the public conscience; the two phenomena meet halfway. Which is why this description is not aimed at anyone in particular but serves only to represent a standard figure on the social chessboard, subject to rules and to making moves as they have evolved in the course of history. Our well-meaning contemporaries take the stand that having intelligence in itself is not enough (there is so much of it around that a little more or less makes no real difference; anyway, everyone thinks he has enough for his own needs), because our first priority is the struggle against stupidity, which means that intelligence must be displayed, made highly visible and operative, and since the Great Author suits this purpose better than an even greater author whom the largest number might not find quite so easy to understand, everyone does his level best to make the visibly Great even greater.

With this understanding, no one could seriously hold it against Arnheim that he was one of the first, experimental, though already quite perfected embodiments of such a public figure, though a certain innate fitness for the role was understood. After all, most writers would like to be Great Authors, but it is the same with them as with mountains; between the Austrian towns of Graz and St. Pölten, for instance, there are many mountains that could look exactly like Monte Rosa, if only they were high enough. The most indispensable condition for being a Great Author is always that one has to write books or plays that will do equally well for high and low. To effect the desired good, one must be an effective writer to begin with; this is the basic principle of every Great Author's life. It is a strange and wonderful principle too, a fine antidote to the temptations of solitude, Goethe's very own principle of effective action: if you will just get things done in a good world, everything else will fall into place. For once a writer has made his effect, his life undergoes a remarkable sea change. His publisher stops saying that a businessman who goes into publishing is a sort of tragic idealist because he could do so much better for himself by dealing in textiles or unspoiled paper. The critics discover him as a worthy subject for their labors, because critics are often not really bad people at heart but former poets who, because times are bad, have to pin their hearts to something that will inspire them to speak out; they are war poets or love poets, depending on the nature of the inward gleanings for which they must find a market, so their preference for the work of a Great Author rather than just any author is quite understandable. There is really only so much work a critic can do, and so the best of this limited output tends to be distributed over the annual publications from the pens of Great Authors, whose works consequently become the savings banks, as it were, of the national cultural economy, in that each of them brings in its train critical commentaries which are in no way mere explications but virtual deposits, and there is correspondingly less capital left over for all the rest. But where this really mounts up is with the essayists, biographers, and instant historians, who relieve themselves all over the great man. Meaning no offense, but dogs prefer a busy street corner to a lonely cliff for their calls of nature, so why should human beings who feel the higher urge to leave their names behind choose a cliff that is obviously unfrequented? Before he knows it, the Great Author ceases to be a separate entity and has become a symbiosis, a collective national product in the most delicate sense of the term, and enjoys the most gratifying assurance life can offer that his prosperity is most intimately bound up with that of countless others.

This may also be why the Great Author is so often noted for his pronounced sense of good form. He resorts to open combat only when his position is threatened; in all other circumstances his conduct is admirably serene and good-natured. He can put up gracefully with any number of trivialities uttered in his praise. Great men of letters do not lightly deign to discuss other writers, but when they do, they seldom flatter a man of true distinction but prefer to encourage one of those unobtrusive talents made up of 49 percent ability and 51 percent inability, which, thanks to this mixture, are very good at everything that needs strength to get done but might be damaged by a strong personality, so that every one of them sooner or later achieves an influential position in the literary world. But with this description we may already have gone beyond what is peculiar to the Great Author alone. The proverb has it that nothing succeeds like success, and nowadays even an ordinary man of letters is likely to have an inordinate fuss made over him long before he has become a Great Author, when he is still a reviewer, columnist, radio scriptwriter, screenwriter, or the editor of some little magazine; some of them resemble those little rubber pigs or donkeys with a hole in their back where you blow them up.

When we see our Great Authors carefully sizing up this situation and doing their best to mold it into an image of an alert population honoring its great personalities, shall we not be grateful to them? They ennoble life as they find it by their sympathetic interest in it. Just try to imagine the opposite, a writer who did none of the above. He would have to decline cordial invitations, rebuff people, assess praise not as a grateful recipient but as a critic, tear up what comes naturally, treat great opportunities as suspect, simply for being so great, and would have nothing of his own to offer in recompense other than processes going on inside his head, hard to express, hard to assess, merely a writer's achievement of which a time that already has its Great Authors has no great need. Would such a man not remain a total outsider and have to withdraw from reality, with all the inevitable consequences?

This was, in any case, Arnheim's opinion.

96

THE GREAT MAN OF LETTERS: FRONT VIEW

A Great Author's problem arises from the fact that even a creative life has to be conducted in a businesslike way, but the language in which it is done is traditionally idealistic, and it was this very blend of business and idealism that played so crucial a part in Arnheim's lifework.

Such anachronistic mixtures turn up everywhere nowadays. Even as our dead, for instance, are being trotted off to their resting place by internal combustion engine, we can't forgo dressing up the top of such a handsome motorized hearse with a medieval helmet and two crossed swords, and that's how it goes with everything; human evolution is a long-drawn-out process. Only two generations ago business letters affected flowery turns of phrase, while today we can already state all sorts of things from love to pure logic in the language of supply and demand, security and discount, at least as well as we can in psychological and religious terms; however, we don't do that yet. That's because our new language is not yet quite sure of itself. The ambitious moneyman finds himself in a difficult spot these days. To place himself on a level with the established powers, he must dress up his activities in great ideas. But great ideas that command instant allegiance no longer exist, because our skeptical contemporaries believe in neither God nor humanity, kings nor morality—unless they believe in all of them indiscriminately, which amounts to the same thing. So the captain of industry, disinclined to forgo greatness, which serves him as a compass, must resort to the democratic dodge of replacing the immeasurable influence of greatness by the measurable greatness of influence. So now whatever counts as great *is* great; but this means that eventually whatever is most loudly hawked as great is also great, and not all of us have the knack of swallowing this innermost truth of our times without gagging a little. Arnheim had been trying conscientiously to find a way.

In such a fix a cultivated man might for instance be reminded of the link between the world of learning and the Church in the Middle Ages. A philosopher who wanted to succeed and influence the thought of his contemporaries had to get along with the Church in those days, which might lead the vulgar freethinker to suppose that such constraints must have kept the philosopher from rising to greatness. But the opposite was the case. Our experts assure us that the result was nothing less than an incomparable Gothic beauty of thought, and if it was possible to make allowances for the Church without harming one's intellectual quality, why shouldn't it be possible to do the same for advertising? Can't a man who wants to get something done get it done under these conditions as well? Arnheim was convinced that it was a sign of greatness in a man not to be overly critical of his times. The best rider on the best horse who is fighting it will not take his hurdles as smoothly as the horseman who manages to move as one with his mount.

Take Goethe, for another example: Now, there was a genius such as the earth is not likely to produce again, but he was also the knighted son of a prosperous business family and, as Arnheim felt, the very first Great Author his nation had ever produced. Arnheim modeled himself on the great poet in many ways. But his favorite story about him was the well-known incident when Goethe, while secretly sympathizing, left poor Johann Gottlieb Fichte in the lurch when the philosopher was fired from the University of Jena for having spoken of the Deity and divine matters "grandly, but perhaps not with the proper decorum," and went about his defense in an "impassioned" manner rather than extricating himself from the affair "in the smoothest possible way," as the urbane master poet observes in his memoirs. Arnheim not only would have done exactly as Goethe did, but would have cited Goethe's example to try to convince all and sundry that this alone was the Goethean, the meaningful way to act. He would hardly have contented himself with the fact that, oddly enough, we are more likely to feel sympathy when a great man does the wrong thing than when a lesser man does the right thing, but would have gone beyond it to point out that an obstinate insistence on principle not only is fruitless but shows a lack of depth and historical irony, what he would also have called the Goethean irony of making the best of it with dignity, showing a sense of humor in action, a mode of conduct that time always proves to have been right in the end. Considering that today, barely two life spans later, the injustice done to the worthy, upright, and slightly excessive Fichte has long since dwindled to a private matter of no consequence to his reputation, while the reputation of Goethe, despite his behaving badly, has suffered equally little in the long run, we must admit that the wisdom of time in fact accords with the wisdom of Arnheim.

And a third example—Arnheim always had quantities of good examples at his disposal—illustrating the deep meaning of the first two: Napoleon. Heine in his *Travel Pictures* describes him in a manner in such perfect accordance with Arnheim's views that we may as well cite his own words, which Arnheim knew by heart:

"Such a mind," Heine wrote, referring to Napoleon—though he might as easily have said it of Goethe, whose diplomatic nature he always defended with the acuity of a lover who knows deep down that he is not really in accord with the object of his admiration— "Such a mind is what Kant means when he asks us to imagine one that works, not intellectually, like our own, but intuitively. The knowledge that our intellect acquires by slow analytic study and laborious deduction, the intuitive mind sees and grasps in one and the same movement. Hence his gift for understanding his time and the moment and for cajoling its spirit, never crossing it, always using it. But since this spirit of the age is not merely revolutionary but is formed by the confluence of both revolutionary and reactionary aspects, Napoleon never acted in a purely revolutionary or counterrevolutionary manner but always in the spirit of both views, both principles, both tendencies, which in him came together, and so he always acted in a manner that was natural, simple, great, never fitful or harsh, always calm and temperate. He never had the need to indulge in petty intrigue, and his coups always resulted from his skill in understanding and moving the masses. Petty, analytical minds incline to slow, intricate scheming, while synthesizing intuitive minds have their own miraculous ways of so combining the possibilities held out by the times that they can take speedy advantage of them for their own ends."

Heine may have meant that a little differently from the way his admirer Arnheim understood it, but Arnheim felt that these words virtually described him as well.

97

CLARISSE'S MYSTERIOUS POWERS
AND MISSIONS

Clarisse indoors . . . Walter seems to have been mislaid somehow, but she has an apple and her bathrobe. The apple and the bathrobe are the two sources from which an unnoticed fine ray of reality streams into her consciousness. What made her think that Moosbrugger was musical? She didn't know. Possibly all murderers are musical. She knows that she wrote a letter on this subject to His Grace Count Leinsdorf; she also remembers what she wrote, approximately, but she has no real access to it.

But was the Man Without Qualities unmusical?

As no good answer came to her, she dropped the question and passed on to other things.

After a while it did come to her: Ulrich is the Man Without Qualities. A man without qualities can't be musical, of course; but he can't be unmusical, either. . . .

He had said to her: You are virginal and heroic.

She reiterated: Virginal and heroic! A glow came into her cheeks. She felt called upon to do something, but she didn't know what.

Her thoughts were driving in two directions, as in a hand-to-hand struggle. She felt attracted and repelled, without knowing toward or by what. This ended in a faint feeling of tenderness that was somehow left over from the struggle and that moved her to go looking for Walter. She stood up and put the apple down.

She was sorry that she was always tormenting Walter. She was only fifteen when she first noticed that she had the power to torment him. All she had to do was to say loudly and firmly that something he had said was not so, and he would flinch, no matter how right what he had said was. She knew he was afraid of her. He was afraid she might go crazy. He had let it slip once and then quickly tried to cover up; but she had known ever since that it was in his mind. She thought it was really lovely. Nietzsche says: "Is there a pessimism of the strong?

An intellectual leaning toward what is hard, horrifying, evil? A deep instinct against morality? A craving for the terrible as the worthy enemy?" When such words came to mind they gave her a sensual thrill in her mouth, gentle and strong as milk, so that she could hardly swallow.

She thought of the child Walter wanted from her. He was afraid of that too. Made sense, if he thought she might one day go mad. It made a tenderness rise up for him, though she violently fought it down. She had forgotten that she meant to go looking for Walter. There was something going on in her body. Her breasts were filling up, the blood flowed thickly through the veins in her arms and legs, there was a vague pressure on her bladder and bowels. Her slim body deepened inside, grew sensitive, alive, strange, step by step; a child lay bright and smiling in her arms; from her shoulders the Mother of God's golden cloak fell in radiant folds to the floor, and the congregation was singing. It was out of her hands: the Lord had been born unto the world!

But no sooner had this happened than her body snapped shut, closing the gap over the image, like a split log ejecting the entering wedge; she was her own slim self again, feeling disgust and a cruel merriment. She was not going to make it so easy for Walter. "Let it be thy victory and thy freedom that long for offspring": she recited Nietzsche to herself. "Thou shalt build living memorials to thyself. But before that, thou must build up thine own body and soul." Clarisse smiled; it was her special smile, licking upward like a slender flame from a fire under a great stone.

Then she remembered that her father had been afraid of Walter. Her mind went back to years ago. It was something she was in the habit of doing; she and Walter would ask each other: "Do you remember . . . ?" and the light of the past flowed magically from the far distance into the present. It was fun, they enjoyed it. It was perhaps like turning around, after having doggedly trudged along a road for hours, to see all the empty distance one has covered transformed into a grand vista, to one's genuine satisfaction; but they never saw it in that light; they took their reminiscing very seriously. And so it seemed to her incredibly titillating and curious that her father, the aging painter, at that time an authority figure in her life, had been afraid of Walter, who had brought a new era into his house, while

Walter was afraid of her. It was like putting her arm around her friend Lucy Pachhofen and having to say "Papa" to him, while knowing that Papa was Lucy's lover, for that was going on during that same period.

Again Clarisse's cheeks flushed. She was intensely absorbed in trying to bring to mind that peculiar whimpering sound, that strange whimpering she had told Ulrich about. She picked up her mirror and tried to make the face, with lips pressed together in fear, that she must have made the night her father came to her bed. She couldn't manage to imitate the sound that had escaped from her breast in that state of temptation. She thought that the same sound must still be there, inside her chest, as it was then. It was a sound without restraint or scruple, but it had never surfaced again. She put down the mirror and looked around warily, touching everything with her eyes to assure herself that she was alone. Then she felt with her fingertips through her robe, searching for that velvety-black birthmark that had so strange a power. There it was, in the hollow of her groin, half hidden on the inside of the thigh and close to where the pubic hairs somewhat raggedly made room for it; she let her hand rest on it, made her mind a blank, and waited for the sensation she remembered. She felt it at once. It was not the gentle streaming of lust, but her arm grew stiff and taut like a man's arm; she felt that if she could just lift it high enough she would be able to smash everything with it! She called this spot on her body the Devil's Eye. It was the spot at which her father had stopped and turned back. The Devil's Eye had a gaze that pierced through any clothing and "caught" men's eyes and drew them to her, spellbound but unable to move as long as Clarisse willed it. Clarisse thought certain words in quotation marks, with special emphasis, just as she heavily underlined them in writing; the words thus emphasized tensed up with meaning, just as her arm was tensed up now; who would even have supposed that one could really "catch" something, someone, with the eye? Well, she was the first person who held this word in her hand like a stone to be flung at a target. It was all part of the smashing force in her arm. All this had made her forget the whimpering sound she had started out to consider; instead, she thought about her younger sister, Marion. When she was four years old, Marion's hands had to be tied up at night, to keep them from slipping, in all innocence, under the covers, only because they were drawn toward a pleasing sensation like two baby bears drawn to a honeycomb in a hollow tree. And some time later Clarisse had once had to tear Walter away from Marion. Her family was possessed by sensuality as vintners are by wine. It was fated, a heavy burden she had to bear. Just the same, her thoughts went on wandering in the past, the tension in her arm relaxed, and her hand rested obliviously in her lap. In those days she had still been on terms of formality with Walter. Actually, she owed him a lot. It was he who had brought the news that there were modern people who insisted on plain, cool furniture and hung pictures on their walls that showed the truth. He read new things to her, Peter Altenberg, little stories of young girls who rolled their hoops in the love-crazed tulip beds and had eyes that shone with sweet innocence like glazed chestnuts. From that time on Clarisse knew that her slender legs, still a child's legs, she had thought, were quite as important as a scherzo by "someone or other."

At the time, they were all staying in a summer place together, a large group; several families of their acquaintance had rented cottages by a lake, and all the bedrooms were filled up with invited friends, male and female. Clarisse had to double up with Marion, and around eleven Dr. Meingast sometimes dropped by on his secret moonlight rounds, for a chat. He—who was now a famous man in Switzerland—had then been the life of the party and the idol of all the mothers. How old was she then?—between fifteen and sixteen, or maybe fourteen and fifteen?—when he had brought his student George Gröschl along, who was only a little older than Marion and Clarisse. Dr. Meingast had been somewhat absentminded that evening, rambling a little about moonbeams, parents who slept through everything and didn't care, and people with a modern outlook; suddenly he was gone, as if he had come only to leave stocky little George, his great admirer, behind with the girls. George was silent, probably too shy to talk, and the girls, who had been talking to Meingast, also kept quiet. But George must have clenched his teeth in the dark and stepped over to Marion's bed. A little light fell into the room from outside, but in the corners, where the bed stood, impenetrable masses of shadow loomed, so Clarisse could not make out what was going on, except that George seemed to be standing upright beside the bed, looking down at Marion; but he had his back to

Clarisse, and there was not a sound from Marion, as though she were not in the room at all. A long time went by. But in the end, while Marion remained motionless, George detached himself from the shadows like a murderer; for a moment his shoulder and side showed pale in the bright patch of moonlight in the middle of the room, as he moved toward Clarisse, who had quickly lain down again and pulled the covers up to her chin. She knew that the secret thing that had been going on at Marion's bed would now happen again and was rigid with suspense as George stood silently by her bedside. His lips seemed pressed unnaturally tight together. Finally his hand came, like a snake, and busied itself with Clarisse. What else he was doing she had no idea, and could make no sense of the little she perceived of his movements, despite her excitement. She herself did not feel aroused—that came later—but at the moment felt only a strong, indefinable, anxious excitement; she kept still like a trembling stone in a bridge over which a heavy vehicle is passing so slowly there seems no end to it; she felt unable to speak, and let it all be done to her. After George had let her go he disappeared without a word, and neither of the two sisters could be sure that the other had experienced the same thing as herself; they had not called to each other for help or asked for sympathy, and years went by before they exchanged a word about the incident.

Clarisse had recovered her apple, gnawed off a little piece, and chewed on it. George had never given himself away or made any acknowledgment of what had happened, except perhaps at first to make stonily portentous eyes now and then. By this time he had turned into a smart rising young lawyer in government service, and Marion was married. Much more, however, had happened with Dr. Meingast. On going abroad, he had shed his cynicism and become what is called, outside the universities, a famous philosopher, always surrounded by a throng of students of both sexes. Walter and Clarisse had recently received a letter from him to the effect that he was about to visit his native land in order to get some work done, undisturbed by his followers. Would they be able to put him up? He had heard that they were living "on the border between nature and the big city."

This news might in fact have been what had triggered Clarisse's line of thought that day. "Oh Lord, what a weird time it was!" she thought, and realized, too, that it had been the summer before the summer with Lucy. Meingast had taken to kissing her whenever he felt like it. "If you please, I shall kiss you now," he said politely before he did it, and he also kissed every one of her girlfriends; there was one of them whose skirt Clarisse had never again been able to look at without having to think of eyelids lowered in false modesty. Meingast had told her about it himself, and Clarisse, who was only fifteen, after all, had said to the fully adult Dr. Meingast, when he told her of his exploits with her young friends: "You're a pig!" She got a kick out of calling him such a crude name to his face—it felt like being booted and spurred—though it did not prevent her from being afraid that she would not be able to resist him either, in the end, and when he asked her for a kiss she did not dare refuse, for fear of seeming silly.

But when Walter kissed her for the first time, she said gravely: "I promised Mama never to do this kind of thing." And that was the difference in a nutshell. Walter talked like an angel and he talked a lot, he was swathed in art and philosophy like the moon swathed in a broad bank of clouds. He read aloud to her. But what he mostly did was look at her constantly, only at her among all her friends, that was all there was between them at first; it was just like having the moon look down on you: all you do is fold your hands. Actually, holding hands was the next step, quietly clasping hands without a word spoken, and what an amazingly strong bond it was! Clarisse felt her whole body purified by the touch of his hand; if he happened to seem absentminded and cool in taking her hand, she felt destroyed. "You can't imagine what it means to me!" she said pleadingly. By that time they were very close, in secret. He taught her a new appreciation of mountains and beetles; all she had ever seen in nature before was a landscape that Papa or one of his colleagues would paint and sell. Now all of a sudden she began to regard her family with a critical eye; she felt all new and different.

Suddenly she had a clear recollection of that business with the scherzo. "Your legs, Miss Clarisse," Walter had said, "have more to do with real art than all of your papa's paintings." There was a piano in the house where they were staying that summer, on which they used to play duets. Clarisse was learning things from him; she wanted to rise above her girlfriends and her family; none of them understood how anyone could spend such lovely summer days playing the piano instead of going out boating or swimming; but she had pinned her hopes on Walter, she had already, even then, decided she would be "his mate," she would marry him, and when he snapped at her for playing a wrong note, she would be boiling inwardly, but her pleasure outweighed the hurt. Walter did snap at her sometimes, in fact, because the spirit is uncompromising; but only at the piano. Music apart, it still happened sometimes that Meingast kissed her, and on one moonlight expedition, when Walter was rowing, she nestled her head on Meingast's chest quite of her own accord as they sat in the stern together. Meingast had such a way with him in these matters, she had no way of knowing what would come of it, while Walter, the second time he grabbed her, right after their piano lesson, at the very last moment when they had already reached the doorway and he pounced on her from behind and kissed her hard, had only given her the unpleasant feeling that she had to struggle for air, to tear herself away from him. Nevertheless, her mind was made up; no matter what happened between her and the other one, she must never let go of this one.

It was a funny thing, all that, anyway; there was something about Meingast's breath that made all resistance melt away—it was like pure, light air that makes you feel happy for no reason—while Walter, who suffered from a halting digestion, as Clarisse had known for some time, just like the halting way he had of making up his mind about anything, had a stuffy kind of breath, a little too hot, a little musty and paralyzing. Such psychosomatic factors had played a strange part all along, and Clarisse could take it in stride, because nothing seemed more natural to her than Nietzsche's saying that a person's body *is* the soul. Her legs had no more genius than her head, they had exactly as much, they *were* her genius; her hand, at Walter's touch, instantly released a stream of intentions and assurances that flowed from head to toe, without a word; and her youth—once it had come to know itself—rebelled against all the convictions and other foolishness of her parents with the simple freshness of a hard young body that despises all the feelings remotely connected with the voluptuous marriage beds and lush Turkish carpets so popular with the morally strict older generation. And so the physical continued to play a part she understood differently from the way others might see it.

But here Clarisse broke off her reminiscences, or it was rather her reminiscences that on the instant, without the bump of a landing, dropped her back into the present. It was all this, and what was to follow, that she had wanted to tell her friend, the Man Without Qualities. Perhaps there was too much of Meingast in it, who had after all disappeared soon after that exciting summer. He had fled abroad; that incredible inward transformation of his had begun that was to make a famous philosopher out of the frivolous womanizer; and thereafter Clarisse had seen him only in passing, when neither of them had been reminded of the past. But as she saw it, her own part in his transformation was perfectly clear to her. A good deal more had happened between them in the weeks before his disappearance. In Walter's absence—and in his jealous presence too, cutting Walter out and driving him to outdo himself—she and Meingast went through emotional storms and even crazier times, in those hours before a storm that can drive a man and a woman out of their minds, followed by the hours after the storm, all passion spent, that are like green meadows after a rain, in the pure air of friendship. Clarisse had let a lot of things be done to her, not unwillingly, but, eager as she was to know everything, the child had fought back in her own way afterward, by telling her licentious friend exactly what she thought of him. And because, in that last period before he left, Meingast's mood had already sobered into friendship and a noble resignation in his rivalry with Walter, she was now convinced that she had drawn onto herself all that had troubled his spirit before he went off to Switzerland, helping him toward that unexpected self-transformation. She was confirmed in this idea by what had happened between Walter and herself immediately afterward. Clarisse could no longer distinguish between those long-gone years and months, but what did it matter just when one thing or another had happened? The point was that when she and Walter had grown close, despite much resistance on her part, there came a dreamy time of long walks and confessions, of taking spiritual possession of one another with countless agonizing yet blissful little orgies of soul-probing to which lovers are tempted when they are still lacking that very amount of resolute courage which they have already lost in chastity. It was just as if Meingast had bequeathed them his sins, to be relived on a higher plane, until their ultimate meaning had been extracted by exhausting it; and they both perceived it thus. And now, when Clarisse cared so little for Walter's love that she often found herself repelled by it, she saw even more clearly that the ecstatic thirst for love that had driven her out of her mind to such a degree could have been nothing other than an incarnation, that is, she knew, a manifestation in the flesh of something not of the flesh: a meaning, a mission, a destiny, such as is written in the stars for the elect.

She was not ashamed, she felt more like crying when she compared the Then and Now, but Clarisse could never cry but pressed her lips together hard, and it turned into something that looked rather more like her smile. Her arm, covered with kisses up to the armpit; her leg, guarded by the Devil's Eye; her pliant body, twisted over and over by her lover's yearning and twisting back like a rope, all harbored the marvelous feeling that goes with love: the sense that every movement is of mysterious importance. Clarisse sat there feeling like an actress during intermission. To be sure, she did not know what lay ahead, but she felt it was the unremitting duty of lovers to always be to each other what they had been in their finest moments. And here was her arm, here were her legs, her head was poised on her body, in awesome readiness to be the first in recognizing the sign that could not fail to appear.

It may be hard to understand what Clarisse meant, but it was all perfectly plain to her. She had written a letter to Count Leinsdorf calling for a Nietzsche Year and also asking for the release of the sex murderer and perhaps his exhibition before the public as a reminder of the calvaries endured by those who are doomed to take upon themselves the widespread sins of all mankind; and now she also knows why she did it. Someone must be the first to speak. She may not have expressed it too well, but no matter, the point was to make a start and end this putting up with everything and letting things take their course. History proves that the world needs such people from time to time—the words *eon to eon* echoed in her mind like two bells one can't see, although they are nearby—people who simply cannot fall into line and go on lying like all the rest and who have to make a nuisance of themselves. So much was clear.

It was also clear that people who make a nuisance of themselves are going to feel the pressure of the world. Clarisse knows that mankind's great geniuses have always had to suffer, and she doesn't wonder that many days and weeks in her life pass under some leaden weight, as if a heavy slab had been laid on them, but she has come through every time so far, and it's the same for everybody; the Church in its wisdom has even instituted formal times of mourning and mortification so as to concentrate all the sadness into a day or a week rather than let a half century be flooded with hopelessness and callousness, as has also been known to happen. More of a problem in Clarisse's life have been certain other phases, all too buoyant and unrestrained, when a word may sometimes be enough to make her go off the rails altogether. At such times she is so beside herself that she can't tell where she is, except that she is definitely not absent; on the contrary, she could be said to be more inwardly present than ever, inside some deep inner space somehow contained inside the space her body occupies in the world, something indefinable in ordinary words—but then, why struggle for words where words don't apply; she will soon be back with the others again in any case, with only a little tickle left in her head, like after a nosebleed. Clarisse realizes that these phases she sometimes goes through are dangerous. Evidently she is being tested and prepared for something special. She tends to think of several things at a time anyway, like a fan opening and shutting, with one fold partly beside, partly underneath the other, and when this gets too confusing it is only natural to wish one could just pull out altogether, with one jerk; lots of people feel like that; they just don't make it, that's all.

So Clarisse enjoys intimations and forebodings as other people pride themselves on their memory or on their strong stomach when they say they could eat splintered glass. Besides, Clarisse has already proved more than once that she has what it takes; she has tested her strength against her father, against Meingast, against George Gröschl. With Walter her struggle was still ongoing, things were still in movement, albeit haltingly. But for some time now Clarisse had been meaning to try her strength on the Man Without Qualities. She could not have said exactly since when; perhaps since the time Walter had come up with that name and Ulrich had accepted it; before that, she had to admit, in those early years, she had never paid him any serious attention, though they had been good enough friends. But "Man Without Qualities" reminded her, for instance, of playing the piano, that is, of all those blue moods, leaps of joy, fits of anger, one races through on the keyboard without their quite being real passions. She felt a kinship with all that. From this point one could only move straight as an arrow to refusing to do anything one could not do wholeheartedly, which took her right back to the deep turbulence in her marriage. A man without qualities doesn't say No to life, he says Not yet! and saves himself for the right moment; she had understood this with her whole body. What if the meaning of all those times when she moved outside herself was that she was meant to become the Mother of God? She remembered the vision that had come to her, not fifteen minutes ago. "Maybe every mother could become the Mother of God," she thought, "if she refuses to give in, to lie, to take action, but only brings out what is deepest inside her as her child? Provided she gets nothing for herself out of it," she added sadly. For the idea was far from being altogether attractive; it was more like having that sense, split between torment and bliss, of serving as a sacrifice for something. For her vision had been like an image appearing between the branches of a tree, with the leaves suddenly flickering like candle flames, but gone in an instant as the branches snap together again; but now her mood was changed for good. The very next moment it occurred to her by chance that the word "birth" was contained in the word "birthmark"—a point that would have been lost on anyone else, but to Clarisse portended no less than that her destiny was written in the stars. The wondrous thought that a woman, both as a lover and as a mother, must take a man into herself made her feel at once yielding and excited. Without knowing its source, she felt it melt away her resistance even as she sensed her power.

But she was still far from trusting the Man Without Qualities. He didn't always mean everything he said. When he insisted that ideas could not be carried out, or that he took nothing quite seriously, he was only covering up; she understood that clearly; they had sniffed each other out and recognized each other by secret signs, while Walter was thinking that Clarisse had her crazy spells. Still, there was something bitterly evil in Ulrich, a devilish bent for going the world's self-indulgent way. He had to be set free. She had to go and get him.

She had said to Walter: Kill him. It didn't really mean anything, she didn't really know what she meant by it, but if anything, it meant that something had to be done to tear him out of himself, at any cost.

She would have to wrestle with him for his soul.

She laughed, rubbed her nose, paced back and forth in the dark. Something had to be done about the Parallel Campaign. What? she didn't know.

98

FROM A COUNTRY THAT CAME TO GRIEF BECAUSE OF A DEFECT IN LANGUAGE

The train of events is a train that lays down its own tracks as it goes along. The river of time carries its own banks along with it. The traveler moves on a solid floor between solid walls, but the floor and the walls are strongly influenced by the movements of the travelers, though they do not notice it. What a stroke of luck for Clarisse's peace of mind that along with all her other notions, this one had not yet occurred to her.

But Count Leinsdorf was also safe from it. He was shielded from this notion by his view of himself as a practitioner of *realpolitik*.

The days rocked along and turned into weeks. The weeks did not stop moving, either, but formed links in a chain. Something was happening every minute. And when something is happening every minute, it is easy to imagine that one is actually getting real things done. The sumptuous reception rooms at the Leinsdorf town residence, for instance, were to be thrown open to the public invited to a festival for the benefit of consumptive children, an event preceded by exhaustive conferences between His Grace and His Grace's majordomo, fixing certain dates by which certain preparations had to be completed. The police simultaneously organized an anniversary exhibition, to which all of high society was invited, and the High Commissioner had called on His Grace personally to deliver the invitation. When Count Leinsdorf arrived, the High Commissioner recognized his volunteer assistant and honorary secretary, who was quite superfluously introduced to him again, giving the High Commissioner a chance to show off his legendary memory for faces; he was said to be acquainted personally with every tenth citizen, or at least to be informed about him. Diotima also came, accompanied by her husband, and all those present awaited the arrival of a member of the Royal and Imperial House, to whom some of them were to be presented, and everyone without exception agreed that the exhibition was a huge success and simply fascinating. It consisted of a great many pictures crowded together on the walls, and mementos of great crimes arranged in glass-fronted cabinets and showcases. These included burglars' tools, forgers' apparatus, lost buttons that had provided clues, and the tragic weapons of notorious murderers, captioned with their respective stories, while the pictures on the walls contrasted with this arsenal of horror by showing edifying scenes of police activities. Here you could see the kindly policeman guiding the little old lady across the street, the solemn policeman looking down at a corpse washed up from the river, the brave policeman flinging himself at the bridle of a shying horse, an allegorical painting of the Police Force as Guardian Angel to the City, the lost child surrounded by motherly policemen at the station, the policeman in flames carrying a young girl out of a burning house, and many, many more, such as "First Aid" and "Alone on the Beat," as well as the portraits of policemen with years of service dating back to 1869, captioned with inspiring accounts of their careers, and framed poems extolling the work of the police force as a whole or its individual functionaries. Its highest official, the ministerial head of the police division that was called, in Kakania, by the psychological designation Ministry for Inner Concerns, in his welcoming speech drew his listeners' attention to these pictures, which, he said, showed the spirit of the police as a true manifestation of the people. The natural admiration for a spirit of such helpfulness and discipline was a fountain of moral renewal in an age such as this, when art and life only too often sank into mindless sensuality and self-indulgence. Diotima, standing beside Count Leinsdorf, felt uneasily that this ran counter to her own efforts on behalf of modern art, and was gazing intently into the art with a gentle yet unyielding expression on her face, to register upon the general atmosphere her dissent from this particular Kakanian official's point of view. Her cousin, watching her from a slight distance with the sentiments proper to an honorary secretary of the Parallel Campaign, suddenly within all this packed crowd felt a gingerly touch on his arm and was surprised to find at his side Bonadea, who had arrived with her husband, the eminent judge, and was using the moment when all necks were craned toward the august speaker, with the Archduke by his side, to work her way close to her fickle lover. This bold move was the fruit of long scheming. Hard hit by her lover's desertion at a time when she was sadly struggling to tie down, as it were, even the freely fluttering fringes of the banner of her lust, all her thoughts in these last weeks had been focused on winning him back. He had been avoiding her, and forcing him to "have it out" with her only put her in the unbecoming role of the pursuer of someone who would rather be left alone, so she had decided to force her way into the circle where he was to be found day after day. She had in her favor, after all, her husband's professional connection with the case of the loathsome killer Moosbrugger, as well as her friend's intention to do something for that murderer, which made her a natural factor in effecting a liaison. She had consequently been making quite a nuisance of herself to her husband lately, with her references to concern in influential circles for the welfare of the criminally insane, and had made him take her along to the opening of the police exhibition, where, something told her, she would at last get to meet Diotima. When the Minister had concluded his speech and the mass of visitors began to circulate, she never budged from the side of her reluctant lover, accompanying him on a tour of the awful bloodstained weapons despite her nearly insurmountable horror of them.

"You said all this sort of thing could be prevented if people only wanted to," she whispered, like an obedient child showing off how earnestly it has been paying attention to something once explained to her. Letting the crowd press her close to him a while later, she smiled and used the opportunity to murmur in his ear: "You once said that in the right circumstances anyone is capable of any weakness."

Her ostentatious insistence on clinging to his side was a great embarrassment to Ulrich, whom she was purposefully steering, despite all he could do to distract her from this aim, toward Diotima, and since he couldn't lecture her in front of all these people on the impropriety of what she was up to, he realized that the day had come when he had no choice but to bring about just what he had always tried to prevent, the acquaintance of these two women with each other. They were already close to a group of which Diotima and His Grace formed the center when Bonadea cried out, in front of a display case: "Oh look, there's Moosbrugger's knife!" And so it was. Bonadea stared at it joyfully, as if she had just come upon Grandma's first party favor in some drawer at home. So Ulrich quickly made up his mind and found a suitable pretext for asking his cousin's permission to present a lady who longed to meet her and whom he knew to be passionately interested in all efforts on behalf of the good, the true, and the beautiful.

So no one could really say that nothing much was happening as the days and weeks rocked along; actually, the police exhibit and all that went with it was the least of it. In England, for instance, they had something far more magnificent, much talked of in society hereabouts: a doll's house that was presented to the Queen, built by a famous architect, with a dining room three feet long, its walls hung with miniature portraits by famous contemporary painters, with bedrooms where hot and cold water came from real taps, and a library that included a little album made entirely of gold, in which the Queen could paste tiny photographs of the royal family, a microscopically printed railway timetable and shipping schedule, and about two hundred tiny volumes in which famous authors had with their own hands written poems and stories for the Queen. Diotima had a two-volume set of the deluxe edition of the English book about it that had only just appeared, with expensive color prints of everything worth seeing, to which rarity she owed an increased participation in her soirees by the highest-ranking personages in society. And there was more, one thing coming so quickly on the heels of another that it was hard to find words to keep up with it all, so that it felt like a flurry of drumbeats in the soul preceding something just around the corner that had not yet come into view. There was, for instance, the first strike ever of the Imperial and Royal Telegraph, conducted in a most disquieting fashion that came to be known as passive resistance, and consisted simply of everyone involved going about their work punctiliously by the book; it turned out that everything could be brought to a standstill far more speedily by the strictest observance of all the official regulations than by the most ruthless anarchy. Like the story of the Captain of Kopenick in Prussia—a man still remembered for conferring that military rank on himself by dint of putting on a secondhand uniform, then stopping a patrol in the street and using it, together with the Prussian virtue of unconditional obedience to orders from anyone in uniform, to liberate the municipal treasury—passive resistance was something that tickled the imagination, but it also subliminally undermined the principles that inspired the disapproval one felt obliged to express. The newspapers reported among other items that His Majesty's Government had signed an agreement with another majesty's government to keep the peace, revive the economy, and work sincerely together to establish and respect the rights of all, and listed the measures to be taken if these were or might be threatened. Section Chief Tuzzi's superior, the Foreign Minister, made a speech, a few days afterward, in which he urged the need for close collaboration among the three continental empires, which could not afford to ignore modern social developments but must, in the joint interests of the dynasties, make common cause against social innovations. Italy was involved in a military campaign in Libya. Germany and England had a problem in Baghdad. Kakania was making certain military preparations in the south, to show the world that it would not allow Serbia to expand to the sea but would permit it only a railway line to the coast. And reported on a par with all the events of this magnitude was the world-famous Swedish actress Vogelsang's confession that she had never in all her life slept as well as on this, her first night in Kakania, and her delight at the policeman who had rescued her from the delirious crowd and then asked permission to press her hand in both of his.

This, then, brings us back to the police exhibition. A great deal was happening everywhere, and people were certainly aware of it. It was regarded as a good thing when we were the ones doing it, and aroused apprehensiveness when it was done by others. Every schoolboy could understand each thing as it happened, but as to what it all meant in general, nobody really knew except for a very few persons, and even they were not sure. Only a short time later it might as well have happened in a different sequence, or the other way around, and nobody would have known the difference, except for a few changes that inexplicably establish themselves in the course of time and so constitute the slimy track made by the snail of history.

In such circumstances a foreign embassy may well be facing a hard task when trying to find out what is actually going on. The diplomatic representatives would gladly have drawn their wisdom from Count Leinsdorf, but His Grace placed obstacles in their way. In his work he found anew day by day the contentment that solid achievement leaves in its wake, and what foreign observers beheld in his countenance was the beaming serenity that comes from operations proceeding in good order. Department One sent a memorandum; Department Two replied; when Department One had been notified of Department Two's reply, it was usually advisable to suggest talking it over in person, and when an agreement had been reached in this fashion, it was decided that nothing could be done about the matter; and so there was always something to do. In addition there were those countless minor considerations that must not be overlooked. After all, one was always working hand in glove with all the various ministries; one did not want to give offense to the Church; one had to take account of certain persons and social considerations; in short, even on those days when one wasn't doing anything in particular, there were so many things one had to guard against doing that one had the sense of being kept frantically busy at all times. His Grace fully appreciated these facts of life.

"The higher a man is placed by destiny," he used to say, "the better he sees that everything depends on only a few simple principles, but above all on a firm will and well-planned activity." Once, when speaking to his "young friend," he went even more deeply into this subject. Apropos of the German struggle for national unity, he admitted that between 1848 and 1866 quite a number of the best brains in the country had had their say in politics. "But then," he went on, "that fellow Bismarck came along, and there was one good thing he did if he did nothing else: he showed them how politics should be done. It isn't done with a lot of talk and clever ideas! Despite his seamy side, he did see to it that ever since his time, wherever the German tongue is spoken, everyone knows that in politics there is no hope to be had from cleverness and speechmaking, only from silent thought and action."

Count Leinsdorf also expressed himself along these lines at Diotima's Council meetings, and the representatives of foreign powers that sometimes sent along their observers had a hard time trying to fathom his meaning. Arnheim's part in it was regarded as worth watching, and so was the position of Section Chief Tuzzi, and there came to be a general consensus that there was a secret understanding between these two men and Count Leinsdorf, the political aim of which was for the present concealed behind lively attention-stealing devices such as Frau Section Chief Tuzzi's pancultural endeavors. Considering how Count Leinsdorf succeeded in hoodwinking even those hardened observers without even trying, there is no denying the gift he felt he had for realism in politics.

But even those gentlemen who on festive occasions wear gold-embroidered foliage and other rank growths on their tailcoats held to the *realpolitisch* prejudices of their game, and since they could discover no solid clues behind the scenes of the Parallel Campaign, they soon turned their attention to something that was the cause of most of the obscure phenomena in Kakania, called "the unliberated national minorities." We all talk as if nationalism were purely the invention of the arms dealers, but we really should try for a more comprehensive explanation, and to this end Kakania makes an important contribution. The inhabitants of this Imperial and Royal Imperial–Royal Dual Monarchy had a serious problem: they were supposed to feel like Imperial and Royal Austro-Hungarian patriots, while at the same time being Royal Hungarian or Imperial Royal Austrian patriots. Their understandable motto in the face of such complexities was "United we stand" (from *viribus unitis*, "with forces joined"). But the Austrians needed to take a far stronger stand than the Hungarians, because the Hungarians were, first and last, simply Hungarians and were regarded only incidentally, by foreigners who did not know their language, as Austro-Hungarians too; the Austrians, however, were, to begin with and primarily, nothing at all, and yet they were supposed by their leaders to feel Austro-Hungarian and be Austrian-Hungarians—they didn't even have a proper word for it. Nor was there an Austria. Its two components, Hungary and Austria, made a match like a red-white-and-green jacket with black-and-yellow trousers. The jacket was a jacket, but the trousers were the relic of an extinct black-and-yellow outfit that had been ripped apart in the year 1867. The trousers, or Austria, were since then officially referred to as "the kingdoms and countries represented in the Imperial Council of the Realm," meaning nothing at all, of course, because it was only a phrase concocted from various names, for even those kingdoms referred to, such wholly Shakespearean kingdoms as Lodomeria and Illyria, were long gone, even when there was still a complete black-and-yellow outfit worn by actual soldiers. So if you asked an Austrian where he was from, of course he couldn't say: I am a man from one of those nonexistent kingdoms and countries; so for that reason alone he preferred to say: I am a Pole, a Czech, an Italian, Friulian, Ladino, Slovene, Croat, Serb, Slovak, Ruthenian, or Wallachian—and this was his so-called nationalism. Imagine a squirrel that doesn't know whether it is a squirrel or a chipmunk, a creature with no concept of itself, and you will understand that in some circumstances it could be thrown into fits of terror by catching sight of its own tail. So this was the way Kakanians related to each other, with the panic of limbs so united as they stood that they hindered each other from being anything at all. Since the world began, no creature has as yet died of a language defect, and yet the Austrian and Hungarian Austro-Hungarian Dual Monarchy can nevertheless be said to have perished from its inexpressibility.

A stranger to Kakanian history might be interested to learn just how so seasoned and eminent a Kakanian as Count Leinsdorf coped with this problem. He began by excising Hungary altogether from his watchful mind; as a wise diplomat, he simply never mentioned it, just as parents avoid speaking of a son who has struck out for independence against their wish and who, they keep expecting, will yet live to regret it; the rest he referred to as the "nationalities," or else as the "Austrian ethnic stocks." This was a most subtle device. His Grace had studied constitutional law and had found a definition accepted more or less worldwide, to the effect that a people could claim to count as a nation only if it had its own constitutional state, from which he deduced that the Kakanian nations were simply national minorities, at most. On the other hand, Count Leinsdorf knew that man finds his full, true destiny only within the overarching communal framework of a nation, and since he did not like the thought of anyone being deprived in this respect, he concluded that it was necessary to subordinate the nationalities and ethnic breeds to an all-embracing State. Besides, he believed in a divine order, even if that order was not always discernible to the human eye, and in the revolutionary modernist moods that sometimes overcame him he was even capable of thinking that the idea of the State, which was coming so strongly into its own these days, was perhaps nothing other than the Divine Right of Kings just beginning to manifest itself in a rejuvenated form. However that might be—as a realist in politics he took good care never to overdo the theorizing, and would even have settled for Diotima's view that the idea of the Kakanian State was synonymous with that of World Peace—the point was that there *was* a Kakanian State, even if its name was a dubious one, and that a Kakanian nation had to be invented to go with it. He liked to illustrate this by pointing out, for instance, that nobody was a schoolboy if he didn't go to school, but that the school remained a school even when it stood empty. The more the minorities balked against the Kakanian school's efforts to bind them into one nation, the more necessary the school, in the given circumstances. The more they insisted that they were separate nations, the more they demanded the restoration of their so-called long-lost historic rights, the more they flirted with their ethnic brothers and cousins across the borders and openly called the Empire a prison from which they must be released, the more Count Leinsdorf tried to calm them down by calling them ethnic stocks and agreed with their own emphasis on their underdeveloped state; only he offered to improve it by raising them up to be part of one Austrian nation. Whatever they wanted that did not fit in with his plan or that was overly mutinous, he blamed in his familiar diplomatic way on their failure so far to transcend their political immaturity, which was to be dealt with by a wise blend of shrewd tolerance and gently punitive restraints.

And so when Count Leinsdorf created the Parallel Campaign, the various ethnicities immediately perceived it as a covert Pan-Germanic plot. His Grace's participation in the police exhibition was linked with the secret police and interpreted as proof positive of his sympathies with that politically repressive body. This was all known to the foreign observers, who had heard all the horror stories about the Parallel Campaign they could want. They kept it in mind while listening to the stories about the reception of the actress Vogelsang, the English Queen's dollhouse, and the striking telegraphers, or when they were asked what they thought of the recently published international agreements; and although the Minister's praise of the disciplinary spirit could be taken as an announcement of a policy if one so desired, they probably felt that to the unprejudiced eye the opening of the police exhibition, despite all the talk about it, had produced nothing worth noticing, though they also had the impression like everyone else that something was brewing in a general way, though it could not yet be pinned down.

99

OF THE MIDDLING INTELLIGENCE AND ITS FRUITFUL COUNTERPART, THE HALFWIT; THE RESEMBLANCE BETWEEN TWO ERAS; LOVABLE AUNT JANE; AND THE DISORDER CALLED MODERN TIMES

It really was impossible to gain a clear idea of what went on when Diotima's Council was in session. The general tendency among the avant-garde in those days was in favor of taking action; people who lived by their brains felt it incumbent upon themselves to take over the leadership from those who lived for their bellies. There was also something known as Expressionism. Nobody could say just what it was, but the word suggests some kind of squeezing-out; constructive visions, perhaps, but inasmuch as the contrast with traditional art revealed them as being destructive, too, we might simply call them structive, which commits one to nothing either way, and a structive outlook sounds pretty good. Nor is that all.

The general orientation was toward the Now and the real world, the inside turning toward the outside, but there was also a movement turning from the outside inward; the intellect and individualism were already seen as outmoded and egocentric, love was once again discredited, and the salutary effect of artistic trash on the masses, when injected into the cleansed souls of men of action, was about to be rediscovered. "What people are" evidently keeps changing as rapidly as "What people are wearing," and both have in common the fact that no one, not even those in the fashion business, knows the real secret of who "these people" are. But anyone trying to run counter to this would look silly, like a person caught between the opposing currents of an electric therapy machine, wildly twitching and jerking without anyone's being able to see his attacker. For the enemy is not those quick-witted enough to take advantage of the given business situation; it's the gaseous fluidity and instability of the general state of affairs itself, the confluence of innumerable currents from all directions that constitute it, its unlimited capacity for new combinations and permutations, plus, on the receiving end, the absence or breakdown of valid, sustaining, and ordering principles.

To find a secure foothold in this flow of phenomena is like trying to hammer a nail into a fountain's jet of water; and yet there is a certain constant in it. What is actually going on when that agile species man calls a tennis player a genius? Something unstated is at work here. And when they attribute genius to a racehorse? Something more is left unsaid. Whether they call a football player a scientist of the game, or admire a fencer's intellectual style, or speak of a boxer's tragic defeat, there is always something undeclared going on. They exaggerate, but the exaggeration is a form of imprecision, the sort of fuzziness of mind that makes the denizens of a small town regard the son of the department store owner as a man of the world. There is bound to be a grain of truth in it, and anyway, why shouldn't the surprises an athletic champion pulls off suggest those we get from a genius, or his strategies seem analogous to those of a seasoned explorer of the unknown? Even though there is something else, something far more important, that is quite wrong with such analogies, of course, this is not perceived, or perceived only with reluctance, by those given to making them. At bottom there is an uncertainty of values, passed over and ignored; it is probably less its idea of genius that makes this era attribute genius to a tennis player or a racehorse than its general distrust for the world of the mind, of the intellect, to which the term rightly belongs.

This might be the moment to bring up Aunt Jane, of whom Ulrich was reminded when he was leafing through some old family albums Diotima had lent him, comparing the faces he saw in them with the faces seen in her house. As a boy, Ulrich had often stayed with a great-aunt who'd had a friend, Aunt Jane, from time immemorial. Jane was not really an aunt, originally. She had come into the house as the children's piano teacher and had not exactly achieved any wonders in that line, either, but she had won their love because it was a principle with her that there was not much point in doing one's piano practice if one was not born for music, as she put it. She got more enjoyment out of seeing the children climb trees, and in this fashion she became an aunt to two generations as well as—through the retroactive effect of the passage of years—her disappointed employer's lifelong friend.

"Ah yes, dear Mucki!" Aunt Jane would say, for instance, full of feeling impervious to time, her voice so charged with indulgence and admiration for little Nepomuk, who was by then an uncle in his forties, that it still lived for anyone who had heard it once. That voice of Aunt Jane's sounded as if it had been dusted with flour; absolutely as if one had dipped one's bare arm into the finest flour. It was a husky voice, crumb-coated, all because she drank lots of black coffee and smoked long, thin, strong Virginia cigars, which, as she aged, had blackened and eroded her teeth. When you looked at her face you might also feel that the sound of her voice had something to do with those innumerable little fine lines that covered her skin like the lines of an etching. Her face was long and gentle, and to the later generations seemed never to have changed, like everything else about Aunt Jane. She wore one and the same dress all her life, even if, as seems likely, it was a series of reproductions of the original; it was a long, tight casing of black ribbed silk from neck to toe, making no allowance for any excessive mobility of the body, with an endless row of little black buttons, like a priest's cassock. At the top there was a low, stiff stand-up collar with turned-down corners, between which her Adam's apple formed active gullies in the fleshless skin of her neck every time she pulled on her cigar; the tight sleeves ended in stiff white cuffs, and for a roof she had a reddish-blond slightly curly man's wig, parted in the middle. With the passing of the years that part showed a little more of the canvas, but more affecting than that were the two spots where the gray temples could be seen from under the bright wig, the only sign that Aunt Jane had not remained the same age all her life.

She might seem to have anticipated by many decades the masculine kind of woman who has since come into fashion, but that is not really the case, because in her manly breast there beat a most feminine heart. She might also be thought to have once been a famous pianist who later lost touch with her time, for that is how she looked. But this was not so either, because she had never been more than a piano teacher, and both that mannish hairdo and her priestly garb could be traced to the fact that as a girl Aunt Jane had been infatuated with the Abbé Franz Liszt, whom she had met socially several times during one short period, and that was when her name had somehow assumed its English form. With that encounter she kept faith, like a lovesick knight wearing his lady's colors into his gray old age without ever having asked for more, and in Aunt Jane's case this was more touching than if it had been some uniform of her own great days she had worn in her retirement.

When the children were considered old enough, they were made privy to Aunt Jane's deep secret, after many solemn admonitions to respect it; much as if it had been a rite of passage. Jane had no longer been a young girl (a fastidious soul takes its time in making such a choice) when she found the man she loved and married, against her family's will; he had of course been an artist, although, because of the rotten luck of small-town, provincial circumstances, only a photographer. But a short time after they were married he was already running up debts like a genius and drinking furiously. Aunt Jane made sacrifices for him, she fetched him home from the tavern, she wept in secret and openly at his knees. He looked like a genius, with an imperious mouth and flamboyant hair, and if Aunt Jane had been able to infect him with the passion of her despair, he would have become, with his disastrous vices, as great as Lord Byron. But the photographer proved recalcitrant to such a transfer of feeling, abandoned Jane after a year of marriage, leaving with her maid, a peasant girl who was pregnant by him, and he died not much later, in misery. Jane cut a lock of hair from his superb head and kept it; she took the child born to him out of wedlock and raised it as her own, under great deprivation; she rarely spoke of her past; a life given over to passion is not an easy one, or easy to talk about.

Aunt Jane's life had held its share of romantic eccentricity. But later on, when the photographer in his earthly imperfection had long ceased to hold her under his spell, the imperfect substance of her love for him had somehow also moldered away, leaving behind only the eternal form of love and inspiration, so that at a great remove in time her experience had become indistinguishable from a truly earthshaking kind of emotion. Aunt Jane's mind was probably not supercharged intellectually, but its form was beautiful. Her attitude was heroic, but such a stance is unattractive only as long as it is falsely motivated; once it has become quite empty of content, it again turns to flickering flames and true faith. Aunt Jane lived on tea, black coffee, and two cups of beef bouillon a day, but no one in that little town stopped and stared after her on the streets when she passed by in her black cassock, because the people knew her, they knew she was a proper lady, they even looked up to her for being a proper lady and having the determination to dress as she pleased, even though they did not know the reasons for it.

So this is more or less the story of Aunt Jane, who died a long time ago, at a great age, and my great-aunt is dead too, and so is Uncle Nepomuk, and what were their lives all about anyway? Ulrich asked himself. But just then he would have given a lot to be able to talk with Aunt Jane again. He turned the pages of the thick old albums with those family photographs that had somehow ended up in Diotima's possession, and the closer he came to the beginnings of that new art of picture-taking, the more proudly, it seemed to him, the subjects faced the camera. There they were, with one foot placed on a pile of cardboard boulders wreathed in paper ivy or, if they were officers, with a saber posed between their straddled legs; the girls had their hands folded in their laps and their eyes opened wide; the emancipated men stood their ground in creaseless trousers that rose up like curling smoke, in coats with a bold romantic sweep to them, as though a gale had blown away the dignified stiffness of the bourgeois frock coat. The time must have been somewhere between 1860 and 1870, when photography had emerged from its earliest stages, when the revolutionary forties were remembered as a wild, chaotic time long gone and life had become subtly different, though no one could say exactly what the new elements were; even the tears, embraces, and confessions in which the new middle class had tried to find its soul in its early days were no more, but as a wave runs out over the sands, this noble impulse had now come to express itself in the way people dressed and in a certain personal buoyancy for which there may be a better word, but for the moment all we have is the photographs. The photographers then wore velvet jackets and handlebar mustaches, to make them look like painters, and the painters designed huge cartoons on which they put whole regiments of important figures through their paces; people in general felt it was just the right time for a technology capable of immortalizing them as well. All that remains to be said is that at no other time could they all have felt so full of genius and stature as the people of this particular period, which produced fewer uncommon individuals—unless it was harder for such individuals to become visible in the midst of so many?— than ever before.

As he turned the pages, Ulrich wondered whether there was some connection between that era, when a photographer could feel like a genius because he drank, wore an open-necked shirt, and, with the aid of the latest techniques, was able to project his sense of his own greatness of spirit onto all those of his contemporaries who posed before his lens, and Ulrich's own time, when only racehorses were truly felt to have genius because of their all-surpassing ability to stretch their legs and contract them again. The two periods look different. The present looks proudly down upon the past, which, if it had happened to occur later, would have looked proudly down upon the present. Yet it mainly amounted to the same thing, because in both cases the major role is played by muddled thinking and an ignoring of the telling differences. A single aspect of greatness is taken for the whole, a distant analogy for a truth, and the flayed hide of a significant word is stuffed with something modish. It works, though not for long. The talkers in Diotima's salon were never entirely wrong about anything, for their concepts were as misty as the outlines of bodies in a steambath. "These ideas, on which life hangs as the eagle hangs on his wings," Ulrich thought, "our countless moral and artistic notions of life, by nature as delicate as mountain ranges of granite blurred by distance." On such tongues as these the ideas multiplied by being turned over and over; it was impossible to discuss one of them for any length of time without suddenly finding oneself caught up in the next.

These were the kind of people who had throughout history regarded themselves as the New Era, a term like a sack in which to catch all the winds of the compass, always serving as an excuse for not placing things in their own objective order but fitting them into an illusory compound with a chimera. And yet it holds a confession of faith, the oddly living conviction that it is up to them to bring order into the world. If we were to judge what they were trying to do along those lines as halfway intelligent, it might be worth saying that it is precisely the other half, the unnamed or—to come straight out with it—the stupid, never exact or complementary part of that middling intelligence that held an inexhaustible power of self-renewal and fruitfulness. There was life in it, mutability, restlessness, freedom to adopt a fresh perspective. They probably had their own sense of how it was with them. They were shaken up by it, it blew in gusts through their heads, those children of a nerve-racked age, aware that something was wrong, each feeling intelligent enough and yet all of them together feeling somehow barren. If they also happened to have talent—and their intellectual woolliness certainly did not exclude this possibility—then what was going on in their heads was like seeing the weather, the clouds, trains, telegraph wires, trees and animals and the whole moving panorama of our dear world, through a narrow, dirt-encrusted window; and no one was very quick to notice the state of his own window, but everyone noticed it about the window next door.

Ulrich had once asked them, for the fun of it, just what they meant by what they were saying. They gave him jaundiced looks, told him he had a mechanistic view of life and was too skeptical, and stated that the most complicated problems must be made to yield the simplest solutions, so that the New Era—once it had shucked the confusing present—would turn out to be simplicity itself. Compared with Arnheim, Ulrich did not strike them as impressive at all, and Aunt Jane would have patted him on the cheek, saying, "I know just how they feel. You put them off with your seriousness."

100

GENERAL STUMM INVADES THE STATE
LIBRARY AND LEARNS ABOUT THE WORLD
OF BOOKS, THE LIBRARIANS GUARDING IT,
AND INTELLECTUAL ORDER

General Stumm had noticed the rebuff to his "comrade in arms" and undertook to comfort him. "What a lot of useless palaver," he said in indignant dismissal of the Council members; then, without any encouragement from Ulrich, he started to talk about himself, with a certain excitement mixed with self-satisfaction:

"You remember, don't you," he said, "that I'd made up my mind to find that great redeeming idea Diotima wants and lay it at her feet. It turns out that there are lots of great ideas, but only one of them can be the greatest—that's only logical, isn't it?—so it's a matter of putting them in order. You said yourself that this is a resolve worthy of a Napoleon, right? You even gave me a number of excellent suggestions, as was to be expected of you, but I never got to the point of using them. In short, I have to go about it my own way."

He took his horn-rimmed glasses out of his pocket and put them on in place of the pince-nez, a sign that he wanted to look closely at someone or something.

"One of the foremost rules for a good general is to find out the enemy's strength," he said. "So I asked them to get me a card to our world-famous Imperial Library, and with the help of a librarian who very charmingly put himself at my disposal when I told him who I was, I have now penetrated the enemy's lines. We marched down the ranks in that colossal storehouse of books, and I don't mind telling you I was not particularly overwhelmed; those rows of books are no worse than a garrison on parade. Still, after a while I couldn't help starting to do some figuring in my head, and I got an unexpected answer. You see, I had been thinking that if I read a book a day, it would naturally be exhausting, but I would be bound to get to the end sometime and then, even if I had to skip a few, I could claim a certain position in the world of the intellect. But what d'you suppose that librarian said to me, as we walked on and on, without an end in sight, and I asked him how many books they had in this crazy library? Three and a half million, he tells me. We had just got to the seven hundred thousands or so, but I kept on doing these figures in my head; I'll spare you the details, but I checked it out later at the office, with pencil and paper: it would take me ten thousand years to carry out my plan.

"I felt nailed to the spot—the whole world seemed to be one enormous practical joke! And I'm telling you, even though I'm feeling a bit calmer about it, there's something radically wrong somewhere!

"You may say that it isn't necessary to read every last book. Well, it's also true that in war you don't have to kill every last soldier, but we still need every one of them. You may say to me that every book is needed too. But there, you see, you wouldn't be quite right, because that isn't so. I asked the librarian.

"It occurred to me, you see, that the fellow lives among those millions of books, he knows each one, he knows where to find them, he ought to be able to help me. Of course I wasn't going to ask him point-blank: Where do I find the finest idea in the world? That sounds too much like the opening of a fairy tale, even I know that much; besides, I never liked fairy tales, even as a child. But what to do? I had to ask him something of the sort in the end anyway. But I never told him why I wanted to know, not a word about our Campaign and having to find the most inspiring aim for it—discretion, you know; I didn't feel I was authorized to go that far. So I finally tried a little stratagem. 'By the way,' I said casually, 'how on earth do you go about finding the right book somewhere in this immense collection . . . ?' I tried to say it as I imagined Diotima might, and I dropped a few pennies' worth of admiration into my voice, and sure enough, he started to purr and fell all over himself with helpfulness, and what was the Herr General interested in finding out?

" 'Oh, all sorts of things,' I said, as if he were prying into state secrets; I was playing for time.

" 'I only meant what subject or what author,' he asked. 'Is it military history?'

" 'Oh no,' I said, 'more on the lines of the history of peace.'

" 'History as such? Or current pacifist literature?'

"No, I said, it wasn't that simple. 'Might there be, for instance, something like a compendium of all the great humanitarian ideas or anything like that?' You remember how much research I've already got my people to do on those lines. He didn't say a word. 'Or a book on realizing the most important aims of all?' I say to him.

" 'Something in theological ethics?' he suggests.

" 'Theological ethics too,' I said, 'but it would have to include something about our old Austrian culture and a bit about Grillparzer,' I specified. My eyes must have been blazing with such a thirst for knowledge that the fellow suddenly took fright, as if I was about to suck him dry altogether. I went on a little longer about needing a kind of timetable that would enable me to make connections among all kinds of ideas in every direction—at which point he turns so polite it's absolutely unholy, and offers to take me into the catalog room and let me do my own searching, even though it's against the rules, because it's only for the use of the librarians. So I actually found myself inside the holy of holies. It felt like being inside an enormous brain. Imagine being totally surrounded by those shelves, full of books in their compartments, ladders all over the place, all those book stands and library tables piled high with catalogs and bibliographies, the concentrate of all knowledge, don't you know, and not one sensible book to read, only books about books. It positively reeked of brain phosphorus, and I felt that I must have really got somewhere. But of course a funny feeling came over me when the man was going to leave me there on my own—I felt both awestruck and uneasy as hell. Up the ladder he scoots, like a monkey, aiming straight at a book from below, fetches it down, and says: 'Here it is, General, a bibliography of bibliographies for you'—you know about that? In short, the alphabetical list of alphabetical lists of the titles of all the books and papers of the last five years dealing with ethical problems, exclusive of moral theology and literature, or however he put it, and he tries to slip away. I barely had time to grab his lapel and hang on to him.

" 'Just a moment, sir,' I cried, 'you can't leave me here without telling me your secret, how you manage to . . .' I'm afraid I let slip the word 'madhouse,' because that's how I suddenly felt about it. 'How do you find your way in this madhouse of books?' He must have got the wrong impression—it occurred to me later that crazy people are given to calling others crazy—anyway, he just kept staring at my saber, and I could hardly keep hold of him. And then he gave me a real shock. When I didn't let go of him he suddenly pulled himself up, rearing up in those wobbly pants of his, and said in a slow, very emphatic way, as though the time had come to give away the ultimate secret: 'General,' he said, 'if you want to know how I know about every book here, I can tell you: Because I never read any of them.'

"It was almost too much, I tell you! But when he saw how stunned I was, he explained himself. The secret of a good librarian is that he never reads anything more of the literature in his charge than the titles and the tables of contents. 'Anyone who lets himself go and starts reading a book is lost as a librarian,' he explained. 'He's bound to lose perspective.'

" 'So,' I said, trying to catch my breath, 'you never read a single book?'

" 'Never. Only the catalogs.'

" 'But aren't you a Ph.D.?'

" 'Certainly I am. I teach at the university, as a special lecturer in Library Science. Library Science is a special field leading to a degree, you know,' he explained. 'How many systems do you suppose there are, General, for the arrangement and preservation of books, cataloging of titles, correcting misprints and misinformation on title pages, and the like?'

"I must admit that when he left me there alone, after that, I felt like doing one of two things: bursting into tears, or lighting a cigarette—neither of which I was allowed to do there. But what do you think happened? As I'm standing there, totally at a loss, an old attendant who must have been watching us all along pads around me respectfully a few times, then he stops, looks me in the face, and starts speaking to me in a voice quite velvety, from either the dust on the books or the foretaste of a tip: 'Is there anything in particular, sir, you are looking for?' he asks me. I try to shake my head, but the old fellow goes on: 'We get lots of gentlemen from the Staff College in here. If you'll just tell me, sir, what subject you're interested in at the moment, sir . . . Julius Caesar, Prince Eugene of Savoy, Count Daun? Or is it something contemporary? Military statutes? The budget?' I swear the man sounded so sensible and knew so much about what was inside those books that I gave him a tip and asked him how he did it. And what do you think? He tells me again that the students at the Staff College come to him when they have a paper to write, 'And when I bring the books,' he goes on, 'they often cuss a bit, and gripe about all the nonsense they have to learn, and that's how the likes of us pick up all sorts of things. Or else it's the Deputy who has to draw up the budget for the Department of Education, and he asks me what material was used by the Deputy the year before. Or it might be the Bishop, who's been writing about certain types of beetles for the last fifteen years, or one of the university professors, who complains that he's been waiting three weeks to get a certain book, and we have to look for it on all the adjoining shelves, in case it's been misplaced, and then it turns out he's had it at home for the last two years. That's the way it's been, sir, for nigh on forty years; you develop an instinct for what people want, and what they read for it.'

" 'Well,' I said, 'be that as it may, my friend, it still isn't so simple for me to tell you what I'm looking for.'

"And what do you think he comes back with? He gives me a quiet look, and nods, and says: 'That happens all the time too, General, if I may say so. There was a lady who came in, not so long ago, who said exactly the same thing to me. Perhaps you know her, sir, she's the wife of Section Chief Tuzzi, of the Foreign Office?'

"Now, what do you think of that? You could have knocked me over with a feather. And when the old fellow caught on, he just went and fetched all the books Diotima has on reserve there, so now, when I come to the library, it's practically like a secret mystical marriage; now and then I make a discreet pencil mark in the margin, or I write a word in, and I know she'll see it the very next day, and she won't have a clue who it is that's inside her own head, when she wonders what's going on."

The General paused blissfully. But then he pulled himself together, his face took on a look of grim seriousness, and he continued: "Now brace yourself and give me your full attention, because I'm going to ask you something. We're all convinced—aren't we?—that we're living in the best-ordered times the world has ever seen. I know I once said in Diotima's presence that it's a prejudice, but it's a prejudice I naturally share. And now I have to face the fact that the only people with a really reliable *intellectual* order are the library attendants, and I ask you—no, I don't ask you; after all, we've talked about this before, and naturally I've thought it over again in the light of my recent experiences. So let me put it this way: Suppose you're drinking brandy, right? A good thing to do in some circumstances. But you keep on, and on, and on, drinking brandy—are you with me?—and the first thing is, you get drunk; next, you get the d.t.'s; and finally, you get conducted with military honors to your last resting place, where the chaplain testifies to your unflinching devotion to duty and so on. Do you get the picture? Good, you've got it, nothing to it. So now let's take water. Imagine drinking water until you drown in it. Or imagine going on eating until your intestines are tied into knots. Or you go on taking drugs—quinine, arsenic, opium. What for? you ask. Well, my friend, I'm coming to the most extraordinary proposition: Take *order*. Or rather, start imagining a great idea, and then another still greater, and then another even greater than that one, and so on; and in the same style, try to increase the concept of order in your head. At first it's as neat and tidy as an old maid's room and as clean as a Horse Guards stable. Then it's as splendid as a brigade in battle formation. Next, it's crazy, like coming out of the casino late at night and commanding the stars: 'Universe, 'ten*shun*, eyes right!' Or let's put it this way: At first order is like a new recruit still falling over his own feet, and you straighten him out. Then it's like dreaming you've suddenly been promoted, over everybody's head, to Minister of War. Next, just imagine a total universal order embracing all mankind—in short, the perfect civilian state of order: that, I say, is death by freezing, it's rigor mortis, a moonscape, a geometric plague!

"I discussed that with my library attendant. He suggested that I read Kant or somebody, all about the limits of ideas and perceptions. But frankly, I don't want to go on reading. I have a funny feeling that I now understand why those of us in the army, where we have the highest degree of order, also have to be prepared to lay down our lives at any moment. I can't exactly explain why. Somehow or other, order, once it reaches a certain stage, calls for bloodshed. And now I am honestly worried that your cousin is carrying all her efforts too far, to the point where she is likely to go and do something that might do her a lot of harm—and I'll be less able than ever to help her! Do you see what I mean? As for the arts and sciences and all they can offer in terms of great and admirable ideas, of course I have nothing but the greatest respect for all that; I wouldn't dream of saying anything against it."

101

COUSINS IN CONFLICT

At about this time Diotima turned to her cousin again. She did it at one of her evenings, coming like a tired dancer through the eddies swirling persistently, unremittingly, through her rooms, to sit down beside him in a pool of quiet where he had parked himself on a little settee against the wall. It was a long time since she had done anything like it. She had avoided seeing him "off duty" ever since those drives in the country together, and as if because of them.

From heat or fatigue, her face looked slightly blotchy.

She propped her hands on the settee, said, "How are you?" and nothing more, even though there was clearly something more needing to be said, and stared straight ahead, with her head slightly bowed. She looked a bit groggy, to borrow a term from the boxing ring, not even bothering to smooth down her dress properly as she sat there, hunched over.

It made her cousin think of tousled hair and bare legs under a peasant skirt. Strip away the frosting, and what was left was a handsome, sturdy creature, and he had to restrain himself from simply taking her hand in his fist, like a peasant.

"So Arnheim isn't making you happy," he said evenly.

Perhaps she should have put him in his place, but she felt strangely moved; after a while, she said: "His friendship makes me very happy."

"I thought his friendship distresses you a little."

"What nonsense!" Diotima pulled herself up and recovered her ladylike poise. "Do you know who really distresses me?" she asked, trying for an easy, chatty tone. "Your friend the General. What does that man want? Why does he keep coming here? Why is he always staring at me?"

"He's in love with you," her cousin replied.

Diotima gave a nervous laugh. She went on: "Do you realize that I shudder from head to foot when I set eyes on him? He makes me think of death."

"An uncommonly life-loving figure of Death, if you look at him without prejudice."

"Evidently I'm not unprejudiced. I don't know why, but I go into a panic every time he comes up to me and informs me that I make 'outstanding' ideas 'stand out' on an 'outstanding occasion.' He makes my skin crawl with an indescribable, incomprehensible, dreamlike fear."

"Of him?"

"Who else? The man's a hyena."

Her cousin had to laugh. She went on with her scolding like a child out of control. "He goes creeping around, just waiting to see our best efforts come to nothing!"

"Which is probably exactly what you are so afraid of. Dear cousin, don't you remember that I foretold the collapse of your undertaking from the first? It can't be helped; you simply have to face it."

Diotima looked at him haughtily. She remembered only too well, even to the words she had spoken to him the first time he came to see her, words that it now hurt her to think about. She had lectured him on what a privilege it was to call upon a whole nation, indeed upon the world, to take up its spiritual mission in the midst of its material-istic concerns. She had wanted nothing outworn, nothing of the old mind-sets, and yet the look she was now giving her cousin was more that of someone who had risen above all that, than of someone who had got above herself. She had considered a Year of the World, a universal rebirth, something to crown all of Western culture; there were times when she had come close, others when her goal seemed to recede from her grasp; she had gone through many ups and downs, and she had suffered. The last few months had been like a long sea voyage, first lifted up by huge waves, then dropped into deep troughs, over and over again, so that by now she could hardly tell what had come first and what later. Now she was sitting here, after her immense efforts, glad that the bench she sat on was not moving, content to do nothing but perhaps watch the smoke curling upward from a man's pipe; so intensely did she feel this that she had, in fact, chosen the image herself—an old man's pipe smoke in the light of the sinking sun. She seemed to herself like someone with great frenzied battles behind him. In a weary tone, she said to her cousin: "I have been through such a great deal; I have changed, I'm afraid."

"In my favor, I hope?"

Diotima shook her head and smiled without looking at him.

"In that case you should know that it's Arnheim who's behind the General, not me!" Ulrich said suddenly. "You've been putting all the blame for bringing in the General on me, all along. But don't you remember what I told you the first time you called me on the carpet about it?"

Diotima remembered. "Keep him away," her cousin had said. But Arnheim had told her to make the General feel welcome. She felt something she could not put into words, as if she were sitting inside a cloud that was quickly rising above her eyes. But the next instant the settee again felt hard and solid under her body, and she said: "I don't know how this General came to us in the first place. I never invited him. And Dr. Arnheim, whom I asked about it, naturally knows nothing about it either. Something must have gone wrong."

Her cousin was not very helpful. "I knew the General years ago, but this is the first time I've seen him in ages," he said. "Of course, he's probably spying here a little for the War Office, but he's sincere about wanting to help you, too. And I have it from his own lips that Arnheim makes quite a point of being attentive to him."

"Because Arnheim takes an interest in everything!" Diotima retorted. "He advised me not to rebuff the General, because he believes in the man's good faith and because he may be useful to us, in his influential position."

Ulrich vehemently shook his head. "Just listen to all the cackling going on around him!" he burst out so sharply that guests nearby turned their heads, to his hostess's embarrassment. "He can take it—

he's rich! He has money, he agrees with every one of them, and he knows that they're all acting as his unpaid press agents."

"Why should he bother?" Diotima asked critically.

"Because of his vanity. He's a monster of vanity. How can I make you see the full extent of it? I mean vanity in the biblical sense: all cymbals and sounding brass to hide a vacuum. A man is vain when he prides himself on having seen the moon rise over Asia on his left while on his right Europe fades away in the sunset—this is how he once described to me his crossing of the Sea of Marmara. The moon probably rises far more beautifully behind the flowerpot on the windowsill of a lovesick young girl than it does over Asia."

Diotima was thinking about where they might go to talk without being overheard. "You find his popularity irritating," she said in a low voice as she led him away through the various rooms, all filled with guests, until she had deftly maneuvered him into the foyer. Here she resumed the conversation with: "Why are you so set against him? You make it so hard for me."

"I make it hard for you?" Ulrich asked with raised eyebrows.

"How can I talk freely with you about everything, as long as you persist in this attitude?" They had come to a stop in the middle of the foyer.

"Please feel free to tell me anything, whatever it is," he said warmly. "You two are in love, I know that much. Will he marry you?"

"He has asked me," Diotima replied without regard to their exposed position as they stood there. She was overcome by her feelings and took no offense at her cousin's bluntness.

"And what about you?" he asked.

She blushed like a schoolgirl. "Oh, for me it's a heavy responsibility," she said hesitantly. "I can't let myself be rushed into doing something unfair. And where the really great things in life are concerned, it doesn't matter so much what one does."

Ulrich was mystified by these words, since he knew nothing of the long nights in which Diotima had learned to overcome the voice of passion and attained that serene evenhandedness of the soul where love floats in the horizontal position of a seesaw equally weighted at both ends. But he sensed that for the moment it would be best to abandon the direct line of straight talk, and took a diplomatic turn:

"I'd be glad to tell you about my attitude to Arnheim, because in the circumstances I shouldn't want you to feel that I'm against him in any way. I think I understand Arnheim quite well. You must realize that whatever is happening in your house—let's call it a kind of synthesis—it is something he has already experienced many times before. Wherever you have intellectual ferment taking the form of convictions, it also appears almost immediately in the form of the opposing convictions. And where it is embodied in a so-called leading intellectual personality, then the moment that personality is not freely saluted on all sides, it feels as insecure as if it were in a cardboard box tossed into the water. We have a tendency in this country to fall in love with noted personalities, like the drunks who throw their arms around a stranger's neck, only to push him away again after a while, for equally obscure reasons. So I have a vivid idea of what Arnheim must be feeling—a form of seasickness, I'd say. And when he remembers in such circumstances what money can do if you know how to use it, he feels firm ground under his feet for the first time after a long sea voyage. He is bound to notice how each suggestion, proposal, wish, service, accomplishment, struggles to enter the orbit of wealth, which is in that sense an image of the mind itself. Ideas striving for power tend to attach themselves to ideas that already have power. I hardly know how to put it to you; the difference between ideas that aim high and those that are merely ambitious is hard to pin down. But once the genuinely great, with its usual material poverty and purity of spirit, is displaced by the mere label of greatness, all sorts of spurious candidates for the label push their way in— quite understandably—and then you also get the kind of greatness that can be conferred by publicity and business acumen. And there you have your Arnheim in all his innocence and guilt."

"You're being very holy all of a sudden," Diotima said acidly.

"You're right, it's none of my business, but that way he has of accepting the mixed effects of inward and outward greatness and trying to make it all look like a model of humanitarianism could in fact exasperate me to a frantic degree of holiness."

"Oh, you are so wrong!" Diotima broke in. "You see him only as a blasé rich man. But Arnheim sees wealth as an absolutely all-pervasive responsibility. He devotes himself to his business as another man might give himself over to a human being entrusted to his care. He deeply needs to make a real difference in the world. If he makes himself available to people, it is because, as he says, a man must keep moving if he wants to be moved. Or was it Goethe who said that? He once explained it to me at length. His point is that to do good, you must, to begin with, *do something*. Of course, I admit that I have also been known to feel that he sometimes mixes too freely with all sorts of people."

As they talked, they were walking back and forth in the empty foyer, with its mirrors and all the coats on the racks. Now Diotima stopped and put her hand on her cousin's arm, saying:

"This man, so highly favored by fate in every way, has the modest notion that a man alone is no stronger than a sick person left on his own. Don't you agree with him there? To be alone is to fall prey to a thousand fantasies." She dropped her eyes as though she were searching the floor for something, even as she felt her cousin's eyes on her lowered eyelids.

"Oh, I suppose I might be talking about myself. I have been so lonely of late. But so are you! I can tell. You have an embittered look; you're not at all happy, are you? Everything you say shows that you're on bad terms with everything in your own life. You're jealous by nature, and you have a chip on your shoulder, you're against everything. I don't mind telling you that Arnheim has complained to me that you refuse to be friends with him."

"Has he actually told you that he wants us to be friends? If so, he's lying!"

Diotima looked up at him and laughed. "There you go again, making a mountain out of a molehill. We both want your friendship. Perhaps we do because you are just as you are. But I'd have to go back a bit to explain: Arnheim came up with such examples as . . ." She hesitated, then thought better of it. "No, that would take us too far afield. In brief, Arnheim says that we have to make use of whatever means our times afford us. The thing is to act on the basis of two different attitudes, never quite revolutionary and never quite antirevolutionary, never quite out of love or out of hate nor out of some particular inclination of our own, but always trying to develop every possibility one has. But that isn't being clever, as you see it; it merely shows a

simple, all-embracing character, someone with a gift for bringing disparate things together by seeing through their superficial differences—the personality of a born leader!"

"And what has that to do with me?" Ulrich asked.

His challenge had the effect of tearing through her reminiscences
of a long conversation about scholasticism, the Church, Goethe and
Napoleon, and the whole fog of cultural ambiguities that had thickened around Diotima's head, and she suddenly saw herself clearly,
sitting beside her cousin on the long shoe cupboard where, in the
heat of argument, she had made him sit down with her; his back was
stubbornly avoiding the coats hanging in rows behind them, which
had badly mussed her hair. As she patted it in place, she replied:

"But you're his exact opposite! You'd like to re-create the whole
world in your own image. You're always opposing everything with
that passive resistance of yours, or whatever that horrid expression
is." She was delighted to tell him just what she thought, for once. But
all this while she kept thinking that they had better not stay where
they were, in case other guests started leaving or coming through the
foyer for some reason.

"You're always so hypercritical," she went on. "I don't recall you
ever having a good word to say about anything, except to praise everything that's intolerable nowadays, out of sheer contrariness. Every
time one tries to hold on to a feeling or an intuition in the midst of
this desert of our godless age, one can count on your fervent defense
of specialization, disorder, all the negative side of life." So saying, she
stood up and gave him to understand, with a smile, that they must
find a better place to sit. It was either rejoining the others or finding
a hiding place where they could go on with their talk. The Tuzzis'
bedroom could be entered even from here, through a door covered
with wallpaper, but Diotima felt it was too intimate a place to take
her cousin, especially as every time the apartment was rearranged for
a reception there was no telling how much of a mess the bedroom
had been left in. So there was no refuge left but one of the two maids'
rooms. The thought that it would be a funny mixture of taking liberties and of her housewifely duty to subject Rachel's room, where she
never set foot, to an impromptu inspection decided her. As they
went there, and even as she apologized for taking him there, and

once they were inside the little room, she intently went on talking to Ulrich:

"I get the feeling that you are always out to undermine Arnheim, every chance you get. Your opposition hurts him. He is an outstanding contemporary, which is why he is and needs to be in touch with present-day realities. While you are always on the point of taking a leap into the impossible. He is all affirmation and perfect balance; you are, frankly, asocial. He strives for unity, intent to his fingertips upon achieving some clear decision; you oppose him with nothing but your formless outlook. He has a feeling for everything that has taken a long time to become what it is; and you? What about you? You act as though the world were about to begin tomorrow. Why don't you answer me? From the very first day, when I told you we had been given a chance to do something truly great, your attitude has been the same. And when I see this chance as a predestined moment that has brought us all together for a purpose, waiting, as it were, with an unspoken question in our eyes, for an answer, you carry on like a brat who wants only to disrupt everything." She was choosing her words with care to gloss over their awkward situation in the maid's room, fortifying her position by giving her cousin the most elaborate scolding.

"If that's how I am, how can I possibly be of any use to you?" Ulrich asked. He had sat down on Rachel's little iron bedstead, an arm's length from Diotima, facing him on the little wicker chair. The answer she gave him was admirable.

"If you ever saw me doing something horrible, something really awful," she said unexpectedly, "I'm sure you'd be an angel about it." She was startled to hear herself say it. She had only meant to point up his love of contradiction by joking that he could be expected to be most kind and considerate when she least deserved it; but a spring had suddenly bubbled up in her unconscious, making her say things that sounded rather silly, and yet it was amazing how they seemed to apply to her and her relationship to this cousin of hers!

Ulrich sensed it. He looked at her without speaking; then, after a pause, he responded with a question: "Are you very much . . . are you madly in love with him?"

Diotima looked at the floor. "What an absurd way to put it! I'm not a schoolgirl with a crush, you know."

But her cousin would not be put off. "I am asking you this for a reason: I am wondering whether you have already come to know that longing that we all have—including even the most detestable creatures among tonight's guests next door—to strip off our clothes, put our arms around each other's shoulders, and sing instead of talking; then you would have to go from one of us to the other and kiss him like a sister on the lips. If this is a bit much, I might let them wear nightshirts."

Diotima answered at random: "What lovely ideas you indulge in."

"But don't you see, I have known what it feels like, myself, though it was a long time ago. And there have been very respectable persons who claimed that this was precisely the way life should be on earth."

"Then it's your own fault if you don't act accordingly," Diotima interrupted. "Besides, there's no need to make it look so ridiculous." She had remembered that her adventure with Arnheim eluded classification and made one long for a life without social differences, where action, soul, mind, and body would all be one.

Ulrich did not answer. He offered his cousin a cigarette. She accepted it. As the cramped little room filled with smoke, Diotima wondered what Rachel would think when she sniffed the evidence of this intrusion. Should they open the window? Or should she explain to the little servant in the morning? Oddly enough, it was precisely the thought of Rachel that decided her to stay; she had been on the point of putting an end to this increasingly awkward tête-à-tête, but the sense of her intellectual superiority and the cigarette smoke that would mystify her maid somehow coalesced into something she was rather enjoying.

Ulrich was watching her. He was surprised at himself for having spoken to her as he did, but he went on with it; he felt a need for companionship. "I'll tell you," he resumed, "under what conditions I might be so seraphic—seraphic is probably not too grand a term for not merely enduring another person but feeling that person if I may put it like this—under his psychological loincloth, without a shudder."

"Unless the other is a woman," Diotima said, in view of her cousin's dubious reputation in the family.

"Not even excepting that."

"You're right. What I call loving the human being in a woman is a great rarity." Diotima felt that Ulrich had been, for some time now, expressing views closer to her own, and yet there was always something amiss and whatever he said never came quite close enough.

"Seriously now," he said stubbornly, leaning forward, his forearm resting on his muscular thighs, his gloomy gaze fixed on the floor. "We still say, nowadays, I love this woman, and I hate this man, instead of saying I find that person attractive or repellent. It would be a step closer to the truth to say that it is I, myself, who arouses in the other the capacity for attracting or repelling me, and even more accurate to say that the other somehow brings out in me the requisite qualities, and so on. We can never know where it begins; the whole thing is a functional interdependence, like the one between two bouncing balls or two electric circuits. We've known all that for a long time now, but we still prefer to regard ourselves as the cause, the primal cause, in the magnetic fields of emotion around us; even when someone admits that he is merely imitating someone else, he makes it sound like an active achievement of his own. And this is why I ask you again whether you have ever been uncontrollably in love, or furious, or desperate. Because it is at such times that you can see clearly, if you are at all perceptive, that in such an overwrought state we behave no differently from a bee on a windowpane or an amoeba in poisoned water: we are caught in a storm of movement, we dash off blindly in every direction at once, we beat our brains out against brick walls, until, by some lucky chance, we find an opening to freedom, which we promptly attribute, as soon as our consciousness has crystallized again, to a calculated plan of action."

"I must say," Diotima objected, "that this is a dismal and demeaning view of emotions that have the power to decide a person's whole life."

"Are you thinking of the boring old argument about whether or not we are masters of our own fate?" Ulrich replied, with a quick glance upward. "If everything is determined by a cause, then no one is responsible for anything, and so on? I must confess that I've never given as much as fifteen minutes of thought to that question in my whole life. It belongs to a period that became obsolete while nobody was looking. It comes from theology, and apart from jurists, who still have a lot of theology and the smell of burning heretics in their nostrils, the only people who still think in terms of causation are those members of your family who are likely to say: 'You are the cause of my sleepless nights' or 'The sudden drop in the price of wheat was the cause of his misfortune.' "

Diotima drew herself up. "Why are you always talking about criminals? Crime seems to hold a special fascination for you. What do you suppose that means?"

"Oh no," her cousin said. "It doesn't mean a thing. A certain degree of excitement, at most. Our ordinary state is an averaging out of all the crimes of which we are capable. But now that the word 'theology' has come up, let me ask you something. . . ."

"Whether I've ever been madly in love or jealous, again?"

"No. Think about this: If God has ordained whatever happens and always knows what will happen, how can a human being commit a sin? It's an old question, but it's still as good as new. What kind of trickster God would it be who sets us up to commit offenses against him, with his own prior knowledge and consent? He doesn't merely know in advance what we are likely to do: there are plenty of examples of such resigned love; oh no, he makes us do wrong! That's the situation in which we find ourselves today, with respect to each other. The self is losing its status as a sovereign making its own laws. We are learning to know the rules by which it develops, the influence of its environment, its structural types, its disappearance in moments of the most intense activity: in short, the laws regulating its formation and its conduct. Think of it, cousin, the laws of personality! It's like talking of a trade union for lonely rattlesnakes or a robbers' chamber of commerce. What with laws being the most impersonal thing in the world, the personality becomes no more than the imaginary meeting point of all that's impersonal, so that it's hard to find for it that honorable standpoint you don't want to relinquish. . . ."

So he spoke, and Diotima took occasion to object: "But, my dear friend, surely one ought to do everything as personally as one can. . . ." Finally, she said: "You really are being very theological today; I've never known that side of your character." Again she sat there like a tired dancer. Such a strong and handsome woman! She somehow felt this herself, in all her bones. She had been avoiding her cousin for weeks, perhaps even months by now. But she rather liked this man of her own age. He looked dashing in evening dress, in the dimly lit room, black and white like a knight templar; there was something of the passion of the Cross in this black and white. She glanced around the modest little bedroom. The Parallel Campaign was far away, she had gone through a great emotional struggle, and here she was in this little room, as plain as duty itself, with only the grace notes of some pussy willows and the unused picture postcards stuck in the frame of the mirror—so it was between these, framed by images of the great city, that the little maid saw her face in the glass! Where did she wash, come to think of it? Ah, in that narrow cupboard, there must be a basin under the lid, Diotima now remembered, and then the thought crossed her mind: "This man wants to and yet he doesn't want to."

She looked at him calmly, with the air of a friendly listener. "Does Arnheim really want to marry me?" she asked herself. He had said so. But then he had not persisted. There was always so much else to talk about. But her cousin too, instead of going on and on in that impersonal fashion, should have asked her: How are you doing, then? Why didn't he ask? She felt that he would understand if she could tell him all about her inner struggles. "Is it a good thing for me?" he had asked her, all too predictably, when she told him how she had changed. The insolence! Diotima smiled.

Both of these men were a bit peculiar, come to think of it. Why did her cousin never have a good word to say for Arnheim? She knew that Arnheim wanted his friendship; but Ulrich too, judging by his own irritable remarks, had Arnheim much on his mind. "And how totally he misunderstands him!" she thought again. There was nothing to be done about it. Besides, at this point it was not only her soul that mutinied against her body, married as it was to Section Chief Tuzzi, but at times her body mutinied against her soul, made to languish, by Arnheim's hesitant and high-strung love, at the rim of a desert where what she saw ahead was perhaps a mirage, only the quivering reflection of her yearning. She would have liked to confide her misery and her helplessness to her cousin. She liked the decisive, one-track mind he usually showed on such occasions. Arnheim's balanced many-sidedness certainly rated higher, but at a moment of decision Ulrich would not waver so much, despite his theorizing, which tended toward an absolute suspension in uncertainty. She sensed this, without knowing why; it was probably part of what she had felt for him from their first encounter. If at this moment Arnheim felt like a huge effort, a royal burden laid upon her soul, too much to bear in every sense, then everything Ulrich was saying tended toward a single effect, that of losing responsibility as one contemplated hundreds of interactions, so that she felt suspiciously free. She suddenly needed to make herself heavier than she was; she couldn't say how, but was immediately reminded of an incident when, as a young girl, she had carried a little boy away from some danger, and how he had kept hitting her in the belly with his knees to make her let him go. The force of this memory—which had occurred to her as unexpectedly as if it had suddenly come down the chimney into this lonely little room—quite threw her off balance. "Madly in love?" she thought. Why did he keep asking her that? As if she were incapable of really letting herself go. Her mind had wandered from what he was saying, so, without any idea whether it would be apropos or not, she simply interrupted him and told him once and for all, without regard to anything he might have been saying, with a laugh (unless her sense of laughing as she spoke was not quite reliable in the sudden, heedless excitement of it): "But I *am* madly in love!"

Ulrich openly smiled at this. "You're quite incapable of it," he said.

She had stood up, her hands on her hair, staring at him in amazement.

"In order to lose control," he specified calmly, "one has to be quite precise and objective. Two selves, aware of how dubious a thing it is these days to be a self, cling to each other—or so I imagine, if it's love at any price and not merely the usual kind of thing and they become so enmeshed with each other that the one feels like the cause for the other one's existence, as they feel themselves changing into greatness and begin to float like a veil. It is incredibly hard, in such a state, to make no false moves, even though one has been making all the right moves for some time. It is simply very hard to feel the right thing in this world! Quite contrary to the general preconception, it almost calls for a certain pedantry. Incidentally, that's just what I wanted to say to you. You flatter me, you know, when you say I could be expected to behave like an angel. A human being would have to be wholly objective—which is almost the same as being impersonal, after all—to be wholly a personification of love. This means being all feeling and sensibility and thought. Now, all the elements that make up a human being are tender, since they yearn toward each other;

only the human being itself is not. So being madly in love is something you might not even want for yourself. . . ."

He had done his best to speak as casually as possible; he even lit another cigarette to keep his face from looking too solemn as he spoke, and Diotima also accepted another from him to hide her embarrassment. She made a comically defiant face and blew the smoke high into the air, to show her independence, because she hadn't quite understood what he was talking about. But their situation as a whole was having a strong effect on her: that her cousin was suddenly saying all these things to her, in this room where they were alone together, without making the slightest move to take her hand or touch her hair, a move so natural in the circumstances, even though they were feeling the magnetic attraction their two bodies exerted on each other in this confined space. What if they . . . , she wondered. But what could one do in this maid's room? She looked around. Act like a whore? But how does one do that? Suppose she started blubbering? Blubbering: that was a schoolgirl expression that had suddenly come back to her. Suppose she suddenly did what he had talked about before, took off her clothes, put her arm around his shoulder, and sang . . . sang what? Played the harp? She looked at him, smiling. It was like being with a wayward brother, in whose company one could do anything that came into one's head. Ulrich was smiling too. But his smile was like a blind window, because now that he had indulged himself in this sort of talk with Diotima he merely felt ashamed of himself. Still, she had an intimation of the possibility of loving this man; it would be something like her idea of modern music, that is, quite unsatisfying and yet full of something excitingly different.

And even though she took it for granted that she was more aware of all this than he was, the thought of it as she stood there facing him sent a hidden glow up her legs, which made her say rather abruptly to her cousin, with the face of a woman who feels the conversation has been running on too long: "My dear, we're really being quite impossible. Do stay here a bit longer while I go ahead and show myself to our guests again."

102

LOVE AND WAR AMONG THE FISCHELS

Gerda waited in vain for Ulrich's visit. He had, in fact, forgotten his promise to see her, or remembered it only when he had other things to do.

"Forget about him," Clementine said, whenever Director Fischel grumbled about it. "We used to be good enough for him, but he's probably setting his social sights higher these days. If you go after him you'll only make matters worse; you're much too clumsy to carry it off."

Gerda missed this older friend. She wished he would come and knew that if he did come, she would wish him away. For all her twenty-three years, nothing had yet happened in her life other than the cautious wooing of a certain Herr Glanz, who had her father on his side, and her Christian-Germanic friends, whom she sometimes regarded as schoolboys rather than real men. "Why doesn't he ever come to see me?" she wondered, whenever she thought of Ulrich. Among her friends, the Parallel Campaign was seen as beyond any doubt the opening salvo in the spiritual destruction of the German people, and she felt embarrassed by Ulrich's involvement in it; she longed to hear his side of it, however, hoping that he would be able to exonerate himself.

Her mother said to her father: "You missed your chance to be in this affair. It would have been a good thing for Gerda, and she'd have had something else to think about; a lot of people go to the Tuzzis'." It had come to light that he had neglected to respond to His Grace's invitation. Now he had to suffer for it.

The young men whom Gerda called her spiritual comrades in arms had settled down in his house like Penelope's suitors, debating what a young man of German blood should do about the Parallel Campaign.

"A financier must be able, at times, to act in the spirit of a Maecenas," Frau Clementine exhorted her husband when he fumed that he had not hired Hans Sepp, Gerda's "spiritual guide," as a tutor, for good money, only to have *this* situation come of it.

Hans Sepp, the graduate student, who had not the slightest prospect of being able to keep a wife, had come into the household as a tutor but, owing to the conflicts that were tearing the family apart, had become its tyrant. Now he was discussing with his friends, who had become Gerda's friends, at the Fischels', how to save the German aristocracy from being ensnared by Diotima—of whom it was said that she made no distinction between persons of her own race and those of an alien race—and caught up in the nets of the Jewish spirit. While in the presence of Leo Fischel this sort of talk was usually tempered with a certain philosophic objectivity, he still heard enough of certain terms and principles for it to get on his nerves. They worried that such a campaign, which was bound to lead to total catastrophe, should have surfaced in an era not destined to bring forth great symbols, and the recurrent expressions "deeply meaningful," "upward humanization," and "free personhood" were enough by themselves to make the pince-nez quiver on Fischel's nose every time he heard them. He had to stand by while there proliferated in his own house such concepts as "the art of living thought," "the graph of spiritual growth," and "action on the wing." He discovered that a biweekly "hour of purification" was held regularly under his roof. He demanded an explanation. It turned out that what they meant by this was reading the poems of Stefan George together. Leo Fischel searched his old encyclopedia in vain for the poet's name. But what irritated him most of all, old-style liberal that he was, was that these green pups referred to all the high government officials, bank presidents, and leading university figures in the Parallel Campaign as "puffed-up little men"; then there were the world-weary airs they gave themselves, complaining that the times had become devoid of great ideas, if there was anyone left who was ready for great ideas; that even "humanity" had become a mere buzzword, as far as they were concerned, and that only "the nation" or, as they called it, "folk and folkways" still really had any meaning.

"The word 'humanity' is meaningless to me, Papa," Gerda said, when he tried to reason with her. "The life seems to have gone out of it. But 'my nation'—now, that's a physical reality."

"*Your* nation!" Leo Fischel began, meaning to say something

about the biblical prophets and his own father, who had been a lawyer in Trieste.

"I know," Gerda interrupted, "but my nation in a spiritual sense is
what I am talking about."

"I'm going to lock you up in your room till you come to your
senses!" Papa Leo said. "And I won't have those friends of yours in
my house. They're undisciplined characters who spend all their time
brooding over their consciences instead of going to work and making
something of themselves."

"I know, Papa, how your mind works," Gerda replied. "Your generation feels entitled to humiliate us just because you're supporting
us. You're all patriarchal capitalists."

Such debates were no rarity, given a father's tendency to worry.

"And what would you live on, if I were not a capitalist?" the master
of the house wanted to know.

Gerda usually cut short any such ramifications. "I can't be expected to know everything; all I know is that we already have scientists, teachers, religious leaders, political leaders, and other men of
action engaged in creating new values."

At this point Bank Director Fischel might bother to ask ironically:
"And by these religious and political leaders I suppose you mean
yourselves?" but he did it only to have the last word; in the end, he
was always relieved that Gerda didn't notice how resigned he was,
how he had learned to expect that her nonsense would always lead to
his giving in. He was finally driven to conclude such arguments more
than once by cautiously praising the reasonableness of the Parallel
Campaign, in contrast to the rabid countermoves advocated in his
own house; but he did it only when Clementine was out of earshot.

What gave Gerda's resistance to her father's admonitions an air of
stubborn martyrdom, something that even Leo and Clementine
vaguely sensed, was that breath of innocent lust wafting through this
house. The young people discussed among themselves many things
about which the elders kept a resentful silence. Even what they
called their nationalism, this fusion of their constantly warring egos
into an imaginary unity they called their Christian-Germanic commune, had, compared with the festering love life of their elders,
something of the winged Eros about it. Wiser than their years, they
disdained "lust" and "the inflated lie about the crude enjoyment of

animal existence," as they called it, but talked so much about su-
prasensuality and mystical desire that the startled listener reacted
willy-nilly by feeling a certain tenderness for sensuality and physical
desires, and even Leo Fischel had to admit that the unbridled ardor
of their language sometimes made the listener feel the roots of their
ideas shooting down his legs, though he disapproved, because in his
opinion great ideas were meant to be uplifting.

Clementine, for her part, said: "You shouldn't simply turn your
back on everything, Leo."

"How can they say 'Property kills the spirit'?" he started to argue.
"Do I lack spirit? Maybe you do, insofar as you take their nonsense
seriously."

"You don't understand, Leo. They mean it in a Christian sense;
they want to leave the old life behind, to have a higher life on earth."

"That's not Christian, that's just crackbrained," Leo said stubbornly.

"What if it is not the realists who see reality, but those who look
inward?" Clementine suggested.

"That's a laugh!" Fischel claimed. But he was wrong; he was crying
inwardly, overwhelmed by the uncontrollable changes all around
him.

These days Director Fischel felt the need for fresh air more often
than he used to; at the end of the day's work he was in no hurry to get
home, and if there was still some daylight he loved to wander a bit in
one of the parks, even in winter. His liking for these city parks dated
back to his days as a junior assistant. For no reason he could see, the
city administration had ordered the iron folding stools freshly
painted in late autumn; now they stood there, bright green, piled up
against each other along the snowy paths, pricking the imagination
with their springtime color. At times, Leo Fischel would sit down on
one of these chairs, all alone and muffled up to the ears at the edge of
a playground or a promenade, and watch the nursemaids with their
charges, flaunting their winter health in the sun. The children played
with their yo-yos or threw snowballs, and the little girls made big
eyes like grown women—ah, Fischel thought, the very same eyes
that in the face of a beautiful woman delight you with the thought
that she has the eyes of a child! It did him good to watch the little
girls at play—in their eyes love still floated as in a pond in fairyland,

where the stork comes to get it later on—and sometimes to watch their governesses too. He had often enjoyed this spectacle in his youth, when he was still standing *outside* life's shop window, without the money to walk in, and all he could do was wonder what fate might have in store for him. What a sorry mess it had turned out to be, he thought, and for an instant he felt as if he were sitting on the green grass amid white crocuses with all the tension of youth. When his sense of reality recalled him to the sight of snow and green paint, his thoughts oddly enough kept coming back to his income. Money means independence, but all his salary went for the needs of the family and the savings required by common sense, so a man really had to do something more, apart from his job, to make himself independent; possibly turn to account his knowledge of the stock exchange, like the top executives at the bank.

But such thoughts came to Leo only while he was watching the little girls at play, and then he rejected them, because he certainly did not feel that he had the necessary temperament for speculation. He was a head of department, with the honorary title of a director and no prospect of rising above this, so he instantly chastened himself with the thought that so toilworn a back as his own was already too hunched over ever to straighten up again. He did not know that he was using such thoughts solely to erect an insurmountable barrier between himself and the pretty children and their maids, who, at such moments in the park, meant the charms of life to him, for he was, even in the disgruntled mood that kept him from going home, an incorrigible family man who would have given anything if only he could have transformed that Circle of Hell at home into a garland of angels around the father-god, the titular bank director.

Ulrich also liked the parks and walked across them whenever he could on his way somewhere, which was now he happened again to run into Fischel, who at the sight of him immediately recollected all he had already had to suffer at home on account of the Parallel Campaign. He expressed his dissatisfaction at his young friend's taking so lightly the invitations of old friends, a point he could make with all the more sincerity since time passing makes even the most casual friendships grow as old as the closest ones.

Fischel's young old friend said that he was truly delighted to see

Fischel again and deplored the foolishness that was keeping him too busy to have done so before.

Fischel complained that everything was going to the dogs and that business was bad. Anyway, the old moral order was losing its grip, what with all the materialism and the hastiness in which everything had to be done.

"And here I was just thinking that I could envy you!" Ulrich countered. "A businessman's work is surely a veritable refuge of sanity? At least it's the only profession resting on a theoretically sound basis."

"That it is!" Fischel agreed. "The businessman serves the cause of human progress, asking only for a reasonable profit. And yet he is just as badly off as everyone else, when it comes to that," he added gloomily.

Ulrich had agreed to walk him home.

On their arrival, they found a mood already strained to the breaking point.

All Gerda's friends were present, and a tremendous battle of words was in full swing. Most of the young people were still at school or in their first or second term at the university, though a few had jobs in business. How they had come to form this group was something they themselves no longer knew. One by one. Some had met in nationalist student fraternities, others in the socialist or Catholic youth movement, and others out hiking with a horde of *Wandervögel*.

It would not be wholly out of order to suppose that the only thing they all had in common was Leo Fischel. To endure, a spiritual movement needs a physical basis, and this physical basis was Fischel's apartment, together with the refreshments provided by Frau Clementine, along with a certain regulation of the traffic. Gerda went with the apartment, Hans Sepp went with Gerda, and Hans Sepp, the student with the impure complexion and all-the-purer soul, though not their leader, because these young people acknowledged no leader, was the most impassioned of them all. They might meet elsewhere occasionally, where the hostess would be someone other than Gerda, but the nucleus of their movement was basically as described.

Still, the source of these young people's inspiration was as remarkable an enigma as the appearance of a previously unknown disease, or a sequence of winning numbers in a game of chance. When the sun of old-style European idealism began to fade and its white blaze darkened, many torches were passed from hand to hand—ideas, torches of the mind, stolen from Heaven knows where, or invented by whom?—and flaring up here and there, they became that dancing pool of fire a little spiritual community. And so there was much talk, those last few years before the great war carried all of it to its foregone conclusion, among the younger generation, about love and fellowship—and the young anti-Semites who met at Bank Director Fischel's felt themselves to be most particularly under the sign of an all-embracing love and fellowship. True fellowship is the work of an inner law, and the deepest, simplest, most perfect, and foremost of these is the law of love. Love, as already noted, not in its base, sensual form, for physical possession is an invention of Mammon that in the end only disrupts the community and strips it of its meaning. And one can't, of course, love just everybody and anybody. But one can respect the character of every individual, as long as that person truthfully strives to keep growing, with an unremitting inner responsibility. And so they fiercely argued about everything, in the name of love.

But on this particular day a united front had formed against Frau Clementine, who was so pleased at feeling young again, and inwardly agreed that married love really did have something in common with interest paid on capital, but drew the line at tolerating harsh criticism of the Parallel Campaign on the grounds that Aryans could create viable symbols only if they kept alien elements out of it. Clementine was just on the verge of losing her temper, and Gerda's cheeks were aflame with round red spots because her mother would take no hint to leave the room. When Leo Fischel had entered with Ulrich, she was pleading in sign language with Hans Sepp to break it off, and Hans said in a conciliating tone: "These days, no one can create anything great!" supposing that he had thereby reduced everything to the customary impersonal formula acceptable to all those present.

Unluckily, Ulrich joined in at this point and asked Hans—poking a little malicious fun at Fischel—whether he did not believe in any kind of progress at all.

"Progress?" Hans Sepp retorted with a patronizing air. "You need only think of the kind of men we had a hundred years ago, before progress set in: Beethoven! Goethe! Napoleon! Hebbel!"

"Hmm," Ulrich said. "The last-named was only just born a hundred years ago."

"Our young friends dismiss numerical precision," Director Fischel gloated.

Ulrich did not pursue this. He knew that Hans Sepp held him in jealous contempt, yet he felt a certain sympathy for Gerda's peculiar friends. So he sat down among them and went on: "We're undeniably making so much progress in the several branches of human capability that we actually feel we can't keep up with it! Isn't it possible that this can also make us feel that there is no progress? After all, progress is surely the product of all our joint efforts, so we can practically predict that any real progress is likely to be precisely what nobody wanted."

Hans Sepp's dark shock of hair turned into a tremulous horn pointed at Ulrich. "There, now you've said it yourself: what nobody wanted! A lot of cackling back and forth, a hundred ways, but no way to go! Ideas, of course, but no soul! And no character! The sentence leaps off the page, the word leaps from the sentence, the whole is no longer a whole, as Nietzsche has already said. Never mind that Nietzsche's egomania is another minus value for existence! Can you tell me one single, solid, ultimate value from which you, for instance, take your bearings in life?"

"Just like that—on demand!" Fischel protested, but Ulrich asked Hans: "Is it really utterly impossible for you to live without some ultimate value?"

"Utterly," said Hans, "but I admit that I am bound to be unhappy as a result."

"The hell you say!" Ulrich laughed. "Everything we can do depends on our not being overly perfectionist, not waiting for the ultimate inspiration. That's what the Middle Ages did, and ignorant they stayed."

"Did they, now?" Hans Sepp retorted. "I'd say that we're the ignorant ones."

"But you must admit that our ignorance is manifestly of a very rich and varied sort?"

A drawling voice was heard muttering at the back: "Variety . . .

knowledge . . . relative progress! All concepts from the mechanistic outlook of an era corrupted by capitalism. There's hardly more to be said. . . ."

Leo Fischel was also muttering to himself; something to the effect that in his opinion Ulrich was being far too indulgent with these juvenile misfits. He took cover behind the newspaper he unfolded.

But Ulrich was enjoying himself. "Is the modern house, with its six rooms, maid's bath, vacuum cleaner, and all that, progress, compared with the old houses with their high ceilings, thick walls, and handsome archways, or not?"

"No!" Hans Sepp shouted.

"Is the airplane progress, compared with the mail coach?"

"Yes!" Director Fischel shouted.

"The machine compared with handicrafts?"

"Handicrafts!" from Hans, and "Machine!" from Leo.

"It seems to me," Ulrich said, "that every step forward is also a step backward. Progress always exists in only one particular sense. And since there's no sense in our life as a whole, neither is there such a thing as progress as a whole."

Leo Fischel lowered his paper. "Would you say that it's better to be able to cross the Atlantic in six days rather than having to spend six weeks on it?"

"I'd be inclined to say that it's definitely progress to have the choice. But our young Christians wouldn't agree to that, either."

The circle of friends sat still, taut as a drawn bow. Ulrich had paralyzed their tongues but not their fighting spirit. He went on evenly: "But you can also say the opposite: If our life makes progress in the particular instance, it also makes sense in the particular instance. But once it has made sense to offer up human sacrifice to the gods, say, or burn witches, or wear powdered wigs, then that remains one of life's valid possibilities, even when more hygienic habits and more humane customs represent progress. The trouble is that progress always wants to do away with the old meaning."

"Do you mean to say," Fischel asked, "that we should go back to human sacrifice after we have succeeded in putting such abominable acts of darkness behind us?"

"Is it darkness, necessarily?" Hans Sepp replied in Ulrich's place. "When you devour an innocent rabbit, that's darkness, but when a cannibal dines reverently and with religious rites on a stranger, we simply cannot know what goes on inside him."

"There certainly must have been something to be said for the ages we have left behind," Ulrich agreed, "otherwise so many nice people would never have gone along with them. I wonder if we could turn that to account for ourselves, without sacrificing too much? And perhaps we are still sacrificing so many human beings today only because we never clearly faced the problem of the right way to overcome mankind's earlier answers. The way in which everything hangs together is extremely obscure and hard to express."

"But to your way of thinking, the ideal aim must always be some sort of bottom line or balanced books, right?" Hans Sepp burst out, against Ulrich this time. "You believe in bourgeois progress every bit as much as Director Fischel, you just manage to express it in the most twisted and perverted words you can find, so that you can't be pinned down." Hans had been the spokesman for his friends. Ulrich turned to look at Gerda's face. He intended to pick up casually where he had left off, ignoring the fact that Fischel and the young men were as ready to pounce on him as on each other.

"But aren't you striving toward some goal yourself, Hans?" he asked doggedly.

"*Something* is striving. Inside me. Through me," Hans rapped out.

"And is it going to get there?" Leo Fischel indulged himself in sarcasm, thereby, as all but himself realized, going over to Ulrich's side.

"I wouldn't know," Hans answered gloomily.

"You should take your exams—that would be progress." Fischel could not refrain from piling it on, so irritated was he, no less by his friend than by these callow youths.

At this moment the room seemed to explode. Frau Clementine cast an imploring look at her husband; Gerda tried to forestall Hans as he struggled for words, which finally came bursting out as yet another attack on Ulrich.

"You may be sure," he shouted, "that basically even you don't have a single idea that Director Fischel couldn't come up with just as well!"

With this parting shot he rushed out of the room, followed by his cohorts, making their bows in angry haste. Director Fischel, bludgeoned by the looks he was getting from his wife, pretended to remember his duties as a host and trudged grumpily into the foyer to speed his guests on their way. Clementine heaved a sigh of relief, now that the air was cleared, then she rose too, and Ulrich suddenly found himself alone with Gerda.

103

THE TEMPTATION

Gerda was visibly upset when they were left alone together. He took her hand; her arm started trembling, and she broke away from him.

"You have no idea what it means to Hans to have a goal," she said. "You make fun of all that; that's cheap enough. It seems to me your mind is more disgusting than ever!" She had been groping for the harshest possible word and was startled by what she had come up with. Ulrich tried to catch hold of her hand again; she pulled her arm close to her side. "That's no longer good enough for us!" She hurled her words with a fierce disdain, but her body swayed toward him.

"I know," Ulrich said sarcastically. "Everything you people do must meet the highest standards. That's exactly what makes me behave the way you've just described so amiably. You probably wouldn't believe how much it meant to me to talk to you quite differently back in the old days."

"You were never any different!" Gerda answered quickly.

"I've always been undecided," Ulrich said simply, searching her face. "Would you be interested in hearing about what's going on at my cousin's?"

Something now flickered in Gerda's eyes that was clearly distinct from her uneasiness at Ulrich's proximity: she was burning to find out all she could on that subject, for Hans's sake, and was trying to hide her eagerness. Ulrich perceived this with a certain satisfaction, and like an animal scenting danger, he instinctively changed course and began to talk of something else.

"Do you still remember my story about the moon?" he asked. "First I'd like to tell you something else like that."

"More of your lies, I'm sure!" she snapped.

"Not if I can possibly help it. . . . You must remember, from the lectures you've attended, how people go about deciding whether something is a law or not? Either you start out with reasons for believing that it is a law, as in physics or chemistry, and even though your observations never quite add up to the precise results you're looking for, they come fairly close in some definite pattern, and you work it out from there. Or else, as happens so often in life, you have no such reasons and find yourself facing a phenomenon about which you can't quite tell whether it is a law or pure chance; that's where things acquire a human interest. Then you translate a series of observations into a series of figures, which you divide into categories to see which numbers lie between this value and that, and the next, and so on; you arrange them in series where the frequency with which something happens shows or doesn't show a systematic increase or decrease, and you get either a stable series or a distributive function. You then calculate the degree of aberration, the mean deviation, the degree of deviation from some arbitrary value, the central value, the normal value, the average value, the dispersion, and so forth, and with the help of all these concepts you study your given phenomenon."

Ulrich laid all this out in so casual a tone that it would have been hard to tell whether he was only just working it out in his own mind or hypnotizing Gerda with a display of science for the fun of it. Gerda had moved away from him, leaning forward in an armchair with a furrow of concentration between her eyebrows as she looked down at the floor. To be spoken to in this matter-of-fact tone, an appeal to her intellect, put a damper on her rebelliousness, which she now felt fading away, together with the self-assurance it had given her. Her schooling had taken her through a few semesters at the university, skimming a vast body of new knowledge that could no longer be contained in the old framework of classic and humanistic studies. Such an education leaves many young people feeling powerless in facing a new time, a new world where the soil can no longer be worked with the old tools. She had no idea where Ulrich's line of reasoning was taking her. She believed him because she was in love with him, and doubted him because she was ten years younger than he and belonged to a new generation keenly aware of its fresh energies; the two conflicting strands of feeling mingled hazily within her as she listened.

"Besides which, you see, we have data that are indistinguishable from those that demonstrate a natural law, yet they have no such basis. Statistical series can sometimes have the same regularity that we associate with natural law. I'm sure you can think of examples you've heard in some sociology lecture, like the statistics about divorce in America, let's say. Or the ratio between male and female births, one of the most stable factors of the kind. Or the number of conscripts annually who try to evade their military service by some form of self-mutilation, also a relative constant, or the suicide statistics; even theft, rape, and bankruptcy occur, as far as I know, at more or less the same annual rate. . . ."

At this point Gerda's resistance tried to break through. "Are you trying to explain progress to me?" she cried out, doing her best to sound sarcastic.

"But of course," Ulrich came back at her, without breaking stride. "It's called the law of large numbers, a bit nebulously. Meaning that one person may commit suicide for this reason and another for that reason, but when a great number is involved, then the accidental and the personal elements cancel each other out, and what's left . . . but that's just it: what *is* left? I ask you. Because you see, what's left is what each one of us as laymen calls, simply, the average, which is a "something," but nobody really knows exactly *what.* Let me add that efforts have been made to find a logical and formal explanation for this law of large numbers, as an accepted fact, as it were. But there are also those who say that such regularity of phenomena which are not casually related to each other cannot be explained at all by conventional logic, and the point has been made, among others, that such phenomena must be analyzed not as individual instances but as involving some unknown laws of aggregates or collectives. I don't want to bother you with the details, which I no longer have at my fingertips anyway, but I would certainly love to know, for myself, whether there are such laws of the collective phenomenon, or whether it is simply by some irony of nature that the particular instance arises from the happening of nothing in particular, and that the ultimate meaning turns out to be something arrived at by taking the average of what is basically meaningless. It would certainly make a radical difference to our sense of ourselves if we knew the answer, one way or another! Whichever it turns out to be, any possibility of leading an ordered life depends on this law of large numbers. If there were no such law of averages, we might have a year with nothing at all happening, followed by one in which you could count on nothing for certain, famine alternating with oversupply, no births followed by too many, and we would all be fluttering to and fro between our heavenly and our hellish possibilities like little birds when someone suddenly comes up to their cage."

"Is all this true?" Gerda asked hesitantly.

"You ought to know it yourself."

"Of course I do, as far as the details go! But what I don't know is whether this is what you meant before, when they were all arguing. What you were saying about progress simply sounded like a deliberate provocation."

"That's what you always think about me. But what do we really know about the nature of our progress? Not a thing. There are all sorts of possibilities for the way things might turn out, and I simply mentioned just one more."

"How things *might* turn out! That's always the way with you; it would never occur to you to wonder how things *should* be."

"You and your friends—always jumping the gun. There's always got to be a supreme goal, an ideal, a program—an absolute. Yet in the end, all that ever comes of it is a compromise, some common denominator. Isn't it tiring and ridiculous to be always reaching for the heights and always ending up settling for some mediocre result?"

It was essentially the same conversation he had had with Diotima, with only superficial differences. Nor did it make much difference which woman happened to be sitting there facing him; a body, introduced into a given magnetic field, invariably sets certain processes in motion. Ulrich studied Gerda, who was not answering his last question. There she sat, a skinny girl, with a little furrow of resentment between her eyes. Another hollow, vertical furrow could be seen in the V of her low-cut blouse. Her arms and legs were long and delicate. She suggested a limp springtime, aglow with a premature summer heat, together with the full impact of the willfulness locked in so young a body. He felt a strange mixture of aversion and detachment at the thought that he was closer to a decision than he had realized and that this young girl was destined to play a part in it. Willy-nilly he suddenly found himself telling her his impressions of the so-called younger generation in the Parallel Campaign, ending with words that took Gerda by surprise:

"These younger people are also very radical, and I'm not popular with them either. But I pay them back in the same coin, because I, too, am radical in my own way, and I can put up with any kind of disorder more easily than the intellectual kind. I like to see ideas not only developed but brought together. I want not only the oscillation but also the density of an idea. This is what you, my indispensable friend, criticize as my tendency to describe only what might be, instead of what ought to be. Well, I do know the difference. This is probably the most anachronistic attitude one can have nowadays, when intellectual rigor and the emotional life are at the farthest remove from each other, but our precision in technology has unfortunately advanced to such a point that it seems to regard the imprecision of life as its proper complement. Why won't you understand? The chances are you're incapable of understanding me, and it's perverse of me to try to confuse a mind so well attuned to the times. Still, Gerda, I sometimes honestly wonder whether I might be wrong, after all. Possibly the very people I can't stand are carrying out what I once hoped to accomplish myself. They may be doing it all wrong, not using their heads, one running this way and the other that way, each spouting an idea that he regards as the only possible idea in the world; each one of them feels tremendously clever, and they all agree in regarding our times as cursed with sterility. But suppose it's the other way around, and every one of them is stupid, but all of them together are pregnant with the future? Every one of our truths seems to be born split into two opposing falsehoods, and this, too, can be a way of arriving at a result that transcends the merely personal. In that case the final balance, the sum total of all the experiments, no longer rests with the individual, who becomes unbearably one-sided, but with the experimental collective. In short, I ask you to make allowances for an old man whose loneliness sometimes drives him to excess."

"You've certainly given me a lot to think about," Gerda said grimly. "Why don't you write a book? That way, you might be able to help yourself and us, too."

"Why on earth should I feel called upon to write a book?" Ulrich objected. "I was born of my mother, after all, not an inkwell."

Gerda was wondering whether a book by Ulrich would really help anyone. Like all the young people in her circle, she overrated the power of the printed word. A total silence had fallen in the apartment since they had stopped talking, as if the elder Fischels had left the house in the wake of their indignant guests. And Gerda sensed the force emanating from the more powerful male body beside her, as she always did, contrary to all her resolutions, when they were alone together; the effort to resist made her tremble. Ulrich noticed it; he stood up, laid his hand on Gerda's frail shoulder, and said to her: "Look at it this way, Gerda. Suppose the moral sphere works more or less like the physical, as suggested by the kinetic theory of gases: everything whirling around at random, each element doing what it will, but as soon as you work out rationally what is least likely to result from all this, that's precisely the result you get! Such correspondences, strange as they are, do exist. So suppose we also assume that there is a certain number of ideas circulating in our day, resulting in some average value that keeps shifting, very slowly and automatically—it's what we call progress, or the historical situation. What matters most about this, however, is that our personal, individual share in all this makes no difference; whether we individually move to the right or to the left, whether we think and act on a high or a low level, in an unpredictable or a calculated fashion, a new or an old style, does not affect this average term, which is all that God and the world care about."

As he spoke he tried to put his arm around her, though it was palpably costing him an effort.

Gerda was furious. "You always begin by philosophizing," she cried out, "and it always turns into the usual rooster's cock-a-doodle-doo!" Her face was aflame, with flecks of color in it. Her lips seemed to be sweating, but there was something attractive about her indignation. "What you make of it is precisely what *we* don't want!"

Now Ulrich could not resist the temptation to ask her, in a low voice: "Is possession so deadly?"

"I don't want to talk about that," Gerda retorted in an equally low tone.

"It's all the same, whether it's a person you own or a thing, I know that," Ulrich went on. "Gerda, I understand you and Hans better than you think. So what is it that you and Hans want? Tell me."

"Nothing! That's just it," Gerda exclaimed triumphantly. "There's no way to state it. Papa also keeps on saying: 'You must make clear to yourself what it is you actually want. Then you will see what nonsense it is.' Well, everything is nonsense when you make it clear to yourself. To be sensible is never to get beyond the commonplace. I know you'll have something to say about that, you and your sensible way of thinking."

Ulrich shook his head. "And what about this demonstration against Count Leinsdorf?" he asked gently, as though he were not changing the subject.

"Oh, so you spy on us!" Gerda exclaimed.

"Call it spying if you like, I don't mind; but tell me about it, Gerda."

Gerda showed some embarrassment. "Nothing special. Just some sort of demonstration by the Young Germans—marching past his residence, yelling 'Shame!' and things like that. The Parallel Campaign is a shame!"

"In what way?"

Gerda shrugged.

"Do sit down again," Ulrich pleaded. "You're making far too much of it. Let's have a quiet talk about it, shall we?"

Gerda obeyed.

"Now listen to me, and tell me if you think I'm on the right track. You say that possession kills. You're thinking of money, to begin with, and of your parents. I agree that they're dead souls. . . ."

Gerda looked offended.

"Very well, let's not talk about money but of 'having' in other ways. Take the man who 'has' himself in hand; the man who 'has' his convictions; the man who lets himself be 'had' by another person or by his own passions or merely his own habits or successes; the man who wants to conquer something, the man who wants anything at all: you reject all that? You want to be nomads, nomads forever on the move, as Hans once called it, if I remember. Moving on toward some other meaning, or state of being? Am I right so far?"

"All you're saying is quite right, in an awful sort of way; the intelligence doing a good imitation of the soul."

"And intelligence is implicated in all that 'having', isn't it? The intelligence is what measures, weighs, classifies, and collects everything, like an old banker. But what about all the things I talked with you about today that have quite a lot to do with our souls?"

"A cold kind of soul."

"You're absolutely right, Gerda. Now all I have to do is to tell you why I'm taking the part of the cold souls or even the bankers."

"Because you're a coward." Ulrich noticed that as she spoke she bared her teeth like a terrified little animal.

"So be it," he replied. "But surely you believe me capable, if nothing else, of being man enough to escape by, if necessary, climbing a lightning rod or down the tiniest foothold on a wall, if I were not so sure that every attempt at breaking out only leads back to Papa."

Gerda had refused to enter into this conversation with Ulrich ever since their last talk on a similar subject. The feelings he was talking about were hers and Hans's alone, and she dreaded, even more than Ulrich's sarcasm, his coming over to her side, which merely left her at his mercy before she could tell whether he meant what he said or was just acting the Devil quoting scripture. From the moment, earlier on, when she had been taken by surprise at the sadness in his words—she was now enduring the consequences of having so briefly let down her guard—she had been visibly engaged in a violent inner struggle. But Ulrich was in a similar fix himself. He was far from taking a perverse pleasure in his power over the girl; he simply did not take Gerda seriously, and since this involved a certain element of dislike, he generally expressed himself freely to her, without regard for her feelings. But for some time now, the more zestfully he took the world's part against her, the more he felt curiously inclined to confide in her, to let her see him as he really was, without deceit or making himself look good, and wanting to see her true inner self as naked as a garden slug. He now looked at her thoughtfully and said: "I feel like letting my eyes rest between your cheeks like clouds in the sky. I don't really know how clouds feel in the sky, but then, I know as much as anybody about those moments when God seizes us like a glove and slowly turns us inside out on his fingers. You and your friends make it too easy for yourselves. You sense the negative side of the world we all live in, and you loudly proclaim that the positive world belongs to your parents and elders, and the world of the shadowy negative to you, the new generation. I don't exactly relish playing the spy for your parents, my dear Gerda, but I put it to you that in choosing between the banker and an angel, the more realistic character of the banker's profession counts for something too."

"Would you like some tea?" Gerda said sharply. "What can I do to make you comfortable here? I want you to see me at my best as the perfect daughter of the house." She had pulled herself together again.

"Then suppose you marry Hans?"

"But I don't want to marry him!"

"You must have some plan or other—you can't go on living forever on your opposition to your parents."

"One of these days I shall leave home, make myself independent, and he and I will remain friends."

"Please, Gerda, let's suppose that you and Hans will be married or something like it; it can hardly be avoided if things keep going the way they are. And now try to imagine yourself brushing your teeth in the morning, and Hans making out the income tax return, in an otherworldly state of mind."

"Do I have to know that?"

"Your Papa would say so, if he had any notion of otherworldly states of mind; most people on life's voyage, I'm sorry to say, know very well how to stow their uncommon experiences so deep in the hold of their ship that they never perceive them at all. But let me ask a simpler question: Will you be expecting Hans to be faithful to you? Marital fidelity is part and parcel of the ownership complex, you know. You would have to accept Hans's finding inspiration in another woman. Indeed, according to your principles, you would have to see it as an enrichment of your own life."

"Don't suppose for a minute that we never discuss these questions ourselves," Gerda replied. "You can't become a new human being overnight; but it is very bourgeois to consider this an argument against making the effort."

"What your father wants is actually something quite different from what you think. He doesn't even claim to know more about all that than you and Hans; he merely says that he can't understand what you're up to. But he does know that power is a very sensible thing. He believes there's more sense in it than in you and him and Hans all rolled into one. What if he were to offer Hans enough money to let him finish his course and get his degree, without having to worry? And if he promised him, after a fair trial period, not that the marriage would take place, but at least that he would not stand in its way on principle? On only one condition: namely, that until the end of the trial period you two stop seeing each other, or keeping in touch, even to the extent you do now?"

"So this is what you're lending yourself to, is it?"

"I merely want to help you understand your father. He is a sinister deity who wields uncanny powers. He thinks he can make Hans see things his way by using money. In his opinion, a Hans with a limited monthly income couldn't possibly go on exceeding every limit of foolishness. But your father may be a dreamer, in his own way. I admire him, just as I admire compromises, averages, dry facts, dead numbers. I don't believe in the Devil, but if I did I should think of him as the trainer who drives Heaven to break its own records. Anyway, I promised him to keep at you until there was nothing left of your fantasies—only reality."

Ulrich was far from saying all this with a clear conscience. Gerda stood facing him as if in flames, the anger in her eyes overlaid with tears. All at once, a way had been opened up for her and Hans. But had Ulrich betrayed her, or did he want to help them? She had no idea, but whichever it was, it was likely to make her as unhappy as it made her happy. In her confusion she mistrusted him, and yet she felt with a passion that there was a sacred bond between them, if only he would admit it.

He now added: "Your father of course harbors a secret hope that I may use the opportunity to win you for myself and change your mind altogether."

"That's out of the question!" Gerda forced herself to say.

"As far as you and I are concerned, I suppose that is out of the question," Ulrich said gently. "But we can't go on like this, either. I've already gone too far." He tried to smile, but felt extreme self-loathing as he did so. He really wanted none of this. He sensed the irresolution in her and despised himself for the cruelty it aroused in him.

At that very instant Gerda stared at him with horrified eyes. Suddenly she was beautiful, like a fire one has approached too closely; almost without form, only a warmth that paralyzes the will.

"You must come to see me," he suggested. "We can't speak freely here." Male ruthlessness shone out of his eyes in a blaze of empty light.

"No," Gerda said defensively. But she averted her eyes, and Ulrich sadly saw—as though by turning away she had again presented herself to his scrutiny—the body of this young girl, neither beautiful nor ugly, breathing hard. He gave a deep and wholly sincere sigh.

104

RACHEL AND SOLIMAN ON THE WARPATH

In the Tuzzi household, charged as it was with a high mission as a gathering place of ideas, there was a light-footed, quick, ardent, un-German creature in service. The little lady's maid, Rachel, was like a chambermaid in Mozart. She opened the front door and stood ready with arms half outstretched to receive the visitor's overcoat. At such times Ulrich sometimes wondered whether she had any idea of his connection with the Tuzzis and tried to catch her eye, but Rachel either turned her eyes away or let them meet his blankly, like two blind little patches of black velvet. He seemed to remember her eyes meeting his with quite a different expression at their first encounter, and several times noticed another pair of eyes, like two big white snails, aiming at Rachel from a dark corner of the entrance hall, Soliman's eyes, but whether this boy might be the reason for Rachel's reserve was an open question, because Rachel responded as little to that gaze as to Ulrich's, and quietly withdrew as soon as she had announced the visitor.

The truth was more romantic than curiosity could suppose. Ever since Soliman had succeeded, with his willful innuendos against Arnheim, in lending that radiant presence a shadowy aura of obscure machinations, tarnishing even Rachel's childlike admiration for Diotima, all her passionate need to outdo herself in correct and devoted service had concentrated on Ulrich. Convinced by Soliman that a strict watch had to be kept on everything that went on in the house, she had become a zealous eavesdropper at keyholes, and while waiting on the guests had overheard more than one private conversation between Section Chief Tuzzi and his wife; nor had Ulrich's position midway between Diotima and Arnheim, as a man they both distrusted and desired, escaped her notice, and this corresponded entirely to her own feeling, wavering between rebellion and remorse, for her unsuspecting mistress. Now she also realized that she had known for a long time that Ulrich wanted something from her. It never entered her mind that he might find her attractive. Driven from home as she had been, and longing to prove to her family back in Galicia how great a success she could make of herself despite all that, she naturally dreamed of striking it lucky, something like an unexpected inheritance, the discovery that she was of noble birth, a chance to save the life of a prince . . . but the simple possibility that a gentleman who came to her mistress's house as a visitor might take a liking to her and want her to be his lover or even his wife would never have occurred to her. And so she simply held herself ready to do Ulrich some great service. It was she and Soliman who had sent the General an invitation when they learned that he was a friend of Ulrich's, though there was no denying they also did it to get things moving; considering what they thought they knew, a general certainly seemed the right person to turn the trick. Rachel, in her obscure, elfin sympathy with Ulrich, inevitably developed an overwhelming identification with him, as she secretly watched every movement of his lips, his eyes, his fingers, as if these were actors to whom she was bound with the passion of someone who sees her own insignificant self brought by them onto a vast stage. The more she realized that this mutual involvement constricted her breathing like a tight dress when crouching at a keyhole, the more depraved she felt for not resisting with greater firmness Soliman's simultaneous dark pursuit of her; this was the reason, of which Ulrich had no inkling, why she met his curiosity about her with that subservient passion for acting the well-trained, model maidservant.

Ulrich wondered in vain why this creature who seemed to be made for tender love play was so chaste that she might be almost a case of that rebellious frigidity not uncommonly found among some fine-boned women. He changed his mind, however, and was even a bit disappointed when he came upon a surprising scene one day. Arnheim had just arrived and gone in to see Diotima; Soliman was squatting on his haunches in the foyer, and Rachel had slipped away again as usual. Ulrich took advantage of the momentary stir caused by Arnheim's arrival to return to the hall for the handkerchief in his overcoat pocket. The light was out again, and Soliman did not realize that Ulrich, in the shadow of the doorway, had not returned to the reception room. Soliman got to his feet stealthily and, with great care, produced a large flower from under his jacket, a lovely white calla lily, which he contemplated for a while, then he set off on tiptoe past the kitchen door. Ulrich quietly followed him until Soliman stopped at Rachel's door, pressed the flower to his lips, and fixed it to the handle by twisting the stem around twice and squeezing its end into the keyhole.

It had not been easy to extract this lily from the bouquet on the way over with Arnheim and hide it for Rachel, and Rachel fully appreciated such attentions. Getting caught and fired would have meant Death and Judgment Day as far as Rachel was concerned, so it was naturally a great nuisance to have to watch out for Soliman all the time, wherever she might be, nor did she like being suddenly pinched in the leg without daring to cry out whenever she passed some hiding place where he might be lying in wait for her. Still, the fact that somebody was taking terrible chances just to be attentive to her, to spy devotedly on her every step and put her character to the test under the most difficult circumstances, could hardly fail to make an impression. The little ape was rushing her quite needlessly and dangerously, and yet, against all her principles and at odds with her crumpled dreams of great things in store, she sometimes felt a guilty craving to make the most of this African king's son whose thick lips were waiting at every turn to serve her, the serving maid, as if made for her alone.

One day, Soliman asked her right out if she was game. Arnheim had gone to the mountains with Diotima and some friends for two days and had left Soliman behind. It was the cook's day off, and Section Chief Tuzzi was taking his meals at a restaurant. Rachel had told Soliman about the cigarette stubs she had found in her room, and Diotima's unspoken question what would the little maid make of it was answered by Rachel's and Soliman's agreeing that something seemed to be afoot in the Council, something that called for the two of them to take some action of their own. When Soliman asked her if she was game, he announced that he meant to take the documents proving his noble birth from where Arnheim had locked them up. Rachel did not believe in these documents, but life amid so many tempting mysteries had given her a craving for something to happen. They decided that she would keep on her maid's cap and frilled apron when Soliman fetched her and took her to Arnheim's hotel, as if she had been sent on an errand there by her employers. When they stepped out on the street, such a smoldering heat rose up from behind the lacy bib of her apron that it almost blurred her vision, but Soliman boldly stopped a cab; he had plenty of money these days, when Arnheim was so often absentminded. This stiffened Rachel's spine too, and she stepped into the carriage in the sight of all the world as if she were charged and employed to ride in style with little black boys. The midmorning streets, with the well-dressed idlers to whom they belonged, flew by, and again Rachel's heart was thumping as if she were a thief. She tried to lean back properly, as she had seen Diotima do, but could not keep her body from bouncing up and down in the rich upholstery as the closed carriage rocked along, while Soliman took advantage of her reclining position to press the broad stamp pads of his lips on hers, risking their being seen through the windows, and a sensation like the simmering of some scented fluid poured from the billowing cushions into Rachel's back.

Nor was the young Moor disposed to forgo the pomp of driving right up to the hotel entrance. The porters in their black silk sleeves and green aprons grinned when Rachel stepped out of the carriage, the doorman peered through the glass door as Soliman paid the fare, and Rachel felt as though the pavement were giving way under her feet. But when no one stopped them as they walked through the vast pillared lobby, she thought that Soliman must enjoy a certain status in the hotel. Again she flushed with embarrassment when she felt the eyes of some armchair loungers following her as she passed by, but going up the stairs, she saw many chambermaids dressed in black with their white caps, like herself, if not perhaps as smartly, and she began to feel quite like an explorer wandering over an unknown, possibly dangerous island, who encounters human beings at last.

Then Rachel found herself for the first time in her life inside the rooms of a distinguished hotel. Soliman immediately locked all the doors and then felt called upon to kiss his little friend again. The kisses these two had been giving each other of late had something of the glow of a child's kiss, intended more for mutual reassurance than as any assault upon the moral fiber, and even now, when they were for the first time alone together in a locked room, Soliman's most pressing concern was to find even more romantic ways of hiding themselves away. He pulled down the blinds and stopped up all the keyholes giving on the corridor. Rachel was much too excited by all these preparations to think of anything other than her own daring and the disgrace of a possible discovery.

Next, Soliman led her to Arnheim's closets and trunks, all open except for one. This was clearly the one harboring the secret. He took the keys from all the open trunks and tried them one by one, with no success, while chattering nonstop, pouring out all his reserves of camels, princes, mysterious couriers, and insinuations against Arnheim. He borrowed one of Rachel's hairpins and tried to pick the lock with it. When this failed him, he ripped all the keys from all the closet doors and drawers, spread them out between his knees as he squatted on the floor, and paused to brood over this collection, trying to think of a fresh expedient. "Now you can see how he hides things from me!" he said to Rachel, rubbing his forehead. "But I may as well show you everything else first."

And so he simply spread the bewildering riches from Arnheim's trunks and closets out before Rachel, who was crouching on the floor, with her hands clasped between her knees, staring at these things with curiosity. The intimate wardrobe of a man accustomed to the choicest of luxuries was something she had never seen before. Her own master was certainly not poorly dressed, but he had neither the money nor the need for the ultrasophisticated concoctions of the best tailors and shirtmakers, the creators of luxuries for home and travel. Even her mistress had nothing to compare with the exquisite things, feminine in their delicacy and complicated in their uses, that belonged to this immensely rich man. Something of Rachel's original awe for the nabob came to life again, even as Soliman puffed himself up with pride in the stunning impression he was making on her as he dragged out everything, showing off all the gadgets and eagerly explaining all the mysteries. Rachel was beginning to tire of the endless display, when she was suddenly struck by an odd coincidence. She realized that things of this kind had been cropping up lately among Diotima's lingerie and household things. They were not as numerous or as expensive as Arnheim's, but compared to Diotima's former monastic simplicity, they were certainly closer to what she was seeing here than to her austere past. Rachel was overcome by the outrageous notion that the link between her mistress and Arnheim might be less spiritual than she had supposed.

She blushed to the roots of her hair.

Never since she had entered Diotima's service had her thoughts wandered into this area. Her eyes had gulped down the glory of her mistress's body without giving any thought to the possible uses of such beauties, like gulping down a powder with its paper envelope. Her satisfaction at being permitted to share the life of persons of such exalted station had been so great that in all this time Rachel, who was so easily seduced, had never thought of any man as a sexual being, but only as someone different in a romantic way, like in a novel. Her high-mindedness had made her a child again, transporting her, as it were, back to the stage before puberty, that time of selfless enthusiasms for the greatness of others. This was in fact how Rachel had come to swallow Soliman's tall stories so willingly, in such a trance of gullibility, that it made the cook laugh at her. But now, as Rachel crouched on the floor and saw the suggestive tokens of an adulterous union between Arnheim and Diotima spread out before her in broad daylight, a long-impending change took place inside her—the awakening from an unnatural state of exaltation into the mistrustful state of the actual world of the flesh.

Gone in a flash was her romanticism; she was a down-to-earth little body with a somewhat irritated notion that even a servant girl had some rights in life. Soliman was squatting beside her before his outspread bazaar, having collected up all the things she had especially admired, and was trying to stuff into her pockets whatever was not too big, as presents from him. Now he leapt up and made another quick attack with a pocketknife on the locked trunk, while rattling on about having to get a lot of money from the bank before Arnheim returned, using his master's checkbook—in money matters the mad little devil had quite lost his innocence—so that he and Rachel could run away together, but not before he had his papers.

Rachel abruptly stood up, firmly emptied her pockets of all the "presents" he had stuffed into them, and said, "Don't talk such non-sense! I have to go now. What time is it?" Her voice sounded deeper. She smoothed her apron and adjusted her cap. Soliman instantly realized that she was through with playing the game, and that she was suddenly much older than he. But before he could reassert himself, Rachel was kissing him good-bye. This time her lips did not tremble but pressed hard into the luscious fruit of his face as she bent over him, forcing the boy's head back and keeping at it so long that he almost choked. Soliman struggled, and when she finally let go he felt as if a taller, stronger boy had been holding him under water, so that his first impulse was to get even with her for an unfair trick played on him. But Rachel had slipped out the door, and the look he sent after her—for that was all of him that caught up with her—as inflamed as the red-hot tip of a burning arrow, gradually faded to a soft ash. Soliman then picked up his master's belongings from the floor to put them back in order; he had now turned into a young man who could look forward to something that had ceased to be unattainable.

105

LOVE ON THE HIGHEST LEVEL IS NO JOKE

Following their excursion to the mountains, Arnheim had gone abroad for longer than usual. "Gone abroad"—as he had come to think of it himself—was certainly an odd expression to use, considering that it should have been "gone home." It was because of this and other such reasons that it was in fact becoming urgently necessary for him to come to a decision. He was haunted by unpleasant daydreams such as had never before entered his disciplined head. One especially persistent one was of seeing himself standing with Diotima on a tall church steeple, where they gazed briefly at the green landscape stretched far below and then jumped off. A vision of forcing his way unchivalrously into the Tuzzis' bedroom at night to shoot the Section Chief obviously came to the same thing. He could perhaps have chosen to finish him off in a duel, but this seemed less natural; the fantasy was already loaded down with too many realistic rituals, and the closer Arnheim approached reality, the more troublesome the increase of inhibitions. Asking Tuzzi simply and openly for the hand of his wife in marriage was conceivable, but what would Tuzzi be likely to say to that? It simply meant opening oneself up to all sorts of ridicule. And even if Tuzzi were to be civilized about it and there was a minimum of scandal, or possibly no scandal at all, divorce having come to be tolerated even in the best circles, there was still the fact that an old bachelor always made himself a bit ridiculous by a late marriage, much like a couple having a baby for their silver wedding anniversary. And if Arnheim really had to do such a thing, he owed it to the firm to marry a prominent American widow at the very least, or a great lady of ancient lineage with connections at court, and not the divorced wife of a middle-class government official. He could not make a move, even if it were merely of a sensual nature, that was not permeated with responsibility. In a time like the present, when responsibility for one's acts or thoughts plays so slight a role, it was by no means mere personal ambition that raised such objections, but a truly suprapersonal need to bring the power fostered by the Arnheims (a formation rooted in simple greed, which it had long since outgrown, however; it now had a mind of its own, a will of its own, it had to keep growing, to solidify its position, lest it sicken, lest it become rusted when it rested!) into accord with the forces and hierarchies of life itself, nor had he ever knowingly made a secret of this to Diotima. An Arnheim was of course free to marry even some peasant if he chose, but free only as regarded his own person; he would still be betraying a cause for a personal weakness.

It was nevertheless true that he had proposed marriage to Diotima. He had done it, if only to forestall the kind of adulterous goings-on that do not consort well with the disciplined conduct of life on a high level. Diotima had gratefully pressed his hand and, with a smile reminiscent of the finest such smiles in the history of art, she had responded to his proposal with the words: "It is never those we embrace that we love most deeply. . . ." After this answer, as equivocal as the seductive yellow deep inside the chaste lily, Arnheim could never bring himself to go once more into the breach. Instead, they went in for general conversations in which the words "divorce," "marriage," "adultery," and the like showed a strange tendency to crop up. More than once, for instance, Arnheim and Diotima talked in depth about the treatment of adultery in contemporary literature, and Diotima felt that this problem was invariably handled without any appreciation for the great values of self-discipline, renunciation, or heroic self-denial, but purely from a sensual point of view. Arnheim's view was precisely the same, unfortunately, so that he could only add that there was hardly anyone left these days capable of fully appreciating the deep moral mystery of the individual. This mystery consisted in having to keep a tight rein on the tendency to self-indulgence. Historic periods of permissiveness have never failed, so far, in making all those who lived in them miserable. All discipline, abstinence, chivalry, music, morality, poetry, form, taboo, had no deeper purpose than to give the correct limits, a definite shape, to life. There is no such thing as boundless happiness. There is no great happiness without great taboos. Even in business, to pursue one's advantage at all costs is to risk getting nowhere. Keeping within one's limits is the secret of all phenomena, of power, happiness, faith, and the key to the task of maintaining oneself as a tiny human creature within the universe. Such was Arnheim's statement of the case, and Diotima could not but agree. It was in a sense a regrettable consquence of such insights that they lent to legitimacy a richness of meaning that is no longer available to most people. But great souls cannot do without legitimacy. At peak moments of perception, one senses how the cosmos turns on an axis of vertical austerity. And the businessman, even as he rules the world, respects kingship, aristocracy, and the church as pillars of the irrational. The legitimate is simple, as all greatness is simple, open to anyone's understanding. Homer was simple, Christ was simple. The truly great minds always come down to simple basics; one must have the courage to admit, in fact, that they always come back to moral commonplaces, which is why it is hardest of all for the truly free spirit to defy tradition.

Such insights, true as they are, are not much help to a man bent on intruding into someone else's marriage. So these two people found themselves in the position of being linked by a splendid bridge with a hole at its center, just a few yards wide, so that they cannot come together. Arnheim was deeply sorry that he had no spark of that desire which is the same, whatever its object, and as likely to catapult a man into a rash business deal as into a rash love affair; his regret moved him to talk at length about desire. According to him, desire was precisely the feeling that best corresponds to the merely intellectual culture of our era. No other feeling aims so unequivocally at its specific object. It strikes and sticks like an arrow, rather than swarming on into ever greater distances like a flock of birds. It impoverishes the soul, just like arithmetic and mechanics and brutality. In this fashion Arnheim spoke with disapproval of desire, even as he felt it struggling like a blinded slave in the cellar.

Diotima took a different tack. She held out her hand to him and beseeched him: "Let us say no more! Words can do much, but there are things beyond words. The real truth between two people cannot be put into words. The moment we speak, certain doors begin to close; language works best for what doesn't really matter; we talk in lieu of living. . . ."

Arnheim concurred. "You're so right. The word, in its arrogance, gives an arbitrary and impoverished form to the invisible movements of our inner being."

"Say no more, please," Diotima repeated, laying a hand on his arm. "I feel that we give each other a moment of life when we are silent together." After a while, she withdrew her hand again and sighed: "There are instants when all the hidden jewels of the soul lie revealed."

"There may come a time," Arnheim complemented this,"—and there are many signs that it is near already—when souls will behold each other without the mediation of the senses. Souls come together when one pair of lips withdraws from the other."

Diotima pursed her lips so that they suggested a crooked little tube such as butterflies dip into blossoms. She was totally besotted.

Like all heightened states of emotion, love brings out a certain madness about the supposed connectedness of things so that any words uttered tended to light up with richly ramifying significance, which manifested itself like a veiled deity before it dissolved in silence. Diotima knew this phenomenon from her lonely hours of lofty meditation, but never before with this intensity to the very edge of barely endurable joy; she was brimming over with uncontrollable feeling, with something godlike inside her that moved as if on skates, and more than once she felt that she was about to crash down in a dead faint.

Arnheim buoyed her up with his great pronouncements. He gave her time to recover, to catch her breath. Then he again spread the safety net of ideal considerations beneath them.

The torment of this expansive joy was that it militated against concentration. It kept emitting tremulous new waves that rippled outward in widening circles but never pressed together to form a current of action. Diotima had after all reached the point of regarding the risks of an affair as the more considerate and civilized alternative to the crude catastrophe of smashed lives, while Arnheim had long since opted morally against accepting such a sacrifice and was ready to marry her. They could have each other, one way or another, at any moment, and they both knew it, but they did not know which form it should take, for their happiness swept their souls, made for it as they were, to such solemn heights that the fear of spoiling everything by some awkward move paralyzed them: a natural state of anxiety for people with a cloud under their feet.

Their minds had never failed to drink in all the grandeur and beauty life had poured out for them, and yet, at its very apex, their joy was strangely curtailed. All the wishes and vanities that had normally filled their lives now lay far beneath them, like toy houses and farmyards deep in the valley, with all the clucking, barking, and other excitements swallowed up in the stillness, leaving only the sense of silent deep space.

"Can it be that we have a mission?" Diotima wondered, surveying the emotional pinnacle on which she found herself with a foreboding of some agonizing and unimaginable turn up ahead. Not only had she experienced lesser degrees of such exaltation herself, but even an emotional lightweight like her cousin had been known to speak of such things, and much had been written about them of late. But if there was any truth to the reports, there were times, every thousand years or so, when the soul was closer to an awakening than usual, born into the real world, as it were, via certain individuals upon whom it imposes tests far beyond mere reading and talking. In this connection, even the inexplicable appearance on the scene of the uninvited General suddenly popped into her mind. And so she murmured to her friend, who was groping for new words as their agitation formed a trembling arc between them: "Two people can understand each other without always finding some rational formula for it."

And Arnheim responded, as his eye met hers straight as a ray from the sinking sun, "You're right. As you said before, the real truth between two people cannot be put into words; every effort of that kind only creates a further obstacle between them."

106

Does modern man believe in God or in the Head of the Worldwide Corporation? Arnheim wavering

Arnheim alone. Deep in thought, he stands at the window of his hotel suite, gazing down on the leafless treetops, their bare branches forming a grille, beneath which the passersby, bright and dark, brushing against each other, form the two serpentine lines of the informal street parade that starts at this hour. A smile of annoyance parts the great man's lips.

Up to now he had never had any difficulty in defining what he considered soulless. What was not soulless these days? It was easy enough to spot the rare exceptions, too. A far-off evening of chamber music came to mind, played by friends visiting his castle in Prussia, young musicians who were rather hard up, and yet whose spirited harmonies rang out on the evening air, amid the fragrance of the northern linden trees; that was soulful. Or to take another case: He had recently refused to go on paying an allowance to a certain artist. He had fully expected that the artist would be angry at him and feel he had been left in the lurch before he had been given a chance to make his reputation; he would have to be told that there were other artists in need of support and all that sort of thing, something Arnheim did not look forward to doing. Instead, this man, the next time he met Arnheim, had merely looked hard into his eyes and then shaken his hand, saying: "You've left me in a tough spot, but I'm sure a man like you never does anything without a good reason." Now, there was a manly soul, and Arnheim was not disinclined to do something for him again, some other time.

So there still was such a thing as soul in many instances, even these days. It had always been a point of importance to Arnheim. But when one has to deal with it directly and unconditionally, a man's sincerity is put to a hard test. Was a time really coming when souls would be able to commune together without the mediation of the senses? Was there any purpose, of the same value and importance as the realistic aims of life, to be accomplished in communing together as he and this marvelous woman had been inwardly driven to do lately? While in his sober senses he never believed it for an instant, yet he was sure that he was encouraging Diotima to believe it.

Arnheim was in a peculiar state of conflict. Moral wealth is closely related to the financial kind; he was well aware of it, and it is easy to understand. For morality replaces the soul with logic; once a soul is thoroughly moral, it no longer has any moral problems, only logical ones; it asks itself whether something it wants to do is governed by this commandment or that, whether its intention is to be understood one way or another, and so on, all of which is like a wildly scrambling mob that has been whipped into shape by a gymnastics coach so that it responds to signals such as Right turn, Arms out, Bend knees, and so on. But logic presupposes repeatable experiences. In a vortex of events that never repeat themselves, we could obviously never formulate the profound insight that A equals A, or that the greater is not the lesser, but would be living in a kind of dream, a condition abhorred by every thinker. And the same is true of morality: if our acts were unrepeatable, then there would be nothing to be expected of us, and a morality that could not tell people what was expected of them would be no fun at all. This quality of repetitiveness that inheres in the workings of the mind and morality inheres also, and to the highest degree, in money. Money positively consists of this quality. As long as it keeps its value, it carves up all the world's pleasures into those little building blocks of purchasing power that can then be combined into whatever one pleases. Money is accordingly both moral and rational; and since we all know that the converse is not the case, i.e., not every moral and reasonable person has money, we may conclude that money is the original source of these qualities, or at least that money is the crowning reward of a moral and rational life.

Not that Arnheim of course thought precisely along the lines that education and religion were the natural consequence of wealth, but he did assume that wealth obliged its owner to have them, while liking to point out that the spiritual powers did not always understand enough of the effective powers in life and were rarely quite free of certain traces of unworldliness. As a man with a large overview, he came to all sorts of conclusions beyond this too. Every act of weighing something, taking account of it or measuring it, presupposes that the object in question will not change in the process; where such a change occurs nonetheless, the mind must be exerted to its utmost to find something unchangeable even within the change, and so money is akin to all the powers of the mind, serving as a model to the world's scientists for dividing up the world into atoms, laws, hypotheses, and curious mathematical symbols, and the technicians use all these fictions to build up a world of new things. All of this was as familiar to this owner of a gigantic industrial complex, who so thoroughly understood the nature of the forces at his disposal, as the moral assumptions of the Bible are to the average reader of novels.

This inward need for the unequivocal, the repeatable, and the solid, upon which the success of all thinking and planning depends—so Arnheim reflected as he stood gazing down on the street from his window—is always appeased by some form of violence. Anyone who wants to build on rock in dealing with human beings has to rely on the baser qualities and passions, for only what is most closely bound up with egotism endures and can always be counted on; the higher aims are unreliable, contradictory, and fleeting as the wind. The man who knew that empires would sooner or later have to be run just like factories gazed upon the swarms of uniforms and proud faces no bigger than nits down there, with a smile that was a blend of superiority and sadness. There could be no doubt that if God returned this very day to set up the Millennium on earth, not a single practical, experienced man would take any stock in it unless the Last Judgment came fully equipped with a punitive apparatus of prison fortresses, police, armies, sedition laws, government departments, and whatever else was needed in order to rein in the incalculable potential of the human soul by relying on the two basic facts that the future tenant of heaven can be made to do what is needed only by intimidation and tightening the screws or else by bribery—in a word, by "strong measures."

But then Paul Arnheim would step forward and speak to the Lord: "Lord, why bother? Egotism is the most reliable factor in human life. It enables the politician, the soldier, the king, to keep order in the world by cunning and force. Mankind dances to its tune, as You and I must admit. To do away with force is to weaken the world order. Our task is to make man capable of greatness, although he is a mongrel cur!" So saying, Arnheim would smile modestly at the Lord, with composure, in token of the importance for every man of recognizing the great mysteries, in all humility. And then he would continue his address as follows: "But money is surely just as safe a means of managing human relationships as physical force, the crude uses of which it allows us to discontinue. Money is power in the abstract, a pliant, highly developed, and creative form, a unique form, of power. Isn't business really based on cunning and force, on outwitting and exploiting others, except that in business, cunning and force have become wholly civilized, internalized in fact, so that they are actually clothed in the guise of man's liberty? Capitalism, as the organization of egotism based on a hierarchy in which one's rank depends on one's capacity for getting money, is simply the greatest and yet the most humane order we have been able to devise, to Your everlasting glory. There is no more precise measure than this for all human action."

And so Arnheim would have advised the Lord to organize the Millennium on business principles and entrust its administration to a leading businessman; a man, it went without saying, who would also have the mental capacities of a philosopher. After all, religion unaided had always got the worst of it in this world, and compared with the insecurity of its existence in times of armed power struggles, there was much to be gained for it under a business administration.

So Arnheim would have spoken, for a deep inner voice told him distinctly that money was as indispensable as reason and morality. But another, equally deep inner voice told him just as sharply that a man must dare to jettison reason, morality, and the whole of his rationalized existence without a backward glance. At those dizzy moments when he felt no greater urge than to plunge, like some errant meteor, into the blazing solar mass that was Diotima, this voice was almost the more powerful. At such times the wild proliferation of his thoughts seemed to him as alien and extraneous as the self-impelled growth of nails and hair. The moral life then looked dead, and a secret aversion to morality and order made him blush. Arnheim was suffering the fate of his whole era. This era worships money, order, knowledge, calculation, measures and weights—the spirit of money and everything related to it, in short—but also deplores all that. Even as it goes on hammering and calculating during working hours, and at all other times carries on like a horde of children driven from one excess to another by the challenge What's next? with its bitter, sickening aftertaste, it cannot shake off an inward warning to repent. It deals with this conflict by a division of labor, assigning to certain intellectuals, the confessers and confessors of their period, dealers in absolutions and indulgences, literary Savonarolas and evangelists, whose presence is the most reassuring to those not personally in a position to live up to their precepts, the task of recording all such premonitions and inward lamentations. Of course, all the lip service and government funds dropped annually by the State into their bottomless cultural schemes are much the same kind of moral ransom money.

This functional split manifested itself inside Arnheim himself as well. Sitting at one of this executive desks checking sales figures, he would have been ashamed to think otherwise than as a businessman and technician; but once it was no longer the firm's money that was involved, he would have been ashamed not to think otherwise, not to insist that mankind must be made capable of self-improvement by some other means than pursuit of the chimera of going by the book, regulations, orders, norms, and all that, with results so devoid of in-

ward meaning and so ephemeral. This Other Way was unquestionably what is called religion, and he had written books about it, in
which he had also called it myth, the return to simplicity, the realm
of the soul, the spiritualization of the economy, the nature of action,
and so on, because it had many aspects, as many, to be specific, as he
found in himself when he was selflessly analyzing himself, as a man
must do when facing the prospect of great tasks. But it seemed to be
fated that this functional split should fail him in the hour of decision.
At the very moment when he longed to entrust himself to the flame
of his passion, or had the urge to be as great and singlehearted as the
heroic figures of old, as untrammeled as only the true aristocrat can
be, as wholly religious as the quintessential nature of love demands;
at the very moment, in short, when he yearned to fling himself at
Diotima's feet without regard to the crease of his trousers or his future, an inner voice held him back. It was the untimely voice of reason or, as he irritably told himself, the instinct for calculating and
hoarding that nowadays stands everywhere in the way of life on the
grand scale, the dream of ecstasy. He hated this voice even as he was
forced to acknowledge its validity. For, assuming that there was a
honeymoon, what form would life with Diotima take after that honeymoon? He would return to his business affairs, and they would
cope with the other tasks of a lifetime together. The year would alter-
nate between financial operations and recuperation in the arms of
nature, in the animal and vegetative part of one's own being. It might
even turn into a great, truly humanistic marriage of action and
repose, of human need and beauty. That would be fine; it was doubtless what he vaguely had in mind as a goal. Arnheim believed that no
one could muster the strength for great financial operations who was
incapable of letting go entirely, of abandoning himself altogether,
beyond all desire, far from the madding crowd, with only a loincloth
to cover his nakedness, as it were. Still, Arnheim was filled with some
savage wordless state of satisfaction, because all this was the opposite
of what he felt first and last for Diotima. Every time he laid eyes on
this Classical beauty with those modern rounded curves, he was
thrown into confusion, felt his strength melting away, unequal to his
need to absorb into his own inner being this poised, self-sufficient
creature so serenely moving in her own orbit. There was nothing loft-
ily humane about this feeling, nothing even merely humane. It was a

taste of the whole cosmic void of eternity. He stared at the beauty of his beloved with a gaze that seemed to have been seeking her for a thousand years and now, having found her, was suddenly unemployed, helpless in a kind of stupor, an almost idiotic amazement. So excessive a demand on emotion left it nearly incapable of responding; it corresponded to nothing so much as a longing for both of them to be shot together from a cannon into intergalactic space!

The tactful Diotima found the right words again even for this condition. In one such moment she recalled that even in his day the great Dostoyevsky had noted a connection between love, idiocy, and inner holiness. But people of our own time, lacking the supportive presence of a devout Russia at their shoulders, probably needed a special dispensation to live by such an idea.

Her words might have come straight from Arnheim's heart.

The moment when they were spoken was one of those times engaged with both self-awareness and object awareness, like a stopped-up trumpet that refuses to emit a sound no matter how hard one blows into it, bringing all the blood to one's head; everything in it was charged with significance, from the tiniest cup on a shelf asserting its presence in the room like one of van Gogh's objects, to the human bodies, swollen and supercharged by the unutterable, which seemed to press into space.

Startled by her own words, Diotima said: "I wish we could just talk in fun. Humor is so wonderful; it floats free beyond desire, completely unconcerned with appearances."

Arnheim smiled at this. He had risen from his chair and started to pace the room. What if I tore her to pieces, he wondered, if I started to roar and dance, if I reached down my throat to tear out my heart for her; could I make a miracle happen? But as he cooled down, he came to a stop.

It was this scene that had just come vividly to mind. His glance again rested icily on the street below. It really would take some sort of redemptive miracle, he thought, the world would have to be populated by a new breed of men, before one could begin to think of putting such thoughts into practice. He dropped the effort of determining how and from what the world was to be redeemed; in any case, everything would have had to be different from the way it was. He went back to his desk, which he had abandoned half an hour since, back to his letters and telegrams, and rang for Soliman to fetch his secretary.

As he awaited the secretary's arrival, already engaged in formulating the first sentences of a statement for dictation on economic conditions, the remembered experience crystallized into a beautiful, richly significant moral form. After all, Arnheim said to himself firmly, a man who is aware of his responsibilities, even when giving his soul away, sacrifices only the interest, never the capital.

107

COUNT LEINSDORF ACHIEVES AN UNEXPECTED POLITICAL SUCCESS

When His Grace spoke of a European family of nations that was to throng joyfully around the venerable Emperor Patriarch, he always tacitly excluded Prussia. Perhaps he was now doing it with more feeling than ever, for Count Leinsdorf was undeniably bothered by his awareness of Dr. Arnheim; every time he arrived at his friend Diotima's he would find either the man himself or traces of his recent presence, and he knew no more than Section Chief Tuzzi what to make of it. As for Diotima, every time she turned her soulful gaze on him, she noticed as never before the swollen veins on His Grace's hands and neck and the faded-tobacco colored skin from which emanated the characteristic smell of an aging man. Even though she never failed to treat the great nobleman with all due reverence, something had gone out of her radiance toward him, something like the change from a summer sun to a winter sun. Count Leinsdorf was not given to fantasies or to music, but ever since Dr. Arnheim had become so persistent a presence it was strange how often he had a faint ringing in his ears, like the kettledrums and cymbals of an Austrian military march, or a visual sensation, whenever he closed his eyes, of a great billowing of black-and-yellow flags, vast numbers of

them, in motion. Similar patriotic hallucinations seemed to be afflict-
ing other friends of the Tuzzis' as well. At least, though Germany was
always spoken of with the utmost respect whenever he happened to
be within earshot, if he ever dropped a hint that the great patriotic
project might eventually take on a certain pointedness against the
brother empire, this respect was irradiated with a heartfelt smile.

His Grace had apparently stumbled upon an important phenomenon within his special field of interest. There are certain family feelings of a special intensity, and one of these was the widespread
dislike of Germany among the European family of states before
1914. Perhaps Germany was spiritually the least unified country, so
that everyone could find something there to suit his own distaste; its
early culture had been the first to fall under the wheels of the new
era, to be shredded into high-flown slogans for the promotion of the
bogus and the commercial; it was also grasping, aggressive, full of
bluster, and dangerously irresponsible, like every great mass in ferment—but all this was ultimately merely European, and might at
most have seemed all-too-European to the Europeans. The world
apparently needs its negative entities, images of the unwanted,
which attract to themselves all the disgust and disharmony, all the
slag of a smoldering fire, such as life tends to leave behind. Out of all
that "could be" there suddenly crystallizes, to the stunned amazement of everyone concerned, the "it is," and whatever drops away
during this disorderly process, whatever is unsuitable, superfluous,
unsatisfying, seems to coagulate into the vibrant universal hatred agi-
tating all living creatures that is apparently so characteristic of our
present civilization, which compensates for all our lack of satisfaction
with ourselves by allowing us to feel that easy dissatisfaction so readily inspired by everyone else. Trying to isolate specific scapegoats for
this displeasure is merely part of the oldest psychotechnical bag of
tricks known to man. Just as the medicine man drew the carefully
prepared fetish from his patient's body, the good Christian projects
his own faults onto the good Jew, whom he accuses of seducing him
into committing advertisements, high interest rates, newspapers, and
all that sort of thing. In the course of time people have blamed their
troubles on bad weather, witches, socialists, intellectuals, generals,
and in the years before the Great War, Austrians saw a most welcome scapegoat of this sort in Prussian Germany. Unfortunately, the

world has lost not only God but the Devil as well. As it projects its unwanted evil onto the scapegoat, so it projects its desired good onto ad hoc ideal figures, which it reveres for doing what it finds inconvenient to do for itself. We let others perform the hard tricks as we watch from our seats: that is sport. We let others talk themselves into the most one-sided exaggerations: that's idealism. We shake off evil and make those who are spattered by it our scapegoats. It is one way of creating an order in the world, but this technique of hagiolatry and fattening the scapegoats by projection is not without danger, because it fills the world with all the tensions of unresolved inner conflicts. People alternately kill each other or swear eternal brotherhood without quite knowing just how real any of it is, because they have projected part of themselves onto the outer world, and everything seems to be happening partly out there in reality and partly behind the scenes, so that we have an illusory fencing match between love and hate. The ancient belief in demons, which made heavenly-hellish spirits responsible for all the good and bad that came one's way, worked much better, more accurately, more tidily, and we can only hope that, as we advance in psychotechnology, we shall make our way back to it.

Kakania was a country exceptionally well qualified for this game with living symbols of what was Wanted or Unwanted; life in Kakania had a certain unreality anyway, so that the most cultivated persons, who regarded themselves as the heirs and standard-bearers of the celebrated Kakanian culture from Beethoven to Lehár, felt it was quite natural to think of the Germans of the Reich as allies and brothers even while cordially detesting them. Seeing them get their occasional comeuppance did not upset anyone here, while their successes always left one a bit concerned about affairs at home. Affairs at home mostly meant that Kakania, a country that had originally been as good as any and sometimes better than most, had in the course of the centuries somewhat lost interest in itself. Several times in the course of the Parallel Campaign it could be perceived that world history is made up much as all other stories are—i.e., the authors seldom come up with anything really new and are rather given to copying each other's plots and ideas. But there is also something else involved which has not yet been mentioned, and that is the delight in storytelling itself; it takes the shape of that conviction so common to authors that they are working on a good story, that passion of authorship that lengthens an author's ears and makes them glow, so that all criticism simply melts away. Count Leinsdorf had this conviction and this passion, and so did some of his friends, but it had been lost in the farther reaches of Kakania, where the search for a substitute had been under way for the longest time now. There the history of Kakania had been replaced by that of the nation; the authors were at work on it even now, formulating it in that European taste that finds historical novels and costume dramas edifying. This resulted in a situation not yet perhaps sufficiently appreciated, which was that persons who had to deal with some commonplace problem such as building a school or appointing a stationmaster found themselves discussing this in connection with the year 1600 or 400, arguing about which candidate was preferable in the light of what settlements arose in the Lower Alps during the great Gothic or Slavic migrations, and about battles fought during the Counter-Reformation, and injecting into all this talk the notions of high-mindedness and rascality, homeland, truth, and manliness, and so on, which more or less corresponded to the sort of stuff the majority were currently reading. Count Leinsdorf, who attached no importance to literature, never ceased to wonder at this circumstance, especially considering how well off, basically, he found all the peasants, artisans, and townsfolk he encountered on his trips through the countryside to visit his Bohemian estates settled by generations of Germans and Czechs. He blamed it on some special virus, the detestable work of agitators, that there would be these sudden outbursts of violent dissatisfaction with each other and with the wisdom of the government, which were all the more puzzling in that these people got on so peacefully and contentedly with everyone in the long intervals between such fits, when nothing happened to remind them of their ideals.

The government's policy, that well-known Kakanian policy for dealing with national minorities, was one of alternating, every six months or so, between taking a punitive line against some mutinous minority and then again wisely giving ground to it; just as the fluid in a U-tube rises on one side when it sinks on the other, so government policy fluctuated vis-à-vis the German minority. This minority played a special part in Kakania, since it tended on the whole to want just one thing: that the State should be powerful. It had clung longer than any other minority to the belief that the history of Kakania must have some meaning, and it was only after it gradually caught on to the fact that in Kakania a man could begin as a traitor and end as a cabinet minister, and could then continue his ministerial career by going in for high treason, that it, too, began to regard itself as an oppressed nationality. It may be that this sort of thing was going on elsewhere too, but in Kakania it needed no revolutions or other upheavals to produce this effect, because here it came about of its own accord, naturally, like the quiet swinging of a pendulum from side to side, simply by virtue of the general vagueness of the ideas involved, until in the end there was nothing left in Kakania except oppressed nationalities, the oppressors being represented by a supreme circle of personages who saw themselves as being constantly baited and plagued by the oppressed. In this high circle people were deeply troubled because nothing was happening, troubled by an absence of history, so to speak, and a strong feeling that something must be done at long last. And if this meant turning against Germany, as the Parallel Campaign seemed inclined to do, it was not an altogether unwelcome eventuality; first of all, because there was that feeling of always being put in the shade by the brothers in the Reich, and second, because persons in government circles were themselves Germans, so there was actually no better way for them to demonstrate Kakania's impartiality than by joining in such a selfless gesture.

It was therefore entirely understandable that in these circumstances nothing could be farther from His Grace's mind than any suspicion that his undertaking was Pan-Germanic. But that it was so regarded could be deduced from the gradual disappearance of the Slavic groups from among the "officially recognized minorities" whose claims should command the attention of the Parallel Campaign committees, and the foreign envoys came to hear such terrible reports about Arnheim, Tuzzi, and a German plot against the Slavic element that some of all this even reached His Grace's ears in the muted form of rumor, confirming his fears that even on those days when nothing special was happening one had to be hard at work to make sure that so many things that were not supposed to happen did not happen. But being a practical politician, he was now slow to make his countermove, though in so doing he unfortunately acted on such a magnanimous calculation that it looked at first like an error in statesmanship. As the Propaganda Committee, in charge of popularizing the Parallel Campaign, did not yet have a chairman, Count Leinsdorf decided to choose Baron Wisnieczky for the post, in special consideration of the fact that Wisnieczky had some years before been a member of a cabinet brought down by the German nationalist parties on suspicion that it was carrying out an insidious anti-German policy. His Grace was in this instance following a scheme of his own. From the very start of the Parallel Campaign it had been one of his ideas to win over precisely those of the German Kakanians who felt less allegiance to their own country than to the German nation. However much the other "ethnic" elements might refer to Kakania as a prison, and however publicly they avowed their love for France, Italy, or Russia, no serious politician could ever put such quasi-exotic predilections on a level with the predilection of certain German Kakanians for the German Reich, which held Kakania in a geographic stranglehold and had been one with it historically until a mere generation ago. It was to these German apostates, whose intrigues hurt Count Leinsdorf most because he was German himself, that he had been referring when he pronounced his well-known dictum: "They'll come along of their own accord!" This dictum had meanwhile attained the rank of a political prophecy in which much confidence was placed by members of the patriotic campaign, signifying more or less that once the other ethnic groups had been won over to patriotism, the German elements would feel constrained to join in, for as everyone knows, it is much harder to hold aloof from something everyone else is doing than to refuse to be first in line. Therefore the way to get the Germans in was to move against them by favoring the other nationalities. Count Leinsdorf had known this for quite a while, and now that the time had come to act, he carried it through and placed Baron Wisnieczky, who was a Pole by birth but a Kakanian by conviction, at the head of the Propaganda Committee.

It would be hard to say whether His Grace was aware that this choice was an affront to the German cause, as his critics later said; the chances are that he thought he was serving the true German interest in this fashion. But the immediate consequence of his move was that the Parallel Campaign was now being intensely attacked in German circles as well, so that it ended up being regarded on the one side as an anti-German plot and being openly resisted as such, while on the other side it had long been regarded as pro-German and had therefore been avoided, with diplomatic excuses, from the outset. The unexpected effect did not escape His Grace's attention, of course, and was a matter of intense concern everywhere. This further tribulation only stiffened Count Leinsdorf's resolve, however, and when Diotima and other leading figures anxiously questioned him about it, time after time, he turned an impenetrable but determined face toward such feeble-spirited creatures and said: "This move has not met with immediate success, I know, but you cannot let a great aim depend on whether or not you achieve instant success with any measure along the way; meanwhile we have achieved a more widespread interest in the Parallel Campaign, and the rest will fall into place if we simply hold firm."

108

THE UNREDEEMED NATIONALITIES AND GENERAL STUMM'S REFLECTIONS ABOUT THE TERMINOLOGY OF REDEMPTION

No matter how many words are spoken at every moment in a great city to express the personal concerns of its inhabitants, there is one word that is never among them: "redeem." All other words, from the most impassioned to the most discriminating, even those dealing with extreme situations, may be assumed to be heard more than once, whether shouted or whispered, expressions such as, for instance: "You're the worst crook that ever lived" or "No other woman could be as beautiful as you," so that these most personal sentiments could in fact be charted in sweeping statistical curves representing their mass distribution throughout the city. But no living man ever says to another: "You can redeem me" or "Be my redeemer." He can be tied to a tree and left to starve, or marooned on a desert island with the woman he had been courting in vain for months, or rescued from being jailed for forging checks, and every word in the dictionary may come pouring from his lips, but as long as he is experiencing real emotion he will never utter the words "redeem," "redeemer," or "redemption," even though these are perfectly acceptable terms as such.

And yet the peoples united under the Crown of Kakania called themselves Unredeemed Nations.

General Stumm von Bordwehr was thinking about it. In his position at the War Office, he had ample knowledge of Kakania's problems with nationalism, because the military were the first to feel the effects, at the budget hearings, of the seesawing policies resulting from the hundreds of conflicting considerations by which the State was hamstrung. Only a little while ago an urgent money bill had had to be withdrawn, to the War Minister's white fury, because an Unredeemed Nationality had demanded in return for its support such concessions as the government could not possibly make without dangerously arousing the yearning for redemption of other nationalities. So Kakania was left naked to its enemies, as the budgetary outlay had been proposed to replace the army's hopelessly obsolete guns—whose range could be compared with the guns of other powers as a knife compares with a spear—with new guns that would be as a spear to a knife compared with those of the other powers. This necessary purchase had now once again been prevented, for who knew how long. To say that this setback made General Stumm consider suicide would be going too far, but a deep depression is sometimes heralded by any number of random, trivial symptoms, and Stumm's brooding over the redeemed and the unredeemed was certainly connected with Kakania's defenseless, disarmed state—to which it was condemned by its intolerable domestic squabbles—the more so because in his semi-civilian status at Diotima's he had been hearing about redemption until he was sick and tired of it.

His first reaction was that the term was one of those verbal inflations not yet classified by linguistic science. So his common sense as a soldier told him, but apart from the fact that his sound instinct had already been disoriented by Diotima—it was after all from her lips that Stumm had heard the word "redemption" for the first time and had been charmed by it, and even today, in spite of the failed artillery bill, the word when uttered by Diotima was still enveloped in a kind of magic, so that the General's first reaction could really more properly be described as the second of his life! And there was another reason why the theory of verbal inflation didn't seem to hold water: it was only necessary to salt the individual units of the word group "redemption" with a small, innocent lack of gravity, and they instantly came trippingly from the tongue. "You've just saved my soul!" or some such; who has not said something of the sort at one time or another, provided of course that it refers to nothing more than the relief after a ten-minute wait or some equally slight inconvenience that has been brought to an end. Now the General realized that it was not so much the words that offended a healthy common sense as their absurd claim to being taken literally. When Stumm asked himself where he had ever come across such talk of redemption or salvation, other than at Diotima's or in politics, he realized that it had been in churches or cafés, in art journals, and in the books of Dr. Arnheim, which he had read with admiration. He now realized that such words refer not to a simple, natural human occurrence but to something abstract, some general complication or other; to redeem and to yearn for redemption is definitely a spiritual transaction.

The General nodded with amazement at the fascinating insights this special duty of his seemed to be bringing him. He switched on the red light over his office door as a signal that he was in conference, and while his officers who came bearing files in their arms turned back from his door with a sigh, he went on with his speculations. The intellectual types he kept running into nowadays wherever he went were chronically dissatisfied, finding fault because there was either too little or too much being done about this or that; to hear them tell it, nothing ever seemed to go as it should. He was becoming quite fed up with them. They were in a class with those miserable specimens susceptible to cold who always find themselves sitting in a draft. When they were not complaining about the preponderance of scientific attitudes, they were excoriating illiteracy, general boorishness or general overrefinement, fanaticism or indifference: whichever way they turned, they found something wrong. Their minds never came to rest, but were fixated on the ceaseless wanderings of that residual element in things that never finds its proper place anywhere. So they ended up convinced that their era was fated to be a spiritual wasteland that could be redeemed only by some special event or some very special personage. It was among the so-called intellectuals that the word "redemption" and its kin came into vogue at this time. They did not see how things could go on unless a messiah came quickly. Depending on circumstances, he would be a medical messiah who would redeem the art of healing from the specialized research teams that pursued their experiments while human beings sickened and died around them, or a messianic poet capable of writing a drama that would sweep millions of people into the theaters despite its ineffable sublimity; besides the belief that every kind of human endeavor needed a messiah to restore it to its pristine purpose, there was of course also the simple and unadulterated longing for a leader sent to put *everything* to rights with his strong right arm. The age before the Great War was a messianic age, and the fact that entire nations wanted to be redeemed in a lump was really nothing special or unusual for its time.

Not that the General regarded this as something to be taken any more literally than anything else people were saying. "If the Redeemer were to come again today," he said to himself, "they would bring down his Government just like any other." Judging by his own personal experience, he supposed that this came of too many people writing too many books and newspaper articles. "How wise of the army to forbid officers to write books without special permission," he thought, and was startled to feel a hot wave of loyalty for the first time in ages. He was obviously starting to think too much! It all came of keeping company with the civilian mind, which had evidently lost the advantage of having a firm perspective on the world. The General saw this clearly now, and it enabled him to understand all that palaver about redemption from yet another angle. The General's mind strayed back to distant memories of his classes in religion and history for support along this new line of thought, and if his welter of ideas could have been lifted bodily out of his head and ironed out, it would have looked more or less as follows: To begin briefly with the ecclesiastical aspect of things, as long as one believed in religion, one could defenestrate a good Christian or a pious Jew from any story in the castle of hope or prosperity, and he would always land on his spiritual feet, as it were, because all religions included in their view of life an irrational, incalculable element they called God's inscrutable will. Whenever a man could not make sense of things, he merely had to remember this rogue element in the equation, and his spirit could rub its hands with satisfaction, as it were. This falling on one's feet and rubbing one's hands is called having a working philosophy of life, and this is what modern man has lost. He must either give up thinking about his life altogether, which is what many people are quite content to do, or else he finds himself strangely torn between having to think and yet never quite seeming to arrive at a satisfactory resolution of his problems. This conflict has in the course of history taken on the form of a total skepticism as often as it has that of a renewed subjection to faith, and its most prevalent form today is probably the conviction that without a spiritual dimension there can be no human life worthy of the name, but with too much of it there can be none either. It is on this conviction that our civilization as a whole is based. It takes great care to provide for education and research, but never too well, only enough money to keep education and research properly subordinated to the great sums expended on entertainment, cars, and guns. It clears the way for talent but sees to it that it should be a talent for business. Every idea is given due recognition, after some resistance, but this always works out so as to benefit equally the opposite idea. It looks like some tremendous weakness and carelessness, but it is probably also a quite deliberate effort to put the spiritual dimension in its place, for if any one of the ideas that motivate our lives were ever carried out seriously, so seriously that nothing would be left of its opposite, then our civilization would hardly be our civilization.

The General had a pudgy little baby fist; he clenched it and whacked the top of his desk with it as if it were a padded glove; a man had to have a strong fist. As an officer, he knew what to think! The irrational element was known as honor, obedience, the Supreme Commander in Chief, Part III of the Service Regulations, and to sum it all up, the conviction that war is nothing but the continuation of peace by stronger measures, a forceful kind of order, without which the world cannot survive. The gesture with which the General had thumped his desk would have been slightly ludicrous if a fist were not as much a spiritual manifestation as an athletic one, a kind of indispensable extension of the mind. Stumm von Bordwehr was a bit fed up with the whole civilian nexus. He had discovered that library attendants were the only people left who had a sound general over-

view of the civilian mind. He had hit upon the paradox of excessive
order, the perfection of which inevitably brought inaction in its train.
He had a funny feeling, something like an insight into why it was the
army where the greatest order was to be found at the same time as
the greatest readiness to lay down one's life. For some indefinable
reason, order seems to bring on bloodshed! This worried him, and he
decided that he must not go on working at such pressure. Anyway, he
wondered mutinously, what is this spiritual dimension? It doesn't
walk around in a bedsheet at midnight, so what can it be but a certain
order we impose on our impressions and experiences? But in that
case, he concluded firmly, on a happy inspiration, if the spirit is nothing more than the order of our experience, then in a properly ordered world we don't need it at all!

With a sigh of relief, Stumm von Bordwehr switched off the "in
conference" light outside his door, stepped up to the mirror, and
smoothed his hair down, in order to efface all signs of emotional
stress before his subordinates came in.

109

BONADEA, KAKANIA; SYSTEMS OF HAPPINESS
AND BALANCE

If there was anyone in Kakania who understood nothing of politics,
and was quite happy that way, it was Bonadea; and yet there was a
connection between her and the Unredeemed Nationalities. Bonadea—not to be confused with Diotima; Bonadea the Good Goddess,
Goddess of Chastity, whose temple by one of those twists of fate
ended up as the scene of orgies; Bonadea, wife of a presiding county
judge or some such legal eminence, and the frustrated mistress
of a man who was neither worthy of her nor sufficiently attached to
her—had a system, which was more than could be said of Kakanian
politics.

Bonadea's system had so far consisted in leading a double life. Her social status was assured in that she belonged to a family of distinction and enjoyed the reputation of a cultivated and notable woman in her own social circle; that she gave way to certain temptations she could ascribe to being constitutionally overexcitable, or having a heart given to folly, since the follies of the heart, like romantic political crimes, enjoy a certain esteem, even when committed under dubious circumstances. Here the heart plays about the same role as honor, obedience, and Service Regulations, Part III, played in the General's life, or as the irrational element in every well-ordered life that ultimately puts to rights whatever baffles the unaided rational mind.

But Bonadea's system had a flaw, in that it split her life into two different conditions, the transition from one to the other of which could not be achieved without paying a heavy price. For however eloquent her heart could be before one of her lapses, it was equally deflated afterward, and she was constantly alternating between a maniacally effervescent state of mind and one that drained away in inky blackness, hardly ever coming into equilibrium. All the same, it was a system, that is, it was no mere play of uncontrolled instincts—the way life used to be seen as the automatic squaring of accounts between pleasure and pain, with a certain profit registered on the side of pleasure, but a system that included quite a number of psychological moves designed to fake these accounts.

Everyone has some such method of jockeying one's psychological accounts in one's own favor, aiming at a minimum balance of pleasure that should ordinarily get one through the day. A person's pleasure in life can also consist of displeasure; such differences in kind don't matter much, since as everyone knows there are as many contented melancholics as there are funeral marches that float as lightly in their element as a dance tune does in its own. The opposite is probably equally valid, in that many normally cheerful persons are no whit happier than many habitually sad ones, because happiness is just as much of a strain as unhappiness, more or less like flying on the principle of lighter or heavier than air. But there is another objection to be made. Would the rich not consider themselves justified in their perennial insistence that the poor need not envy them, because the happiness to be got out of money is illusory? Money merely sets a man the problem of working out another system of life, the pleasure surplus of which can at best be no greater than any other. According to this principle, the family without a roof over its head, provided it survives an icy winter night, should theoretically be just as happy with the first rays of the morning sun as the rich man who has to get out of his warm bed. In practice it comes down to this, that everyone bears his burden with the patience of a donkey, since a donkey whose strength slightly exceeds the demands of his burden is happy enough. And this is, in fact, the soundest available definition of personal happiness, as long as we restrict ourselves to donkeys. In reality, however, personal happiness (or equilibrium, contentment, whatever we may choose to call the innermost reflex aim of the personality) is self-contained only as a stone is in a wall, or a drop of water in a river, which are permeated by the forces and tensions of the whole. What a person does and feels is a negligible part of what he must assume many others normally do and feel with him. A human being never lives only in his own equilibrium but depends on that of the surrounding strata of humanity, so that the individual's little pleasure factory is affected by a most complicated moral credit system, about which more will have to be said later on, being as much a part of the community's psychic balance sheet as of the individual's.

Since Bonadea's efforts to win her lover back were unsuccessful, making her think that Diotima's intellect and energy had robbed her of Ulrich, she was consumed with jealousy; and yet, as is the way with weak personalities, her admiration for her rival provided a certain justification and compensation for her loss, which partially reconciled her to it. In this condition she had managed for some time now to be received by Diotima occasionally, on the pretext of having some modest contribution to offer to the Parallel Campaign, without achieving an entrance into the circles that frequented the house; on this point she imagined there must be a certain understanding between Diotima and Ulrich. So she felt herself to be a victim of their cruelty, and since she also loved them, the illusion of an ineffable purity and selflessness flowered inside her. In the mornings, when her husband had left the house—a moment she could hardly wait for—she often sat down at her mirror like a bird ready to groom its feathers. She tied, curled, and twisted her hair until it took on a form

not unlike Diotima's Grecian knot. She combed out and brushed little curls into place, and if the total effect was a bit silly, she never
noticed, because the face that smiled back at her from the mirror did
bear a faint resemblance to the goddess. The poise and beauty of her
idol, and the latter's sense of fulfillment, then rippled upward inside
her like the tiny, shallow, warm waves of a mysterious if not yet
deeply consummated union, much like sitting at the ocean's rim dabbling one's feet in the surf. What she did was akin to an act of religious worship—from the times when primitive man crept bodily into
the masks of the gods down to the rites and ceremonies of civilization, so carnal a joy of faithful mimicry has never quite lost its
power!—and had all the greater hold on Bonadea because of her
compulsive love of clothes and adornments. When Bonadea studied
her appearance in a new dress in her mirror, she could never have
imagined a time to come when leg-of-mutton sleeves, little curls
framing the forehead, and long bell-shaped skirts would be replaced
by knee-length skirts and hair cut like a boy's. Nor would she have
argued against it; her brain was simply incapable of imagining such a
possibility. She had always dressed like a lady and contemplated the
latest fashions, every six months, with reverence, as though she were
face-to-face with eternity. Even though an appeal to her intelligence
could have brought her to admit that such things were transitory, it
would in no way have lessened her reverence for them. The tyranny
of the mundane entered her bloodstream unnoticed, and the times
when one turned down the corner of one's visiting cards, or sent
one's friends New Year's greetings, or slipped off one's gloves at a
ball, were so long gone by the time one did *not* do any of these things
that they might as well have been a hundred years in the past: that is,
wholly unimaginable, impossible, and outdated. Which is why Bonadea without her clothes on was such a comical sight, stripped as she
was of all her ideological protection too, the naked victim of an inexorable compulsion that was sweeping her off her feet with the inhuman force of an earthquake.

But her periodic Fall from Civilization amid the vicissitudes of a
dull reality had been missing from her life of late, and ever since
Bonadea had been devoting such ritualistic care to her appearance,
the illegitimate portion of her life, for the first time since she was
twenty, was being lived as if she were a widow. In general, women

who are overly careful of their appearance may be presumed to be leading relatively chaste lives, because the means become the ends, just as great sports figures often make poor lovers, all-too-martial-looking officers make bad soldiers, and exceptionally intellectual-looking men are often blockheads. But with Bonadea it was not only a matter of where she chose to invest her energies but the amazing intensity with which she had turned to her new life. She penciled her eyebrows with a painter's loving care and enameled her forehead and cheeks for a heightened effect that reached beyond naturalism and mere reality into the style of religious art. Shaking her body into place inside a pliant corset, she suddenly felt a sisterly affection for her large breasts, which she had hitherto regarded as an embarrassing, because overly feminine, handicap. Her husband was quite taken aback when he tickled her neck with a finger and was told: "Please don't, you're spoiling my coiffure!" or when he tried to take her hand and she said: "Not now, I'm wearing my new dress!" But the power of sin had slipped from its physical mooring in the body and was drifting like a nova across the sky in the transfigured new world of a Bonadea who, in this unaccustomed softer radiance, felt released from her "excitability" as though the scales of some leprous disease had fallen away from her. For the first time since they were married, her spouse wondered whether there might be some third party threatening his domestic peace.

All that had happened was merely a phenomenon from the realm of vital systems. Clothes, when abstracted from the flow of present time and their transmogrifying function on the human body, and seen as forms in themselves, are strange tubes and excrescences worthy of being classed with such facial decorations as the ring through the nose or the lip-stretching disk. But how enchanting they become when seen together with the qualities they bestow on their wearer! What happens then is no less than the infusion, into some tangled lines on a piece of paper, of the meaning of a great word. Imagine a man's invisible kindness and moral excellence suddenly looming as a halo the size of the full moon and golden as an egg yolk right over his head, the way it does in old religious paintings, as he happens to be strolling down the avenue or heaping little tea sandwiches on his plate—what an overwhelming, shattering sensation it would be! And just such a power to make the invisible, and even the nonexistent, *visible* is what a well-made outfit demonstrates every day of the week.

Such things are like debtors who repay our investment in them with fantastic interest, and in that sense all things are indebted to us. For it is not only clothes that have such power, but convictions, prejudices, theories, hopes, faith in something or other, ideas, even thoughtlessness insofar as it is its quality of self-reflexiveness that gives it a sense of its own rightness. All these, by endowing us with the properties we lend them, serve the aim of presenting the world in a light that emanates from ourselves, and this is basically the task for which everyone has a method of his own. With great and varied skills we create a delusion that enables us to coexist serenely with the most monstrous things, simply because we recognize these frozen grimaces of the universe as a table or a chair, a shout or an outstretched arm, a speed or a roast chicken. We are capable of living between one open chasm of sky above our heads and another, slightly camouflaged chasm of sky beneath our feet, feeling as untroubled on earth as if we were in a room with the door closed. We know that our life is ebbing away both outward into the inhuman distances of cosmic space and downward into the inhuman microspace of the atom, while we go on dealing with a middle stratum, the things that make up our world, without troubling ourselves at all over the fact that this proves only a preference for impressions received in the middle distance, as it were. Such an attitude is considerably beneath our intellectual level, but that alone proves what a large part our feelings play in our intelligence. Our most important psychological machinery is, in fact, kept in motion to maintain us in a certain equilibrium, and all the emotions, all the passions in the world are nothing compared with the immense but wholly unconscious effort human beings make just to preserve their peace of mind. This works so well that there seems no point in drawing attention to it. But looked at closely, it does seem to be an extremely artificial state of mind that enables a man to walk upright among the circling constellations and permits him, surrounded as he is by an almost infinite unknown, to slip his hand with aplomb between the second and third buttons of his jacket. Not only does every human being, the idiot as much as the sage, apply his special skills to make this happen; all these personal stratagems are also cleverly built into society's moral and intellectual systems for maintaining its inner equilibrium, so that they serve the same purpose on a larger scale. This interlocking of systems resembles that of nature itself, where all the magnetic fields of the cosmos affect those of the earth without anyone noticing it, because the result is simply whatever happens on earth. The consequent psychological relief is so great that the wisest of men and the most ignorant of little girls, if left undisturbed, feel very clever and pleased with themselves.

But such states of satisfaction that might also be called compulsive states of feeling and volition, in a sense, are sometimes followed by the contrary; to resort again to the terminology of the madhouse, there is a sudden great flight of ideas worldwide, which leaves in its wake a repolarization of all human life around new centers and axes. The final cause of all great revolutions, which lies deeper than their effective cause, is not the accretion of intolerable conditions, but the loss of cohesion that bolstered the society's artificial peace of mind. There is an applicable saying by a famous early scholastic, "*Credo ut intelligam,*" which might be freely translated into a prayer for our times as "O Lord, please grant my spirit a production credit!" since every human creed is probably only a special instance of the credit system. In love as in business, in science as in the long jump, one has to believe before one can win and score, so how can it be otherwise for life as a whole? However well founded an order may be, it always rests in part on a voluntary faith in it, a faith that, in fact, always marks the spot where the new growth begins, as in a plant; once this unaccountable and uninsurable faith is used up, the collapse soon follows; epochs and empires crumble no differently from business concerns when they lose their credit.

And so this reflection on the principle of psychic equilibrium leads us from the beautiful example of Bonadea to the sad case of Kakania. For Kakania was the first country in our present historical phase from which God withdrew His credit: the love of life, faith in itself, and the ability of all civilized nations to disseminate the useful illusion that they have a mission to fulfill. It was an intelligent country, it housed cultivated people who, like cultivated people all over the globe, ran around in an unsettled state of mind amid a tremendous whirl of noise, speed, innovation, conflict, and whatever goes to make up the optical-acoustical landscape of our lives; like everybody else, they read and heard every day dozens of news items that made their hair stand on end, and were willing to work themselves up over them, even to intervene, but they never got around to it because a few minutes afterward the stimulus had already been displaced in their minds by more recent ones; like everyone else, they felt surrounded by murder, killings, passion, self-sacrifice, and greatness, all somehow going on within the Gordian knot that was forming around them, but they could never break through to these adventures because they were trapped in an office or somewhere, at work, and by evening, when they were free, their unresolved tensions exploded into forms of relaxation that failed to relax them. There was the special problem for persons of cultivated sensibilities, at least for those who did not devote themselves so single-mindedly to love as Bonadea: they no longer had the gift of faith or credit, nor had they learned to fake it. They no longer knew what their smiles, their sighs, their ideas, were for. What exactly was the point of their thoughts, their smiles? Their opinions were haphazard, their inclinations an old story, the scheme of things seemed to be hanging in midair, one ran into it as into a net, and there was nothing to do or leave undone with all one's heart, because there was no unifying principle. And so the cultivated person was someone who felt steadily mounting up a debt that he would never be able to pay off, felt bankruptcy inexorably approaching; and either inveighed against the times in which he was condemned to live, even though he enjoyed living in them like anyone else, or else hurled himself with the courage of those who have nothing to lose at every idea that promised a change.

It was the same as anywhere else in the world, of course, but when God cut off Kakania's credit, He did it in so special a style that whole nations had their eyes opened to the high cost of civilization. Like bacteria they had been sitting pretty in their culture medium, without bothering their heads about the proper curvature of the sky above or anything, when suddenly things tightened up. Although men are not normally aware of it, they must believe that they are something more than they are in order to be capable of being what they are; they need to feel this something more above and around them, and there are times when they suddenly miss it. What is missed is something imaginary. Nothing at all had happened in Kakania, and formerly it would have been thought of as the old, unobtrusive Kakanian way of life, but this nothing had become as disturbing as getting no sleep or seeing no sense in anything. And so it was easy enough for the intellectuals, once they had persuaded themselves that an ethnically homogeneous culture was the answer, to make the Kakanian ethnic minorities believe it, as a kind of substitute for religion or for the ideal of the Good Emperor in Vienna, or simply as a way of understanding the incomprehensible fact that there are seven days in the week. There are so many inexplicable things in life, but one loses sight of them when singing the national anthem. It would naturally be at such a moment that a good Kakanian could have joyfully answered the question of what he was by saying: "Nothing," meaning that Something that could make of a Kakanian everything he had never yet been! But the Kakanians were not so stiff-necked a people and contented themselves with a compromise, in that every nationality tried only to do with every other nationality whatever suited its own purposes. It is naturally hard in these circumstances to empathize with grievances not one's own. After two thousand years of altruistic teachings, we have become so unselfish that even if it means you or I have to suffer, we are bound to take the part of the other fellow. But it would be wrong to think of the notorious Kakanian nationalist rivalries as particularly savage. It was more a historical process than a real one. The people actually quite liked each other; even though they did crack each other's heads and spit in each other's faces, it was done as a matter of higher cultural considerations, as when a man who normally wouldn't hurt a fly, for instance, will sit in court under the image of Christ Crucified and condemn another man to death. It is only fair to say that whenever their higher selves relaxed a bit, the Kakanians breathed a sigh of relief and, born consumers of food and drink as they were, looked with amazement upon their role as the tools of history.

110

MOOSBRUGGER DISSOLVED AND PRESERVED

Moosbrugger was still in prison, waiting for further psychiatric examinations. It felt like a solid stack of days. Each day made itself distinctly felt when it came, of course, but toward evening it already began to merge with the stack. Moosbrugger certainly registered the presence of convicts, guards, corridors, courtyards, a glimpse of blue sky, a passing cloud or two, food, water, and now and then an official checking up on him, but these impressions were too feeble to be lasting. He had no watch, no sun, no work, to tell him the time. He was always hungry. He was always tired, from pacing around his seven square yards, which is far more tiring than wandering freely for miles. He was bored with everything he did, as if he had to keep stirring a pot of glue. But when he considered it as a whole, it seemed to him that day and night, his cleaning his plate and again cleaning his plate, inspections and checkups, all droned along one after the other without a break, and he found that entertaining. His life clock had gone out of order; it could be turned ahead or back. He liked that; it was his sort of thing. Things long past and fresh happenings were no longer kept apart artificially, and when it was all the same, then what they called "at different times" no longer stuck to it like the red thread they tie to a twin baby's neck so they can tell it from the other one. All the irrelevancies vanished from his life. When he pondered this life of his, he talked with himself inwardly, slowly, laying equal stress on every syllable; in this way life sang a different tune from the one heard every day. He often let his mind linger on a word for a long time, and when he finally moved on, without quite knowing how, after a while the word would turn up again somewhere else. It tickled him to think how much was happening for him that nobody knew about. The sense of being inwardly at peace with himself that sometimes came to him is hard to describe. Anyone can conceive of a man's life flowing along like a brook, but what Moosbrugger felt was his life flowing like a brook through a vast, still lake. As it flowed onward it continued to mingle with what it was leaving behind and became almost indistinguishable from the movements on either side of it. Once, in a half-waking dream, he had a sense of having worn this life's Moosbrugger like an ill-fitting coat on his back; now, when he opened it a bit, the most curious sort of lining came billowing out silkily, endless as a forest.

He no longer cared what was going on outside. Somewhere a war was going on. Somewhere there was a big wedding. Now the King of Belukhastan is coming, he thought. Everywhere soldiers were being drilled, whores were walking their beat, carpenters were standing among rafters. In the taverns of Stuttgart the beer came pouring from the same curving yellow taps as in Belgrade. On the road there were always the police demanding to see your papers. Then they stamped them. Everywhere there are bedbugs or no bedbugs. Work or no work. The women are the same everywhere. The doctors in all the hospitals are the same. When a man leaves his work in the evening the streets are full of people with nothing to do. It's all the same, always and everywhere; nobody has any new ideas. When Moosbrugger saw his first plane overhead in the blue sky—now, that was something! But then there was one plane after another, and they all looked alike. The sameness of things out there was different from the way his thoughts were all alike in being wonderful. He couldn't figure it out, and anyway it had always got in his way. He shook his head. To hell with the world, he thought. Or to hell with him and let them hang him: whatever happened, what did he have to lose . . . ?

And yet he sometimes would walk as if absentmindedly to the door and quietly try the place where the lock was on the outside. Then an eye would glare through the peephole and an angry voice come from the corridor, calling him names. Such insults made Moosbrugger move quickly back into his cell, and it was then that he felt locked up and robbed. Four walls and an iron door are nothing when you can freely walk in and out. Bars on an unfamiliar window are nothing special, and a plank bed or wooden table always in its place is quite in order. It's only when a man can't do what he wants with them that something crazy happens. Here things, made by human beings to serve them, slaves whose appearance one doesn't even bother to notice, suddenly get uppity. They block one's way. When Moosbrugger noticed these things giving him orders he had a good mind to smash them, and it was a struggle to convince himself that it was beneath him to fight these minions of the law. But his hands were twitching so hard he was afraid he was going to have a fit.

Out of the whole wide world they had picked these seven square yards, and Moosbrugger was pacing them, back and forth. The minds of the sane people out there, incidentally, who were not locked up, worked much the same as his own. They who had taken such a lively interest in him not so long ago had quickly forgotten him. He had been put in this place like a nail driven into the wall; once in, nobody notices it anymore. Other Moosbruggers were taking their turn; they were not himself, not even the same person every time, but they served the same purpose. There had been a sex crime, a grim story, a horrible murder, the act of a madman, of a man not quite responsible, the sort of thing to watch out for, but then the police and the courts had done their job. . . . Such vague and vacuous generalizations and memory tags loosely held the now-desiccated remains of the incident somewhere in their wide net. Moosbrugger's name was forgotten, the details were forgotten. He might have been "a squirrel, a hare, or a fox," the public remembered nothing specific about him, there remained only dim, wide areas of overlapping general notions, like the gray shimmer in a telescope focused at too great a distance. This failure to make connections, the cruelty of a mind that shuffles concepts around without bothering about the burden of suffering and life that weighs down every decision, was what the general mind had in common with that of Moosbrugger; but what was in his crazed brain a dream, a fairy tale, that flawed or odd spot in the mirror of consciousness which does not reflect reality but lets the light through, was lacking in society as a whole, unless some individual, in his obscure excitement, showed a hint of it here and there.

And what did concern Moosbrugger specifically, this particular Moosbrugger and none other, the one temporarily stored on these seven square yards of the world—the feeding, surveillance, authorized treatment, final disposal of the case by life or death sentence— was all in the hands of a relatively small group of people with a wholly different attitude. Here eyes on duty spied on him, voices came down hard on him for the slightest misstep. Never did fewer than two guards enter his cell. He was always handcuffed when they took him through the corridors. They acted with the fear and caution that had to do with this particular Moosbrugger within this limited area but was in strange contrast with the treatment accorded to him in general. He often complained about these strict measures. But when he did, the captain, the warden, the doctor, the priest, whoever heard him, turned a frozen face on him and told him he was being treated according to regulations. So regulations had taken the place of the interest the world had once taken in him, and Moosbrugger thought: "You've got a long rope around your neck and you can't see who's pulling it." He was roped to the outside world but, as it were, around the corner, out of sight. People who mostly never gave him a thought, who did not even know he existed, or to whom he meant at best no more than what some chicken on a village street means to a university professor of zoology— they were all in it together, preparing the doom that he felt tugging at him in some ghostly way. Some skirt in an office was typing a memo for his record. A registrar was ingeniously classifying it for filing. Some high functionary of the court was drawing up the latest directive for implementing his sentence. Psychiatrists were debating how to draw the line between the purely psychopathic constitution in certain cases of epilepsy and its manifestations when combined with other syndromes. Jurists were analyzing the factors that mitigated culpability in relation to factors that might modify the sentence. A bishop denounced the unraveling of the moral fabric, and a game warden's complaint to Bonadea's husband, the judge, about the excessive increase in foxes was reinforcing that eminent legal mind's bias in favor of reinforcing the inflexibility of the law.

It is such impersonal matters that go into the making of personal happenings in a way that for the present eludes description. When Moosbrugger's case was shorn of all its individual romantic elements, of interest only to him and to the few people he had murdered, not much more was left of it than what could be gathered from the list of references to works cited that Ulrich's father had enclosed in a recent letter to his son. Such a list looks like this: AH. AMP. AAC. AKA. AP. ASZ. BKL. BGK. BUD. CN. DTJ. DJZ. FBvM. GA. GS. JKV. KBSA. MMW. NG. PNW. R. VSvM. WMW. ZGS. ZMB. ZP. ZSS. Addickes ibid. Beling ibid., and so on. Written out, these would read: Annales d'Hygiène Publique et de Médicine légale, ed. Brouardel, Paris; Annales Médico-Psychologiques, ed. Ritti . . . etc.,

582 · THE MAN WITHOUT QUALITIES

etc., making a list a page long even when reduced to the briefest of abbreviations. The truth is not a crystal that can be slipped into one's pocket, but an endless current into which one falls headlong. Imagine every one of these abbreviations trailing a dozen or hundreds of printed pages, for each page a man with ten fingers writing it, and for each of his ten fingers ten disciples and ten opponents with ten fingers each, and at every fingertip a tenth of a personal idea, and you have a dim notion of what the truth is like. Without it not even that well-known sparrow can fall off the roof. Sun, wind, food brought it there, and illness, hunger, cold, or a cat killed it, but none of this could have happened without the operation of laws, biological, psychological, meteorological, physical, chemical, sociological, and all the rest, and it is much less of a strain to be merely looking for such laws than to have to make them up, as is done in the moral and judicial disciplines.

As for Moosbrugger himself, with his great respect for human knowledge, although he had, unfortunately, so small a portion of it: he never would have understood his situation completely even had he known exactly what it was. He had a dim sense of it. He felt that he was in an unstable condition. His big, powerful body was not as solid as it looked. Sometimes the open sky peered right into his skull. Just as it had, so often, in the old days on the road. And though he sometimes wished he could shake it off, he was never free, these days, of a certain solemn exaltation that streamed toward him, through the prison walls, from all the world. So there he sat, the wild, captive threat of a dreaded act, like an uninhabited coral island in a boundless sea of scientific papers that surrounded him invisibly on all sides.

111

TO THE LEGAL MIND, INSANITY IS AN
ALL-OR-NOTHING PROPOSITION

Still, a criminal's life can often be a picnic compared with the strenuous brainwork he imposes on the pundits of the law. The offender simply takes advantage of the fact that the transitions in nature from health to sickness are smooth and imperceptible, while to the jurist it is a case of "The arguments *pro* and *contra* freedom of the will or insight into the wrongful nature of the act so tend to cut across and cancel each other out that no system of logic can lead to other than a problematic verdict." A jurist has logical reasons for bearing in mind that "in regard to one and the same act there is no admissible possibility that it can arise from a mixture of two different mental states," and he will not permit "the principle of moral freedom in relation to physically conditioned states of mind to be lost in a vague mist of empirical thought." He is not beholden to Nature for his concepts, but penetrates Nature with the flame of his thinking and the sword of moral law. A heated debate on this point had broken out in the committee, of which Ulrich's father was a member, convoked by the Ministry of Justice to update the penal code; however, it had taken some time and several reminders from his father to bring Ulrich to the point of studying, like a good son, his father's position paper with all its enclosed documentation.

Ulrich's "affectionate father," as he signed even the most embittered of his letters, had declared and proposed that a partially insane person should be acquitted only when there was sufficient evidence that his delusory system contained ideas that, were they not delusory, would justify the act or exempt it from liability to punishment. Professor Schwung, on the other hand—possibly because he had been the old man's friend and colleague for forty years, which must after all lead to a violent difference of opinion sooner or later—had declared and proposed that such an individual, in whom the state of being responsible for his actions and not being responsible for his

actions must occur in constant alternation, since from a legal point of
view they could not coexist simultaneously, should be acquitted only
if and when there was evidence, with respect to that specific act of
the will, that at the precise moment of this act of the will the offender
had been unable to control himself. So much for the point at issue.
The layman can readily see that it may be no less difficult for the
criminal not to overlook any moment of sane volition at the instant he
performs the act in question than not to overlook any thought that
might perhaps make him liable to punishment; but the law is not
obliged to make thinking and moral conduct a bed of roses! And as
both these learned jurists were equally zealous on behalf of the law's
dignity, and neither could win a majority of the committee over to his
side, they began by charging each other with error, and then in swift
succession with illogical thinking, deliberate misunderstanding, and
a lapse of standards. They did this at first within the privacy of the
irresolute committee, but then, when the meetings came to a halt,
had to be adjourned, and finally suspended indefinitely, Ulrich's father wrote two pamphlets, entitled "Paragraph 318 of the Penal
Code and the True Spirit of the Law" and "Par. 318 of the Penal
Code and the Muddied Wellsprings of Our Jurisprudence," which
Ulrich found among the enclosures with his father's letter, together
with the critical review of them published by Professor Schwung in
the journal *The Legal Scholar*.

These pamphlets were full of "and"s and "or"s, because the question of whether these two views could be combined by an "and" or
must be kept apart by an "or" had to be "cleared up." When after a
long interval the committee finally reassembled, it, too, had split into
an "and" and an "or" faction. There was also another fraction, which
supported the simple proposal to let the degree of culpability and
responsibility rise and fall in proportion to the rise and fall in the
degree of the psychological effort that would suffice, in the given
pathological circumstances, to maintain self-control. This grouping
was opposed by a fourth faction, which insisted that before all else
there must be a clear and definite decision as to whether a criminal
could be said to be responsible for his actions at all; logically, where
there was a lessened responsibility for an action, there had first to be
a responsibility, and even if the criminal was only in part responsible
for his actions he must still suffer the penalty with his entire person,

because the guilty part was not otherwise accessible to the workings of the law. This met with opposition from yet another faction, which, while granting the principle, pointed out that nature did not follow it, in that nature produced half-crazy people upon whom the benefits of the law could be conferred only by modifying their punishment, in view of the circumstances, without at all condoning their guilt. This led to the formation of a "soundness of mind" faction as opposed to a "full responsibility" faction, and it was only when these also had split up into enough splinter groups that those aspects of the problem came to light which had not yet occasioned a difference of opinion.

Naturally, no professional man of our time bases his arguments on those of philosophy and theology, but as perspectives—empty, like space, and yet, like space, telescoping the objects in it—these two rivals for the last word of wisdom persist everywhere in invading the optics of each special field of knowledge. And so here, too, the carefully avoided question of whether a human being could be regarded as a free agent, that good old problem of the freedom of the will, provided the focus for all the differences of opinion, although it was not under consideration. For if a man is morally free, he must, in practice, be subjected by punishment to a compulsion in which no one, in theory, believes. If, on the other hand, he is regarded not as free but as the meeting ground for inexorably interlocking natural processes, then one cannot consider him morally accountable for what he does, even though one can effectively discourage him from doing it by inflicting punishment on him. This problem gave rise to still another faction, which proposed that the culprit be divided into two parts: a zoologic-psychological entity, which did not concern the judge, and a juridical entity, which, though only a fiction, was legally free and accountable. Fortunately, this proposal remained confined to theory.

It is hard to be brief in doing justice to justice. The commission consisted of about twenty legal pundits who were capable of adopting several thousand different points of view among themselves, as can easily be calculated. The laws to be updated had been in operation since the year 1852, so that on top of everything else they had proved highly durable, not lightly to be replaced by anything else. In any case, the fixed institution of the law cannot keep up with every brain wave of currently fashionable tendencies, as one participant rightly pointed out. The conscientiousness with which the commission's task had to be performed is best appreciated in the light of the fact that statistically, about seventy out of every hundred people who commit crimes that damage society may be sure of slipping through the meshes of the law. How clear this makes our duty to give all the more rigorous thought to the 25 percent or so who get caught! This situation may of course have improved slightly, and besides, it would be wrong to see the real purpose of this report as making fun of the ice flowers that logic brings so exquisitely to bloom in the heads of our legal pundits; this has been done already by innumerable people whose mental climate tends toward slush. On the contrary, it was masculine strictness, arrogance, moral soundness, impregnability, and complacency, all qualities of temperament and largely virtues that, as we say, we hope never to lose, which prevented the learned members of the commission from making an unprejudiced use of their intelligence. They dealt with men as boys, in the manner of elderly schoolteachers in charge of a pupil who needed only to be willing to learn and pay attention in order to "do well"—and thereby simply evoked the prerevolutionary sentiments of the generation before their own, that of 1848. No doubt their understanding of psychology was about fifty years out of date; that easily happens when one has to till one's own fields of expertise with the borrowed tools of a neighbor, and the deficiency is usually made good as soon as circumstances permit. The one thing that remains permanently behind the times, especially because it prides itself on its steadfastness, is the human heart, most of all that of the conscientious man. The mind is never so hard, dry, and twisted as when it has a slight chronic heart condition.

This ultimately led to a furious outburst. When the various skirmishes had worn down all the participants and kept the work from getting on, more and more voices were raised to suggest a compromise, which would look much as all formulas do when designed to cover up an unbridgeable gap with fine phrases. There was a tendency to agree on the familiar definition that termed "of sound mind" those criminals whose mental and moral qualities make them capable of committing a crime, but not those who lacked such qualities; a most extraordinary definition, which has the advantage of making it very hard for criminals to qualify, so that those who do would almost be entitled to wear their convict's uniform with the aura of an academic degree.

But at this point Ulrich's father, facing the threatening lull of the Jubilee Year, and a definition as round as an egg, which he regarded as a hand grenade aimed at his own person, took what he called his sensational turn to the social school of thought. The social view holds that the criminally "degenerate" individual must be judged not morally but only insofar as he is likely to harm society as a whole. Hence the more dangerous he is, the more responsible he is for his actions, with the inescapable logical consequence that those criminals who seem to be the most innocent, the mentally sick, who are by nature least susceptible to correction by punishment, must be threatened with the harshest penalties, harsher than those for sane persons, so that the deterrent factor of the punishment be equal for all. It might fairly be expected that Professor Schwung would have a hard time finding an objection to this social view of the matter. This expectation was borne out, which was why he resorted to expedients that drove Ulrich's father in turn to leave the path of jurisprudence, which was threatening to lose itself in the sands of controversy within the committee, and appeal to his son to turn to account those connections with high and even the highest circles, which he owed to his father, in his father's good cause. For instead of making any attempt at a sober refutation, his colleague Schwung had at once fastened maliciously on the term "social" to denounce it, in a new publication, as "materialistic" and suspect of being infected with "the Prussian idea of the State."

"My dear son," Ulrich's father wrote, "of course I immediately pointed out the Roman precedent for the social school of legal theory, which is by no means Prussian in origin, but this may be of no use against such a denunciation and defamation calculated with diabolical malice to create in *high quarters* the predictably loathsome impression only too easily linked there with the thought of materialism and Prussia. These are no longer the kind of allegations against which a man can defend himself. Rumors are being spread, so vague that they are hardly likely to be carefully scrutinized in *high quarters*, where being forced to deal with them at all may be held

against their innocent victim quite as much as against the unscrupulous slanderer. I, who have all my life scorned to use backstairs methods, now see myself driven to ask you . . ." And so on, and so the
letter ended.

112

ARNHEIM SETS HIS FATHER, SAMUEL, AMONG THE GODS AND DECIDES TO GET ULRICH INTO HIS POWER. SOLIMAN WANTS TO FIND OUT MORE ABOUT HIS OWN ROYAL FATHER

Arnheim had rung for Soliman. It was a long time since he had felt
like talking with the boy, and now that he did, the rascal seemed to
be wandering around in the hotel somewhere.

Ulrich's opposition had finally succeeded in wounding Arnheim.

Arnheim had of course not been blind to the fact that Ulrich was
working against him. Ulrich did it impersonally, with an effect like
that of water on fire, salt on sugar, undermining Arnheim's influence
almost without conscious intent. Arnheim felt sure that Ulrich even
took advantage of Diotima's reliance on him to drop unfavorable or
satiric remarks about Arnheim.

Nothing of the kind had happened to him in ages. His usual
method for keeping the upper hand failed him here. The effect of a
great man who is his own man is like that of a great beauty; deny it,
and it is a punctured balloon, or a Greek statue on which someone
has put a hat. A beautiful woman loses her looks when she ceases to
please, and a great man when ignored may become an even greater
one but ceases to be a great public figure. Not that Arnheim realized
it in these terms, but he thought: "I can't stand opposition, because
only the intellect thrives on it, and I despise anyone who is all
intellect."

Arnheim took it for granted that he could find a way to neutralize his opponent. But he wanted to win Ulrich over, to influence him, teach him, compel his admiration. In order to make this easier, he had talked himself into feeling a deep and paradoxical affection for Ulrich, though he would not have known how to account for this. He had nothing to fear from Ulrich, and there was nothing he wanted from him; he knew that neither Count Leinsdorf nor Section Chief Tuzzi was a friend, and otherwise things were going, if slowly, just as he wanted them to go. Ulrich's countereffect paled beside Arnheim's effect; all that was left of it was a wispy protest, which seemed to accomplish nothing except perhaps to delay Diotima's resolve by faintly paralyzing that marvelous woman's purpose. Arnheim had subtly pried it out of her and now could not help smiling when he thought of it. Was it a wistful smile or a malicious one? Such distinctions, in matters of this kind, are of no consequence. It was only fair, he thought, that his enemy's criticism and resistance should work unconsciously in his, Arnheim's, favor. It was the victory of the deeper cause, one of those marvelously lucid, self-resolving complications of life. It was destiny, Arnheim felt, that seemed to bring him and the younger man together and made him yield points to Ulrich, who did not understand. For Ulrich resisted all his blandishments; he seemed moronically insensitive to his own social advantage, either not noticing or not appreciating this offer of friendship.

There was something that Arnheim called Ulrich's wit. What he meant by it was, in part, this failure of a brilliant man to recognize his own advantage and to adjust his mind to the great aims and opportunities that would bring him status and a solid footing in life. Ulrich acted on the absurd contrary idea that life had to adjust itself to suit his mind. Arnheim called Ulrich's image to mind: as tall as himself, younger, without the softening of contour he could not fail to notice on his own body; something unconditionally independent in his look—something Arnheim attributed, not without envy, to Ulrich's coming of ascetic-scholarly stock, which was his idea of Ulrich's origins. The face showed less concern about money and appearances than a rising dynasty of experts in the processing of waste had permitted their descendants to feel. Yet there was something missing in this face. It was life that was missing here; the marks of experience were shockingly absent! As Arnheim perceived this in a flash of surreal clarity, he was so disturbed by it that it made him realize all over again how much he cared about Ulrich—why, here was a face almost visibly headed for disaster! He brooded over the conflicting sense of envy and anxiety this made him feel; there was a sad satisfaction in it, as when someone has taken a coward's refuge in a safe port. A sudden violent upsurge of envy and disapproval drove to the surface the thought he had been both seeking and avoiding, that Ulrich probably was a man capable of sacrificing not only the interest but all the capital of his soul, if circumstances called for it. Strangely enough, it was this, in fact, that Arnheim also meant by Ulrich's wit. At this moment, recalling the expression he had coined, it became perfectly clear to him: the idea that a man could let himself be swept away by passion, beyond the limits of the atmosphere where he could breathe, struck Arnheim as a witty notion, a joke.

When Soliman at last came sidling into the room and stood facing his master, Arnheim had almost forgotten why he had sent for him, but he found it soothing to have a living and devoted creature close by. He paced up and down the room, with a stern expression, and the black disk of the boy's face turned this way and that, watching him.

"Sit down!" Arnheim ordered; he had turned on his heel when he reached the corner and kept standing there as he spoke: "The great Goethe, somewhere in *Wilhelm Meister*, has a maxim charged with much feeling to guide our conduct in life: 'Think in order to act, act in order to think.' Can you understand this? No, I don't suppose you can understand it. . . ." He answered his own question and fell silent again. This prescription holds all of life's wisdom, he thought, and the man who wants to oppose me knows only half of it: namely, thinking. This, too, could be what he had meant by "merely witty." He recognized Ulrich's weakness. Wit comes from witting, or knowing; the wisdom of language itself here pointed to the intellectual origins of this quality, its ghostly, emotionally impoverished nature. The witty man is inclined to outsmart himself, to ignore those natural limits the man of true feeling respects. This insight brought the matter of Diotima and the soul's capital substance into a more pleasing light, and as he was thinking this, Arnheim said to Soliman: "This maxim holds all the wisdom life can give, and it has led me to take away your books and make you go to work."

Soliman said nothing and made a solemn face.

"You have seen my father several times," Arnheim said suddenly. "Do you remember him?"

Soliman responded to this by rolling his eyes so that the whites showed, and Arnheim said pensively, "You see, my father almost never reads a book. How old do you think my father is?" Again he did not wait for an answer and added: "He is already over seventy and still has a hand in everything in the world that might concern our firm." Arnheim resumed pacing the room in silence. He felt an irrepressible urge to talk about his father, but could not say everything that was on his mind. No one knew better than he that even his father sometimes lost out in a business deal; but nobody would have believed him, because once a man has the reputation of being Napoleon, even his lost battles count as victories. So there had never been any way for Arnheim of holding his own beside his father other than the one he had chosen, that of making culture, politics, and society serve business. Old Arnheim seemed pleased enough at the younger Arnheim's great knowledge and accomplishments, but whenever an important decision had to be made, and the problem had been discussed and analyzed for days on end, from the production angle and the financial angle and for its impact on the world economy and civilization, he thanked everyone, not infrequently ordered the exact opposite of what had been proposed, and responded to all objections with only a helpless, stubborn smile. Even the directors often shook their heads dubiously over this way he had, but then sooner or later it would always turn out that the old man had somehow been right. It was more or less like an old hunter or mountain guide having to listen to a meteorologists' conference but then always ending up in favor of the prophecies delivered by his own rheumatism; not so very odd, basically, since there are so many problems where one's rheumatism happens to be a surer guide than science, nor does having an exact forecast matter all that much in a world where things always turn out differently from what one had expected, anyway, and the thing is to be shrewd and tough in adapting oneself to their waywardness. So Paul Arnheim should have had no trouble in understanding that an old hand at the game knows a great deal that cannot be foreseen theoretically, and can do a great deal because of his knowledge; still, it was a fateful day for him when he discovered that old Samuel had intuition.

"Do you know what is meant by intuition?" Arnheim asked, from deep in his thoughts, as though groping for the shadow of an excuse to speak of it. Soliman blinked hard, as he always did when he was being cross-examined about something he had forgotten to do, and Arnheim again caught himself up. "I'm feeling a bit on edge today," he said, "as you can't be expected to know, of course. But please pay close attention to what I am about to tell you: Making money often gets us into situations in which we don't look too good, as you can imagine. All this having to watch your arithmetic and make sure you get a profit out of everything, all the time, runs strictly counter to the ideal of a great and noble life such as was possible for a man to aim at in happier times long ago. In those days they could make of murder the noble virtue of bravery, but it seems doubtful to me that something of the sort can be done with bookkeeping: there is no real goodness, no dignity, no depth of feeling in it. Money turns everything into an abstraction, it is so coldly rational; whenever I see money I can't help thinking—I don't know whether you can follow me here—thinking of mistrustful fingers testing it, of loud arguments and much shrewd manipulation, all equally repulsive to me."

He broke off and fell back into his solitary musing, as he thought of those uncles who had patted him on the head when he was a child, saying what a good little head he had on his shoulders. A good little head for figures. How he hated that kind of attitude! Those shining gold coins reflected the mind of a family that had worked its way up in the world. Feeling ashamed of his family was beneath him; on the contrary, he made a point of acknowledging his origins with a fine modesty, especially in the highest circles, but he dreaded any show of the calculating family mind as though it were a taint, like speaking with too much intensity and gesturing with hands aflutter, which would make him impossible among the best people.

This was probably the root of his reverence for the irrational. The aristocracy was irrational—this might be taken as a witticism reflecting on the intellectual limitations of the nobility, but not as Arnheim meant it. It had to do with the fact that as a Jew he could not be appointed an officer in the Army Reserve, nor could he, as an Arnheim, occupy the lowly position of a noncom, so he was simply declared unfit for military service, and to this day he refused to see only the absurdity of this without duly appreciating the code of honor behind it. This recollection moved him to enrich his speech to Soliman with some further remarks.

"It is possible"—he picked up the thread, for despite his distaste for pedantry he was a methodical man, even in his digressions—"it is possible, even probable, that our noble families were not always paragons of what we today consider a noble bearing. To assemble all those huge landed estates upon which their titles of nobility came to be based, their forebears must have been no less calculating and sharp in their dealings than today's men of business; it is even possible that the modern businessman conducts his affairs with far more honesty. But there is a force in the earth itself, you know, something in the soil, in hunting, in warfare, in faith, in tilling the land—in short, in the physical life of people who used their heads far less than their arms and legs; it was nature itself that gave them the strength to which they ultimately owed their dignity, their nobility, their disinclination to demean themselves in any way whatsoever."

He wondered whether he had not allowed his mood to trick him into going too far. What if Soliman missed his master's meaning and misunderstood the words to suggest that he was entitled to think less highly of the upper classes? But something unexpected happened. Soliman had been fidgeting on his seat for a while, and he now interrupted his master with a question.

"If you please, sir," Soliman asked, "about my father: is he a king?"

Arnheim gave him a startled look. "I don't know anything about that," he said, still somewhat sternly, though inwardly a little amused. But as he gazed at Soliman's serious, almost resentful face, he found it touching. It pleased him to see the boy taking everything so seriously. He is a dimwit, he thought, and really a tragic case. Somehow he equated witlessness with a heavy feeling of well-being. In a gently didactic manner, he went on to give the boy something more of an answer to his question. "There is hardly any reason to assume that your father is a king. More likely he had a hard living to earn, because I found you in a troupe of jugglers on a beach."

"How much did I cost?" Soliman persisted.

"My dear boy, how can you expect me to remember that today? It couldn't have been much. But why worry about that now? We are born to create our own kingdom. Next year sometime I may let you take a commercial course, and then you could make a start as a trainee in one of our offices. Of course it will depend on you what you make of it, but I shall keep an eye on you. You might, for instance, aim at eventually representing our interests in places where the colored people already have some influence. We'd have to move with care, of course, but being a black man might turn out to have certain advantages for you. It is only in doing such work that you can come to understand fully how much these years under my immediate supervision have done for you already, and I can tell you one thing now: you belong to a race that still bears some of nature's own nobility. In our medieval tales of chivalry, black kings always played a distinguished role. If you cultivate what you have of spiritual quality—your dignity, your goodness of heart, your openness, your courageous love of the truth, and the even greater courage to resist intolerance, jealousy, resentment, and all the petty nervous spitefulness that stigmatizes most people nowadays—if you can do that, you will certainly make your way as a man of business, because we are called upon to bring the world not only our wares but a better life."

Arnheim had not talked so intimately with Soliman in a long time, and the idea that any onlooker might think him a fool made him uneasy, but there was no onlooker, and besides, what he was saying to Soliman was only the surface layer covering far deeper currents of thought he was keeping to himself. What he was saying about the aristocratic mind and the historic rise of the nobility was moving, deep inside him, in the opposite direction to his spoken words. Inwardly he could not repress the thought that never since the beginning of the world had anything sprung from spiritual purity and good intentions alone; everything was far more likely to spring from the common dirt, which in time sheds its crudeness and cleans itself up and eventually even gives rise to greatness and purity of thought. The rise of the nobility was not based on conditions pregnant with a lofty humanism, he thought, any more than was the growth of the garbage-moving business into a worldwide corporation, and yet the one had blossomed into the silver age of the eighteenth century, and the other had led directly to Arnheim. Life was facing him, in short, with an inescapable problem best formulated in the dilemma: How much common dirt is necessary and acceptable as the soil in which to propagate high-mindedness?

On another level, his thoughts had meanwhile intermittently pursued what he had been saying to Soliman about intuition and reason, and he suddenly had a vivid memory of the first time he had told his father that he—the old man—did business by intuition. Intuition was fashionable at the time with all those who could not justify what they did by logic; it was playing the same role, more or less, as is played today by having "flair." Every false or ultimately unsatisfactory move was credited to intuition, and intuition was used for everything from cooking to writing books, but the elder Arnheim had not heard of it, and he actually let himself go so far as to look up in surprise at his son, for whom it was a moment of triumph. "Making money," he said to his father, "forces us to think along lines that are not always in the best style. Still, it will probably be up to us men of big business to take over the leadership of the masses the next time there's a turning point in history, whether we are spiritually ready or not. But if there is anything in the world that can give me the courage to face such a burden, it is you; you have the vision and willpower of the kings and prophets of the great old days, who were still guided by God. Your way of tackling a deal is ineffable, a mystery, and I must say that all mysteries that elude calculation are in the same class, whether it is the mystery of courage or of invention or of the stars!" It was humiliating to see old Arnheim, who had been looking up at him, drop his eyes again, after his son's first sentences, back to his newspaper, from which he did not raise them on any subsequent occasion when the younger man talked of business and intuition. Such was the characteristic relationship between father and son, and on a third level of his thoughts, on the same screen with these remembered images, as it were, Arnheim was analyzing it even now. He regarded his father's superior gift for business, though it always depressed him to think of it, as a kind of primitive force that would forever elude the son, a more complicated man; this relieved him of having to keep striving in vain to emulate the inimitable, and at the same time provided him with letters patent of his own noble descent. This brilliant double maneuver turned money into a suprapersonal, mythical force for which only the most primitive originality could be a match, and it also set his forebear among the gods, quite as had the ancient heroes, who undoubtedly also thought of their mythical forefather, with all the awe he inspired, as just a shade more primitive than themselves.

But on a fourth level of his mind he knew nothing of the smile that hovered over that third level, and rethought the same idea in a serious vein, as he considered the role he still hoped to play on this earth. Such levels of thought are of course not to be taken literally, as if superimposed on each other like actual layers of the soil, but are merely meant to suggest currents of thought, flowing from various directions and perpetually crisscrossing under the influence of strong emotional conflicts. All his life, Arnheim had felt an almost morbidly sensitive dislike of wit and irony, a dislike probably motivated by a not inconsiderable hereditary tendency to both. He had suppressed this tendency because he felt it to be ignoble, a quality of the intellectual riffraff, yet it unaccountably popped up at this very moment, when he was feeling his most aristocratic and anti-intellectual, with regard to Diotima: just when his feelings were on tiptoe, ready to take flight, as it were, he felt a devilish temptation to give sublimity the slip by making one of those pointed lethal jokes about love he had heard often enough from the lips of low-ranking or coarse characters.

As his mind rose again to the surface through all these strata of thought, he abruptly found himself gazing at Soliman's gloomily listening face, like a black punchball on which unintelligible words of wisdom had come raining down like so many blows. What an absurd position I am getting myself into! Arnheim thought.

Soliman looked as if he had fallen asleep on his chair with his eyes wide open; as his master reached the end of that one-sided conversation, the eyes set themselves in motion, while the body refused to stir, as though still waiting for the word to wake up. Arnheim saw it and saw in the black boy's gaze the craving to hear more about whatever intrigues could have brought a king's son to be a valet. This gaze, lunging at him like claws outstretched for their prey, momentarily reminded Arnheim of that gardener's helper who had made off with pieces from his collection, and he said to himself with a sigh that he would probably always be lacking in the natural acquisitive instinct. It suddenly occurred to him that this would also sum up, in a word, his relation to Diotima. Painfully moved, he felt how, at the very summit of his life, a cold shadow separated him from everything he had ever touched. It was not an easy thought for a man who had just stated the principle that a man must think in order to act, and who had always striven to make all greatness his own and to trans-

form whatever was less than great with the stamp of his own distinguished imprint. But the shadow had slipped between him and the
objects of his desire, despite the willpower he had never lacked, and
Arnheim surprised himself by thinking that he could see a connection between that shadow and those shimmers of awe that had cast
their veils over his youth, as if, mishandled in some way, they had
turned into an almost imperceptible skin of ice. Why this ice did not
melt even when confronted with Diotima's unworldly heart he could
not tell; but, like a most unwelcome jab of a pain that had only been
waiting for a touch to awaken it, there came the sudden thought of
Ulrich. It came with the realization that the same shadow rested on
the other man's life, but with so different an effect! Within the range
of human passions, that of a man jealous of another man's personality
is seldom accorded the recognition its intensity has earned for it, and
the discovery that his uncontrollable irritation with Ulrich resembled, on a deeper level, the hostile encounter of two brothers unaware of each other's identity gave him a rather pleasant jolt.
Arnheim compared their two personalities from this angle with a
new interest. Ulrich had even less of the crude acquisitive instinct for
advantages in life, and his immunity to the sublime acquisitive instinct for status and recognition, whatever it was that mattered, was
downright infuriating. This man needed none of the weight and substance of life. His sober zeal, which was undeniable, was not a self-
serving passion; it came close to reminding Arnheim of the
self-effacing manner in which his own staff did their work, except
that Ulrich's selflessness came with such a flourish of arrogance. One
might call him a man possessed who was not interested in possessing
anything. Or perhaps a man fighting for a cause who had taken a vow
of poverty. He could also be regarded as a man given entirely to
theorizing, and yet this, too, fell short, because one could certainly
not call him a theorist. Arnheim recalled having pointed out to Ulrich
that his intellectual capacities were no match for his practical ones.
Yet from a practical point of view, the man was utterly impossible.

So Arnheim's mind turned this way and that, not for the first time,
but despite the day's mood of self-doubt, he could not possibly grant
Ulrich superiority over himself on any one count; the crucial difference must be attributable to some deficiency of Ulrich's. And yet the
man had such an air of freshness and freedom, which, Arnheim re-

luctantly admitted to himself, reminded him of that "Secret of Integrity" which he knew himself to possess, though this other man somehow shook his faith in it. How else would it have been possible, on a purely rational plane, to attribute, however uneasily, the same "wit" to this rootless phantom of a man as Arnheim had learned to fear in an all-too-expert realist such as his father? "There's something missing in the man," Arnheim thought, but as though this were merely the obverse of that truth, it occurred to him at almost the same moment and quite involuntarily that "the man has a soul!"

The man had reserves of soul as yet untapped. As this intuition had taken him by surprise, Arnheim was not ready to say just what he meant by it, but as time goes on, every man, as he knew, finds that his soul, by some irreversible process, has turned into intelligence, morality, and lofty ideas; in his friendly enemy this had not yet run its course, and he still had some of his original store of it, something with an indefinable ambiguous charm, which manifested itself in peculiar combinations with elements from the realm of the soulless, the rational, the mechanical—everything that could not quite be regarded as part of the cultural sphere itself.

While he was turning all this over in his mind and immediately adapting it to the style of his philosophical works, Arnheim had incidentally not had a moment in which to credit any of it to Ulrich's account, not even as the single solitary credit to be granted to him, so strong was his sense of having made a discovery of his own, something he alone had created; he felt like a maestro spotting a fine voice that had not yet fulfilled its potential. This glow of discovery only began to cool when he caught sight of Soliman's face; Soliman had obviously been staring at him for quite a while, and now believed the time had come again to be able to ask him more questions. His awareness that it was not given to everyone to organize his own mind with the aid of such a mute little semi-savage enhanced Arnheim's joy at being the only one to know his enemy's secret, even if there still were a few points to be cleared up as to their implications for the future. What he felt was the love of the usurer for the victim in whom he has invested his capital. Perhaps it was the sight of Soliman that suddenly inspired him to draw into his own orbit, at any cost, the man whom he had come to see as a different embodiment of the adventure that was his own self, even if he had to adopt him as a son!

He smiled at this overhasty enthusiasm for a notion that would take time to mature, and instantly cut short Soliman, whose face was twitching with a tragic need to know more, saying: "That's all for now. Take the flowers I ordered to Frau Tuzzi. If there's anything else you want to ask, we can deal with it some other time."

113

ULRICH CHATS WITH HANS SEPP AND GERDA IN THE JARGON OF THE FRONTIER BETWEEN THE SUPERRATIONAL AND THE SUBRATIONAL

Ulrich had no idea what to do in response to his father's request that he pave the way for a personal talk with His Grace and other high-ranking patriots as a partisan of the sociopragmatic approach to crime and punishment. So he went to see Gerda, to put it all out of his mind. Hans was with her, and Hans instantly took the offensive.

"So now you're standing up for Director Fischel?"

Ulrich dodged the question by asking whether Hans had it from Gerda.

Yes, Gerda had told him.

"What about it? Would you like to know why?"

"Do tell me," Hans demanded.

"That's not so easy, my dear Hans."

"Don't call me your dear Hans."

"Well then, my dear Gerda," Ulrich said, turning to her, "it's far from simple. I've talked about it so exhaustively already that I thought you understood."

"I understand you perfectly, but I don't believe a word of it," Gerda answered, trying hard to soften the blow of her siding with Hans against him by the conciliatory way she said it and looked at him.

"We don't believe you," Hans said, instantly aborting this turn to amiability in the conversation. "We don't believe that you can mean it seriously. You picked it up somewhere."

"What!? I suppose you mean something one can't really put into words . . . ?" Ulrich had instantly realized that Hans's impertinence had to do with what Ulrich and Gerda had discussed in private.

"Oh, it can be put into words, all right, provided one means it."

"I don't seem to have the knack. But let me tell you a story."

"*Another* story! You seem to go in for telling stories like Great Homer himself!" Hans was taking an even ruder and more arrogant tone. Gerda gave him a pleading look. But Ulrich would not let himself be put off, and went on: "I was very much in love myself once, when I was just about the same age as you are now. Actually, I was in love with being in love, with my changed condition, rather than with the woman in the case, and that was when I found out all about the things you, your friends, and Gerda make such great mysteries of. That's the story I wanted to tell you."

They were both startled that it turned out to be so short a story.

"So you were very much in love once . . . ?" Gerda asked haltingly, and hated herself in that instant for having asked the question in front of Hans, with the shivering curiosity of a schoolgirl.

But Hans broke in: "Why are we talking about that sort of thing in the first place? Why don't you tell us instead what your cousin is really up to, now that she has fallen in with all those cultural bankrupts?"

"She is searching for an idea that will give the whole world a splendid image of what our country stands for," Ulrich replied. "Wouldn't you like to help her out with some suggestion of your own? I'd be glad to pass it on to her."

Hans gave a scornful laugh. "Why do you act as if you didn't know that we intend to disrupt the whole show?"

"But why on earth are you so much against it?"

"Because it is an incredibly vicious scheme against all that's German in this country," Hans said. "Is it possible that you really don't know what a strong opposition is developing? The Pan-German League has been alerted to your Count Leinsdorf's machinations. The Physical Culture Clubs have already lodged a protest against this affront to German aspirations. The Federation of Arms-bearing Student Corps throughout our Austrian universities is formulating an appeal against the threat of Slavification, and the League of German Youth, of which I am a member, will not put up with it, even if we have to take to the streets!" Hans had drawn himself up tall and re cited this speech with a certain pride. But he could not resist adding: "Not that any of this makes any difference. These people all make too much of externals. What matters is that there's no way of getting anything done to anyone's satisfaction in this country!"

Ulrich asked him to explain.

The great races of mankind had all begun by creating their own mythology. Well, was there such a thing as a great myth of Austria? Hans asked. Did Austria have an ancient religion of its own, or a great epic poem? Neither the Catholic nor the Protestant religion had originated here; the art of printing and the Austrian tradition of painting had all come from Germany. The reigning dynasty had come from Switzerland, Spain, Luxembourg; the technology from England and Germany; our most beautiful cities, Vienna, Prague, Salzburg, had been built by Italians or Germans; the army was organized on the Napoleonic model. Such a country had no business trying to take the lead. Its only possible salvation had to be union with Germany. "Satisfied?" Hans concluded.

Gerda was not sure whether to be proud of him or ashamed. Her attraction to Ulrich had been flaring up again of late, even though the natural human need to be someone in her own right was much better served by her younger friend. This young woman was strangely torn between the contradictory inclinations to grow old as a virgin and to give herself to Ulrich. The second of these inclinations was the natural consequence of a love she had felt for years, though it never burst into flame but only smoldered listlessly inside her, and her feelings were like those of someone infatuated with an inferior, in that her soul was humiliated by her body's contemptible craving for submission to this man. In strange contrast with this, though perhaps tied to it as simply and naturally as a yearning for peace, she suspected that she would never marry but would end up, when all the dreams were over, leading a solitary, quietly busy life of her own. This was not a hope born of conviction, for Gerda had no very clear idea of herself, only a foreboding such as the body may have long before the mind is alerted to it. The influence Hans had on her was part of it. Hans was a colorless young man, bony without being tall or strong, who tended to wipe his hands on his hair or his clothes and peer, whenever possible, into a small round tin-framed pocket mirror because he was always troubled by some new eruption of his muddy skin. But this, with the possible exception of the pocket mirror, was exactly how Gerda pictured the early Roman Christians, forgathering in their underground catacombs in defiance of their persecutors. It was not an exact correspondence of details that she meant, after all, but the basic general feeling of terror shared with the early Christian martyrs, as she saw them. Actually, she found the well-scrubbed and scented pagans more attractive, but taking sides with the Christians was a sacrifice one owed to one's character. For Gerda the lofty demands of conscience had thereby acquired a moldy, slightly revolting smell, which went perfectly with the mystical outlook Hans had opened up to her.

Ulrich was quite conversant with this outlook. We should perhaps feel indebted to spiritualism for satisfying—with its funny rappings from the Beyond so suggestive of the minds of deceased kitchen maids—that crude metaphysical craving for spooning up, if not God, then at least the spirits, like some food icily slipping down one's gullet in the dark. In earlier centuries this longing for personal contact with God or His cohorts, said to occur in a state of ecstasy, did, despite the subtle and sometimes marvelous forms it took, make for a mixture of crude earthliness with experiences of an exceptional and ineffable condition of psychic awareness. The metaphysical was thus the physical, embedded in this intuitive state, a mirror image of earthly longings, believed to reveal whatever the concepts of those times encouraged people to expect that they would see. But it is just such concepts that change with the times and lose their credibility. If nowadays anyone told a story of God speaking to him personally, seizing him painfully by the hair to lift him up to Himself, or slipping into his breast in some numinous, intensely sweet way, no one would take any of these details embodying the experience literally, least of all God's professional functionaries, who, as children of a scientific age, feel an understandable horror of being compromised by hysterical and maniacal adherents. Consequently we must either regard such experiences, of frequent and well-recorded occurrence in the Middle Ages and in classical antiquity, as delusions and pathological phenomena, or face the possibility that there is something to them, something independent of the mythical terms in which it has hitherto been expressed: a pure kernel of experience, in other words, that would have to pass strict empirical tests of credibility, whereupon it would of course become a matter of overriding importance long before anyone could deal with the next question, what conclusions to draw from this with regard to our relationship to the Beyond. And while faith based on theological reasoning is today universally engaged in a bitter struggle with doubt and resistance from the prevailing brand of rationalism, it does seem that the naked fundamental experience itself, that primal seizure of mystic insight, stripped of all the traditional, terminological husks of faith, freed from ancient religious concepts, perhaps no longer to be regarded as a religious experience at all, has undergone an immense expansion and now forms the soul of that complex irrationalism that haunts our era like a night bird lost in the dawn.

An absurd splinter of this manifold movement was in fact represented by the social circle or vortex in which Hans Sepp was playing his part. If one were to tabulate the ideas that ebbed and flowed within that company—though this would be against their principles, as they were against numbering and measuring things—the first one would have been a timid and quite Platonic call for trial or companionate marriage, in fact for the sanctioning of polygamy and polyandry; next, when it came to art, they favored the most abstract, aiming at the universal and the timeless, then called Expressionism, which disdained mere appearances or the shell, the banal externals of things, the faithful, "naturalistic" delineation of which had oddly enough been regarded as revolutionary only one generation earlier. Cheek by jowl with this abstract aim of capturing the essential vision of the mind and the world, without bothering about externals, there was also a taste for the down-to-earth and limited kind of art, the so-called regional and folk arts, the promotion of which these young people regarded as a sacred duty to their Pan-Germanic souls; these and others were just some of the choice straws and grasses picked up beside the road of time to be woven into a nest for the human spirit, most particularly the most luxuriant ideas of the rights, duties, and creative promise of the young, which played so great a role that they must be considered in more detail.

The present era, they argued, was blind to the rights of young peo-

604 · THE MAN WITHOUT QUALITIES

ple; a person had virtually no rights until he or she had come of age. Fathers, mothers, or guardians could dress, house, feed such a person as they liked, reprimand or punish and even, according to Hans Sepp, wreck the child's life, so long as they did not overstep some far-off provision of the law, which granted to a child no more protection than it did to a domestic animal. The child is owned by its parents as a chattel and is, by virtue of its economic dependence on them, a piece of property, a capitalist object. This "capitalist dehumanization of the child," which Hans had picked up somewhere in his reading and then elaborated for himself, was the first lesson he taught his astonished disciple, Gerda, who had until then felt quite well taken care of at home. Christianity had somewhat lightened the wife's yoke, but not that of the daughter, who was condemned to vegetate at home by being forcibly kept away from real life. After this prelude, he indoctrinated her in the child's right to educate itself according to the laws of its own personality. The child was creative, it was growth personified and constantly engaged in creating itself. The child was regal by nature, born to impose its ideas, feelings, and fantasies on the world; oblivious to the ready-made world of accidentals, it made up its own ideal world. It had its own sexuality. In destroying creative originality by stripping the child of its own world, suffocating it with the dead stuff of traditional learning, and training it for specific utilitarian functions alien to its nature, the adult world committed a barbaric sin. The child was not goal-oriented—it created through play, its work was play and tender growth; when not deliberately interfered with, it took on nothing that was not utterly absorbed into its nature; every object it touched was a living thing; the child was a world, a cosmos unto itself, in touch with the ultimate, the absolute, even though it could not express it. But the child was killed by being taught to serve worldly purposes and being chained to the vulgar routines so falsely called reality! So said Hans Sepp. He was all of twenty-one when he brought his doctrines to the House of Fischel, and Gerda was no younger. In addition, Hans had been fatherless for a long time by then, and felt free at all times to bully his mother, who was supporting him and the rest of her children by keeping a small shop, so that there seemed to be no direct cause for his philosophy of the child as helpless victim of tyranny.

Gerda, absorbing these teachings of Hans, accordingly wavered between a mild pedagogical urge to raise a future generation in their own light, and putting them to more immediate and direct use in her war upon Leo and Clementine. Hans Sepp, however, stood more firmly on his principles and on his slogan "Let us all be children!" That he clung so fiercely to a child's embattled stance might have originated in an early craving for independence, but he basically owed it to the fact that the language of the youth movement then coming into vogue was the first that helped his soul to find its tongue, and it led him, as any true language does, from one word to the next, each word saying more than the speaker had actually intended. And so the original call for a return to childhood gave rise to the most important insights. For the child should not go counter to its nature, renouncing it for the sake of becoming a father or a mother, which means only becoming a bourgeois, a slave of this world, tied hand and foot, and turned into a "useful" object. What ages people is their social conformism; the child resists being turned into a citizen, and so the objection that a twenty-one-year-old is not supposed to behave like a child is swept away, because this struggle goes on from birth to old age and is ended only when the conventional world is overturned by the world of love. This was the higher aspect of Hans Sepp's doctrine, on all of which Ulrich had been kept informed by Gerda.

It was he who had discovered the link between what these young people called their love, or, alternatively, their community, and the consequences of a peculiar, wildly religious, unmythologically mythical (or merely infatuated) state, and it touched him deeply, though they did not know it, because he confined himself to making fun of its manifestations in them. In the same vein he now answered Hans by asking him point-blank why he would not take advantage of the Parallel Campaign for advancing the cause of his "Community of the Purely Selfless."

"Because it's out of the question," Hans replied.

The resulting conversation between them would have been as baffling to an uninitiated listener as an exchange in criminal street slang, although it was no more than the pidgin of social infatuation. So what follows is more the gist of what was said than a literal transcription of it. The Community of the Purely Selfless was what Hans called it; despite this, it was not devoid of meaning; the more selfless a person feels, the brighter and intenser the things of this world appear; the more weight a person sheds, the more he feels uplifted; everyone has probably experienced this at one time or another, though such experiences must not be confused with mere gaiety, cheerfulness, lightheartedness, or the like, which are simply substitutes for it, serving a lower or even some corrupt purpose. Perhaps the real thing should be called not a state of uplift but rather a shedding of one's armor, that armor in which the ego was encased. You had to distinguish between the two walls pressing in on the human being. Man succeeds in getting over the first rampart every time he does something kind and unselfish, but that is only the lesser rampart. The greater wall equals the selfhood of even the most unselfish person; this is original sin as such; with us, every sensation, every feeling, even that of self-surrender, is more a taking than a giving, and there is hardly any way of shaking off this armor of all-permeating selfishness. Hans ticked off specifics: Knowledge is simply the appropriation of something not our own. We kill, tear, and digest our "object" as an animal does its prey. A concept is a living thought killed, never to stir again. A conviction is an impulse of faith, frozen into some unchanging lifeless form. Research confirms the known. Character is inertia, the refusal to keep growing. To know a person amounts to no longer being moved by that person. Insight is one-way vision. Truth is the successful effort to think impersonally and inhumanly. Everywhere, the instinct to kill, to freeze, to clutch, to petrify, is a mixture of self-seeking with a cold, craven, treacherous mock-selflessness. "And when," Hans wanted to know, even though the innocent Gerda was all he had experienced, "when has love ever been anything but possession, or the giving of oneself as its quid pro quo?"

Ulrich cautiously and with qualifications professed to agree with all these none too coherent assertions. He allowed that even suffering and renunciation yielded a slight profit for the ego; a faint, as it were grammatical cast of egotism shadowed all we did as long as there was no predicate without a subject.

But Hans would have none of that! He and his friends argued endlessly about the right way to live. Sometimes they assumed that everyone had to live first and foremost for himself and only then for all the others; or else they agreed that a person could have only one true friend, who, however, needed his own one friend, so that they saw the community as a circular linking of souls, like the spectrum or other chains of being; but what they most liked to believe was that there was such a thing as a communal soul; it might be overshadowed by the forces of egotism, but it was a deep, immense source of vital energy, its potential unimaginable and waiting to be tapped. A tree fighting for its life in the sheltering forest cannot feel more unsure of itself than sensitive people nowadays feel about the dark warmth of the mass, its dynamism, the invisible molecular process of its unconscious cohesion, reminding them with every breath they take that the greatest and the least among them are not alone. Ulrich felt the same. While he perceived clearly that the tamed egotism on which life is built makes for an orderly structure, compared with which the single breath of all mankind is no more than the quintessence of murky thinking, and while for his part he preferred keeping to himself, he could not help feeling oddly moved when Gerda's young friends talked in their extravagant fashion of the great wall that had to be surmounted.

Hans now reeled off the articles of his faith in a drone interspersed with bursts of vehemence, his eyes staring straight ahead without seeing anything. An unnatural crack ran through the cosmos, breaking it in two like the two halves of an apple, which consequently start to shrivel up. Which was why, nowadays, we had to regain by artificial and unnatural means what had once been a natural part of ourselves. But this split could be healed by opening up the self, by a change of attitude, for the more a person could forget himself, blot himself out, get away from himself, the more his energy could be freed for the common good, as though released from a bad chemical combination; and the closer he drew to the community, the more he would realize his true self, because, as Hans saw it, true originality was not a matter of empty uniqueness but came from opening oneself up, degree by degree, to participation and devotion, perhaps all the way to the ultimate degree of total communion with the world achieved by those dissolved in selflessness.

These propositions so devoid of content set Ulrich to wondering how they might possibly be substantiated, but all he did was to ask Hans coolly just how all this opening up of one's self and so forth might be done in actual practice.

Hans came up with some prodigious words for it: the transcendent

ego in place of the sensual ego, the Gothic ego instead of the naturalistic one, the realm of being rather than the realm of phenomena or
appearances, the unconditional experience, and similar formidable
expressions, which had to do duty for his sense of the indescribable
reality he envisioned, as they all too often must, incidentally, to the
detriment of the cause they somehow manage to enhance nonetheless. And because this condition of which he had occasional, perhaps
even frequent, glimpses never stayed in focus for more than a few
brief instants of meditation, he went even further and claimed that
transcendence nowadays simply did not manifest itself other than
sporadically, in flashes of an extracorporeal vision that was naturally
hard to pin down, except perhaps in the traces it left in great works of
art, which led him on to the symbol, his favorite word both for art
and for other supernaturally towering signs of life, and finally to the
Germanic gift, peculiar to those who carried even a smattering of
Germanic blood in their veins, for creating and envisioning said
things. Using this sublime variant of "good old days" nostalgia made
it easy for him to suggest that a lasting perception of the essence of
things was a thing of the past and denied to the present time, an assertion from which the whole debate had after all sprung.

Ulrich found this superstitious claptrap rather irritating. He had
been wondering for a long time what it was that Gerda actually saw in
Hans. There she sat, with her pale look, taking no active part in the
conversation. Hans Sepp had a grandiose theory of love, in which she
probably found the deeper meaning of her own existence. Ulrich
now gave the conversation a new turn by stating—not without a protest against having to carry on this kind of talk in the first place—that
the highest intensity of feeling of which a person was capable did not
arise out of one's usual egotistical appropriation of whatever came
one's way or, as Hans and his friends felt, out of what is called self-
enhancement through self-surrender, but was actually a state of rest,
of changelessness, like still waters.

At this Gerda brightened up and asked what he meant.

Ulrich told her that Hans had actually been talking all this time,
even when he went out of his way to disguise it, about love and nothing but love; saintly love, solitary love, the love that overflows its
banks of desire, the love always described as a loosening, a dissolu-

tion, indeed a reversal of all earthly bonds, in any case no longer a
mere emotion but a transformation of a person's whole way of thinking and perceiving.

Gerda looked at him as though she were trying to decide whether
this man who knew so much more than she did had somehow discovered this too, or whether this man she was secretly in love with and
who sat beside her without revealing much of himself was emitting
some strange sympathetic radiation that draws two people together
even when their bodies do not touch.

Ulrich felt her probing look. It was as though he were speaking
some foreign tongue in which he could go on fluently, but only superficially, because the words had no roots inside him.

"In this state," he said, "in which one oversteps the limits normally
imposed on one's actions, one understands everything, because the
soul accepts only what is already part of it; in a sense, it already knows
all that's coming its way. Lovers have nothing new to say to each
other; nor do they actually recognize each other; all that a lover
recognizes is the indescribable way in which he is inwardly activated
by the beloved. To recognize a person he does not love means drawing that person into the sphere of his love like a blank wall with the
sunlight on it. To recognize some inanimate object doesn't mean de
coding its characteristics one by one; it means that a veil falls away or
a barrier is lifted, somewhere beyond the world of the senses. Even
the inanimate, unknown as it is, enters trustfully into the shared life
of lovers. Nature and the spirit peculiar to love gaze into each other's
eyes, two versions of the same act, a flowing in two directions, a
burning at both ends. Awareness of a person or thing apart from oneself then becomes impossible, for to take notice is to take something
from the things noticed; they keep their shape but turn to ashes inside; something evaporates from them, leaving only their mummies.
For lovers there is no such thing as a truth—it could only be a blind
alley, the finish, the death of something that, while it lives, is like the
breathing edge of a flame, where light and darkness lie breast-to-
breast. How can any one thing light up, in recognition, where all is
light? Who needs the beggarly small change of security and proof
where everything spills over in superabundance? And how can one
still want anything for oneself alone, even the beloved itself, once

one knows how those who love no longer belong to themselves but must give themselves freely, four-eyed intertwined creatures that they are, to everything that comes their way?"

Anyone who has mastered the idiom can run on in this vein without even trying. It is like walking with a lighted candle that sheds its tender rays on one aspect of life after another, all of them looking as if their usual appearance in the hard light of common day had been a crude misrepresentation. How impossible it becomes, for instance, to apply that verbal gesture "to possess" to lovers, once one remembers the etymology (from *potis* and *sedere*, i.e., *pos-sess* equals "to sit upon," "be-set"). Does it show desires of a higher order, to aim at "pos-sessing" principles, the respect of one's children, ideas, oneself? But this clumsy ploy of a heavy animal subduing its prey with the full weight of its own body is still, and rightly, the basic and favorite term of capitalism, showing the connection between the possessors of the social world and the possessors of knowledge and skills, which is what it makes of its thinkers and artists, while love and asceticism stand apart in their lonely kinship. How aimless this pair appears, how devoid of a target, compared with the aims and targets of normal life. But the terms "aim" and "target" derive from the language of the marksman. To be without aim or target must have meant, originally, not to be out to kill. So merely by tracking down the clues in language itself—a blurred, but revealing trail!—one can see how a crudely changed meaning has everywhere usurped the function of far subtler messages now quite lost to us, that ever-perceptible but never quite tangible nexus of things. Ulrich gave up pursuing this idea out loud, but Hans could not be blamed for thinking that all he had to do was tug at a certain thread to unravel the whole fabric; the world had merely lost its instinct for the right thread to pull. He had been repeatedly interrupting Ulrich and finishing his sentences for him.

"If you choose to look at all this with a scientific eye, you'll see nothing more in it than any bank teller might. All empirical explanations are deceptive, they never take us beyond the level of crude sensory data. Your need to know would like to reduce the world to nothing more than the so-called forces of nature twiddling their thumbs." These were Hans's objections, his interpolations. He alternated between rudeness and passion. He felt that he had done a poor job of stating his case, and blamed his failure on the presence of this interloper between him and Gerda, for had he been alone with Gerda, eye-to-eye with her, the same words would have risen sky ward like a shimmering fountain, like spiraling falcons. He knew it, he felt that this was one of his days. He was also surprised and annoyed to hear Ulrich talking so fluently and so intently in his place.

Actually, Ulrich was not speaking as a scientist at all but was saying far more than he would have been prepared to defend, although he was not saying anything he did not believe. He was carried away by a suppressed fury. To run on like this he had to be in a curiously elevated, a rather inflamed frame of mind, and Ulrich's mood was somewhere between this state and the one induced by seeing Hans, with his greasy, bristling hair, his muddy skin, his repellent emphatic gestures, and his foaming torrent of speech in which some filmy fragment of his true self hung trapped, like the skin from a flayed heart. But strictly speaking, Ulrich had been suspended all his life between two such aspects of this subject, always ready to expound it as he was doing, half believing what he was saying but never going beyond such verbal games, because he did not really take them for real, and so his discomfiture was keeping step with his pleasure in this conversation.

Gerda ignored the mocking asides that he injected into his talk from time to time as a kind of self-parody, overwhelmed as she was by her sense of his opening himself up at last. She looked at him with a touch of anxiety. He's much softer than he'll ever admit, she thought, with a feeling that broke down her own defenses, as if a baby were groping at her breast. Ulrich caught her eye. He knew almost everything that was going on between her and Hans, because in her worry she needed to relieve her heart by at least throwing out hints of her problems, and that made it easy enough for Ulrich to fill in the rest. She and Hans regarded the act of physical possession, the normal preoccupation of young lovers, as a despicable surrender to capitalist urges; they thought they despised physical passion altogether, but they also despised self-control as a middle-class virtue, so what it came to was their always clinging to each other in a nonphysical or semiphysical way. They tried to "accept" each other, as they called it, and felt that trembling, tender merging of two people lost in each other's eyes, slipping into the invisible currents that ripple through each other's heads and hearts, and feeling, at the apparent moment of mutual understanding, that each holds the other inside himself and is at one with the other. At less exalted times they were satisfied with ordinary mutual admiration, seeing in great paintings or dramatic scenes the parallels to their own condition and marveling, when they kissed, at the thought that—as the saying goes—millennia were gazing down upon them. They did kiss, even though they regarded the crude physical sensations of love, that spasm of the bodily self, as no better than a stomach cramp, but their limbs did not pay too much attention to their ideals and pressed hard against each other on their own. Afterward they both felt bewildered. Their budding philosophy was not proof against their heady sense of nobody watching, the dim lights, the furiously mounting attraction of two young bodies nestling close together, and Gerda especially, who as the girl was the more mature of the two, felt the craving to consummate their embrace with the innocent intensity a tree might feel on being prevented from budding in the springtime. This arrested lovemaking, as bland as the kisses of little children and as interminable as the aimless fondlings of the old, always left them feeling shattered. Hans found it easier to take because he could always regard it afterward as a successful test of his convictions.

"It isn't for us to have and to hold," he lectured her. "We are nomads who must keep moving onward, step after step." And when he noticed that Gerda's whole body was quivering with frustrated desire, he made no bones about calling it a weakness, if not actually a residue of her non-Germanic genes, and felt like Adam walking with his God, his manly heart having once more resisted his erstwhile rib's tempting of his faith. At such moments Gerda despised him. Which was probably why she had told Ulrich so much about it, at least in the beginning. She suspected that a full-grown man would do both more and less than Hans, who would bury his tear-stained face in her lap like a child after he had insulted her. Since she was just as proud of her experiences as she was bored with them, she let Ulrich in on all this in the anxious hope that he would find something to say that would put an end to the agonizing beauty of it.

Ulrich, however, seldom spoke to her as she wished he might; instead, he cooled her off with his sardonic tone, because even though it made Gerda more reserved, he knew too well that she longed to submit to him, and that neither Hans nor anyone else had the power over her mind he could have if he chose. He justified himself with the thought that any other real man in his place would have the same effect on Gerda, that of a blessed relief after that woolly-minded dirty little tease Hans. But even as he was thinking it over, suddenly seeing it all in perspective, Hans had collected himself and started a fresh attack.

"All in all," he said, "you've made the biggest possible mistake by trying to express as a concept something that occasionally elevates an idea somewhat above the level of the merely conceptual. But I suppose that's what makes the difference between one of you intellectual people and the likes of us. First," he added proudly, "one must learn to live it before one can, perhaps, learn to think it." When Ulrich smiled at this, he flashed out like a bolt of lightning: "Jesus was a seer at the age of twelve, without first getting his doctorate."

This provoked Ulrich into breaking the silence he owed to Gerda by giving Hans a piece of advice that betrayed his knowledge of facts he could have learned only from her. "I don't know why," he said, "if you want to live it, you don't go all the way. I would take Gerda in my arms, forget all the qualms of my rational mind, and keep her locked in my arms until our bodies either crumbled to ashes or became transformed into the fullness of their own being in a way that is beyond our power of comprehension!"

Hans, feeling a stab of jealousy, looked not at him but at Gerda, who turned pale with embarrassment. Ulrich's words about locking her in his arms had touched her like a secret promise. At the moment she didn't care at all how "the other life" was to be imagined, and she felt sure that Ulrich would do everything just as it should be done, if he really wanted to. Hans, incensed at Gerda's betrayal, argued against Ulrich's proposal, which could not be carried out successfully, he said, because the time was not ripe. The first souls to take flight would have to take off from a mountain, just like the first airplanes, and not from the lowlands of a period like the present. Perhaps there must first come a man who would release mankind from its bondage before it could achieve the heights. It was not unthinkable that he might be the man himself, but that was his own affair, and apart from this, the present low level of spiritual development was incapable of producing such a man.

Now Ulrich remarked on the proliferation of redeemers these

days—indeed, every self-respecting chairman of a social club seemed to be eligible. If Christ were to come again tomorrow, he would certainly fare worse than the first time. The better newspapers and book clubs would find him vulgar, and the great international press would hardly be likely to welcome him to its columns.

With this they were back where they had started, the discussion had come full circle, and Gerda sank back into herself.

Yet something had changed; without giving any outward sign of it, Ulrich had tripped himself up a little. His thoughts had parted company with his words. He looked at Gerda. Her body was angular, her skin looked dull and tired. That faint breath of old-maidishness that hung over her had suddenly become apparent to him, although it had probably always been the major factor holding him back from ever coming to the point with this girl who was in love with him. Of course, Hans also had something to do with it, what with the semiphysical nature of his communal utopia, which had an old-maidish quality of its own. Ulrich did not feel attracted to Gerda, but even so he was inclined to continue his dialogue with her. This reminded him that he had invited her to come to see him. She gave no sign of either remembering this invitation or of having forgotten it, and he got no opportunity to ask her about it privately. It left him with an uneasy sense of regret as well as of relief, such as one feels when one skirts a danger recognized too late.

114

THINGS ARE COMING TO A BOIL. ARNHEIM IS
GRACIOUS TO GENERAL STUMM. DIOTIMA
PREPARES TO MOVE OFF INTO INFINITY.
ULRICH DAYDREAMS ABOUT LIVING ONE'S
LIFE AS ONE READS A BOOK

His Grace had urged Diotima to find out about the famous Makart pageant, which had brought all Austria together in the 1870s in a burst of national fervor; he still had vivid memories of the richly draped carriages, the heavily caparisoned horses, the trumpeters, and the pride people took in their medieval costumes, which lifted them out of their humdrum daily lives. It was this that had brought Diotima, Arnheim, and Ulrich to go through the materials on the period at the Imperial Library, from which they were now emerging together. As Diotima, her lip curling with disdain, had predicted to His Grace, what they had come up with was quite impossible; such frippery could no longer make people forget the monotony of their existence. They were still on the library stairs when the beauty informed her companions that she felt like making the most of the sunny day and the year 1914—which in the few weeks of its existence had already left the moldering past so far behind—by walking home. But they had no sooner stepped out into the light of day when they bumped into the General, on his way in. Proud to be discovered on such a mission of high learning, he instantly offered to turn back and enlarge Diotima's entourage by joining it. This made Diotima realize after only a few steps that she was tired and wanted a cab. With no such vehicle in sight, they all stopped in front of the library, which faced a trough-shaped rectangular square, three sides of which were formed by splendid ancient façades, while on the fourth the asphalt street in front of a long, low palace shimmered like an ice rink, with cars and carriages rushing past, none of which responded to the four people waving and signaling to them like survivors of a shipwreck, until they tired of it and forgot about giving anything but the occasional halfhearted signal in the direction of the traffic.

Arnheim had a big book under his arm. He was pleased with this gesture, both condescending and respectful toward the life of the mind. He greeted the General eagerly: "How nice to see you coming to the library too; men of position nowadays so seldom seek out the life of the mind in its own house."

General Stumm replied that he was quite at home in this library.

Arnheim was impressed. "Almost all we have nowadays is writers, and hardly anyone who reads books anymore," he went on. "Do you realize, General, how many books are printed annually? I think it's over a hundred books a day published in Germany alone. Over a thousand periodicals are founded every year. The whole world is writing! Everyone helps himself to ideas as though they were his own, all the time. Nobody feels any responsibility toward the situation as a whole. Ever since the Church lost its influence, there is no central authority to stem our general chaos. There is no educational model, no educational principle. In these circumstances it is only natural that feeling and morality should drift without an anchor, and the most stable person begins to waver."

The General felt his mouth turning dry. It wasn't as though Dr. Arnheim was actually addressing him in person; he was a man standing in the square and thinking out loud. The General thought of how many people talk to themselves in the street, on their way to somewhere; civilians, of course, because a soldier who did such a thing would be locked up, and an officer would be sent to the psychiatric clinic. Stumm felt embarrassed at the thought of standing there philosophizing in public, as it were, smack-dab in the middle of the Imperial Residential capital. Apart from the two men, there seemed to be only one other, a mute figure of bronze standing on a stone pedestal in the sunny square. The General had only just noticed this monument and did not remember whom it represented, so that he had to apologize for his ignorance when Arnheim asked him.

"And to think that he was put here to be venerated," the great man remarked. "But that's how it is. Every moment of our lives we move among institutions, problems, and challenges of which we have barely caught the tail end, so that the present is constantly reaching into the past. We keep crashing through the floor, if I may put it so, into the cellars of time, even while we imagine ourselves to be occupying the top floor of the present."

Arnheim smiled. He was making conversation. His moving lips flickered in the sunshine, and the lights in his eyes kept changing like those on a signaling steamer. Stumm was growing uneasy; he found it hard to keep acknowledging so many and such unusual turns in the conversation while being served up to the world, in full uniform, on this platter of a square. Grass was growing in the cracks between the cobblestones; it was last year's grass but looked implausibly fresh, like a corpse left lying in the snow; it was, in fact, most peculiar and disturbing that grass should be growing here between the stones, when only a few steps farther on the asphalt was being polished, in keeping with the times, by the passing cars. The General began to be troubled by a nervous fear that if he had to go on listening much longer he might suddenly go down on his knees and eat grass in front of the whole world, without knowing why. He looked around for Ulrich and Diotima for protection.

These two had taken shelter where a thin veil of shade had spun itself around the corner of the wall, and seemed to be involved in an argument, though their voices were too low to be understood.

"You make it sound hopeless," Diotima was saying.

"What do you mean?" Ulrich asked, without real interest.

"There is still such a thing as individuality."

Ulrich tried to catch her eye sideways. "Good heavens, we've been all over this already."

"You have no heart, or you wouldn't always talk like this," she said softly. The sun-heated air was rising from the stone pavement up between her legs, which were encased in long skirts like those of a robed statue, inaccessible and to all intents nonexistent. She showed no awareness of it. It was a caress that had nothing to do with anyone, any man. Her eyes turned pale, but that might have been merely the effect of her reserve in a situation where she was exposed to the glances of the passersby. Turning to Ulrich, she said with an effort:

"When a woman has to choose between duty and passion, what can she rely on if not her character?"

"You don't have to choose," Ulrich replied.

"You go too far; I wasn't speaking of myself," his cousin whispered.

As he did not reply, they both stared across the square for a while in a hostile silence. Then Diotima asked: "Do you think that what we call our soul might emerge from the shadows where it usually keeps itself?"

Ulrich gave her a puzzled look.

"In the case of unusual, specially gifted persons," she added.

"Am I to understand that you're interested in establishing a rapport with the Beyond?" Ulrich asked incredulously. "Has Arnheim introduced you to a medium?"

Diotima was disappointed in him. "I would never have thought you capable of such a misunderstanding," she said reproachfully. "When I speak of emerging from the shadows, I mean from the unreality, from that flickering concealment in which we sometimes sense the presence of the unusual. It is spread out like a net that torments us because it will neither hold us nor let us go. Don't you think that there have been times when it was otherwise? When the inner life was a stronger presence, when there were individuals who walked in the light or, as people used to say, walked in holiness, and miracles could happen in reality because they *are* an ever-present form of another reality, and nothing else!"

Diotima surprised herself by the firmness with which it seemed possible to say this sort of thing, without any special elation, as though she were walking on solid ground. Ulrich felt secretly infuriated, but actually he was deeply shocked. Has it come to this, he thought, that this giant hen can talk the way I do? Again he saw Diotima's soul in the shape of a colossal chicken pecking at his own soul, in the shape of a little worm. He was seized by the primal childhood terror of the giantess, mixed with another strange sensation; there was a certain gratification in being spiritually consumed, as it were, in mindless accord with a kinswoman. Their unanimity was a silly coincidence, of course; he did not believe that there was any magic in being related by blood, nor could he possibly have taken his cousin seriously even if he were dead drunk. But he had been changing lately, mellowing perhaps; his characteristic inner readiness to move to the attack was giving way to a need for tenderness, dreams, kinship, whatever, which also manifested itself in sudden outbreaks of the ill will that was its opposite.

Which prompted him to make fun of his cousin now: "If that's how you feel," he said, "then you ought to go all the way and become Arnheim's lover, openly or in secret, as soon as possible."

"You shouldn't say such things; I've given you no right!" Diotima rebuked him.

"But I must speak of it. Until now I wasn't sure what was going on between you and Arnheim. But now I understand, and you look to me like a person who is seriously thinking of flying to the moon. I would never have thought you capable of such madness."

"I've told you that I'm capable of going to extremes." Her upward gaze was meant to be audacious, but the sun made her screw up her eyes, so that she seemed to be twinkling at him.

"These are the ravings of starved love," Ulrich said, "which pass off when hunger is appeased." He wondered what Arnheim's plans might be with regard to her. Did he regret his proposal, and was he covering his retreat by putting on some sort of act? But then he could simply leave and not come back; a man who had been in business all his life would surely have the necessary callousness for that? He remembered noticing certain signs in Arnheim that indicated passion in an older man; his face was sometimes a grayish yellow, slack and tired, like a room with the bed still unmade at noon. The most likely explanation was the havoc caused by two almost equally strong passions fighting each other to a standstill. But since he was incapable of imagining the passion for power in the degree to which it ruled Arnheim, he could not conceive of the measures love had to take in order to fight it.

"You're an odd sort of man," Diotima said. "Always different from what one would expect. Wasn't it you who spoke to me of seraphic love?"

"You regard that as a possibility?" Ulrich asked absentmindedly.

"Not as you described it, of course."

"So Arnheim loves you seraphically?" Ulrich began to laugh softly.

"I wish you wouldn't laugh." Diotima almost hissed at him.

"You don't understand," he apologized. "It's only the excitement. You and Arnheim are sensitive people. You love poetry. I'm sure that you are sometimes touched by a breath . . . a breath of something: the question is just what that is. And now you want to get to the bottom of it, with all the thoroughness of your idealism."

"Aren't you always saying that one must be precise and thorough?" Diotima countered.

It was too much. "You're mad!" he said. "Forgive my saying so, but you are mad. And you of all people mustn't be."

Meanwhile Arnheim had been telling the General that for the last two generations the world had been undergoing the most profound revolution of all: the end of the soul was in sight.

It gave the General a stab. What the devil, here was yet another problem to think about. To be honest, he had thought until this moment, despite Diotima, that there was no such thing as the soul. At military school and in the regiment, nobody gave a hang about this kind of preacher's talk. But here was this manufacturer of guns and tanks, talking about the soul as though he could see it standing there. The General's eyes began to itch and to roll around gloomily, goggling at the translucent air around them.

But Arnheim was not waiting to be asked for particulars; words flowed from his lips, from that pale pink slit between his clipped mustache and his little pointed beard. As he phrased it, the soul had started to shrivel and age ever since the Church began to crumble, around the beginning of the bourgeois era. Since then it had lost God and all solid values and ideals until the present, when men had actually reached the point of living without morals, without principles, without real experiences, in fact.

The General could not quite see why one could not have experiences if one had no morals. Whereupon Arnheim opened the big volume bound in pigskin that he was holding, revealing an expensive facsimile of a manuscript so valuable that even a mortal of Arnheim's extraordinary standing could not be permitted to take the original out of the building. The General saw the depiction of an angel with wings spread horizontally across two pages, against a background of dark earth, golden sky, and marvelous colors layered like clouds; he was looking at a reproduction of one of the most moving and splendid of early medieval paintings, but since he did not know this, while he did know all about bird-hunting and depictions of it, he could only conclude that a creature with wings and a long neck that was neither human nor a snipe must be an aberration to which his companion wished to draw his attention.

Arnheim was pointing his finger at it and saying pensively: "Here you see what that great lady who is creating the Austrian Campaign is trying to bring back into the world. . . ."

"I see, I see," Stumm said, realizing that he had failed to appreciate this thing for what it was and that he had better watch his step.

"The great expressiveness, and with such utter simplicity," Arnheim went on, "bears witness to what our age has lost forever. What is our science compared with this? Patchwork. Our art? Extremes, without a mediating substance to hold them together. We lack the magic key to unity, and this, you see, is why I am so deeply moved by this Austrian plan to set the world an example of unification, of a shared idea, even though I do not quite believe it can be done. I am a German. Everything in the world today is loud and crude, and Germany is the loudest. In every country the people are straining themselves morning, noon, and night, whether at work or at play, but in Germany they start earlier and stop later than anywhere else. In all the world the spirit of cold calculation and brute force has lost touch with the soul, but we in Germany have the most businessmen and the strongest army in the world." He looked around the square with delight. "Here in Austria, things have not yet gone so far. The past is still with you, and the people have kept something of their original intuitiveness. If the German spirit can still be saved from rationalism, this is the only place left from which a start can be made. But I am afraid," he added with a sigh, "we can hardly succeed. A great idea nowadays encounters too much resistance; great ideas just barely help to prevent each other from being misused. We are living in a state of moral truce, as it were, armed to the teeth with ideas."

He smiled at his own joke. Then something more occurred to him: "You know, the difference between Germany and Austria we have just touched on always reminds me of billiards. Even at billiards everything goes wrong if you try to do it all by calculation instead of with feeling."

The General had guessed that he was supposed to feel flattered by the reference to a moral armed truce, and he wanted to show that he had been paying attention. He did know something about billiards, so he said, "I play snooker myself, and skittles too, but I never heard that there's a difference between the Austrian and the German styles of play."

Arnheim shut his eyes and gave it some thought. "I myself never play billiards," he said after a moment, "but I know that you can play the ball high or low, from the right or from the left; that you can strike the second ball head-on or merely graze it; that you can hit it hard or lightly, bluff a little—or a lot—and there must be many more such options. Now, if you imagine each of these elements with all their inherent gradations, you have an almost infinite number of possible combinations. To state them theoretically, I should have to take into account, besides the laws of mathematics and statics, the mechanics of solids, plus the laws of elasticity; I would have to know the coefficients of the materials, the influence of the temperature, the most precise means of measuring the coordination and gradation of my motor impulses, of estimating distances exactly, like a nonius, how to combine the various factors with better than the speed and accuracy of a slide rule, to say nothing of allowing for margins of error, fields of dispersal, and the fact that the aim, which is the correct coincidence of the two balls, is in itself not clearly definable but only a collection of barely adequate data round an average value."

Arnheim spoke slowly, and in a way that compelled attention, as though pouring a liquid drop by drop from a vial to a glass; he did not spare his interlocutor a single detail.

"And so you see," he continued, "that I should need to have all the qualities, and do all the things, I cannot possibly have and do. You must be enough of a mathematician to see that it would take a lifetime to plan a single carom shot in that fashion; it boggles the mind! And yet I step up to the table with a cigarette between my lips, a tune in my ear, and my hat on, as it were, and hardly bothering to look over the board, I take my cue to the ball and the problem is solved! General, this is the sort of thing that happens all the time in real life. You are not only an Austrian, you are a military man, so you're bound to understand me: politics, honor, war, art, all the crucial processes of life, take place beyond the scope of the conscious rational mind. Man's greatness is rooted in the irrational. Even we businessmen don't really operate by calculation—not the leading men, that is. The little fellows may have to count their pennies; we learn to regard our really successful moves as a mystery that defies analysis. A man who doesn't care deeply about feeling, morality, religion, music, poetry, form, discipline, chivalry, generosity, candor, tolerance—believe me, such a man will never make a businessman of real stature. This is why

I have always admired the military, especially the Austrian military, based as it is on age-old traditions, and I am truly delighted that Frau Tuzzi can count on your support. It is a relief to me to know it. Your influence, with that of our younger friend, is extremely important. All great things rest on the same principles; great obligations are a blessing, General."

To his own surprise he suddenly found himself spontaneously shaking Stumm's hand, then he ended by saying: "Hardly anyone realizes that true greatness has no rational basis; I mean to say, everything strong is simple."

Stumm von Bordwehr held his breath; he was not sure he understood a word of it all, and wished he could rush back into the library and spend hours reading up on all these points that the great man had paid him the compliment of making to him. At last, out of this March gale whirling in his mind, there came a piercing ray of lucidity. What the hell, he thought, this fellow wants something from me! He looked up. Arnheim was still holding the book in both hands but was now turning his attention seriously to hailing a cab. His face was slightly flushed with animation, like that of a man who has just been trading ideas with another. The General was silent, like a man awed by a portentous thought. If Arnheim wanted something from him, then General Stumm was free to want something from Arnheim too, to the advantage of His Majesty's service. This perception opened such vistas of possibility that Stumm put off thinking about just what it all really meant. But if the angel in the book had suddenly lifted up a wing to give clever General Stumm a glimpse of what was hidden underneath, the General could not have felt more bewildered and overjoyed.

Over in Diotima's and Ulrich's corner, the following question had meanwhile been posed: Should a woman in Diotima's difficult position make a gesture of renunciation, or let herself be swept into adultery, or take a third, mixed course, such as belonging physically to one man and spiritually to another, or perhaps physically to neither? For this third solution there was as yet no libretto, as it were, only some great harmonic chords. Diotima still wanted it understood that she was absolutely not speaking of herself but speaking only of "a woman"—every time Ulrich tried to fuse the two together he got a warning glance from her.

And so he also chose a devious course. "Have you ever seen a dog?" he asked. "You only think you have. What you see is only something you feel more or less justified in regarding as a dog. It isn't a dog in every respect, and always has some personal quality no other dog has. So how can we ever hope, in this life, to do 'the right thing'? All we can do is something that's never *the* right thing and is always both more and less than that. Has a tile ever fallen off the roof in precise accord with the law of falling bodies? Never. Even in the lab, things never behave just as they should. They diverge from the ideal course in all possible directions, while we keep up a fiction that this is to be blamed on our faulty execution of the experiment, and that somewhere midway a perfect result is obtainable.

"Or else you find certain stones, and because of the properties they have in common they are all regarded as diamonds. But suppose one of them comes from Africa and another from Asia, one is dug out of the ground by a black man and the other by an Oriental. What if these differences in circumstances were to matter so much that they cancel out what the objects have in common? In the equation 'diamond plus circumstances is still diamond,' the use value of the diamond is so great that it makes the value of the circumstances negligible. But it's possible to imagine spiritual circumstances in which the situation is reversed.

"Everything partakes of the universal and also has something special all its own. Everything is both true to type and refuses to conform to type and is in a category all its own, simultaneously. The personal quality of any given creature is precisely that which doesn't coincide with anything else. I once said to you that the more truth we discover, the less of the personal is left in the world, because of the longtime war against individuality that individuality is losing. By the time everything has been rationalized, there's no telling how much of us will be left. Nothing at all, possibly, but then, when the false significance we attach to personality has gone, we may enter upon a new kind of significance as if embarking upon a splendid adventure.

"So how do you decide? Should 'a woman' go by the law? Then she may as well go by the laws of society. Conventional morality is a perfectly valid average and collective value, to be literally adhered to, without deviations, wherever it is acknowledged. But no individual case can be decided on moral grounds alone; morality is irrelevant to it in the precise degree that it shares in the inexhaustible nature of the universe."

"That was quite a speech," Diotima said. She took a certain satisfaction in the loftiness of discourse being imposed upon her, but intended to gain the upper hand by not talking in equally wild generalities. "But what is a woman to do, given the circumstances, in real life?"

"Let things happen," Ulrich answered.

"What things?"

"Whatever happens. Her husband, her lover, her renunciation, her mixed feelings."

"Do you have any idea what you are saying?" Diotima asked, feeling painfully reminded of how her high resolve possibly to give up Arnheim had its wings clipped every night by the mere fact that she slept in Tuzzi's bed. Ulrich must have sensed some of this, because he asked her bluntly: "Would you try your luck with me?"

"With you?" Diotima drawled, then decided to save face by taking a humorous tack. "If this is an offer, just what is it you have in mind?"

"I'll tell you," Ulrich replied seriously. "You read a great deal, don't you?"

"Of course."

"What is it you do, then? I'll tell you: You leave out whatever doesn't suit you. As the author himself has done before you. Just as you leave things out of your dreams or fantasies. By leaving things out, we bring beauty and excitement into the world. We evidently handle our reality by effecting some sort of compromise with it, an in-between state where the emotions prevent each other from reaching their fullest intensity, graying the colors somewhat. Children who haven't yet reached that point of control are both happier and unhappier than adults who have. And yes, stupid people also leave things out, which is why ignorance is bliss. So I propose, to begin with, that we try to love each other as if we were characters in a novel who have met in the pages of a book. Let's in any case leave off all the fatty tissue that plumps up reality."

Diotima felt called upon to argue the case; she wanted to direct the conversation away from this too-personal vein, and she also wanted to show that she understood something of the problems that had been touched upon.

"All well and good," she said, "but art is supposed to afford us a vacation from reality, so that we can return to it with our energies restored."

"And I am opinionated enough to say that there should be no time off," her cousin retorted. "What sort of a life is it that we have to drill holes in it called holidays; would we punch holes in a painting because it makes too strenuous demands on our sense of beauty? Should we look forward to taking time off from eternal bliss in the next world? Even the thought of time taken off my life by having to sleep sometimes seems unacceptable to me."

"Ah, there it is." Diotima seized her opportunity. "You see how unnatural it all is, what you're saying. What human being doesn't need to rest and take a break? It's a perfect illustration of the difference between you and Arnheim. Yours is a mind that will not acknowledge the shadow on things, the dark side, while his has developed out of the fullness of human experience, with sunshine and shadow intermingled."

"Of course I exaggerate," Ulrich admitted coolly. "You will see it even more clearly as we go into more detail. Think of the great writers, for instance. We can model our lives *on* them, but we can't squeeze life out of them, like wine out of grapes. They have given so solid a form to what once moved them that it confronts us like pressed metal even between the lines. But what have they actually said? Nobody knows. They themselves never knew all of it at a time. They're like a field over which bees fly back and forth; they themselves are flying back and forth, as it were. Their thoughts and feelings show all the gradations between truth and even error, as can be demonstrated if necessary, and changeable natures that come close to us at will and then elude us when we try to observe them closely.

"There is no detaching an idea in a book from its context on the page. It catches our eye like the face of a person looming up in a crowd as it is being swept past us. I suppose I'm exaggerating a little again, but tell me, what happens in our lives that is any different from this? Leaving the precise, measurable, and definable sensory data out of account, all the other concepts on which we base our lives are no more than congealed metaphors. Take as simple a concept as manliness, and think how it keeps wavering among its many possible variants. It's like a breath that changes shape at every exhalation, with nothing to hold on to, no firm impression, no logic. So when we simply leave out in art whatever doesn't suit us and our conceptions, we're merely going back to the original condition of life itself."

"My dear friend," Diotima said, "you don't seem to be talking about anything in particular." Ulrich had paused for a moment, and her words fell into that pause.

"Yes, I suppose so. I hope I haven't been talking too loudly."

"You've been talking fast, in a low voice, and at length," she said, with a touch of sarcasm. "Without saying a word of what you meant to say. Do you realize what you've just explained to me all over again? That reality should be abolished! It's true that when I heard you make this point the first time, on one of our trips into the country, I think, it made a lasting impression—I don't know why. But how this is to be done is something you haven't yet revealed, I'm sorry to say."

"Clearly, I'd have to go on talking for at least as long again to do so. But do you really expect it to be that simple? If I'm not mistaken, you spoke of wanting to fly away with Arnheim into some kind of transcendent state. Something you regard as another kind of reality. What I have been saying, on the other hand, is that we must try to recover unreality. Reality no longer makes sense."

"Oh, Arnheim would hardly agree with you there," Diotima said.

"Of course not. That's just the difference between him and me. He is trying to make the fact that he eats, sleeps, is the great Arnheim, and doesn't know whether to marry you or not, mean something, and to this end he has been collecting all the treasures of the mind throughout his life." Ulrich suddenly paused, and the silence lengthened.

After a while he asked, in a different tone: "Can you explain to me why I should be having this conversation with you, of all people? Suddenly I'm reminded of my childhood. You won't believe this, but I was a good child, mild as the air on a warm moonlit night. I could fall madly in love with a dog, a pocketknife . . ." But then he left this statement unfinished too.

Diotima looked at him, wondering what he could mean. She again remembered how he had once hotly advocated "precision of feeling," while just now he was taking the opposite view. He had accused Arnheim of insufficiently clean-cut intentions, while now he favored "letting things happen." And she was troubled by the fact that Ulrich was advocating an intense emotional life without any "time off," compared with Arnheim's ambiguous suggestion never to let oneself in for single-minded hatred or *total love!* These thoughts left her uneasy.

"Do you really believe that there is such a thing as boundless feeling?" Ulrich asked her.

"Oh yes, there is such a thing as boundless emotion," Diotima said, the ground firm under her feet again.

"You see, I don't quite believe that," Ulrich said absently. "Strange how often we talk about it, but we certainly do our best to avoid it throughout our lives, as if we were afraid of drowning in it."

He noticed that Diotima was not listening. She was uneasily watching Arnheim, who was looking around for a cab.

"I'm afraid we ought to rescue him from the General," she said.

"I'll go and get a cab and take the General off your hands," Ulrich offered, and at the moment he turned to go, Diotima laid her hand on his arm and said kindly, as if to reward him for his trouble: "Any feeling that isn't boundless is worthless."

115

THE TIP OF YOUR BREAST IS LIKE
A POPPY LEAF

In accordance with the law that periods of great stability tend to be followed by violent upheavals, Bonadea, too, suffered a relapse. Her attempts to get on closer terms with Diotima had failed, and her fine scheme to get even with Ulrich by making friends with her rival, leaving Ulrich out in the cold—a fantasy she had spent much time in spinning out—had come to nothing. She had to swallow her pride and come knocking on his door again, but when she was there her beloved seemed to have arranged for constant interruptions, and her stories to account for her coming to see him again even though he did not deserve it were wasted on his impervious friendliness. She was longing to make a terrible scene but committed to behaving with absolute propriety, so that in time she came to hate herself for being so good. At night her head, heavy with unappeased cravings, sat on her shoulders like a coconut with its mat of monkeylike hair growing freakishly inside the shell, and she came close to bursting with helpless rage, like a drinker deprived of his bottle. She privately called Diotima every name she could think of, such as fraud and insufferable pompous bitch, and came up with cynical glosses on that noble femininity which was the secret of Diotima's charm. Her aping of Diotima's style, which had delighted her for a while, had now become a prison from which she broke out into an almost licentious freedom; her curling iron and mirror lost the power to turn her into an idealized image of herself, and the artificial state of mind it had supported collapsed as well. Even sleep, which Bonadea had always reveled in despite her chronic inner conflicts, sometimes kept her waiting when she had gone to bed, an experience so new to her that she thought she must be sick with insomnia, and felt what people usually feel when they are seriously ill, that her spirit was deserting her body, leaving it helpless like a wounded soldier on the battlefield. As she lay there in her vexations as if on red-hot sand, all that high-minded talk of Diotima's, which Bonadea had so admired, seemed to her infinitely beside the point, and she honestly despised it.

When she found it impossible to go to Ulrich yet again, she thought of another scheme to bring him back to his senses. It was of course the culmination of the plan that came to her first: a vision of herself effecting an entrance at Diotima's when that siren had Ulrich with her. Bonadea regarded all his visits with Diotima as transparent pretexts for carrying on their flirtation rather than actually doing something for the public good. So it was up to Bonadea to do something for the public good—and this gave her the opening gambit of her plan as well: no one was paying any attention to Moosbrugger anymore, and he was going to his doom, while all the others were pontificating about it. Bonadea never stopped to wonder that it was Moosbrugger once more who came to her rescue in her hour of need. Had she bothered to think about him at all, she would have been horrified, but all she was thinking was that if Ulrich cared so much about Moosbrugger, she would see to it that he would at least not forget the man. As she mulled over her plan, she remembered two things Ulrich had said when they were talking about the murderer: namely, that everyone had a second soul, which was always innocent; and that a responsible person could always choose to do otherwise, but an irresponsible person had no such choice. From this she somehow concluded that she wanted to be irresponsible, which would mean that she would also be innocent, which Ulrich was not, and which he needed to be, for his own salvation.

So motivated, and dressed as for a social occasion, she spent several evenings wandering up and down past Diotima's windows, and never had long to wait before they lit up along the whole front, betokening something going on inside. She had told her husband that she was invited out but would not stay too long, and in the course of a few days, while she was still trying to screw up her courage, her lies and her strolls in front of a house where she had no business to be unleashed a growing impulse that would soon drive her up those steps to the front door. What if she was seen by some acquaintance, or even by her husband if he should pass that way by chance, or what if she was noticed by the doorman, or by a policeman, who might decide to question her—the more often she went out on this expedition, the greater the risks, and the more probable that if she hesitated too long an incident would occur. Now, it was true that Bonadea had more than once slipped into doorways or places where she did not want to be seen, but on those occasions she had been fortified by the thought that it had to be; this time she was about to intrude where she was not expected and could not be sure of her reception. She felt like an assassin who has started out with none too clear an idea of what it would be like, and is then swept by circumstances into a state in which the actual pistol shot or the glitter of vitriol drops flying through the air no longer adds much to the excitement.

Without any such dramatic intentions, Bonadea nevertheless felt similarly benumbed by the time she actually found herself pressing the doorbell and walking inside. Little Rachel had slipped over to Ulrich and told him that someone was waiting out in the hall to see him, not mentioning that this someone was a heavily veiled unknown lady—who, when Rachel shut the door to the salon behind him, flung the veil back from her face. At the moment she was absolutely convinced that Moosbrugger's fate depended on her taking instant action, and she received Ulrich not like a lover plagued by jealousy, but gasping for breath like a marathon runner. With no effort, she lied that her husband had told her yesterday that Moosbrugger would soon be past saving.

"There's nothing I hate so much," she ended, "as this obscene kind of murderer. But even though it goes against my grain, I've taken the risk of being regarded as an intruder here, because you must go straight back to the lady of the house and her very influential guests and get their help if you still want to get anything done." She had no idea what she expected to come of this. Perhaps that Ulrich would be deeply moved and would thank her, then call Diotima, who would then take Bonadea into some private place to talk, away from the other guests. Or else Diotima might be drawn to the hall by the sound of voices, and Bonadea was ready to let her see that she, Bonadea, was far from being the person least qualified to take an interest in Ulrich's noble causes. Her eyes were moist and flashing, her hands trembled, her voice rose out of control. Ulrich, deeply embarrassed, smiled desperately to quiet her down and gain time while he found a way to talk her into leaving as quickly as possible. It was a ticklish situation and could have ended with Bonadea's having a screaming or crying fit, if Rachel had not come to his aid. Little Rachel had been standing close by all this time, with wide-open, shining eyes. When the beautiful stranger, trembling all over, had asked to speak to Ulrich, the maid had instantly divined the romantic nature of the affair. She managed to hear most of what was said, and the syllables of Moosbrugger's name fell on her ear like pistol shots. The sadness, passion, and jealousy throbbing in this lady's voice moved her powerfully, although she knew nothing of what was behind it. She guessed that the woman was Ulrich's mistress, and it doubled her infatuation with him. It was as though the two of them had burst into full-throated song together and made her want to lift up her own voice and join in, or do something to help. And so, with a glance enjoining secrecy, she opened a door and invited the pair into the only room not being used for the gathering this evening. It was Rachel's first conscious act of disloyalty to her mistress, and she knew what would happen if she was found out, but life was so exciting, and romantic passion such an untidy state of mind, that she had no chance to think twice about it.

When the gaslight flamed upward and Bonadea's eyes gradually took in her surroundings, her legs almost gave way under her, and her cheeks flushed red with jealousy: they were inside Diotima's bedroom. There were stockings, hairbrushes, and much else lying around, whatever is left in view when a woman must change hastily from head to foot for a big party and the maid has not had time to put things away or has left it till the next morning, as in this case, because the room was due for a thorough cleaning then anyway; on big-party evenings the bedroom was used to store furnishings from the other rooms where the space was needed. So the air was heavy with the smell of all this furniture jammed together, and of powder, soap, and scent.

"What a silly thing for the girl to do," Ulrich said with a laugh. "We can't stay here. Anyway, you shouldn't have come. There's nothing to be done for Moosbrugger."

"So I shouldn't have bothered, is that it?" Bonadea echoed him almost inaudibly. Her eyes strayed all over the place. How could the girl have even thought of taking Ulrich into the most private room in the house, she wondered in anguish, if she had not done it often before? Yet she could not bring herself to confront him with this proof of his infidelity, but chose instead to say dully: "How can you sleep in peace when such injustice is being done? I haven't been able to sleep at night, which is why I decided to come looking for you." She had turned her back on the room and stood staring out the window into the opaque, glassy darkness outside, at what might be treetops or some deep courtyard down below. Upset as she was, she had enough sense of orientation to know that she was not looking out on the street, and when she considered that here she was in her rival's bedroom, standing in a flood of light in the uncurtained window beside her faithless lover, as on a stage in front of an unseen audience, it threw her mind into turmoil. She had taken off her hat and thrown her coat back; her forehead and the warm tips of her breasts touched the cold windowpane; tenderness and tears moistened her eyes. Slowly she freed herself from the spell and turned back to her friend, but her eyes still held some of that soft, yielding darkness she had gazed into, and were deeper than she knew.

"Ulrich," she said with feeling, "you're not a bad man! You only pretend to be. You go to a lot of trouble to be as good as you can be."

These incongruously perceptive words of Bonadea's made the situation precarious again; for once, they were not the ridiculous desire of a woman to mask her body's demands for consolation with an overlay of lofty sentiment, but the beauty of that body itself claiming its right to the gentle dignity of love. Ulrich went up to her and put his arm around her shoulder; together they turned and looked into the darkness outside. A faint glimmer of light from the house was dissolving in the infinite darkness beyond so that it looked like a dense mist softening the air, and Ulrich felt as if he were staring out into a mildly chilly October night, though it was late winter; the whole city seemed wrapped in a vast woolen blanket. Then it occurred to him that one could just as well say that a woolen blanket resembled a night in October. He felt a gentle uncertainty on his skin and drew Bonadea closer.

"Will you go back to them now?" Bonadea asked.

"And save Moosbrugger from injustice? No; I don't even know whether injustice is being done to him. What do I really know about him? I saw him once, just a glimpse in a courtroom, and I've read a few things that were written about him. It's as though I had dreamed that the tip of your breast is like a poppy leaf. Does that give me the right to think it is any such thing?"

He stopped to think. So did Bonadea. He was thinking, "One human being, when you think of it, means nothing more to another one than a string of similes." Bonadea's thinking concluded with: "Come, let's get away from here."

"That's impossible," Ulrich told her. "They would wonder about my disappearance, and then if something should leak out about your coming here, it could cause quite a scandal."

Again they both fell silent, staring out the window together, into something that could have been a night in October, a night in January, a woolen blanket, sorrow, or joy, though they didn't attempt to define it.

"Why do you never do the natural next thing?" Bonadea asked.

He suddenly remembered a recent dream. He was one of those people who seldom have dreams, or at least never remember their dreams, so that it gave him a queer feeling to have this unexpected memory opening up and letting him in. In the dream, he had kept trying to cross a steep mountainside and was driven back, again and again, by violent dizzy spells. Without trying to interpret it, he now knew that the dream was about Moosbrugger, who never actually appeared in it. Since a dream image often has several meanings, it was also a physical representation of his mind's useless struggles to make some headway, as recently manifested again and again in his conversation and in his affairs, struggles that exactly resembled walking without a path to follow and being unable to get beyond a certain point. He could not help smiling at the ingenuous concreteness of the dream imagery for this: smooth rock and slippery earth underfoot, the occasional lone tree to hold on to or to aim for, the abrupt increase in the steepness of the grade as he went. He had tried and failed to make it on a higher and a lower route and was growing sick with vertigo, when he said to someone with him, Let's give it up; there's the easy road down there in the valley that everyone takes! The meaning was obvious. Incidentally, it occurred to Ulrich that the person with him might very well have been Bonadea. It was quite possible that he had also dreamed of her nipple as a poppy leaf—some unconnected thing that might, to the groping touch, easily seem broad and jagged, the dark purplish hue of a mallow, floating like a mist from some as yet unlit cranny in the dream world.

Now he experienced a moment of that special lucidity that lights up everything going on behind the scenes of oneself, though one may be far from being able to express it. He understood the relationship between a dream and what it expresses, which is no more than analogy, a metaphor, something he often thought about. A metaphor holds a truth and an untruth, felt as inextricably bound up with each other. If one takes it as it is and gives it some sensual form, in the shape of reality, one gets dreams and art; but between these two and real, full-scale life there is a glass partition. If one analyzes it for its rational content and separates the unverifiable from the verifiable, one gets truth and knowledge but kills the feeling. Like certain kinds of bacteria that split an organic substance into two parts, mankind splits the original living body of the metaphor into the firm substance of reality and truth, and the glassy unreality of intuition, faith, and artifact. There seems to be nothing in between; and yet how often a vaguely conceived undertaking does succeed, if only one goes ahead without worrying it too much! Ulrich felt that he had at last emerged from the tangle of streets through which his thoughts and moods had so often taken him, into the central square where all streets had their beginning. And he touched on all this in answering Bonadea's question as to why he never did the natural next thing. She probably did not understand his answer, but this was decidedly one of her good days; after thinking it over, she slipped her arm more firmly into his and summed it all up by saying: "Well, in your dreams you don't think either; you only live through some story or other." This was almost true. He squeezed her hand. Suddenly her eyes filled with tears again. They coursed slowly down her cheeks, and from her skin, bathed in those salty tears, there arose the indefinable scent of desire. Ulrich breathed it in and felt a great longing for this slippery nebulous state, for surrender and forgetfulness. But he pulled himself together and led her tenderly to the door. At this moment he felt sure that there was still something ahead of him and that he must not fritter it away in halfhearted attachments.

"You must go now," he said gently, "and don't be angry with me because I don't know when we can see each other again. I have a great deal to work out for myself just now."

And wonder of wonders! Bonadea put up no resistance and said nothing in anger or wounded pride. Her jealousy was gone. She felt that she was herself part of a story. She felt like taking him in her arms, guessing that he needed to be brought down to earth again, and was tempted to make the sign of the cross over his forehead for his protection, as she did with her children. It was all so romantic that it never occurred to her that it could be the end. She put on her hat and kissed him, and then she kissed him again through her veil, so that the threads seemed to glow like red-hot wires.

With the help of Rachel, who had been guarding the door and listening, Bonadea managed to slip away unseen, even though the party was breaking up and people were coming out. Ulrich pressed a big tip into Rachel's hand and complimented her on her presence of mind, making Rachel so ecstatic that her fingers unconsciously kept clutching his hand with the money. He had to laugh; when she blushed scarlet at this, he patted her on the shoulder.

116

THE TWO TREES OF LIFE AND A PROPOSAL TO ESTABLISH A GENERAL SECRETARIAT FOR PRECISION AND SOUL

That evening at the Tuzzis', there had been fewer guests than formerly; attendance at meetings of the Parallel Campaign was falling off, and people tended to leave earlier. Even the last-minute appearance of His Grace—who incidentally looked worried and preoccupied, and was in a bad mood, in fact, because he had received disturbing news about the nationalist intrigues against his work—could not prevent the party from breaking up. People lingered on for a bit in the expectation that he had brought some special news, but then, when he gave no sign of having anything of the kind to report and paid scant attention to the remaining guests, even the last of them left. By the time Ulrich reappeared, he was shocked to see the rooms almost empty. Shortly afterward only the "innermost circle" was left, joined by Section Chief Tuzzi, who had meanwhile come home.

His Grace had reverted to a favorite topic: "Of course we can regard an eighty-eight-year-old monarch of peace as a symbol; it gives us so much to think about. But it must be given a political content as well. Without that, it is only too natural for people to lose interest. In other words, as far as I am concerned, I've done all I could. The German Nationalists are furious with me for appointing Wisnieczky, whom they regard as a Slavophile, and the Slavs are furious because, as far as they're concerned, when he was in the government he was a wolf in sheep's clothing. All that only goes to show that he is a true patriot who stands above parties, and I wouldn't think of dropping him! However, we must supplement this with all possible speed on the cultural front, so that people have something positive to go on. Our public-opinion survey of what the various population sectors want is moving far too slowly. An Austrian Year or a World Year of Austria is a splendid idea, of course, but I must say that every symbol must in due course turn into something real; that is to say, I can let myself be deeply moved by a symbol without necessarily understanding it, but after a while I am bound to turn away from the mirror of my heart and get something else done, something I have meanwhile found needs doing. I wonder if I have managed to make my point? Our admirable friend the lady of the house is doing her utmost, and the discussions that have been held in this house for months have been most fruitful, I'm sure, but attendance is falling off nevertheless, and I have a feeling that we shall soon have to decide on something definite. I don't know what it will be: perhaps a second steeple on St. Stephen's, or an Imperial and Royal Colony in Africa; it doesn't matter what—it's sure to turn into something else at the last moment anyway. The main thing is to harness the inventiveness of the participants in time, before it all dribbles away."

Count Leinsdorf felt that he had spoken to the point. Arnheim now took the floor on everybody else's behalf. "What you say about the need, at times, to fructify thought by taking action, even if only pro tem, is most realistic and is true to life in general. You will be interested to know that there is a new mood, corresponding to what you say, among those of us meeting here regularly. We are no longer being swamped with an endless stream of considerations; almost no new proposals are being put forward now, and the older proposals are hardly ever mentioned, or at any rate nobody is fighting for them in any persistent way. Everyone seems to realize that in accepting the invitation to take part in this campaign he has obligated himself to come to an agreement, so that any acceptable proposal would now stand a good chance of being approved."

"And how are we coming along, my dear fellow?" said His Grace, turning to Ulrich, whom he had spotted meanwhile. "Can we see our way to winding it up?"

Ulrich had to admit that it was not so. An exchange of views can be drawn out on paper to everyone's pleasure for far longer than in person, and even the influx of proposed reforms had not abated, so that he was still founding organizations and referring them, in His Grace's name, to the various government departments whose readiness to deal with them had, however, shown a marked decline lately. This was what he had to report.

"No wonder," His Grace commented, turning to the others. "There's no dearth of patriotism among the population, but one would have to be as well informed as an encyclopedia to satisfy all the people on every point they bring up. Our government departments simply can't cope, which proves that the time has come for us to intervene from above."

"In this connection"—Arnheim spoke up again—"Your Grace might be interested to note that General von Bordwehr has been attracting increasing interest in the Council of late."

Count Leinsdorf looked at the General for the first time. "In what way?" he asked without in the least bothering to mask the rudeness of his question.

"Oh, how very embarrassing! I never intended anything of the kind," Stumm von Bordwehr demurred bashfully. "The role of the soldier in the council chamber can only be a modest one; that's always been a principle with me. But Your Grace may remember that at the very first meeting, only doing my duty as a soldier, so to speak, I suggested that if the Committee had no better idea, they might remember that our artillery has no up-to-date guns and our navy, for that matter, has no ships—not enough ships, that is, to defend the country if that should ever have to be done—"

"And?" His Grace interrupted him and shot a surprised, questioning look at Diotima that made no secret of his displeasure.

Diotima shrugged her beautiful shoulders in resignation; she had almost become hardened to the fact that wherever she might turn, the pudgy little General popped up like a nightmare, as if sponsored by some sinister forces.

"And lately, you see," Stumm von Bordwehr hastened to say before his modesty could get the better of him in the face of his success, "voices have been raised that would support such a proposal if someone were to come forward with it. It is being said, in fact, that the Army and the Navy are a concept behind which all could rally, and a great concept too, after all, and His Majesty would be pleased as well. Besides, it would be an eye-opener for the Prussians—no offense, I hope, Herr von Arnheim."

"Not at all, General. The Prussians wouldn't be at all disconcerted by it." Arnheim waved this aside with a smile. "Besides, it goes without saying that whenever such Austrian concerns come up I am simply not present, even while I most humbly take the liberty of listening in anyway. . . ."

"Well then, in any case," the General concluded, "opinions have in fact been expressed that the simplest thing would be not to keep talking much longer but to settle for a military solution. For myself, I'd be inclined to think that this could be done in combination with something else, some great civilian concept, perhaps, but as I say, it's not for a soldier to interfere, and views to the effect that nothing better is likely to come out of all this civilian thinking have just been voiced in the most intellectual quarters."

Toward the end of the General's speech, His Grace was listening with a fixed stare, and only involuntary twitchings in the direction of twiddling his thumbs, which he could not quite suppress, betrayed the strain of his painful inner workings.

Section Chief Tuzzi, whose voice was not usually heard on these occasions, now slipped in a comment, speaking slowly and in a low tone: "I don't believe the Ministry of Foreign Affairs would have any objections."

"Aha, so the departments have been in touch on this subject already?" Count Leinsdorf asked ironically, in a tone betraying his irritation. Unshaken, Tuzzi replied affably: "Your Grace is joking. The War Department would sooner welcome universal disarmament than have any truck with the Ministry of Foreign Affairs." He went on to tell a little story. "Your Grace must have heard about the fortifications in the southern Tyrol that have been built during the last ten years at the insistence of the Chief of the General Staff. They are said to be perfectly splendid, quite the latest thing. They have of course also been equipped with electrically charged barbed wire and huge searchlights that get their current from underground diesel engines; no one could say that we're behind the times in this. The only trouble is that the engines were ordered by the Artillery, and the fuel is pro-

vided by the War Ministry's Department of Works, according to regulations, which is why the fortifications can't be made operational,
because the two authorities can't agree on whether the match that
has to be used to start the engine should be regarded as fuel and
supplied by the Department of Works, or as a mechanical part for
which the Artillery is responsible."

"How delightful!" Arnheim said, though he knew that Tuzzi was
confusing a diesel engine with a gas engine and that even with gas it
was a long time since matches had been used. It was the kind of story
that circulates in government offices, full of enjoyable self-depreca-
tion, and the Section Chief had told it in a tone of tolerant amusement. Everyone smiled or laughed, none more appreciatively than
General Stumm. "Of course, it's the civilians in the other departments who are really to blame," he said, to take the joke a little further, "because the minute we order something not regularly
provided for in the budget, the Finance Ministry loses no time in
reminding us that we don't know the first thing about the workings of
constitutional government. So if war were to break out—God forbid!—before the end of the fiscal year we would have to telegraph
the commanding officers of these fortifications at dawn, on the first
day of mobilization, empowering them to buy matches, and if there
were none to be had in those mountain villages, the war would
have to be conducted with the matches in the pockets of the officers'
orderlies."

The General had probably gone a little too far in his elaboration of
the joke; as its humor thinned out, the dire seriousness of the problems facing the Parallel Campaign became apparent again. His
Grace said pensively: "As time goes on . . . ," but then he remembered that it is wiser in a difficult situation to let the others do the
talking, and did not finish. The six persons present were silent for a
moment, as though they were all standing around a deep well, staring
down into it.

"No," Diotima said, "that's impossible."

What? all eyes seemed to ask.

"We would only be doing what Germany is accused of: arming for
war." Her soul had paid no attention to the anecdotes, or had forgotten them already, arrested at the moment of the General's success.

"But what is to be done?" Count Leinsdorf asked gratefully, but still troubled. "We must look for some temporary expedient, at the very least."

"Germany is a relatively naïve country, bristling with energy," Arnheim said, as though he felt called upon to apologize to his lady on behalf of his country. "It has been handed gunpowder and schnapps."

Tuzzi smiled at this metaphor, which struck him as more than daring.

"There's no denying that Germany is regarded with growing distaste in those circles to which our Campaign is meant to appeal." Count Leinsdorf did not pass up the opportunity to slip this in. "And even, I am sorry to say, in those circles it has already appealed to," he added, for a wonder.

Arnheim surprised him by stating that he was not unaware of it. "We Germans," he said, "are an ill-fated nation. Not only do we live in the heart of Europe; we even suffer the pains of this heart. . . ."

"Heart?" Count Leinsdorf asked involuntarily. He would have been prepared for "brain" and would have more readily acceded to this. But Arnheim insisted on heart. "Do you remember," he asked, "that not so long ago the City Council of Prague awarded a very large order to France, although we had also made a tender, of course, and would have filled our order more efficiently and more cheaply? It is simply an emotional prejudice at work. And I must admit that I fully understand it."

Before he could go on, Stumm von Bordwehr was happy to elucidate. "All over the world," he said, "people are struggling desperately, but in Germany they're struggling even harder. All over the world a lot of noise is being made, but even more in Germany. Business has lost touch with traditional culture everywhere, but most of all in Germany. Everywhere the flower of youth is stuck into barracks as a matter of course, but the Germans have more barracks than anyone else. And so we are bound, in a way, as brothers, not to hang back too far behind Germany," he concluded. "If all this sounds a bit paradoxical, I hope you'll all excuse me, but such are the complications faced by the intellect nowadays."

Arnheim nodded in agreement. "America may be even worse than we are," he added, "but America is at least utterly naïve, without our intellectual conflicts. We Germans are in every respect the nation at

the center of things, where all the world's currents crisscross. More
than any other we need a synthesis. And we know it. We have a sense
of sin, as it were. But admitting this frankly, at the outset, I think it is
only fair to acknowledge that we also suffer for the others, that we
take their faults upon ourselves, so to speak, and that in a sense we
are being cursed or crucified, however you might want to put it, on
behalf of the whole world. A change of heart in Germany would
probably be the most significant thing that could happen. I rather
suspect that some vague idea of this is present in that conflicted and,
as it seems, somewhat impassioned opposition to us of which you
have just spoken."

Now Ulrich joined in: "You gentlemen underestimate the pro-
German elements. I am reliably informed that any day now there is
going to be a fierce demonstration against our campaign by those
who consider us anti-German. Your Grace will see the people of
Vienna demonstrating in the streets. There is to be a protest against
the appointment of Baron Wisnieczky. Our friends Tuzzi and Arnheim are assumed to be acting in collusion, while you, sir, are said to
be working to undermine the German influence on the Parallel
Campaign."

Count Leinsdorf's eyes now reflected something between the impassivity of a frog's gaze and the irritability of a bull's. Tuzzi looked
up slowly at Ulrich's face and gave him a warm, questioning look.
Arnheim laughed heartily and stood up, trying to catch the Section
Chief's eye with an urbane, humorous glance as a way of deprecating
the absurd insinuation about the two of them, but as he could not
connect with him he turned to Diotima instead. Tuzzi had meanwhile taken Ulrich by the arm and asked where he had got his information. Ulrich told him it was no secret but a widely accepted rumor
he had heard at a friend's house. Tuzzi brought his face closer, forcing Ulrich to turn slightly aside from the others, and with this effect
of privacy he suddenly whispered: "Don't you know yet why Arnheim is here? He is an intimate friend of Prince Mosyutov and very
much persona grata with the Czar. He keeps in touch with Russia
and is supposed to influence this Campaign in a pacifist direction.
Unofficially, of course, on his Russian Majesty's private initiative, as
it were. A matter of ideology. Something for you, my friend," he concluded in a mocking tone. "Leinsdorf has no inkling of it."

Section Chief Tuzzi had this information through official channels. He believed it because he saw pacifism as a movement that was in keeping with the outlook a beautiful woman would have, which would explain Diotima's being so enraptured with Arnheim and Arnheim's spending more time in Tuzzi's house than anywhere else. Before this he had come close to being jealous. He could believe in "intellectual affinities" up to a point, but he did not care to use devious methods to find out whether this point had been passed or not, so he had forced himself to go on trusting his wife. But while this was a victory of his manly self-respect over mere sexual instincts, these could still arouse enough jealousy in him to make him see for the first time that a professional man can never really keep an eye on his wife unless he is willing to neglect his work. Though he told himself that if an engine driver could not keep his woman with him on the job, a man at the controls of an empire could afford even less to be a jealous husband, it went against his character as a diplomat to settle for the noble ignorance in which this left him, and it undermined his professional self-assurance. So he was most thankful to be restored to his old self-confidence by this harmless explanation for everything that had worried him. There was even a little bonus in his feeling that it served his wife right that he knew all about Arnheim, while she saw only the human being and never dreamed that he was an agent of the Czar. Now Tuzzi again enjoyed asking her for little scraps of information, which she undertook to provide with a mixture of graciousness and impatience. He had worked out a whole series of seemingly harmless questions, the answers to which would enable him to draw his own conclusions. The husband would have been glad to take the "cousin" into his confidence, and was just wondering how to go about it without exposing his wife, when Count Leinsdorf again took the lead in the conversation. He alone had remained seated, and nobody had noticed anything of the struggle going on inside him as the problems piled up. But his fighting spirit seemed to be restored. He twirled his Wallenstein mustache and said slowly and firmly: "Something will have to be done."

"Have you come to a decision, Count?" they asked him.

"I haven't been able to come up with anything," he said simply. "Still, something must be done." He sat there like a man who does not intend to move from the spot until his will is done.

The effect was so powerful that everyone present felt the futile straining after an answer rattling inside him like a penny in a piggy bank that no amount of shaking will get out through the slot.

Arnheim said: "Now, really, we can't let ourselves be influenced by that sort of thing."

Leinsdorf did not reply.

The whole litany of proposals intended to give the Parallel Campaign some content was gone over again.

Count Leinsdorf reacted like a pendulum, always in a different position but always swinging the same way: This can't be done because we have to think of the Church. That can't be done, the freethinkers won't like it. The Association of Architects has already protested against this. There are qualms about that in the Department of Finance.

So it went, on and on.

Ulrich kept out of it. He felt as if the five persons taking their turn to speak had just crystallized out of some impure liquid in which his senses had been marinated for months now. Whatever had he meant by telling Diotima that it was necessary to take control of the imaginary, or that other time, when he had said that reality should be abolished? Now she was sitting here, remembering such statements of his, and probably thinking all sorts of things about him. And what on earth had made him say to her that one should live like a character in a book? He felt certain that she had passed all that on to Arnheim by now.

But he also felt sure that he knew what time it was, or the price of eggs, as well as anyone. If he nevertheless happened, just now, to hold a position halfway between his own and that of the others, it did not take some queer shape such as might result from a dim and absent state of mind; on the contrary, he again felt flooded by that illumination he had noticed earlier, in Bonadea's presence. He recalled going with the Tuzzis to a racecourse last fall, not so long ago, when there was an incident involving great, suspicious betting losses, and a peaceful crowd had in a matter of seconds turned into a turbulent sea of people pouring into the enclosure, not only smashing everything within reach but rifling the cash boxes as well, until the police succeeded in transforming them back into an assemblage of people out for a harmless and customary good time. In such a world it was absurd to think in terms of metaphors and the vague borderline shapes life might possibly, or impossibly, assume. Ulrich felt that there was nothing amiss with his perception of life as a crude and needy condition where it was better not to worry too much about tomorrow because it was hard enough to get through today. How could one fail to see that the human world is no hovering, insubstantial thing but craves the most concentrated solidity, for fear that anything out of the way might make it go utterly to pieces? Or, to take it a step further, how could a sound observer fail to recognize that this living compound of anxieties, instincts, and ideas, such as it is, though it uses ideas at most in order to justify itself, or as stimulants, gives those ideas their form and coherence, whatever defines them and sets them in motion? We may press the wine from the grapes, but how much more beautiful than a pool of wine is the sloping vineyard with its inedible rough soil and its endless rows of shining wooden stakes. In short, he reflected, the cosmos was generated not by a theory but— he was about to say "by violence," but a word he had not expected leapt to mind, and so he finished by thinking: but by violence and love, and the usual linkage between these two is wrong.

At this moment violence and love again did not have quite their conventional meaning for Ulrich. Everything that inclined him toward nihilism and hardness was implied in the word "violence." It meant whatever flowed from every kind of skeptical, factual, conscious behavior; a certain hard, cold aggressiveness had even entered into his choice of a career, so that an undercurrent of cruelty might have led to his becoming a mathematician. It was like the dense foliage of a tree hiding the trunk. And if we speak of love not merely in the usual sense but are moved by the word to long for a condition profoundly different, unto the very atoms that make up the body, from the poverty of lovelessness; or when we feel that we can lay claim to every quality as naturally as to none; or when it seems to us that what happens is only semblances prevailing, because life— bursting with conceit over its here-and-now but really a most uncertain, even a downright unreal condition—pours itself headlong into the few dozen cake molds of which reality consists; or that in all the orbits in which we keep revolving there is a piece missing; or that of all the systems we have set up, none has the secret of staying at rest:

then all these things, however different they look, are also bound up with each other like the branches of a tree, completely concealing the trunk on all sides.

These two trees were the shape his life had taken, like a two-pronged fork. He could not say when it had entered into the sign of the tree with the hard, tangled branchwork, but it had happened early on, for even his immature Napoleonic plans had shown him to be a man who looked on life as a problem he had set himself, something it was his vocation to work out. This urge to attack life and master it had always been clearly discernible in him, whether it had manifested itself as a rejection of the existing order or as various forms of striving for a new one, as logical or moral needs or even merely as an urge to keep the body in fighting trim. And everything that, as time went on, he had called essayism, the sense of possibility, and imaginative in contrast with pedantic precision; his suggestions that history was something one had to invent, that one should live the history of ideas instead of the history of the world, that one should get a grip on whatever cannot quite be realized in practice and should perhaps end up trying to live as if one were a character in a book, a figure with all the inessential elements left out, so that what was left would consolidate itself as some magical entity—all these different versions of his thinking, all in their extreme formulations against reality, had just one thing in common: an unmistakable, ruthless passion to influence reality.

Harder to recognize because more shadowy and dreamlike were the ramifications of the other tree that formed an image for his life, rooted perhaps in some primal memory of a childlike relationship to the world, all trustfulness and yielding, which had lived on as a haunting sense of having once beheld the whole vast earth in what normally only fills the flowerpot in which the herbs of morality send up their stunted sprouts. No doubt that regrettably absurd affair of the major's wife was his only attempt to reach a full development on this gentle shadow side of his life; it was also the beginning of a recoil that had never stopped. Since then, the leaves and twigs always drifting on the surface were the only sign that the tree still existed, though it had disappeared from view. This dormant half of his personality perhaps revealed itself most clearly in his instinctive assumption that the active and busy side of him was only standing in for the real self, an assumption that cast a shadow on his active self. In all he did—involving physical passions as well as spiritual—he had always ended up feeling trapped in endless preparations that would never come to fruition in anything, so that as the years went by his life had lost any sense of its own necessity, just as a lamp runs out of oil. His development had evidently split into two tracks, one running on the surface in daylight, the other in the dark below and closed to traffic, so that the state of moral arrest that had oppressed him for a long time, and perhaps more than was strictly necessary, might simply be the result of his failure to bring these two tracks together.

Now, as he realized that this failure to achieve integration had lately been apparent to him in what he called the strained relationship between literature and reality, metaphor and truth, it flashed on Ulrich how much more all this signified than any random insight that turned up in one of those meandering conversations he had recently engaged in with the most inappropriate people. These two basic strategies, the figurative and the unequivocal, have been distinguishable ever since the beginnings of humanity. Single-mindedness is the law of all waking thought and action, as much present in a compelling logical conclusion as in the mind of the blackmailer who enforces his will on his victim step by step, and it arises from the exigencies of life where only the single-minded control of circumstances can avert disaster. Metaphor, by contrast, is like the image that fuses several meanings in a dream; it is the gliding logic of the soul, corresponding to the way things relate to each other in the intuitions of art and religion. But even what there is in life of common likes and dislikes, accord and rejection, admiration, subordination, leadership, imitation, and their opposites, the many ways man relates to himself and to nature, which are not yet and perhaps never will be purely objective, cannot be understood in other than metaphoric or figurative terms. No doubt what is called the higher humanism is only the effort to fuse together these two great halves of life, metaphor and truth, once they have been carefully distinguished from each other. But once one has distinguished everything in a metaphor that might be true from what is mere froth, one usually has gained a little truth, but at the cost of destroying the whole value of the metaphor. The extraction of the truth may have been an inescapable part of our intellectual evolution, but it has had the same effect of boiling down a liquid to thicken it, while the really vital juices and elements escape in a cloud of steam. It is often hard, nowadays, to avoid the impression that the concepts and the rules of the moral life are only metaphors that have been boiled to death, with the revolting greasy kitchen vapors of humanism billowing around the corpses, and if a digression is permissible at this point, it can only be this, that one consequence of this impression that vaguely hovers over everything is what our era should frankly call its reverence for all that is common. For when we lie nowadays it is not so much out of weakness as out of a conviction that a man cannot prevail in life unless he is able to lie. We resort to violence because, after much long and futile talk, the simplicity of violence is an immense relief. People band together in organizations because obedience to orders enables them to do things they have long been incapable of doing out of personal conviction, and the hostility between organizations allows them to engage in the unending reciprocity of blood feuds, while love would all too soon put everyone to sleep. This has much less to do with the question of whether men are good or evil than with the fact that they have lost their sense of high and low. Another paradoxical result of this disorientation is the vulgar profusion of intellectual jewelry with which our mistrust of the intellect decks itself out. The coupling of a "philosophy" with activities that can absorb only a very small part of it, such as politics; the general obsession with turning every viewpoint into a standpoint and regarding every standpoint as a viewpoint; the need of every kind of fanatic to keep reiterating the one idea that has ever come his way, like an image multiplied to infinity in a hall of mirrors: all these widespread phenomena, far from signifying a movement toward humanism, as they wish to do, in fact represent its failure. All in all, it seems that what needs to be excised from human relations is the soul that finds itself misplaced in them. The moment Ulrich realized this he felt that his life, if it had any meaning at all, demonstrated the presence of the two fundamental spheres of human existence in their separateness and in their way of working against each other. Clearly, people like himself were already being born, but they were isolated, and in his isolation he was incapable of bringing together again what had fallen apart. He had no illusions about the value of his philosophical experimentation; even if he observed the strictest logical consistency in linking thought to thought, the effect was still one of piling one ladder upon another, so that the topmost rungs teetered far above the level of natural life. He contemplated this with revulsion.

This could have been the reason he suddenly looked at Tuzzi. Tuzzi was speaking. As though his ear were receiving the first sounds of the morning, Ulrich heard him say: "I am in no position to judge whether our time is devoid of great human and artistic achievements as you say; I can only assure you that foreign policy is nowhere else so hard to determine as in this country of ours. It is fairly safe to predict that even in our great Jubilee Year, French foreign policy will be motivated by the desire to settle scores and by colonialism, the English will be pushing their pawns to advantage on the world's chessboard, as their game has been characterized, and the Germans will be pursuing what they call, not always unambiguously, their Place in the Sun. But our old Empire is so self-contained that it's anyone's guess in what direction we may be driven by circumstances." It was as though Tuzzi were trying to put on the brakes, to utter a warning. That whiff of unintended irony came only from the naïvely factual tone in which he dryly presented to them his conviction that to want for nothing in this world was highly dangerous. The effect on Ulrich was to perk him up, as if he had been chewing on a coffee bean. Meanwhile Tuzzi kept harping on his warning note, and he ended by saying:

"Who can take it upon himself, today, even to think of putting great political ideas into practice? It would take a criminal or a gambler courting bankruptcy. You surely wouldn't want that? The function of diplomacy is to keep what we have."

"Keeping what we have leads to war," Arnheim countered.

"It may, I suppose," Tuzzi conceded. "All one can do, probably, is to choose the most favorable moment for being led into it. Remember Czar Alexander II? His father, Nicholas, was a despot, but he died a natural death. Alexander was a magnanimous ruler who began his reign by instituting sweeping liberal reforms, so that Russian liberalism turned into Russian radicalism, and Alexander survived three attempts to assassinate him, only to succumb to a fourth."

Ulrich looked at Diotima. There she sat, upright, alert, serious, voluptuous, and corroborated her husband: "That's right. From what I have seen of the radical temper in our own discussions, I would say that if you give them an inch they'll take a mile."

Tuzzi smiled with the sense of having won a small victory over Arnheim.

Arnheim looked impassive where he sat, his lips slightly parted, like a bud opening. Diotima, a silent tower of radiant flesh, gazed at him across the moat between them.

The General polished his horn-rimmed glasses.

Ulrich spoke with care: "That's only because those who feel called upon to act, in order to restore some meaning to life, have one thing in common: they despise 'mere' thinking just at the point where it could lead us to truths rather than simple personal opinions; instead, where everything depends on pursuing those views to their inexhaustible wellspring, they opt for shortcuts and half-truths."

Nobody spoke in answer. And why should anyone have answered him? What a man said was only words, after all. What mattered was that there were six people sitting in a room and having an important discussion; what they said or did not say in the course of it, their feelings, apprehensions, possibilities, were all included in this actuality without being on a level with it; they were included in the same way the dark movements of the liver and stomach are included in the actuality of a fully dressed person about to put his signature to an important document. This hierarchical order was not to be disturbed; this was reality itself.

Ulrich's old friend Stumm had now finished cleaning his glasses; he put them on and looked at Ulrich.

Even though Ulrich had always assumed that he was only toying with these people, he suddenly felt quite forlorn among them. He remembered feeling something like it a few weeks or months before, a little puff of Creation's breath asserting itself against the petrified lunar landscape where it had been exhaled; he thought that all the decisive moments of his life had been accompanied by such a sense of wonder and isolation. But was it anxiety that was troubling him this time? He could not quite pin his feeling down, but it suggested that he had never in his life come to a real decision, and that it was high time he did. This occurred to him not in so many words but only as an uneasy feeling, as though something were trying to tear him away from these people he was sitting with, and even though they meant nothing to him, his will suddenly clung to them, kicking and screaming.

Count Leinsdorf was now reminded by the silence in the room of his duties as a political realist, and said in a rallying tone: "Well then, what's to be done? We must do something final, even if it's only temporary, to save our campaign from all those threats against it."

This moved Ulrich to try something preposterous.

"Your Grace," he said, "there is really only one real task for the Parallel Campaign: to make a start at taking stock of our general cultural situation. We must act more or less as if we expected the Day of Judgment to dawn in 1918, when the old spiritual books will be closed and a higher accounting set up. I suggest that you found, in His Majesty's name, a World Secretariat for Precision and Soul. Without that, all our other tasks cannot be solved, or else they are illusory tasks." He now added some of the things that had crossed his mind during the few minutes he had been lost in thought.

As he spoke, it seemed to him not only that everybody's eyes were popping out of their sockets in sheer amazement, but also that their torsos were lifting up from their backsides. They had expected him to follow their host's example and come up with an anecdote, and when the joke failed to materialize he was left sitting there like a child surrounded by leaning towers that looked slightly offended at his silly game. Only Count Leinsdorf managed to put a good face on it. "Quite so," he said, though surprised. "Nevertheless, we are obliged now to go beyond mere suggestions and offer some concrete solution, and in that respect I must say that Property and Culture have left us badly stranded."

Arnheim felt he must save the great nobleman from being taken in by Ulrich's jokes.

"Our friend is caught up in an idea of his own," he explained. "He thinks it is possible to synthesize a right way to live, just like synthetic rubber or nitrogen. But the human mind"—here he gave Ulrich his most chivalrous smile—"is sadly limited in being unable to breed its life forms as white mice are bred in the laboratory; on the contrary, it takes a huge granary to support no more than a few families of mice." He immediately apologized for indulging in so daring an analogy, but was in fact quite pleased with himself for coming up with something in the aristocratic Leinsdorf style of scientific large-scale land management, while so vividly illustrating the difference between ideas with and without the responsibility for carrying them out.

But His Grace shook his head irritably. "I take his point quite well," he said. "People used to grow naturally into the conditions of their lives as they found them, and it was a sound way of coming into their own; but nowadays, with everything being shaken up as it is, everything uprooted from its natural soil, we will have to replace the traditional handicrafts system, even in the raising of souls, as it were, by the intelligence of the factory." It was one of those remarkable statements His Grace occasionally voiced, to his own and everyone else's surprise, all the more so as he had merely been staring at Ulrich with a dumbfounded expression the whole time before he began to speak.

"Still, everything our learned friend is saying is totally impracticable, just the same," Arnheim said firmly.

"Oh, would you say so?" Count Leinsdorf said curtly, full of fighting spirit.

Diotima now tried to make peace. "But, Count," she said, as if asking him for something one doesn't put into words: namely, to come to his senses. "We've long since tried everything my cousin says. What else are these long, strenuous talks, such as the ones we had this evening, about, after all?"

"Indeed?" the annoyed peer huffed. "I had an idea from the first that all these clever fellows won't get us anywhere. All of that psychoanalysis and relativity theory and whatever they call all that stuff is pure vanity. Every one of them is trying to make his own special blueprint of the world prevail over all the others. Let me tell you, even if our Herr Doktor did not express himself as well as he might have, he's basically quite right. People are always trying on something new whenever the times begin to change, and no good ever comes of it."

The nervous strain caused by the abortive meanderings of the Parallel Campaign had now broken through to the surface. Count Leinsdorf had, without being aware of it, switched from twisting his mustache to fretfully twiddling his thumbs. Perhaps something else had also come to the surface: his dislike of Arnheim. While he had been astonished when Ulrich brought up the word "soul," he was quite pleased with what followed. "When a fellow like Arnheim bandies that word about," he thought, "that's a lot of flimflam. We don't need it from him—what else is religion for?" But Arnheim, too, was upset; he had gone white to the lips. Up to now, Count Leinsdorf had spoken in that tone only to the General. Arnheim was not the sort of man to take it lying down. Still, he could not help being impressed with Count Leinsdorf's firmness in taking Ulrich's part, which painfully reminded him of his own divided feelings about Ulrich. He felt at a loss, because he had wanted to talk things out with Ulrich but had not found an opportunity to do so before this fortuitous clash in front of all the others, and so, instead of turning on Count Leinsdorf, whom he simply ignored, he addressed his words to Ulrich, with every sign of intense mental and physical agitation to a degree quite out of character for him.

"Do you actually believe what you have just been saying?" he asked sternly, with no regard to considerations of civility. "Do you believe it can be done? Are you really of the opinion that it is possible to live in accordance with some analogy? If so, what would you do if His Grace were to give you a free hand? Do tell me, I beg you!"

It was an awkward moment. Diotima was oddly enough reminded of a story she had read in the papers a few days before. A woman had received a merciless sentence for giving her lover an opportunity to murder her aged husband, who had not "exercised his marital rights" for years but would not agree to a separation. The case had caught Diotima's attention by its quasi-medical physical detail, and held it by a certain perverse fascination; it was all so understandable that one was not inclined to blame any of the persons involved, limited as they were in their ability to help themselves; it was only some unnatural general state of affairs that gave rise to such situations. She had no idea what made her think of this case just at this moment. But she was also thinking that Ulrich had been talking to her lately about all sorts of things that were "up in the air," and always ended up by annoying her with some outrageous suggestion of a personal kind. She had herself spoken of the soul emerging from its insubstantial state, in the case of a few privileged human beings. She decided that her cousin was just as unsure of himself as she was of herself, and perhaps just as passionate too. All of this was interwoven just now—in her head or in her heart, that abandoned seat of the noble Leinsdorfian amity—with the story of the condemned woman, in a way that caused her to sit there with parted lips, feeling that something terrible would happen if Arnheim and Ulrich were allowed to go on like this, but that it might be even worse if anyone interfered and tried to stop them.

During Arnheim's attack on him, Ulrich had been looking at Tuzzi. It cost Tuzzi an effort to hide his eager curiosity in the brown furrows of his face. He was thinking that all these goings-on in his house were now coming to a head, propelled by their inherent contradictions. Nor had he any sympathy for Ulrich, whose line of talk went quite against Tuzzi's grain, convinced as he was that a man's worth lay in his will or in his work, and certainly not in his feelings or ideas; to talk such nonsense about mere figures of speech, he felt, was positively indecent.

Ulrich might have been sensing some of this, because he remembered telling Tuzzi that he would kill himself if the year he was "taking off" from his life were to pass without results. He had not said it in so many words but had made his meaning painfully clear, and he now felt ashamed of himself. Again he had the impression, without being able to account for it, that his moment of truth was at hand. Suddenly Gerda Fischel came to mind; there was a dangerous possibility of her coming to see him, to continue their last conversation. He realized that even as he had only been toying with her, they had already reached the limit of what words could do, and there was only one last step: he would have to fall in with the girl's unexpressed longings, ungird his intellectual loins, and breach her "inner ramparts." This was crazy; he would never have gone this far with Gerda had he not felt safe with her on this point. He was feeling a strangely sober, irritated exaltation, when he caught sight of Arnheim's angry face and heard himself accused of having no respect for reality, followed by the words "Forgive my saying so, but such a crass Either/Or as yours is really too juvenile," but he had lost the slightest inclination to answer any of it. He glanced at his watch and, with a smile of appeasement, said it had grown much too late for going on with the subject.

In so saying he had regained his contact with the others. Section Chief Tuzzi even stood up, and barely masked this discourtesy by pretending to do something or other. Count Leinsdorf, too, had meanwhile calmed down; he would have been pleased to hear Ulrich put the Prussian in his place but did not mind his doing nothing about it. "When you like a man, you like him, that's that," he thought, "no matter how clever the other fellow's talk may be." And with a daring, though quite unconscious approach to Arnheim's idea of the Mystery of the Whole, he continued cheerfully, as he looked at Ulrich's expression (which was, at the moment, anything but intelligent): "One might even say that a nice, likable person simply can't say or do anything really stupid."

The party quickly broke up. The General slipped his horn-rims into his pistol pocket, after having tried in vain to stick them into the bottom of his tunic; he had not yet found a proper place for this civilian instrument of wisdom. "Here we have an armed truce of the intellect," he said to Tuzzi, like a pleased accomplice, alluding to the speedy dispersal of the last guests.

Only Count Leinsdorf conscientiously held them all back for another moment: "What is the consensus, then?" And when no one found anything to say, he added peaceably: "Oh well, we shall see, we shall see."

117

A DARK DAY FOR RACHEL

Soliman's sexual awakening and his decision to seduce Rachel made him feel as cold-blooded as a hunter sighting game, or a butcher sharpening his knives for the slaughter, but he had no idea how to go about it and what, exactly, a successful seduction was; in short, the more he had a man's will, the more it made him feel the weakness of a boy. Rachel also had her sense of the inevitable next step, and ever since she had so self-forgetfully clung to Ulrich's hand, that evening of the incident with Bonadea, she was quite beside herself, afloat in a state of acute erotic distraction that was also raining flowers on Soliman, as it were. But conditions just then were not favorable and made for delays. The cook had taken sick, Rachel's time off had to be sacrificed, the heavy social schedule in the house was keeping her busy, and although Arnheim continued to visit Diotima often enough, it was as though they had decided that the two youngsters needed watching, for he seldom brought Soliman, and when he did, they saw each other only briefly, in the presence of their employers, with the proper blank and sullen looks on their faces.

At this time they almost learned to hate each other, because they made one another feel the misery of being kept on too short a leash. Soliman was also driven by his mounting ardor to violent escapades; he planned to slip away from the hotel at night unbeknownst to his master, so he stole a bedsheet, which he tried to cut up and twist into a rope ladder; when he made a mess of it, he threw the tortured bedsheet down a light shaft. Then for a long time he vainly studied ways and means to clamber up and down a housefront, using windowsills and the carved figures on the façade, and on his daytime errands examined the city's fabled architecture solely for the hand- and footholds it might offer a cat burglar. Meanwhile Rachel, who had been told of all these plans and setbacks in hasty whispers, would think that she saw the black full moon of his face on the pavement below, looking up at her, or that she heard his chirping call, to which she attempted a shy response, leaning far out her window into the empty night, until she had to admit that the night was indeed empty. She no longer regarded this romantic muddle as a nuisance but surrendered herself to it with a yearning wistfulness. The yearning was actually for Ulrich; Soliman was the man one didn't love but to whom one would give oneself nonetheless, as she never doubted; the fact that they had been kept apart lately, that they had hardly spoken to each other except in stolen whispers and were both in disfavor with their employers, had much the same effect on her as a night full of uncertainty, mystery, and sighs has on all lovers: it concentrated her fantasies like a burning glass, whose intense ray is felt less as a pleasant warmth than as a heat one cannot stand much longer.

In this regard, Rachel, who did not waste any time fantasizing about rope ladders and climbing walls, was the more practical-minded. The nebulous dream of an elopement soon dwindled to a plan for a single night together, and when this could not be arranged, a stolen quarter of an hour would have to do. After all, neither Diotima nor Count Leinsdorf nor Arnheim—staying on together for another hour or two after some crowded and unproductive meeting

with the best minds in town, while they all worried about the progress of their "business," without need of further attentions from their
staff—ever considered that such an hour "at liberty" consists of four
quarter hours. But Rachel had thought about it, and since the cook
was still not quite recovered and had permission to retire early, the
young maid was so overburdened that there was no telling where she
might be at any given time, even as she was spared much of her regular duty as a parlor maid. Experimentally—more or less as a person
afraid of committing suicide outright will go on making halfhearted
attempts until one of them succeeds by mistake—she had smuggled
Soliman into her room several times already, always prepared with
some story of having been on duty if he was caught, while hinting to
him that there were other ways to her bedroom than climbing the
walls. So far, however, the young lovers had not gone beyond yawn-
ing together in the front hall while spying out the situation, until one
evening, when the voices inside the meeting room had been heard
endlessly responding to each other, monotonous as the sounds of
threshing, Soliman used a lovely expression he had read in a novel
and said that he could stand it no longer.

Even inside her little room it was he who bolted the door, but then
they did not dare turn on the light but stood there blindly facing each
other as though the loss of sight had deprived them of all their other
senses as well, like two statues in the park at night. Soliman naturally
thought of pressing Rachel's hand or pinching her leg to make her
shriek, his way of conducting his male conquest of her thus far, but
he had to refrain from causing any noise, and when at last he made
some clumsy pass at her, there was only Rachel's impatient indifference in response. For Rachel felt the hand of fate on her spine, pushing her ahead, and her nose and forehead were ice cold, as though
she had already been drained of all her illusions. It made Soliman
feel quite at a loss too; he was all thumbs, and there was no telling
how long it would take them to break the deadlock of their rigid posture face-to-face in the dark. In the end, it had to be the civilized and
more experienced Rachel who took the part of the seducer. What
helped her was the resentment she now felt in place of her former
love for Diotima; ever since she had ceased to be content to enjoy
vicariously her mistress's exaltations and was involved in her own
love affair, she had greatly changed. She not only told lies to cover up

her encounters with Soliman, she even pulled Diotima's hair when she combed it, to revenge herself for the vigilance with which her innocence was being guarded. But what enraged her most was something in which she had formerly delighted: having to wear Diotima's cast-off chemises, panties, and stockings, for even though she cut these things down to a third of their former size and remodeled them, she felt imprisoned in them, as though wearing the yoke of propriety on her bare body. But this lingerie now gave her the inspiration she needed in this situation. For she had told Soliman earlier about the changes she had been noticing for some time in her mistress's underthings, and now she could break their deadlock by simply showing him.

"Here, you can see for yourself what they're really up to," she said in the darkness, showing Soliman the moonbeam frill of her little panties. "And if they're carrying on together like this, then they're certainly also making a fool of the master about that war they're cooking up in our house." And as the boy gingerly fingered the fine-textured and dangerous panties, she added somewhat breathlessly, "I bet that your pants are as black as you are, Soliman; that's what they're all saying." Now Soliman vengefully but gently dug his nails into her thigh, and Rachel had to move closer to free herself, and had to do and say one thing and another, all of which produced no real result, until she finally used her sharp little teeth on Soliman's face (which was pressed childishly against her own and at every movement she made kept on clumsily getting itself in the way), as if it were a large apple. At which point she forgot to feel embarrassed at what she was doing, and Soliman forgot to feel self-conscious, and love raged like a storm through the darkness.

When it was over, it dropped the lovers with a thud, vanished through the walls, and the darkness between them was like a lump of coal with which the sinners had blackened themselves. They had lost track of time, overestimated the time they had taken, and were afraid. Rachel's halfhearted final kiss was a mere annoyance to Soliman; he wanted the light switched on, and behaved like a burglar who has his loot and is now wholly intent upon making his getaway. Rachel, who had quickly and shamefacedly straightened her clothes, gave him a look that was fathomless and aimless at once. Her tousled hair hung down over her eyes, and behind them she saw again all the great images of her ideal self, forgotten until this moment. Her fantasies had been filled with her wish not only for every possible desirable trait in herself but also for a handsome, rich, and exciting lover—and now here in front of her stood Soliman, still half undressed, looking hopelessly ugly, and she didn't believe a single word of all the stories he had told her. She might have liked to take advantage of the dark to cradle his tense, plump face in her arms a little while longer before they let go of each other. But now that the light was on, he was only her new lover, a thousand possibilities shrunken into one somewhat ludicrous little wretch, whose existence excluded all others. And Rachel herself was back to being a servant girl who had let herself be seduced and was now beginning to be terrified of having a baby, which would bring it all to light. She was simply too crushed by this transformation even to give a sigh. She helped Soliman to finish dressing, for in his confusion the boy had flung off his tight little jacket with all those buttons, but she was helping him not out of tenderness but only so that they could hurry downstairs. She had paid far more than it was worth, and to be caught out now would be the last straw. All the same, when they had finished, Soliman turned round and flashed her a dazzling smile that turned into a whinny of self-satisfaction. Rachel quickly picked up a box of matches, turned out the light, softly drew the bolt, and whispered, before opening the door: "You must give me one more kiss." For that was the right way to do things, but it tasted to both of them like toothpowder on their lips.

Back down in the front hall, they were amazed to find they still had time. The voices on the other side of the door were running on as before. By the time the guests were dispersing, Soliman had disappeared, and half an hour later Rachel was combing her mistress's hair with great attentiveness and almost with her former humble devotion.

"I am glad that my little lecture seems to have done you some good," Diotima said with approval, and this woman who in so many ways never quite achieved any real satisfaction kindly patted her little maid's hand.

118

SO KILL HIM!

Walter had changed out of his office suit into a better one and was knotting his tie at Clarisse's dresser mirror, which despite its irregularly curving art nouveau frame showed a shallow, distorted image in its cheap glass.

"They're absolutely right," he said gruffly. "The famous campaign is nothing but a fake."

"But what's the point of marching and screaming?" Clarisse said.

"What's the point of anything these days? Marching together, at least they're forming a procession, feeling each other's physical presence. And at least they're not *thinking*, and at least they're not *writing*; something may come of it."

"Do you really think the campaign is worth all that indignation?"

Walter shrugged his shoulders. "Haven't you read that resolution by the German faction in the paper? Haranguing the Prime Minister about defamation and unfairness to the German population and so on? And the sneering proclamation of the Czech League? Or the little item about the Polish delegates returning to their voting districts? For anyone who can read between the lines, that one's the most revealing story, because so much depends on the Poles, and now they've left the government in the lurch! This was no time to provoke everyone by coming out with this patriotic campaign."

"This morning in town," Clarisse said, "I saw mounted police go by, a whole regiment of them. A woman said they're being kept in reserve somewhere."

"Of course. There are troops standing by in the barracks too."

"Do you suppose there'll be trouble?"

"Who can tell?"

"Will they run the people down? How awful, all those horses' bodies jammed in among the people . . ."

Walter had undone his tie and was reknotting it all over again.

"Have you ever been mixed up in anything of this kind?" Clarisse asked.

"As a student."

"Never since then?"

Walter shook his head.

"Didn't you say just now that if there's trouble, it will all be Ulrich's fault?"

"I said nothing of the kind," Walter protested. "He takes no interest at all in politics, unfortunately. All I said was that it's just like him to start up something of this sort; he's involved with the people who are responsible for all this."

"I'd like to come into town with you," Clarisse announced.

"That's out of the question. It would upset you too much." Walter spoke with great firmness. He had heard all sorts of things in the office about what might happen at the demonstration, and he wanted to keep Clarisse away from it. It wouldn't do at all to expose her to the hysteria of a large crowd; Clarisse had to be treated with care, like a pregnant woman. He almost got a lump in his throat at the word "pregnant," even though he did not actually pronounce it, so unexpectedly had it come to mind, warming him with the thought of motherhood, however foolishly, considering his wife's ill-tempered refusal of herself. Well, life is full of such contradictions, he told himself, not without some pride, and offered: "I'll stay home, if you'd rather."

"No," she said. "You should be there, at least."

She wanted to be left to herself. When Walter had told her of the upcoming demonstration and described what it would be like, it had made her think of a huge serpent covered with scales, each in separate motion, and she had wanted to see this for herself, but without the fuss of a long argument about it.

Walter put his arm around her. "I'll stay home too?" he repeated, in a questioning tone.

She brushed his arm off, took a book from the shelf, and ignored him. It was a volume of her Nietzsche. But instead of going, Walter pleaded: "Let me see what you're up to."

The afternoon was ending. A vague foretaste of spring made itself felt in the house, like birdsong muted by walls and glass; an illusory scent of flowers rose from the varnish on the floor, the upholstery, the polished brass doorknobs. Walter held out his hand for her book. Clarisse clutched it with two hands, one finger between the pages where she had opened it.

And now they had one of their "terrible scenes," of which this marriage had seen so many. They were all on the same pattern. Imagine a theater with the stage blacked out, and the lights going on in two boxes on opposite sides of the proscenium, with Walter in one of them and Clarisse in the other, singled out among all the men and women, and between them the deep black abyss, warm with the bodies of invisible human beings. Now Clarisse opens her lips and speaks, and Walter replies, and the whole audience listens in breathless suspense, for never before has human talent produced such a spectacle of son et lumière, sturm und drang. . . . Such was the scene, once more, with Walter stretching out his arm, imploring her, and Clarisse, a few steps away from him, with her finger wedged between the pages of her book. Opening it at random, she had hit on that fine passage where the master speaks of the impoverishment that follows the decay of the will and manifests itself in every form of life as a proliferation of detail at the expense of the whole. "Life driven back into the most minute forms, leaving the rest devitalized . . ." was what she remembered, though she had only a vague sense of the general drift of the context over which she had run her eye before Walter had again interrupted her; and yet, despite the unfavorable circumstances, she had made a great discovery. For although in this passage the master spoke of all the arts, and even of all the forms taken by human life, his examples were all literary ones, and since Clarisse did not understand generalizations, she saw that Nietzsche had not grasped the full implication of his own ideas—for they applied to music as well! She could hear her husband's morbid piano playing as though he were actually playing there beside her, his exaggerated pauses, choked with emotion, the halting way his notes came from under his fingertips when his thoughts were straying toward her and when—to use another of the master's expressions—"the secondary moral element" overwhelmed the artist in him. Clarisse had come to recognize the sound Walter made when he was full of unuttered desire for her, and she could see the music draining out of his face, leaving only his lips shining, so that he looked as though he had cut his finger and was about to faint. This was how he looked now, with that nervous smile as he held his arm stretched out toward her. Nietzsche, of course, could not have known any of this, and yet it was like a sign that she had been led to open the book, by chance, at the place touching on this very thing, and as she suddenly saw, heard, and grasped it all, she was struck by the lightning flash of inspiration where she stood, on a high mountain called Nietzsche, which had buried Walter although it reached no higher than the soles of her feet. The "practical philosophy and poetry" of most people, who are neither originators nor on the other hand unsusceptible to ideas, consists of just such shimmering fusions of someone else's great thought with their own small private modifications.

Walter had meanwhile stood and was coming toward Clarisse. He had decided to forget the demonstration he had intended to join and stay home with her. He saw her leaning back against the wall in repugnance as he approached her, yet this deliberate gesture of a woman shrinking from a man unfortunately did not infect him with the same abhorrence but only aroused in him those male urges that might have been precisely what she shrank from. For a man must be capable of taking charge and of imposing his will on whoever resists him, and the need to prove his manhood suddenly meant just as much to Walter as the need to fight off the last shreds of his youthful superstition that a man must amount to something special. One doesn't have to be something special! he thought defiantly. It was somehow cowardly not to be able to get along without that illusion. We are all inclined to excesses, he thought dismissively. We all have something morbid, some horror, withdrawal, malevolence, in our makeup; each one of us could do something that he alone could do, but what of it? He resented the mania for fostering the extraordinary in oneself instead of reabsorbing those all too corruptible outgrowths and, by assimilating them organically, injecting some new life into the bloodstream of the civilization, which was far too inclined to grow sluggish. So he thought now, and he was looking forward to the day when music and painting would no longer mean anything more to him than a refined form of amusement. Wanting a child was part of this new sense of mission; the dominant desire of his youth to become a titan, a new Prometheus, had ended in his coming to believe, somewhat overemphatically, that one must first become like everyone else. He was now ashamed of having no children; he would have liked at least five, if Clarisse and his income had permitted it, so that he could be the center of a warm circle of life; he wanted to surpass in mediocrity that great mediocre mass of humanity which transmits life itself, paradoxical as his desire was.

But whether he had taken too long to think, or had slept too late before starting to dress and beginning this conversation, his cheeks were glowing now, and Clarisse showed that she instantly understood why he was moving closer to her book; and this fine attunement to each other's moods, despite the painful signs of her aversion to him, immediately subdued the brute in him and broke down the simplicity of his impulse.

"Why won't you show me what you're reading? Can't we just talk?" he pleaded, intimidated.

"We can't 'just talk'!" Clarisse hissed at him.

"You're hysterical!" Walter exclaimed. He tried to get the book, open as it was, away from her. She stubbornly clung to it. After they had been wrestling over it silently for a while, Walter started wondering, "What on earth do I want the book for?" and let go. At this point the incident would have been closed if Clarisse had not, at the very moment she was released, pressed herself up against the wall even more fiercely than before, as though she had to force her body backward through a stiff hedge to escape some threat of violence. She was fighting for breath, her face white, and hoarsely screamed: "Instead of amounting to something yourself, you just want to make a child to do it for you!"

Her lips spat these words at him venomously, and all Walter could do was gasp his "Let's talk!" at her again.

"I won't talk; you make me sick!" Clarisse answered, suddenly in full possession of her voice again, and using it with such sharpness that it crashed like heavy china to the floor, midway between them. Walter took a step backward and stared at her in amazement.

Clarisse did not really mean it. She was merely afraid of giving in, from good nature or recklessness, and letting Walter bind her to him with swaddling bands, which must not happen, not now when she was ready to settle the whole question once and for all. The situation had come *to a head.* She thought of this term, heavily underlined—it was the one Walter had used to explain why the populace was demonstrating in the streets; for Ulrich, who was linked to Nietzsche by dint of having given her the philosopher's works as a wedding present, was on the other side of the conflict, the side against which this spear*head* would be directed, if there was trouble. Now Nietzsche had just given her a sign, and if she was standing on a high mountain, what was a high mountain other than the earth coming to a point—to a *head?* The way things were interrelated was truly amazing, like a code that hardly anyone could decipher; even Clarisse didn't have too clear a perception of it, but that was just why she needed to be alone and had to get Walter out of the house. The wild hatred that flared up in her face at this point in her thoughts was an expression of a physical rage in which she as a person was only vaguely involved, a kind of pianist's *furioso* such as Walter also had at his fingertips, so that he too, after having stared at his wife in bewilderment, suddenly went white in the face, bared his teeth, and, responding to the loathing of him she had expressed, shouted: "Beware of genius! You in particular, just watch out!"

He was screaming even louder than she had been, and his dark prophecy, which had burst from his throat with a force beyond any he knew himself to have, so horrified him that everything turned black as though there had been an eclipse of the sun.

Clarisse was in shock, too, and struck dumb by it. An emotion with the impact of a solar eclipse is certainly no trifle, and whatever had brought it on, at the heart of it was the quite unexpected explosion of Walter's jealousy of Ulrich. Why was he driven to call Ulrich a genius? All he had meant was hubris, the pride that comes before the fall. Images from the past came to his inner eye: Ulrich returning home in uniform, that barbarian who had already been carrying on with real women when Walter, who was the older, was still writing poems to statues in the park. Later on, Ulrich the engineer bringing home the latest reports on the exact sciences, the world of precision, speed, steel; for Walter, the humanist, it was another invasion by the Mongol horde. With his younger friend, Walter had always felt the obscure uneasiness of being the weaker man, both physically and in initiative, although he had seen himself as the life of the mind incarnate while the other stood merely for raw will. Wasn't Walter always being moved by the Beautiful or the Good, while Ulrich stood by shaking his head? Such impressions leave their mark, they confirm and define the relationship. Had Walter succeeded in seeing that passage in the book for which he had wrestled with Clarisse, he would certainly not have understood it as she did; to her the decadence Nietzsche described as driving the will to life away from the whole and into the realm of detail fitted Walter's tendency to brood over the problems of the artist, while Walter would have seen it as an excellent characterization of his friend Ulrich, beginning with his overestimation of facts, in accord with the modern superstition of empiricism, which led directly to the barbaric fragmentation of the very self that was what made Ulrich a man without qualities, or qualities without a man, according to Walter's diagnosis, which Ulrich, in his megalomania, had had the gall to accept wholeheartedly.

It was this that Walter had meant by denouncing Ulrich as a "genius," for if anyone was entitled to call himself a solitary original it was Walter himself, and yet he had given this up in order to rejoin the rest of the human race in fulfilling its shared mission; in this he was a whole generation ahead of his friend. But as Clarisse did not utter a sound in answer to his violent outburst, he was thinking: "If she says one word in his favor now, I couldn't stand it!" and he shook with hatred, as though it were Ulrich's arm shaking him.

In his fury he imagined himself snatching up his hat and dashing out the door to rush blindly through the streets, the houses bending in the wind as he ran. Only after a while did he slow down and look into the faces of the people he was passing; as they met his stare in a friendly fashion, he began to calm down. At this point he tried, to the extent his consciousness had not been swallowed up altogether by his fantasy, to explain himself to Clarisse. But his words only shone in his eyes instead of coming from his lips. How was a man to describe the joy of being with his own kind, with his brothers? Clarisse would say he was not enough of an individual. But there was something inhuman about Clarisse's towering self-confidence, and he'd had enough of trying to live up to its arrogant demands. He ached to take refuge with her within some broader human order, instead of this lonely drifting in a boundless delusion of love and personal anarchy. "Underneath everything one is and does, and even when one happens to be in opposition to one's fellowmen, one needs to feel that one is basically moving toward union with them" was more or less what he would have liked to say to her now. For Walter had always been lucky in getting along with people; even in the midst of an argument they felt his attraction, and he theirs, and so the somewhat banal notion that there is, inherent in the human community, something that keeps things in balance, that rewards soundness and always comes through in the end, had become a solid conviction in his life. The example came to mind of the kind of person who could make birds come flying to him of their own accord, and who often had a rather birdlike look about them. For every human being there was some animal mysteriously akin to him, he felt; it was a theory he had once worked out for himself, though not scientifically. He believed that musical people are intuitively aware of a great deal that is beyond the ken of science, and from childhood on, Walter's animal kinship had undoubtedly been with fish. Fish had always held a powerful attraction for him, though mixed with dread, and at the start of his school vacations he always acted as if possessed; he would stand for hours at the water's edge angling for fish, pulling them out of their element and laying their corpses beside him on the grass, until it all ended with a fit of revulsion close to panic. Fish in the kitchen, too, were among his earliest passions. There the bones from the filleted fish were put into a boat-shaped receptacle, glazed green and white, like grass and clouds, and half full of water, where, for some reason having to do with the laws of the kitchen, the fish skeletons were kept until after the meal had been prepared, when the fish bones went into the garbage. This dish drew the boy like a magnet; he would always find childish excuses for hovering over it for hours at a time, and when anyone asked him outright what he was doing there, he was struck dumb. When he thought about it now, the answer that occurred to him was that the magic of fish lay in their belonging wholly to one element, never to more than one. Again he saw them as he had often seen them in the deep mirror of the water, moving not as he did both on the earth and within a second, intangible element (and at home in neither the one nor the other, Walter thought, spinning out the image this way and that: one belongs to the earth, with which one shares no more than the bare space occupied by the soles of one's feet; the rest of one's body is upright in air that it merely displaces, that gives no support but lets one fall). The fishes' ground, their air, food, and drink, their recoil from enemies as well as their shadowy advances in love and their grave, were all one, wholly enclosing them; they moved within the element that moved them, something a human being can experience only in a dream or in the longing to return to the sheltering tenderness of the womb (the belief in this universal longing was just coming into fashion). But in that case, why did he rip the fish from their element and kill them? Why did he get such an unutterable, awesome thrill out of that? Well, he did not want to know the answer. He, Walter, could admit that he was an enigma. But Clarisse had once said that fish were the aquatic bourgeoisie. Walter winced at this insult. As he kept hastening through the streets in his ongoing fantasy, looking into the faces of the passersby, it was turning into good fishing weather, not actually raining, but some moisture was coming down, and the streets, as he now saw for the first time, had already been darkly glistening for a while. The men were all dressed in black, with bowler hats but no collars and ties, which did not surprise him, as they were not middle class but were evidently coming from a factory, walking in easy groupings, while others, who had not yet finished their day's work, were hastily pushing through these clusters, just as Walter himself was doing, and it all made him feel very happy, except for those bare necks that reminded him of something troubling and not quite right. Suddenly the rain came pouring down, the people scattered and ran as something came slashing through the air, a flash of white, fish raining down, and then a trembling, tender single voice that seemed to have nothing to do with anything called a little dog by name!

These last images were so independent of him that they took him entirely by surprise. He had not been aware that his thoughts had gone dreaming on their own, drifting along with incredible speed on a flood of images. He raised his eyes and found himself staring into his young wife's face, which was still twisted with dislike. He felt deeply unsure of himself, remembered that he had been about to register a complaint, in detail and at length; his mouth was still open. But he had no idea whether minutes had passed since then, or seconds, or only milliseconds. Yet he also felt a warmth of pride, as after an ice-cold bath an ambiguous shuddering of the skin signalizes more or less: "Look at me, see what I can stand." There was shame as well at such an eruption of buried feeling, when he had been on the point of praising everything that knows its place, keeps a tight rein on itself, and is content with its modest part as a link in the great scheme of things, as being far superior to the deviant—and here his inner-most convictions lay prone with their roots up in the air, mired in life's volcanic mud. Mainly he felt terrified, sure that something horrible was about to befall him. This fear had no rational basis; he was still thinking in images and was obsessed with the notion that Clarisse and Ulrich were intent on tearing him out of his picture. He made an effort to shake off his waking dream and find something to say that would pull the conversation which his loss of control had brought to a a standstill back onto a sensible track, and actually had something on the tip of his tongue, but a suspicion that his words came too late, that meanwhile something else had been said and done without his being aware of it, restrained him, and then, in the midst of catching up with the time-lapse, he suddenly heard Clarisse saying to him:

"If you want to kill Ulrich, why don't you? You're a slave of conscience. An artist can't make good music when he's saddled with a conscience."

It took a long time for this to sink in. Some things are soonest understood by means of one's own answer to them, and Walter was holding back his answer for fear of betraying his absence of mind. And in this moment of indecision he understood, or let himself be persuaded, that Clarisse had actually put into words the source of the terrifying fugue of ideas he had just been through. She was right: if Walter could have had his wish, it would often have been none other than to see Ulrich dead. That sort of thing is not too uncommon in a friendship (which does not dissolve as easily as love) when there is something in it that threatens a person's self-esteem. Nor was there real murder in his heart, for the moment he imagined Ulrich dead, his old boyhood love for his lost friend instantly revived, at least in part, and just as in the theater the civilized inhibition against a monstrous act is temporarily suspended by some pumped-up emotion, Walter almost felt that the thought of a tragic solution ennobled even the intended victim. He felt rather uplifted, despite his physical timidity and his squeamishness at the thought of seeing blood. While he would have liked to see Ulrich's arrogance broken down, he would have done nothing toward bringing even this about. But thoughts are not logical by nature, however much we like to think they are; only the unimaginative resistance of reality alerts us to the paradoxes inherent in the poem called man. So perhaps Clarisse was right in saying that too much of a civilized conscience got in an artist's way. All of this was going through Walter's head as he faced his wife with a baffled, reluctant expression.

"If he hampers you in your work," Clarisse repeated with zeal, "then you have the right to get him out of the way." She seemed to offer this as a stimulating and entertaining idea.

Walter wanted to hold out his hands to her, and although his arms felt pinned to his sides, he seemed to have come closer to her. "Nietzsche and Christ only failed because they were halfhearted in the end," she whispered in his ear. What awful nonsense she was talking. How could she drag Christ into this? What was that supposed to mean—that Christ failed because he was halfhearted? Such analogies were merely embarrassing. And yet Walter felt an indescribable prompting issuing from those moving lips of hers. Evidently his own hard-won resolution to make common cause with the majority was being steadily undermined by the irrepressible need to be someone in his own right. He laid hands on Clarisse and held her fast with all his strength, so that she could not move. Her eyes met his like two tiny disks. "How can you let such ideas enter your head?" he said, over and over, but got no answer. He must have unconsciously drawn her closer to him, for Clarisse now set the nails of her outspread ten fingers on his face like a bird's claws, keeping it from getting any closer to hers. She's crazy, Walter felt, but he couldn't let her go. An ugliness beyond all comprehension distorted her face; he had never seen a lunatic in his life, but this, he thought, must be what they looked like.

And suddenly he groaned: "You're in love with him!" It was not a particularly original remark, nor was this the first time they had argued the point; it was only that he did not want to believe that Clarisse was mad but preferred to believe that she loved Ulrich. This act of self-sacrifice was perhaps not quite uninfluenced by the fact that Clarisse, whose thin-lipped Early Renaissance beauty he had always admired, now for the first time looked ugly to him, an ugliness possibly related to her face being no longer tenderly veiled by love for him but stripped bare by the brutal love for his rival. Here was a sufficiency of complications, trembling between his heart and his eye as something quite new to him, full of meaning both general and personal. But what if his groaning out "You're in love with him!" in that subhuman voice was a sign of his being already infected by Clarisse's madness? The thought gave him a start.

Clarisse had gently freed herself from his grasp but then moved close to him of her own accord and said several times, in answer to his question, as though she were chanting something: "I don't want a child from you! I don't want a child from you!" kissing him lightly and quickly as she spoke.

Then she was gone.

Had she really also said, "He wants a child from me?" Walter could not be sure, but he heard it as a sort of possibility. He stood at the piano, jealous to the bursting point, sensing a breath of something warm and something cold blowing on him from either side. Were these the currents of genius and madness? Of surrender and of hatred? Of love and rationality? He could imagine himself leaving the way open for Clarisse and of laying his heart down on the road for her to walk over, and he could also imagine himself annihilating her and Ulrich with the power of words. He could not decide whether to rush off to Ulrich or begin composing his symphony, which might in this moment become the eternal struggle between the earth and the stars, or whether it might be a good idea to cool himself off first in the water-nymph pool of Wagner's forbidden music. By dint of these considerations, the indescribable state in which he had found himself began to clear up.

He opened the piano and lit a cigarette, and while his thoughts were scattering farther afield, his fingers on the keyboard were beginning to play the billowing, spine-melting music of the Saxon wizard. After this slow discharge of emotion had been going on for a while, he came to realize that he and his wife had both been in a state in which they could not be held responsible for their actions; embarrassing as it was, he knew it was too soon to go after Clarisse and make her understand. Now he needed to be with other people. He clapped on his hat and went off to town to carry out his original intention and immerse himself in the general excitement, if he could find it. As he walked he felt as though he were a captain bringing with him a demonic fighting force to link up with the others. But once he was on the trolley to town, life resumed its ordinary appearance. That Ulrich would have to be among the opposing forces, that

Count Leinsdorf's town house might be stormed by the marchers, that he might see Ulrich hanging from a streetlamp or being trampled by an onrushing mob or, alternatively, being defended by Walter and brought, trembling, to safety—these possibilities were at most fleeting shadows on the bright daylight pattern of the orderly train ride, with its set ticket prices, regular stops, and warning bells, a pattern with which Walter, his breathing now restored to a calmer rhythm, felt so much at home.

119

A COUNTERMINE AND A SEDUCTION

It now looked as though things were coming to a head, and even for Director Leo Fischel, who had been patiently biding his time and laying his countermine against Arnheim, the moment of satisfaction came. Too bad that Frau Clementine happened to be out, so that he had to content himself with walking into his daughter Gerda's room, in his hand the afternoon paper that usually carried the latest news of the Stock Exchange. He settled himself comfortably in a chair, pointed to an item on the page, and asked genially: "Well now, my child, do you know to what we are indebted for the presence of that highbrow financier among us?"

At home he never referred to Arnheim in any other terms, to show that as a serious man of business he was not impressed by his womenfolk's admiration for this rich windbag. Hatred may not give a man second sight, but there's often a grain of truth in a Stock Exchange rumor, and the hint of one in the news item, combined with Fischel's dislike of the man, instantly made him see the whole picture.

"Well, my dear, do you?" he repeated, trying to catch his daughter's eye and hold it in the triumphant beam of his own. "He wants to get control of the Galician oil fields, that's what!"

With this Fischel got up again, grabbed his paper as one might grab a dog by the scruff of his neck, and walked out, because it had just occurred to him that there were several men he might call to check his information. He felt as though what he had just learned from the paper was what he had been thinking all along—which shows that news from the Stock Exchange has quite the same effect as the higher forms of literature—and he now approved of Arnheim as a sensible man of whom nothing less should have been expected, quite forgetting that he had till then been calling him nothing but a windbag. He could not be bothered to elucidate to Gerda the meaning of his announcement; every further word would only have weakened the impact of the facts, which spoke so eloquently for themselves. "He wants control of the Galician oil fields!" With the weight of this blunt statement on his tongue he left the scene, thinking only: "The man who can afford to play a waiting game always wins in the end." This is axiomatic on the Stock Exchange, among other such truths, which most perfectly complement the eternal verities.

Gerda waited until he was out of her room to give vent to her feelings—she would not give her father the satisfaction of seeing her disconcerted or even surprised—but now she hastily flung open the closet, grabbed her hat and coat, and straightened her hair and dress at the mirror, where she sat still for a bit, doubtfully studying her face. She had decided to rush directly to Ulrich with her father's disclosure, which she thought Ulrich of all people should hear as soon as possible, since she knew enough about what was going on in Diotima's circle to realize its importance to him. She sensed a world of feeling coming into motion, like a crowd that has been hesitating on the brink of something for a long time. Up to this point she had forced herself to behave as if she had forgotten Ulrich's invitation, but her first impulses had no sooner begun to detach themselves from the dark mass of feeling and slowly to move forward than the ones farther back were irresistibly impelled to run and push forward, and while she hesitated to make up her mind, her mind made itself up without paying any attention to her.

"He doesn't love me!" she told herself while studying her face, grown even more haggard in the last few days, in the mirror. "How could he love me, when I look like this," she thought listlessly, and added at once, in defiance: "He's not worth it; it's all in my imagination anyway."

She sat there in utter discouragement, feeling drained, feeling also that for years they had both worked hard at complicating something that was basically quite simple. Meanwhile Hans was only adding to her nervous strain with his immature attempts at making love to her. She treated him harshly and sometimes, of late, contemptuously, which only made Hans more violent, behaving like a boy who threatens to do himself in, and when she had to calm him down, he fell back to putting his arms around her and touching her in his vague way, so that her shoulders grew bony and her skin turned dull. All these torments she had put behind her when she opened her closet to take out her hat, and her anxiety in front of the mirror only led to her jumping up again and rushing out, without in the least getting rid of the anxiety itself.

When Ulrich saw her coming in, he saw everything; to top it off, she had even tied on a veil such as Bonadea wore to visit him. Gerda was trembling in every limb and tried to mask her condition by assuming an unnaturally casual manner, which only made her seem absurdly stiff.

"The reason I came, Ulrich, is that I've just had some important information from my father."

"How peculiar," Ulrich thought; "she's never called me by my first name before." Her forced tone of intimacy infuriated him, but he tried to keep her from seeing this by attributing her theatrical behavior to her wish to make her visit look less portentous, more like a normal, if slightly belated, occurrence, though the effort it cost her was bound to have the opposite effect on him, suggesting that her intentions were clearly to go to the limit.

"We've been close friends for a long time," she explained, "and the only reason we never used first names was to avoid the implications." It was a rehearsed entrance, and she was prepared to surprise him with it.

But Ulrich cut it short by putting an arm around her and giving her a kiss. Gerda gave way like a melting candle. Her breathing, her fingers fumbling for him, were those of a person who has lost consciousness. He was instantly moved to behave with the ruthlessness of a seducer who senses the vacillation of a soul being dragged along by its body like a prisoner in the grip of his captors. From the windows a faint glimmer of wintry afternoon light entered the darkening room, where he stood outlined against one of these bright rectangles with the girl in his arms, her head was yellow and sharply contoured against the soft pillow of light, and her complexion had an oily shine, so that the whole effect was corpselike. He had to overcome a slight revulsion as he kissed her slowly everywhere on her bare skin between her hair and her neckline until he came to her lips, which met his in a manner reminiscent of the frail little arms a child puts around a grownup's neck. He thought of Bonadea's beautiful face, which, in the grip of passion, resembled a dove with its feathers ruffled in the claws of a bird of prey, and of Diotima's statuesque loveliness, which he had never enjoyed; how strange that instead of the beauty these two women had to offer he should be looking at Gerda's homely face, grim with passion.

But Gerda did not remain in her waking swoon for long. She had meant to shut her eyes for only a fleeting moment but lost all sense of time while Ulrich was kissing her, as if the stars were standing still in the infinite; as soon as he began to pause in his labors, however, she awakened and got firmly to her feet again. These were the first kisses of real, not merely would-be passion she had ever given and, as she thought, received, and the reverberations in her body were as extraordinary as though this moment had already made a woman of her. It is a process much like having a tooth pulled: although immediately afterward there is less of one's body than before, one actually feels more complete because a source of disquiet has been definitively removed. Hence, when Gerda felt the inner resolution of this chord, she pulled herself up, full of fresh determination.

"You haven't even asked me what I came to tell you," she said.

"That you love me," Ulrich said in some embarrassment.

"Oh no; only that your friend Arnheim is making a fool of your cousin, carrying on like a lover when what he's really after is something quite different," and Gerda told him what her papa had found out.

The news in all its simplicity made a deep impression on Ulrich. He felt obliged to warn Diotima, who was sailing with wings outspread into a ludicrous disappointment. For despite the malicious satisfaction he took in dwelling on this image, he felt sorry for his beautiful cousin. But most of all he was overcome with heartfelt appreciation for Papa Fischel, although he was on the verge of doing him a great wrong; he sincerely admired the man's reliable old-fashioned business sense, with its decorative border of fine sturdy convictions, which had hit on the simplest explanation for all the mysteries surrounding that modish Great Mind. Ulrich's mood had been altered, leaving far behind the tender demands made on him by Gerda's presence. He couldn't believe that only a few days ago he had been able to think that he could open his heart to this girl. Surmounting the inner ramparts, he thought, is what Hans calls his sacrilegious notion of two lovesick angels coming together, and he savored, as though he were running his fingers over it in his mind, the wonderfully smooth, hard surface of the matter-of-fact form life had taken on nowadays, thanks to the good sense of Leo Fischel and his like. All he could find to say was "Your papa is a wonder."

Gerda was so full of the importance of her news that she had expected something more—she didn't know exactly what, but something like the moment when all the instruments in the orchestra, winds and strings, strike up in unison—and Ulrich's indifference was a painful reminder of how he had always made a point of siding with the average, the ordinary, the matter-of-fact aspect of things to deflate her. She had tried to see this as a prickly kind of making advances, something not altogether alien to her own young girl's ways, but now, "when they had really begun to love each other," as her somewhat childish formula went, she felt it as a clear warning that the man to whom she was giving herself so recklessly was not taking her seriously enough. It was a blow to her new self-confidence, and yet she was also oddly pleased by "not being taken seriously enough." It was a relief, compared with the strain in keeping up her relationship with Hans, and while she did not understand Ulrich's praise of her father, it somehow restored an order of things she had disturbed by hurting Papa Leo because of Hans. This mild sense of making a somewhat unusual reentry into the bosom of her family by way of losing her virtue so distracted her that she gently resisted the pressure of Ulrich's arm and said to him: "Let's understand each other first as human beings, and the rest will take care of itself." These words came from a manifesto of her group, the so-called Community in Action, and was all that was left at the moment of Hans Sepp and his circle.

But Ulrich had put his arm around her again because, knowing that he had something important to do since hearing the news about Arnheim, he first had to finish this episode with Gerda. He was not at all reconciled to having to go through everything the situation called for, but he immediately put the rejected arm around her again, this time in that wordless language which, without force, states more firmly than words can do that any further resistance is useless. Gerda felt the virility of that arm all the way down her spine. She had lowered her head, with her eyes fixed on her lap as though it held, gathered as in an apron, all the thoughts that would help her to reach that "human understanding" with Ulrich before anything could be allowed to happen as a crowning act. But she felt her face looking duller and more vacuous by the moment until, like an empty husk, it finally floated upward, with her eyes directly below the eyes of the seducer.

He bent down and covered this face with the ruthless kisses that stir the flesh. Gerda straightened up as if she had no will of her own and let herself be led the ten steps or so to Ulrich's bedroom, leaning heavily on him as though she were wounded or sick. Her feet moved, one ahead of the other, as if she had nothing to do with it, even though she did not let herself be dragged along but went of her own accord. Such an inner void despite all that excitement was something Gerda had never known before; it was as if all the blood had been drained from her; she was freezing, yet in passing a mirror that seemed to reflect her image from a great distance she could see that her face was a coppery red, with flecks of white. Suddenly, as in a street accident when the eye is hypersensitive to the whole scene, she took in the man's bedroom with all its details. It came to her that, had she been wiser and more calculating, she might have moved in here as Ulrich's wife. It would have made her very happy, but she was groping for words to say that she was not out for any advantage and had come only to give herself to him; yet the words did not come, and she told herself that this had to happen, and opened the collar of her dress.

Ulrich had released her. He could not bring himself to help undress her like a fond lover and stood apart, flinging off his own clothes. Gerda saw the man's tall, straight body, powerfully poised between violence and beauty. Panic-stricken, she noticed that her own body, still standing there in her underthings, was covered with gooseflesh. Again she groped for words that might help her, that might make her less of a miserable figure where she stood. She longed to say something that would turn Ulrich into her lover in a way she vaguely imagined as dissolving in infinite sweetness, something one could achieve without having to do what she was about to do, something as blissful as it was indefinable. For an instant she saw herself standing with him in a field of candles growing out of the earth, row upon row to infinity, like so many pansies, all bursting into flame at her feet on signal. But as she could not utter a single word of all this, she went on feeling painfully unattractive and miserable, her arms trembling, unable to finish undressing; she had to clamp her bloodless lips together to keep them from twitching weirdly without a sound.

At this point Ulrich, who saw her agony and realized that the whole struggle up to now might come to nothing, went over to her and slipped off her shoulder straps. Gerda slid into bed like a boy. For an instant Ulrich saw a naked adolescent in motion; it affected him no more, sexually, than the sudden blinking of a fish. He guessed that Gerda had made up her mind to get it over with because it was too late to get out of it, and he had never yet perceived as clearly as in the instant he followed her into bed how much the passionate intrusion into another body is a sequel to a child's liking for secret and forbidden hiding places. His hands encountered the girl's skin, still bristling with fear, and he felt frightened too, instead of attracted. This body, already flabby while still unripe, repelled him; it made no sense to do what he was doing, and he would have liked nothing better than to escape from this bed, so that he had to call to mind everything he could think of that would help him to see it through. In his frantic haste he summoned up all the usual reasons people find nowadays to justify their acting without sincerity, or faith, or scruple, or satisfaction; and in abandoning himself to this effort he found, not, of course, any feeling of love, but a half-crazy anticipation of something like a massacre, a sex murder or, if there is such a thing, a lustful suicide, inspired by the demons of the void who lurk behind all of life's images. This reminded him of his brawl with the hoodlums that night he met Bonadea, and he decided to be quicker this time. But now something awful happened. Gerda had been gathering up all her inner resources to alchemize them into willpower with which to resist the shameful terror she was suffering, as though she were facing her execution; but the instant she felt Ulrich beside her, so strangely naked, his hands on her bare skin, her body flung off all her will. Even while somewhere deep inside her she still felt a friendship beyond words for him, a trembling, tender longing to put her arms around him, kiss his hair, follow his voice to its source with her lips; and imagined that to touch his real self would make her melt like a fragment of snow on a warm hand—but it would have to be the Ulrich she knew, dressed as usual, as he appeared in the familiar setting of her parental home, not this naked stranger whose hostility she sensed and who did not take her sacrifice seriously even as he gave her no time to think what she was doing—Gerda suddenly heard herself screaming. Like a little cloud, a soap bubble, a scream hung in the air, and others followed, little screams expelled from her chest as though she were wrestling with something, a whimpering from which high-pitched cries of *ee-ee* bubbled and floated off, from lips that grimaced and twisted and were wet as if with deadly lust. She wanted to jump up, but she couldn't move. Her eyes would not obey her and kept sending out signals without permission. Gerda was pleading to be let off, like a child facing some punishment or being taken to the doctor, who cannot go one step farther because it is being torn and convulsed by its own shrieks of terror. Her hands were up over her breasts, and she was menacing Ulrich with her nails while frantically pressing her long thighs together. This revolt of her body against herself was frightful. She perceived it with utmost clarity as a kind of theater, but she was also the audience sitting alone and desolate in the dark auditorium and could do nothing to prevent her fate from being acted out before her, in a screaming frenzy; nothing to keep herself from taking the lead in the performance.

Ulrich stared in horror into the tiny pupils of her veiled eyes, with their strangely unbending gaze, and watched, aghast, those weird motions in which desire and taboo, the soul and the soulless, were indescribably intertwined. His eye caught a fleeting glimpse of her pale fair skin and the short black hairs that shaded into red where they grew more densely. It occurred to him that he was facing a fit of hysteria, and he had no idea how to handle it. He was afraid that these horribly distressing screams might get even louder, and remembered that such a fit might be stopped by an angry shout or even by a sudden, vicious slap. Then the thought that this horror might have been avoided somehow led him to think that a younger man might persist in going further with Gerda even in these circumstances. "That might be a way of getting her over it," he thought, "perhaps it's a mistake to give in to her, now that the silly goose has let herself in too deep." He did nothing of the sort; it was only that such irritable thoughts kept zigzagging through his mind while he was instinctively whispering an uninterrupted stream of comforting words, promising not to do anything to her, assuring her that nothing had really happened, asking her to forgive him, at the same time that all his words, swept up like chaff in his loathing of the scene she was making, seemed to him so absurd and undignified that he had to fight off a temptation to grab an armful of pillows to press on her mouth and choke off these shrieks that wouldn't stop.

At long last her fit began to wear off and her body quieted down. Her eyes brimming with tears, she sat up in the bed, her little breasts drooping slackly from a body not yet under the mind's full control. Ulrich took a deep breath, again overcome with repugnance at the inhuman, merely physical aspects of the experience. Gerda was regaining normal consciousness; something bloomed in her eyes, like the first actual awakening after the eyes have been open for some time, and she stared blankly ahead for a second, then noticed that she was sitting up stark naked and glanced at Ulrich; the blood came in great waves back to her face. Ulrich couldn't think of anything better to do than whisper the same reassurances to her again; he put his arm around her shoulder, drew her to his chest, and told her to think nothing of it. Gerda found herself back in the situation that had driven her to hysteria, but now everything looked strangely pale and forlorn: the tumbled bed, her nude body in the arms of a man intently whispering to her, the feelings that had brought her to this. She was fully aware of what it all meant, but she also knew that something horrible had happened, something she would rather not focus on, and while she could tell that Ulrich's voice sounded more tender, all it meant was that he regarded her as a sick person, but it was he who had made her sick! Still, it no longer mattered; all she wanted was to be gone from this place, to get away without having to say a word.

She dropped her head and pushed Ulrich away, felt for her camisole, and pulled it over her head like a child or someone who did not care how she looked. Ulrich helped her to dress, he even pulled her stockings up over her legs, and he also felt as though he were dressing a child. Gerda was a bit unsteady on her feet when she stood up. She thought of how she had felt earlier in the day when she left home, the home to which she was about to return, and felt, in deep misery and shame, that she had not passed the test. She did not utter a word in answer to anything Ulrich was saying. A very distant memory came back to her, of Ulrich once saying, as a joke on himself, that solitude sometimes led him into excess. She did not feel angry at him. She simply wanted never again to hear him say anything whatsoever. When he offered to get her a cab she only shook her head, pulled her hat on over her ruffled hair, and left him without a glance. Seeing her walk away with her veil now sadly trailing from her hand, he felt awkward as a schoolboy. He probably should not have let her go in this state, but he could think of no way to stop her, half-dressed as he was because he had been attending to her, unprepared even to confront the serious mood in which he was left, as though he would have to get fully dressed before he could decide what to do with himself.

120

THE PARALLEL CAMPAIGN CAUSES A STIR

When Walter reached the center of town he sensed something in the air. There was no visible difference in the way people moved on the sidewalks or in the carriages and streetcars, and if there was something unusual here and there it faded out before one could tell what it was; nevertheless, everything seemed to be carrying a little sign pointing in one direction, and Walter had barely walked a few steps before he felt such a sign on himself as well. He followed the indicated direction and felt that the Department of Fine Arts official he was, as well as the struggling painter and musician, and even Clarisse's tormented husband, were all giving way to a person who was none of the above. The very streets, with all their bustle and their ornate, pompous buildings, seemed to be in an analogous "expectant state," as though the hard facets of a crystal were being dissolved in some liquid medium and about to fall back into an earlier, more amorphous condition. However conservative he was in rejecting innovations, he was also always ready in his own mind to condemn the present, and the dissolution of the existing order that he was now sensing was positively stimulating. As in his recent daydream, the crowds he ran into had an aura of mobility and haste, and a unity that seemed more unforced than the usual group spirit based on intellect, morality, and sound security measures; more that of a free, informal community. They made him think of a huge bunch of flowers just after it has been untied, opening freely without, however, falling apart; and of a body unclothed, standing free, smiling, naked, having no need of words. Nor was he troubled when, quickening his pace, he ran into a large contingent of police standing by; he enjoyed the sight, like that of a military camp in readiness for the alarm to be given; all those red uniform collars, dismounted riders, movements of small units reporting their arrival or departure, stirred his senses into a warlike mood.

Beyond this point, where a cordon was about to be drawn across the street, the scene was more somber. There were hardly any women on the sidewalks, and even the colorful uniforms of the army officers who normally were seen hereabouts when off duty had somehow been swallowed up by the prevailing uncertainty. There were still many pedestrians like himself coming downtown, but the impression they gave was more that of chaff and litter in the wake of a strong gust of wind. Soon he saw the first groups forming, apparently held together not only by curiosity but just as much by indecision whether to follow the unusual attraction farther or to turn around and go home.

Walter's questions elicited a variety of answers. Some said that there was a great patriotic parade; others thought they had heard of a protest march against certain dangerously nationalistic activists, and opinions were equally split as to whether the general uproar was caused by the Pan-Germans protesting against the government's coddling of the Slavic minorities, as most people thought, or by loyal supporters of the government urging all patriotic Kakanians to march shoulder-to-shoulder in its defense against such continual disorders. They were all tagalongs like himself and knew nothing more than he had already heard rumored at the office, but an irrepressible itch to gossip led Walter on to speak to people, and even though they mostly admitted to having no idea, or laughed the whole thing off as a joke, including their own curiosity, the farther he went the more everyone seemed to be in agreement that it was high time *something* was done, though no one volunteered to tell him just what that should be. As he kept on, he noticed more often on the faces he met something senseless that overflowed and drowned out reason itself, something that told him that no one cared any longer what was happening, wherever they were being drawn to, as long as it was something unusual that would "take them out of themselves," if only in the attenuated form of a common general excitement, suggesting a remote kinship with long-forgotten states of communal ecstasy and transfiguration, a sort of developing unconscious readiness to leap out of their clothes, and even their skins.

Trading speculations and saying things that were not at all in character, Walter fell in with the rest, who were gradually transforming themselves from small crumbling groups of people, just waiting, and other people walking aimlessly along, into a procession that advanced toward the supposed scene of events, still without any definite intent yet visibly growing in density and energy. Emotionally they were still at the stage where they were like rabbits scampering about outside their burrows, ready to scurry back inside at the slightest sign of danger, when from the front of the disordered procession, far ahead and out of sight, a more definite sort of excitement came rippling back toward the rear. Up there a group of students, young men anyway, who had already taken some sort of action and had returned from "the battlefield," joined the vanguard, and sounds of talking and shouting too far away to be understood, garbled messages, and waves of excitement were running through the crowd and, depending on the listeners' temperaments or what scraps of information they snatched up, spread indignation or fear, the itch to fight or some moral imperative, causing the gathering mob to thrust forward in a mood guided by the kind of commonplace notions that take a different form inside every head but are of so little significance, despite being uppermost in the consciousness, that they join in a single vital force that affects the muscles more than the brain. In the midst of this moving throng Walter also became infected and soon found himself in that stimulated but vacuous state rather like the early stages of drunkenness. Nobody really knows the exact nature of the change that turns individuals with a will of their own into a mob with a single will, capable of going to the wildest extremes of good or evil and incapable of stopping to think anything through, even if most of the individuals involved have spent their lives dedicated to moderation and prudence in the conduct of their private affairs. A mob in a state of mounting excitement for which it has no outlet will probably discharge all that energy into the first available channel, and those among its participants who are the most excitable, sensitive, and most vulnerable to pressure, those at the extreme ends of the spectrum who are primed to commit sudden acts of violence or rise to unprecedented levels of sentimental generosity, are most likely to set the example and lead the way; they are the points of least resistance in the mass, but the shout that is uttered through them rather than by them, the stone that somehow finds its way into their hands, the emotion into which they burst, is what opens the way along which the others, who have been generating excitement among themselves to the point where it must be discharged, then come surging in a frenzy, giving to what happens the character of mob action, which is experienced by those involved in it as both compulsion and liberation.

What makes such agitated behavior interesting, incidentally, observable as it is among spectators of any sporting event or among crowds listening to speeches, is not so much the psychology of the emotional release it affords as the question of what it is that primes people to get themselves into such a state in the first place. Assuming that life makes sense, even its senseless manifestations would have some meaning and would not necessarily look like mere demonstrations of mental deficiency. Walter happened to know this better than most and could think of all sorts of remedies for it, so that he was constantly struggling against being swept along by this tidal wave of communal passion, which, demeaning as it was, nevertheless raised his spirits sky-high. The thought of Clarisse flashed through his mind. What a good thing she isn't here, he thought; she'd be crushed flat. A stab of grief kept him from pursuing his thought of her—with it had come the all-too-distinct impression she had given him of being raving mad. Maybe I'm the one that's mad, he thought, because it's taken me so long to notice it. I soon will be, if I go on living with her. I don't believe it, he thought, but there's no doubt about it. Right between my hands her darling face turned into a hideous mask, he thought. But he couldn't think it all through properly; his mind was awash with despair. He could only feel that despite his helpless anguish for her, it was incomparably finer to love Clarisse than to be running with the pack here—and to escape his fears, he pressed himself deeper into the ranks of the marchers.

Meanwhile Ulrich had arrived at the Palais Leinsdorf, though by another route. As he turned into the gate he noticed a double guard at the entrance and a large detachment of police stationed inside the courtyard. His Grace welcomed him with composure, while apparently aware of having become a target of popular disfavor.

"I think I once told you that anything favored by a good many people is sure to turn out to be worthwhile. Well, I have to take that back. Of course, there are exceptions," he said.

His Grace's majordomo now arrived with the latest bulletin: the demonstrators were approaching the Palais, and should he arrange to have the gate and shutters locked? His Grace shook his head. "What an idea!" he said kindly. "They'd like nothing better; it would allow them to think we're afraid of them. Besides, we've got all those men down there from the police looking out for us." Then, turning to Ulrich, he said indignantly: "Let them come and smash our windows! I told you all along that all that intellectual chatter would get us nowhere." Behind his façade of dignified calm, a deep resentment seemed to be working within him.

Ulrich had just walked over to the window when the marchers arrived. They were flanked by police, who dispersed the onlookers lining the avenue like a cloud of dust raised by the firm tread of the marchers. A little farther back, vehicles could be seen wedged in the crowd, while its relentless current flowed around them in endless

black waves on which the foam of upturned faces seemed to be dancing. When the spearhead of the mob came within sight of Count
Leinsdorf's windows, it looked as though it had been slowed down by
some command; an immense ripple ran backward along the column
as the advancing ranks jammed up, like a muscle tightening before
launching a blow. The next instant this blow came whizzing through
the air, in the weird form of a massed shout of indignation made visible by all those wide-open mouths before their roar was heard. In
rhythmical succession the rows of faces snapped open as they arrived
on the scene, and since the noise of the those in the rear was blotted
out by the louder noise of those in the front, the spectacle could be
seen repeating itself continually in the distance.

"The maw of the mob," Count Leinsdorf said, just behind Ulrich,
as solemnly as if it were some familiar phrase like "our daily bread."
"But what is it they're actually yelling? I can't make it out, with all
that din."

Ulrich said he thought they were mostly screaming "Boo!"

"Yes, but there's something more, isn't there?"

Ulrich did not tell him that among the indistinct dancing sound
waves of boos, a clear, long-drawn-out "Down with Leinsdorf!"
could often enough be heard. He even thought he had heard several
outcries of "Hurray for Germany!" interspersed with "Long live Arnheim!" but could not be absolutely sure, because the thick glass of
the windows muffled the sounds.

Ulrich had come here as soon as Gerda left him, because he felt it
was necessary to tell Count Leinsdorf, if no one else, the news that
had come to his ears, which exposed Arnheim beyond all expectation. He had not yet had a chance to speak of it. As he looked down at
the dark surge of bodies beneath the window, thoughts of his own
days in the army made him say to himself: "It would take only one
company to make a clean sweep of the square." He could imagine all
those gaping mouths turning into a single frothing maw suddenly
succumbing to panic, growing slack and drooping at the edges, lips
slowly sinking over teeth; his imagination transformed the menacing
black crowd into a flock of hens scattering before a dog rushing into
their midst. All his anger had contracted again into a hard knot, but
the old satisfaction in watching moral man retreat before brute violent man was, as always, a two-edged feeling.

"Are you all right?" Count Leinsdorf was asking. He had been pacing the floor behind Ulrich and had actually received the impression from some odd movement of Ulrich's that he had cut himself, though there was no sharp-edged object anywhere in the vicinity. When he received no answer he stood still, shook his head, and said: "We must not forget, after all, that it is not so very long since His Majesty's generous decision to let the people have a voice in the conduct of their own affairs; so it is understandable that a degree of universal political maturity that would be worthy of our Sovereign's magnanimity is still lacking. I believe I said as much at our very first meeting."

This little speech made Ulrich drop any notion of telling His Grace or Diotima about Arnheim's machinations; despite his antagonism to Arnheim he felt closer to him than to the others, and his memory of himself setting upon Gerda, like a big dog on a howling little one, a memory he now realized had been haunting him all along, troubled him less when he thought of Arnheim's infamous conduct toward Diotima. The episode of the screaming body staging a dramatic scene for a captive audience of two embarrassed souls could also be seen from the farcical side, and the people down there in the street at whom Ulrich was still staring spellbound without taking the slightest notice of Count Leinsdorf were also staging a farce. It was this that fascinated him. They did not really want to attack or rip anyone apart, although they looked as if they did. They made a serious show of being enraged, but it was not the kind of seriousness that drives men into a line of fire, not even that of a fire brigade! They're only going through some kind of ritual, he thought, some time-hallowed display of righteous indignation, the half-civilized, half-barbaric legacy of ancient communal rites no individual need take wholly seriously. He envied them. How appealing they are, even in this state where they are doing their best to be as unappealing as possible, he thought. The warm defense against loneliness that a crowd provides came radiating up from below, and here he was, fated to stand up here, outside its protective shelter—he felt this vividly, for an instant, as if he were looking up from down there and seeing his own image behind the thick pane of glass set in the wall of the building. It would have been better for him and his fate, he felt, had he been able to fly into a rage at this moment, or, on Count

Leinsdorf's behalf, give the alarm to the guard, or alternatively had he been capable of feeling close to the people as their friend; a man who plays cards with his fellows, bargains with them, quarrels with them, and enjoys the same pleasures they do is free to order them shot, too, when the occasion calls for it, without its seeming to be anything unnatural. There is a way of being on good terms with life that allows a man to go about his business with no second thoughts, in a live-and-let-live fashion, Ulrich was thinking. It may have a peculiarity of its own but is no less dependable than a natural instinct, and it is from this that the intimate scent of a healthy personality emanates, while whoever lacks this gift for compromise with life and is solitary, unyielding, and in dead earnest makes the others feel uneasy and unnerves them, as a caterpillar might, not because it is dangerous but because it is repellent. He felt a depressing aversion for the unnaturalness of the solitary man and his mental games, such as may be aroused by the sight of a turbulent crowd in the grip of natural, shared emotions.

The demonstration had been growing more intense. Count Leinsdorf was pacing the room in some agitation, with an occasional glance through the second window. He was in distress, though he would not show it; his eyes protruded like two little marbles from among the soft furrows of his face, and he stretched his arms now and then before he crossed them again behind his back. Ulrich suddenly realized that it was he, who had been standing at the window the whole time, who was being taken for the Count. All the eyes down there seemed focused on his face, and sticks were being brandished at him. A few steps beyond, where the street curved from view as though it were slipping into the wings, the performers were already beginning to take off the greasepaint, as it were; there was no point in looking fierce for no one in particular, so they naturally let their faces relax, and some even began to joke and laugh as if they were on a picnic. Ulrich noticed this and laughed too, but the newcomers took him for the Count laughing and their rage rose to a fearsome pitch, which only made Ulrich laugh all the more and without restraint.

But all at once he broke off in disgust. With his eyes still moving from the threatening open-mouthed faces to the high-spirited ones farther back, and his mind refusing to absorb any more of this spectacle, he was undergoing a strange transformation. I can't go on with this life, and I can't keep on rebelling against it any longer, either, was what he felt, while keenly aware of the room behind him with the large paintings on the wall, the long Empire desk, the stiff perpendicular lines of draperies and bell ropes, like another, smaller stage, with him standing up front on the apron, in the opening between the curtains, facing the drama running its course on the greater stage outside. The two stages had their own way of fusing into one without regard for the fact that he was standing between them. Then his sense of the room behind him contracted and turned inside out, passing through him or flowing past him as if turned to water, making for a strange spatial inversion, Ulrich thought, so that the people were passing behind him. Perhaps he had passed through them and arrived beyond them at some zero point, or else they were moving both before and behind him, lapping against him as the same ever-changing ripples of a stream lap against a stone in their midst. It was an experience beyond his understanding; he was chiefly aware of the glassiness, emptiness, tranquillity of the state in which he found himself. Is it really possible, he wondered, to leave one's own space for some hidden other space? He felt as though chance had led him through a secret door.

He shook these dreams off with so violent a motion of his whole body that Count Leinsdorf stood still in surprise. "Whatever is the matter with you today?" His Grace asked. "You're taking it much too hard. I must stick to my decision: the Germans will have to be won over by way of the non-Germans, whether it hurts or not." At these words Ulrich was at least able to smile again, and was grateful to see the Count's face before him, with all its knots and furrows. He was reminded of that special moment just before a plane lands, when the ground rises up again with all its voluptuous contours out of the map-like flatness to which it had been reduced for hours on end, and things revert to their familiar earthly meanings, which seem to be growing out of the ground itself. At the same moment the incredible idea flashed through his mind to commit some crime, or perhaps it was an unfocused passing image, for he was not thinking of anything in particular. It might have had some reference to Moosbrugger, for he would have liked to help that fool whom fate had chanced to bring his way as two people come to occupy the same park bench. But all this "crime" really amounted to for him was the urge to shut himself out, to abandon the life he had been living companionably with others. His "dissident" or even "misanthropic" attitude, his so variously justified and well-earned position, had not "arisen" from anything, there was nothing to justify it, it simply existed, he had held it all his life, though rarely with such intensity. It is probably safe to say that in all the revolutions that have ever taken place in this world, it has always been the thinking men who have come off worst. They always begin with the promise of a new civilization, make a clean sweep of every advance hitherto achieved by the human mind as though it were enemy property, and are overtaken by the next upheaval before they can surpass the heights previously attained. Our so-called periods of civilization are nothing but a long series of detours, one for every failure of a movement forward; the idea of placing himself outside this series was nothing new for Ulrich. The only new element was the increasing force of the signs that his mind was coming to a decision and that he was, in fact, ready to act on it. He did not make the slightest effort to come down to specifics. For some moments he was content to be permeated with the feeling that this time it would not be something general or theoretical, the sort of thing he had grown so tired of, but that he must do something personal, take an action that would involve him as a man of flesh and blood, with arms and legs. He knew that at the instant of committing his undefined "crime" he would no longer be in a position to defy the world openly, but only God knew why this should arouse in him such a sensation of passionate tenderness. It was somehow linked with his strange spatial experience of a while ago, a faint echo of which he could bring back at will, when what was happening on this side and on the other side of the window fused into one to form an obscurely exciting relationship to the world that might have suggested to Ulrich—if he could have taken the time to think about it—the legendary voluptuousness that overcame mythical heroes on the point of being devoured by the goddesses they had wooed.

Instead, he was interrupted by Count Leinsdorf, who had meanwhile fought his own inner struggle through to a decision.

"I must stay at my post and face down this insurrection," His Grace began, "so I can't leave. But you, my dear fellow, must really go to your cousin as quickly as possible, before she has time to be frightened and possibly moved to say something to some reporter that might not be quite the thing at this moment. You might tell her . . ." He paused to consider his message. "Yes, it will be best if you say to her: Strong remedies produce strong reactions. And tell her, too, that those who set out to make life better must not shrink, in a crisis, from using the stake or the knife." He stopped again to think, with an almost alarming look of resolution, as his trim little beard rose and then sank to a downward, vertical position every time he was on the verge of saying something but paused to reconsider. In the end, his innate kindliness broke through and he said: "But tell her not to worry, not to be afraid of the troublemakers. The more of a case they have, the more quickly they adjust themselves to the realities when they are given a chance. I don't know whether you've noticed this, but there has never yet been an opposition party that didn't cease to be in opposition when they took over the helm. This is not merely, as you might think, something that goes without saying. It is, rather, a very important point, because it is, if I may say so, the basic reality, the touchstone, the continuity in politics."

121

TALKING MAN-TO-MAN

When Ulrich arrived at Diotima's, Rachel, who let him in, told him that Madame was out but that Dr. Arnheim was there, waiting for her. Ulrich said he would wait too, not noticing that his little ally of the other night had blushed scarlet at the sight of him.

Arnheim, who had been at the window, watching what unrest there still was in the streets, crossed the room to shake hands with Ulrich. His face lit up at seeing Ulrich unexpectedly, for he had wanted to speak with Ulrich but had hesitated to seek him out; however, he did not want to rush into things, and could not immediately think of a good opening. Ulrich was also reluctant to start off with the

Galician oil fields, and so both men fell silent after their first words of greeting and ended up walking over to the window together, where they stared mutely at the flurries of movement down below.

After a while, Arnheim spoke:

"I really don't understand you. Isn't it a thousand times more important to come to grips with life than to write?"

"But I haven't been writing," Ulrich said crisply.

"I'm glad to hear it." Arnheim adjusted to the fact. "Writing, like the pearl, is a disease. Look down there. . . ." He pointed two of his beautifully manicured fingers at the street, with a movement that for all its rapidity had the air of a papal blessing about it. "See how they come along, singly and in clusters, and from time to time a mouth is torn open and something inside makes it yell something. The same man under different circumstances would write something; I agree with you on that."

"But you are a famous writer yourself, aren't you?"

"Oh, that doesn't mean anything." But after saying this, gracefully leaving the question open, Arnheim turned to face Ulrich, confronting him as it were broadside, and standing chest-to-chest with him, said, carefully spacing his words:

"May I ask you something?"

Ulrich could not say no to that, of course, but as he had instinctively moved back a little, this rhetorical courtesy served to rope him in again.

"I hope," Arnheim began, "that you will not hold our recent little difference of opinion against me but rather credit it to my keen interest in your views even when they seem—as they do often enough—to run counter to mine. So let me ask you whether you really meant what you said—to sum it up, if I may: that we must live with a tight rein on our conscience. Is this a good way of putting it?"

The smile Ulrich gave him in answer said: I don't know; let me wait and see what more you have to say.

"You spoke of having to leave life in a free-floating state, like a certain kind of metaphor that hovers inconclusively between two worlds at once, as it were, did you not? You also said some extremely fascinating things to your cousin. I would be mortified if you were to take me for a Prussian industrial militarist who is unlikely to understand that sort of thing. But you say, for instance, that our reality and our history arise only from those aspects of ourselves that don't matter. I take this to mean that we must change the forms and patterns of what happens, and that it doesn't matter much, in your opinion, what happens meanwhile to Tom, Dick, and Harry."

"What I mean," Ulrich interjected warily and reluctantly, "is that our reality is like a fabric being turned out by the thousands of bales, technically flawless in quality but in antiquated patterns no one bothers to bring up-to-date."

"In other words," Arnheim broke in, "I understand you to say that the present state of the world, which is clearly unsatisfactory, arises from our leaders' concern with making world history instead of turning all our energies to permeating the world of power with new ideas. An even closer analogy to our present state of affairs is the case of the manufacturer who keeps turning out goods in response to the market, instead of regulating it. So you see that your ideas touch me very closely. But just because of this you must see that these ideas at times strike me, a man continually engaged in making decisions that keep vast industries going, as positively monstrous! Such as when you demand that we give up attaching any meaningful reality to our actions! Or propose that we abandon the 'provisionally definitive' character of our behavior, as our friend Leinsdorf so gracefully phrases it, when, in fact, we can do no such thing!"

"I demand nothing at all," Ulrich said.

"Oh, you demand a great deal more! You demand that we live our lives in a scientific, experimental way," Arnheim said with energy and warmth. "You want responsible leaders to regard their job not as making history but as a mandate to draw up reports on experiments as a basis for further experiments. A perfectly delightful idea, of course. But how do wars and revolutions—for instance—fit in with that? Can you raise the dead when your experiment has been carried out and taken off the schedule?"

Ulrich now succumbed after all to the temptation to talk, which is not so very different from the temptation to go on smoking, and conceded that one probably had to tackle everything one wanted to do effectively with the utmost seriousness, even when one knew that in fifty years every experiment would turn out not to have been worthwhile. But such a "punctured seriousness" was nothing so very unusual, after all; people risked their lives every day in sport and for nothing at all. Psychologically, there was nothing impossible about a life conducted as an experiment; all that was needed was the determination to assume a certain unlimited responsibility. "That's the crucial difference," he concluded. "In the old days, people felt as it were deductively, starting from certain assumptions. Those days are gone. Today we live without a guiding principle, but also without any method of conscious, inductive thinking; we simply go on trying this and that like a band of monkeys."

"Splendid!" Arnheim admitted freely. "But allow me one last question. Your cousin tells me that you're taking a great interest in the case of a dangerous psychopath. I happen to understand this very well, incidentally. We really don't know how to handle such cases, and society's method of dealing with them is disgracefully hit-or-miss. But in the circumstances—which leave us no choice but either to kill an 'innocent' man or to let him go on killing innocent people—would you let him escape the night before his execution, if you could?"

"No!" Ulrich said.

"No? Really not?" Arnheim asked with sudden animation.

"I don't know. I don't think so. I might of course talk myself out of it by claiming that in a malfunctioning world I have no right to act freely on my own personal convictions; but I shall simply admit that I don't know what I would do."

"That man must surely be stopped from doing further harm," Arnheim said pensively. "And yet, when he is having one of his seizures, he is certainly a man possessed by the demonic, which in all virile epochs has been felt to be akin to the divine. In the old days such a man would have been sent into the wilderness. Even then he might have committed murder, but perhaps in a visionary state, like Abraham about to slaughter his son Isaac. There it is! We no longer have any idea of how to deal with such things, and there is no sincerity in what we do."

Arnheim might have let himself be carried away in uttering these last words without quite knowing what he meant by them; his ambition might have been spurred on by Ulrich's not mustering up enough "heart and rashness" to answer with an unqualified "yes" when asked whether he would save Moosbrugger. But although Ulrich felt this turn of the conversation to be almost an omen, an unexpected reminder of his "resolve" at Count Leinsdorf's, he resented Arnheim's flamboyance in making the most of the Moosbrugger problem, and both factors made him ask dryly, but intently: "Would you set him free?"

"No," Arnheim replied with a smile, "but I'd like to propose something else." And without giving him time to put up resistance, he added: "It's a suggestion I've been wanting to make to you for some time, to make you give up your suspicions of me, which, frankly, hurt my feelings; I want you on my side, in fact. Do you have any conception of what a great industrial enterprise looks like from the inside? It is controlled by two bodies, the top management and the board of directors, usually capped by a third body, the executive committee, as you in Austria call it, made up of representatives of the first two, which meets almost every day. The board of directors naturally consists of men who enjoy the confidence of the majority shareholders. . . ." Here he paused for the first time, to give Ulrich a chance to speak if he wished, as though testing to see whether Ulrich had already noticed something. "As I was saying, the majority shareholders have their representatives on the board and the executive committee." He prompted Ulrich. "Have you any idea who this majority is?"

Ulrich had none. He had only a vague general concept of finance, which to him meant clerks, counters, coupons, and certificates that looked like ancient documents.

Arnheim cued him in again. "Have you ever helped to elect a board of directors? No, you haven't," he answered his own question. "There would be no point in trying to imagine it, since you will never own the majority of shares in a company." He said this so firmly that Ulrich very nearly felt ashamed of being found wanting in so important a respect; and it was in fact just like Arnheim to move in one easy stride from his demons to his board of directors. Smiling, he continued: "There is one person I haven't mentioned yet, the most important of all, in a sense. I spoke of the majority shareholders, which sounds like a harmless plural but is in fact nearly always a single person, a chief shareholder, unnamed and unknown to the general public, hidden behind those he sends out front in his place."

Ulrich now realized that he was being told things he could read in the papers every day; still, Arnheim knew how to create suspense.

He was sufficiently interested to ask who was the majority shareholder in Lloyd's of London.

"No one knows," Arnheim replied quietly. "That is to say, there are those in the know, of course, but one doesn't usually hear it spoken of. But let me get to the point. Wherever you find two such forces, a person who really gives the orders and an administrative body that executes them, what automatically happens is that every possible means of increasing profits is used, whether or not it is morally or aesthetically attractive. When I say automatically I mean just that, because the way it works is to a high degree independent of any personal factor. The person who really wields the power takes no hand in carrying out his directives, while the managers are covered by the fact that they are acting not on their own behalf but as functionaries. You will find such arrangements everywhere these days, and by no means exclusively in the world of finance. You may depend on it that our friend Tuzzi would give the signal for war with the clearest conscience in the world, even if as a man he may be incapable of shooting down an old dog, and your friend Moosbrugger will be sent to his death by thousands of people because only three of them need have a hand in it personally. This system of indirection elevated to an art is what nowadays enables the individual and society as a whole to function with a clear conscience; the button to be pressed is always clean and shiny, and what happens at the other end of the line is the business of others, who, for their part, don't press the button. Do you find this revolting? It is how we let thousands die or vegetate, set in motion whole avalanches of suffering, but we always get things done. I might go so far as to say that what we're seeing here, in this form of the social division of labor, is nothing else than the ancient dualism of conscience between the end that is approved and the means that are tolerated, though here we have it in a grandiose and dangerous form."

In answer to Arnheim's question whether he found all this revolting Ulrich had shrugged his shoulders. The split in the moral consciousness that Arnheim spoke of, this most horrifying phenomenon of modern life, was an ancient fact of human history, but it had won its appalling good conscience only in recent times, as a consequence of the universal division of labor with all its magnificent inevitability.

Ulrich did not care to wax indignant over it, especially as it gave him, paradoxically, the funny and gratifying sensation one can get from tearing along at a hundred miles an hour past a dust-bespattered moralist who is standing by the wayside, cursing. When Arnheim came to a stop, Ulrich's first words were: "Every kind of division of labor can be developed further. The question is not whether it repels me but whether I believe that we can attain more acceptable conditions without having to turn back the clock."

"Aha, your general inventory!" Arnheim interjected. "We have organized the division of labor brilliantly but neglected to find ways of correlating the results. We are continuously destroying the old morality and the soul in accordance with the latest patents, and think we can patch them up by resorting to the old household remedies of our religious and philosophical traditions. Levity on such a subject"—he backed off—"is really quite distasteful to me, and I regard jokes on the whole as in dubious taste anyway. But then, I never thought of the suggestion you made to us all in the presence of Count Leinsdorf, that we need to reorganize the conscience itself, as a mere joke."

"It *was* a joke," Ulrich said gruffly. "I don't believe in such a possibility. I would sooner be inclined to believe that the Devil himself built up the European world and that God is willing to let the competition show what he can do."

"A pretty conceit," Arnheim said. "But in that case, why were you so annoyed with me for not wanting to believe you?"

Ulrich did not answer.

"What you said just now," Arnheim calmly persisted, "also contradicts those adventurous remarks of yours, some time ago, about the means toward attaining the right way in life. Besides, quite apart from whether I can agree with you on the details, I can't help noticing the extent to which you are a compound of active tendencies and indifference."

When Ulrich saw no need to reply even on this point, Arnheim said in the civil tone with which such rudeness must be met: "I merely wished to draw your attention to the degree to which we are expected, even in making economic decisions, on which after all everything depends, to work out the problem of our moral responsibility on our own, and how fascinating this makes such decisions." Even in the restraint with which this reproof was expressed there was a faint suggestion of trying to win him over.

"I'm sorry," Ulrich said, "I was totally caught up in what you've been saying." And as though he were still pursuing the same line of thought, he added: "I wonder whether you also regard it as a form of indirect dealing and divided consciousness in keeping with the spirit of the times to fill a woman's soul with mystical feelings while sensibly leaving her body to her husband?"

These words made Arnheim color a little, but he did not lose control of the situation. "I'm not sure I know what you mean," he said quietly, "but if you were speaking of a woman you love, you couldn't say this, because the body of reality is always richer than the mere outline sketch we call principles." He had moved away from the window and invited Ulrich to sit down with him. "You don't give in easily," he went on in a tone of mingled appreciation and regret. "But I know that I represent to you more of an opposing principle than a personal opponent. And those who are privately the bitterest opponents of capitalism are often enough its best servants in the business world; I may even say that to some extent I count myself among them, or I wouldn't presume to say this to you. Uncompromising, passionately committed persons, once they have seen that a concession must be made, usually become its most brilliant champions. And so I want in any case to go ahead with my intended proposal: Will you accept a position in my firm?"

He took care to say this as casually as he could, trying by speaking rapidly and without emphasis to lessen the cheap surprise effect he could be only too sure of causing. Avoiding Ulrich's astonished gaze, he simply proceeded to go into the details without making any effort to indicate his own position.

"You wouldn't, of course, have the necessary training and qualifications at first," he said smoothly, "to assume a leading position, nor would you feel inclined to do so, therefore I would offer you a position at my side, let us say that of my executive secretary, which I would create especially for you. I hope you won't take offense at this: it is not a position I can see as carrying an irresistible salary, to begin with; however, in time, you should be able to aim for any income you might wish. In a year or so, I am sure that you will understand me quite differently from now."

When Arnheim had finished, he felt moved in spite of himself. Actually, he had surprised himself by going so far in making this offer to Ulrich, who only had to refuse in order to put Arnheim at a disadvantage, while if he accepted, there wasn't much in it for Arnheim. Any idea that this man he was talking to could accomplish something that he himself could not do on his own had vanished even as he spoke, and the need to charm Ulrich and get him into his power had become absurd in the very process of finding articulate expression. That he had been afraid of something he called this man's "wit" now seemed unnatural. He, Arnheim, was a man of some consequence, and for such a man life has to be simple! Such a man lives on good terms with other great men and circumstances, he does not act the romantic rebel or cast doubt on existing realities; it would be against his nature. On the other hand, there are, of course, all the things of beauty and ambiguity one wants in one's life as much as possible. Arnheim had never felt as intensely as he did at this moment the permanence of Western civilization, that marvelous network of forces and disciplines. If Ulrich did not recognize this he was nothing but an adventurer, and the fact that Arnheim had almost let himself be tempted to think of him as— At this point words failed him, unformulated as they still were at the back of his mind; he could not bring himself to articulate clearly, even in secret, the fact that he had considered taking Ulrich on as an adopted son. Not that it really mattered; it was only an idea like countless others one need not answer for, probably inspired by the kind of moodiness that afflicts every man of action, because a man is never really satisfied, and perhaps he had not had this idea at all, in so dubious a form, but only some vague impulse that could be so interpreted; still, he shied away from the memory, and only kept painfully in mind that the difference between Ulrich's age and his own was not all that great; and behind this there was a secondary, shadowy sense that Ulrich might serve him as a warning against Diotima! How often he had already felt that his relationship to Ulrich was somehow comparable to a secondary volcanic crater that emits the occasional warning or clue to the strange goings-on in the main crater, and he was somewhat troubled that the eruption had now occurred and his words had come pouring out and were making their way into real life. "What's to be done," flashed through his mind, "if this fellow accepts?" It was in such suspense that an Arnheim had to wait for the decision of a younger man who mattered only insofar as Arnheim's own imagination had lent him significance. Arnheim sat there stiffly, his lips parted in a hostile expression, thinking: "There'll be a way of handling it, in case there's still not a way of getting out of it."

Even while his feelings and thoughts were running their course in this fashion the situation had not come to a standstill; question and answer followed each other without pause.

"And to what qualities of my own," Ulrich asked dryly, "do I owe this offer, which can hardly be justified from a businessman's point of view?"

"You always misjudge this sort of thing," Arnheim replied. "To be businesslike in my position is not the same as counting pennies. What I stand to lose on you is quite immaterial compared to what I hope to gain."

"You certainly pique my curiosity," Ulrich remarked. "Very seldom am I told I represent a gain of any kind. I might perhaps have developed into a minor asset in my special subject, but even there, as you know, I have been a disappointment."

"That you are a man of exceptional intelligence," Arnheim answered, in the same quiet tone of unshakable confidence to which he was outwardly clinging, "is surely something of which you are fully aware without my having to tell you. Still, we may have keener and more dependable minds already working for us. It is actually your character, your human qualities, that, for certain reasons, I wish to have constantly at my side."

"My qualities?" Ulrich could not help smiling at this. "That's funny: I have friends who call me a man without qualities."

Arnheim let slip a faint gesture of impatience that said, more or less: "Tell me about it, as if I didn't know." This twitch that ran across his face all the way to the shoulder betrayed his dissatisfaction, even while his words flowed on as programmed. Ulrich caught the fleeting grimace, and he was so ready to be provoked by Arnheim that he now dropped all restraint against bringing everything out into the open.

They had meanwhile risen from their chairs, and Ulrich moved back a few steps to see his effect all the better as he said:

"You have asked me so many pointed questions, and now there is something I would like to know before I make my decision. . . ." When Arnheim nodded he went on in a frank and matter-of-fact tone: "I've been told that your interest in our Parallel Campaign and everything connected with it, Frau Tuzzi and my humble self thrown in for good measure, has to do with your acquiring major portions of the Galician oil fields."

Despite the failing light, Arnheim could be seen to have turned pale; he walked slowly up to Ulrich, who thought he had brought some rude answer upon himself and regretted his own rash bluntness, which had given the other man a way to break off the conversation when it became inconvenient for him to go on with it. So he said, as affably as he could: "Please don't misunderstand me. I have no wish to offend you, but there is surely no point in our conversation unless we can speak our minds with brutal frankness."

These few words and the time it took him to cover the short distance enabled Arnheim to regain his composure. As he reached Ulrich he smiled, placed his hand—actually, his arm—on Ulrich's shoulder, and said reproachfully: "How can you fall for such a typical Stock Exchange rumor?"

"It reached me not as a rumor but as information from someone who knows what he is talking about."

"Yes, I know, I've heard that such things are being said, but how can you believe it? Of course I'm not here purely for pleasure; it's too bad, but I can never get away entirely from business affairs. And I won't deny that I have talked with some people about these oil fields, though I must ask you to keep this confidential. But what has this to do with anything?"

"My cousin," Ulrich resumed, "hasn't the remotest idea of your interest in oil. She has been asked by her husband to find out whatever she can about the reasons for your stay here, because you are regarded as a confidant of the Czar, but I am convinced that she is not doing justice to this diplomatic mission because she is so sure that she herself is the one and only reason for your continued visit with us."

"How can you be so indelicate?" Arnheim's arm gave Ulrich's shoulder a friendly little nudge. "There are always secondary strings to everything, everywhere, but despite your sardonic intention you have just expressed yourself with the naked rudeness of a schoolboy."

That arm on his shoulder made Ulrich unsure of himself. To stand there in this quasi embrace was ridiculous and unpleasant, a miserable feeling, in fact. Still, it was a long time since Ulrich had known a friend, and perhaps this added an element of bewilderment. He would have liked to shake off the arm, and he instinctively tried to do so, even while Arnheim, for his part, noticed these little signals of Ulrich's restiveness and did his utmost to ignore them. Ulrich, realizing the awkwardness of Arnheim's position, was too polite to move away and forced himself to put up with this physical contact, which felt increasingly like a heavy weight sinking into a loosely mounded dam and breaking it apart. Without meaning to, Ulrich had built up a wall of loneliness around himself, and now life, by way of another man's pulse beat, came pouring in through the breach in that wall, and silly as it was, ridiculous, really, he felt a touch of excitement.

He thought of Gerda. He remembered how even his old friend Walter had aroused in him a longing to find himself once more in total accord with another human being, wholly and without restraint, as if the whole wide world held no differences other than those between like and dislike. Now that it was too late, this longing welled up in him again, as if in silvery waves, as the ripples of water, air, and light fuse into one silvery stream down the whole width of a river. It was so entrancing that he had to force himself to be on his guard and not to give in, lest he cause a misunderstanding in this ambiguous situation. But as his muscles tightened he remembered Bonadea saying to him: "Ulrich, you're not a bad man, you merely make it hard for yourself to be good." Bonadea, who had been so incredibly wise that evening and who had also said: "After all, in dreams you don't think either, you simply live them." And he had said: "I was a child, as soft as the air on a moonlit night . . . ," and he now remembered that at the time he had actually had a different image in mind: the tip of a burning magnesium flare, for in the flying sparks that tore this tip to shreds he thought he recognized his heart; but that was a long time ago, and he had not quite dared to make this comparison and had succumbed to the other; not in conversation with Bonadea, incidentally, but with Diotima, as he now recalled. All the divergences of life begin close together at their roots, he felt, looking at the man who had just now, for reasons not entirely clear, offered him his friendship.

Arnheim had withdrawn his arm. They were standing once more in the window bay where their conversation had begun; on the street below, the lamps were already giving a peaceful light, though there was still a lingering sense of the excitement of earlier in the day. From time to time clusters of people passed by in heated talk, and here and there a mouth would open to shout a threat or some wavering "hoo-hoo," followed by guffaws. One had the impression of semiconsciousness. And in the light from this restless street, between the vertical curtains framing the darkened room, he saw Arnheim's figure and felt his own body standing there, half brightly lit up and half dark, a chiaroscuro sharpening the intense effect. Ulrich remembered the cheers for Arnheim he thought he had heard, and whether or not the man had anything to do with what had happened, in his Caesar-like calm as he stood pensively, gazing down on the street he projected himself as the dominant figure in this momentary light-painting, and he also seemed to feel the weight of his own presence in every glance cast upon him. At Arnheim's side one understood the meaning of self-possession. Consciousness alone cannot impose order on all the world's swarm and glow, since the keener it is, the more boundless the world becomes, at least for the moment; but that consciousness of self that is self-possession enters like a film director who artfully composes a scene into an image of happiness. Ulrich envied the man his happiness. In that instant nothing seemed easier than to do him some violence, for in his need to present an image at center stage this man conjured up all the old tags of melodrama. "Draw your dagger and fulfill his destiny!" Though the words came to mind only in the ranting tone of a ham actor, Ulrich had unconsciously moved so that he stood halfway behind Arnheim. He saw the dark, broad expanse of neck and shoulders before him. The neck in particular was a provocation. His hand groped in his right pocket for a penknife. He rose up on tiptoe and then once more looked over Arnheim's shoulder down on the street. Out there in the twilight, people were still being swept along like sand by an invisible tide pulling their bodies onward. Something would of course have to come of this demonstration, and so the future sent a wave ahead, some sort of suprapersonal fecundation of humanity occurred, though as always in an extremely vague and slipshod manner—or so Ulrich perceived it as it briefly held his attention, but he was tired to the point of nausea at the thought of stopping to analyze it all. Carefully he lowered his heels again, ashamed of the mental byplay that had caused him to raise them just before, though he did not attach too much importance to it, and he now felt greatly tempted to tap Arnheim on the shoulder and say to him: "Thank you. I'm fed up and I would like something new in my life. I accept your offer."

But as he did not really do this, either, the two men let the answer to Arnheim's proposal go by default. Arnheim reverted to an earlier part of their conversation. "Do you ever go to see a film? You should," he said. "In its present form, cinematography may not look like much, but once the big interests get involved—the electrochemical, say, or the chromochemical concerns—you are likely to see a surging development in just a few decades, which nothing can stop. Every known means of raising and intensifying production will be brought into play, and whatever our writers and aesthetes may suppose to be their own part in it, we will be getting an art based on Associated Electrical or German Dyes, Inc. It's absolutely terrifying; you'll see. Do you write? No, I remember I've asked you that. But why don't you write? Very sensible of you. The poet and philosopher of the future will emerge out of journalism, in any case. Haven't you noticed that our journalists are getting better all the time, while our poets are getting steadily worse? It is unquestionably a process in accordance with the laws of nature. Something is going on, and for my part I haven't the slightest doubt what it is: the age of great individuals is coming to an end." He leaned forward. "I can't see your face in this light; I'm firing all my shots in the dark." He gave a little laugh. "You've proposed a general stocktaking of our spiritual condition: Do you believe in that? Do you really suppose that life can be regulated by the mind? Of course you don't; you've said so. But I don't believe you in any case, because you're someone who would embrace the Devil for being a man without his match in the world."

"Where's that quotation from?"

"From the suppressed preface to *The Robbers*."

Naturally from the suppressed preface, Ulrich thought. He wouldn't bother with the one read by everyone else.

" 'Minds that are drawn to the most loathsome vices for their aura of greatness . . .' " Arnheim continued to quote from his capacious memory. He felt himself to be the master of the situation once more, and that Ulrich, for whatever reasons, had given ground; the antagonistic edge was gone; no need to bring up that offer again; what a narrow escape! But just as a wrestler knows when his opponent is slackening off and then gives it all he's got, so he felt he needed to let the full weight of his offer sink in, and said: "I believe you understand me better now. Quite frankly, there are times when I am keenly aware of being alone. The new men think too much in purely business terms, and those business families in their second or third generation tend to lose their imagination. They produce nothing but impeccable administrators and army officers, and they go in for castles, hunting parties, and titled sons-in-law. I know their kind the world over, fine, intelligent individuals among them, but incapable of coming up with a single idea concomitant with that basic state of restlessness, independence, and possibly unhappiness I referred to with my Schiller quotation just now."

"I'm sorry I can't stay and talk more," Ulrich said. "Frau Tuzzi is probably waiting in some friend's house for things to quiet down out there, but I have to go now. So you suppose me capable, despite my ignorance of business, of that restlessness which is so good for business by making it so much less narrowly businesslike?" He had turned on the light in preparation for saying good-bye, and waited for an answer. With majestic cameraderie, Arnheim laid his arm on Ulrich's shoulder, a gesture that seemed to have proved its usefulness by now, and answered: "Do forgive me if I seem to have said rather too much, in a mood of loneliness. Business and finance are coming into power, and one sometimes asks oneself what to do with this power. I hope you won't take it amiss."

"On the contrary," Ulrich assured him. "I mean to think your proposal over quite seriously." He said it in a rush, which could be interpreted as a sign of excitement. This left Arnheim, who was staying on to wait for Diotima, rather disconcerted and worried that it might not be too easy to find a face-saving way of making Ulrich forget the offer.

122

GOING HOME

Ulrich decided to walk home. It was a fine night, though dark. The houses, tall and compact, formed that strange space "street," open at the top to darkness, wind, and clouds. The road was deserted, as if the earlier unrest had left everything in a deep slumber. Whenever Ulrich did encounter a pedestrian, the sound of his footsteps had preceded him independently for a long time, like some weighty announcement. The night gave one a sense of impending events, as in a theater. One had a notion of oneself as a phenomenon in this world, something that appears bigger than it is, that produces an echo, and, when it passes lighted surfaces, is accompanied by its shadow like a huge spastic clown, rising to full height and the next moment creeping humbly to heel. How happy one can be! he thought.

He walked through a stone archway in a passage some ten paces long, running parallel to the street and separated from it by heavy buttresses; darkness leapt from corners, ambush and sudden death flickered in the dim cloister; a fierce, ancient, grim joy seized the soul. Perhaps this was too much; Ulrich suddenly imagined with what smugness and inward self-dramatization Arnheim would be walking here in his place. It killed the pleasure in his shadow and echo, and the spooky music in the walls faded out. He knew that he would not accept Arnheim's offer, but now he merely felt like a phantom stumbling through life's gallery, dismayed at being unable to find the body it should occupy, and was thoroughly relieved when before long he passed into a district less grand and less oppressive.

Wide streets and squares opened out in the blackness, and the commonplace buildings, peacefully starred with lighted rows of windows, laid no further spell on him. Coming into the open, he breathed this peace and remembered for no special reason some childhood photographs he had recently been looking at, pictures showing him with his mother, who had died young; from what a distance he had regarded the little boy, with the beautiful woman in an old-fashioned dress happily smiling at him. There was that overpowering impression of the good, affectionate, bright little boy they all felt him to be; there were hopes for him that were in no way his own; there were the vague expectations of a distinguished, promising future, like the outspread wings of a golden net opening to enfold him. And though all this had been invisible at the time, there it was for all to see decades afterward in those old photographs, and from the midst of this visible invisibility that could so easily have become reality, there was his tender, blank baby face looking back at him with the slightly forced expression of having to hold still. He had felt not a trace of warmth for that little boy, and even if he did take some pride in his beautiful mother, he had on the whole the impression of having narrowly escaped a great horror.

Anyone who has had the experience of seeing some earlier incarnation of himself gazing at him from an old photograph, wrapped in a bygone moment of self-satisfaction, as if glue had dried up or fallen out, will understand Ulrich's asking himself what sort of glue it was that seemed to hold for other people. He had now reached one of those green spaces bordered by trees, a break in the Ringstrasse, which follows the line of the ancient city walls, and he might have crossed it in a few strides, but the broad strip of sky above the trees made him turn aside and follow where it was leading, seeming to come closer and closer to the festoons of lights so intent upon their privacy in the distant sky above that wintry park, without actually getting any nearer to them. It's a kind of foreshortening of the mind's perspective, he thought, that creates the tranquil sense of the evening, which, from one day to the next, gives one this firm sense of life being in full accord with itself. Happiness, after all, depends for the most part not on one's ability to resolve contradictions but on making them disappear, the way the gaps between trees disappear when we look down a long avenue of them. And just as the visual relationships of things always shift to make a coherent picture for the eye, one in which the immediate and near at hand looks big, while even the big things at a distance look small and the gaps close up and the scene as a whole ends by rounding itself out, so it is with the invisible connections which our minds and feelings unconsciously arrange for us in such a way that we are left to feel we are fully in charge of our affairs. And just this is what I don't seem to be able to achieve the way I should, he said to himself.

A wide puddle blocked his way. Perhaps it was this puddle, or perhaps it was the bare, broomlike trees on either side, that conjured up a country road and a village, and awakened in him that monotonous state of the soul halfway between fulfillment and futility which comes with life in the country, a life that had tempted him more than once to repeat the "escape" he had made as a young man.

Everything becomes so simple, he felt. One's feelings get drowsy, one's thoughts drift off like clouds after bad weather, and suddenly a clear sky breaks out of the soul, and under that sky a cow in the middle of the path may begin to blaze with meaning; things come intensely alive as if there were nothing else in the world. A single cloud drifting past may transform the whole region: the grass darkens, then shines with wetness; nothing else has happened, and yet it's been like a voyage from one seashore to another. Or an old man loses his last tooth, and this trifling event may become a landmark in the lives of his neighbors, from which they date their memories. Every evening the birds sing around the village in the same way, in the stillness of the setting sun, but it feels like something new happening every time, as though the world were not yet seven days old! In the country, he thought, the gods still come to people. A man matters, his experiences matter, but in the city, where experiences come by the thousands, we can no longer relate them to ourselves; and this is of course the beginning of life's notorious turning into abstraction.

But even as he thought all this, he was also aware of how this abstraction extended a man's powers a thousandfold and how, even if from the point of view of any given detail it diluted him tenfold, as a whole it expanded him a hundredfold, and there could be no question of turning the wheel backward. And in one of those apparently random and abstract thoughts that so often assumed importance in his life, it struck him that when one is overburdened and dreams of simplifying one's life, the basic law of this life, the law one longs for, is nothing other than that of narrative order, the simple order that enables one to say: "First this happened and then that happened. . . ." It is the simple sequence of events in which the overwhelmingly manifold nature of things is represented, in a unidimensional order, as a mathematician would say, stringing all that has occurred in space and time on a single thread, which calms us; that celebrated "thread of the story," which is, it seems, the thread of life itself. Lucky the man who can say "when," "before," and "after"! Terrible things may have happened to him, he may have writhed in pain, but as soon as he can tell what happened in chronological order, he feels as contented as if the sun were warming his belly. This is the trick the novel artificially turns to account: Whether the wanderer is riding on the highway in pouring rain or crunching through snow and ice at ten below zero, the reader feels a cozy glow, and this would be hard to understand if this eternally dependable narrative device, which even nursemaids can rely on to keep their little charges quiet, this tried-and-true "foreshortening of the mind's perspective," were not already part and parcel of life itself. Most people relate to themselves as storytellers. They usually have no use for poems, and although the occasional "because" or "in order that" gets knotted into the thread of life, they generally detest any brooding that goes beyond that; they love the orderly sequence of facts because it has the look of necessity, and the impression that their life has a "course" is somehow their refuge from chaos. It now came to Ulrich that he had lost this elementary, narrative mode of thought to which private life still clings, even though everything in public life has already ceased to be narrative and no longer follows a thread, but instead spreads out as an infinitely interwoven surface.

When he resumed his homeward progress, reflecting on this insight, he remembered Goethe writing in an essay on art that "Man is not a teaching animal but one that lives, acts, and influences." He respectfully shrugged his shoulders. "These days," he thought, "a man can only allow himself to forget the uncertainties on which he must base his life and his actions as much as an actor who forgets the scenery and his makeup, and believes that he is really living his part." The thought of Goethe, however, brought back the thought of Arnheim, who was always misusing Goethe as an authority, and Ulrich suddenly remembered with distaste his extraordinary confusion when Arnheim had placed an arm on his shoulder. At this point he had emerged from under the trees and was back on the street, looking for the best way home. Peering upward for a street sign, he almost ran full tilt into a shadowy figure emerging from the darkness, and had to pull up short to avoid knocking down the prostitute who had stepped in his way. She held her ground and smiled instead of revealing her annoyance at his having charged into her like a bull, and Ulrich suddenly felt that her professional smile somehow created a little aura of warmth in the night. She spoke to him, using the threadbare words commonly thrown out as bait, which are like the dirty leavings of other men. She had a child's sloping shoulders, blond hair was showing under her hat, and her face looked pale, even indefinably appealing under the lamplight; beneath her nighttime makeup there was the suggestion of a young girl's freckled skin. She was much shorter than Ulrich and had to look up into his face, yet she said "baby" to him again, too numb to see anything out of place in this sound she uttered hundreds of times in a night.

Ulrich found it touching somehow. He did not brush her off but stopped and let her repeat her offer, as though he had not understood. Here he had unexpectedly found a friend who, for a slight charge, would put herself entirely at his disposal, ready to do her best to please him and avoid anything to put him off. If he showed himself willing, she would slip her arm in his with a gentle trustfulness and faint hesitation, as when old friends meet again for the first time after a separation not of their own making. If he promised to double or treble her usual price, and put the money on the table beforehand, so that she need not think about it but could abandon herself to that carefree, obliging state of mind that goes with having made a good deal, it would be shown that pure indifference has the merit of all pure feeling, which is without personal presumption and functions minus the needless confusion caused by interference from private emotions. Such thoughts went through his mind, half seriously, half flippantly, and he could not bring himself altogether to disappoint the little person, who was waiting for him to strike a deal; he even realized that he wanted her to like him, but clumsily enough, instead of simply exchanging a few words with her in the language of her profession, he fumbled in his pocket, slipped approximately the amount she would have asked into her hand, and walked on. For the space of a moment he had briefly pressed her hand—which had oddly resisted, in her surprise—firmly in his, with a single friendly word. But as he left this willing volunteer behind, he knew that she would rejoin her colleagues, who were whispering nearby in the dark, show them the money, and finally think of some gibe at him to give vent to feelings she could not understand.

The encounter lived on in his mind for a while as though it had been a tender idyll of a minute's duration. He did not romanticize the poverty of his fleeting friend or her debasement, but when he imagined how she would have turned up her eyes and given the fake little moan she had learned to deliver at the right moment, he couldn't help feeling without knowing why that there was something touching about this deeply vulgar, hopelessly inept private performance for an agreed price; perhaps because it was a burlesque version of the human comedy itself. Even while he was still speaking to the girl he had thought fleetingly of Moosbrugger, the pathological comedian, the pursuer and nemesis of prostitutes, who had been out walking on that other, unlucky night just as Ulrich was this evening. When the housefronts on that street had stopped swaying like stage scenery for a moment, Moosbrugger had bumped into the unknown creature who had awaited him by the bridge the night of the murder. What a shock of recognition it must have been, going through him from head to toe: for an instant, Ulrich thought he could feel it himself. Something was lifting him off the ground like a wave; he lost his balance but didn't need it, the movement itself carried him along. His heart contracted, but his imaginings became confused and overran all bounds, until they dissolved in an almost enervating voluptuousness. He made an effort to calm down. He had apparently been living so long without some central purpose that he was actually envying a psychopath his obsessions and his faith in the part he was playing! But Moosbrugger was fascinating, after all, not just to himself but to everyone else as well. Ulrich heard Arnheim's voice asking him: "Would you set him free?" and his own answer: "No! Probably not." Never ever, he now said to himself, and yet he had the hallucinatory image of an act in which the movement of reaching out in some extreme state of excitement and that of being moved by it fused into an ineffable communion, in which desire was indistinguishable from compulsion, meaning from necessity, and the most intense activity from blissful receptiveness. He fleetingly recalled the opinion that such luckless creatures as Moosbrugger were the embodiments of repressed instincts common to all, of all the murders and rapes committed in fantasies. Let those who believed this make their own peace with Moosbrugger, let them justify him to reestablish their own morality, after they had satisfied their dark urges through him! Ulrich's conflict was different; he repressed nothing and could not help seeing that the image of a murderer was no stranger to him than any other of the world's pictures; what they all had in common with his own old images of himself: part crystallization of meaning, part resurgence of the nonsense beneath. A rampant metaphor of order, that was what Moosbrugger meant for him. And suddenly Ulrich said: "All of that—" and made a gesture as though thrusting something aside with the back of his hand. He had not merely thought it, he had said it out loud, and reacted to hearing himself speak by pressing his lips together and finishing his statement in silence: "All of that has to be settled, once and for all!" Never mind what "all of that" was in detail; it was everything he had been preoccupied with, tormented by, sometimes even delighted with, ever since he had taken his "sabbatical"—everything that had tied him up in knots, like a dreamer for whom all things are possible except getting up and moving about; all that had led him from one impossible thing to another, from the very beginning until these last minutes of his homeward walk. Ulrich felt that he would now at long last have to either live like everybody else, for some attainable goal, or come to grips with one of his impossible possibilities. He had reached his own neighborhood, and he quickened his pace through the last street with a peculiar sense of hovering on some threshold. The feeling lent him wings, it moved him to take action, but as it was unspecific, again he was left with only an incomparable sense of freedom.

This might have passed off like so much else, but when he turned the corner into his own street he thought he saw all the windows of his house lit up, and shortly afterward, when he reached his garden gate, he could have no doubt about it. His old servant had asked for permission to spend the night with relatives somewhere; Ulrich had not been home since the episode with Gerda, when it was still daylight, and the gardener couple, who lived on the ground floor, never entered his rooms; yet there were lights on everywhere—intruders must be in the house, burglars he was about to take by surprise. Ulrich was so bewildered, and so disinclined to shake off the spell he was under, that he walked straight up to the house without hesitation. He had no idea what to expect. He saw shadows on the windows that seemed to indicate there was only one person moving about inside, but there could be more, and he wondered whether he might be walking into a bullet as he entered—or should he be prepared to shoot first? In a different state of mind Ulrich would probably have gone looking for a policeman or at least investigated the situation before deciding what to do, but he wanted this adventure to himself, and did not even reach for the pistol he sometimes carried since the night he had been knocked down by the hoodlums. He wanted . . . he didn't know what he wanted; he was willing to see what happened!

But when he pushed open the front door and entered the house, the burglar he had been looking forward to with such mixed feelings was only Clarisse.

123

THE TURNING POINT

Ulrich's recklessness might from the beginning have been motivated in part by an underlying faith in some harmless explanation for everything, that shying away from believing the worst that always leads one into danger; nevertheless, when his old servant unexpectedly came up to him in the hall, he almost knocked him down. Fortunately, he stopped himself in time, and was told that a telegram had come, which Clarisse had signed for and was now holding for him upstairs. The young lady had arrived about an hour ago, just as he, the old man, had been about to leave, and she would not let herself be turned away, so that he had preferred to stay in and give up his night out this once, for if he might be permitted to say so, the young lady seemed to be rather upset.

Ulrich thanked him and went up to his rooms, where he found Clarisse lying on the couch, on her side with her legs drawn up. Her straight, slim figure, her boyish haircut, and the charming oval of her face resting on one hand as she looked at him when he opened the door all made a most seductive picture. He told her that he had taken her for a burglar.

Clarisse's eyes flashed like rapid bursts of machine-gun fire. "Maybe I am a burglar!" she said. "That old fox your servant did his best to make me leave. I sent him off to bed, but I know he's been lurking out of sight downstairs somewhere. Your house is lovely!" She held out the telegram to him without getting up. "I was curious to see what you're like when you come home to be by yourself," she went on. "Walter's gone to a concert. He won't be back till after midnight. But I didn't tell him I was coming to see you."

Ulrich ripped open the telegram and read it while only half listening to Clarisse's words. He turned suddenly pale and read the startling message over again, unable to take it in. Although he had failed to answer several letters from his father asking him about the progress of the Parallel Campaign and the problem of "diminished responsibility," a longish interval had passed, without his noticing it, since any further reminders had come—and now this telegram, obviously drafted in advance with meticulous care by his father himself, informed him punctiliously, and in a funereal tone that did not quite succeed in repressing all reproach, of his own death. There had been little enough affection between them; in fact, the thought of his father had almost always been rather disturbing to Ulrich, and yet, as he now read the quaintly sinister text over again, he was thinking: "Now I am all alone in the world." He did not mean it literally, nor would that have made any sense, considering how things had been between them; what he meant was that he felt, with some amazement, that he was floating free, as though some mooring rope had snapped, or that his state of alienation from a world to which his father had been the last link had now become complete and final.

"My father's dead," he said to Clarisse, holding up the telegram with a touch of unintended solemnity.

"Oh!" Clarisse said. "Congratulations!" And after a slight, thoughtful pause she added: "I suppose you're going to be very rich now?" and looked around with interest.

"I don't believe he was more than moderately well off," Ulrich replied distantly. "I've been living here quite beyond his means."

Clarisse acknowledged the rebuke with a tiny smile, a sort of little curtsy of a smile; many of her expressive movements were as abrupt and disproportionate in a small space as the theatrical bow of a boy who must demonstrate before company how well he has been brought up. She was left alone for a few moments while Ulrich excused himself to go and make preparations for the trip he would have to take. When she had left Walter after their violent scene she had not gone far; outside the door to their apartment there was a seldom-used staircase leading up to the attic, and there she had sat, wrapped in a shawl, until she heard him leave the house. It made her think of the lofts in theaters for the stage machinery, where ropes run on pulleys, and there she sat while Walter made his exit down the stairs. She imagined that actresses might sit on the rafters above the stage between calls, wrapped in shawls, watching the stage from above, enjoying a full view of everything that was going on, just as she was now. It fitted in with a favorite notion of hers, that life was a dramatic role to be played. There was no need to understand one's part rationally, she thought; after all, what did anyone know about it, even those who might know more than she did? It was a matter of having the right instinct for life, like a storm bird. One simply spread out one's arms—and for her that included words, tears, kisses—like wings and took off! This fantasy offered some compensation to her for being no longer able to believe in Walter's future. She looked down the steep staircase Walter had just descended, spread her arms, and kept them raised in that position as long as she could; perhaps she could help him in that way! A steep ascent and a steep descent are strong complementary opposites and belong together, she thought. "Joyful world aslant" was what she named her wingspread arms and her gaze down the stairwell. She changed her mind about sneaking out to watch the demonstrators in town; what did she care about the common herd; the fantastic drama of the elect had begun!

And so Clarisse had gone to see Ulrich. On the way a sly smile would sometimes appear on her face, whenever it occurred to her that Walter thought her crazy each time she let slip any sign of her greater insight into what was going on between them. It tickled her vanity to know that he was afraid of having a child by her even while he impatiently longed for it. "Crazy" to her meant being something like summer lightning, or enjoying so extraordinary a degree of health that it frightened people; it was a quality her marriage had brought out in her, step by step, as her feelings of superiority and control grew. She did realize, all the same, that there were times when other people did not know what to make of her, and when Ulrich reappeared she felt she ought to say something to him that would be in keeping with an event that cut so deeply into his life. She leapt up from the couch, paced through the room and the adjoining rooms, and then said: "Well, my sincere condolences, old fellow!"

Ulrich looked at her in astonishment, although he recognized the tone she fell into when she was nervous. Sometimes she's so hopelessly conventional, he thought; it's like coming upon a page from another book bound in with what one is reading. She had not bothered to watch her words with the appropriate expression but had flung them at him sideways, over her shoulder, which heightened the effect of hearing, not a false note exactly, but the wrong words to the tune, giving the uncanny impression that she herself consisted of many such misplaced texts.

When she received no answer from Ulrich, she stopped in front of him and said: "I have to talk with you!"

"May I offer you some refreshment?" Ulrich said.

Clarisse only fluttered her hand at shoulder height to signal no. She pulled her thoughts together and said: "Walter is dead set on having a child. Can you understand that?" She seemed to be waiting for an answer. But what could Ulrich have said to that?

"But I don't want to!" she cried out violently.

"Well, no need to fly into a rage," Ulrich said. "If you don't want to, it can't happen."

"But it's destroying him!"

"People who are always expecting to die generally live a long time! You and I will be shriveled ancients while Walter will still have his boyish face under his white mane as Director of his Archives."

Clarisse turned pensively on her heel and walked away from Ulrich; at a distance, she wheeled to face him again and "fixed him" with her eye.

"Have you ever seen an umbrella with its shaft removed? Walter falls apart when I turn away from him. I'm his shaft and he's . . ." She was about to say "my umbrella" but thought of something much better: "my shield," she said. "He sees himself as my protector. And the first thing that means is giving me a big belly. Next will be the lectures on breast-feeding the infant because that is nature's way, and then he'll want to bring up the child in his own image. You know him well enough to know all that. All he wants is to have the rights to everything and a terrific excuse for making bourgeois conformists out of both of us. But if I go on saying no, as I have been, he'll be done for. I mean simply everything to him!"

Ulrich smiled incredulously at this sweeping claim.

"He wants to kill you," Clarisse added quickly.

"What? I thought that was your suggestion to him."

"I want the child from you!" Clarisse said.

Ulrich whistled through his teeth in surprise.

She smiled like an adolescent who has misbehaved with deliberate provocation.

"I wouldn't do something so underhanded to such an old friend," Ulrich said slowly. "It goes against my grain."

"Oh? So you're a man of high scruple, are you?" Clarisse seemed to attach some special significance of her own to this that Ulrich didn't understand. She gave it some thought and then returned to the attack: "But if you are my lover, he's got you where he wants you."

"How do you mean?"

"It's obvious; I just don't know quite how to put it. You'll be forced to treat him with consideration. We'll both be feeling sorry for him. You can't just go ahead and cheat on him, of course, so you'll have to try to make it up to him somehow. And so on and so forth. And most important of all, you'll be driving him to bring out the best that's in him. You know perfectly well that we are stuck inside ourselves like statues in a block of stone. We have to sculpt our way out! We have to force each other to do it."

"Maybe so," Ulrich said, "but aren't you getting ahead of yourself? What makes you think any of this will happen?"

Clarisse was smiling again. "Perhaps I am ahead of myself," she said. She sidled up to him and slipped her arm confidingly under his, which hung limply at his side and made no room for hers. "Don't you find me attractive? Don't you like me?" she asked. And when he did not answer, she went on: "But you do find me attractive, I know it; I've seen it often enough, the way you look at me, when you come to see us. Do you remember if I've ever told you that you're the Devil?

That's how I feel. Try to understand, I'm not calling you a poor devil: that's the kind who wants to do evil because he doesn't know any better. You are a great devil: you know what's good and you do the opposite of what you'd like to do! You know the life we lead is abominable, and so you say mockingly that we must go on with it. And you say, full of your high scruples, 'I won't cheat on a friend,' but you only say that because you've thought a hundred times, 'I'd like to have Clarisse.' But just because you're a devil you have something of a god inside you, Ulo! A great god. The kind who lies to try to keep from being recognized. You do want me. . . ."

She had gripped both his arms now, standing before him with her face lifted up to his, her body curving back like a plant responding to a touch on its petals. In a moment her face will be drenched with that look, like the last time, Ulrich thought apprehensively. But nothing of the kind happened; her face remained beautiful. Instead of her usual tight smile there was an open one, which showed a little of her teeth between the rosy flesh of her lips, as though about to bite. Her mouth took on the shape of a double Cupid's bow, a line echoed in the curve of her eyebrows and again in the translucent cloud of her hair.

"For a long time now you've been wanting to pick me up with those teeth in that lying mouth of yours and carry me off, if only you could stand to let me see you as you really are," Clarisse had continued. Ulrich gently freed himself from her grip. She dropped down on the couch as if he had put her there, and pulled him down after her.

"You really shouldn't let your imagination run away with you like this," Ulrich said in reproof.

Clarisse had let go of him. She closed her eyes and supported her head with both hands, her elbows resting on her knees; now that her second attack had been repelled, she decided to resort to icy logic.

"Don't be so literal-minded," she said. "When I speak of the Devil, or of God, it's only a figure of speech. But when I'm alone at home, or walking in the neighborhood, I often think: If I turn to the left, God will come; if I turn to the right, the Devil. Or when I'm about to pick something up with my hand, I have the same feeling about using the right or the left hand. When I tell Walter about it he puts his hands in his pockets, in real panic. He's happy to see a flower in bloom, or even a snail, but don't you think the life we lead is terribly sad? No God comes, or the Devil either. I've been waiting for years now, but what is there to wait for? Nothing. That's all there is, unless art can work a miracle and change everything."

At this moment there was something so gentle and sad about her that Ulrich gave way to an impulse to touch her soft hair with his hand. "You may be right in the details, Clarisse," he said. "But I can never follow your leaps from one point to another, or see how it all hangs together."

"It's quite simple," she said, still in the same posture as before. "As time went on, an idea came to me. Listen!" She straightened up and was suddenly quite vivacious again. "Didn't you once say yourself that the way we live is full of cracks through which we can see the impossible state of affairs underneath, as it were? You needn't say anything, I've known about it for a long time. We all want to have our lives in order, but nobody has! I play the piano or paint a picture, but it's like putting up a screen to hide a hole in the wall. You and Walter also have ideas, and I don't understand much of that, but that doesn't work either, and you said yourself that we avoid looking at the hole out of habit or laziness, or else we let ourselves be distracted from it by bad things. Well, there's a simple answer: That's the hole we have to escape through! And I know how! There are days when I can slip out of myself. Then it's like finding yourself—how shall I put it?— right in the center of things as if peeled out of a shell, and the things have had their dirty rind peeled off too. Or else one feels connected by the air with everything there is, like a Siamese twin. It's an incredible, marvelous feeling; everything turns into music and color and rhythm, and I'm no longer the citizen Clarisse, as I was baptized, but perhaps a shining splinter pressing into some immense unfathomable happiness. But you know all about that. That's what you meant when you said that there's something impossible about reality, and that one's experiences should not be turned inward, as something personal and real, but must be turned outward, like a song or a painting, and so on and so forth. Oh, I could recite it all exactly the way you said it." Her "so on and so forth" recurred like some wild refrain as Clarisse's torrent of words flowed on, regularly interspersed with her assertion "You can do it, but you won't, and I don't know why you won't, but I'm going to shake you up!"

Ulrich had let her go on talking, only shaking his head from time to time when she attributed to him something too unlikely, but he could not bring himself to argue with her and left his hand resting on her hair, where his fingertips could almost sense the confused pulsation of the thoughts inside her skull. He had never yet seen Clarisse in such a state of sensual excitement and was amazed to see that even in her slim, hard young body there was room for all the loosening and soft expansion of a woman's glowing passion; this sudden, always surprising opening up of a woman one has known only as inaccessibly shut away in herself did not fail to have its effect on him. Although they defied all reason, her words did not repel him, for as they came close to touching him in the quick and then again angled off into absurdity, their constant rapid movement, like a buzzing or humming, drowned out the quality of the tone, beautiful or ugly, in the intensity of the vibrations. Listening to her seemed to help him make up his mind, like some wild music, and it was only when she seemed to have lost her way in the maze of her own words and could not find her way out that he shook her head a little with his outspread hand, as though to call her back and set her straight.

But the opposite of what he intended happened, for Clarisse suddenly made a physical assault on him. She flung an arm around his neck and pressed her lips to his so quickly that it took him completely by surprise and he had no time to resist, as she pulled her legs up under her body and slid over to him so that she ended up kneeling in his lap, and he could feel the little hard ball of one breast pressing against his shoulder. He caught barely anything of what she was saying; she stammered something about her power of redemption, his cowardice, and his being a "barbarian," which was why she wanted to conceive the redeemer of the world from him and not from Walter. Actually, her words were no more than a raving murmur at his ear, a hasty muttering under her breath more concerned with itself than with communication, a rippling stream of sound in which he could only catch a word here and there, such as "Moosbrugger" or "Devil's Eye." In self-defense he had grabbed his little assailant by her upper arms and pushed her back on the couch, so that she was now struggling against him with her legs, pushing her hair into his face and trying to get her arms around his neck again.

"I'll kill you if you don't give in," she said loud and clear. Like a boy fighting in affection mixed with anger, who won't be put off, she struggled on in mounting excitement. The effort of restraining her left him with only a faint sense of the current of desire streaming through her body; even so, Ulrich had been strongly affected by it at the moment of putting his arm firmly around her and pressing her down. It was as if her body had penetrated his senses. He had after all known her for such a long time, and had often indulged in a bit of horseplay with her, but he had never been in such close, head-to-toe contact with this little creature, so familiar and yet so strange, its heart wildly bouncing, and when Clarisse's movements quieted down in the grip of his hands, and the relaxation of her muscles was reflected tenderly in the glow of her eyes, what he did not want to happen almost happened. But at this instant he thought of Gerda, as though it were only now that he was facing the challenge to come to terms with himself.

"I don't want to, Clarisse," he said, and let her go. "I need to be by myself now, and I have things to do before I leave."

When Clarisse grasped his refusal, it was as though with a jolt her head had shifted gears. She saw Ulrich standing a few steps away, his face contorted with embarrassment, saw him saying things she did not seem to take in, but as she watched the movement of his lips she felt a growing revulsion. Then she noticed that her skirt was above her knees, and jumped up off the couch. Before she understood what had happened, she was on her feet, shaking her hair and her clothes into place, as if she had been lying on the grass, and said:

"Of course you have to pack now; I won't keep you any longer." She was smiling again, her normal vaguely scoffing smile that was forced through a narrow slit, and wished him a good trip. "By the time you're back we'll probably have Meingast staying with us. He wrote to say he was coming, and that's actually what I came to tell you," she added casually.

Ulrich hesitantly held her hand. She was rubbing his playfully with a finger. She would have given anything to know what in the world she had been saying to him; she must have said all sorts of things, because she had been so worked up that now she had forgotten it all! She did have a general idea of what had happened, and she didn't mind, for her feelings told her that she had been brave or ready to sacrifice herself, and Ulrich timid. She wanted only to part as good friends and not to leave him in any doubt about that. "Better not tell Walter about this visit, and keep what we were talking about between ourselves for the time being," she said lightly. She gave him her hand once more at the garden gate and declined his offer to accompany her beyond it.

When Ulrich went back into the house he was preoccupied. He had to write some letters to let Count Leinsdorf and Diotima know he was leaving and had to attend to various other details, because he foresaw that taking over his inheritance might keep him away for some time. He stuffed various personal articles and a few books into the traveling cases already packed by his servant, whom he had sent off to bed, but when he had finished he no longer felt like going to bed himself. He was both exhausted and overstimulated after his eventful day, yet instead of canceling each other out, these two states of feeling only heightened each other so that, tired as he was, he felt unable to sleep.

Not really thinking, but following the oscillations of his memories, Ulrich began by acknowledging that he could no longer doubt his impression, at various times, that Clarisse was not merely an unusual person but probably already mentally unbalanced—and yet, during her attack just now, or whatever one might call it, she had said things that were too close for comfort to much that he had occasionally said himself. This should have started him really thinking hard, but it only brought the unwelcome reminder, in his half-drowsy state, that he still had much to do. Almost half of the year he had taken off to think was gone, without his having settled any of his problems. It flashed through his mind that Gerda had urged him to write a book about it. But he wanted to live without splitting himself into a real and a shadow self. He remembered speaking to Section Chief Tuzzi about writing. He saw himself and Tuzzi standing in Diotima's drawing room, and there was something theatrical, something stagy, about the scene. He remembered saying casually that he would probably have to either write a book or kill himself. But the thought of death, thinking it over at close range, so to speak, did not in the least correspond to his present state of mind either; when he explored it a little and toyed with the notion of killing himself before morning instead of taking the train, it struck him as an improper conjunction at the moment he had received the news of his father's death! Half asleep as he was, the figures of his imagination raced through his mind; he saw himself peering down the dark barrel of a gun, where he saw a shadowy nothing, the darkness veiling the depths beyond, and mused on the rare coincidence that the same image of a loaded gun had been his favorite metaphor in his youth, when his will was all charged up, waiting to take aim and let fly at some unknown target. His mind was flooded with images such as the pistol and standing with Tuzzi. The look of a meadow in the early morning. A winding river valley filled with dense evening mists, as seen from a moving train. The place at the far end of Europe where he had parted from the woman he loved—he had forgotten what she looked like, but the image of the unpaved village streets and the thatched cottages was as fresh as yesterday. The hair under the arm of another loved woman, all that was left of her. Snatches of forgotten melodies. A characteristic movement. The fragrance of flower beds, unnoticed at the time because of the charged words being forced out by the profound emotion of two souls, and coming back to him now when the words and the people were long forgotten. He saw a man on various paths, almost painful to look at, left over like a row of puppets that had had their springs broken long ago. One would think that such images are the most transient things in the world, but there are moments when all one's life splits up into such images, solitary relics along the road of life, as though the road led only away from them and back to them again, as though a man's fate were obeying not his ideas and his will but these mysterious, half-meaningless pictures.

But while he was moved almost to tears by the pointlessness, the uselessness, of all the efforts he had ever taken pride in, his sleepless, exhausted state gave rise to a feeling, or perhaps one should say that a marvelous feeling diffused itself around him. The lights Clarisse had turned on in all the rooms while she was alone were still on, and an excess of light flowed back and forth between the walls and the objects, filling the space between with an almost living presence. It was probably the tenderness inherent in any painless state of exhaustion that changed his total sense of his body; this ever-present though unheeded physical self-awareness, vaguely enough defined in any case, now passed over into a more yielding and expansive state. It was a loosening up as though a tourniquet were coming undone, and since neither the walls nor the objects underwent any real change and no god entered the rooms of this unbeliever, and since Ulrich himself by no means allowed his clear judgment to become clouded (unless his fatigue deceived him into thinking so), it could only be the relationship between himself and his surroundings that was undergoing such a change. The transformation was not objective; it was a subjective expanse of feeling, deep as groundwater, on which the senses and the intelligence, those pillars of objective perception, normally supported themselves but on which they now were gently separating or merging—the distinction lost its meaning almost as soon as he made it.

"It's a change in attitude; as I change, everything else involved changes too," Ulrich thought, sure that he had himself well under observation. But one could also say that his solitude—a condition that was present within him as well as around him, binding both his worlds—it could be said, and he felt it himself, that this solitude was growing greater or denser all the time. It flowed through the walls, flooded the city, then, without actually expanding, inundated the world. "What world?" he thought. "There is none!" The notion no longer seemed to have any meaning. But Ulrich's good judgment was still sufficiently in charge to make him recoil at once from such an exaggeration; he stopped hunting for more words and moved instead toward a state of full wakefulness. After a few seconds he gave a start. Day was breaking, its gray pallor mingling with the swiftly withering brightness of the artificial light.

Ulrich jumped to his feet and stretched. Something remained in his body that he could not shake off. He passed a finger over his eyelids, but something remained of that gentleness, that fusion of his vision and the things it beheld. And suddenly he recognized in a way hard to describe a sort of draining away of his strength, as though he had lost any power to go on denying that he was again standing exactly where he had stood years before. He shook his head, smiling. "An attack of 'the major's wife,' " he called it mockingly. There was no real danger of that, his rational mind told him, since there was no one with whom he could have repeated that old foolishness. He opened a window. The air outside was neutral, ordinary everyday morning air in which the first sounds of the city's life were striking up. He let its coolness rinse his temples, as the civilized European's distaste for sentimentality began to fill him with its hard clarity and he made up his mind to deal with the situation, if necessary, with the utmost precision. And yet, standing for a long time at the window, staring out into the morning without thinking of anything, he still had a sense of all the feelings that were slipping gleamingly away.

His servant's sudden entrance, with the solemn expression of the early riser, to wake him up, took Ulrich by surprise. He took a bath, rapidly did a few vigorous exercises, and left for the railroad station.